SONS
of the
EAGLE

K.A. Higgs

For my brother Max,
I miss you every day.

This book is dedicated to my daughters, Nicky and Stephi, I love you so much and I am very proud of you both. With love to my husband Steve, thank you for everything you do for me and for the wonderful years we've had together. Thanks to my sister, Nikki, for her great design for the cover of this book. For my Mum, I hope you are in a happier place. To Peter, for being my lovely Dad, thank you for letting me delve into your memories, something I know you were sometimes not comfortable with, but you always came through for me, and lastly Julius, my grandfather.

THE EMPRESS ELISABETH HOSPITAL, AUSTRIA, 1919

Julius peered through the gloom. As his eyes became accustomed to the darkness he saw a bed on the far side of the room illuminated by a single candle that cast ghostly shadows across the ceiling as its small flame flickered in the breeze from a half open window. Julius wheeled himself into the room but came to an abrupt stop and clasped his hand over his mouth as the foulest stench overwhelmed him, so foul that he began to retch. He had smelt the nauseous odor before, but never had it been so strong as in the confines of this hospital room. It was the smell of putrid, rotting flesh, of gangrene.

Julius had seen gangrene many times during the war, the first indication of the mortification of decaying flesh was common amongst wounded soldiers. It was the smell that engendered the greatest fear in every man. In this room, although masked by hospital disinfectants, the smell pervaded the chamber like a harbinger of death and for the first time Julius wondered if he had been right to come.

He shivered, the open window made the air chilly and damp. Julius felt the stillness and coldness travel over his body whilst the shadows on the ceiling danced above him like ethereal spirits warning him to depart.

Julius' senses told him to leave and he would have fled at that moment, but the silence was broken by the sound of someone breathing heavily. The hairs on the back of his neck stood on end as an unfamiliar guttural voice echoed around the room as the occupant of the bed spoke. "I knew you would come, Julius, I knew you would not stay away. You are a fool, why could you not have left me alone?"

The speaker gasped in tortured breaths, as though the effort to speak was using all his energy. Fascinated, but at the same time appalled at what he might find, Julius approached the bed. As his eyes met the horrific scene in front of him Julius Mayer wept. The tears ran down his face as he came face to face with the ultimate horror of his worst nightmare.

The Town Square
Kosice, Eastern Bohemia.
Tuesday, December 31ˢᵗ 1899

"Julius, take your sister's hand, we do not want to lose her in this crowd"

Julius scowled as he grabbed his sister's hand roughly whilst he looked around, hoping he wouldn't be seen by any of his classmates holding a little girl's hand. It wasn't fair, his older brothers had managed to escape their parents as soon as they had arrived at the town square, but he had not been so lucky and now he was stuck with his younger sister and his parents. Papa had been right though, it was certainly a big crowd. Julius thought the whole town must be here as he watched his parents greet their friends and acquaintances.

He was always proud to be with his father, whom he adored. Julius' father was a Colonel in the Austro-Hungarian Army and was often away at army headquarters in Vienna or with his regiment, so the family treasured the time when he was home with them. Father had called all his children, Karl, Franz, Julius and their younger sister Irmy into his study that afternoon and told them they would be witnessing the arrival of a new century that evening and they would all be allowed to stay up very late and celebrate with their parents in the streets of their home town of Kosice in Eastern Bohemia. Papa had tried to explain to his children that they were very blessed, not everyone witnessed a new century in their lifetime and they should relish the moment and never forget it. At the tender age of nine Julius was not sure what a new century meant, all he knew was that he could stay up late and see the fireworks display.

The crowds sauntered around the square, everybody was wearing greatcoats, hats and gloves to ward off the freezing weather that was so prevalent at this time of year. Snow lay on the ground as people stamped the cobblestones to ward off the cold and great swirls of gray mist danced in the gaslight as everybody's breaths met the frigid coldness of the night air. There were puppet shows, magicians and acrobats providing entertainment and the children laughed when the magicians produced coins out of their ears and the acrobats tumbled around the square.

The air was filled with the smell of foods being cooked on glowing braziers while mulled wine and hot chocolate were dispensed to the grateful crowd.

Julius had never seen anything so exciting in all his young life. He watched as his mother kept furtively looking in the direction of the Cathedral of St. Elizabeth while trying to converse with her friends. Julius knew why his mother was so apprehensive, he had heard her arguing with Papa that afternoon. Mama was a devout Catholic, she attended Mass every day at the cathedral, and Julius had heard his parents heatedly discussing this evening's celebrations. Mama had wanted to attend church as the new year arrived, but Papa had declined her request, saying she should spend it with her family, she could go to church tomorrow. Julius knew his mother was torn by this decision, but, as always, Papa was not a man to refuse.

Mama turned to Julius and placed a coin in his hand, "take Irmy and get yourself something to eat and some hot chocolate, you must keep warm, but don't go far, the new century is nearly here" Julius accepted the money gratefully and he and Irmy pushed through the crowd towards the food stalls. They decided to buy some hot chestnuts that were being cooked over a wood fire. The blaze warmed them as they were handed the chestnuts in a funnel of rolled up newspaper and though they were very hot they agreed that nothing had ever tasted so good.

If he was honest, Julius would have to admit that of all his siblings he was closest to his sister. Irmy was only a year younger than he was, and, being the baby of the family, and the only girl, was probably more spoilt than her brothers. If ever they were trying to gain some privilege or other from their parents, especially their father, it was always Irmy who was pushed into the room first to plead their case. Despite this, and to Irmy's credit, she was a sweet and amiable girl, who everybody liked.

Karl, their eldest brother, was fifteen. He seemed very old to the two younger children, and since he was off to Vienna in the summer to start his army training he obviously felt himself superior now and they rarely saw him as he was always out with his friends. Franz was twelve and he and Julius remained close, though he too was starting to think about his future in the army. All the boys attended a local military school and they knew that one day they would all be soldiers in His Majesty's Austro-Hungarian Army.

After buying their hot chocolate Julius and Irmy returned to their parents. Many of the revelers were becoming rowdy as the evening progressed and Julius was glad to be back in the safety of his parent's company. Suddenly the crowd started counting down from sixty, Mama leaned down to Julius and explained they were counting down the last seconds of the old century in order to welcome the new one. Julius nodded somberly, the hairs were standing up on the back of his neck as he started to realize what Papa had meant by this being a momentous occasion. He joined in with the crowd as they shouted the numbers, Papa whisked Irmy up into his arms as Mama put her arm around Julius, "10,9,8,7,6,5,4,3,2,1" and there was a great roar when the church bells rang out. Everybody was jumping up and down and kissing, Julius thought he would get lost in the crowd, as they jostled with each other, caught up in the excitement of the moment.

Julius turned his face upwards as the fireworks lit up the sky in a display which seemed to go on forever. Out of the corner of his eye Julius noticed his mother crossing herself and looked to see his father's reaction, but he was too busy with Irmy in his arms as he shook hands with friends or quickly kissed ladies on their cheeks. Julius thought the noise of the crowd and the fireworks would deafen him, but everybody was so happy and jubilant, this had to be the best night of his life, even better than going to Vienna and seeing the soldiers on parade.

Eventually the crowds began to disperse and Julius suddenly felt very tired, he had never stayed up this late in his young life. Karl and Franz rejoined the family and Julius groaned inside when he realized that they would have to walk home as, due to the crowds, they had not used the carriage that night. He was jealous to see Irmy fast asleep in her father's arms being carried home.

When they arrived at their house Danusia, their Polish nanny, was there to greet them. Julius had never been so pleased to see her as she gently guided him and Irmy upstairs and without even a wash put them to bed between sheets which she had thoughtfully warmed with a bedpan. As she tidied his clothes Julius could hear Danusia quietly singing one of her Polish lullabies and he thought he was in heaven.

Just as he was drifting off to sleep he was aware that Papa was sitting on his bed. With a great effort he opened his sleepy eyes and smiled at his father. "So, my son, did you enjoy this evening?"

Julius nodded, too exhausted to speak.

"Good, you know Julius, this evening was an historic moment for all of us, and an experience you should never forget. It is the beginning of a new century, the year is 1900, who knows what the next few years will bring, I hope it will be a wonderful time for you"

Julius smiled as Papa rose, pulled the sheets up closely around his young son, and turned down the light. As Julius drifted off to sleep, he thought about what his father had said, he wasn't sure he had understood everything, but if his father had asked him what his future might be he knew what the answer would have been, he was going to be a soldier, just like Papa.

The next summer, at the age of sixteen, Karl joined the Austro-Hungarian Army. Julius had never felt so envious of anyone in his life as he did of Karl the day he left to join the army cadet school in Vienna, the capital of the Austro-Hungarian Empire. The army was then known as the Kaiser and Konig Army, or the K+K Army after their Emperor Franz Josef who was the Kaiser (Emperor) of Austria and the Konig (King) of Hungary. As they said their farewells to Karl at Kosice station Julius watched the happy smiling face of his brother waving from the departing rail carriage as his mother tearfully waved goodbye to her eldest son.

In the ensuing years Julius continued his studies at school, he was encouraged to do well and he knew his school results would help with his entrance into the army.

One evening he was sitting at the desk in the nursery doing his homework when Irmy, who was sitting by the fire sewing, let out a long, deep sigh. Julius turned in his seat to look at his sister. Irmy was now thirteen and she had grown up in the last few months. She was tall, almost as tall as her brothers, with a willowy figure and beautiful ash blonde hair which she now wore dressed on top of her head. She was also very pretty, with a lively, witty mind. "Julius, did you always know that you wanted to go into the army?" she asked, still looking down intently at her needlework.

"Of course" replied Julius, "I don't think I have ever considered doing anything else, why do you ask?"

"Oh I don't know, I suppose I was just thinking of my future and what lies ahead of me".

4

"You are a bit young to be thinking of your future, surely. Anyway, you know what your future is. You will be a beautiful young woman of society and all the young men of Kosice will be lining up at our front door, begging Papa for your hand in marriage"

Irmy frowned at her brother, "there speaks a man, perhaps I want more than that. Perhaps I want to do something with my life rather than settling for a life of domesticity" Irmy argued.

"Well I hate to disillusion you" answered Julius, "but Papa would never let you do anything else, and anyway, well brought up young ladies, yes, even ones like *you*" he joked, "all they do *is* get married and have children, and things like that do not change. Anyway, what is it you were thinking of doing that is going to change your life?"

Irmy stared into the fire and was quiet for a while until she replied in a small voice "I want to help people. I want to care for sick people, maybe as a nurse. Mama takes me to the Alms Hospital to help distribute food parcels to the ill and needy. There is so much that I could do, it would be wonderful to care for them"

Julius stared with his mouth open. Women simply did not have these ambitions, and certainly not those who came from a family like theirs. His parents would be amazed to hear their daughter talking like this, he was not even sure that he was enjoying the conversation. He knew his sister's stubborn persistence once she had an idea in her mind and decided to temper her obvious ambition.

"Irmy, you know Mama and Papa would never countenance such an idea, and if I were you I would not bring up the subject with them. Perhaps you could press Mama to take you more often to the hospital and help out in that way, but as to taking up medicine as a profession, you know our parents would absolutely refuse to let you. Just keep your feelings to yourself, you are still young and will probably have changed your mind by this time next year"

Irmy did not answer but continued to stare into the fire. Julius went over to her, knelt before her and looked into her face. Her eyes were full of tears and she looked so unhappy that Julius realized she was very serious about her ambition. He wished he hadn't been so flippant in his reply to her.

"Tell you what" he said, taking her trembling hands in his, "this will be our secret and if you ever want to talk about it

5

you know I am always here to listen, but I am afraid I have to be honest with you and say I cannot see Mama and Papa agreeing to any of this" When he saw that his words didn't seem to make her any happier he tried to cheer her up by adding, "who knows, they say things are changing with the new century and maybe they will change for you. Failing that, if I were you, I would find a nice doctor to marry!"

With that Irmy burst out laughing and tugged her brother's hair in fun. Julius was pleased to see her usual good humor return, but she and Julius would have many such conversations in the years to come and Irmy found much solace in the confidences she shared with her brother.

The years passed quickly. Entry into the army was easy, especially for someone as bright as Julius, and, coming from a military family, as he did, certainly helped. Franz had also gone into the army and now Julius was the only son left at home. As the time grew nearer for him to go he began to feel a certain uneasiness. Maybe it was leaving his mother and Irmy, or maybe just the mere fact that it would be the first time, at the age of sixteen, that he would leave the safety and security of Kosice and go off into the world on his own.

Julius stood on the same station platform, as his brothers had before him, saying goodbye to his mother and sister. Frau Mayer had been a soldier's wife for over twenty-five years, but with each son that had departed it had become harder for her to bear. Now, in June 1906, it was the turn of her beloved Julius, perhaps her favorite, if she ever admitted to having a favorite. Irmy had started to cry, she felt the parting as much as her mother. Julius took his sister to one side and gave her an affectionate farewell hug.

"Oh Julius, what am I going to do without you?" she said through her tears, "Who can I talk to now, who will listen to my stupid ravings and make me laugh at myself?"

"I will be back on leave before you know it" replied Julius "and whilst I am away I will expect you to write to me at least once a week so that I will not feel homesick. Promise me you will, and do not forget *all* your dreams, who knows, one day they may come true!"

Irmy smiled, "Oh I think I have come to terms with my dreams, but I am still going to look for that doctor!"

Brother and sister laughed with each other and, with a last hug for his mother, Julius jumped into his carriage. He was

6

still laughing and blowing kisses to them as the train pulled
out of the station and out of their view.

II

Julius settled into a window seat of the train carriage. He felt the excitement of the long journey ahead, but he had felt sad watching his mother and sister grow smaller and smaller into the distance as the train had left the station. It was the first time he had left home completely on his own and as he sat in his carriage, surrounded by strangers, he felt very lonely for the first time in his life. Was he feeling homesick already? He hoped not. He wondered if his brothers had felt the same on their journeys off into the unknown. They had never mentioned it, but of course they wouldn't. Were soldiers meant to feel homesick? Julius wrestled with these unhappy thoughts as his train steamed through the countryside, trundling its way towards Vienna and the army. He had always wanted to go into the army, had never thought of anything else, but now the reality was here he felt uneasy, even a little scared.

He sighed to himself and looked around the carriage at his fellow passengers. There was a young mother with a child of about four who was constantly asking his mother questions that she chose to ignore as she read her book. Next to Julius was an elderly gentleman with little round spectacles that were obviously not very effective as he held his newspaper just under his nose to read, and opposite Julius was a young man, about his own age. He was sturdily built, with a shock of bright red hair and an angelic smile that somehow never left his face. He had an open book on his lap, but was not reading it as he gazed out of the window at the moving landscape. Watching these strangers in his carriage made him feel lonelier than ever.

Julius dozed as he succumbed to the hypnotic sound of the rhythms of the train. He was roused out of his slumber by the steward opening the compartment door and informing its occupants that lunch was being served in the dining car. Julius felt very hungry, he had hardly eaten any breakfast that morning, despite Danusia's coaxing, as he had been so excited and apprehensive.

He decided to hurry to get his lunch before a line had formed, exactly the same time as Julius jumped up from his seat the boy who had been sitting opposite him did the same. The boy had forgotten his book on his lap and it fell down onto Julius' feet. Both of them went down to retrieve

8

the book at the same time, resulting in a painful crash of heads. They both fell about laughing as they rubbed their sore heads.

"Sorry about that" laughed the boy, "it is lucky we have both got thick heads. Were you going to get some lunch? because if you were perhaps we could go together, travelling on your own on a train journey can get pretty lonely and I would appreciate the company" Julius readily agreed, impressed by the boy's friendliness and openness, and grateful for the companionship.

As they walked to the dining car the boy introduced himself as Nikolas Manz who came from Presov, a town north of Kosice. After they had been shown to their table the boys ordered Svickova, a beef dish with Knedliky which were dumplings, a staple food in most Bohemian households. The food was excellent and as their train continued its journey to Vienna the boys fell into an easy conversation about their lives and backgrounds.

Julius was amazed to discover that Nikolas had a very similar life to his own. His father, too, was a Colonel in the Imperial Army, stationed in Prague. He had a younger brother, ten years younger than himself and to cap it all he was on his way to Vienna to join the K+K Army. Julius felt much happier as he had a companion on the train, and now he would know at least one other person in Vienna apart from his father. The boys continued chatting all the way back to the carriage after their lunch. Once seated Julius felt sleepy after his meal so he had a nap, while Nikolas read his book.

They dined together again that evening and as they stood out in the corridor whilst the valets prepared their sleeping compartments for the night Nikolas, looking out of the window at the gloom of the evening and the stars bright in the dark blue sky, said to Julius, "did you feel scared when you left home this morning, or homesick at all?" Julius, who was also looking out of the window, turned to look at his new friend, but he could not see his face, it was turned away from him. He didn't know what to say. Should he admit to his inner turmoil this morning, would Nikolas think him a baby if he did, or should he be dishonest and laugh off the thought of such a thing? For a moment he was confused, not knowing what to say, then he summoned up his courage and replied, "If you mean not eating any breakfast this morning, feeling close to tears as I watched my mother and sister from the train and feeling like I wanted to be sick, yes I suppose you could say I was all those things"

There was an awfully long silence as Nikolas did not reply, but continued staring out of the window. At last Nikolas turned to face Julius, still with the angelic smile on his face, which now turned into a booming laugh, "Oh well that is all right then, because I went one better than you and was actually physically sick in the station convenience, I am glad I am not the only one!"

Both boys started to laugh and Julius was grateful that he had met Nikolas Manz, a sentiment he was to repeat often in the years to come.

As their train steamed into Vienna's central station the boys leaned out of their window to get a better view. The journey had been long and the boys were looking forward to putting their feet on terra firma once more. They had passed the time happily enough, chatting about anything that came into their minds. They had played with the little boy, as his mother seemed determined to ignore him throughout the journey. When they had told him they were going to Vienna to become soldiers his eyes had opened very wide and after that he was continually asking them questions about military life, questions they could only answer through their experiences of being in an army family. Even the old man became friendlier as the journey progressed, telling them the best places to visit in Vienna.

The station was teeming with people. As the boys unloaded their baggage and helped the mother and boy down from their carriage they were hit by the tremendous noise that bombarded them from everywhere. Everyone was rushing about in various directions, from beautifully dressed elegant Viennese gentry to ragged dirty children begging a few hellers from passers-by.

Julius had been here many a time, but always with his mother or his father, never on his own. Then he had felt protected and safe as his parents swiftly organized their escape from this confusing melee, now he did not even know which exit to take.

Luckily his father had sent him a detailed map of how to get to his new barracks and he now fished it out of his pocket. He grinned as Nikolas waved a similar paper in front of him "Colonels!" They both laughed together. Picking up their luggage they threaded their way through the crowds of people towards their exit and out onto the Alserbachstrasse. The boys had a few hours before they had to report to their barracks so instead of taking the tram they decided to walk and watch the sights and sounds of Vienna by themselves for the first time.

Julius' spirits rose as they wandered through the streets of Vienna. He had always loved this city and to know he was to live here for at least the next six months made him very happy. Hazy sunshine covered the city that morning, and as they neared the center they were struck by all the military personnel that thronged the streets. The Austro-Hungarian army was one of the largest armies in the world and it appeared to Julius that most of its soldiers were in Vienna that morning. He especially loved to see the horses, beautiful noble beasts, groomed to perfection, proudly strutting along the street, their riders ramrod straight upon their backs. Julius couldn't wait to be one of those soldiers, riding through the streets of Vienna.

Julius commented on the beauty of Vienna to which Nikolas shook his head. "You would never say that if you had seen Prague. Vienna is too brash and full of its own splendor, Prague is much slower, with an understated elegance, full of romanticism and optimism" Julius eyed his friend warily, surprised at his eloquence in describing the Bohemian capital. Nikolas laughed, "You have never been there. One day maybe you will go there and then you will see that I am right"

They approached their barracks underneath a large stone archway that led into a huge cobbled square. As at the train station, everything was a mass of noise and people, though this was mixed with a large selection of horses all waiting to be mounted by their riders. All the horses were decorated with polished harnesses, saddles, and gleaming bridles and their coats and manes had been brushed until they shone. All the soldiers massed in the square wore full dress uniforms, with feathered helmets, and their long black boots had been polished until you could see a reflection in them.

Suddenly all was quiet as a bellowing shout was heard from the other end of the vast courtyard. At the second shout all the soldiers, as one, mounted their horses and made ready for departure. At the third shout a bugle was sounded and the riders travelled forward in perfect formation and exited out of an even larger archway at the other end of the square.

Julius and Nikolas stood with their mouths open; the spectacle had been so wonderful and exciting to watch. As the last of the riders vacated the arch young stable lads raced forward with shovels to clear up the mess left by the horses and everything was strangely silent and dreamlike after the pomp and splendor they had just seen.

The boys literally jumped in the air as a loud bellowing voice instantly pulled them out of their quixotic state, "And what have we here then?" the voice bellowed, "a couple of lads looking for some cheap horse shit?"

The boys turned round to be confronted by an enormous man, in full dress uniform, staring down fiercely at them from the end of his nose. "What's the matter then lads, cat got your tongue?" Julius could feel the man's breath on his face as he leaned over to look Julius straight in the eyes.

"N-no Sir" Julius stammered, he felt himself going bright red as the sweat trickled down his face.

"Well come on lad, who are you, what are you doing here?" he roughly asked.

"Cadet Officer Mayer reporting for duty, sir", Julius heard himself whisper.

By the tone of his voice the man obviously did not believe them, "and what about you copper knob?" he asked unkindly of Nikolas, "don't tell me, you're an officer cadet too, and what might your name be?"

"Cadet Officer Manz, sir" Nikolas replied as he stared down at his feet.

"Well Cadet Officer Manz" he sneered, "when you enter an army barracks you check in first at the sentry post by the main gate, otherwise we could get any delinquent walking in here off the street, which is what I took you two to be, *UNDERSTAND*?"

Again the boys nodded their heads, although Julius was insulted at the man's allusion to him looking like a delinquent. He was quite tempted to point out to this ogre that they would have reported to the sentry post if indeed there had been anybody in it at the time, but it had been empty. Presumably the occupant had sneaked out to watch the departing procession. Julius decided to keep his silence, not only was he sure that the absent sentry guard would receive a swift punishment from this officer, but he also decided that anything he uttered would only infuriate the

12

man more, a circumstance he really did not want to experience.

The officer continued to stare at the boys for what, to them, seemed like an eternity and then asked them for their papers. After reading them thoroughly, he ordered them to report to the West barracks and abruptly dismissed them.

The boys quickly picked up their bags and swiftly went in the direction of the man's pointing finger. They could still feel his icy stare on their backs as they rounded a corner and ran down an alley between two buildings. At the end of the alley they stopped to catch their breath.

"What a bastard" gasped Nikolas, whose face was as red as his hair. He leant against the wall trying to catch his breath. "He was only a bloody sergeant. One day, when I am a Colonel, or even a General, I am going to have his guts for garters. He scared the life out of me; I hope there are not too many more around like him!"

Julius looked at his friend with a conspiratorial smile on his face, "well all I can say is I am glad I wore brown trousers today!" both boys grinned at each other as they started off to try to find the West barracks.

After having to ask directions a couple of times they eventually found the West barracks. The complex itself was vast, the largest one in Vienna. The buildings of red stone all looked very similar and it was difficult to differentiate one building from another. The boys were sure they had passed one doorway at least three times before they arrived at their destination. They entered the building through a heavy paneled wooden door and found themselves in a large lobby that had ornate sweeping staircases in each of its corners leading up to the upper floors. Hanging from the ceilings were two crystal chandeliers and the dark wooden floor was polished and gleaming. Between the two staircases, against the back wall, was a large desk where a young soldier was sitting, writing. He looked up from his work as Julius and Nikolas closed the door noisily behind them.

"Good afternoon, gentlemen, can I help you?" he asked politely. Julius breathed a sigh of relief, he had begun to wonder if all army personnel were as revolting as the officer they had met in the courtyard, but this man was courteous enough. Julius and Nikolas approached the desk and showed the man their papers. He read them thoroughly and then looked up at the two boys.

"Well, welcome to the Austro-Hungarian Army, Cadet Mayer, Cadet Manz. You know one another?"

"Well no, not really" replied Julius "that is, we met on the train, and decided to report here together"

The soldier leaned back in his chair and looked at the two boys, "Good, now let us see where they have put you" He opened a large book and ran his finger down a few pages until he found their names, "Cadet Officer Manz, you are allocated to dormitory six on the second floor. The batman for that room is Private Smid, he will see to all your personal needs. Tomorrow morning you will report to uniform stores to receive your uniform. Uniform stores are in the North barracks. All meals are served in the barracks dining room which is through that door" he pointed to a door to the left of the lobby. "Your senior officer is Colonel Weber. Your Sergeant Major is Sergeant Major Hoffman. He will see to all your basic training for the next six months. Here is a map of the barracks. You will find this a confusing place for the first few weeks but soon you will find your way around quite easily"

After the trouble they had finding the West barracks Julius was not sure he would ever be able to find his way around the place. The soldier continued "Now, Cadet Mayer, let us see about you" he looked up from his papers with a smile on his face "well it seems you are in luck, you are also in dormitory six, and as I am sure you were paying full attention to what I was saying to Cadet Manz, I don't have to repeat myself again, do I?"

"No, Sergeant" replied Julius, trying to hide his delight at sharing the same dormitory as Nikolas.

"As you may, or may not know, there is to be a parade for the Emperor through the streets of Vienna tomorrow" Now they understood the spectacle they had seen in the courtyard upon their arrival, "Sergeant Major Hoffman is out at present practicing the route for tomorrow so it is possible you may not see him this afternoon. If not please be sure you present yourself for dinner at seven o'clock sharp this evening in the dining-room. As you have no uniform, evening dress is required. Any questions?"

"No Sergeant" the boys replied in unison.

"Very well, dismissed" and with that they picked up their bags and began to ascend one of the staircases in search of their room on the second floor.

When they opened the door of dormitory six they found a large room that had four beds, two each side of the room. Each bed was laid with crisp white linen and a large feather filled duvet. Beside each bed was a bedside cabinet. By the door was a wooden table, surrounded by four chairs. At the far end of the room, against the wall, was a wide dresser that contained a large amount of drawers and on top there were porcelain basins and numerous towels. Flanking the dresser on either side were two enormous wardrobes of dark heavy wood and next to the right hand wardrobe was a door. As the boys dumped their bags on the floor the door opened and there appeared the strangest looking little man Julius had ever seen. He had a young, boyish looking face, almost like that of a pixie, but his skin was brown and leathery, with little eyes that twinkled with humor. He was fairly small in stature, and his fair hair stood on end on his head, adding to his comical appearance. When he noticed the presence of the boys his face was split in two by a wonderful wide smile that went from ear to ear.

"Afternoon, gentlemen, can I help you?" he asked in a rough country accent that suited him exactly. The boys introduced themselves.

"You must be Private Smid," said Julius, "pleased to meet you. I am Cadet Mayer and this is Cadet Manz"

Julius didn't know what else to say as Private Smid stood in the middle of the room, eyeing him up and down, still with the enormous grin on his face. Julius decided that he should start the conversation.

"Could you tell us if our trunks have arrived yet?" Danusia had packed his large trunk days earlier and it had been sent on ahead of him.

"Yes sir" replied Smid, "I took the liberty of unpacking for you and all your clothes are in the left hand wardrobe, I've sent your dress suits to be pressed for tonight"

Julius had trouble following the little man's conversation, his accent was so broad he was difficult to understand. He was trying to decide where Smid came from when the little man carried on, "I'll take you round now, if you don't mind, show you where things are. As you are the first to arrive you can choose which beds you would like. Through that door there is the communal bathroom. Baths are restricted to two

15

baths per week for each person. The water closet is out in the hall two doors down on your left, you'll find pots under your bed for during the night. Emptying them is not my job, nor is tidying up or cleaning up after you. As you are sharing a room with other people you will find it easier if you keep everything clean and tidy. Either of you been to boarding school?" Both boys shook their heads "Pity" murmured Smid, "you can always tell the ones who have been to boarding school"

Both boys grinned at each other behind Smid's back; obviously they had gone down in his estimation, as they hadn't been to boarding school. Julius felt he was back home being lectured to by his mother or Danusia.

"Your bedside tables are for your personal belongings. Each one has a lock and the key is in the top draw. No photographs on top, please, keep them in your cupboard. Anything else I can help you with?"

Julius had been concentrating so hard following this speech that he couldn't think of anything to say, but he was sure as soon as the little man had gone out of the door he would think of a hundred things he wanted to ask him. As both boys had no questions Smid took his leave of them, saying he would be back later to see the next arrivals and if they ventured out of their room to take some identification with them as security was rigorous at the moment, because of the Emperor's visit. Julius wanted to ask if that included the sentry box, but held his tongue.

After Smid left the room Julius jumped on one of the beds, claiming it for himself. He lay on the comfortable white duvet and surveyed his new home. Nikolas went up to the wardrobes and opened the heavy wooden doors.

"Good heavens" he exclaimed, "I have never seen my clothes hung so neatly, and look at this" he opened one of the drawers of the dresser, "all our clothes are wrapped in tissue paper, I think I am going to like having old Smid around. He reminds me of a genial elf!"

Julius swung his legs onto the floor and retrieved his bag to start unpacking his things into the bedside table. He brought out a photograph of his family, taken the last time they had all been at home together, when Karl and Franz had had the same leave. Nikolas came over to have a look at it. He let out a long low whistle, "You didn't say how pretty your sister was"

16

Julius looked at his new friend, not sure whether he was pleased or annoyed that Nikolas had noticed Irmy, "Sorry, you have no chance, unless you decide to change professions and become a doctor" and he laughed to himself at his private joke, leaving Nikolas with a confused look on his face.

Once they had unpacked the boys lay on their beds deciding what to do next. They were contemplating going for a walk to see if the procession had returned when the door burst open and two boys walked into the room. One boy was very tall, and was probably the most handsome boy that Julius had ever met. He had a shock of white blonde hair that fell across his forehead above piercing blue eyes and finely honed cheekbones. He introduced himself as Josef von Kutz from Vienna. The other boy was very different from his companion, being short and stocky. He had a pimply, friendly face and he exuded a boundless, nervous energy, as though he couldn't stay in one place more than a few minutes at a time. He was very different to von Kutz, who had the lazy elegance of one who was very sure of himself. The boy shook hands with Julius and Nikolas. "Hello there, my name is Viktor Leitner, from Salzburg, pleased to meet you, been here long?"

The boys all continued in idle chatter, Julius and Nikolas filling in the new arrivals on the various rules around the place. As Josef and Viktor began to unpack Julius and Nikolas decided to leave them to it and take a wander around.

"Any idea where I might find this Smid?" asked Josef as they left the room.

"Probably on a toadstool somewhere" replied Nikolas over his shoulder. The boys hurried off down the corridor laughing loudly, leaving Josef and Viktor wondering if they were sharing with a couple of lunatics.

When Julius returned to his room later that afternoon he found a letter waiting for him. It was from his brother, Karl, now with his regiment in Linz, in northern Austria. Julius felt a rush of affection for his eldest brother. They had not been very close when young, Karl was six years older than Julius, but he was touched that his brother had written to him on his first day in the army. The letter was full of memories of Karl's first days in Vienna and bits of advice on how to avoid getting himself into trouble. The letter ended with Karl informing him that he had recently asked permission of his colonel to become engaged to the daughter of a senior officer in the army. Her name was Anna and they were to be married next year. Karl wrote that he had also written to Mama and Papa and hoped that they would like their prospective daughter-in-law. Julius read the letter in some amazement. Karl, to be married? He was only twenty-two, why he would want to be saddled with a wife already, he simply could not understand. The thought of marriage appalled him, still it was up to Karl he supposed, though he was definitely never going to be married himself.

With that thought he stuffed the letter into his bedside cabinet and started to get himself ready for the meal that evening. Josef and Viktor were already starting to change. By the time Julius and Nikolas had returned they had unpacked all their belongings, found Smid and were sharing Nikolas' joke about the toadstool.

"Rum looking fellow that Smid, but you have to admit he is efficient" drawled Josef.

Josef looked very handsome in his evening dress, Julius dreaded to think what he would look like in his uniform.

When they were all ready they went down to the dining room. As they went through the door they found themselves with about twenty more new recruits standing around, obviously all unsure as to what they should do. As the clock struck seven in strode the most imposing colossus of a man that Julius had ever seen. He was in full dress uniform that added to the effect, and within him one could sense an air of absolute honesty and duty, someone you would not want to cross swords with too often.

"Good evening gentleman, my name is Colonel Weber, I am sorry I was not here to greet you in person this afternoon, but I had duties elsewhere" His voice, though not loud, dominated the room, you could have heard a pin drop as he continued, "firstly I would like to welcome you to His Majesty's Imperial Army. Over the next six months at least I will be your commanding officer for your initial training period. I won't pretend the next few months will be easy, they won't, they will be damned hard. At times, perhaps many times, you will regret joining the army, you will want to give it all up, but let me tell all of you" and he scanned all the eager young faces in front of him "you are here to work hard, very hard, but in the end you will realize why we have worked you so hard. You will see that all the aches, pains, late night studies, tears, yes even tears, have all been

18

worth it, for then you will be officers in the greatest army in the world.

The man who will be overseeing your training period is Sergeant Major Hoffman, and I have asked him here tonight so that I might introduce him to you, Sergeant Major" A small bull of a man stepped forward, very neatly dressed and standing rigidly to attention. He saluted his senior officer, then turned to the cadets.

"Good evening, gentlemen, I hope we will all be working well together. I am here to mold you into the very best soldiers I can, and believe me I will, by whatever, and I mean *whatever*, means it takes. All I ask for is your total dedication, then I am sure we will succeed in making you exemplary soldiers for the Austro-Hungarian Army" with that he turned to his senior officer.

"Now, we have said our little sermons," continued Colonel Weber, "so let us enjoy ourselves this evening. You are lucky, your training should have started tomorrow morning, but, due to the Emperor's procession, your army life will not start until the day after tomorrow. Tomorrow morning you will all report to uniform stores to collect your uniforms, after that I have obtained special permission for you to go into the city to watch the procession. You will not be allowed to wear your uniforms for this as I will not be able to inspect you first. Obtain your pass outs from the sentry on the main door, and you will be back in the barracks by seven o'clock tomorrow night, dressed for dinner. I will have no excuses for tardiness, being new to the city is no excuse, do I make myself clear?" There was a murmur of assent from the assembled recruits.

"Do I make myself clear?" repeated Colonel Weber, in a louder voice.

"Yes, Sir" came the correct reply in unison.

"Good, I will be coming round to talk to you during the evening, so any questions you have to ask, please ask then. Lastly let me introduce Corporal Venner, while I and Sergeant Major Hoffman are away tomorrow, taking part in the procession, should you need anything then find Venner, and that will be so in the future" and from behind the colonel stepped a very thin, unprepossessing man, who looked even smaller than he really was beside his superior officers. The Colonel then dismissed Hoffman and Venner and they marched out of the mess door.

"Now, let us eat, be seated gentlemen"

19

Weber proceeded to the top table with various officers and the recruits were left to seat themselves. They all sat with their roommates, so Julius sat with Nikolas, Josef and Viktor. The room was filled with the hum of idle chatter until there was silence for grace which was said by Colonel Weber.

The food was good and as the meal progressed Julius began to chat with his other neighbors at the long tables. They were a very mixed bunch, mostly Czechs, Slovaks and Austrians, but from very varied backgrounds. Some came from military backgrounds, like himself and Nikolas. Some had professional backgrounds, like Viktor, whose father was a banker, and some from moneyed families, like Josef, who was the youngest son of a count, who evidently did not approve of his son's military career.

"So why did you join the army?" enquired somebody after Josef had recounted his story. Josef fingered the stem of his glass and appeared to be pondering his answer, then he looked up with his lazy hooded eyes and a ghost of a smile appeared on his face. "Why did I join the army? Well I thought of the one thing that would most annoy my father, that would send him into the biggest rage, that he would hate more than anything else, and this was it. You see I loathe my father and I think I rather did it to annoy him more than anything else, I just walked in one day and signed the papers and here I am"

The conversation stopped and everyone around him stared at Josef in disbelief. Obviously some were annoyed by his utterances, most of them had joined the army because of a great sense of patriotism for their Emperor and their country, and certainly did not like Josef's reasons for joining. Julius looked at his new roommate and wondered if Josef was teasing them. He struck Julius as the sort who liked to be the centre of attention, even if it meant being outrageous, but he wasn't so sure when he saw the look on Josef's face. He couldn't quite work it out, he was either a very good actor, or the look of hurt and despair on his handsome face was very real. Everybody by this time was looking very uncomfortable. Julius was afraid the situation was going to turn quite ugly when, to his relief, they noticed that Colonel Weber was approaching their table and they all stood to attention, Josef notably slower than the others.

After talking to the rest of the table the colonel turned to Julius, "Welcome, young Mayer, I taught your brother,

Franz, he is a good soldier, you have a lot to follow haven't you? but I'm sure you will not let me down. Saw your father today, says he will try to get to see you in the next couple of weeks. He is in the parade tomorrow, did you know?" Julius shook his head and he felt his face go redder and redder as the other boys stared at him at this show of familiarity by their senior officer. With that Weber walked off to another table and everybody resumed their seats.

"Well we all know who's going to get the top marks now don't we" somebody offered and some of the cadets smirked. Although Julius knew it was all harmless banter he wished at that moment he was the son of a lawyer with no older brothers.

As everybody climbed the stairs to retire Nikolas whispered in Julius' ear, "do you think Josef was serious down there?"

"I don't know" replied Julius in a low voice, "by the look on his face at the time I would say there was some vestige of truth in what he said"

"Well he seems very odd to me. What a strange reason for joining the army. Still, we must not judge a person on the first day, but I hope he lightens up a little. I am really glad we managed to room together, let's hope we can say the same about Josef" he added.

Julius lay in his bed that night reflecting on his first day in the army. He listened to all the unfamiliar sounds around him, so different from home. The banging of doors, the calls of the night sentries, the gentle snoring coming from Viktor in the opposite bed. He moved his head and watched Nikolas who was fast asleep. Even in sleep his new friend had an angelic smile on his face, like a contented child. As he sat up to turn off the gas lamp above his bed he could see Josef lying on his back. He was still awake, lying motionless, looking up at the ceiling, lost in his own thoughts. Now there *is* a strange one, Julius mused, he is a lot deeper than he would have us believe. No doubt we will find out what he's really like over the next few months, and with that thought Julius fell off into a heavy, dreamless sleep.

III

When reveille sounded at six o'clock the next morning, Julius woke with a start, trying to remember where he was. He looked around at his roommates as they tried to rouse themselves from their slumber. Smid came in beaming his wide smile, "Come on young gentlemen, let's be having you"

"What time of day do you call this?" groaned Josef.

"Time you were out of your bed, cadet" boomed a voice from the doorway and in strode Sergeant Major Hoffman, looking immaculate in his full dress uniform, even at that early hour of the morning. The boys all jumped out of their beds. "And, after today, if you are not out of bed as soon as you hear reveille you will be washing down the latrines, do I make myself clear?"

"Yes Sergeant Major" replied the boys together. Julius thought they must look a very strange lot all standing to attention in their pajamas.

"Good" replied Hoffman, "you are expected down for breakfast in half an hour, good day" the boys all breathed a large sigh of relief as he left the room.

Julius was eager to get to uniform stores to try on his uniform so they all washed quickly in the basins full of ice cold water in their rooms, dressed and proceeded downstairs for breakfast. Julius felt too excited to eat but forced himself to eat a Buchteln, a warmed jam filled doughnut and a cup of scalding hot Mokka coffee. Julius noticed that several of the new recruits were giving Josef a wide berth after the night before, but whether he noticed, or even cared, he didn't show it.

After breakfast they were told to assemble in one of the classrooms on the second floor where Corporal Venner supplied every cadet with a book of Army and Barrack Regulations. They were each given times to report for their uniform fittings then dismissed back to their rooms. As they were leaving Corporal Venner added "Gentlemen, just remember you are in His Majesty's Imperial Army now. You may not be in uniform when you go into the city today but you are expected to behave yourselves. No heavy drinking or high spirits please and remember you all have to be back here by seven this evening, dressed for dinner"

Julius and his roommates returned to their room where they started to make their beds and clean up the mess they had left when going down for breakfast. Smid appeared carrying their dress suits, all freshly pressed. "Do you ever sleep Smid?" asked Nikolas, "you must have been up for ages to have sorted those out already".

Smid grinned "Wanted to get these done so I can get off to see the procession. Well done, I'm glad to see you've tidied up, but in future that has to be done before you go down to breakfast. You'll find that's one of the rules in that book you've been given this morning. By the way, I suggest you read the book well, they'll test you on it by the end of the week" and with that he went out of the room, chuckling to himself.

"Do you think he's serious?" asked Viktor with a worried look on his face.

"Who knows" replied Josef, "but I suggest we make the most of today, it will probably be the last time we enjoy ourselves for a while. How about I show you country bumpkins around my city after the procession?"

Julius looked uncomfortably at Nikolas. They had already agreed to explore the city together and he wasn't sure he wanted Josef's company. Josef struck him as the sort of person who would always take over and want his own way. However he couldn't refuse the invitation without being rude. "Yes, why not" he replied, "you game Viktor?" he added as he wasn't sure that Viktor had been included in the invitation. With that settled they all set off for their uniform fitting.

Julius loved his uniform. He was supplied with a blue tunic that had pointed breast pockets, a stand up collar with yellow braiding and a shirt, whose collar had to show above his tunic collar. He was fitted with the red trousers of a cavalry officer with ordinary boots and military dress riding boots. The greatcoat, which reached down to his calves, was brown with a dark collar. He had a shako, a cylindrical military cap, embossed with the badge of the Emperor and also a black kepi, a flat-topped cap, to wear with his undress uniform. Also issued was an 1869 cavalry saber to wear on his left side. When all this was added to the various accessories that accompanied a military uniform, Julius had acquired an extensive new wardrobe.

As Julius had suspected Josef struck an impressive figure in his uniform, but he himself did not realize how perfectly his uniform suited him. Not one given to any vanity Julius was not aware of how handsome he was becoming. He had dark, brooding good looks, which were even more enhanced when a smile covered his face, which was often, for Julius was generally a happy, easygoing boy. Added to that he had a fine muscular figure that ideally suited the Imperial uniform. Even Josef had to remark "I am not going into the city with you Mayer when you have that uniform on, I won't get a look in with the girls with you about."

Julius reddened at the casual mention of girls but did not pursue the conversation.

At just before eleven Julius and his companions had positioned themselves on the famous Ringstrasse to await the Imperial procession. The Ringstrasse had been commissioned by the Emperor Franz Josef over fifty years before. It had at last been finished some twenty years ago and was now the political and artistic centre of Vienna. It housed some of the most beautiful buildings of the capital and today it seemed as if all of Vienna was thronging its streets. It was a wonderful sunny summer's day and there was a carnival atmosphere among the Viennese citizens. The Emperor was known to encourage these processions, he knew his people loved the pageantry and pomp of the occasion and they were good for the morale of the army.

At eleven o'clock there was the sound of a cannon salvo and the Imperial cavalcade came into view. Heading the procession was a bearer carrying the standard of the Austro-Hungarian Empire, the two headed eagle, the gold statue shining brightly in the sunshine. The crowds cheered and waved as their Emperor appeared.

Franz Josef rode on a magnificent gray horse. He was dressed in full military dress uniform and his breast was completely covered with a myriad of medals and decorations. Although not a large man and approaching his eightieth year, he sat up straight and dignified in his saddle and looked every inch the King and Emperor he was. His long reign had been one of turbulence and grief. There had been attempts on his own life, and in 1889 his son and heir, Prince Rudolf, had committed suicide at his hunting lodge at Mayerling. After her son's death the Empress Elisabeth spent less and less time in Vienna and in 1897 she had been assassinated in Switzerland.

24

Behind the Emperor rode four riders all attired in full military dress uniform. Julius strained to see if he could see the Archduke Franz Ferdinand, a man about whom he had heard a lot but had never seen. On the death of the Emperor's son, Archduke Charles Louis, the Emperor's brother, had become the heir to the throne but he had died in 1896, leaving his son, the Archduke Franz Ferdinand, as heir to the Habsburg dynasty. Franz Ferdinand was not a popular figure within the Empire. He was known as a brutal, overbearing man, and even to Julius, watching from the crowd, it was easy to see which rider was Franz Ferdinand. He rode with a pompous air about him, looking down on the populace with an arrogant and haughty disdain of his surroundings. Julius had often heard his father and brothers relate the shortcomings of the heir to the throne, especially his hostility to most countries within the Austro-Hungarian Empire, chiefly Hungary, Bohemia and Moravia and especially Serbia, plus an undiplomatic animosity towards Germany. Whilst all soldiers swore absolute allegiance to their Emperor Franz Josef, Julius knew his father worried about the accession of the Archduke.

The Emperor and his retinue passed by to loud acclaim from the crowd and then proceeded the various regiments of the Army. Not far behind the Emperor Julius spotted his father, impeccable in his uniform, riding by. Julius' beamed with pride at the sight of his father sporting his Habsburg beard and moustaches, looking very distinguished as he rode by. After last night's ribbing Julius didn't point out his father to Josef and Viktor, but proudly showed him to Nikolas, who at least understood his situation. Nikolas grinned, "Well, he is better looking than you, but I suppose that's not difficult."

The procession carried on for the next hour and when the last of the riders were out of view the crowds started to dissipate, off to enjoy their public holiday. Julius was already regretting his meager breakfast, and they all declared themselves ready for something to eat. It was decided to have an early lunch before the restaurants started to fill up with the citizens of Vienna. They argued about the best place to eat until Josef told them to follow him, he knew of somewhere perfect where they could eat. Julius and Nikolas met this statement with some skepticism but they had no alternative but to follow Josef who was already striding off down the street.

Julius' fears were confirmed when they turned down the Operngasse and stooped outside the Hotel Sacher. Julius only knew it by reputation, he had never been there, but it was known as a discreet location for the aristocracy and gentry of Vienna, certainly not a place for four young boys to consider frequenting. His mother would have died if she had known he was even thinking of entering its doors. Julius hesitated on the pavement.

"Come on you lot" beckoned Josef.

"How do you know we will get in there, we are a bit young you know" said Julius.

Josef laughed, "Oh we will get in all right, come on" and disappeared through the doors.

"Come on" said Nikolas, "if we don't like it we can always leave."

Julius didn't want them to think he was being churlish so he followed his friends in. They found themselves in a sumptuous foyer, richly furnished and lit by shining chandeliers. Josef was talking to an expensively dressed middle aged woman at the far end of the room. He beckoned them over.

"Anna, may I introduce Nikolas Manz, Julius Mayer and Viktor Leitner, gentlemen, Frau Anna Sacher, the proprietress of this establishment"

All the boys bowed in introduction and Julius noticed to his amazement that Frau Sacher was smoking a small cigar.

"Welcome to my hotel, gentlemen, I have a table waiting for you in my restaurant, though I hope in the future you will be back to sample all our other facilities" and she and Josef laughed together. Julius blushed at her implication but Nikolas and Viktor looked on in fascination at the alluring woman in front of them. She took a step towards Julius and stroked the side of his face. "Especially this one, Josef you may have a rival for female attentions. He may not be as pretty as you but he's definitely going to be all man" and she looked straight into Julius' eyes. If Julius had been red before he was sure he was now a dark shade of purple in his embarrassment. The other boys all laughed good-naturedly, although Josef obviously did not find the joke so funny.

The meal in the hotel was excellent. They all decided on Bauernschmaus, a plate of hot meats with Sauerkraut and dumplings and they finished it off with Sachertorte, a thick chocolate cake, which had first been prepared by Anna

Sacher's father-in-law, and was now a famous delicacy in Vienna. As they were drinking their coffee Viktor asked Josef, "so how do you know Frau Sacher? you seem to be on pretty intimate terms"

Josef leant back in his chair, "well I've been coming here for quite a few years. My father used to bring me here when I was quite young. When he disappeared upstairs for his fun and games with one of his mistresses, he would leave me to look after myself so Frau Sacher used to take pity on me and keep me company"

Another one of his stories wondered Julius who asked "Why would he bring you here, didn't he think that at some point you might tell your mother about his liaisons?"

"That is the thing about my father, you see, it is a question I have often asked myself. I have never quite worked out whether he brought me knowing I would tell my mother and therefore humiliate her even more than he has done in the past or to show me what a man of the world he was with all his various women. Basically he only cares about one person, and that is himself. He probably did not even think about why he brought me here, he just did it on a whim"

Poor Josef, thought Julius, fancy having a father like that. No wonder he is so cynical about the world.

"Did you ever tell your mother?" asked Viktor.

"No, I never did, even from a young age something told me not to tell her. Sometimes I wish I had told her, then she might have stood up to the bastard, but I think she always knew about him and chose to ignore it anyway. So, enough of my ramblings, everybody ready to explore the city?"

Julius, Nikolas and Viktor all dug into their pockets for their money in order to pay the bill, but Josef waved his hand in the air, "don't worry about that, the meal is with the compliments of my father, a welcome to Vienna for you"

"Are you sure?" said Viktor "we do not want to get you into trouble"

"My father has accounts all over Vienna, there has to be one advantage of having him as a father and this is it. Do not worry, I do this all the time and he never says a thing. Probably doesn't even realize, they send him the bills and he just pays without even looking at them. Stop looking so worried, honestly. Look, if he asks me to settle the bill at a later date you can pay me then, all right? but I promise you, he won't"

They still were not sure but as there seemed to be no more argument they thanked Josef and left their table. Julius did not like it but had to admit to himself some relief as he had worked out the bill would have taken a substantial amount of his monthly allowance.

"I'm beginning to see some advantages of having Josef around" grinned Nikolas as they walked out of the restaurant. As they left the hotel Frau Sacher was talking to a group of men, but halted her conversation to come over to them.

"I hope you enjoyed the hospitality of my hotel, gentlemen, be sure to come back as often as you like, especially when you have your uniforms. I love a man in uniform" and she winked at Julius. He had the feeling that she was teasing him so he developed a great interest in his shoes. They all said their farewells and went out onto the street.

"Where now?" said Nikolas, "We haven't got much time left"

"How about the Prater?" asked Josef.

Julius was relieved. He had been wondering where Josef would direct them next, but thought the idea of the Prater was an excellent one. The Prater was a large funfair in the northeast of the city. Julius had been there often with his family when they had visited Vienna. The funfair had sideshows and booths and there were beer gardens on the site, but best of all was the giant Ferris wheel in the park. It had only been built about ten years ago and whenever they went to the Prater he and Irmy had loved to ride on the wheel, going up into the air and pretend they were flying, they were so high up.

As it was quite a distance across the city they took a tram car, which were prevalent in Vienna. As it was a public holiday the carriages were packed and so was the Prater when they got there. Nikolas and Viktor were eager to try the famous Ferris wheel they had heard so much about. The line was very long, but eventually they were riding to the top with its magnificent views across Vienna. When the ride had finished they sauntered along the booths and watched some of the side-shows and travelling troupes of acrobats giving impromptu performances for a few coins in a proffered hat. They had some steins of beer and Viktor bought himself several sausages from the wurst stands. It was a marvel to watch Viktor, for he never stopped eating. The atmosphere was one of carnival and gaiety on a beautiful summer's day.

Julius had begun to understand why Josef had suggested the Prater. As they walked around he was eyeing the girls and flirting with them shamelessly. Many responded to his smiles and Julius marveled at his audacity, especially as most of them were with their elders.

Nikolas and Josef had decided to go for another ride on the wheel so Julius and Viktor sat on the grass by the ride to await their return. After his meal and several beers Julius felt drowsy in the hot afternoon sun and was drifting off to sleep when he realized that Viktor was talking to him.

"Sorry, did you say something, I was nearly dropping off there"

"No, nothing important, you go back to sleep" replied Viktor.

"No, I am awake now, what is it?" and he hauled himself up into a sitting position.

"I just wondered, you are from a military background, what makes a good soldier?"

Julius thought about this for a while before replying, "I really don't know. I suppose dedication, loyalty, courage, all of them, maybe none of them, I really could not say, why do you ask?"

"I just hope I'm going to be good enough, that I'm capable of making the grade. I really want to do well, not just for myself, but for my family as well. My father was not too enthusiastic about my joining the army, he wanted me to join him and my elder brother in the family banking business, but I always yearned for a military career. Besides, my brother has always been the intelligent one and I did not want to face having to live in his shadow for the rest of my life. I just hope I have made the right decision. I mean there is you and Nikolas, you already have a military bearing, you have been surrounded by it all your lives. Then there is Josef who has enough confidence for a whole regiment, but seems not to care much anyway and then there is me who wants to succeed so much, but I do not know if I can"

Julius thought of his reply carefully. "Viktor, just because Nikolas and I come from military backgrounds does not mean we are going to be better soldiers than you. We may have a head start in some departments, but you do not strike me as stupid. You will catch up quickly enough. As for Josef, all the confidence in the world does not make a good soldier. I asked my father once what sort of men made the

29

best soldiers, in his opinion. His answer was 'the ones that fight with their hearts, you can have the best brain in the land, but if you do not fight with your heart, you have lost already'. I think if you stick to that, you will make a pretty good soldier"

"Thank you, Julius. Your father sounds like a fine man"

"He is" replied Julius, "and remember if you ever get stuck with something, and you think we can help, Nikolas and I are always there for you. Now, I know what will cheer you up, how about another wurst?"

As they left the Prater Julius looked back at the packed fair, still busy even in the late afternoon. It had been a wonderful day, one he would remember and cherish for a very long time.

They started to run to catch the tram at the end of the street, rushing to get back in time for dinner. Tomorrow he and his new friends would start their training in earnest, the start of his new life as a soldier in His Majesty's Imperial Army.

IV

Julius had never worked so hard, or felt so weary, during those first few weeks of training. Every day was so full he didn't know if he was coming or going. There was classroom work, endless books to read and learn, numerous tests that left his head swimming. They would look back in history at various battles and would be asked why a certain general had decided this, or why had a division advanced at that time. Julius had to learn how to wear and maintain his own uniform, clean and protect the various firearms he would use. He had to master riding a horse with precision in a march, something he practiced until, although used to riding, his inner thighs bled with the hours spent in the saddle. They had to understand how to send signals and communicate with other regiments. Everything was drummed into him until he thought his head would burst with so many new things to learn.

Then there was the physical side. Every morning, straight after breakfast, he was on the courtyard doing exercises to start the day, exercises that had his chest screaming for air and feeling sick. On other days they were taken out into the countryside and had to run for miles on rough terrain, sometimes with full packs on their backs. As the weather got colder they were made to run through several ice-cold streams until Julius felt he would never be able to feel his nether regions again. In the middle of marching drills they would suddenly be given a command and they would have to drop to the floor and do numerous press ups until Julius thought he would pass out.

Most nights Julius and his friends would crawl up the stairs to their beds, with no energy to even complain, fall straight off to sleep, to be woken, in what seemed to be only minutes later, by reveille. Julius had never thought he could feel as tired as he did then. He was doing quite well in his schoolwork, but the physical side worried him. However, as the months went on he realized, along with the others, that physically he was getting much stronger and the constant exercise did become easier.

His one enjoyment at that time were the letters from his mother and Irmy. Irmy especially wrote lively and interesting letters. Julius was ashamed to admit to himself that his letters back to her in those first few months must have been a great disappointment as he just could not summon up the energy to write more than a few scribbled lines in reply.

One letter made him smile. Irmy opened with her usual gossip about their friends in Kosice then she added, 'Danusia has been acting very strangely lately, she kept bursting into tears and would not tell Mama or I what the problem was. Mama and I contrived to waylay her one afternoon and get the truth out of her. Well, after a lot of weeping and wailing it seems that now you are gone into the army and I am growing up Danusia thinks that Mama has no further need for her and that she will send her away! I have to confess I had to hide a little smile behind my hand, Julius, because I would have liked to have pointed out to Danusia that none of us have needed a nanny for at least the last five years at least, so why the worry now? but of course I did not. Anyway, Mama managed to calm her down and persuade her that she was not going to send her away and how could she possibly survive without Danusia's company now that all her sons had left home? Unfortunately for Mama the result of this is that since then Danusia has relished her new role of 'companion' to Mama and is constantly hovering over Mama to see to her every whim! I think Mama is at the end of her tether, she now spends most of her day trying to find things to occupy Danusia.

I have to tell you that this has been a blessing for me too. You see Mama is so glad to have some peace and quiet occasionally that she now sends Danusia to the hospital with me, instead of accompanying me herself. This is wonderful as I now go where I like, helping wherever I want to, as Danusia is unaware that Mama would only let me go into certain wards. I am truly happy!

I know you are going to tell me off for using Danusia in this way, but I do not think it harms anyone and I am really gaining a lot of experience at the hospital.

I will end now, your friend Nikolas seems especially nice and I don't mind your terrible little letters. Do you remember the ones Franz sent when he was first in Vienna? they were worse than yours. Just as long as you write longer ones when your initial training is over. Will you stay in Vienna or go somewhere else? Did you know Franz is in Graz now? So many questions, I am sorry, your affectionate sister, Irmy.

Julius smiled as he reread his sister's letter. He had needed it that day as it had probably been the worst day since his arrival into the army.

At breakfast Sergeant Major Hoffman had informed them that they were to have a new sergeant for marching drills. This was probably the most unpopular lesson for all the cadets. Walking up and down the cobbled courtyard for hours on end, being shouted at and moaned at constantly was not anybody's idea of fun. So imagine Julius and Nikolas' consternation on arriving at the parade ground to be confronted with the ogre they had met on their first day. As they stood to attention they desperately hoped that he would not remember them, but as the sergeant walked down the ranks inspecting his new trainees he stopped in front of Julius and Nikolas.

"Well, well, well, what have we here, the shit shovelers" there were sounds of stifled laughter from the other cadets standing in line.

"Nice to see you again, I've got a good memory, don't you think?"

Julius and Nikolas stared straight ahead, hardly daring to breathe, "well we will see today if you are any good won't we?" and with that he sauntered off down the line, commenting on uniforms and the condition of guns and swords as he went. Julius noticed that he didn't have a good word to say to anybody. When he had finished his inspection he introduced himself as Sergeant Brunner, and ordered the men to get into lines to begin marching drill.

Julius had never known such a hard taskmaster as Sergeant Brunner. He had them marching endlessly up and down for most of the day until Julius thought he would never be able to get his boots off that night as his feet were so swollen. He introduced complex marching routines that were impossible to master easily, and as soon as the cadets thought they had managed it, he would change the marching pattern, to audible groans from the recruits. He picked on every cadet, whether they were good or bad, but worst of all he had obviously decided that Viktor was to be his victim for that day.

Viktor was the first one to admit that marching drills were not his forte. Whilst Julius was used to marching, as it had been an everyday activity at his school, and managed it quite well, Viktor had never been able to quite master the skill of the patterns of the drill. It had become a joke

33

amongst his roommates who all said they couldn't wait to see him on a dance floor and watch how many toes he trod on. But today none of them thought it a joke as Sergeant Brunner mercilessly bullied Viktor, who became steadily worse through the day the more he was harassed. When eventually they were dismissed at the end of a very long day they dragged themselves up to their room, too tired to even wash and think about going down to dinner. Viktor was unusually quiet, which worried Julius. Of the four of them it was Viktor who always kept their spirits up, who made them laugh with his irrepressible sense of humor.

"You are not going to let that old bastard get to you, are you?" asked Nikolas.

"You heard what he said. I was useless, not fit to wear his Majesty's uniform, and the trouble is he was right, I was terrible out there today"

"Did you ever stop to think that Brunner might have something to do with that?" asked Josef, lying on his bed, his eyes closed.

"What do you mean?"

"Well, I admit you are not the best I've ever seen, but you're not that bad. No worse than most of us out there, but you were bad today because Brunner made you terrified and put you off, no other reason"

"Fine, so I'm scared of him, how is that going to help me?"

Josef opened his eyes and raised himself up onto his elbows, "don't let him intimidate you, that is what he wants, that is what he revels in; he enjoys seeing you get upset. Stand up to him, once he sees you are not scared of him he will leave you alone"

"That is easy for you to say, but in case you haven't noticed I am not endowed with your obvious sense of superiority or your smug confidence"

Julius sensed an argument brewing, but Josef just smiled condescendingly and fell back onto the bed and closed his eyes.

Trying to diffuse the situation Julius added, "look Viktor, to a certain extent Josef is right. A man like Brunner thrives on people's insecurities, in plain language, he is a bully. You must try and not let him get to you or every time we have drills you will get worse, not better. When Nikolas and I first had a run in with him, I remember Nikolas saying he would get the bastard back when he was his superior officer and that is how you have to think. Just imagine, one day you will be his superior, then you will have the upper hand"

At last a smile spread over Viktor's face, "I like that idea, I like it a lot. Maybe you are right. I am sorry Josef, I am just tired after today" Josef raised his arm in salute as he lay as though asleep on his bed.

"What do you think Nikolas, shall we send Brunner to thirty days solitary confinement when we are both generals?" asked Viktor as he turned round to look at Nikolas who lay collapsed and disheveled in an untidy heap on his bed. He was gently snoring, still with a smile on his face. Viktor looked at Julius and grinned his thanks and both of them lay down on their beds to succumb to an exhausted sleep.

Brunner did not cease his persecution of Viktor in the next few weeks, but Viktor seemed to cope with him better. When they had any spare time Nikolas and Julius would try to help him learn the marching patterns in their room, which helped. At these times Josef would lie on his bed commenting and criticizing. A few times Julius noticed Viktor's clenched fists by his sides, but by now the three were used to Josef's indolent ways and accepted them. In fact, although Josef was never to endear himself to the other recruits, in his own way he showed himself to be loyal and generous and the four boys very quickly became firm friends.

The only misgivings Julius had after joining the army were religious ones. Every Sunday soldiers were allowed to go to church to attend Mass. On his first Sunday Julius jumped out of bed to attend the service. "Come on you lot" he called to the others, "time to get up"

Josef opened one sleepy eye and muttered, "Sorry old boy, only go on Saints Days, Easter and Christmas, now leave me to sleep" and he pulled the covers over his head.

Julius looked at his two other companions. "Same here" grunted Viktor, "not very religious family, I'm afraid".

Julius turned hopefully to Nikolas, "sorry" he said, "but as my dear Mama is not here to watch over me I think I would prefer my first lie in for a long time" Nikolas was right, if you did not attend church you were allowed to lie in.

Julius did not know what to do; he would have dearly liked to have stayed with his friends but he knew his conscience would not allow it, so off he went to Mass. When he came back he found them all still in bed debating whether to rise or not.

"Enjoy yourself Julius?" asked Josef, "going to be accepted into the kingdom of Heaven now, while we all burn in hell!" Julius threw a pillow at him and no more was said on the subject.

By the third Sunday Julius could stand the temptation no longer and remained in his nice warm bed long after the bells for Mass were rung. I will go next week, he thought to himself, I will just allow myself one lie in and then I will go to confession.

Although full of good intentions Julius did not go to Mass for some weeks, and when, after about six weeks of being in the barracks, he was given special permission to go and have dinner with his father, his conscience was in turmoil. He dreaded his father bringing up the subject, as he knew he could not lie to him.

He met his father in his quarters expecting to eat with him in the Mess. He was pleased to see his father, he had not seen him for many months. When his father explained that he had booked a table at a local restaurant for them he was even happier as it meant they would be completely on their own for the first time in many a year.

Julius felt very proud walking into the restaurant with his father, the two in army uniform striking a handsome picture together. It was a restaurant that Julius had been to before with his family when he had been on holiday in Vienna and the maitre d' obviously knew his father well.

"Colonel Mayer, how nice to see you again, your table is ready for you" he peered at Julius, "do not tell me, not another handsome son in uniform, you must be very proud" and with a flourish of his hand he led Julius and his father to their table. As they passed through the crowded restaurant Colonel Mayer acknowledged some acquaintances, among them several ladies. Julius began to wonder about his father, so often alone for long periods of time here in Vienna. Was he like Josef's father? he had never thought of the possibility before. He shrugged off the unpleasant feeling as being overly imaginative and sensibly put this down to hearing of Josef's family exploits. Not everybody acted like that, and he decided his father did not, and if he was honest with himself, he did not want to know about it, even if he did.

Colonel Mayer jolted Julius out of his reverie, "Julius, are you here at all? I know you are worked particularly hard in your first few months of training but I did not think you would be falling asleep before we have even ordered the meal"

"Sorry, father, I was miles away" replied Julius, and, to change the subject, asked his father if he had any news of his family. After Colonel Mayer had told Julius of all the contents of the various letters he had received he started to talk about Karl's engagement.

"Well your mother seems pleased about it, but I am not so sure. I think your brother is too young, but his mind seems made up and, as he has his colonel's permission, they are to be married in Linz next spring. Your mother is determined to go with Irmy, and I will go, if I can get leave. Mind you I do not know how he is going to support a wife on a lieutenant's pay, at least I was a captain when I married your mother"

As he picked up his menu the Colonel reached inside his pocket and pulled out a pair of spectacles and placed them on his nose as he started to read. Julius stared with an open mouth. His father looked up at him, "what are you staring at Julius, never seen a pair of spectacles before? I only need them for reading, anything wrong in that?"

As he had never seen his father in a pair of spectacles they appeared somewhat comical to Julius and it occurred to him that his father was not getting any younger. He realized it had probably dawned on his father too, by the brusque manner in which he had spoken to him. Julius did not know how old his father was. Karl was twenty-two now, and he knew his father had not been young when he had married his mother. To Julius, his father had never changed over the years, but that evening he noticed how tired he looked, almost unwell.

"Are you all right father? you seem out of sorts"

Colonel Mayer looked up from his menu at his son, "I am well Julius, maybe it is having to wear spectacles, or maybe it is the realization that my body does not respond quite as easily as it used to. I suppose it comes to us all, and though you are young and carefree now, it will even come to you. The reality of becoming old, it is not a good feeling, believe me"

Julius frowned, "are you sure that is all?"

"There are other things. Things that I cannot talk about, I am sure you will understand. Army worries, but nothing that will affect you. Enjoy yourself while you are carefree

Julius, because all too soon you will have to grow up and take on all the responsibilities that goes with that."

Julius was troubled by his father's despondency but knew better than to pursue the conversation so he began to tell his father about his new roommates. His tales of his training exploits cheered up his father, especially hearing about Sergeant Brunner.

"Did you know he taught Karl? no, well it is just as well he has not worked out that you are his brother, because they did not get on well at all, very much like the experiences of your friend Viktor. Mind you if you were to ask Karl today he would tell you that Sergeant Brunner was one of the best teachers that ever had. His methods may be unkind but he has good results from them, maybe you should tell Viktor that, it might help"

When Julius mentioned Josef Colonel Mayer sat up in his seat with narrowed eyes. "von Kutz you say? not any relation to Count von Kutz I hope" when Julius replied in the affirmative and related the story of Josef and his family his father continued, "well I hope he is better than his father. Frightful man who thinks that his money can buy him anything. I hear he always has a different young woman on his arm. I should think he hates the idea of his son in the army. I do not really know the story but it is rumored that the Count was in the army but only for a short time when he was dismissed under a cloud. There was some sort of scandal that was hushed up pretty quickly by his family. Now he will not have anything to do with the military and pointedly ignores any of us socially"

With his interest aroused Julius tried to push his father further but his father would not be pressed and ended by saying that as he did not know all the pertinent details he would do well to keep quiet about it, for his friend's sake.

They finished their meal amiably enough, talking about this and that. It was while they were drinking their schwarzer coffees and brandy that Julius' father asked the dreaded question, "and have you been going to Mass, Julius?" Julius stared down into his coffee that he was stirring vigorously. He felt his face redden, but when he looked up at his father he found a large grin on his face and a mischievous twinkle in his eye.

"What is so funny, father?" asked Julius.

"Julius, Julius, I have sat opposite each of my three sons and asked them the same question and each time they have found something on the table that is very interesting to look at whilst they turn bright red, and you are no exception. Let us understand each other completely, my son. I appreciate your reluctance to disobey your mother, but I also accept that you are now on your own, a young man starting his army life. There are few such men who find going regularly to Church as the priority of their life. This I understand, but your mother would not. All I ask of you is that you keep the fact that you do not go to Mass regularly from your mother, it would upset her too much. You will still be going with your regiment on occasions, and on holidays and saints days, and what your mother does not know will not hurt her"

"Are you not annoyed with me father?"

"Son, I realized a long time ago that I was not as religious as your mother. It does not mean I am not religious at all, I am. I believe in God, I just do not believe that I have to go to church regularly to talk to him. It also does not mean that when I am troubled or confused that I do not go to Church, or ask my priest to hear my confession, because I do. All I ask is that you are the same. Never lose your faith, it will give you strength and guidance when nothing else can and I would also ask when you go home to Kosice that you attend Mass regularly there. Are we in agreement?"

Julius was amazed at how candid and honest his father had been with him and he was proud to think his father could talk to him in this manner, it made him feel very grown up.

"Yes father, agreed. I will not let you down and I will remember what you have said"

Julius felt a great weight had been lifted from his shoulders as though the sharing of his guilt had somehow alleviated it.

Julius returned to his barracks in high spirits that evening and marveled that he could feel even more respect for his beloved father than he had done before.

V

The first six months of initial training went very quickly, before he knew it Julius was getting ready to go home for his Christmas leave. He was looking forward to seeing his mother and Irmy. Franz had managed to obtain leave as well and it would be good to see him again.

One afternoon, in December, he returned from a shopping trip into the city where he had obtained several Christmas presents for his family. He pushed open the door with his foot and deposited his parcels onto his bed. Looking round he found that Josef was sitting writing at the table. "Josef, I did not see you there, where is everybody?"

Josef looked up from his papers, "Nikolas and Viktor were invited out by the cadets in room ten; they have gone off into town somewhere. They left the address on your pillow, in case you wanted to join them"

"So why did you not go with them?" asked Julius.

A cynical smile crossed Josef's face, "I had the impression that I was not included in the invitation, I am not the most popular boy in the class you know" Julius started to protest at this but Josef silenced him "do not be hypocritical Julius, I hope you of all people will be honest with me. I know I am not liked here, the trouble is I am not sure if I really care, which is probably worse. I think I do have some of my father in me after all. Now, let us change the subject, did you get all your presents?" Julius began to show Josef some of his shopping.

"Do you know what I shall be doing this Christmas, Julius. I will be sitting with my mother, bored to death, staring at the four walls of my home"

"What about your family, don't you all meet at Christmas?"

"Good Lord, no. Both my elder brothers are married and prefer to stay with their families and I cannot say I blame them. My father might grace us with his presence to go to church. He likes to be seen as the good family man, but after that he will be off to see one of his mistresses, leaving mother and I trying to make polite conversation all day, but ignoring the fact that he is not there"

Poor Josef, thought Julius, he does seem to be a very lonely person, what a life he has, beneath all his bravado he is like a confused little boy. Julius was amazed to hear himself say, "look, would you like to spend Christmas with my family,

40

you would be very welcome" and immediately after saying it, regretted offering the invitation. Much as he felt sorry for Josef he was not sure he would fit in with his family, he would probably think they were beneath him, Josef could be very superior at times. Josef looked at Julius and an enormous smile spread across his face. The effect of the smile completely changed him, it occurred to Julius that it was the first time he had seen a genuine smile on Josef's face since he had met him.

"I know you regret asking me already Julius, but I would just like to say that I think that is the nicest thing anyone has said to me, and although, thankfully for you, I will have to decline your kind invitation, much as I would like to spend Christmas with you, I appreciate you asking me. I will never forget the kindness you have shown me today, never"

Julius felt embarrassed by this little speech and felt obliged to add, "are you sure you won't come?"

"Yes, I am sure, I always think my one saving grace is that I do love my mother and I would not leave her to spend Christmas on her own. It would break her heart, especially as I do not know when I will get another Christmas leave in the future"

With that settled Julius tried to persuade Josef to come with him to join Nikolas and Viktor but he declined, adding sarcastically "I am not up to dining with country bumpkins tonight" That is the trouble with Josef, thought Julius, as he made his way out of the barracks and into the city, he always has to have the last word on everything.

A week later, the four boys were sitting round the table in their room trying to study. They were discussing a Napoleonic battle and were arguing about the validity of certain tactics used during the engagement when Viktor said, "I know this is changing the subject somewhat but what do you think about buying Smid a Christmas present. I mean, he looks after all of us pretty well and I thought it would show him how much we appreciate all his hard work"

"What a good idea" replied Nikolas, "but what do we buy him. I haven't a clue as to his likes and dislikes, plus I have to say my allowance is pretty low at the moment, having bought all my Christmas presents"

"God, yes, that's true" said Julius, "but I think we should get him something, even if it has to be something small. Has anyone any suggestions?"

"Fairy dust?" suggested Nikolas and they all groaned. The jokes about Smid were never ending between them.

"Tell you what," said Josef, "I have permission to go into the city tomorrow, shall I get something for Smid while I am there?"

"Well yes, but what?" ventured Viktor.

"Leave it to me" said Josef, and seeing the skeptical looks on their faces he added, "I promise I will not bankrupt you, and I will try to find something that Smid would appreciate, trust me"

As the other boys had little choice they agreed to Josef getting Smid's present, though they all had reservations as to the suitability of Josef buying it.

The next afternoon Julius, Nikolas and Viktor returned to their room after a particularly grueling lesson with the Horse Master. They had had to ride without a saddle as this was supposed to increase the bond between man and horse by using their bodies to command the beast. Julius enjoyed the lesson tremendously although he could feel the soreness of his inner thighs as he climbed the stairs and knew he would still be feeling the pain tomorrow. As they entered the room the boys found Josef lying on his bed, reading.

"You smell like you have had a good day, I do hope you are all allowed a bath tonight"

The boys gingerly tried to pull off their riding boots.

"Any luck with Smid's present?" asked Viktor, "I think we will need something to humor him when he smells this room"

Josef pointed to a parcel on the table. "There it is, tell me what you think"

The boys limped over to the table and were dismayed to see it was printed with the name Knize, a well-known and very expensive tailoring shop that supplied clothes and accessories, mainly to the aristocrats at the Imperial Court. Nikolas unwrapped the parcel carefully and found an exquisite green and tan tooled leather case that, when opened, revealed a lining of velvety soft kid leather. Placed into pockets of the leather was a pair of beautiful silver backed hair brushes, a silver comb, a silver shaving brush and a pair of silver nail clippers. The three boys looked in wonder at the handsome present and then turned to Josef.

"It is wonderful Josef, but this would probably cost us a years income, we cannot possibly afford it" said Viktor.

"Now how did I know you were going to say that? I think old Smid will be very pleased with that, and I think he is worth it. I know you are going to complain but I bought it on good old Papa's account, he honestly won't even notice it on his bill. I am sure he will not mind when he knows it is being given to such a worthy fellow, a man who has looked after his beloved son so well"

His sarcasm was not lost on the boys and they knew that whenever they were out with Josef and he had put things on his father's bill that the Count had not contacted Josef for any recompense.

"Very well, we accept," said Nikolas "but if your father does ask you to settle the bill, you are to tell us so we can give you our share"

"He won't, and if he did we could not possibly repay him," laughed Josef.

The boys decided to give Smid his present the morning of the day they were to be dismissed for their leave. They were up early packing their bags, eager to be off as they had been given permission to leave the barracks at noon. After breakfast they were to assemble in the second floor classroom in order to receive their first six monthly reports and to find out if they had passed all their exams in order to stay on for further training. It was an anxious time for everybody. Viktor especially was very nervous.

"I know I have failed" he lamented, "I know I have"

"Stop worrying," countered Josef, "you will be fine, if anybody should be worrying, it is me" but you won't be, thought Julius, and that is the difference.

Nikolas had gone to find Smid to ask him to come to their room on some pretext or other, and presently they appeared, Smid moaning at Nikolas about his incapability of finding anything for himself. Smid stopped short as he entered the room to be confronted by Julius, Viktor and Josef lined up behind the table with big grins on their faces.

"What are you up to, gentlemen, you look very pleased with yourselves"

Viktor had been nominated their spokesman, so he stepped forward, "Smid, we all know you have to put up with a lot from us, and at times you think we do not appreciate all your work on our behalf, but we would like you to accept this festive present from all of us to say thank you and we do not know what we would do without you"

Throughout this speech Smid had been going redder and redder in the face. Now he looked at the boys and said in a very husky voice, "well, sirs, I don't really know if I am allowed to accept a gift from you, after all I am only carrying out my duties for the Imperial Army"

Nikolas raised his eyes to the ceiling and said, "So let us call it a gift for services *beyond* the call of duty, Smid, you deserve it"

Smid approached the table and proceeded to unwrap the parcel. When the tissue paper came away he gasped at the beautiful object in front of him and his hands were trembling as he opened it up to reveal its contents. "Oh no sirs, I cannot possibly accept this, this is too good for me" and he left the case lying on the table, but remained staring down at it. Julius felt his embarrassment on receiving such a gift and motioned behind his back for the others to leave the room. They all quietly left the room with Julius saying, "please take it Smid, we would be honored if you accepted it with the same spirit in which it was bought for you" as he turned back to look into the room Julius saw Smid holding the case and caressing it as though it were a precious baby and was startled to see tears running down the little man's face.

Julius' uneasiness left him as he sat down to breakfast and thought about the morning in front of him. He was confident enough in his own abilities to assume that he would pass this part of his training. He knew he had done fairly well in his exams and he had progressed enormously with his physical training over the last six months. He was also optimistic about his friends. Nikolas had proved to be a natural soldier, Viktor would get through by sheer hard work, and Josef would probably scrape through even though he had hardly tried. Julius could not imagine what he could achieve if he put his mind to it.

He knew some would not survive the initial training, it was very rare that all cadets were successful in their first six months. Julius remembered his brothers relating the awful stories of cadets who found that their career with the Imperial Army was over after the arduous months that they had endured. He had made many friends amongst the cadets and hoped none of them would fail.

To take his mind off his gloomy thoughts he looked forward to his leave. He had found out that Nikolas had to stay a night in Kosice on his way home as, by the time their

44

train reached the city, there would not be a connecting train to Presov until the next afternoon. He was amazed to learn that his friend was contemplating staying in a hotel that night. Julius had informed him that he would do no such thing, but would stay the night with his family, who would love to meet him. He had written to Mama to ask her if Nikolas could stay and she had replied she would not hear of him doing anything else. She and Irmy could not wait to meet Julius' new friend of whom they had heard so much. So it was all agreed and Julius was looking forward to taking Nikolas home to meet his family. The only sad thing was that Franz was not due to arrive until after Nikolas had gone home as he was sure the two of them would have taken to each other famously.

Everybody was reluctant to rush to the classroom that morning, but eventually they were all assembled and they stood to attention as Colonel Weber, Sergeant Major Hoffman and Corporal Venner entered the room. Colonel Weber began with a stirring speech about their commitment over the last six months. It went over Julius' head, all he wanted was for his senior officer to get on with it and let him know his fate and that of his friends.

After what seemed an age Colonel Weber concluded, "Sergeant Major Hoffman will now read out a list of cadets who will go on for further training. If your name is not read out I would like to see you in my office as soon as you are dismissed. To the successful cadets I would like to congratulate you all, you are now Sons of the Eagle and you can be very proud, but do not become too complacent, this is just the beginning. When you come back from your leave it will be to work even harder so do not think you can drop your standards just because you have got through these initial stages. I hope you all have an enjoyable Christmas leave and we will see you in the New Year" with that he saluted the cadets and marched out of the room.

As Hoffman began to read the list Julius felt his mouth go dry and his stomach began to turn somersaults. He did not feel very confident now and he closed his eyes to try and concentrate on hearing his name. When he did hear his name he experienced a tremendous sense of relief. He had a huge smile on his face that he could not get rid of, even as he noticed two or three cadets with their heads down, who were close to tears. He looked across at his friends and realized that in his excitement he had not listened for their names and therefore did not know their fates. He was reassured when he saw they all wore smiles on their faces, and even Josef looked pleased with himself. Julius looked at the unsuccessful cadets and his heart went out to them. Now he understood when his brothers had mentioned the awful way the results were announced; it was an appalling way to learn your fate, in full view of your classmates. The unsuccessful cadets left the room, their heads down, while everybody else congratulated each other and shook hands. Some were even seen to shake hands with Josef in their excitement.

"This is definitely something we will have to celebrate when we come back after Christmas" said Josef, "what do you think?"

Everybody agreed and they all adjourned to their rooms to collect their bags and begin their journeys home. They said goodbye to Josef in their room as he only lived a half hour walk from the barracks. As they were leaving Smid entered the room. He looked a little embarrassed but managed to say, "I know you might think me rude, but I was lost for words back there. I would just like to say that I accept your gift with grateful thanks and was deeply touched by it" and then added with his impish smile, "but don't think I'm going to let you get away with being untidy in your room, because you can think again!"

"Well said Smid" said Viktor, "we are glad you liked it and we really are grateful for everything you do for us, and no further word will be said on this, is that all right?"

"Fine" replied Smid, "now you young sirs had better be off or you will miss your trains, merry Christmas to you all"

Julius, Nikolas and Viktor travelled together to the station, Viktor to catch his train to Salzburg, Julius and Nikolas to Kosice. With a shake of hands they parted to find their platforms, and Julius and Nikolas were soon settled into their carriage, looking forward to going home.

As Julius had anticipated his mother and Irmy took to Nikolas straight away. He had never found anybody who did not like his friend. On their journey to Kosice Julius had remarked to Nikolas that with all the excitement he had not even found out where or how Smid was to spend his Christmas leave. Nikolas had replied that Smid was going to see his married sister and various nieces and nephews at their home in Styria. This was so typical of Nikolas, who always took the trouble to find out about people, to show he was interested in them. Even when his excited mother bombarded Nikolas with many questions about their life in Vienna that left Julius cringing with embarrassment, he replied to them all with a patience and tact that Julius knew he himself did not possess. Irmy obviously enjoyed Nikolas' company and he had a feeling that Irmy rather dazzled his young friend as he became tongue-tied when talking to her. Julius was sure he could see his friend blushing every time she turned to converse with him.

Danusia had decided to cry into her apron as soon as Julius had walked through the door. He could not believe it, when, after enveloping him with one of her enormous hugs, she proceeded to embrace Nikolas as well, calling him Julius' 'little' friend. Nikolas of course laughed this off with his usual good humor and endeared himself to Danusia by telling her that he felt he knew her already as Julius spoke about her so often. This was of course not strictly true and Julius raised his eyes to heaven as his friend looked at him over Danusia's shoulder. He was also thanking God that Josef had not accepted his invitation, think how *he* might have endured Danusia's reception!

The evening passed very pleasantly, Frau Mayer's cook had excelled herself. The food was all the more wonderful after months of mess food, which though good, could not touch home cooking. After the ladies had retired Julius and Nikolas enjoyed a late night brandy in front of the fire that was burning in the parlor. They began talking about their fellow roommates. Viktor, it was agreed, was an affable chap, but it was very easy to tease him, something that Julius and Nikolas did often, especially when Julius and Nikolas spoke in Czech or Slovak to each other. Viktor and Josef both made it very clear that they disliked this practice and thought it very underhand which made the two boys speak it even more. Whilst the language in the barracks was German they found it easy to talk in private to each other in Czech, a language which Viktor and Josef could not understand. Julius and Nikolas were almost reduced to tears as they laughed about the time when Viktor had been really irate as Nikolas had continually talked in Czech. He believed that something was being hidden from him. Little did he know that Nikolas was just reciting an old Czech nursery rhyme to vex him. Josef was more complex, a strange fellow who, even after they had lived with him for six months, was still a very closed book.

As Julius poured another brandy, Nikolas said "I think this will be my last Christmas in Presov. My father wants my mother and brother to move to Prague. He is permanently stationed there now and feels he has seen little of my brother growing up and the move would rectify that"

"How do you feel about your family moving?" enquired Julius.

"Oh, I do not feel it has much to do with me any more, now I have joined the army. Besides, as you know, being an army family makes you feel as if you really do not have roots of any kind. Although we have lived in Presov for some years it is not where my parents came from originally, indeed, I should think my father has been longer at his postings than the time he has been in Presov"

Julius stared into the dancing flames of the fire and reflected how true this was. Although Kosice had been his birthplace, he did not regard it with any great feeling. Perhaps, as Nikolas had said, it was because it had never been a complete home with his father away so much. He reflected that this was probably the fate of every army family. Since moving to Vienna he had begun to consider himself to be more Austrian than anything else, probably because he had been brought up by Austrian parents. He thought of Karl and his approaching nuptials and wondered if Karl and his wife would follow the same path as his mother and father before him. Julius reflected that although he had had a wonderful childhood and had extraordinary parents it was not a path that he himself was willing to follow.

The two boys sat in companionable silence for a little while longer and then decided that it was time to retire. Julius could not resist teasing his friend about his sister as they climbed the stairs to bed and was delighted to see the back of Nikolas' neck turn a startling shade of red as he entered his room.

After lunch the next day Julius went with Nikolas to the station. He saw Nikolas into his carriage and with a farewell wave, started to walk down the platform towards the main exit. As he walked through the archway he thought he heard his name and turned round. He was delighted to see, through the mists of departing steam engines, his brother Franz walking towards him. Julius ran back to greet him and the two brothers embraced in welcome. "What are you

48

doing here?" asked Julius, "you are not expected until tomorrow"

"I was lucky and managed to get leave a day earlier, so here I am. What are you doing here? you could not have known of my changed plans"

Julius explained that he had been seeing his friend off to Presov and the brothers walked home discussing all the various news of the moment. Julius was pleased to see that Franz had the same embarrassing greeting from Danusia, whilst Mama and Irmy rushed around getting Franz's room ready for his early arrival.

The next day was Christmas Eve and the family participated in the usual Christmas Eve dinner and the opening of presents in the evening. Everybody was delighted with Julius' presents from Vienna and he was pleased he had taken so much time in choosing them. From his parents he received a beautiful pair of pearl cufflinks set in rose gold.

"Mama, they are wonderful" enthused Julius as he kissed his mother.

"You know your father and I always buy our sons a special present for passing their exams at the end of their initial training. Your father was so confident of your passing that he, Irmy and I chose them when he was last here on leave. Well done Julius, we are proud of you" and she smiled at her sons, "we are proud of all our sons" She became a little tearful and Franz went over to give her a hug.

"What is the matter, Mama, you should not be distressed on such a night as this"

Frau Mayer playfully pushed her son away, and dabbing a white linen handkerchief to her eyes replied, "I am not unhappy, just sad. All my sons have left me now, all I have left is Irmy, and one day she will leave me to be married. Do not listen to me, I am just a silly old woman"

Looking at his mother in the firelight Julius thought she looked anything but old. She had always been a pretty woman but she also possessed an elegance and serenity which simply did not diminish with the years. If anything the advancing years enhanced these qualities in his mother and he always thought of her as one of the most charismatic women that he had ever met. His thoughts were disturbed by a howl that sounded like a wounded dog that was followed by Danusia running out of the room with tears running down her face.

49

"Now look what I have started with my stupid ramblings, I have upset Danusia. I will have to go to her and try and calm her down. Please excuse me"

As Frau Mayer rose from her chair her two sons jumped up from their seats and Franz rushed to open the door for his mother. Frau Mayer looked up at her son and placing a hand on his chest said, "I may be some time, Danusia can be a little difficult lately" and with a little smile on her face added, "I really must remember to keep my maudlin thoughts to myself when Danusia is around or I will never get to see you while you are home" With that she left the room.

"Poor Mama" laughed Irmy, "I know I should not laugh but I think Danusia is getting worse and dear Mama always keeps her patience with her. I do not know how she does it"

"She had a lot of practice raising the four of us," replied Franz, "I do not think we were the easiest of children to cope with on her own." The three siblings spent the rest of the evening discussing childhood memories of who had been the naughtiest child for Mama. Julius, much to his chagrin, received the credit for vexing Mama most of the time, an opinion he hotly disputed despite his brother and sister insisting otherwise.

Just before midnight Frau Mayer rejoined her children and together they all proceeded to St. Elizabeth's for Midnight Mass. Julius thought this service the most beautiful of the year. Even the Cathedral appeared welcoming, lit up with hundreds of candles for the celebration of Christ's birth. Julius did not feel guilty about attending the Mass, as he had been to church the previous week with other members of his barracks, and his priest had listened to his confession. On the way home from the station the other day he and Franz had discussed his talk with their father. He was relieved to find that indeed his brothers were following the same course as he in regard to attending church. Maybe his father had been right when he had said that he did not have to attend church regularly to keep his faith.

He found himself quite moved by the service as he joined in with his family, an emotion that he never remembered experiencing before. As they left the Cathedral several friends of the Mayers came up to convey their Yuletide greetings and to shake hands with the family. The night was bitterly cold and their breaths created large clouds of mist as it met the icy night air.

"I think we will have snow soon" commented Frau Mayer as she surveyed the night sky and pulled her fur collar closer around her to ward off the chill air. Good, thought Julius, who loved the snow. The Mayer's carriage arrived at the Cathedral steps and Julius and Franz helped their mother and sister up into their seats and they swiftly drove home, Mama eager to escape the freezing night.

When Julius awoke on Christmas morning he was delighted to see through his frost encrusted window that it had started to snow. Mama went to church in her carriage, accompanied by Danusia, recovered from her hysterics of the previous evening. Irmy, Franz and Julius decided to walk to the Cathedral in the falling snow. It was wonderful to walk through the cold with snowflakes falling on them, they felt like children again.

By the time the service had ended the snow was falling very heavily, and despite Mamas pleadings they decided to walk back to the house. Kosice looked like a wonderland, covered in sparkling white snow and everybody they encountered hailed them with a Christmas greeting. As they progressed towards the house Julius bent down and scooped up a round of snow which he pitched at his brother. The snowball landed squarely on the back of Franz's neck and fell down into his collar. Franz turned round with a look of absolute amazement on his face, which turned into a wide grin as he too scooped up some snow and returned it to Julius. The battle was on and with shrieks of laughter the two brothers, with Irmy joining in, starting running after each other with handfuls of snow and throwing them with deadly accuracy. They ran through many streets as the skirmish progressed and eventually Julius and Franz fell into a heap on a corner manfully trying to stuff snow down each other's collar. They eventually looked up to find Irmy doubled over with tears of laughter running down her cheeks.

"What is so funny?" asked Julius.

"The two of you, of course", replied Irmy through her laughter, "I was just thinking what you look like. Two officers of His Majesty's Imperial Army having a snowball fight in the middle of the town, looking like two little schoolboys, it is very funny"

Julius and Franz looked at each other and as one thought the same thing. They both reached up and grabbed their sister, pulling her to the ground, and proceeded to rub her face with the snow.

When they eventually reached home Frau Mayer was none too pleased with the disheveled state of her children. She scolded Franz and Julius for their childishness and was especially displeased that they had let their sister be a party to their frivolous antics. As she called the maids to prepare hot baths for them she admonished them for causing the servants so much extra work on the Lord's birthday. As they stood in a row to receive their mother's scolding they stared down at the carpet but after Mama had left the room they looked at each other and started to laugh.

"Well I think it was worth a lecture from Mama" grinned Irmy, "because that is the most fun I have had for a very long time"

Julius found his time at home to be fully occupied. He looked up old school friends, tried to spend time with Mama, went for long walks in the snow covered woods with Irmy and Franz and went to the local lake, which was frozen over, to skate. Irmy loved to skate and was especially pleased when she was escorted by her brothers as it amused her to watch all her friends pretend to fall over in front of one of her brothers in order to attract their attention. Julius noticed quite a few young men taking Irmy for a circuit of the lake, but was relieved to see she showed no particular inclination for any of them. His sister was now nearly sixteen and possessed the same elegant air as her mother. She was obviously noticed by the local young men but he felt she was far too young to have any interest in that direction.

On one occasion Julius relieved Danusia of her chaperoning duties and accompanied Irmy to the hospital. He was interested to see just how deep his sister's interest in medicine was. He himself did not like hospitals. He hated the smell of them, he felt there was a pervading sense of gloom as soon as you entered their doors.

Irmy looked very efficient as she went around the wards and whilst he had been prepared to scoff at his sister for 'playing' nurses the visit completely changed his mind. As Irmy moved amongst the patients he realized she had a real gift, they responded to her and she displayed an understanding and a caring attitude that impressed him greatly.

On the way home Julius thought that Irmy was particularly quiet, "what is the matter, Irmy, is there something worrying you?"

"It is just that you have not said much since leaving the hospital. You think I am silly don't you, working there, you think I am not very good with the patients. Well let me tell you, Julius Mayer, I love tending to the sick, and nothing you can say will put me off spending my afternoons there, I enjoy them too much"

Julius held up his hands to this diatribe, "Irmy, it is not me you have to convince. I have supported you in this all along, and this afternoon only further convinced me that you have a genuine aptitude for nursing, but I say again, Mama and Papa will never allow it"

Irmy let out a large sigh as they walked along, "I know, but I feel so frustrated sometimes. I am sorry Julius, I should not take it out on you. I know my ambitions are hopeless and without our parents consent I can never hope to train to be a nurse. I get so annoyed with life sometimes. You heard Mama the other night, all she thinks about is my getting married, as if that is my only destiny"

"You must not blame Mama for that. She is like all mothers, it has probably never occurred to her that there is any other future for you than to be married. Have you tried to broach the subject with her?"

"No I have not, I am not stupid, Julius. If Mama and Papa had even a suspicion of my wanting to be a nurse they would stop my visits to the hospital straight away. I could not bear that, it is my one solace in all this"

"You do not know that for sure" consoled Julius.

Irmy stopped walking and turned to her brother. She looked him straight in the eye and said, "Julius, with your hand on your heart, can you honestly tell me it would not be otherwise?"

Julius tried to avert his eyes from his sister's steadfast gaze, but her eyes held his. He knew she needed his honesty, not a hope of something that could not possibly happen. "No, I have to agree with you, they would certainly stop your visits to the hospital, I am sorry Irmy"

Irmy put her arm through her brother's and started to walk down the street. Julius detected a slight tremble in her voice as she replied, "Then we are agreed, I say nothing to Mama and Papa, and I carry on as I have been doing for what seems no special purpose because there is no happy ending for me"

Julius started to open his mouth to speak when Irmy turned to him and said, "and if you tell me one more time to find a doctor, I will probably strike you"

Julius looked at her and saw a glint of mischief in her eyes and was pleased to see that at least she could be humorous about her predicament.

Brother and sister amicably strolled home together in silence, both lost in their own private thoughts, Julius trying desperately to think of a solution to his sister's problem. He knew if he brought up the subject with either of his parents he would in all probability be jeopardizing Irmy's visits to the hospital, as she had already said, but he heartily wished he could do something for her. He felt so sorry for his sister, but, despite all his efforts, by the time they had reached home he still had not thought of a solution that would help her.

Leave passed far too quickly for Julius. It was all too soon when Julius stood with his brother on the platform waiting for the trains that would take them back to their postings in Vienna and Graz. They had persuaded Mama and Irmy not to come to the station with them as the snow still lay heavily on the ground. It would have been far too cold for them to stand on the station to say their farewells. These had been said at home, with Danusia, true to form, loudly crying and dear Mama and Irmy stoically trying not to shed any tears as they departed, whilst vainly reminding Julius and Franz to write home more frequently. As Julius had more than an hour to wait for his train he walked round to Franz's platform to see him off. The two brothers embraced and Franz leapt onto his train.

Seeing his brother's carriage disappear out of the station was especially sad for Julius as he had no way of knowing when he would see his brother again. He had always been closer to Franz than he had Karl, maybe as they were nearer in age, they were more like each other than their elder brother. Julius knew that now they were all in the army the chances of them being together again was very remote and this made him feel quite despondent.

He sauntered back up the platform and in the station buffet bought himself a Mokka and palacinky, a fruit filled pancake, to try and make himself feel better. Just as he was deciding whether to have a second palacinky he looked up to see a familiar cherubic face, topped with bright red hair entering the cafe. He started to smile, although Nikolas and he had arranged to meet it was not certain if his friend could make the rendezvous, as this depended on connecting trains running to schedule, something that could not be relied on.

Nikolas' arrival cheered him up immensely, for as well as his farewell to his brother he had not been looking forward to the long journey back to Vienna on his own. They shook hands in greeting, Julius picked up his bags and the two friends proceeded to the platform to join the train to Vienna and return to army life.

VI

When they arrived back at the barracks everybody was discussing their leave, except for Josef who never even mentioned his holiday. Julius, Nikolas and Viktor felt it wiser not to ask him about it. Viktor regaled them with stories of beautiful Salzburg and endless skiing in the snow, something that sounded wonderful to Julius, who had never had the opportunity to try this sport. Viktor had even mentioned, quite shyly, of forming an attachment to a local girl, something that was quite strange to Julius as Viktor had not seemed in the least bit interested in girls. Julius was even more amazed when violet, scented letters started arriving for Viktor. Julius felt that Viktor had regretted mentioning the girl, because the leg pulling he received from his roommates was endless and caused Viktor to often rush downstairs to collect the post so as to escape the teasing of his friends.

Colonel Weber had not been wrong when he had stated that things would not be easier on their return. Although routine army procedures came as second nature by then the cadets were given more specialized training as this would be an indication as to which direction their futures might take once they were given their commissions. They were taught horsemanship, given weapons training, prepared for army maneuvers, as next year they would join the main army carrying out army exercises in the Austrian Alps. They were taught a form of shorthand and also how to read coded messages and to prepare their own codes in times of conflict. The lessons were varied and long, but very interesting, and Julius thoroughly enjoyed them. They were being treated more as men now, not boys, since they had finished their first six months training and passed their tests to remain in the Imperial Army.

One task Julius did not look forward to was clerical work. Every cadet had to do some clerical work as part of his duties but Julius hated it. He disliked being stuck in an office doing paperwork, or running errands for senior officers, delivering letters, or, as he scathingly put it, just being everybody's slave. Whilst his friends endured it with stoic patience Julius always dreaded getting his timetable from Corporal Venner and seeing the odious duty before him. He was especially displeased as on these occasions

56

Colonel Weber would take him under his wing, he presumed because he knew his father, and would undertake to take Julius everywhere with him. Although Julius liked and respected his senior officer this produced a large amount of sarcastic comments and derision from his fellow cadets, and this added to his detestation of the duty.

He returned to his room one day, after a day of office duty which had seen Colonel Weber march onto the parade ground to talk to his men with Julius duty bound to follow the Colonel a few paces behind like a grateful hound, much to the amusement of the other cadets. Julius had never felt so embarrassed and was so annoyed by this experience that he had excused his duties at the earliest possible moment and fled to the sanctuary of dormitory six.

He kicked open the door and fell onto his bed, burying his head under the pillow, in order to blot out his awful day. He heard a movement nearby and surfaced from the bolster to find Smid standing over him, a concerned look on his face.

"You all right, sir, are you unwell?" enquired Smid.

"Oh go to hell, Smid, I do not need you patronizing me as well, thank you" Julius replied rudely.

Smid's gentle face contorted into an expression of extreme hurt and he turned to leave the room.

Julius immediately regretted his outburst and as Smid reached the door cried out, "Smid, I am sorry, I should not have spoken to you like that, come back and say you forgive my rudeness"

Julius watched as Smid's hand rested on the doorknob and realized by the little man's stance how much he had offended him. Smid returned to face Julius and said, with a very dignified air, "I know I am here to serve your needs, but I am also a soldier in His Majesty's Imperial Army, and I was only trying to help you as you seemed troubled"

Julius sat up on his bed and looked at Smid, "I know Smid, I am truly sorry about the way I spoke to you, it was unforgivable of me. I should not have taken my temper out on you and I promise it will never happen again"

Smid looked somewhat mollified by this speech and a trace of a smile began to appear on his face. Encouraged, Julius sought to appease Smid further by asking after his family. "Nikolas tells me you have a sister, does that mean you have nieces and nephews?"

"Yes, sir" replied Smid, "I have three nieces and three nephews"

"My that is quite a brood!" exclaimed Julius, "how do you remember all their names?"

Smid smiled, "with difficulty, I can tell you, but they are good children and are always pleased to see their uncle, I am happy to say"

Smid became quite animated talking about his family, it was a side to him that Julius had never seen before. Julius asked Smid if his family had liked the Christmas present that he and his roommates had given him.

"Oh yes" said Smid, "they were very impressed. I have left it with my sister to look after"

"Didn't you like it Smid? you know you could have exchanged it for something else if you had wanted to"

Smid looked alarmed and hastily said, "It was wonderful, don't get me wrong, but you see I am keeping it for my old age"

Julius raised his eyebrows as he could not understand the little man's meaning.

"You see I know it is worth a lot of money, so, so my sister suggested that I put it away and if I need to I could, well sort of, well what I mean to say is, well, sell it if I fall on hard times when I have to leave the army"

Smid looked very embarrassed at having been cornered into confessing that his ultimate aim was to sell his present and he stared down at the floor in his confusion. Julius felt for the man's discomfort, "do not worry Smid, your secret is safe with me, I would not dream of telling the others. The present was given to you to do with what you will and if in the end you have to sell it, well I think it was still a present given to a worthy recipient. I hope it will make you very happy"

Smid looked up with one of his face splitting smiles, evidently relieved at not having offended Julius and hastily departed the room.

Julius lay back on his bed and stared up at the ceiling. The events of the day fell into insignificance compared to his conversation with Smid. You just do not know how lucky you are, thought Julius, until you realize that some poor beggar is relying on a shaving kit to supplement his old age, a present that Josef only bought to get back at his father. It was a sobering thought.

58

One morning after Viktor had once again run down to intercept the mail, he returned with a letter from Irmy. Julius had been anxious for a letter from his sister as she and Mama had travelled to Linz to attend Karl's wedding and he was eager to know the details of the marriage. He had sent a gift and a letter to his future sister-in-law, but as yet had received no reply, which he thought rather strange, if not discourteous.

It was a long letter from Irmy, written with her usual animation, though he found its contents rather disconcerting. After a few lines of writing Irmy proceeded 'now you know, Julius, that I try to find good in everybody, but I am afraid I have to write and say that I simply did not take to our new sister. That Karl is madly in love with her there is no doubt, but I am afraid I found her, an only daughter you will remember, to be spoilt and overbearing. From the moment we arrived she virtually ignored Mama and myself, she obviously liked to be the centre of attention. Only when Papa arrived did she show any kind of warmth towards us, but then Papa is a man, is he not? I am sure you will understand my meaning, Julius' Julius did, but he was not sure that his young sister should. Irmy continued 'mother took all this in her stride, telling me I was being over sensitive, but I could tell she secretly agreed with me. All Anna did prior to the wedding was to whine and complain. Nothing was to her satisfaction, she would only have the best of everything. I can still recall her high-pitched voice incessantly saying 'I must be perfect for my wedding' 'I', you will note, not everything'. She has very expensive tastes, I wonder how she will survive on a lieutenants pay? a point I overheard Papa mentioning to Mama.

I have to confess she is very pretty, if you like her sort of looks' Julius had to smile at this, his sister had plainly not taken to Anna at all. Irmy then wrote, 'I know you will think this is all very beneath me, but I cannot voice my opinion to Mama as she would think it disloyal. I hope you do not mind me writing of my displeasure to you. Personally I think Karl is going to have his hands full with his new wife.

The wedding was lovely, and Mama and I had a little weep (though was I weeping for Karl?) Karl looked especially handsome in his uniform, and yes, Anna was a very beautiful bride, though it pains me to admit it. I was thankful that we interrupted our journey in Vienna to buy new outfits for the wedding, as the guests were all very fashionable. What a pity we did not see you on our visit, but as Papa pointed out we had seen you at Christmas, though that seems such a long time ago now, does it not?' Julius had been upset to find that he was not allowed leave to visit his mother and sister whilst they had been in Vienna, but as they had only been in the capital for two days, he understood he was not entitled to special privileges just because he had relatives visiting the city.

Julius smiled at his sister's bluntness, which endeared her so much to him. As she grew older she was becoming more outspoken and this bothered him a little, not for his own sake, but for hers, should she upset the wrong person. He would not change his sister, but few people were as tolerant as he, especially where a woman was concerned.

Her letter worried him. If only half of what she wrote was true, his brother could well endure a difficult life with such a demanding wife, but there was nothing he could do. Maybe Irmy had not exaggerated too much. It probably explained the reason why Anna had not written to thank him for her wedding present. With his meager allowance he had bought her a small brooch depicting an edelweiss, the flower of the mountains, set with diamonds and pearls, albeit small ones. Although costly for him, it probably had been received with derision and consigned to the back of her jewel box, if Irmy's assessment of their new sister was true. He realized he was making assumptions but he was probably very near the truth as he was never to receive a thank you note from Anna Mayer.

The summer months in Vienna were particularly hot that year, the city was very quiet and lethargic as most of the wealthy citizens had departed to their summer residences. Most of the army who were stationed in the city had decamped to the mountains for summer maneuvers. All the cadets watched with envy as the soldiers and horses made ready for their departure. The cadets were to stay behind but were placated by the promise that next summer they were to join the army's annual exercise. The barracks were dull after the departure of the main army and lessons were very boring in the oppressive heat and dust of the city.

To relieve the young cadet's boredom and to increase their understanding of horsemanship Colonel Weber had arranged for the cadets to be taken to watch the magnificent Lipizzaner stallions at the nearby Winter Riding

School, located near the Imperial State Apartments. The entire Hofburg Quarter of Vienna was full of some of the most breathtaking edifices in the city, but Julius found the interior of the Riding School one of his favorite buildings. Around the performing arena were two storeys of graceful galleries, supported by carved columns of white stone. In these galleries spectators sat to watch the displays in the arena below. Suspended from the high ceilings were elaborate chandeliers that added to the elegance of the scene below. At one end of the building was the court box which had an arch that supported an enormous carved relief of the Habsburg coat-of-arms, the double headed eagle. It was here that members of the royal family would sit when they came to watch the equestrian demonstrations at the school. To the rear of the court box hung a large portrait of Emperor Karl VI, the founder of the Spanish Riding School, and as each rider entered the stadium they would raise their hat to the portrait as a sign of respect.

The riders all wore the same uniform, a black bicorn hat decorated with gold braid, coffee colored tunics, pale leather gloves and buckskin trousers, with long black riding boots that came up over the knee. In keeping with tradition they used a saddle with a red and gold embroidered cloth bearing the Habsburg arms, but despite all the flamboyance of the surroundings, these paled into insignificance, once the Lipizzaner stallions started their displays. The intricate steps, more like a ballet performance, were explained to the cadets who soon became familiar with the different patterns and movements achieved by the graceful horses.

Julius never tired of watching these displays, the ultimate demonstration of horsemanship. He watched in awed respect as the horses leapt through the air with their hind legs and forelegs bent under their bellies in a movement known as the croupade. Then there was the levade, when the horses stood on their hind legs with their hocks nearly brushing the ground. Spectators gasped as the horses leapt into the air and kicked their hind legs out behind them or halted between two upright posts and trotted on the spot with perfect precision.

The ultimate treat for the cadets was to go to the neighboring Stallburg Palace that provided the stabling for the Lipizzaners and to actually be close to these magnificent beasts. They would discuss their training with their grooms, and sometimes help with their stabling, Julius had to admit it was one of the events he most looked forward to in his busy training schedule.

The heat of the summer months turned into the golden hues and cooler breezes of autumn. The main body of the army returned to Vienna, and Julius was pleased to be able to see his father again, as he had been away from the city for three months. Julius went to see his father soon after his return and was glad to hear that Colonel Mayer had seen both his brothers on army maneuvers and that both had been well.

"I don't suppose Karl appreciated being separated from his bride so soon after his marriage Papa" observed Julius.

His father gave a rather loud snort which sounded very derisive, "Well he should not have married if he did not want to be parted from his wife. He knew what life would be like in the army when he entered into marriage, so forgive me if I show little sympathy for your brother's predicament" Julius had never known his father speak with such vehemence about his brother, and his tone startled him. He wanted to ask further about Karl but kept his silence as he could sense his father's annoyance of the subject. His father was quiet for a while, then added absent-mindedly, "I just hope you and Franz have more sense than to marry so young. Stupid thing" His father's voice trailed off and he appeared to be in deep thought.

Julius wondered if something had occurred between his elder brother and his father but knew better than to ask. He resolved to ask Irmy if she knew anything the next time he wrote to her.

Irmy wrote back that she had not heard of any upset between their father and Karl, but added petulantly that she would be the last person to know, even if there had been. All cadets had once again been given leave for Christmas, but they were much shorter than last year. Julius wondered if it was really worth his going home, for as soon as he had endured the journey home it would only be a few days before he would have to return to Vienna. However he knew he would make the effort as he could not disappoint Mama and Irmy. As Nikolas' family had now moved to Prague he could not even look forward to his friend's company on the train journey. He was to travel to Kosice with his father as he also had leave at Christmas.

One night, shortly before their leave began, Josef entered their room, "we have permission to go into the city tonight" said Josef, "how about making it my treat?

"You mean your father's treat, don't you?" Julius retorted.

"Probably" replied Josef, "does this mean your conscience will not allow you to join us this evening?" Julius immediately regretted his sarcasm, he had not meant to be abrupt with Josef.

"Sorry, Josef. I did not mean to be rude. I would love to accept your invitation, if you are still willing"

Josef treated them to a wonderful dinner. After their meal they went to a coffee house for a coffee and a glass of schnapps. Coffee houses were very fashionable in Vienna. They were a meeting place for businessmen, artists, writers, politicians or anybody who wanted to drink coffee and watch the world go by. The smart coffee houses always supplied newspapers and periodicals and some even supplied foreign newspapers. Josef sarcastically commented that the people who picked up these newspapers, probably could not read a word of another language, they just did it to make themselves appear cultured.

The coffee house Julius and his friends were in also boasted several bridge tables, and for a while they stood and watched the intricacies of this popular card game. Josef had played bridge since a boy and he had endeavored to teach his roommates the rudiments of the game. Julius, especially, had enjoyed learning to play and vowed that when he had more free time he would concentrate on playing the game properly.

The boys ordered their coffee and schnapps and sat down at a secluded table in the corner. When their order arrived, with the obligatory glass of water, they started to discuss their plans for Christmas.

"God I hope my father does not make an appearance this Christmas" commented Josef, "I cannot stand the atmosphere when he is in the house, it only upsets my mother"

"I know this is personal, Josef" said Viktor, "and tell me to mind my own business if you want to, but don't you ever worry that your father will cut you off some day and not give you a penny. I mean you make your dislike of him pretty well known"

A malicious smile crept onto Josef's face, "that is the beauty of my relationship with my father, there is absolutely nothing he can do about me and he knows it. You see my mother has definitely had the last laugh on my father, a fact he cannot bear. My mother comes from a very wealthy family, probably as wealthy as my father's. She was the only daughter and my grandfather adored her. He did not want her to marry my father, they hated each other on sight and perhaps, even then, the old man could see what an ogre my father was. Anyway, he gave way to my mother and allowed her to marry my father. She believed she was in love with him, and perhaps she hoped she could change him, he was known for his evil ways, even then.

In time, my grandfather was proved right, and despite my mother giving him three sons my father became more and more dissolute. My grandfather stood by helplessly watching the way my mother was treated. I can remember him in our house, pleading with her to leave him, but she never would, she would never leave her children. My mother doted on me, being the youngest, and my father hated me, maybe because she gave me all her attention, I think by then she had given up on my father. I became the pawn in the middle of his endless games, he knew he could always blackmail my mother by using me.

My grandfather saw what was happening and I started to spend more and more time at his house. He was a wonderful man, but sadly, when I was about ten he became very ill and I was told he was dying. My father rejoiced in this as he knew my grandfather's money would then be inherited by my mother, and as her husband, it would then be his. I even heard him boasting about it when my mother told him of my grandfather's illness. I think that is what finally spurred my mother into action. Soon after he had been told of his illness, my grandfather, my mother and his lawyers drew up a new will. My grandfather's money was left to me, with trustees looking after it until I am twenty-five.

The wonderful thing was that, due to my grandfather employing some very clever lawyers, it was all perfectly legal, there was not a thing my father could do about it and he cannot touch my money" Josef smiled triumphantly, "I cannot tell you the satisfaction we felt the day my mother and I witnessed my father's anger when the will was read. I thought he was going to have a seizure, but unfortunately he didn't"

The boys had listened to Josef's story in amazement.

64

"What do your brothers think about it all?" asked Nikolas.

"Oh they are all right. They will receive my father's fortune anyway, and although they dislike him too, they know not to rock the boat, or they might find themselves disinherited. We get on quite well actually, and my mother has promised them that if ever they need help, the money is there. That is one of the things she agreed upon with my grandfather. I get an annual allowance from the trustees now and inherit the bulk when I am twenty-five. I am going to have a big party then, so make a date in your social calendar. Now you see why my father hates me as much as I hate him. He has no hold over me and he hates that fact more than anything else. I suppose I don't help matters as I feel I have to remind him of it every time I see him, just in case he has forgotten, you understand"

Nikolas picked up his glass of schnapps, "well I would like to propose a toast, to Josef's grandfather, God bless him"

The other boys picked up their glasses and smiled at each other. They repeated the toast together.

"Josef's grandfather, God bless him"

VII

Julius enjoyed the journey home with his father. It was the first time he had had his father's company entirely to himself and they passed the time in idle conversation relishing their time together.

Christmas was very subdued without Franz and Julius could tell that something was bothering his parents, but they did not discuss their problems with him. The Christmas celebrations passed by and all too soon Julius was packing for his journey back to Vienna.

The afternoon before his return he was leaving the house to go out to meet some of his old school friends in the local beer keller. He was passing the parlor door when it opened and Irmy furtively beckoned him into the room. His interest aroused, he quickly entered the room while Irmy looked out of the door as though suspicious of anybody lurking in the hallway.

"What is it?" asked Julius, "why are you acting so mysteriously?"

"I have to talk to you Julius. I overheard Mama and Papa talking this morning and I have to tell someone what I heard, or I shall burst"

Julius laughed at his sister's exuberance, but sat down as she was obviously desperate to relate the result of her eavesdropping. "Are you sure you should be telling me this, after all it was Mama and Papa's private conversation"

"Julius stop being so sanctimonious, you know you want to hear what I have to say"

Irmy sat down to compose herself. Julius tried to suppress a smile as he looked at his sister. She looked like an actor, ready to deliver the key speech of a play. "I was passing their bedroom this morning and I had stopped to tie up the lace of my boot".....

"Oh Irmy stop, I cannot take this. You stopped to listen to our parent's conversation, do not try to convince me otherwise, now get on with your story, I am feeling very thirsty and my friends are waiting for me at Sebastians"

"You are no fun Julius, army life has made you too serious. Anyway, you will never guess, Papa has received a letter from Karl asking him for money, quite a considerable amount I gather from the way Papa was talking. Evidently he is in debt to several tradesmen in Linz and has hugely overspent himself. Papa is furious, he was blaming Anna, saying that she has far too extravagant tastes and that it is up to Karl to curb his wife's expensive lifestyle. There, I knew that I would shock you"

Julius was indeed shocked, he could not believe what his sister was telling him. It was obviously true and it explained a lot of his father's outbursts lately, but he still could not believe it. Karl had been married for less than a year, how could they have got into so much trouble in such a short time? "and did you manage to hear whether Papa was going to help Karl"

"Well no, unfortunately just as Mama and Papa were about to discuss that Hanne appeared in the corridor with fresh bed linen so I had to leave, but I could hear that Mama was very upset. I told you that Anna was a bad influence, now do you agree that I was right?"

Julius did not answer his sister, he was too deep in thought about his brother. Poor Karl, to get himself so deeply in debt that he had to ask Papa for help, he must be in a bad way.

After this news he did not feel like joining his friends so he and Irmy went for a long walk in the woods. They discussed their brother's predicament and agreed that even if Papa did help his son out this time, it was unlikely that he would help him in the future and then where would Karl go for help? It was a very unhappy situation.

Julius travelled back to Vienna on his own as his father's leave was to last for another two weeks. It was a lonely journey, Julius was not sure when he would be home again, at least not for another year, and because he was on his own his thoughts kept returning to Karl. He knew his brother must have been desperate to have turned to his father for money. He must have some very large debts to have to ask his father for help. Karl had always been such a studious, dependable boy that he had to agree with Irmy, although he did not like to speak ill of someone he had never met, he had to suppose that Anna must have some bearing on the situation. He was also concerned for his parents, the news must have come as a shock for them, especially Mama. She had not looked too happy when he had said his farewells to her, but he hoped that had as much to do with her saying goodbye to him as worrying about her eldest son.

He was glad to be back in the barracks, amongst his friends, looking forward to the coming year. He was enjoying his life in the army now and was coping with his training well. His marks continued to be of a high standard and the cadets were encouraged to think to the future as to which branch of the army they eventually wanted to enter. Julius had mixed feelings about this. He and Nikolas favored the artillery, but were drawn to the dragoon regiments. In discussions with Colonel Weber and Sergeant Major Hoffman Julius was advised to keep his options open until they had experienced the full extent of their training. "Do not worry if you think you are forever changing your mind" said Weber, "every time you experience something new you will probably say to yourself, this is what I want to do, that is until you encounter the next new assignment. You have plenty of time to make up your mind. Do not rush to make a decision"

The cadets were eagerly looking forward to the summer maneuvers, which were to take place in the months of June, July and August. It was something of a relief to be getting away from the heat and dust of summer in the city, up into the cool mountain air of the Austrian Alps. Like the numerous parades and processions, Emperor Franz Josef always encouraged these summer diversions as he felt they were good for morale and kept his troops from becoming bored in times of peace. Apart from the odd skirmish and uprisings to deal with, these were the only times when the army could prepare for conflict, if it ever arose.

Julius' company of cadets were to leave for Salzburg at the beginning of June. There they would work together for a month on combat training, then for the next two months they would be assigned to regiments where they would be acting as commissioned officers in their own units. Julius knew that this was a very important time for all of them. They would be closely observed and their actions scrutinized minutely for a final report, which would result in finding out if they were possible officer, and indeed army, material.

The month of May was spent in preparing for their departure. They were lectured on field army procedures, advised on uniform requirements, given an idea of what tasks they would have to perform and shown how, within their assigned regiments, they would be carrying out mock battles, the winning of which was everything. There was great rivalry between different regiments and units and if a cadet was to let anybody down and thereby lose a battle or impede an advancement, then their life would not be worth living. Many cadet faces turned a pale shade of gray at these lectures, the worry being that they would be the ones to let the side down, a fear that hung over all of them.

Early June found the cadets at Vienna station boarding their train for the journey to Salzburg, their base for the next month. Before their departure from the barracks Colonel Weber had given them a stirring speech about how they were representing His Majesty on this trip and that he was sure that they would see how all the hard work of the past two years would seem worth it, once it was put into practice. "I doubt that very much" murmured Josef, "Nothing can be worth all that hard work" Colonel Weber heard the distant whisper and looked in Josef's direction, but Josef, with his usual nonchalance, just looked straight back at the Colonel, who returned to his speech.

"I know you are all capable of being fine soldiers and are not about to let myself, or Sergeant Major Hoffman, down. Just remember everything you have been taught, use your common sense and above all, listen to your senior officers, and you should not go far wrong. Maneuvers are taken very seriously, they are not simply grown men playing games, which is what you may think. They are our only way of knowing how the army would react in time of conflict, indeed how you as individuals would react, which is probably just as significant. I do not need to tell you that the next few months are very important for you, especially in regard to your futures in this army, but I will also say to you, enjoy yourselves, it will be a wonderful time for you all, one you will probably never forget, your first experience of active life in His Majesty's Imperial Army. As you know you are to travel to Salzburg with Sergeant Major Hoffman and Corporal Venner. I will join you at the beginning of July, when you are assigned to your various regiments. I will see you then gentlemen, dismissed" All the cadets jumped out of their seats to salute their senior officer, then he strode out of the room.

The stowing of all the baggage seemed endless, but finally they were seated in their carriages, pulling out of the station. The mood was one of excitement and expectation and there was general banter and leg pulling as the journey progressed. Viktor especially was excited about returning to his hometown. He regaled them all with stories of its beauty and the wonderful sights that he would show them once they were there.

As the train travelled towards their destination the air noticeably freshened. Even Nikolas had to admit that the landscape as they approached Salzburg was breathtaking, as were the commanding mountains that could be seen in the distance, on the horizon. Salzburg was a typical Austrian alpine city. Clean, neat with a sparkling purity that was very noticeable after months spent in Vienna.

The cadets were allocated rooms in the local barracks, and there were twenty cadets assigned to each dormitory. Every room had valets to serve them, but all four boys missed Smid. The barracks were clean and spartan and on their first night they sat down to a welcoming alpine meal which included Tiroler Grostl, beef with onions, potatoes and caraway, followed by a delicious Apfel Strudel. Whether it was the alpine air, the food or the fatigue of their journey, they all slept deeply that night until the sound of reveille interrupted their dreams.

Their first days were spent getting to know their new surroundings and being shown on maps where the impending maneuvers were to take place. They went on long route marches through the hills around the city. Although the sun shone brightly every day it was not overwhelmingly hot as it could be in Vienna at that time of year, so these expeditions were very pleasant, with the magnificent scenery adding to the enjoyment.

Several hours were spent in the classroom discussing battle tactics, signaling, coding and decoding messages. The ciphers were something that Julius found especially interesting, he excelled at decoding at great speed and preparing codes himself. He was careful not to bring attention to his interest however. He knew if you showed too much of an aptitude in this department it was what you ended up doing most of the time, something he did not relish as he preferred to be more active, his office duties haunted him too much.

There was also leisure time as the main body of the Army was not due to arrive until the end of the month. Although they all missed the camaraderie of their own room in Vienna, the four boys still tended to spend time together. Viktor took great pride in taking them round his city, showing them all the sights he had talked so much about.

One evening they obtained permission from Sergeant Major Hoffman to go to Viktor's house for dinner. They duly arrived outside a handsome, large building, located in one of the best areas of the city. Even Josef was seen to stand with his mouth open, not only at the opulence of the house, but also because Viktor had never hinted that his family was this wealthy, which they obviously were. Viktor had told them his father was a banker but never alluded to how rich he was. Julius' estimation of his friend rose as he realized how modest and unassuming he was, never boasting about his family, which he surely could have, so very unlike Josef.

Herr and Frau Leitner were delightful hosts, clearly very proud of their son. They were introduced to Viktor's brother, Felix, an older version of Viktor, and to his two little sisters, aged five and six. The two girls leapt on their brother with affection as soon as they saw him and did not let him go until their nanny dragged them away to their beds.

The dinner was excellent, served by a regiment of servants, too numerous to count. The greatest astonishment to Julius was Josef's behavior that night. Julius thought that Josef might at least have been a little scathing of Viktor's family. After all they were what people like Josef would refer to as 'moneyed' wealth because Viktor's father had to work for his living, as opposed to Josef's family who were aristocracy and had inherited wealth. However Josef was courteous, well mannered and struck up an instant rapport with Herr Leitner, as indeed did all the guests. Julius felt guilty about his thoughts of Josef at Christmas, but then reflected that this household was very different to his own. Herr Leitner was an urbane, intelligent man and Julius reflected that Viktor was very lucky to have such a father.

As they all walked back to their barracks that evening Nikolas said to Viktor, "you sly old dog, you never told us you were rich and lived in a house like that"

"You never asked" replied Viktor, "anyway, my father keeps a tight rein on my allowance, he has the money, not me. I am not allowed to use his accounts like old moneybags over there" and he inclined his head towards Josef who was walking ahead of them, seemingly lost in thought. Josef stopped and turned to face his friends. "Maybe you do not have as much money as me, I do not know, but there is one way in which you are far richer than me, in fact you all are. You have fathers that you love and that love you in return, just appreciate that" and with that he turned on his heel and walked off quickly towards the barracks. The three boys stared at his disappearing figure marching off down the street.

"I will never understand that fellow, as long as I live" observed Viktor, "but I think underneath all that bravado is a very unhappy man who *has* got a heart, something I never thought I would hear myself say" and with that thought they all proceeded back to their barracks.

Josef was his old self by the time the other three joined him for bed that night, but Julius was to observe, perhaps rather unkindly, that Josef's attitude to Viktor definitely softened after that evening and he believed it had more to do with the size of Viktor's house than Josef liking him better.

The month in Salzburg passed rapidly, with the cadets given so many different facts and conflicting orders that they were sure they would not know what to do once they were assigned to their units. The end of June found Julius packing again, making ready for their departure to go up into the mountains. The anticipation and excitement was great as they assembled to hear their allocation to regiments for the next two months. Sergeant Major Hoffman read out the orders. "When you reach your designated assignments you will be detailed to work with a captain. For the next two months you will be acting as a commissioned lieutenant alongside this officer. You will learn from him, watch him at work, observe how he operates within the army so that when your time comes you will be able to accept your commission with some experience of the job. It is very important that you make decisions for yourself, you are not there just to be his shadow, you are to be an active member of your unit, do I make myself clear?" Hoffman then proceeded to read out the assigned duties. Julius was assigned to the Horse Artillery under a Captain Schneider. Nikolas and Viktor were also assigned to other Horse Artillery units whilst Josef was to work with the Cavalry. It was strange to say farewell to his three friends. They had been virtually inseparable for the last two years, but Julius hoped he would meet them up in the mountains, and he knew it was to be for only two months.

The journey to the mountains did not take long and Julius walked up into a large clearing in a forest on the mountainside to be met by the sight of row upon row of dark brown tents pitched in perfect symmetrical lines. The camp was a hive of activity with hundreds of soldiers settling into their home for the next two months. Julius stopped a passing soldier to ask him where he could find the quartermaster's tent. The soldier looked at him in total miscomprehension, shrugged his shoulders and carried on his way. Julius turned to the three other cadets who had travelled with him from Salzburg and who were also assigned to this section.

"I wonder what's wrong with him?" asked Julius.

A voice from behind him laughed and said, "even if you didn't recognize his uniform, I would have thought you could have smelt a Hungarian" Julius turned round to be confronted by a young soldier. He was so shocked by the young man's speech that he forgot to reprimand him for his rudeness. It was true he had not recognized the uniform but he had not realized that Hungarians were to be included in the exercises, despite which the boy had no right to be talking as he did.

The soldier directed them to the quartermaster's tent, where Julius found out the location of Captain Schneider, his mentor for the next two months.

Captain Schneider turned out to be a solemn, taciturn man, in his early thirties, who was content to make sure Julius did his job, but beyond that kept himself very much to himself. Over the next few weeks, despite often trying to engage him in idle conversation, Julius found out little more about Schneider than he had learnt on his first day, and that was not much. However he was an excellent teacher, serious but fair. Julius had to grudgingly admit that although his time on maneuvers was not exactly filled with amusement he learned a lot from Schneider. Julius shared a tent with the captain and he spent all his spare time reading, or writing letters home as Schneider seemed disinclined to join in any shared activities.

Julius loved the outdoor life. At first the altitude had him reaching for breath, but gradually his lungs got used to the thin air and he coped with the exercises well. The mock battles were his favorite. All units were issued with different colored armbands so that during forays you could tell who your enemy was. The one thing Schneider taught him was patience, something Julius did not have an abundance of, but he learnt to bide his time, that rushing in was not always the best policy.

On one occasion when their objective was to take a hill to the west of their camp, Schneider had him and their men lying in concealment, without daring to move for over six hours, until he decided the time was right to attack, which reminded Julius of his hunting days with his father and brothers. The strategy was a good one as the 'enemy' were so sure by that time that the threat of attack was over that they had relaxed their defenses and the taking of the hill had been easy.

Although they were not always triumphant on these skirmishes, their unit was one of the most successful and Julius knew this was often due to Schneider's, and sometimes their superior officers, intelligent tactics. "Always have a plan, a back up to that plan and always make sure your men are fully aware of those plans, then you are halfway there" said Schneider in one of his more verbose moments. It was sound advice, which Julius stored away for future use.

In one area Julius knew he impressed his senior officers in his company, and once again it was his aptitude for ciphering. Julius developed a system for signaling to each other whilst in hiding in order to communicate without sound. Again it was something he had used whilst hunting when he had wanted to say something to his brothers but could not make a sound in case they scared off their prey. The signaling he devised was very rudimentary, but it worked and was used on more than one occasion during exercises. He was often used to decode messages sent from other 'friendly' units. Although he had tried to avoid this task beforehand, he quite enjoyed it on the 'battlefield' as this meant he remained close to the commanding officers and had a first hand experience of how and why decisions were made.

The two months were not all spent in fighting mock battles. Units were sent off into the mountains for several days, with sparse survival packs, to follow a map in order to get to a specific destination in an allotted time. Units were penalized if they arrived late at a station. Soldiers carried heavy packs on their backs and the marches were often fast and grueling to get to a checkpoint in time. Julius enjoyed sleeping outdoors, lying on a thin bedroll, staring up at the stars.

74

One night he was drifting off to sleep when he felt something hovering over him, casting a large shadow. He knew it to be human and worried that this might be a test of some sort to simulate an enemy attack. Julius kept his eyes closed but swiftly reached up and grabbed the form above him around the neck and, with an almighty effort, pulled the assailant over himself. He then leapt onto the sprawling body in front of him, hitting it with all his might. Suddenly through his blind panic he heard a familiar voice crying out, "Julius you stupid pig, it's me, for God's sake what are you trying to do?"

Julius stopped his attack and as his eyes became used to the dark night a vision of a shock of red hair appeared before him, but the cherubic smile was not there. "Nikolas, you idiot, I might have hurt you, what were you doing creeping up on me like that?"

By now several other soldiers were awake, moaning at Julius and Nikolas about the noise they were making, so Julius got up and walked over to a clearing with his friend. Nikolas was trying to tidy himself up and even in the gloomy night-light Julius could see Nikolas' right eye beginning to close up. Seeing the hurt he had inflicted on his friend Julius forgot his anger and expressed his concern for Nikolas' injuries. Nikolas at last managed a grin, "it is as much my fault as yours, I just thought I was going to give you a bit of a fright, that was all. God knows how I am going to explain away this eye; do you think they will believe that I walked into a tree or something?"

Julius laughed with his friend. It was good to have some merriment, he realized he had missed the humor during his weeks with the dour Captain Schneider.

The two friends carried on talking for a while, discussing their experiences over the last few weeks. Nikolas was camped just over the hill and when he had heard that his friend's unit was nearby he had thought to pay them a visit, but with his eye beginning to close up rapidly, he was now regretting his decision.

Nikolas walked back to Julius' bedroll in order to pick up his hat. With one of his beatific smiles, which made him wince with pain as it affected his swollen eye, he walked off in the direction of his camp, ruefully declaring "I will not forget this Julius, I will get you back one day"

Julius smiled, watching Nikolas' departing figure, and realized how much he was missing his friend.

75

Although Julius enjoyed his time in the mountains he was disturbed by his first experiences with the different levels of army life. He found many of the senior officers offhand and some had a total indifference to the men who served underneath them. They appeared to have no interest in the reason for being on maneuvers, which Julius presumed was to drill their men in all aspects of warfare and survival. Instead they were content to delegate their duties to their junior officers and enjoy sitting on their backsides all day, accepting the accolades when their particular unit did well, or alternatively blaming their junior officers when their men performed badly.

Worse than the conduct of his senior officers was the conduct of soldiers towards their fellow combatants. As it was in the Empire itself, within the Austro-Hungarian Army at least fifteen different languages were regularly used. Amongst its men were more then eleven different racial groups, all clinging to their own ethnic identities, which created disarray among the ranks. Although these nations served under one umbrella, the Austro-Hungarian Army, they all held some antipathy for each other. For some this was just a mild dislike, but for many it was a determined hatred, which created large schisms within the foundations of the army. As Julius had seen on his first day at camp, with the young soldier's contempt of the Hungarian soldier, the men were quite open in their animosity of one another. It deeply worried him as he wondered if there was a time of real conflict whether these men could fight together as a cohesive team.

All his life he had been brought up to believe in the glory of the Empire and the Imperial Army as a magnificent fighting force, a flag bearer for other nations in Europe, but he had to admit that his first experience had been disappointing and he was shocked by the dissent within the army. He even had to admit that he had been subjected to some prejudice as he was seen as a Bohemian, though he regarded himself as an Austrian national first. He had never presumed his nationality in anyway interfered with his allegiance to the Emperor.

These thoughts troubled him greatly and he wished he could talk to his father, or his brothers of his fears. He was aware for the first time in his life what a sheltered existence he had led so far.

Julius realized he had a lot of growing up to do, and quickly, if he was to survive in the army he now viewed with more than a little despondency.

VIII

Once back in Vienna Julius' gloom lifted a little. Maybe it was being back with his friends again and in the welcoming atmosphere of his barracks in Vienna. He tried to ascertain if his friends felt the same way as him about the morale of the soldiers, but whether they simply did not see things the way he did, or thought it was a subject best left unmentioned, no one broached the subject and so Julius decided to keep his thoughts to himself. He felt that he could not even discuss his worries with Nikolas, which was strange as he thought he could talk about anything with his best friend. The only subject they did all criticize was the conduct of some of their senior officers, although this became a very muted conversation when Julius and Nikolas suddenly realized they were talking about officers who were the same rank as their fathers, and henceforth found the discussion very uncomfortable.

On their return to Vienna every cadet had a private interview with Colonel Weber and Sergeant Major Hoffman to ascertain how they had carried out their duties whilst on maneuvers. Julius was embarrassed to receive a glowing report from Captain Schneider as he thought that he had not got on too well with him. He was aware that Schneider thought him far too flippant at times and on their farewell Julius had had the impression that the captain was glad to see the back of him. Despite this he had written him a very flattering report and Julius was grateful to the dour captain for not letting his personal opinion of Julius mar his professional opinion of him. It was something he would remember for the future, when he would be judging cadets himself.

His marks on exercises were also quite good and his senior officers appeared to have formed a good opinion of him. Julius smiled to himself at this as he felt that several of the officers who had written the report had probably not even met him, or if they had they had never personally watched him on maneuvers. Once again he thanked Schneider's good accounts of him as he was sure that it was only after reading them that they could have written their own reports. Colonel Weber and Sergeant Major Hoffman congratulated him on his progress, they were obviously pleased with him. They then told him that he had been put forward for winter training. This meant he would go back to the mountains in the winter to learn to ski, endure survival courses in the snow and be taught how to engage in combat in the extreme conditions that snow could bring. Julius was delighted when he heard this. He had always wanted to learn to ski, loved the snow and despite his previous experiences looked forward to some more months in the mountains.

He returned to his room to await the others to see how they had fared with their reports. He did not have to wait long for Nikolas to return. Julius was sitting at the table, writing a letter to Irmy, when the door opened very slowly and Nikolas entered, his head down, obviously upset.

"What is the matter?" asked Julius, "something wrong?" It did not occur to Julius that Nikolas' report had been bad. He knew he was too good a soldier to have failed.

"They did not pass me" Nikolas slumped down on a chair opposite Julius and looked as if he was about to cry. Julius stared open mouthed. He could not believe it.

"But why, there must be some mistake"

"No, no mistake" whispered Nikolas.

"Did they give you a reason? there, there must be a reason" stuttered Julius.

"Oh, they told me why. You remember that night on the hill, when I came to find you while we were on survival training?" Julius nodded, dreading what was to come next.

"Well, I did not exactly get permission to come and see you and when I returned with a black eye they presumed I had been fighting with a fellow soldier. It all went down on report and now Weber and Hoffman know and they have deferred my marks and I have to go through all the exercises again"

Nikolas raised himself from his chair and went to lay down on his bed. Julius did not know what to say. He felt so sorry for his friend. He sat on Nikolas' bed and placing his hand on his friend's shoulder said, "look how about I go to Colonel Weber now and tell him the whole story, maybe that would help"

Nikolas sat up, "would you? I would really appreciate that, but it might get you into trouble you know"

Julius swallowed hard, he knew the implications but felt he had to help Nikolas. He picked up his hat and smiling at his friend went out of the room, dreading the confrontation he was about to have.

When he was halfway down the corridor he heard his name called. He turned round to see Nikolas leaning out of the doorway. "Julius, I always said I would get you back for my black eye" a great big smile spread over his face, "the joke is on you, stupid, I would have loved to have seen Weber's face when you tried to explain yourself. He would not have known what you were talking about, he would have thought you ready for the asylum!" and with that he ungraciously stuck out his tongue at Julius. Julius let out an enormous yell and running at full speed launched himself into his room.

"You bastard, Manz, you are going to get two black eyes now"

He chased Nikolas round the room, into the corridor, down the stairs and out of the barracks building, past a very startled soldier sitting at his desk in the lobby. The chase continued for quite a while until they found themselves in the barracks stables where Nikolas held up his hands, panting furiously, and gasped "Pax, pax, I am sorry, Julius, I just couldn't resist it. You should have seen your face. I have never seen anything so funny" and he collapsed, laughing, into some straw. Julius by this time had come to see the funny side of things and he too fell into the straw, laughing. After they had recovered their breath they lay quietly for a while.

"I suppose you did get a good report after all then?" asked Julius.

"Jolly good actually", replied Nikolas, "I think they are going to keep me for a little while longer"

"More is the pity" countered Julius, with a sly look at his friend.

Julius and Nikolas hauled themselves up and dusted the straw from their uniforms. As they were walking out, Julius spied something on the cobbled floor of the stables. He put out his foot in front of his friend causing him to trip and topple over onto the floor straight into a pile of horse manure. Nikolas lay as though comatose before looking up at Julius.

"Pax?" laughed Julius, looking down at his friend, "I don't think so" and ran out of the stable door.

When Nikolas arrived back at the dormitory Viktor and Josef had joined Julius. "What is that smell?" asked Viktor as Nikolas undressed. Nikolas and Julius looked at each other and burst out laughing, "you do not want to know" said Nikolas, "but let us just say I think I deserved this one" Viktor and Josef looked puzzled so Julius changed the conversation by asking them about their reports. Both had received good assessments, so were in ebullient moods, and it transpired that they had all been put forward for winter training so they were very happy. "I cannot wait" said Viktor, "and as I can ski already at last I can excel at something over you three"

Returning to classes was rather mundane after their time in the mountains, but the cadets soon adjusted back to barracks life. As their training progressed Julius and his group were treated with more respect than before and even hardened officers like Sergeant Brunner gave the cadets more consideration than they had done previously.

Irmy wrote regularly to Julius, but she had no news of Karl. Julius thought he detected some dejection in her writing. He felt sorry for his sister, with all her brothers now away from home the companionship of Mama and Danusia, however much she loved them, must seem a bit stifling for her. Of course she did have friends her own age, but Julius had noticed that lately she had been quite scathing about them, writing that all they talked about were 'boys, marriages and babies' which she found very boring. Julius had smiled at her comments, and thought to himself that that was probably what most girls of Irmy's age did talk about, but then he had to admit that his sister was not like most girls of her age. He had received a few letters from Franz but had had no correspondence from Karl or his new wife.

The previous night he had been out to dinner with his father and had found him very preoccupied. He had wanted to ask his father about Karl and to relate to him his thoughts about the morale that he had encountered in the summer, but his father's mood warned him not to broach the subject. His father appeared so ill at ease and self absorbed that they had not finished their meal and Julius had returned early to his barracks, worried about his father's state of mind, hoping that Karl had not inflicted any more unhappiness on his parents.

The next day Julius was lying on his bed talking to Josef and Nikolas, who were sitting at the table, writing letters, when suddenly the door burst open and Viktor appeared, out of breath and very excited.

"Have you heard the news?" he panted.

"What news, what are you talking about?" asked Josef.

"We have formally announced the annexation of Bosnia and Herzegovina"

"What do you mean 'we', what are you talking about Viktor?"

"I mean the Emperor and the government have announced that Bosnia and Herzegovina are now part of the Austro-Hungarian Empire. The news is all over the city, everybody is talking about it"

"I hope we said please before we told them they are now with us" Josef flippantly remarked.

"Shut up, Josef. This could be serious" Julius sat up on his bed. He now knew the reason for his father's preoccupation the night before. He had known about this and was worried by it.

"What do you mean serious, Julius. How?"

"Because some people are going to object. The days are gone when countries could just simply take over other countries with no objections raised. There are treaties these days, which people are meant to abide by, believe me this could mean trouble"

"Does that mean we are in for a fight?" asked Viktor excitedly, "that would be wonderful"

"For God's sake, be quiet Viktor" retorted Julius sharply, "this is not a game you know and anyway, if there was a conflict it would be doubtful if we would be a part of it, we are only cadets after all and are barely halfway through our training"

Nikolas, Viktor and Josef eyed their friend warily after his outburst but Julius was not in the mood for their foolish chatter and lay back on his bed lost in his thoughts. He wished he could talk to his father, but knew he could not. He worried in case his father might become involved, and then thought about his two brothers who may well have to fight should it come to it.

During the month of October, after the announcement, Vienna was a hive of activity and rumor. The newspapers were full of the stories of the diplomatic developments over the annexation and throughout the city it seemed that nothing else was talked about. The move to include Bosnia and Herzegovina in the Austro-Hungarian Empire had angered France, Britain and Russia. Serbia was particularly outraged as this action infringed on the rights of their fellow Slavs. As Russia was a close ally of Serbia, Russia intervened, stating that the Empire had broken the spirit of the agreement between their two countries. Throughout all the negotiations and political rhetoric, the army was put on war alert and there was great upheaval as the organization for possible mobilization was put into motion.

During all the disruption Julius kept his thoughts to himself. His friends welcomed the idea of war and the whole barracks were imbued with the idea of confrontation. Their intended trip to the mountains was postponed for the time being which was disappointing, but the cadets took this as a sign that indeed they would be put to use if there was a war. Julius had given up trying to influence his fellow cadets and resigned himself to the inevitable.

If Russia backed Serbia, which appeared very likely as the Romanov nation believed that they had been slighted by Austro-Hungary, then Germany would have to support her ally, Austro-Hungary. Instead of this being a small conflict in the Balkans, as had at first been prophesied, by the end of 1908 war across the continent appeared very likely. All Christmas leave was cancelled which added to Julius' depression as he had been looking forward to seeing Mama and Irmy. He managed to get a message to his father that he would like to see him and received a note back asking him to attend his quarters the next evening. When Julius went to Colonel Weber's office to ask his senior officer for permission to go and see his father Weber told him to sit down and offered him the chair in front of his desk.

"Is there something wrong Cadet Mayer, that you want to see your father so urgently?"

Julius felt embarrassed by the question and could feel his face going red, "No Sir" he lied, "I just felt while things are somewhat calmer I would go and see my father. With all Christmas leave cancelled and everybody talking of a possible conflict in the New Year, I felt I should go and see him now, as I have no idea when I will see him in the future"

Colonel Weber held Julius with a steady gaze, which did not leave his face. Julius felt that this man could read his mind, knew exactly what he was thinking, and was confused as to what to say next. He wrenched his eyes from the Colonel's stare and looked down at the ground. After what seemed a very long silence Colonel Weber frowned, then said, "very well, Cadet Mayer, you have leave to go and see your father tonight, please give him my regards, dismissed"

Julius jumped up from his chair, saluted and turned to march out of the office. As he opened the door he heard Colonel Weber say his name and he turned back to face him. The Colonel leaned back in his chair and folded his arms, "Cadet Mayer, I am your senior officer, I am not only here to oversee your training, but also to see to your welfare and well-being whilst you are a cadet. If you ever need anybody to talk to, and your father may not always be available, remember my door is always open, understood?"

"Yes, sir, thank you sir" Julius bolted out of the room feeling even more confused.

Colonel Weber sat at his desk and stared at the door for a long time.

When Julius arrived at his father's quarters he was met by his father's batman who informed Julius that his father would be with him shortly, then he left the room. Julius took off his kepi and greatcoat and walked around his father's rooms. They were spartanly furnished, rooms typical of a single military man, which, he reflected, was what his father was here in Vienna. The only color in the room was provided by Mama and Irmy's tapestries and embroidery, lovingly stitched for his father, most of them decorated with quotes from the Bible and some with wildfowl and hunting scenes, which were Colonel Mayer's favorites.

On the mantelpiece, above a blazing fire, were assorted pictures of the family. He was surprised to find a wedding picture of Karl and Anna, it was lying flat on the shelf and Julius wondered if it had been placed in that way deliberately. He had not seen it before as none of the family had sent him a photograph of the event. He stared at the sepia image of his brother and his new wife, she was certainly a beauty. He also looked at a photograph of the whole family together, similar to the one that was still in his bedside table. He smiled as he remembered the badinage and jollity when they had been posing for that picture. It was imperative that you stayed still for a length of time while the photographer was taking the picture, but they had one by one all started to giggle and could not keep a straight face, despite the photographer's pleadings that in the end turned to exasperation. Mama had tried to calm them all down, but in the end even she was finding it difficult to keep a smile from her face. Julius presumed that was why he liked this picture so much, you could see the merriment in his family's eyes and the ghosts of smiles that were on their faces, all except Papa who kept a stoical Habsburg stance throughout.

He was still smiling at his memories when his father entered the room, glasses on the end of his nose and a large sheaf of papers in his hand. Julius was shocked at his father's appearance, he looked very tired and haggard, and he instantly regretted disturbing him when he was so busy.

"Julius, my boy, good to see you. I am afraid I cannot spare you much of my time. I have a meeting in an hour and I have to make sure all the paperwork is correct before I go" Colonel Mayer sat down at his desk and proceeded to quickly peruse the paperwork.

"I am sorry, father, I did not realize you were so busy" Julius picked up his coat and hat and walked towards the door, "I can see you another time, what I wanted to talk you about will wait for another day"

"Julius" his father's voice made Julius stop in his tracks. It transported him back to his childhood when the somber tone of that voice created such fear in him as he knew his father was about to berate him or one of his brothers for some mischief. Julius turned round, feeling like a sulky child waiting for his punishment.

"Julius, come here now. I shall be a few minutes. I have two more pages to look at and then my attention will be yours. Sit down and stop behaving like a spoilt child"

Julius resented being called a child, but the way his father had spoken to him made him feel like one and for a moment he was desperately trying to stem the tears that were welling up inside him. Eventually his father stacked his papers together and went and sat with Julius. He watched his son for a while as he sat dejectedly, with his head down.

"Julius I am sorry I spoke to you in that way, there is really no excuse, except to explain that circumstances are very fraught at the moment, Sleep seems to be eluding me lately and consequently I seem to have little patience these days. Now what is it you wanted to see me about?"

Julius reflected that his feelings were very insignificant in the light of all that was happening around him and his family. He felt very stupid to have brought them to his father at a time like this. He did not know what to say, he found himself tongue-tied.

"Come on Julius, we have always been able to talk to each other I think, so what is stopping you now?"

Julius hesitated, then said, "I have to admit I have been troubled, father, but now, sitting here with you, it all seems rather petty and inconsequential"

"Well why don't you let me be the judge of that, you obviously felt strongly enough about it to come and see me"

"I really do not know where to start"

"How about at the beginning" his father smiled encouragingly, "that is always a good place to start"

So Julius told his father the whole story. He recounted the maneuvers in the mountains, his experiences of racism within the army, his feelings about certain senior officers and his misgivings about the present furor over the annexation of Bosnia and Herzogevina.

"I know I am going to let you down by saying this father, but when they first announced the possibility of war, I felt really frightened. At first I tried to persuade myself it was because I have not finished my training and therefore feel I am not ready for combat, but I think it was something more basic than that, I think I am just scared"

Whilst Julius had delivered this speech he had not been able to look at his father, but now he had confessed his innermost feelings he looked up at him. His father was staring at him with an expressionless face and he could not fathom his feelings. His father had lit a cigar, which he now sucked on and blew out great clouds of smoke, which he watched as they curled and danced up towards the ceiling.

"Have you told anybody of your feelings, your friends, Colonel Weber?"

"No, I would not dare, I feel I am being disloyal, but the feelings still remain"

"Good" replied his father. He leaned forward in his chair towards Julius, "remember Julius, in this army, indeed in many walks of life, there is always someone who is trying to climb above you, sometimes by any means possible. You could tell someone something today and they may not even acknowledge they were listening to you, but sometime in the future, maybe many years from now, they may well use that information against you, just remember that.

Now to what you have told me. My son, all you have said is true. In some ways I am very proud of you that at such a young age you have noticed these things, but I have to tell you that such occurrences have been going on in this army for many years, and will continue to do so probably for another hundred years. It is not something that you or I can

86

change, though God knows I have tried. The only way we can help the situation is by doing our jobs well, and becoming exemplary officers who do not allow such things to happen in our regiment, do you understand?"

"I think so" said Julius, "you mean that as long as we stay true to ourselves and lead by example, maybe we can make a difference, even if it is only a small one, but we cannot change everything overnight"

Colonel Mayer smiled and tapped Julius' head, "I am so pleased you have your mother's brain in there, instead of mine. Do you remember when we went out to dinner just after your arrival in Vienna? and I was rather morose that evening? well I had come from a disciplinary hearing involving an ethnic situation. It is very depressing to know that there is such dissent amongst your own soldiers, before they even start fighting the enemy. If there is a solution, I do not know it. Maybe bright young things like you might make a difference, who knows. As to your opinion of some senior officers, in an army as large as ours not everyone will be a good officer, there are some very bad officers, but that is true of any army. When you receive your commission just try and be the best officer you can, that is all the Emperor asks of you. If you can go to bed at night and sleep without a conscience then you know you are fulfilling your expectations.

As to being frightened, I suppose several of the young cadets have been rushing about desperate to join the fighting have they? Well I suppose that is only to be expected, but that does not mean they are wrong, Julius. You are right to be frightened, war is an ugly thing, and I hope to God that it does not come to that, but some people do not think as deeply as you do, all they see is victory and triumph, not the possibility of failure"

Julius felt alarmed, "do you think that if war does come, then we will fail?"

"No of course I do not, but we should never forget that there is always that possibility, however great an army we possess, look at Napoleon for example. All I am saying is do not condemn people because they are not worried by the prospect of war, but at the same time realize that your feelings are true as well, you would be surprised how many soldiers are feeling just as scared as you are at the moment, and some quite senior as well"

"Really?" asked Julius incredulously.

"Really, but you probably will not find any of them admitting to it. Now I am sorry Julius I really must go. I hope I have helped you in some way, I am afraid your answers only lie within yourself; it is for you to sort them out and come to terms with them if possible. Have you been to confession lately?"

Julius grinned, "It is funny father, but ever since we have had this crisis we have all been going to Mass regularly"

"There, you see what I mean. Everyone sorts out their feelings in their own individual way, and I suspect for a lot of people, even those desperate for a fight, the comfort of the Church means a lot to them. Never be scared of the confessional, Julius, do not think of yourself as disloyal. Remember your priest cannot repeat your confidences and I cannot always be here to listen to you"

Julius looked up sharply, wondering how his father had read his mind. When he had been to Mass he had not entered the confessional as he felt that it was treasonous to repeat his misgivings in this way, although he had longed to talk to somebody and he had sought out his father as a substitute for confession.

"I am glad you came to talk to me, and perhaps I can understand you better than a priest as I am a fellow soldier and your father, but promise me if you cannot see me go and see your priest, he will give you comfort, I assure you, and remember be careful who you confide in, heed my warning"

Julius embraced his father, donned his topcoat and hat and left the room. As he turned round to wave goodbye his father was already engrossed in his paperwork.

Christmas and New Year were very somber affairs in the barracks. New rumors circulated daily as to the nearness of war, then that there was to be a climb-down by the government, then that the Russians had capitulated. Every day there was a different story until everybody was heartily sick of waiting around and despondency settled over the city. Julius did not see his father at this time, though his visit had helped him come to terms with his self doubts and he took his father's advice and went to confession and this helped him a little.

News came, early in January 1909, that Serbia had called up her reservists and that there had been threatening speeches against the Austro-Hungarian Empire made in the Belgrade parliament. Tension was high everywhere but still the government persisted in pursuing a diplomatic end to the hostilities. January dragged into February with still no progress being made.

The cadets were in their classroom one morning, listening to a lecture. Training had been difficult after the New Year as most instructors had been preparing for war and the cadets found it difficult to concentrate on their lessons with so much upheaval around them. Colonel Weber marched into the classroom and all the cadets stood to attention.

"Gentlemen, I have just received this announcement from the Emperor's office which I think will prove of interest to all of you"

Julius felt sure that it was a declaration of war and his stomach felt as if it was tied in knots. "The Emperor and his government have received a communiqué from the governments of Russia and Serbia. They concede to the Austro-Hungarian government the rights to the provinces of Bosnia and Herzegovina. Gentlemen, the victory is ours"

All the cadets threw their hats up and jumped in the air, the feeling of jubilation filled the room. Julius was ecstatic, but he still was not sure whether it was due to the fact that the Empire had acquired two new provinces and had stood up to the might of the Russias, or because almost certain war had been averted.

IX

After the frenzy of the last three months barracks life settled down to what was almost a dull routine. Julius' good humor returned, he knew he had learnt a lot in the last few months, especially about himself, he realized he was growing up. The next month would see him celebrate his nineteenth birthday and he felt he was a very different person to the boy who had arrived in Vienna nearly three years ago.

With his physical training he had grown in stature and was now a tall, muscular young man who turned many young girl's heads in the streets of Vienna. Julius was still oblivious to the effect he had on members of the opposite sex, only really noticing when Josef would point out a pretty young girl smiling in his direction. Julius was often curious to know if Josef had had any experience of women, but was too shy to ask him. Josef obviously knew how to flirt, but Julius wondered if his knowledge of women went beyond that. Julius himself had started to wonder about relationships with women but his army career would temper that ambition for a while. Viktor still received his violet perfumed envelopes, but he had shown no inclination to see the writer of the letters when they had been in Salzburg, so Julius had presumed there could not be much in the relationship. Nikolas continued to be shy and nervous whenever he even looked at a girl. Julius recalled how self-conscious he had been with Irmy, though he would never make fun of his friend about such a sensitive subject.

Just before his birthday he had received a letter from Irmy, which held an urgent request. It was one that he did not really want to comply with, but he knew that he would have to as he did not want to let her down. There was to be a ball at the City Hall in Vienna. Years ago the Emperor held Grand Balls at the Opera House on the Ringstrasse. They were huge affairs and the noblest aristocracy and senior military personnel clamored for an invitation to these prestigious events. The Emperor and his family always attended the Ball and it was seen as one of the high points in the Viennese social calendar. At the end of the last century the Emperor had chosen to cancel the Opera Ball, but the aristocracy of the city still tried to emulate those glittering affairs by organizing balls of their own.

Many people thought that after the circumstances of the past few months that the Ball would be cancelled. However Irmy wrote that Papa had had an invitation to the Ball, which was a very great honor, and that he wished Irmy to accompany her mother to Vienna. Here Irmy continued, with obvious guile, 'Mama is so excited, but there is a problem. I would love to go to the ball, nothing would please me more, but I could not possibly go unaccompanied. Papa suggested that you might like to come with us Julius and that would be wonderful, if you will agree. What more could I ask than to have my handsome brother escort me?'

Julius smiled to himself at her blatant form of flattery. She went on 'of course I will understand if you wish to refuse the invitation and I will stay in my hotel room while Mama and Papa go to the ball, but I would like to go nonetheless'

Julius shook his head at his sister's emotional blackmail. He had no inclination to go to the ball and he did not envisage such a night as any enjoyment for himself, but he knew he would go, for Irmy's sake. He understood that she had a rather dull life and was often frustrated by her desires to become a nurse and the ball would be wonderful for a girl of her age.

Because of the cancellation of Christmas leave he had not seen his sister for nearly fifteen months, she was eighteen now and he knew his parents were considering her marriage prospects. It worried him to think of Irmy in a marriage that stifled her imaginative and ambitious nature. Yes, he would accompany Irmy to the ball, not that he relished the evening himself, but because he knew it would make her happy.

He duly wrote back to his sister, then braced himself to tell his roommates of his invitation to the ball. He knew they would not let the event go by without a certain amount of leg pulling.

"He will be asking us to bow before him soon, once he starts getting acquainted with royalty" joked Nikolas, on hearing the news.

"I want you to tell me about all the food that is served" laughed Viktor, who still always thought of his stomach first. Julius realized that Josef was being unusually quiet, "come on Josef, it is not like you to forgo the chance of poking fun at me"

"Well I feel it would be rather hypocritical of me as I am going to the ball as well"

"You sly dog" said Viktor "when were you going to tell us about this?"

Julius looked to see if Josef was at all embarrassed by his disclosure, or at being caught out, but he appeared as unconcerned as ever, "actually I wasn't going to tell you, I could imagine the comments I would get, but after hearing that Julius was to be at the ball and there was a good chance he would see me I thought I had better come clean. I am going at the request of my mother who wishes me to accompany her for the evening"

"What about your father?" asked Nikolas.

"Oh she cannot rely on him, he probably would not turn up, preferring to be with one of his mistresses" replied Josef, staring at the floor.

Julius tried to alleviate the somber gloom that had descended on Josef. "Well I am glad you are going Josef. I really do not want to go myself, but my sister feels she cannot go unaccompanied, and I do not want to disappoint her"

The afternoon of the ball provided a hive of activity in dormitory six. On hearing the news that Julius and Josef were to attend the Ball Smid had become overcome with the excitement of it all. He took it as a personal triumph that two of his young gentlemen had been honored with an invitation to the prestigious event, and proceeded to check and double check that they were both immaculately dressed for the evening ahead.

Viktor and Nikolas were lying on their beds making facetious remarks about their friends as Julius and Josef attempted to shave without cutting themselves on their cut-throat razors.

Julius observed his two friends in his mirror, "if you two do not shut up I am going to use this razor on your throats"

"Do not rise to them Julius, they are only jealous" rejoined Josef, which produced peals of laughter from Viktor and Nikolas.

"Jealous?" exclaimed Viktor, "I would rather do a few days drill work with old Brunner than have to suffer the evening you are going to have. Too refined for me I am afraid"

There was a loud bang as their door was kicked open and there appeared in the doorway their dress uniforms apparently floating in mid air, on top of which could be seen a few tufts of hair sticking up. Nikolas leapt off his bed to help poor Smid who was carefully carrying the uniforms as though he held the Imperial Jewels. Nikolas stopped in his tracks as Smid shouted, "No don't come near me, don't touch anything!"

Smid carefully laid the uniforms on a bed and proceeded to hang them in the wardrobe, carrying each item as though it were made of fragile glass.

"Sorry to have shouted at you sir" he apologized, "but I have spent hours pressing these and you could have easily spoilt all my work"

Nikolas good-naturedly shrugged his shoulders and returned to his bed where he continued to watch the scene before him.

"Smid we really do appreciate all your work, but you know you pressed those uniforms yesterday, there was no need to do them today as well" said Josef.

"I know you think I am being finicky, Sir, but I looked at them this morning and knew I could make a better job"

Julius and Josef proceeded to dress carefully in their uniforms, with Smid fussing over every garment that they put on. At last they were ready. Both men were striking figures in their regimental dress uniforms, both handsome, though both having very different looks, one so dark and one so fair. As they stood for Smid to see to last minute touches Viktor and Nikolas got up from their beds and started to walk theatrically around them as though making a military inspection.

Viktor let out a long low whistle, "Very nice gentlemen, you will do. You are both a vision fit for an Emperor, or in Josef's case, any young girl that catches his eye" Josef grinned, then stuck out his tongue at Viktor.

"Oh, I am not so sure" laughed Nikolas, "it would help if they were better looking. I mean the uniform looks well on them, it is a shame about their ugly faces" Both Julius and Josef went to make a grab for Nikolas but were stopped as Smid shouted, "Gentlemen, remember your uniforms, please!"

The two men went to get their gloves from the dresser, "I wonder what the new uniform will be like, I hope it is not too much of a drastic change" observed Julius. Their class had been informed, only that week, that the Emperor had agreed to a new uniform for the Austro-Hungarian Army, which would be issued that summer. There had been much consternation in the ranks about this new uniform. Rumour had it that the cavalry had appealed to the Emperor himself to keep their red madder trousers as this was a part of the uniform that was supposedly to be changed.

Josef donned his cape, he was to go to his mother's house before the ball and Julius was to meet his family at their hotel in the city, not far from the barracks.

Julius turned to Viktor and Nikolas, "well goodbye you two, how are you going to amuse yourselves this evening?"

Viktor and Nikolas looked at each other, and Nikolas said innocently, "Oh, we are going to the City Hall to watch the idle rich arrive at their ball"

Julius stared at them with an open mouth, "You cannot be serious"

Viktor chuckled, "oh but we are, we thought while we were there we could beg a few heller off the aristocracy to supplement our meager allowance"

"Do you not mean a few krone, Viktor" corrected Nikolas, "such people as attend the Ball would probably not know what a heller was" and the two men dissolved with laughter. Julius and Josef decided to ignore their banter and with Smid still fussing over them like a mother hen, they departed for the ball.

Frau Mayer's maid admitted Julius into her suite of rooms and informed him that Irmy and his mother would be joining him shortly. Julius walked around the room and was adjusting his watch to the clock on the mantelpiece when he heard someone behind him enter the room.

He was not prepared for the vision that met him as he turned round. Julius had not seen his sister for over a year, and in that time she had grown from an adolescent girl into a beautiful young woman. She stood before him, very composed and elegant, reminding Julius of their mother. Her hair was dressed attractively on the top of her head. Irmy wore a shimmering white dress over which there was an overdress of diaphanous white material that crossed over her bosom and fell shorter than her dress. The delicate material was decorated with sequins and glowed in the lights of the room. She was wearing a pearl choker and beautiful pearl drop earrings, which Julius knew to be their mother's.

"Julius what is the matter?" asked Irmy, "is something wrong? you do not like my dress, please say you like it. Mama and I sent to Vienna for the pattern and our dressmaker made it up for me. Is it not the fashion? Oh I knew I was wrong to have chosen this style"

Julius, seeing Irmy was working herself into an apoplexy, rushed over to his sister. "Irmy, calm yourself, I am just amazed. I leave a naive young girl in Kosice and here in Vienna I meet a beautiful young woman, it is quite a shock"

Irmy disarmingly looked up at her brother, "do you mean that Julius, or are you just being kind?"

"I swear on our parent's life Irmy, I have never seen you looking so lovely. My only worry is keeping all the young men away from you tonight. Good Lord, Josef!"

"Julius, what are you talking about" asked Irmy.

Julius recovered his composure, "take no notice of me Irmy, but I would like you to be careful tonight, Viennese men are not like our friends in Kosice"

Irmy laughed, "well thank you for your compliments and your concern, but I am sure I can take care of myself. Anyway I have something to tell you, a secret, I am bursting to tell you" but Irmy was unable to confide her secret to Julius for at that moment Frau Mayer entered the room looking her usual elegant and serene self in a ball gown of deep blue. "Julius I was not told you had arrived, my how you have grown and you look so handsome"

Julius kissed his mother and commented on his sister's favorable appearance. "I know, she looks so lovely tonight, I do not think it will be hard to find a husband for Irmy, do you Julius?"

Julius grinned as he saw Irmy's eyes raised to the ceiling. Shortly afterwards Colonel Mayer arrived to complete their party and he was also impressed with his daughter. As they were leaving the suite on the way to their carriage he exclaimed "I think we will be the most envied men at the ball tonight Julius, with such beautiful companions"

"Yes indeed" replied Julius as he took his sister's arm.

The ride to City Hall was a long one as the carriages lined up to deposit their passengers at the door. As they arrived Julius and his father alighted first in order to help Mama and Irmy down from the carriage. As Julius again took Irmy's arm to escort her into the ball he looked up to see two familiar faces amongst the crowd that were gathered to see the guests arrive and perhaps catch a glimpse of the Imperial Family. Viktor started to wave and pull funny faces but Julius was amused to see Nikolas staring with his mouth open as he watched Irmy walk by.

Once inside the building Julius was struck by the cacophony of sound that assailed them as they entered. The sight reminded him of the railway station in Vienna, a state of ordered chaos, but this was a far richer scene as the jewels and tiaras of some of Vienna's richest families sparkled in the thousands of candles burning to light up the interior of the Hall.

Colonel Mayer took charge as he seemed to know where they were to be seated and his family dutifully followed him through the crowded assembly. As they sat down at their table Julius looked around to see if he could see Josef, but the Hall was too crowded to have any hope of seeing anybody that he might know.

Irmy was very excited and looked around in wonderment at the cream of Viennese society that paraded about them. She and Mama spent several minutes commenting on the hairstyles and the dresses of the various ladies that passed by in an endeavor to find their seats.

At last most people were seated and everybody waited in anticipation for the arrival of the Royal Family and their entourage. Julius looked up to see, on the other side of the room, Josef enter with a woman who was obviously his mother. Julius had never seen such a beautiful woman as the Countess von Kutz. He could see where Josef got his looks from. She had his high cheekbones and blonde hair and held herself with such a natural poise and elegance that all eyes were drawn to her as she sat down at her table with Josef. Josef looked around, but didn't see Julius, or did not care to, thought Julius wryly.

A few minutes later there was the sound of raised voices and a large, obese man blundered in, closely followed by several stewards who were remonstrating with him. Julius thought he had probably been drinking as the man was uncertain on his feet. He had the appearance of a habitual toper with a bright red, bloated face, which held mean little eyes that were having difficulty in focusing.

"My God" whispered Colonel Mayer, "what is he doing here?"

"Who is he father?" asked Julius, his curiosity aroused.

"That, Julius, is your friend's father, the infamous Count von Kutz"

Julius turned back to watch the man he had heard so much about, but had never met. He had often wondered what

96

Count von Kutz was like, but never in his imagination had he ever pictured such a vile figure as the one before him. He just could not imagine this man even being remotely related to Josef or the beautiful woman that he had observed just a few minutes ago.

"How on earth did he get like that?" pondered Colonel Mayer, "I have not seen him for several years. He was quite a good-looking young man when I knew him, now look at him, heaven knows what sort of life he leads now"

Julius watched in fear as he saw Count von Kutz approach his wife's table. He shouted something at Josef who promptly jumped up and in one deft move locked his father's arm behind his back and marched him out. Julius looked on in admiration at Josef's prompt action in defusing what was a very embarrassing situation and rose to follow his friend to offer him some assistance.

"Sit down Julius" Colonel Mayer spoke very quietly, but Julius knew better than to disobey that voice, and so sat down again. Colonel Mayer looked across the table at his son, "I admire your loyalty, Julius, and I also admire the way your friend dealt with such an ugly situation, but running after him in front of all these people will only prolong the attention on Countess von Kutz and her son. Leave it be now, you will be able to help the situation in a far better way later on, believe me"

Julius sulked at his fathers' words, as he felt he should be helping Josef. He was about to ask his father what his words meant when there was a loud trumpet fanfare which heralded the arrival of the royal party and everybody rose in their seats to greet the Royal family.

Society always hoped that Franz Josef would attend these affairs, but once again they were to be disappointed. In the royal procession was the Emperor's nephew and heir Franz Ferdinand with his wife. The Archduke Franz Ferdinand had not helped his popularity by entering into a morganatic marriage with his wife, a move viewed with open distaste, especially by Austrian aristocracy. As he proceeded through the room everybody whom he passed either bowed or curtsied. Julius noted that the greeting for the couple was not as warm as it would have been for the Emperor. It was unlikely that they noticed as they swept through the room without a look at the assembled throng. They stared straight ahead and walked with urgency to get to their seats as quickly as possible.

When the royal party was seated the rest of the room resumed their seats and the ball commenced. An orchestra began to play the waltz and soon the dance floor was full of swirling colors, from the women's beautiful dresses to the many uniformed officers who added to the brilliance of the evening.

Colonel Mayer escorted his daughter onto the floor for their first dance and Julius followed with his mother. Julius' dancing skills were very basic, his experience being confined to the tea dances in Kosice many years ago, but his mother danced so gracefully that Julius found himself enjoying the dance as they waltzed around the floor. As he and Mama approached the far side of the dance floor Julius was able to snatch a quick look at Josef's table. He was pleased to see the blonde head of his friend deep in conversation with his mother, though he could also see that the rest of their table was vacant. He hoped this was because they had all progressed to the dance floor, not for any other reason.

As the music stopped, Julius and Frau Mayer found themselves standing very near Colonel Mayer and Irmy. Julius started to guide his mother back to their table but was caught by his father's hand on his arm. He turned to see his father, indicating with his eyes, that he should follow him and found himself walking towards Josef and his mother whose table was still deserted. As they approached the table Josef jumped up to greet them and on seeing Julius his face opened into a large smile.

Colonel Mayer bowed and introduced himself and Mama to Countess von Kutz.

"Countess von Kutz, may I have the honor of introducing myself. I am Colonel Mayer and this is my wife" The two women inclined their heads towards each other, "And this is my son, Julius, who I am sure you have heard of, and my daughter Irmy. We are delighted to make your acquaintance at last"

Countess von Kutz surveyed the scene in front of her. Close to her Julius felt he had never seen such a lovely creature in all his life. She possessed the most wonderful eyes, eyes that seemed to bore into his very soul when she looked at him. He felt himself blushing and quickly began to stare at the floor. He heard Josef introducing his mother to his parents and was alarmed to hear his friend ask Irmy for the honor of a dance. Julius looked at Irmy to try and warn her not to accept the invitation but was dismayed to hear Irmy

98

consenting to his request. He watched his sister take Josef's arm and be escorted onto the dance floor, with a knowing smile at Julius as she passed him.

Countess von Kutz invited Julius and his parents to join her at her table and they continued in idle chatter whilst Julius watched Irmy and Josef in animated conversation as they whirled around the dance floor. Julius was even more disturbed when Josef detained his sister for a second dance and was wondering whether to cut in on the pair when he realized that Countess von Kutz was talking to him. He turned to her and was surprised to find himself alone with Josef's mother. He had not noticed that his parents had repaired to the dance floor themselves, so engrossed had he been in watching Irmy.

"They make a very handsome couple, do they not, my son and your sister?" commented Countess von Kutz.

Julius tried to hide his embarrassment, "Yes, very" he faltered. He was at a loss for words and tried desperately to think of something to say and was relieved to find the Countess leading the conversation.

"I am glad that I have had this opportunity to speak to you alone, Julius, may I call you Julius?" Julius nodded wide-eyed, mesmerized by the beauty in front of him.

"I just wanted to thank you for the friendship you have given my son over the last few years. Josef is a very complex boy, as I am sure you know. He does not make friends easily but I know the friendship he has formed with you, Nikolas and Viktor means a great deal to him. More than I am sure he makes obvious to you" They both smiled as they acknowledged the complicated personality that was Josef. "I hope you will always think well of my son Julius. Under that bluff exterior is a warm, caring young man who over the years has learned to mask his feelings under what I think, at times, is mistaken for arrogance, am I right?"

Julius opened his mouth but could not think of the right words to say. He was looking straight into the Countess' deep blue eyes that held a whole gamut of emotions. He looked closely at her lovely face and saw small lines around her mouth and on her brow that expressed an unhappiness and misery that she hid with her calm and elegant exterior. Even her lovely limpid eyes held a sadness that could not be touched.

"Would you thank your parents for their act of kindness in coming to our table this evening. Although it was a pleasure to meet them, I know it was also an act of charity in our embarrassing situation and I am most grateful to them. It is nice to know there are honorable people in this world" she ended sadly.

The music had stopped and gratefully Julius saw Josef escorting his sister back to the table. Grateful because Irmy was no longer dancing with his friend, but also because he was finding it increasingly difficult to talk to the Countess, so overpowered was he at the closeness of such an exquisite creature. Julius rose as Irmy approached the table. He could hear her tinkling laughter as she shared some amusement with Josef.

"Julius, you did not tell me you had such a beautiful and witty sister" laughed Josef.

"I will wager he hardly mentions me at all, and if he does it is in all likelihood to mock his little sister" added Irmy, with a mischievous twinkle in her eye.

Julius was about to protest as Josef replied, "no, not at all, I assure you, I was only teasing Julius. He speaks of you often and obviously has a deep affection for you. He probably omitted to tell me of your beauty and wit on purpose. I think he believed I would be a terrible influence on you if we were ever to meet"

Josef and Irmy laughed heartily at Julius' discomfort. Irmy seeing her brothers' embarrassment hastily changed the subject and suggested that she and Julius share the next dance as the orchestra began to play again. Julius bowed to Countess von Kutz and added, "it was an honor to meet you, madam. Josef, I will see you later, I hope"

Josef grinned, "who knows Irmy, maybe we may have another dance this evening, but only if your brother will allow it"

Julius pulled a face at his friend's laughing countenance and as Josef bowed he led Irmy onto the dance floor.

As he danced with Irmy Julius wondered whether to warn his sister as to Josef's somewhat mischievous nature but decided against this cause of action. To tell her would probably increase her interest in Josef, not deter it. As though reading her brother's mind Irmy looked up at her brother, "I found Josef very amusing company, Julius, but I was not completely won over by his good looks or his suave nature you know. I have lived too long with three elder brothers to be swayed by a pair of blue eyes and a few well intentioned compliments"

100

Julius laughed at his sister's audacity and her accurate assessment of Josef and was cheered by her words. As much as he cared for his friend and truly liked him, he had no desire to see his beloved sister form an attachment to him, an attachment that was so wholly unsuitable.

"Julius, I have something to tell you, but you must swear that you will not breathe a word of this to anybody else. At least not for a little while anyway"

Julius was intrigued by his sister's enigmatic manner. As he looked down at her she would not meet his eyes and looked furtively round the room as though someone might be overhearing their conversation.

"Is this the secret you were telling me about at the hotel. Must I even keep it from Mama and Papa?"

Irmy's head pulled up and she looked at Julius with real fear in her eyes, "*especially* not Mama and Papa, promise me Julius"

Julius felt he should not be agreeing to such a pledge, but his curiosity overcame his doubts as he swore his silence to Irmy.

"Julius I have such news, I am engaged!"

Julius stopped dancing in the middle of the floor and gazed at his sister with such an incredulous expression that several of the surrounding dancers also stopped to see what the matter was.

"Julius, please, you are bringing attention to ourselves. Start dancing again before you stop everybody else dancing" Irmy put her arm on her brothers and they began to dance again.

"I am sorry Irmy. You could have been a bit more subtle. Engaged? what on earth are you talking about? and our parents do not know. What on earth have you been up to now?"

Irmy laughed, "do not distress yourself Julius. I have done nothing that would shame me, well apart from hiding my engagement from Mama and Papa, and I promise you they will know soon enough"

"Yes, maybe, but will they be happy about it, that is the question?"

The music had stopped, but Julius suggested they stayed for another dance as he had to hear the rest of Irmy's story and this was the only place where they could talk freely. As they circled the dance floor Julius was oblivious to his surroundings as Irmy continued to excitedly recount all the details of her romance.

"His name is Richard Beck, and you will never guess, he is a doctor! He came to the hospital about eight months ago. He is training to be a surgeon and he has a one year contract at the hospital under Professor Krebs. You know Professor Krebs? no? well he is an eminent surgeon and he has many students who come from all over Austria, Germany and Bohemia to study under him. It is a great privilege to be picked by Professor Krebs, so Richard is very lucky. Anyway we met, at the hospital and kept meeting on the wards and I have met him occasionally for coffee...."

Julius looked at his sister, as her face blushed a deep red color and guessed at her nervousness.

"Irmy, don't tell me you have met this Richard outside the hospital, on your own? Without Mama or Danusia in attendance?"

"Oh Julius you can be so straight-laced at times. How else could I have got to know him better? It was only in Hoffmeyers Coffee House, never completely on my own. I wanted to get to know him before I introduced him to Mama. If Mama had met him earlier she would have scared him away by asking him about his prospects. She would have been ordering my wedding dress before he had stepped foot in the doorway!" Julius had to grin at this picture of his mother, as he had to admit to himself it would have been a very likely scenario.

"He is wonderful, Julius. I do love him and I want you to like him, that is very important to me"

"I promise I will try, when do I have the pleasure of meeting this scoundrel who has stolen my little sister's heart? I cannot wait to tell him that it would not have mattered if he had two heads, you would still have fallen in love with him because he is a doctor"

Irmy laughed, "that is not true, and you know it. Richard is due in Vienna in two weeks to attend a conference with the Professor and he is to ask Papa for my hand in marriage then. I hope you can meet him too. He is a very liberal man, you know. He has said that after we are married he is happy for me to train to be nurse. Is that not wonderful?"

Julius received this news with some reservations. Although his sister was obviously very happy with her new found love he doubted whether their parents would receive the news with absolute enthusiasm, especially not with the thought of their only daughter working for her living. He felt that his sister was not being totally honest about Richard Beck, that she was hiding something from him that he would not like to hear about his future brother-in-law. He resolved to find out what that was.

"And what are the good Herr Doktor Beck's prospects may I ask?"

"Julius you sound like my Papa, not my brother" Irmy hesitated before she continued, "Richard is actually quite wealthy. He has his own private income. I believe he would not have to work if he did not want to. His family comes from Prague, which is where he will return to practice when his year in Kosice has finished"

Maybe that was the trouble, if Irmy did marry this man she would be living in Prague, a long way from Kosice, a fact that Mama would find hard to bear.

The music finished and Julius agreed with his sister that it was time they returned to their parent's table. As they left the floor Irmy turned to her brother, "Remember, Julius, not a word to anyone, you promised"

They made their way back to their parent's table, side-stepping all the various people walking to and from the dance floor. Just as they approached their table Irmy looked up at her brother, "there is one more thing I have to tell you, Richard is thirty years old"

Julius felt the floor come up towards him as his brain assimilated his sister's remark. Irmy had quickly taken her seat next to Papa and was looking as demure as ever, but she kept giving her brother a nervous glance as he resumed his seat. Thirty years old! Twelve years older than his sister. A large age difference that he felt was too much for an eighteen-year-old girl, why he was positively an old man! So that was the news Irmy had been trying to hide from him. She herself must know their difference in ages would be a large obstacle to Papa's consent to their marriage.

He had promised not to say a word to their parents and he would not go back on his word. Indeed he felt it was best not to say anything to his parents. If he did they would then know he knew more about the nature of Irmy's visits to the hospital than he had admitted. He then might find himself in serious trouble for not telling Colonel Mayer of his misgivings.

The rest of the evening passed very quickly. Julius decided to leave Irmy and her betrothal to be sorted out between his father and Richard Beck. That Irmy believed herself in love with the fellow there was no doubt. He did not want to make any hasty decisions until he had met Herr Doktor Beck himself and so decided not to dwell too long on the future. Irmy was asked for several dances by various young men and Julius was pleased to see her having so much fun as she danced around the floor, looking lovelier than he had ever seen her before.

After their supper Josef and his mother approached their table. Josef, with a mischievous smile on his face mockingly asked Julius if he could have the pleasure of his sister's company for the next dance. Julius was only too happy to comply with his wishes, secretly smiling to himself as he knew of the total disinterest that Irmy had for his friend, however much he flirted with his sister. After Irmy and Josef had departed for the dance floor Julius found himself in the embarrassing situation of once more being alone with the Countess. He felt the only thing to do was to ask Josef's mother for a dance and was bewildered to find himself leading this exquisite vision around the dance floor.

Julius had no knowledge of the scene around him, it was as if there was no music and all he was aware of was the flashing colors and lights darting around his head as he danced around the floor. The only vision in focus was the beautiful face of Countess von Kutz as she smiled benignly at him and the smell of her perfume, the scent of fresh spring flowers that filled the air. He was sweating profusely and his legs felt like they did not belong to him. He had a most uncomfortable feeling in his body that he felt sure he should not be experiencing for his friend's mother. Julius was not even aware of the music stopping until he heard the countess' gentle voice suggesting they return to their seats. Julius courteously led Josef's mother back to her seat and with a curt bow left the Countess at her table. He returned across the ballroom to his parents. He wished that the floor would swallow him up, so embarrassed was he by the affect the alluring Countess von Kutz had had on him. He flushed even deeper to think of the thoughts he had imagined about Josef's mother as they had circled the dance floor. On returning to his seat his parents commented on how quiet he had become. He was confused as he knew that he had fallen a little in love with the Countess von Kutz that evening.

Julius bade farewell to his mother and sister at their hotel. They were to leave for Kosice the next day and Julius had to be back at the barracks. As he kissed his sister goodbye he saw the appeal in her eyes and knew she was reminding him of his promise. He nodded to her and smiled as he said, "I hope you have had a wonderful time Irmy. I would not be surprised if quite a few young men fell in love with you this evening" Julius was pleased to see the panic in his sister's eyes as she turned to see if their parents had heard the irony in his voice but they were deep in conversation and had not heard his comments.

When he returned to his room Nikolas and Viktor were wide-awake, anxious to hear about his evening. He was telling them about the royal party when Josef entered the room. Josef seemed in a happy mood as he tried to rib Julius about Irmy but gave up when he realized this was having no affect. "You made quite an impression on my mother Julius, she was quite taken with you I think"
Julius felt himself blushing but hoped his roommates did not guess the reason why. Nothing was said about the incident with Josef's father.

The next day Josef took Julius to one side and thanked Julius for his family's show of respect the night before. "I would also like to thank you for not telling Nikolas and Viktor. I do not really care for myself. I am used to him, but he still manages to upset my mother and I would not like the incident to be common knowledge around here"
"No one will hear of it from me Josef, I promise. It is your business and I think we should both forget it as soon as possible"
Josef smiled at his friend and the two of them never mentioned the fracas at the Ball ever again.

X

The next month was Julius' nineteenth birthday. The day was spent in class but in the evening Josef had offered to take everybody out to celebrate.

Through the years Julius, Nikolas and Viktor had come to enjoy these forays into Viennese nightlife. Julius had become used to Josef's eccentric behavior and was bemused to remember his naiveté when Josef had first taken them to the Sacher Hotel. Now, in his maturity, he had learned to accept Josef's somewhat cavalier attitude and they all enjoyed his generosity, especially when sampling the social life of Vienna.

Often Josef's name had gained them entry into some establishments that the three other boys would never have dreamed of being able to enter without the patronage of their roommate. That Josef still enjoyed trying to shock them was still very evident but having lived nearly three years in the capital of the Austro-Hungarian Empire in one of its most vibrant and exciting periods the three country boys now displayed a confidence and learning which was far removed from the shy and nervous cadets who had entered the army in 1906.

As they embarked into the city that evening all four were looking forward to an enjoyable night. Julius, Viktor and Nikolas were impatient to know where they were going but Josef would only reply with an enigmatic smile and a mysterious "wait and see"
Julius eyed his friend warily, he was not sure he liked all the mystery and he knew he could not trust Josef.

His misgivings were heightened when Josef led them to a largely residential area of the city and stopped outside a house in a side street. The house was in a terrace, modestly elegant with stone steps leading up to an ornate front door. On either side of the door were two tall squared windows hung with dark red drapes through which could be seen large chandeliers that were lit in the evening gloom giving a warm and inviting look to the house. It was certainly not the place that Julius had envisaged being taken to on his birthday. The normality of the place only increased his suspicions of Josef.

Josef climbed the steps, followed somewhat reluctantly by his friends. He tapped on the door and Julius was

106

surprised to see a panel in the door open and two beady eyes appear. No words were spoken but the door opened to reveal a large, round oriental man who bowed to them as Josef ushered them inside. As soon as they were through the door it was shut with a resounding thud. The entrance of the house was tastefully furnished in rich welcoming colors of cream and burgundy and beyond the entrance hall was a large sweeping staircase, lit by chandeliers and decorated with portraits that lined the wall up to the next floor. As the boys looked around the hallway they were led by the oriental man into another room, equally well furnished, around which were positioned large vases of flowers that gave a heavy scent to the air. The oriental man then bowed and left the room, closing the double doors behind him, never having spoken a word.

Josef took off his greatcoat and collapsed onto one of the many sofas and chairs that littered the salon and lay there, his hands behind his head, observing his friends with a mischievous grin on his face.

"If you don't tell me this minute what we are doing here Josef, I for one am leaving" spat out Nikolas, obviously as uncomfortable with his surroundings as his companions.

"If this is another one of your stupid jokes Josef, you are going to regret it" said Viktor, "what is this place, it is clearly not a normal house, we could tell that by our greeting, so what is it?"

Josef sat up, the smile gone from his face, the first look of concern on his countenance. "Calm down, you will thank me for this, just wait and see"

"No, I am sorry Josef, I agree with Viktor and Nikolas, you tell us what you are up to or we are leaving now" Julius sat down to face Josef, who was trying to avoid looking at him.

Josef became distracted then took a deep breath as he seemed to come to a decision. "Well I thought as you were now nineteen, and not altogether experienced with females, I would give you" he looked up at Nikolas and Viktor who were staring at him with open mouths, dreading what was coming next, "well all of you really, a helping hand"

Julius stared in disbelief at his friend, knowing what was coming next but wanting to hear it from Josef's own mouth, "and by helping hand you mean....."

Josef stared straight back at his friend, his confidence seeming to return to him as he smiled, "can't you guess, this is what our mothers would call 'a house of ill repute' though I have to say a very high class one, only the best for my friends you know"

Nikolas moved to grab Josef but was held back by Viktor. "You bloody idiot, Josef" shouted Nikolas, "who the hell do you think you are?"

Josef jumped up to avoid Nikolas who was still struggling with Viktor in an effort to get to Josef. Josef ran behind the sofa, using the furniture to create a barrier between himself and Nikolas. Julius remained seated, absolutely at a loss as to what to say. His thoughts were wildly racing around inside his head, but he knew he should calm things down before an enraged Nikolas tore Josef apart, limb by limb.

"Stop it, all of you" he shouted. At the sound of his voice Nikolas calmed down and even Josef looked towards him as the authority in his voice seemed to take effect.

"Sit down all of you. Now let us get this right, Josef. For my birthday you have brought us here to, how shall I put it, sleep with some prostitutes?"

"Well I would not put it quite like that you know" faltered Josef.

"How would you put it then" sneered Viktor.

"Look, as I told you, this place is very discreet. The aristocracy of Vienna frequent these hallowed rooms. The girls are *not* prostitutes. They are very high class and very clean, I can assure you of that"

"Now that *is* a comfort" interrupted Nikolas, sarcastically.

"If I had known your reaction was going to be this extreme, I would never have brought you here. I honestly thought you would like the idea. This is where I first, well, you know, and you will all be treated very well. To be absolutely honest with you I would say this is the perfect place for your first time, believe me, I know. Do not tell me you have never wondered about it?"

All three boys looked at the floor in their embarrassment at the obvious answer to Josef's question. Viktor suddenly said, "my God, we are in uniform, what if someone saw us coming in here, we will be court-martialed"

Josef laughed, "not unless they want half of the officers in the Austro-Hungarian army on trial as well. This is a well-known place amongst our peers and superiors. I told you, everyone is very discreet. So what do you say, do you accept my present, this is not a cheap place you know"

Viktor got up, "whilst I hope you planned this with the very best intentions Josef, I for one do not feel I can accept. This would be too impersonal, not to say embarrassing for me, what did you expect us to do, slap you on the back and thank you for being such a wonderful friend?"

Julius could see that Josef was hurt by Viktor's reply. Whilst he knew Josef liked to try and humiliate his friends, he also realized, perhaps for the first time, that Josef was also looking for their approval. He felt that Josef had planned this evening with the intention of pleasing his friends, of receiving their approbation, and now was truly upset by their reactions. However Julius had to agree with Viktor, the idea was abhorrent to him, but he had to admit that mixed with his dislike of the situation was also a great feeling of fear. He knew he was scared, but also more than a little curious to know what might have happened had he agreed to the assignation.

Nikolas, Viktor and Julius picked up their coats and moved towards the door, whilst Josef pleaded with them to stay, at least for a little while longer. Just as they reached the double doors they were flung open and three women, all dressed in bedroom lingerie appeared. The three boys came to an abrupt halt, not knowing what to do next. To avoid any rudeness, and with resignation, the boys retreated back into the salon and sat together on one of the sofas, steadfastly stuck together as though their closeness provided a barricade for themselves.

The three women were very pretty, not at all as Julius had expected. He had expected cheap, overly made up creatures, much as he had seen on the street corners of Vienna, offering their wares in coarse and vulgar accents. These women would have graced any parlor in Vienna. They were all dressed similarly in negligees, edged with lace, slightly diaphanous, which exposed a tantalizing glimpse of the curves of their bodies through their under garments. Their only makeup was a slight rouging on their faces and lipstick, which heightened the whiteness of their teeth as they smiled. All wore their hair hanging down their backs caught with a ribbon, reminding Julius of Irmy in her younger days. He shook himself as he became aware of himself staring at them as they moved into the room. They elegantly seated themselves and one of them said in a clear crystal voice, "I do hope you were not thinking of leaving us gentlemen, that would be a great shame, for all of us"

"No but I was" said Josef, "I will see you all later, back at the barracks, have fun" and despite the look Nikolas gave him Josef picked up his greatcoat and quickly vacated the room, giving them all a knowing smile as he departed. God help me, I will kill him later, thought Julius. He wished he had the courage to get up and leave, but the allure of the women in front of him was proving too much and part of him very much wanted to stay.

The women tried to start a conversation, which was very difficult, especially as Nikolas became tongue tied whenever he was asked anything, and the one time he did manage to utter something it came out sounding like a cat being strangled.

Wine was bought by the oriental man and after a few glassfuls everyone appeared to relax, even Nikolas. Julius was appreciative of the way the girls began to put them at their ease, though he had to wryly admit to himself that this was after all what they were being paid to do.

Without realizing what was happening, each girl picked her partner, and after some more wine Julius found himself ascending the great staircase. As he climbed he felt the faces of all the people in the portraits following him up the stairs and he had to close his eyes as he imagined one of the portraits becoming Mama and he knew then he had definitely had too much wine.

The bedroom was as luxuriantly furnished as the rooms below, though decorated in rich colors of gold and green. It was dominated by an enormous four-poster bed, which Julius pointedly ignored in his embarrassment. The girl introduced herself as Lise and Julius was grateful of the fact that she busied herself about the room for a while, letting him get used to the idea of being alone in a bedroom with a woman for the very first time. As she moved about she talked to Julius, asking him innocuous questions, telling him a bit about herself until Julius started to feel more at ease.

Julius was always to be thankful for the way Lise treated him that evening. She had obviously known he was a virgin and had taken things very slowly so that he was not embarrassed. She had encouraged him to undress her, which he had done with shaking fingers, but she never once gave any indication that she noticed his fumbling or his blushing. She had a beautiful body and Julius' first sight of a naked woman was one he was to remember for the rest of his life. That it also created feelings in other parts of his body was clearly apparent but Lise only smiled in encouragement as she undressed him with a deftness and rapidity that amazed him.

Finally naked he felt an overwhelming sense of sheer and absolute exhilaration, such as he had never felt before, mixed with a sense of fear of not knowing what to do next. At that moment he would have seized the beckoning flesh that stood before him but Lise held her hands to his chest to stop him. She told him they would take things very slowly. "You must learn to explore the human body, to learn about it, then you will obtain the ultimate enjoyment from it" Slowly she showed him how to feel her body, and though embarrassed by the places she was allowing him to touch, Julius was swept away by the wonderful feelings that were rapidly spreading through his body. As he explored her sweet smelling skin he felt Lise's breath quicken as she began to moan under his touch, telling him what to do, her body swaying to his caress, until she exclaimed in delight and her body shook with the pleasure. Amazed at the reaction to his touch Julius exalted at the enjoyment he was obviously giving her. He wanted to take her lovely body into his arms but still she stopped him and then proceeded to stand before him and touch every part of his torso until he felt he would scream with the ecstasy of it all. Even when she caressed his private parts, although shocked that a woman would touch him in such a place, he could not help but moan with the pleasure of it as he became hotter and hotter until he thought he would burst. At last she took him by the hand and led him to the bed where they came together in such perfect harmony that Julius thought if his life were to end at that moment he would be content.

As they lay in satisfied fulfillment Julius looked down at their entwined bodies and realized that this was the most natural thing in the world. All his schoolboy fantasies and adolescent dreams had never prepared him for this. He had been brought up to believe it was something you did as a duty and for the procreation of children, he had never realized it could also be so enjoyable. That he had also been brought up to believe this was also something that was only done within the confines of marriage was something he chose not to think about.

They made love again, this time swiftly, as though they knew their time together was fleeting and would soon be over.

As Lise helped him to dress they said little but there were constant smiles between them as they came close, or touched. As he left her room she said "I know you think I say this to everybody, but I don't, I promise you. Tonight may have been your first time, but I know you are going to make some young lady a caring husband, and I am very envious. Thank you for tonight, it was nice for me as well, you know, and I can honestly say that does not happen too often"

Julius left the house without even enquiring whether his friends were still there or not. He needed to be on his own. He had to admit the night had been wonderful. He thought of Lise and realized that throughout their lovemaking they had never even kissed, no thoughts of affection had crossed his mind. It had been pure lust, but a wonderful lust, one he would remember all his life. As enjoyable as it had been he was aware that if you could combine that lust with love it would be an overwhelming and wonderful thing that must be preserved at all costs.

On his walk home through the dark Viennese streets on his nineteenth birthday, the moon shining brightly in the sky, surrounded by her twinkling stars, he made a pact with himself that when he found his lifelong partner, the woman he wanted to spend the rest of his life with, he would make sure that their relationship held that sort of power, for with it he was sure, nothing could go wrong.

XI

The four boys never discussed Julius' birthday amongst themselves. It was something that was tacitly understood between them all. It had happened, they were not ashamed of the event, but it was not something that any of them were able to talk about openly with each other. That it had changed them was undeniable, but it was a very subtle change. Josef accepted that they had benefited from the evening but took no offence that his friends did not openly thank him. He took enjoyment from the fact that the evening had eventually turned out to be a success and was pleased to be back in favor with all of them. Besides, other events were to occupy their thoughts over the next couple of months.

A few days after Julius' birthday Colonel Weber had entered their classroom with important news. All the cadets were due to have finished their officer training in June of that year, 1909. However due to the Balkan crisis it had been presumed that the course would have to be extended into the New Year so that the cadets could carry out their winter exercises in the Alps, an important part of their training. Colonel Weber announced to an excited class that it had been decided that final exams would be taken in the coming summer and the successful cadets would gain their commissions then. The new officers would be assigned to their various regiments but would be released from their duties to take part in winter exercises later on in the year.

The news was received by the cadets with enthusiasm, mixed with a large amount of alarm. The change in proceedings meant that final exams would take place in just over two months. Most cadets had been particularly lax in their studies as they had thought they would not have exams for almost another year. Some cadets were dismayed by the prospect of the approaching exams, none more so than Viktor. On returning to their room after classes he fell onto his bed with his head in his hands bemoaning the fact that he would never be able to revise in such a short time.

"I think you are overreacting, Viktor" said Julius, trying to mollify his friend, "most of the exams contain all the things we have experienced over the past three years, there is nothing new. You have always done well in previous tests, so why are you worrying now? We will all work together over the next two months, continually revise, and you will see that we will all be ready for the exams, and pass them with flying colors"

Viktor managed to smile at Julius, "that is what I hate about you the most Mayer, you are always so full of damn optimism"

True to their words the boys settled down to work really hard over the next few weeks. Every evening saw them grouped around the table in their room testing each other, reading their copious manuals and revising late into the night. Even Josef took the approaching exams seriously. His friends were amazed to note that he was not going out into the city at all, but stayed in their room, studying with the others. Every morning the cadets would drag themselves to their various tasks with weary bodies and red eyes from poring over their books into the early hours of the morning. At times Julius felt he could not absorb any more facts into his tired brain. Then somebody would mention some problem or other that sent them all diving into their books again trying to find the relevant answers.

It was in the middle of this study period that Julius was descending the stairs to enter the mess for breakfast when he was hailed by one of the porters who held a hand written letter for him. Julius recognized his father's writing and was alarmed as to why his father would be sending an urgent letter to him by messenger. The note was very short and entailed a brief request, which Julius recognized as an order, to report to his father's rooms that evening. Julius was annoyed at the dismissive tone of the note, added to which he should be in his rooms that night, revising for his exams. The time he would spend with his father he felt could be better spent in the barracks.

He found Sergeant Major Hoffman and informed him of his father's request. He hoped that Hoffman would deny him permission to leave the barracks that evening, but in his heart Julius knew that he would not go against the wishes of a colonel. Hoffman even added, "I think it would be a good idea to visit your father, Mayer. The break away from your studies will do you good, too much studying can be as harmful as too little, you know"

Colonel Mayer's note had requested Julius to be in his rooms at seven o'clock that evening. As the clock was chiming on the colonel's mantelpiece Julius was ushered into his father's rooms by his batman. Colonel Mayer was seated in one of his armchairs and whilst not looking openly hostile Julius felt a definitely icy feel to his father's greeting. "Well at least you are prompt, sit down Julius, I wish to discuss something of importance with you"

Julius removed his greatcoat and sat on the sofa opposite his father. He had the feeling his father had orchestrated this positioning. His father was sitting upright, slightly higher than his son, and Julius noticed too that he was in full uniform, which was not necessary in the privacy of his rooms.

Julius looked at his father, taking in the graying hair and moustaches that somehow added to his authoritarian demeanor, the powerful body that remained remarkably slender, despite the gaining years. Not for the first time did Julius wonder about his father's age, and how much longer he could remain in the Imperial Army. The thought of his father not in the army alarmed Julius. He could not imagine any other place for his father and though he felt sure his mother would welcome her husband's retirement, he knew the thought of it would break his father's heart. He supposed one day this fact would be an inevitability, but pushed it to the back of his mind, as he was sure his father often did.

Julius realized that his father was looking at him intently and felt uncomfortable under his father's gaze.

"I am glad you could come tonight, I imagine you are working hard for your exams, I heard that your commission had been brought forward. How do you think you will fare?"

Julius started to discuss the exams and his choice of regiments with Colonel Mayer. Throughout the conversation he had the uneasy feeling that this was not the reason he had been summoned and started to speculate on what the real reason was. Suddenly it became only too clear. The colonel rested back into his seat and observing the reaction of his son said, "There is another reason I especially wanted you here tonight. We are to be joined at eight o'clock by a Herr Doktor Richard Beck, does that name mean anything to you Julius?"

Julius felt his mouth go dry and he looked away to avoid the steady regard of his father. He tried to gather his thoughts as to what to say next but was at a loss as he had no idea how much his father knew of his knowledge of Irmy's engagement. He decided not to say a word and was relieved when, after a long silence, his father began to speak again.

"You are very quiet Julius, perhaps you are tired from your studying, is that it?" His father's sarcasm was not lost on Julius, so he decided to be honest with him. He told his father what he knew about Richard Beck, which after all was only what Irmy had told him at the ball.

"Did you not think to tell me about their proposed engagement, or was I to be the last person to know?"

"It really was not like that father. Irmy swore me to secrecy, and you know how dogmatic Irmy can be when she sets her mind to something. She told me that Doktor Beck was coming to see you in the next few weeks so I thought there was no harm in not telling you. Besides which, since hearing about my commission exams, I have been so busy that I really have not thought on the matter too much"

Colonel Mayer seemed to dwell on what Julius had told him, then said, "very well Julius, I will give you the benefit of the doubt. To be honest I did not know if you had any idea of your sister's future marriage. However, knowing how close the two of you are, I could not believe that Irmy had not at least divulged some of her feelings to you"

Julius went red as he realized how his father had tricked him into his confession and then smiled at the artfulness of his parent.

Colonel Mayer smiled in understanding as he said, "you may think us old and world weary, Julius, but your mother and I have always been able to see through the schemes of you and your siblings. It is something you learn when you become a parent. As to honoring your promise to Irmy, I can respect you for that. I know how assertive she can be, in fact I feel quite sorry for Herr Doktor Beck, do you think he realizes what a high spirited young lady he is about to become engaged to?"

"So you are to give your consent, Papa? I think there is something you ought to know first..."

Colonel Mayer held up his hand to halt Julius' speech, "do not worry yourself Julius. No man was to become engaged to my only daughter before I found out everything there was to know about him. If I were to be honest with you I do not think I could have found a more suitable husband for your sister if I had gone looking for him myself. By all accounts he is very comfortably situated, very studious and well thought of in the medical world. His letter to me, asking for this meeting, was very courteous and written with a well-educated hand. Your mother has met him in Kosice and sent me a letter highly commending him, she was most impressed. I think, dependent of course on our mutual agreement, that your sister will soon be a married woman"

Julius did not know what to say. His father had obviously already made up his mind without even meeting the man. He felt dismayed that his father had not even mentioned Irmy's feelings. He had sounded more as if he was entering into a business contract, rather than the marriage of his daughter. Julius knew better than to argue with his father, but he added, "Father, do you know how old Herr Doktor Beck is?"

"Of course I do, why should that matter?"

"He is a lot older than Irmy, and you yourself said that she is a strong willed, independent girl"

"The age gap is but a little more than that between myself and your mother, and I think you will agree that our marriage is a very happy one, would you not?" The Colonel fixed Julius with a baleful stare, daring him to refute him, which of course he could not. "Besides" his father carried on, "you yourself have just offered the very reasons why someone older than Irmy will be ideal for her. She needs someone to moderate her impetuous nature. To my mind her mother, and to some extent her brothers, have all indulged her for far too long. What she needs now is someone who is not going to spoil her or put up with her headstrong, independent ideas"

Julius had to look at the floor to hide the smile that was creeping on to his face. He noted that his father had not included himself in the list of people who had made Irmy so headstrong. It was well known within the family that she could get anything she wanted out of her father just by fluttering her eyelashes at him. He was also smiling as he knew that Richard Beck had agreed to Irmy training to be a nurse after their marriage, something he knew would outrage his parents. However he was not about to tell his father this. If Irmy was to achieve her long desired ambition he was not about to divulge her secret though the temptation was great, just to see the look on his father's face when he heard the news.

The door opened and his father's batman announced Herr Doktor Richard Beck as Colonel Mayer and Julius rose to greet their visitor. Richard Beck was not at all how Julius had envisioned him. He was very tall, well over six feet, very slender to the point that he looked almost emaciated. He had a sallow, gaunt face, topped with a shock of dark hair. From behind a pair of small round spectacles peered a pair of dark, almost black eyes that radiated the intelligence of the man to whom they belonged. Julius was reminded of a monkey that he had seen at the Schonbrunn Zoo. He had gone to the zoo with Nikolas and both had been fascinated by one monkey who had sat on a branch, absolutely still, looking at the people who were staring in at him through the wires of his cage. Julius and Nikolas had stood for some while, trying to stare out the monkey, but it would not be disturbed. It just sat on its branch staring back at the two of them, its little, dark, unblinking eyes glittering in the sunlight.

Colonel Mayer's batman took the doctor's coat. Julius noticed how well cut and expensive his suit was, however it seemed to hang straight down from his shoulders giving the impression it was not touching the thin body that it covered. After shaking hands the three men sat down and Julius was surprised to see Herr Doktor Beck taking charge of the situation and starting the conversation. Julius began to realize this was no ordinary man. He exuded a confidence and a superiority that Julius was not sure he liked. He struck Julius as somewhat arrogant; a sentiment that was often used to describe Josef, but one knew that under all his bravado Josef was using his arrogance to hide far deeper feelings. With Richard Beck Julius felt this was not the case. The man before him was the real man, not a person affected by nerves or emotions.

Julius let his father and Richard Beck carry on their conversation. He had not much that he could offer to the formal introductions that were being voiced and he preferred to sit back and observe his future brother-in-law. He was amazed that his sister, his witty and beautiful Irmy had become attracted to such a man. He may have admirable qualities, he was sure he must have, but he just could not visualize Irmy engaged to him. He had no doubt she felt in love with him, that had been obvious at the Opera Ball. Julius had imagined a laughing, suave, handsome man who had swept her off her feet, rather than this rather serious, dour man seated in front of him. For a moment he was reminded of Captain Schneider, except that Richard Beck spoke a lot more. In fact that was another

118

thing that was puzzling Julius, observing the scene in front of him. Richard Beck appeared to be conducting the interview, not his father, and his father was accepting the situation as he sat in his chair seemingly rapt in Herr Doktor Beck's address.

Noticing that Julius was not taking part in the conversation Richard Beck turned to him to affably say, "I am pleased to meet you at last Cadet Mayer. Irmy has spoken so much of you that I feel I know you already. I hope you are happy with our engagement, I feel very honored that a woman such as Irmy has seen fit to bestow her affections on me. I know I am a very lucky man"

It was a very pretty speech and one Julius could tell was sincere. Although the rest of the evening continued in much the same vein Julius left his father's rooms that night deciding to accept Irmy's choice of husband. However he was still not sure if he would ever completely warm to Herr Doktor Richard Beck.

When Julius returned to the barracks Nikolas was asleep and he woke him up as he noisily entered the room. "Where are the others? I thought you were all studying tonight"

Nikolas sat up, his red hair sticking up in all directions as he roused himself from the drowsiness of his sleep. "They decided to follow Hoffman's advice and have a break from their studies, so they have gone into the city. I felt so tired that I thought I would have an early night, which I was enjoying until somebody came crashing through the door. Did you not have a good evening with your father?"

"Sorry, yes, no, oh I don't know. I have a lot on my mind"

"Well, either share it with me or be quiet so I can go back to sleep" Nikolas collapsed back onto his pillow, but still continued to watch his friend.

"It is nothing crucial really. It is just, well, I met Irmy's fiancé tonight and..."

"Fiancé?" shouted Nikolas as he sat bolt upright in his bed with a stricken look on his face, "fiancé" he repeated, "what do you mean fiancé? Irmy is engaged, when, to whom, why" the words tumbled out of Nikolas' mouth and Julius saw in that brief moment how much his news had affected his friend. That Nikolas had always shown an interest in Irmy had been evident since the time they had met in Kosice at Christmas but Julius had not understood the extent of Nikolas' feelings. He now felt ashamed of the callous way he had broken the news to his friend. He had

119

had no idea just how much Nikolas had admired his sister.

He decided not to admit that he had known about the engagement since the Opera Ball, and to save his friends' feelings he decided to lie. "You are as surprised as I am, I only found out this evening. To a doctor, would you believe? Strange fellow, not at all the sort I would imagine Irmy with. Look here Nikolas I am sorry, I had no idea you thought about Irmy in this way"

Nikolas hung his head, "I do not know how I feel to be honest with you. I really do like her, Julius, but I thought that she was only being nice to me because I was your friend, but I hoped that she liked me a little"

"Believe you me Nikolas, she liked you, Irmy would soon have let you know if she did not like you, friend or no friend of mine. Why did you not say something? Who knows, I might have been able to help" Julius grinned, "I could not think of a better brother-in-law"

"Now you are being stupid Julius. I thought I would just bide my time. We are still young, cadets, and Irmy is even younger. I just thought in time, as the years progressed and we got to know each other better, that something might possibly happen. Now it seems I am too late"

Julius felt for his friend and tried to find the words to console him, "They are only engaged, he is a bit of a rum fellow. Maybe Irmy will change her mind and then you can dash in like a knight in shining armor and console your damsel in distress. Failing that we can hope that Herr Doktor Richard Beck falls under the wheels of a tram"

Nikolas looked shocked as he said "Julius that is a terrible thing to say about anyone, take it back this instant. I expect you to go to confession this week after saying something like that"

Julius started to undress and after a wash climbed into his bed. He noticed that Nikolas was still wide awake, his cherubic face lit in the half light, his eyes focused on some far distant thought that Julius could only too easily guess at. Julius turned off his lamp and was amazed to hear in the darkness a little voice say, "maybe fall under a tram and receive a knock on his head so that he loses his memory, and thus the desire to marry Irmy"

Julius chuckled as he said, "Looks like I will not be the only one going to confession this week, goodnight Nikolas"

The next few weeks proved very hectic for the cadets and in June they all congregated in the barracks classrooms to sit their final exams. The results would be the culmination of three years of extremely hard and varied work. The ultimate hope was that these young men would emerge as exemplary officers of the Austro-Hungarian Army who would choose the army as their career for life, that they would honor the title, Sons of the Eagle.

Julius reflected on how much he had learned in the last three years, and not just the physical aspect of soldiering, marching, horsemanship, and exercise. He also had to learn the cerebral side where the strategies of warfare were learned, as well as the economics of running a regiment, transportation of men and ultimately the leading of men.

He had also become used to the caring and use of various firearms and guns, so very different from his former hunting days in Kosice. The power of some of the armies' big guns was awesome. It was somehow gruesome to sit in a classroom and work out the sighting and trajectory of a gun, its ammunition capacity, where it could be positioned to ultimately kill an opposing force. However they all knew that it was necessary knowledge if one was to survive in open warfare.

Throughout his cadetship Julius had the distinct impression that they were little boys, playing soldiers in the schoolroom. He knew things would be very different once all their training was put into practice within the army and he could not wait to begin. He had enjoyed his time as a cadet, but he felt he now wanted to experience the real thing, and he knew he was ready.

As they had hoped the exams gave them hardly any trouble. It was supposed that if you had endured the three years of training you were ready for army life and the tests were merely a summary of their work. Although some exams were harder than others nobody appeared to have any real trouble with them. On the final day of tests all the occupants of dormitory six were quite confident of their results, even Viktor. To celebrate they decided to have a night in the city, to take the opportunity to unwind after their weeks of revision. The evening was a great success as they dined in one of the best restaurants in Vienna, courtesy of Count von Kutz. Julius was pleased they were not in uniform as the champagne flowed freely and the boys became very drunk. In their drunkenness they began to recall their adventures over the past three years and surprised themselves on how much they had shared together.

Their laughter and banging of the table began to diminish slightly as it slowly dawned on all four of them that this would probably be one of their last evenings together. Soon they would receive their commissions and be assigned to their regiments.

In their inebriated state they all became quite maudlin as they realized that things were about to change and they knew they did not want to alter this aspect of their lives.

"Well, I think," slurred Josef, "we should all raise our glasses and make a pledge. That wherever we are in the world, whatever we are doing, we will always look after each other if we need help, you know like those Musketeer people in that novel"

Nikolas roared with laughter, "I think you mean the Three Musketeers, which does not seem quite right as there are four of us"

"Oh whatever" waved Josef, now drunker than ever, "there were four in the end, I think. Anyway Manz, do not stop me. For the first time in my life I am going to be sentimental. I know it is because I am drunk, so you had better listen carefully, because I will never repeat this again, especially when I am sober. I would just like to say" and here he grabbed Viktor around the neck and pulled him towards himself where he held him in a vice like grip, despite his protestations. "I would just like to say thank you, thank you for being my friends. I have never had good friends before. I would just like to say thank you, not only for being my friends, but for also putting up with me. I know I can be a bit of a bastard at times, but you know my mother loves me, if nobody else does"

Julius winked at Nikolas, "do you know I think he wants to thank us, do you get that impression?"

"Ssshh" continued Josef, dramatically putting a finger up to his lips. "I would just like to say I love you all. I know when I am sober in the morning I am going to deny this conversation entirely"

With that statement Josef let go of his grip on Viktor, who was still locked in his arm and collapsed on to the table, where he lay as if asleep.

"Josef that was touching" Nikolas replied, whose speech was even more indistinct than Josef's, "so touching, that I am taking you to the asylum first thing in the morning"

122

Julius knew his friend was very drunk as he had started to point his finger as he spoke as though trying to put a point across. This was something he always did when he was inebriated.

"But I am really sorry to have to agree with Josef, something you know I very seldom do. Even in my drunken stupor I know what I am saying, you are my best friends and I am going to miss you. I cannot imagine not being with you all in dormitory six"

Julius thought that Nikolas was about to burst into tears as he watched his impish face begin to pucker up and his eyes begin to water. He was relieved when Nikolas added, "but not your snoring, or your smelly feet, especially not your smelly feet, no definitely not your smelly feet" then he slumped back into his chair.

Julius, who was dangerously close to joining his friends in their drunken stupor, lifted up his glass and proclaimed, "well I would like to propose a toast, to the best friends a man could have and I agree with Josef. Wherever we are in the world should any of our friends need us then I hope we will be there for them. To lasting friendship"

Julius and Viktor raised their glasses and even Josef woke up from his slumber, lifted his head and then his glass and joined in the toast. Nikolas waved his glass around in the air that unfortunately caused his champagne to spill onto a passing waiter. He was heard to be muttering above the mutual toast "smelly feet and snoring, I have to say I will not miss them"

Soon after this they were asked quite politely, considering the state they were all in, to leave the restaurant. This proved somewhat difficult as Viktor had to virtually carry the now almost comatose Josef. Meanwhile Julius was trying to guide Nikolas through the tables to the door without him falling over, whilst Nikolas tried to tell every diner how much he loved his friends, despite their smelly feet and their snoring.

Finding themselves in a disheveled heap on the pavement outside the restaurant Viktor grinned at Julius and said, "I wish I could see the reception Count von Kutz receives next time he dines in that restaurant"

"Could not care a less old boy" came Josef's muffled voice from Viktor's shoulder where he rested like a small child.

"Come on Viktor" said Julius, "as you and I seem the least inebriated of our party I think it is our solemn duty to guide

these ingrates back to the barracks without being arrested"
This proved more difficult than he had at first presumed. Any hansom cab that they hailed drove on by when they saw the condition of Nikolas and Josef.

Eventually they saw that their only option was to walk home, not an easy task with Josef and Nikolas leaning on their friends like dead weights and virtually having to be dragged through the streets. Luckily it was a warm evening and the moon was full so their journey home was fairly well lit.

Julius and Viktor decided to take a shortcut through some of the back streets of Vienna as time was approaching when they were due back at the barracks. Viktor was sure he knew the way and Julius dutifully followed, relieved at anything that would shorten the length of time he would have to half carry Nikolas home. Julius was a fit, strong man, but Nikolas was equally muscular and Julius was finding his strength starting to sap with the effort of supporting his friend. Viktor was finding it even harder. Although strong himself, Josef was nearly a head taller than he was which was making it difficult for Viktor to keep his friend upright. Every so often Nikolas or Josef would start to sing bawdy drinking songs or mutter away to themselves in their drunken state. Viktor turned back to look at Julius. "If Josef tells me he loves me one more time I swear I am going to leave him here on the roadside. That and his dreadful singing, I do not think I can take much more" Julius noticed the red, sweaty face of his friend and realized how much effort it was for Viktor to carry Josef.
"Do you want to swap bodies for a while?"
"No thank you, if I stop I will never start again, let's keep going"

Several streets later Julius knew they were nearing the barracks. They turned into a very badly lit side street, with a few houses and a row of small shops. Julius looked up as he heard what he thought was a scream or a shout for help. He saw a crowd of about six men attacking what looked like a large bundle of rags lying in the road. Julius realized the bundle was a person who was being attacked by the group, some with sticks, though most of them were kicking viciously with their boots. Viktor saw the assault as well and without thinking they dropped their drunken friends and with a shout started running down the street to aid the person who was being beaten.

Later on both Julius and Viktor knew it had been a very foolish course of action. The two of them were ostensibly rushing to see off a crowd that greatly outnumbered them. A very idiotic thing to do in hindsight, but at the time a swift decision made to help someone in trouble. However the element of surprise worked in their favor because the attackers looked up and seeing the two men running and shouting down the street decided to run off before there was a chance of any confrontation.

When Julius and Viktor approached the place of the attack they saw that the victim was an elderly man, probably in his seventies. He was lying in the road, his eyes closed, blood pouring from several cuts to his face and head, his clothes were covered in dust and badly torn. At first they had the awful feeling that he might be dead. Viktor knelt down and as he softly spoke to him the old man opened his eyes and a small ghost of a smile appeared on his face.

"Thank you, my son" he whispered, "thank you"

"Are you hurt?" asked Viktor, "do you think you can stand up, we ought to get you out of the road"

Viktor and Julius carefully helped him up but he was obviously badly hurt as his face creased into lines of pain as he awkwardly raised himself off the floor. Julius noticed the small black skull cap that covered the back of his head as he rose from the floor and realized why this poor man had been attacked, he was Jewish. Carefully they helped him onto the pavement.

"I think you should go to the infirmary, sir, so that they can look at your injuries" said Viktor.

The old man waved his hand in dismissal and with a weak voice replied, "No, no I will be fine, my daughter and her husband live in the next street. I will go there and she will tend to my aches and pains" He smiled a sweet, gentle smile which illuminated his whole face, "thank you for coming to my rescue, not everybody would rush to help an old Jew" He cocked an eyebrow at them as he slyly added, "but perhaps you would not have helped me had you known I was a Jew?" He said it rather provocatively but Julius realized it was also said with some sadness of an inevitable fact that this man lived with. Both Viktor and Julius protested at his insinuation and he quickly apologized for his rudeness, "I am sorry, but when you are my age you tend to have a rather jaundiced view of the world" He shrugged his shoulders as if this was the way of life.

Viktor and Julius offered to see him to his daughter's house, but he declined their offer and they watched his departing, frail figure as it limped up the street and disappeared around the corner.

Now feeling very sober they walked back to their friends, who were still lying fast asleep on the pavement where they had been dropped, oblivious to the drama that had just occurred. Julius and Viktor pulled up their loads who murmured in protestation at being moved. As they walked off towards the barracks, still supporting their friends, Julius asked Viktor "Why do people do that, attack someone just because of their religion?"

"You could talk all night on that subject and still not find an answer, and it really is not as simple as that you know. Jews are not popular people, especially here in Vienna; do you not remember the anti-Semitic riots at the university only a few years ago?"

"Well yes, but that still does not give people the right to set upon innocent people in the streets. We are meant to be living in a civilized society you know"

"My father has a lot of dealings with Jews, being a banker. He actually quite admires them, he says they are hardworking, very clever, and absolutely ruthless in business, maybe that is what people dislike about them"

"What do you mean?" asked Julius.

"Just that people are envious of a lot of Jews because they are rich, but not only that. A lot of them became rich by, as I said, using ruthless means. There is no such thing as sentiment for a Jew in business, and a lot of people resent that way of doing things. The Jews have been persecuted for a very long time. Think of the moneylenders in mediaeval times and peoples dislike for them has not decreased over the years"

"Well I think it is wrong. No one should be persecuted for their religion, or their nationality for that matter. Look at the divisions it creates in our own army"

"I agree with you Julius, even Catholics have been persecuted in the past, but we are not going to change things. For every person that thinks like us there are probably ten who think otherwise"

126

"I suppose you are right, even that old man, who the persecution is aimed at, seems to accept it as an inevitability for his race"

"Exactly, it happens now and no doubt will happen in the future. As human beings we have to live with that fact"

They were now approaching the barrack gates and trying to lighten the somber mood they had talked themselves into. Viktor added, "maybe we could arrange the persecution of certain cadets who get so drunk they have to be carried home"

The route back to their room was uneventful. The sentry on duty chose to turn a blind eye to the fact that they were somewhat late and to the sight of two cadets being carried home by their friends, he had seen it all before. Josef and Nikolas were deposited on their beds where they proceeded to snore all night. When they awoke the next morning they had the most horrendous headaches which Julius and Viktor took great delight in worsening with tales of greasy foods, lots of shouting and several unnecessary banging of doors.

The next few days produced lots of activity within the West barracks. Whilst awaiting the results of their exams Colonel Weber and Sergeant Major Hoffman interviewed all the cadets as to their choice of regiment and to the suitability of their choice. Julius and Nikolas had decided to apply to an artillery division. This was not in the hope of being posted together as both agreed this was unlikely, but because this was where their greatest interest had been throughout their training.

Julius saw the artillery as one of the most essential elements of an army. The engineering of guns, their capacities, their mobilization all fascinated him. He enjoyed learning the details of all the different guns available to the army, as well as the designs for new ones that the army tested.

Colonel Weber and Sergeant Major Hoffman listened patiently as Julius explained to them why the artillery was his choice. After his interview Colonel Weber looked across the table at him and said, "I must say Cadet Mayer that I am surprised by your wish to enter the artillery division. However as you have so eloquently explained to us why it is your choice I think you may rest assured that Sergeant Major Hoffman and I will be putting through a recommendation that you join the artillery. While you are here, and in the privacy of this room, I think it would be all right for me to tell you that you have done very well in your exams. Indeed, you have excelled throughout your years of training. I am sure your father must be very proud of you. Well done, I hope to hear in the future that you have lived up to our great expectations of you, I am sure you will. Dismissed Cadet Mayer"

Julius stood up and saluted his senior officer. Colonel Weber and Sergeant Major Hoffman both rose and shook hands with him. Julius, somewhat embarrassed by Weber's glowing words murmured, "Thank you sir, thank you both"

Hoffman smiled at his protégé and said, "well done, sir, good luck for your future"

Outside Weber's office Julius stopped for a while. As he had stepped through the door, he had experienced a feeling of an overwhelming finality, that this was the end. The end of training, the end of the camaraderie that was so unique among the cadets, the end of being a boy and thus becoming a man. All at once he felt quite sad, but also elated at the challenge that was before him. One thing he did understand at that moment was that his life was about to drastically change. The last three wonderful years were to be savored and remembered with great joy and affection for the rest of his life, for they were to never come again.

When the cadet's results were finally posted up Julius found he had the highest marks of his class. This produced much backslapping and shaking of hands from his fellow students. Although they still teased Julius and called him 'Weber's favorite' they had all come to appreciate that Julius was an excellent cadet. His hard work and good humor had won over even his sternest critics. Julius was highly embarrassed by his marks and tried to avoid seeming too arrogant about his results. Nikolas, Viktor and Josef were very proud of their roommate. All of them had done well in the exams, even Josef, surprising himself with his excellent mark.

Now that their results were known the cadets started to prepare to leave their home of the last three years. There was much excitement as they performed the official passing out parade for officers where they swore the Oath of Allegiance to the Emperor and received their promotions.

Once they had been notified of their new regiments all cadets were allowed a three week leave before starting their new lives. The cleaning out of their room proved to be a frightful task. Even after hours of sorting through drawers

128

and cupboards the occupants of dormitory six were no nearer completing their task than they had been when they had started several hours previously.

"How did we manage to accumulate so much rubbish?" asked Viktor, sitting amongst a pile of assorted sports equipment.

"How did I manage to have so many odd socks?" lamented Nikolas, as he endeavored to clear his chest of draws.

At that moment Smid appeared in their doorway. Smid had been unusually quiet in the last few days. The boys could only guess why but had to presume it had something to do with their approaching departure. They all had to admit that it was going to be a very hard wrench for them too. Smid had looked after them all for such a long time that they could not imagine life without him. From the very beginning Smid had been there for them. Not only helping to make their lives run smoothly but he was there to listen, to help if he could. He always acted with a dignity and grace that an aristocrat would have been proud of.

Since that first Christmas the boys had always bought a Yuletide present for Smid. Although Julius had never divulged Smid's secret to the others, it warmed his heart to think that long after they had left the barracks they would still be helping Smid. They were often amazed at how he had put up with their antics. Unless they had been openly rude or discourteous to him, which was very rare, he took all their high spirits with a good heart and humor. Now as he stood in the doorway of their room his sadness was etched clearly on his face as the reality of the future was spread before him in the chaos that was dormitory six.

Julius thought he was about to cry. He watched the little man, who thought he was not being observed, shake off his despair and make a determined effort to recover his composure. He strode confidently into the room, "I said to you young gentlemen, wait for me, but do you listen to Smid? No, and look what happens, this" and he spread his arms to encompass the untidy room, "what are you going to do without me to look after you I really do not know. You have to have a system, gentlemen. Who do you think has the most experience in a situation like this? Smid, that's who. Now let's get you organized and we will have this room sorted out in no time"

True to his words Smid soon had them arranging their things as he barked out orders, sounding like a nanny in a kindergarten. Within a couple of hours dormitory six was almost back to its former self. Trunks were packed and a great pile of unwanted belongings stacked up in the corridor outside their room. The hours of activity had obviously done Smid a lot of good. By the time they had finished his face splitting smile had returned and he was cheerfully humming tunes to himself as he finished layering their clothes in copious sheets of tissue paper into their trunks. All four boys were now lying on their beds, exhausted by their burst of domesticity. As Smid went to leave he made a large tut tutting noise as he regarded their prone bodies, "I really don't know, and this is the future of our great Imperial Army, well, well, well"

Josef lazily opened one eye; "If I had the energy, Smid, I would throw this pillow at you, so go away in case I decide to anyway"

Smid chuckled to himself, he had long ago learnt to ignore Josef's sarcasm as much as the others did. Just as Smid opened the door Josef called to him, "Thank you for all your help Smid, it was really appreciated. If I ever decide to leave the army, how about considering coming to work for me?"

Smid appeared to consider this for a moment, then regarded Josef with a completely blank expression and said, "I'm sorry sir I would have to decline your kind offer. I fear you could not pay enough money to compensate me for having to look after you" With another of his wide grins he dived out of the room closely followed by Josef's pillow.

The next day the cadets were informed of their new regiments and postings. Julius and Nikolas could not believe their luck when both were posted to the 7th Artillery Division in Prague. As they perused the list even Viktor and Josef had to admit how lucky they were.

"I told you, you Bohemians all stick together," laughed Viktor. He had been posted to the Dragoons in Graz whilst Josef was in the Cavalry and was to stay in Vienna.

"Well I suppose Mama will be pleased that I am to remain in Vienna" was his only comment on reading his assignment, but Julius noted some trepidation in his voice.

Julius felt sorry for Josef. He knew wherever Nikolas or Viktor had been assigned their future would hold no worries for them. They were both amenable, likeable fellows who made friends easily and who were popular with their peers and superiors. Josef was a different story however. He knew it would be hard for his friend, though Josef himself would never admit it. He did not make friends easily as was evident amongst their own class of cadets. Julius knew the real Josef, but that was only after having lived with him for the last three years, and at times he was still able to infuriate everyone quite easily. Although Julius thought it might have been a good idea for Josef to have been stationed away from Vienna, and thus away from his hated father, maybe in another way it was helpful he was staying. If he found conflict amongst his brother officers at least he had his mother and his various acquaintances in Vienna to turn to. Away from Vienna could be a very lonely place for Josef.

Julius thought briefly of the Countess von Kutz. He had sometimes remembered the Opera Ball in quiet moments over the last few months. He could clearly visualize her beautiful face and recall the scent of spring flowers, and then resolved to dash the images from his mind. Such thoughts of his friend's mother, however innocent, were contemptible, but still they would come to him from time to time. He would also wonder why it was Josef's mother he kept remembering rather than the youthful and pretty Lise who had shared so much with him and who had opened his mind to things that he had only dreamed of before. To him that was the greatest mystery of all.

On their final evening the cadets assembled in the mess for their last dinner together. After this evening they would all be second lieutenants in the Imperial Army, commissioned officers at last. Sergeant Major Hoffman appeared briefly to congratulate them all on their commissions and to wish them well in their future life in the army. As he finished his speech one of the cadets stood up to ask for three cheers for the sergeant major. The small but powerfully built man stood to attention as he received the acclaim and applause of his trainees. They all agreed it was well deserved. Hoffman had been an excellent teacher, hard but fair with a genius for instilling in his charges the absolute surety that they were capable of achieving anything they set their minds to. When you had been running for miles, your feet a mass of blisters and raw skin, with every muscle in your body aching and your throat screaming out for the drink of water that you were not allowed, Hoffman would come along and make you stand up and carry on despite your pain. He gave you the confidence to believe that you could make it, and invariably you did. As he left the cadets felt they were not just saying to goodbye to their mentor, but also to an old friend.

The evening proceeded in high spirits. The chefs had excelled themselves for the cadets final meal, starting with leberknodelsuppe, a clear broth soup with liver dumplings followed by traditional wiener schnitzel, breaded veal cooked to succulent perfection. The meal ended with a delicious mohr im hemd, a rich, steamed chocolate pudding served with a hot chocolate sauce. All this was washed down with champagne, allowed especially for the evening.

As they were finishing their meal Josef leaned across to Julius and Nikolas and artfully said, "you had better enjoy your meal gentlemen, from now on you will have to start getting used to your Bohemian peasant food again" Nothing Josef could say that evening could spoil the air of bonhomie that abounded, not even with the other cadets. As the evening wore on, and after the drinking of a lot of champagne, they were even seen to be socializing with Josef, an occurrence that did not happen too often.

The last act of the evening entailed lifting Julius up in a chair onto four cadet's shoulders and carrying him around the room in a triumphant procession. Several times he was sure they were going to drop him, but they ignored all his cries for help until he was dropped unceremoniously from his lofty height onto the floor to great cheers from everybody. How they all found their way back to their rooms they were not quite sure. The next morning Julius awoke to find himself feeling very sore and covered in bruises, a fact his roommates found most amusing.

The time had come to say goodbye. It was so difficult, none of them could think of the right words to say. They really didn't want to say anything, because when they did they knew it would bring the reality of the end that they all dreaded.

To avoid the inevitable leave-taking the boys summoned Smid to their room. The roommates had wanted to give Smid something personal for his final gift. They had decided to have their photograph taken together, which they had mounted into a beautiful silver frame decorated in the avant-garde Jugendstil design at the local Wiener Werkstatte studios. Julius was not sure he liked the modern design of the frame. Josef had persuaded them that this was becoming very popular and in time Smid's frame would be worth far more than had been paid for it. As Julius, Viktor and Nikolas had no idea about art they had bowed to Josef's superior knowledge and had bought the frame, it was certainly a beautiful piece of workmanship,

The little man had come into the room his head bent down. This time he could not hide his feelings and the tears were running down his leathery face and splashing down onto his uniform jacket, creating a large dark patch on his breast. None of the boys knew what to say. Julius felt that his throat had a small ball stuck in it as he tried to stem the tears that were in his eyes at the sight of Smid. Julius opened his mouth to speak but no sound would come out and it was Viktor who had to step forward to rescue the situation.

"Smid" his voice trembled, "Smid, we just felt, well we, er, had worked out what to say and now I cannot remember a thing. Basically, you know, what we wanted to say was thank you. Thank you for everything, for looking after us, for putting up with us, we know we did not make your life easy at times. We wanted to tell you we will miss you dreadfully and well" here Viktor struggled to find his words as the emotion overcame him. All of them, even Josef, were near to tears and were trying not to look at each other, "and I really cannot say anymore, this is all too much. I think you know how we feel about you Smid, it is just very difficult to put into words at this moment, but I am sure you know"

Viktor went over to the table and picked up the present which he placed in Smid's hands. Smid still stood in the middle of the room, his head bent, they had not seen his face since he had walked into the room. He was still crying and his little body shook as it reacted to his sobs.

"This is for you, a little something to say thank you, though nothing could repay you for all that you have done for us"

Smid looked at the package in his hands. Then in a painfully thin voice, trembling with emotion, he said, "I say this every time, sirs, but you really should not buy these presents for me, but I will accept this gladly as this is the last" he paused to regain his composure, "the last time we shall be together and I will take it to remember you by. Thank you, all of you, and God bless"

Smid turned to leave the room.

"You are not going to open it now Smid?" asked Josef.

For the first time Smid brought his head up to face them all. His eyes were red from crying and his mouth dropped at the corners in a mask of misery, "No, if you don't mind sirs, I would rather not. I think it would be too much for me, I will say goodbye now. I don't think I will be seeing you off later; you don't want an old fool like me embarrassing fine young men like yourselves, now do you? It has been a pleasure to know you. I hope you will think of me sometimes, I know I will never forget you"

With that the sadness seemed too much for the little man and he turned to leave the room.

Suddenly he turned, ran back to them and embraced each one in turn, something that was definitely against the rules, but which none of the occupants of the room gave a damn about. They were now all very upset, and long after the little man had departed the four boys stood around the room in total silence, each one coming to terms with their misery. They knew they had not only just said goodbye to Smid, but had also said goodbye to each other and their life for the last three years.

XII

Julius returned to Kosice with a heavy heart. He knew his life was now changing dramatically. Though he looked forward to being a commissioned officer at last, he still had the feeling that a great weight had descended on him and it would not go away. He realized this was partly due to a fear of his unknown future, but also a great sadness for the life he now had to leave behind.

His leave passed pleasantly enough. He visited some old friends who still lived in Kosice, listened to Mama and Irmy's gossiping, even enjoyed Danusia's over zealous attention, but still the cloud of gloom hovered over his head. Even his relationship with Irmy had subtly changed. Being in love suited her, she glowed with an inner radiance and happiness that was quite breathtaking. Julius sadly reflected that with her engagement a part of the special bond that they had was gone.

Richard was away from the city at the time of his visit so they did not have the pleasure of his company. His name was mentioned frequently in Irmy's conversation and of course every time she mentioned her future Richard was a part of it, and this annoyed Julius intensely. Though he tried to rationalize this as sadness at losing his sister to another man he also had to admit to himself that maybe this was the reason why he did not particularly like Herr Doktor Richard Beck. The fact worried him, as he genuinely wanted to like his sister's choice of husband. He did not confide his feelings to Irmy, he knew it would hurt her too much.

When he was asked his thoughts on first meeting Richard, he had carefully chosen his words in reply, so as not to leave himself feeling too much of a hypocrite. Papa, Mama and Danusia liked Richard, however after the meeting he had had with his father in Vienna he wondered how much this was to do with his bank balance and his standing, as to the man himself. So Julius kept his thoughts to himself, which added to his depression. He felt elated when the time approached for his leave to end and he could travel to Prague to take up his new posting and meet up again with Nikolas.

Julius left for Prague a few days before he was due to report to his new barracks. He had arranged to stay with Nikolas and his family, as his friend was eager to show

Julius his new home. Julius had decided he would like to look around the city before concentrating on his new responsibilities.

As the train pulled into the station Julius pulled out the map that Nikolas had sent him, on it were written detailed instructions of how to reach the Manz family home. Jumping off the train, his bags in hand, Julius set about locating his exit from the station.

The first thing he noticed was the difference between Prague and Vienna station. Prague station was very busy, but with an orderly, quiet procession, unlike the mayhem and noise that always greeted you in Vienna. He was amazed when the first person he approached to ask the way actually stopped and gave him detailed instructions and advice. This was so unlike Viennese locals, who were always in too much of a hurry to stop and help a stranded visitor.

Making his way to the exit he needed Julius heard a familiar voice that made him look up, "so you managed to find your way here then"

"Nikolas" beamed Julius, who dropped his bags and embraced his friend, "it is so good to see you, what are you doing here?"

Nikolas smiled his wide, angelic smile "You told me which train you were to catch so I came here in the hope of meeting you. As Josef would say, I could not let a country bumpkin get lost in the big city, now could I?"

The two men walked out of the station in companionable silence, happy to be in each other's company. Julius looked around him at the city that was to be his new home. He quickly understood what Nikolas had meant all those years ago about the understated elegance of Prague. It certainly did not have the stateliness or boldness of Vienna, but as he walked through her streets on that warm summer morning he began to fall in love with Prague, it was a romance that would stay with him for the rest of his life.

He marveled at the beautiful buildings, the cobbled streets, the slower pace of the city that made him feel as if he had returned to a time gone by. Every time they ventured down another street Nikolas would point out features of buildings, certain shops and landmarks, as if he were talking about a cherished friend, that these sights were personal to only him, and Julius shared with his friend his enthusiasm for the city.

136

Nikolas decided that they should stop at a local beer hall for a drink and something to eat. The beer hall was noisy and busy but Nikolas and Julius found a table and were soon chatting amiably about their leave and the prospect of their new posting. Julius ordered red cabbage soup followed by Uzene, smoked pork with potato dumplings, and Nikolas had Hovezi with houskove knedlicky, beef with sliced bread dumplings. The food was excellent, and was enhanced by the drinking of several glasses of Staropramen beer, a local Bohemian brew.

At the end of their meal both men felt happy and relaxed, and for the first time in several weeks Julius began to experience a sense of well being and excited anticipation for his future. After some prompting he had related much of his misgivings about Irmy to Nikolas. Although Julius had wanted to discuss his sister with Nikolas he felt it disloyal, given the fondness that his friend had for Irmy. However Nikolas, as magnanimous as ever, had waved aside his own emotions on the subject. "I do not want you to stop talking about Irmy just to spare my feelings. What has happened, has happened, and luckily your sister is blissfully unaware of any sentimental thoughts I might have had about her, so there is no harm done. Life does go on Julius, it was a stupid notion on my part to believe she would even look at me, let alone care anything for me"

Julius looked at his friend over the rim of his glass and slyly said, "but I will let you know if I hear of any tram accidents" to which Nikolas roared with laughter. Despite his good humor Julius did not believe for one moment that Nikolas no longer harbored any secret desire for Irmy. He had seen the truth in his eyes as he had delivered his careful speech and Julius had known Nikolas long enough to know that he had not meant a word of it.

Nikolas suggested they go on to his house, but Julius was feeling rather inebriated after their long and enjoyable lunch. Having no desire to be slightly tipsy on meeting Nikolas' mother for the first time he suggested that they have an extended walk home in order for him to sober up a little. Nikolas agreed, but stipulated that they could not be too long, as his mother would be expecting them. After a little thought Nikolas guided Julius through several winding, cobbled streets until they were in a large square that was surrounded by various colorful Gothic and Renaissance buildings, all beautifully decorated and preserved. The square was busy with people walking around, shopping, chatting or sitting on benches, simply happy to watch the world go by. The afternoon was pleasantly warm and the populace were reveling in the heady atmosphere of a lovely summer's day. Julius observed several military personnel, and was interested to notice some in the new pike-gray uniform that he and Nikolas were to be issued with in the next few days. He was not sure he liked the new livery, he thought it looked quite dull. He noticed with some surprise that cavalry officers still wore red trousers, so their petition to the Emperor had been a success.

He felt Nikolas pulling at his arm and he was led to the front of a large building above which a high tower stretched up towards the sky. Nikolas explained that this was the Old Town Hall. On its wall, below the tower, there was what he thought was a large, ornate clock. On the outer edge were Arabic numerals and there were Roman numerals within the inner circle, all worked in gold, it was quite unlike any clock he had ever seen before. The apparatus itself was decorated in bright colors of blues, amber and gold, and the whole facade shone brightly in the afternoon sun. Flanking the clock, two on each side, were figures of three men and a skeleton

Intrigued Julius turned to Nikolas to ask him what this instrument was. He was amazed to see that they were now surrounded by a large crowd of people, all with their faces turned upwards towards the building, expectantly waiting for something to happen. Nikolas smiled, put his finger to his lips and said, "Wait, then you will see"
As though in answer the figure of the skeleton to the right of the clock, pulled on a rope in its right hand. Two windows above the clock opened and two figures of saints moved in procession and behind them several more figures appeared and proceeded slowly round. Nikolas whispered that the figures were St Peter and St. Paul leading ten of the Apostles.

As the doors of the windows closed a cock was heard to crow, a bell started to ring, and the clock chimed the hour. Julius noticed that the other figures beside the clock were now moving. Nikolas explained these were, Vanity, admiring himself in a mirror, a Turk representing Lust, who shook his head from side to side, a Jewish moneylender watching his money bag who symbolized Greed and the skeleton representing Death. Julius was amazed by the display

138

before him and longed to see it again. He would have gladly stayed for another hour in order to repeat the experience was it not for the thought of offending Nikolas' mother. Nikolas explained that the clock was the famous Astronomical Clock, Julius had of course heard of it, but had not realized it would be so awe inspiring. The face of the clock represented the orbits of the sun and the moon around the earth and portrayed the movements of the sun through the twelve signs of the zodiac. The old Arabic numbers around the perimeter of the clock represented old Bohemian time. Julius listened astonished as Nikolas described all the intricacies of this complex piece of machinery.

"I did not know you could be so knowledgeable Nikolas, maybe you are not quite as stupid as you look"

Nikolas took this bantering with good humor as he replied, "I probably am as stupid as I look, but from the first time I saw the astronomical clock it has always fascinated me and I made it my business to find out all about it. It is amazing to think it was made in the fifteenth century, so much intricacy of movement does not seem possible for so long ago"

The two men stood for some time observing the clock until they decided it was time for them to return to Nikolas' house.

The Manz household greeted Julius warmly. Frau Manzova was exactly as Nikolas had described her to his friend. She was the image of her son, with bright red hair, a round pleasant face and the same Manz smile. Her blue eyes held the same twinkle of merriment as her son's and she welcomed Julius into her home as though she had known him all her life. She and Nikolas were obviously very close as she good-humouredly chided her son for his late return. Julius felt he ought to defend his friend and attempted to lay the blame for their tardiness on himself.

"I am really sorry if we offended you, Frau Manzova, that was not our intention. I am afraid I persuaded Nikolas to show me the astronomical clock and my fascination caused us to be late"

Frau Manzova laughed a soft tinkling laugh, a feminine version of her sons. She laid her hand on Julius' arm as she said, "take no notice of me Julius, I may call you Julius? Please take no notice of our bantering. I mean no harm by it and Nikolas knows I am only teasing him, don't you Nikolas?"

Nikolas smiled as Frau Manzova led them into the parlor for afternoon tea, which she dryly observed should more appropriately be called early evening tea.

As they were seated chatting to Nikolas' mother and drinking their tea they heard a loud crash in the hall that prompted Julius to rise from his seat as he thought there had been an accident. He looked at Nikolas to see if he was going to investigate the noise but Nikolas and his mother had remained seated with a look of resignation on their faces.

"I would sit down if I were you Julius," said Nikolas, "or you might be knocked down by the whirlwind that is about to enter the room"

Julius had just resumed his seat when the door burst open and a young boy of about nine or ten literally fell into the room. There was no mistaking who he was, Georg Manz looked exactly like his older brother, with the same shock of red hair and angelic smile. It amused Julius to look upon this young boy and realize that this was exactly how Nikolas would have looked at the same age. He was dressed in military school uniform that was in a state of total disarray. It was covered in dust, scuffed at the elbows and his shirt hung down below his jacket. Georg ran over to his mother, without even a glance at Julius and began remonstrating with her in a high-pitched voice.

"Mama, whatever they say it was not my fault. I did not start it, it was that Gustav Reidel, he is always trying to cause trouble for me..."

"Georg!" Frau Manzova did not shout at her son, but her tone conveyed instantly that he should stop his tantrum immediately. This he did, standing in front of his mother, his head down and his face turning bright red.

"Georg, I am ashamed of you, not only do you come rushing into the room without greeting our guest, but also that you should enter in such a state. I will hear the reasons for the untidiness of your uniform in a minute. Before that would you please welcome our guest with the manners I know you possess" Frau Manzova turned to Julius, "Julius, I would like to introduce my younger son, Georg. Georg, this is Nikolas' friend, Julius Mayer"

Georg, still with his head down, walked across the room to Julius and held out his hand in greeting. Julius, trying to keep the smile from his face, rose to shake hands with Georg.

"Pleased to meet you, sir" Georg said in a small voice as they shook hands.

"I am very pleased to meet you too, Georg, I have heard a lot about you from Nikolas"

"Really?" Georg slightly raised his head to look up through his eyelashes at Julius, who could see the boy was close to tears from his mother's scolding.

"That is better, now Georg come here, I am interested to hear how your uniform came to be in such a state"

Georg returned to his mother and related at some length the fight he had had at school, which of course was absolutely not his fault. Nikolas and Julius tried to avoid looking at each other whilst Georg was telling his account of the events for fear they would burst into laughter. Julius marveled at the artful way the young boy told his version of the story with such an air of innocence you almost believed him. He wondered how Frau Manzova managed to keep a straight face as she said, "very well Georg. I have heard your side of the story, so I will go to see your headmaster tomorrow and demand to see this boy you have been fighting with, and hear his version of events"

Julius watched as he saw the color drain from Georg's face as he opened his mouth to speak, then quickly shut it again, wisely deciding silence was best. Frau Manzova dismissed her son, telling him to ask the maid to run him a bath and to clean himself up as quickly as possible.

Georg left the room without even a glance at Julius and Nikolas but with a very worried look on his face. As the door closed Frau Manzova let out a long sigh, "Of course, he was not telling the truth, what am I to do with him Nikolas?"

"He is not as bad as all that, Mama, he is just a typical nine year old boy, I was not exactly an angel myself if you recall"

"No, you were not" laughed Frau Manzova, "however I cannot remember having to go to the school about you as often as I do for Georg"

"Did you mean it about going to the school tomorrow, or were you trying to frighten the boy"

"I was, I hope it will encourage him to tell me the truth of the matter, but I am sure I will receive a letter from his headmaster about this. It is not the first time he has been in trouble for fighting, what am I to do with him?" she looked across at Julius, "I am so sorry Julius, you do not want to be a part of our family troubles on your first night with us. Georg is really a good boy, I think we have spoilt him rather, him being the baby of our family. I also think that Nikolas is a difficult person to follow, don't you" and Frau Manzova looked fondly at her elder son.

"I think you may be right Frau Manzova" and he grinned at Nikolas, who was turning red at his mother's display of affection, "but please do not be worried for me. I grew up in a household of boys. With three of us in our house I am sure my mother saw every display of misbehavior imaginable. Please believe me I am quite used to it"

Frau Manzova seemed to be assuaged by Julius' little speech but Georg did not appear for dinner that evening and Frau Manzova intimated that this was his punishment for his misconduct at school.

The next few days Nikolas showed Julius as much as he could of the city of Prague. On their first morning the boys had risen early, a thing they did from habit, having been three years in the army, and used to six o'clock reveille. They had breakfasted alone as Nikolas' mother and brother were still in their beds, then set off to explore the city. Nikolas took Julius to the Strahov Monastery that stood on a hill above the city. From the monastery walls they had a wonderful panoramic view of Prague.

The early rise had been worth it for as they stood on the hillside in the early morning light, the view was astounding. The whole city lay spread out before them, covered in an eerie early morning mist, which made the city appear to be floating in mid air. As the sun rose in the sky and cast its soft golden rays over the landscape the mist began to evaporate revealing the true colors of the scenery. It looked as though a painter was quickly applying his brush to the scene. All the buildings were rendered in a variety of colors, blues, greens, yellows and reds all enhanced by the early morning sun. Julius had the impression that he was looking down on a mediaeval town, rather than a modern city.

From their high vantage point they could see the layout of the buildings and streets. Nikolas pointed out the spire of the St. Vitus cathedral that stood within the walls of Prague Castle and they could see the River Moldau winding its way through the heart of the city. It was an auspicious start to Julius' introduction to Prague. For the next few days they wandered around its streets, sampling the restaurants and beer halls, seeing the many sights. In the evening they

142

would return to the hospitality of the Manz household, who proved to be an entertaining, witty and loving family. By the end of his visit Julius felt as if he had known them for years.

On the night before they were due to report to their barracks Colonel Manz visited his home. Colonel Manz was stationed in Prague, his office was in the Army headquarters that were housed in a magnificent building in the Loreto Square, not far from Prague Castle.

Colonel Manz was not at all how Julius had expected him to be. He was a tall, thin man who looked somewhat younger than his own father, but who carried the same authoritarian demeanor of a senior Habsburg Army officer. It was easy to see that Nikolas and his brother took after their mother more than their father. However, as they ate a very enjoyable meal, Julius found that Colonel Manz had the same dry sense of humor that so endeared him to Nikolas.

Julius soon realized that Colonel Manz was not here to meet his son's friend, although he was very courteous, it was obvious he had been called home to deal with his wayward younger son. Julius felt sorry for Georg as he saw him take the dreaded steps towards his father's study and heard the heavy door close behind the boy. He knew how Georg was feeling as he could remember the same scenario from his own childhood days. They did not see Georg emerge from the room, but he was not seen at the dinner table that night, and they could only guess at the punishment that he had received.

Later, when Colonel Manz had returned to his barracks and Frau Manzova had retired to her bedroom, the two men sat discussing their own previous misdemeanors.

"I would not lose any sleep over Georg if I were you" offered Nikolas, "that little imp will have forgotten his punishment in a few days and I guarantee he will be in trouble again in the very near future"

"Is he really that bad? even I managed to keep myself out of trouble if I knew I had caused my father to be angry"

Nikolas laughed, "I am afraid Georg has little fear of punishment. Maybe Mama is right, maybe he has been spoiled, but I have to admit he is an endearing little soul who you cannot be mad with for too long. My mother seems to think that my living here in Prague might be a good influence for him, though I have my doubts"

Julius raised his eyebrows at his friend's remark, "so do I. Maybe I should tell her of some of our escapades in Vienna, that would soon change her mind"

"And turn her hair white" chuckled Nikolas, "anyway I would blame it all on Josef, he was such a bad influence you know"

Both men were quiet for a while, they had hardly mentioned their cadet life or their two friends since Julius had arrived in Prague. Perhaps it was too painful a subject for both of them, maybe they could not yet come to terms with the fact that they would not soon be boarding the train to Vienna to be reunited with Viktor and Josef.

"I am going to miss those two scoundrels," reflected Julius "I wish we could all have been posted here, together"

Nikolas reflected on this statement, then added, "Maybe, maybe not, things like that do not last for ever. We were very lucky to share a room, to like each other's company, but all good things come to an end they say. Besides which we will never lose their friendship, we will keep in touch and what was our pledge? always to help each other wherever we are in the world"

"I thought you were too drunk to remember that"

"I remember that bit, it is the rest of the evening that is a complete mystery to me. Didn't you say you asked your brother to look up Viktor when he got to Graz?"

Julius had indeed written to Franz asking him, if he could, to welcome Viktor when he arrived to take up his commission. Franz and Julius wrote regularly to each other, though they had not seen each other for several years. In his latest letters Franz had been mentioning a local farmer's daughter whom he had become attached to. When Julius had asked him if he was proposing marriage Franz had replied that he did not intend to make the same mistake as his elder brother and marry too young. That he had formed quite an affection for this girl was very evident in his letters. Karl had not written in years and although Julius wrote occasionally to his elder brother he had had no replies from him. On his last visit home Irmy had informed him that she presumed that Papa had paid off his debts, but she did not know for sure. Karl wrote to their mother about twice a year with a very dutiful, boring letter that told them nothing about his welfare or happiness. Julius reflected it was a very sad state of affairs.

Nikolas and Julius retired early that night. The next day they would report to their new barracks as Second Lieutenants Manz and Mayer. Julius lay awake for some hours that night contemplating the new phase of his life that he was now entering.

Julius' first few days as a commissioned officer were very frantic. He spent the whole time rushing from one post to another, having orders barked at him, then rushing off to find another location. He had been assigned to barracks to the North of the city. He was pleased to find he shared a room with Nikolas. When they had dropped their bags into their sparsely furnished rooms they were ordered to report to uniform stores to pick up their uniforms. The new uniform was a pike-gray color and was made of a drill material for summer and wool for winter. The tunic jacket was single breasted with a fly front, a stand up collar and the two patch breast pockets had a three-pointed flap. Most personnel were issued with a kepi, with a black leather peak and flaps. Being assigned to the Horse Artillery Julius received a shako that was worn with a gray cover and black horsehair plume and a woolen side cap to wear when off duty. As he was to be mounted personnel he was issued with gray breeches that were worn with ankle boots and leather gaiters or long black riding boots. The greatcoat was made of gray wool with a gray velvet collar and he was also issued with a cloak. The new uniform, though not as dashing as the old one, suited Julius' physique perfectly, and the color complimented his dark coloring. As he deposited his new equipment in his room a young corporal came in and ordered Julius and Nikolas to report to their new commanding officer, Colonel Reichart.

On entering his office Nikolas and Julius were made to stand to attention for a long time before the Colonel even deigned to look up from his paperwork and acknowledge their presence in the room. The Colonel, sitting behind his desk, was a small, dapper man with sparse black hair that was greased back onto his head with hair oil. When he eventually did raise his eyes to look at them Julius had the impression that he was looking at an emaciated skull. The colonel's face was painfully thin, with the skin drawn tightly over the bones. Set into the macabre profile was a pair of shining, black eyes that were so lively they looked incongruous amid the pallid complexion of their host. When he addressed them in a strong, rough Austrian accent, it was with a curt speech of welcome and a long list of his rules and regulations within the barracks.

From first meeting this man it was apparent there was to be no camaraderie between him and his junior officers. He would treat them with disdain and they would accept this as part of army life. Whilst Colonel Weber's task had been nurturing and training young boys to become disciplined army men, and as such to be almost a father figure to his trainees, he had done it with an authority and fairness that had earned him the loyalty and respect of all the cadets. Julius very quickly knew that Colonel Reichart was a very different man to Colonel Weber. There would be no acknowledgement of the fact that they had both done well in their exams, or that he was receiving two excellent cadets into his regiment. They were there to do a job and as long as they did it well, he held no other interest in them.

They were brusquely dismissed as Colonel Reichart took up his pen and resumed his paperwork, as though they were no longer in his office.

"Now there is a happy soul" remarked Nikolas, as they made their way to the stables where they had been told to report next. "Thank God we do not have to meet him often, do you think there is any humor in the man?"

"I doubt it" replied Julius, "I think we may have been somewhat spoiled with Colonel Weber, so I guess this is our welcome to the real world"

Julius soon forgot Colonel Reichart as he entered the stable block. Since a young boy he had always loved horses, and the smell of the stables filled him with a happy feeling of being near to those noble creatures. The stable block was large, housing about forty horses. Most of them were in their stalls, but some were in the central aisle being brushed down by their grooms. Mixed with the scent of the horses were the sounds of the busy stable, the soft neighs of the horses, and the crash of metal shoes grating on the cobbled floor as the horses impatiently stamped on the floor.

Julius and Nikolas walked up and down the stalls looking at the mixed array of mounts. Julius was pleased he had joined a mounted regiment. Within the cadets in Vienna there had been heated discussions as to how long the horse would remain a viable part of army life. It was true that automotive vehicles were now becoming increasingly popular, but Julius could not believe that one day they would supersede the horse, as some people argued. The horseless carriage or automobile seemed to be only destined for the very rich as they were very expensive. Julius had read in a newspaper that a man in America was now producing horseless carriages on a production line. The price that he charged for them was very reasonable so that many people could afford to buy one. Indeed there were autobuses on the streets and even utility vehicles such as ambulances were becoming motorized. The automotive vehicle may be becoming popular, but nothing could surpass the maneuverability of a horse, or so Julius hoped.

A young private led them to an office in the corner of the stables where a sergeant looked up their names and led them to the horses to which they had been assigned. Nikolas had a beautiful gray mare, called Stahle, or Steel and Julius found he had been allocated a handsome black stallion called Gespenster, or Phantom. He was certainly a large horse standing at least sixteen hands high with a glossy, dark coat and long tail. He kept hitting Julius with it as he swished it to and fro over his back, ostensibly to get at the numerous flies that swarmed above his flanks. As he watched, the horse pinned back his ears and showed the whites of his eyes. He fixed Julius with a baleful stare and Julius had the unnerving feeling that the horse had been hitting him on purpose. Julius could see he had a very headstrong partner, and looked forward to the challenge of keeping Phantom in check.

"He is a headstrong one sir, think you can handle him?" asked the sergeant.

Julius grinned, "I think I will manage, I will let you know when I have ridden him a few times"

Over the next few weeks Julius rode Phantom a lot, preparing himself for the numerous parades and sentry duties that were all part of army life. Phantom was a very recalcitrant horse, and quite a few times he was unseated. Julius would leave his training sessions feeling so exhausted that he could hardly drag himself back to his room. However, in the end, there developed a tacit respect between rider and horse, and although Phantom would never be an easy horse to master they became quite a team together. One day when a session had gone really well and even some of the grooms had applauded his horsemanship Julius was leading Phantom back to his stall when the sergeant appeared beside him.

147

"How do you feel now, Sir, happy with your mount?"

"Well I think we are getting somewhere at last," said Julius patting Phantom on his flank as he was led away by one of the grooms. "I believe you did not think I would get this far, am I right sergeant?"

The sergeant looked around to see who was in their vicinity and then said in a whispered voice, "well, sir, and you understand, this is strictly between you and me. If anybody should ask me I will deny this conversation took place, are we in agreement?"

"Of course, please carry on" Julius was intrigued and was trying not to smile at the secretive way the man was acting.

"We were given strict instructions to assign Phantom to you. He is known as a troublemaker, that horse. You would not have been the first rider who couldn't handle him"

"But who gave you such an order?" Julius was now even more puzzled.

"Colonel Reichart, of course. Rumor has it that you were the top cadet, is that right?" Julius nodded, "so this was his way of deflating your ego. He hoped you wouldn't be able to get along with Phantom, but you did, so that showed him didn't it?"

"I suppose so," said Julius, "but why are you telling me this, and why on earth would Colonel Reichart act like that?"

"Well I was impressed by the way you handled Phantom. Horses are my life and I like to acknowledge a good horseman when I see one. As to Colonel Reichart, for a start he is an Austrian" Julius chose to ignore this hint of xenophobia so the sergeant carried on, "well he came up the hard way sir, and he does not take to clever boys coming into the army, thinking they know everything"

"But I am not like that, am I?"

"I know that, sir, and you know that, but to be pre-warned is always an advantage I say. As I said this conversation never took place" and with that the man walked off to his duties, leaving Julius with a lot of thinking to do.

Although they shared a room Julius and Nikolas rarely saw each other except maybe at night and not always then if they had a night guard duty. Their duties were very separate and although at first they both found this strange they soon settled into their new way of life.

Julius began to enjoy himself, once his initial nerves were suppressed. He found the work varied and enjoyable. From guard duties to marching drill with the new men in his

148

company to route marches through the countryside around the city this new life was certainly different to the one that he had lived in Vienna. It was gratifying to at last be treated like an adult and with the respect that an officer was due. Although he found the attitude to his duties far less strict than when he had been a cadet with that also came the onus of far more responsibility. If anything went wrong the only person he could answer to was himself. There would be no discussion if there were a misdemeanor, no classroom analysis of why things went wrong. The punishment would be swift and to the point, and Julius was very aware of this new aspect of his army life.

Surprisingly Josef wrote to Julius and Nikolas often. Although they had all agreed to write to each other Julius had feared that it would be Josef who would not bother to put pen to paper, so he was pleasantly surprised when letters arrived frequently from Vienna. Josef wrote entertaining letters, very sarcastic and witty, mainly about his new army acquaintances. Julius had worried that Josef would have a hard time with his new regiment. If his letters were to be believed, he did not enjoy himself as much with his new brother officers, but he was enduring life and seemed to be out on the town a lot. He had even visited their old barracks to see Smid, which pleased Julius.

Viktor wrote about once a month, he had met Franz in Graz, and had liked him very much. As was to be expected he had settled well into his new home and was obviously well suited to the disciplines of army life. Irmy's letters still gave Julius a great source of enjoyment, even if they did often refer to Richard. Her marriage was to be in the spring of next year. She wrote that she was to be married in the cathedral in Kosice after which she would begin her married life with Richard in Prague. 'I cannot believe it' wrote Irmy, 'I will be living near you, it will be wonderful, or do you not wish to be encumbered with a silly younger sister? but I forget myself, I will be a mature married woman then. Frau Beckova, it does sound nice, does it not?' Julius gazed out of the window as he suppressed the thoughts that had come into his head at this sentence. 'There is one more thing I must tell you, though I am sure Papa will write to you about this in the near future. On Papa's last leave he realized that Mama has become very upset of late at the thought of my moving to Prague after my marriage. After much discussion between ourselves Papa has resolved that once I am

149

married he will sell the house in Kosice and move Mama and Danusia to Prague. I think it will be a wonderful idea. I have to admit that I was a little scared at the prospect of moving to a new city not knowing a soul. (I know you will be there, but you will be busy with your army duties, and you may well be posted elsewhere in the future) Having Mama near me will be a great comfort. I think I might have been quite lonely especially with Richard being at the hospital at odd hours. Of course Mama would have been lonely without me in Kosice, so really we are helping each other. Papa says that the journey to Prague from Vienna is no different than travelling to Kosice so he is happy with the arrangement as well. So what do you think, Julius, will you be happy with all your family around you in Prague?'

Julius did not know quite what to think. He had become used to being apart from his family for long periods of time, much as he supposed his brothers and father were. He had to admit he was envious at times when Nikolas could leave the barracks for a few hours to see his parents and Georg. He was pleased for Irmy, as he knew it would help her to have Mama near her, but how they would all feel when they found out that Irmy was to begin nursing training was another thing. In fact the more he reflected, the more he thought it would be quite an enjoyable time. He could watch the fur fly as his parents realized that their plans to curb their willful daughter were not going to go exactly as they had planned.

It was with some surprise that Julius and Nikolas received their orders for winter training camp. In the few months that they had been in Prague life had been so full that they had not had time to think about their future. As no senior officers had mentioned winter training they thought that the idea had been abandoned. Both viewed it as a mixed blessing. The timing was not fortunate, they had just begun to get into their routine within the regiment. They were at last beginning to feel they were getting to know their men and becoming part of a team rather than being newcomers who had to be endured. However the thought of being reunited with Josef and Viktor was very pleasing and Julius had always wanted to learn to ski, and here was his chance.

At the beginning of November they began to pack for their stay in the mountains. They were to be there for three months and it was with a particularly heavy heart that Julius

150

said his farewells to Phantom. The sergeant promised to take care of him and exercise him regularly. This was little compensation for Julius, for although he had only been riding Phantom for three months, he felt he was saying goodbye to an old friend.

The journey by train took them to the north-western region of Austria, to the town of Lienz. From there they took a narrow gauge railway trip up into the isolated mountain regions of the Hohe Tauern, the highest mountain range in Austria. Their journey ended at Heiligenblut, a beautiful village nestling beneath the highest peak of Austria, the Grossglockner. It was situated beside the river Moll, which began its life at the foot of a mighty glacier near the summit. The winter camp was to be situated higher up into the mountains, behind Heiligenblut.

The first thing that struck Nikolas and Julius was the freshness and coldness of the air. Whilst their journey had ascended up into the mountains the temperature had noticeably dropped as the countryside around them changed from the sparse greenery of winter into the romantic scenery of white snow as far as the eye could see, only broken by the majestic evergreen trees that stood in their proud dignity, as if defying the cold clutches of winter to envelop them. The magic was enhanced when they looked towards the peaks of the mountains that dominated the view. It looked as though great white gods sat there looking down on the minute forms of humanity that dared to encroach upon their peace.

Julius found the effect of the mountains very humbling, feeling he was privileged to be allowed into their lofty domains. The sun was starting to set and the village was almost deserted. Nikolas and Julius were wondering how to find directions to their camp when they heard somebody shouting. They saw two men on horseback riding into the village, leading two horses behind them. Both riders were instantly recognizable and Julius and Nikolas started running down the snow covered street to meet them. As Josef came up to them he brought his horse to an abrupt halt, and with a swaggering movement jumped off his horse and proceeded to greet them with a low sweeping bow.
"Good afternoon, sirs, your steeds await you"
To see those deep blue eyes beneath the sweeping lock of blonde hair underlined with a roguish smile was the perfect greeting. Even Viktor, who had by now joined the party,

was laughing as from his mount he said, "Only Josef would have greeted you like that. Life in the cavalry has not instilled any sense in him, has it gentlemen?"

All four men embraced in greeting, happy to be together once again. As they walked back down the road to retrieve their bags that they had dropped in their hurry to meet their friends Nikolas asked, "how did you know we were here? your timing was excellent"

Viktor looked at him and with a straight face and in a theatrical voice said, "we watched the stars last night. They showed us that two great soldiers from the lost city of Prague would be coming at this time to annoy us"

Nikolas jumped onto Viktor and tripped him up onto the snow, "at least in Prague we have sensible men in the army, not like you Austrian simpletons"

Leaving Viktor and Nikolas grappling in the snow Julius and Josef walked on, leading their horses. "So how did you know we were coming?" asked Julius

"Quite simple really, from our camp we have a panoramic view of the whole of the Heiligenblut basin. All we had to do was look for the train through our field glasses and then we could assess what time you would get here"

"So how was it that you two managed to get the job of greeting us?"

"I think you will find things very different at this camp. Life is very relaxed, it is not meant to be run on strict military lines. We are here to learn about all aspects of mountain life, skiing, walking, survival, need I go on? We told them that you were old friends of ours and asked if we could bring the horses down to you, simple as that"

Julius looked across at his friend; he did not seem to have changed much but Julius felt he detected some strain in Josef's face "how are you getting on? Thank you for your letters, I would never have thought you could write so fluently"

"I think I will take that as a compliment" observed Josef, "as to how I am getting on. I am all right, I suppose. Life is definitely different in the regular army"

Julius was not sure whether Josef was referring to the difference in being a cadet to an officer, or different in the fact that he was not now surrounded by his friends but he decided not to pursue the conversation. He had the feeling that Josef did not want to further the discussion at that moment and he knew he would have plenty of time to talk

152

to him in the next few months. Viktor and Nikolas joined them, brushing the snow off their uniforms. After they had stowed their bags onto the horses, they took a leisurely and scenic ride into the mountains, to their home for the next three months.

Their camp was a settlement of about twenty log cabins nestled into the side of the mountain. At the far end of the camp were the stables for the horses and after leaving their mounts in the care of the grooms Josef and Viktor showed them to their cabin. They were once again sharing together, evidently the choice of roommates being left to the young officers themselves. The cabins were very clean and spartan, with every man having to clean and tidy his own cabin. The men bemoaned the absence of Smid, but found themselves enjoying the privacy the lack of a valet allowed them. There was a stove in the middle of the room that they had to maintain themselves. The fire provided a welcoming heat for the room, giving it a warm and cozy feel.

On their beds were additions to their uniforms, essential items of warmer clothing for the cold Alpine conditions. There were fur lined boots, gloves and hats, white alpine coats, camouflage in the snow, and special snow shoes, shaped like oval pieces of board. Viktor explained you strapped them to your boot and they made walking in the snow easier. The relaxed atmosphere of the camp was endorsed by the fact that there was to be no official greeting by their superior officers. They would all meet each other at the informal dinner that evening.

Julius felt as if he was encountering a school reunion as he greeted his class of cadets that evening. The food was very basic fare, but enjoyable nonetheless. When Nikolas and Julius were approached by the senior officer, Major Hals, they both jumped up to salute him. His reply was a very ineffectual return salute and a wave of the hand requesting them to resume their seats.

Major Hals was a great bear of a man, whose body seemed to fill the entire room. He had a large, open face underlined by an enormous white handlebar moustache. His skin was ruddy with a leathery complexion that gave evidence to the many years he had spent in the mountains. He did not have a military demeanor, obviously finding the strictness of military regimen something of an anathema. The major appraised them both with his ice cold blue eyes, then smiled as he said, "I think I shock you a little gentlemen" He sat down opposite them, his great stature enveloping them both as he said "let me explain something to you, it is something I tell everyone who joins me here. I have been up here for many years, my duty is to train everybody how to live and survive in these mountains. Never underestimate the terrain around you, it is dangerous and is far stronger than any mere man. What I have to do is show you how to live *with* the mountains, not on them. To do this your first priority is to survive, not to be a soldier but to be a man learning about the elements around you, do you understand? You cannot salute your senior officer as you are racing down a mountainside trying to outrun an avalanche of snow, now can you?"

Everybody laughed nervously at the Major's humor. "Now when it comes to army matters, then we will be serious. When you learn about warfare and survival in a battle situation in the mountains, then you can salute me all you like, because that is when being a soldier will come into its own. However for the next few weeks you can forget that you are in the army, for I am going to try and show you all I know about this unforgiving land. Your army training will be at a later date" The major held up a horny, callused hand and then said, "and that is the end of my lecture gentlemen. I hope you enjoy your time here. Tomorrow you will start your skiing lessons, so I will see you tomorrow night carrying your cushions for your sore behinds and nursing your various bruises. Goodnight gentlemen"

Julius started to rise from habit, then checked himself just in time as he realized no one else had stood up as the major departed the dining room. Julius reflected what a strange fellow the Major was, but decided he liked the man. It was going to be a very interesting three months.

XIII

After breakfast and several cups of strong black coffee the soldiers assembled outside their cabins to meet their new instructors. It was very early in the morning, Julius thought he would never see such a beautiful sight as the sun rising over the crests of the mountains, causing the snow topped summits to reflect the mellow hues of the warming sun. Julius felt he was on top of the world, watching the very beginning of creation.

All the soldiers were dressed in their winter apparel. They had found it tedious to dress, there were so many layers to put on and they felt bulky and cumbersome. Once outside however they were glad of the extra warmth that the clothing afforded them. The early morning proved to be bitterly cold and their faces, which were the only part of their bodies exposed to the elements, soon began to feel stretched and numb and started to sting as the freezing temperatures took their effect.

All the soldiers were put into teams, Viktor was put into a separate team as he could already ski, but his team was to stay with the learner skiers to help them with their first few days of tuition.

They travelled further up into the mountains until they found themselves in a beautiful valley, filled with virgin snow. Their instructor had explained that this was a good place to learn as the slopes were very gentle and the sides of the valley provided a good shelter. Before they started their lesson they learnt how to put on their skis. This was not as easy as it sounded, the skis were heavy and curved at one end. In the middle of the ski were leather straps that had to be tied around the foot and secured by the heel of the boot to the ski. To get the attachment right was crucial, and it took most of the morning for the trainees to get the hang of it. After this they all stood in a line. With the aid of thick, heavy wooden poles, which had a circular metal wheel attached to them at one end, they were shown how to push themselves off and start to traverse the snow.

The exhilaration of moving across the snow, albeit very slowly, was wonderful for the first few moments. As he built up speed, which seemed to him frighteningly fast, Julius suddenly realized that he did not know how to stop himself. In his panic he threw up his ski poles into the air which

155

made him lose complete control and he fell onto his back with a resounding crash and lay there, looking up at the clear blue Alpine sky. When he looked around him he saw that all of his group were in the same position as he was, which soothed his hurt pride somewhat.

As he struggled to raise himself up off the snow, with the encumbrance of his skis, he heard the delicate swishing noise of skis on snow. Several instructors elegantly skied past him and came to a perfect stop right in front of the mass of bodies lying on the mountain snow.

"Gentleman you have just had your first lesson" shouted one of the instructors. "Firstly, always learn how to stop before you start to ski"

Very funny thought Julius, who still lay sprawled on the snow, "secondly, when you do get into trouble, never panic, as soon as you panic, you are lost. Waving your sticks in the air will not help, if anything they will contribute to upsetting your balance. Now we will show you how to get up"

With a display of amazing agility he showed them the correct way to rise from the snow onto their skis, using the weight of their bodies to propel themselves upwards. It looked very easy, but for some minutes the class looked like a group of failed contortionists as they tried to master the technique.

The lesson proceeded and by the time they had stopped for a quick lunch of bread and wurst with water Julius, Josef and Nikolas felt that at least they were managing to stay upright, which to them was progress. They had to admit they were having a lot of fun, even if they had to put up with Viktor's superior attitude, he was relishing the fact that at last he could do something at which he excelled his three friends.

By the end of the day they were all covered in bruises, but Julius did feel he was at last accomplishing something. He could travel a little way without falling over, he had learnt not to panic when he felt his skis running away with his legs and he had become very adept at learning how to stop. He had decided from very early on, that if he did not master anything else, this was the one thing he was going to make sure he did well.

The days passed by rapidly. It was very noticeable that some days they would go out on the slopes and feel they had finally mastered skiing, only to find the next day that their technique was terrible. Viktor explained that a large part of this was because when you first learn to ski, you think you have really mastered the intricacies of the art. However this makes you too confident, therefore you rush things and make unnecessary mistakes. They knew Viktor was right, every time they built up their confidence they would become arrogant with their success and do rash things.

"No one is ever that good that they can stop thinking about what they are doing on a pair of skis" remarked Viktor, "you must concentrate the whole time on what you are doing. You never know what conditions you will find over the next slope on a mountain and you must be ready for anything"

It was sound advice that Julius, Nikolas and Josef adhered to, and after the first few weeks up in the mountain their progress increased rapidly. Although there were still many bruises from numerous falls and they found aching muscles where they never even knew they had muscles, they started to really enjoy themselves. They even began to feel that they might become competent skiers by the end of their training.

Viktor thrived at the camp, it was obvious that the mountains were where he was happiest. After the first few days of training, he and the other cadets who could already ski were taken off high up into the mountains onto the glaciers to receive further training. Viktor would come back tired, but very happy from these trips with a big smile on his face and recall his adventures. His friends were quite jealous as he recounted his expeditions. As experienced skiers they often stayed out overnight, setting up camps on the mountain, where they built fires to keep themselves warm. All the trainees had been told that depending on their progress this would happen in the latter stages of their course, but after hearing Victor's exploits they were impatient to experience this for themselves.

One night Viktor came back to the cabin, very excited. He told them that he had gone up to the glacier that day with a Colonel Bilgeri. Colonel Bilgeri was a famous skier attached to the Imperial Army. He had taken a group, which included Viktor, to show them a new turn that had just been developed by an Austrian called Arlberg. The new turn enabled a skier to gain much faster speeds down the slopes than had previously been achieved. It was not just the learning of the new turn that had so excited Viktor, it seemed that the Colonel had also been experimenting with his skis. He had shown Viktor a new move that he had developed whereby a skier, using two poles would bring the front tips of his skis together in a 'v' shape, thereby slowing the skier down. As he was relating these events to his three roommates, Viktor was virtually dancing round the room, with a broad smile on his face, unable to contain his excitement. Julius, Nikolas and Josef although enjoying their skiing, could not get caught up in Victor's enthusiasm.

Josef lay on his bed watching his friend's antics as he observed, "I do not know about you two, but I am getting worried about our friend here. To get so excited about a move in skiing seems a little strange to me. Maybe the mountain air has affected him, they say people who live in the mountains are a little odd"

"I know you are laughing at me Josef, but I am not going to let you spoil my good humor. If you were an experienced skier you would understand how marvelous today was, but as you are not I will not even begin to explain it to you"

Nikolas laughed, "Take no notice of us Viktor, we are only jealous because we cannot wait to advance up into the mountains ourselves. At dinner tonight Major Hals said that as we have progressed so well we will probably start our survival training next week"

"That is wonderful news," replied Viktor generously, "though I think the survival training is going to be very hard, according to my instructors"

Survival training did prove to be very hard. True to his word Major Hals started them on the next stage of their course the following week. The training was varied and very strenuous. Hopefully all the trainees would end up being able to survive on the mountains for at least a week. This would be in small groups, as was planned, or even on their own, if the situation should arise.

For the next few weeks the young officers were made to walk long distances in the snow with heavy packs on their backs, wearing boots or board snow shoes. They were led for long distances on routes around the mountain villages, using their skis to 'walk' on, pushing one ski, and then the other over the snow in a perpetual motion.

They had to learn how to set up camp on the slopes, direct themselves using a compass by day and navigate by the stars at night. They were taught to make use of the wild animals that were found on the mountains, to hunt for them and lay traps, as gunfire was unwise higher up the slopes for fear of avalanches. They learnt how to dig holes in the snow, wrap themselves up in a blanket and climb in the hole to keep themselves warm should they find themselves stranded and exposed to the elements.

At times Julius disliked the snow and the limitations it made for him, he knew if it had not been for the encouragement of his friends, he would not have survived that first week. As the weeks progressed Julius was not sure that things got any easier, but he did find he was able to cope better with the harshness of the terrain. He was able to withstand the urge to drop to his knees and say 'no more' although the thought still often crossed his mind.

The training was hard on everybody and all the trainees were feeling the strain as the weeks proceeded. Tempers started to fray and there was a noticeable shortage of patience amongst the men. The instructors took all this with a good grace and although they drove their men hard it was to make sure they were fit enough and ready to tackle any situation.

The three months passed by rapidly. Before they knew it Julius, Nikolas, Josef and Viktor were once again contemplating having to say farewell to each other and returning to their regiments. Although the training had at times been difficult they had enjoyed being together again. They had also noticed how much they had changed, even in the few short months that they had been officers. Their boyish humor remained, but with it came evidence of their new responsibilities and the appreciation that they were all growing up.

In keeping with his relaxed attitude with the trainees Major Hals let the young men choose their own teams for the week long trek into the mountains, which was to be the climax of the course. The trainees were equipped with maps, sparse provisions and given a route to follow for one week. In that time they were to find out if they could survive the elements in the unforgiving terrain. Whenever they had been out before it was with an instructor, but this time they were to be on their own, the only stipulation was that at least one member of each party was an experienced skier.

Each soldier was provided with a rucksack that held provisions, an ice pick, a small shovel, a blanket, a mirror for signaling and a flare in case of emergencies. Major Hals explained that there would be a permanent guard on the camp who would look out for distress flares and watch for any mirror signaling during the day. He told them to take things easy, and not to be too adventurous.

"If you stay on the route on your map, you should not encounter too much trouble. We would not send novice recruits like you into any dangerous parts of the mountain. Your only worry will be avalanches, snow falls or if you injure yourselves"

"And that is *all* we have to worry about!" whispered Josef, sarcastically.

"Gentlemen, we are relying on you to be sensible. This is an exercise aimed at finding out about yourselves as much as anything else. If you are successful this week, remember next time you return to the mountains, it will be to lead your own men up here, so learn from this experience for the future"

It was with a feeling of trepidation that the four roommates prepared their rucksacks for the week ahead. They were glad that they were going together, but they all felt the enormity of the task in front of them.

"They would not send us out there if they did not think we were up to the task" reasoned Nikolas.

"And let us not forget that Viktor can show us how to stop if we need to" offered Julius, trying not to laugh. Viktor would still try and extol the virtues of his new skiing lessons, even when they made it quite plain to him that he was beginning to bore them on the subject.

Viktor sprang to his own defense "You may thank me for my experience one day, but I promise not to utter another word on the subject. My lips are sealed"

"Permanently I hope, that would be wonderful" countered Josef.

Once on their way, Julius began to enjoy himself, despite his earlier misgivings. The last few months of constant exercise had built up his muscular physique and his body was accustomed to the constant movement that skiing demanded. His stamina had increased and he now skied well, maybe not with Victor's aptitude, but he was able to feel confident about the next few days. As they progressed through a snow-covered valley, silent but for the sound of their skis on the snow, he felt content with himself. At that moment he could not think of anything better than to be traversing this beautiful landscape with his

160

three closest friends, looking forward to their shared time together in the week ahead.

Viktor led the party, as he was the best skier and map-reader. Along the route they scooped up snow into their water bottles to provide them with much needed refreshment. They had been supplied with a few meager provisions but they were expected to provide their own food. Nikolas and Julius were the best hunters, both having hunted from an early age. They were detailed to go and set some traps, whilst Josef and Viktor started a fire and set up camp for their first night. Their luck was in, for whilst they were setting their traps Nikolas spied a hare a little distance from them. Keeping perfectly quiet Nikolas reached inside his boot and pulled out his knife. With one deft movement he hurled the knife at the hare. The hare started to run off, with the knife embedded in its side, but its life was short as the mortal wound took effect. With great whoops and cries Nikolas ran to retrieve his knife and his prey. They had all believed that all they were going to eat that night was their dry provisions from their rucksacks so the hare was an unexpected bonus.

Nikolas was feted that evening as they ate the succulent meat of the hare. They all agreed it tasted as good as the best steak in the most expensive restaurant in Vienna. The campsite was well sheltered and the four men sat around the fire reminiscing about the old days, and talking about their new lives. Josef was recounting the many drunken nights they had enjoyed together and lamenting that at the winter camp no alcohol was allowed.

"Being an officer does not seem to have affected your social calendar," said Julius, "if your letters are to be believed"

"Certainly not" replied Josef, "in fact being an officer seems to make me even more popular with the ladies, if that is possible" he added smugly. "By the way, talking of ladies I went to the house a few weeks ago and they all send their love to you. I think you all made quite an impression there" Josef laughed as he saw the mixed reaction of his friends to his statement. It was one of embarrassment overcome by some pride in the fact that they had been remembered in such a way. "Have any of you managed to be similarly accommodated in your new regiments?"

Despite his attempt at some manners, Julius knew exactly what Josef was trying to ask in his roundabout way. Now they were officers it was common knowledge in the mess how and where to obtain the favors of certain women in the city. He and Nikolas had even discussed the possibility of going one night, but had never plucked up the courage to do so. Julius was amazed when Nikolas confessed all this to Josef, but ended by claiming that so far they had not had time to go.

"What do you three do without me?" chuckled Josef, "I know, next time we all get leave why not come and stay with me in Vienna. It would be wonderful to be back there together again"

Julius was not sure about this venture, but Viktor and Nikolas were so enthusiastic about the idea, that he had not the heart to put them off. He tried to change the subject, but realized his error as he said, "Josef, how is your mother, well I hope?"

He hoped his reaction was not too obvious in the light of the campfire as he felt the color creeping into his face as he mentioned the Countess von Kutz. He was glad that Josef did not realize that a vision of his mother's face had confusingly leapt into his mind as it always did when he thought of his night with Lise. Josef's face clouded over as he said, "yes she is well, but it is sad to see a woman as unhappy as my mother. Let us hope when your sisters marry they make a better choice than my mother did"

Julius quickly looked at Nikolas, knowing he was thinking of Irmy, but his friend did not betray any emotion as he stared into the fire. Julius could sense the unhappiness of his friend and Nikolas remained very quiet for the rest of the evening.

When they awoke the next morning their fire had gone out and it was freezing. They collected their belongings quickly, eager to be moving again, to restore some feeling to their stiff joints which were numbed by the cold. On checking their traps they were delighted to find they had caught two hares overnight, and so, with the prospect of another good evening meal, they set off onto the next part of their journey.

Viktor was a hard taskmaster as he knew that if they were to cover the distance outlined on their map they would have to keep a steady progress throughout the day. He only allowed them to stop for a few minutes for a lunch of dried biscuits and water before he had them on their feet again and, with compass in hand, was directing them to follow him. By the time they struck camp on the second night they were exhausted, but knew that the chores, such as setting

162

traps and building a fire had to be done before they could succumb to the fatigue they all felt. There was no campfire discourse that night, for as soon as they had eaten they had all fallen fast asleep.

The next morning Viktor said that the days trek would not be as arduous as the previous one. There was less distance to travel and easier terrain to cross to achieve their third campsite. They were disappointed to find that no animal had been lured into their traps, so they hoped they would be able to catch something during the day or at their new campsite.

The morning was fresh and clear and they enjoyed the leisurely trek through the valleys and slopes of the alpine range. As they stopped to rest Nikolas suddenly called to the others to look behind them. They were concerned to observe the sight of a blackening sky, which looked ominous and threatening as it raced across the afternoon sky towards them.

"What do you think Viktor?" asked Josef, "you know more about the weather conditions up here. Do you think it is coming our way?"

Viktor scanned the sky, "I have to be honest with you, it is not a welcome sight. That sky looks to me as though it is bringing some very bad weather, and a large amount of snow. I do not mean to alarm you, but I think it would be a good idea to look for some form of shelter in case that catches up with us"

The finding of a shelter was not so easy, the valley they were in consisted of plain undulating slopes with no natural forms of protection around.

"I suggest we ski on a little further and hope there is something over that ridge" proposed Viktor.

Glad to take his advice Julius, Nikolas and Viktor followed their friend. They skied as fast as they could into the next valley, all the time looking over their shoulders as the angry black cloud chased them and seemed to be catching them up. Julius noticed the wind becoming stronger as it whirled around their bodies impeding their progress across the snow. As they crested the ridge they could see that Viktor was shouting something at them but they could not hear what he was saying, the wind was now so forceful. Josef waved his hand at Viktor, showing him that he should carry on and they would follow him.

The wind was now extremely strong and Julius was alarmed to see flecks of snow whipping past his face as they raced along. The snow began to fall heavily and visibility was getting less and less.

Julius was losing sight of Josef and Viktor who were in front of him, as the wind slammed the snow into his eyes and face. He suddenly looked up as he collided with Josef and then felt a knock in his back as Nikolas came to a halt behind him. Through the thickening snow he could just make out Viktor frantically pointing at something to the left of them. They all nodded to let Viktor know they were with him and understood that they were to follow him. Julius did not know what Viktor was pointing at but he reasoned that he was the most knowledgeable person there and that their priority was to stick together.

Their progress was very slow now, mainly due to the force of the wind that screamed around their bodies and the heavy fall of snow, hindering any speed that they tried to muster. In some ways this helped as they stayed close together and were all visible to one another.

The trek felt interminable; Julius felt the strength draining from his legs and arms as he willed himself to carry on. He kept his head down, trying to keep the end of Josef's skis in his sight. Every so often he would push his head upwards against the wind and the snow to make sure they were all still together. He wanted to drop to the floor and give up, his body screamed at him to stop, to ease the pain that was sucking the air out of his lungs, causing his heart to beat so fast he could hear it racing in his chest. Several times, he stumbled, as did Josef and Nikolas and each time they helped each other raise themselves again to carry on, knowing if they stopped it would be the end for all of them.

After what seemed like hours, Viktor stopped in his tracks. The relief at stopping was tremendous, but Julius knew if he did not move soon, he could not command his aching legs to start again. Viktor moved off to the left making sure they were all following him, the walk was steep and in their fatigue they all started to slide backwards on their skis. With a last superhuman effort they reached the top of a ridge. Through the blinding snow and screaming wind Julius could just make out the shadowy forms of a few trees, looking like forbidding spirits beckoning him to join them. They all slid down the other side of the ridge, towards the trees and Julius was overjoyed to see a large

164

overhanging rock behind the trees that he hoped would afford them some shelter.

The sight of their sanctuary spurred them on as they raced towards the trees and they charged underneath the rock and collapsed onto the snow. Looking above him as he lay on the floor Julius could see that although the snow still swirled about them in its potent fury the ledge of rock did offer them some protection. The group of about six trees in front of them slowed down the force of the wind somewhat, although it still roared around them. Julius felt hot and clammy, despite the freezing snow on his clothes, and as he lay there his eyes closed in the pure joy of knowing he could now stop and sleep.

He found himself being shaken furiously and he reluctantly opened his eyes to see Viktor kneeling over him. He was shouting, but his words were being carried away by the force of the wind. He pulled Julius up by his jacket and put his face right up against Julius' face.

"Don't be a bloody idiot, haven't you learnt anything?" he shouted, "get your skis off, take off your rucksack and get further back against the rock and do it quickly before I kick your arse"

Julius shook himself out of his lethargy, he knew Viktor was right, they had to prepare themselves to sit out the storm. If he had lain down and just gone to sleep he would certainly not have woken again, though looking around at their situation he was not sure they would survive anyway. He tried to shake off his feelings of doom as he attempted to take his skis off.

He looked around him and could just make out Viktor forcing Nikolas and Josef to take off their rucksacks and throw them to the back of the ledge as they started to release their bindings. This was not easy because they had to take their gloves off. Julius knew they could only take their gloves off for a certain amount of time before their hands would become frozen and possibly frostbitten. Every so often they would put their gloves back on and try to warm their hands. Their main problem was their leather bindings. In the snow they had become wet and were very difficult to untie, especially with numb fingers. At last Julius managed to undo his skis and went further into the rock face only to be pushed back out by Viktor to pick up his skis and carefully stow them. Josef was having trouble with his ski bindings, so they all took it in turns to remove their gloves and try to undo them.

Eventually they were under the rock, huddled together. The storm was still howling and after being hot and sweaty from their trek they were all shivering as the cold started to creep through their clothing and into their bodies. Viktor crawled round and crouched in front of his friends, who huddled closer to him to try and understand what he was saying.

"We will never survive like this, we will all perish in the cold. We must get our blankets out of the rucksacks and wrap them firmly round us. Then we must all embrace each other as firmly as possible, using our body heat to warm each other"

As the snow whirled around Julius could just see the ghost of a smile that had appeared on his friend's face, which seemed incongruous in their present situation, "and when I mean embrace, I mean embrace. Just pretend we are back in Vienna, on the night of Julius' birthday, that is what I mean by embrace. Understand?"

Julius, Josef and Nikolas all nodded their heads vigorously, they understood perfectly.

With great difficulty, as their shivering racked their bodies, they got their blankets out of their rucksacks and wrapped them tightly around themselves, like swaddling clothes. Then they all lay together, hugging each other as firmly as possible, the warmth of their bodies endeavoring to withstand the snow and wind that lashed about them, the elements taunting them to give themselves up to their icy clutches.

XIV

When Julius awoke it was to absolute silence, and for a moment he believed he had been dreaming or that he had indeed succumbed to the storm and had forfeited his life. In panic he opened his eyes and was relieved to find himself staring into Nikolas' face, which held such a look of peace and contentment, like that of a sleeping child, that his fears were once more aroused, this time for his friend, as he thought he was not breathing. Julius' anxiety was allayed when Nikolas let out a gentle snore and Julius realized he was lying firmly wrapped in the arms of his friend. He felt very cold and as he tried to extricate himself from Nikolas' arms he saw that they were covered in a layer of snow that tumbled over them as he moved. The rush of snow onto his face woke Nikolas, who yawned, then opened his eyes and stared at Julius. Aware of their position and situation Nikolas smiled his wonderful cherubic smile and said, "Hello, darling, was the night wonderful for you too?"
Julius shrieked with laughter, not just from Nikolas' joke but also from the sheer joy of knowing they had survived the storm and were still alive. His laughter woke Viktor and Josef, who were also entwined around each other. The four men grinned at each other and laughed with the sheer elation that life brought them, their laughter echoing across the snow covered valley.

They lay in their makeshift beds, discussing the night and reflecting on the good fortune of finding the overhanging rock and the trees. They were allowing themselves the time for their stiff joints to ease under the heat of the morning sun that was bathing the mountain, but also to adjust themselves to the tremendous feeling of contentment that swept over them. They had come through an horrendous nightmare together and survived to tell the tale. Although good friends before, they knew that the sharing of such an experience would somehow bond them together for the rest of their lives, it was something no other person would be able to share with them. To face death together, and know they had helped each other overcome the lure of death's icy embrace, and lived, was not something that could be put into words, but something which they all felt as they lay on the mountain, just happy to be alive.

The valley they were in held no evidence of the terrible storm it had endured the night before. The mountainside was restored to its picturesque beauty, the sun sparkled on the virgin snow and the skies above were a beautiful clear blue with not a cloud to mar them. The four men attempted to rise from their bed but it took quite a while before the stiffness in their bodies allowed them to walk a little way to try and ease their aches and pains. The exertion of the previous day was all too obvious and they were very tired. Viktor suggested that they try and find some food, and that they should really try and find out where they were and endeavor to get back to the main camp.

"I would imagine after last night's storm that the exercise has been abandoned. They are probably starting out now to try and find all of us. Let us hope that the others had the same luck we did"

Josef, who was rolling up his blanket, looked up at Viktor and said, "Let us hope they all had someone in their party like you Viktor. You know you saved our lives last night, something I will never forget. Without you pushing us on, encouraging us, bullying us even, we would never have survived. I know I am speaking for the others when I say thank you. It does not sound much, but I think you know how we all feel about you"

Viktor blushed deeply and started to mumble that they had all worked as a team when his three friends went over to him and they all embraced together. When they let go they all had tears in their eyes, and it was left to Josef to lighten the situation.

"I would just like to say if it ever gets around Viennese society that I spent the night in Viktor's arms, I will know who to come looking for!"

With their rucksacks on their backs and their skis once more strapped to their boots they scanned the map trying to work out their position. Viktor thought he knew which direction they had taken the night before and with the aid of his compass and a look at the mountaintops around him he decided which direction they should take. No one chose to argue with him. After last night they would have followed him to the end of the world if he had asked them. Nikolas suggested they send up a flare, but Viktor thought it was better not to.

"We are all right, just short of food. We should be able to make it back to camp unharmed. We do not know what happened to the others last night. Some may be injured or in difficulties and they will need help far more than we do. I suggest we press on for the day, and if we have not found the camp by tomorrow morning, then we can use our flares" They all agreed that this was the most sensible course of action and started off.

The journey was hard, their limbs were aching from yesterday's exertions and, as they were not on the designated course they had been allocated, the terrain was difficult for Julius, Nikolas and Josef, who were relatively inexperienced skiers. Viktor helped them along, giving them advice if they came to a particularly difficult part of the landscape. He was stopping quite frequently, to give them time to rest, and also to consult his map and compass.

They began to feel very hungry as the day wore on. They had exhausted their supply of dry provisions and the lack of food was not helping them to maintain the stamina they needed. As they approached late afternoon Nikolas suggested that maybe they should think about setting up camp for the night. Viktor, who had been reading his map, looked up with a smile on his face, "I do not think we will need to, my friend. I thought the terrain was beginning to look familiar, look over there, what do you see?"

They all looked over to their right at an enormous mountain peak that dominated the skyline. "Now what does that look like to you?"

"The Grossglockner!" shouted Nikolas.

"I believe so" said Viktor, "which, if I am right, means that over that ridge there should be......"

"Home" grinned Julius.

"Food" shrieked Nikolas.

"A bath" laughed Josef.

Their energy revived by the thought of being back at the camp by nightfall, they all picked up their ski poles and raced over the mountain.

As they skied into the encampment they were hailed by other soldiers as a door to one of the cabins opened and Major Hals appeared.

"So you have returned, what happened to you all?"

Julius, Nikolas, Josef and Viktor all poured out their story to the Major, who was pleased at the way they had survived the storm.

"So I send out boys and they come back men. Now do you see why I tell you how dangerous it can be up here? You

169

were very lucky yesterday, but you did well, I am proud of you"

Josef stepped forward and nobly outlined Viktor's contribution to their salvation. Major Hals looked at Viktor, who was turning red again. "Well done Lieutenant Leitner, you have done well. We will talk of this later, but for now you are tired and hungry. I am sure you are longing for a bath. We have been boiling water all day for our returning heroes, so there is plenty of hot water for you all. Then you can eat"

Once back in their cabin, the men discarded their mountain gear, and went to the bathhouse for their baths. Julius had to agree that it was the best bath he had ever had in his life as he lay in the hot water, letting its heat seep into his bones, relishing in the realization that at last he was feeling warm again.

Dressed, and their spirits high, they made their way to the main cabin for their meal. They opened the door, loudly laughing and joking with each other, but soon stopped as they saw the expressions on the faces of the other soldiers already sitting at the tables. They knew straight away that something was very wrong.

"What is the matter?" asked Julius, afraid of what the answer was going to be.

"We have just heard," volunteered a young officer, "we were missing one of our groups. They have just been found. Two are dead, and the two surviving soldiers have broken arms and legs and severe frostbite. They are in a very bad way and it is not known whether they will survive the journey down from the mountain"

Julius and his friends looked at one another, as the shock of the news sunk in. The deaths of their comrades appalled them, but there was also the appreciation of how close they had been to the same fate. The evening meal was a very somber affair, and when they went to bed that night the four friends all prayed before going to sleep.

The death of their classmates affected everybody at the camp. The two survivors and their dead companions had been brought down from the mountain, but it was not known whether the two injured men would survive their ordeal.

That Sunday all the camp assembled at the beautiful church in Heiligenblut and special prayers were said for the two dead soldiers and for the return to health of their two friends. It was a sad ending of their time in the mountains and as Julius, Nikolas, Josef and Viktor packed for the return to their regiments they regretted, after going through so much together, that they were parting in such a sad way. They realized their experience on the mountain had imbued in them all an intense appreciation of life, and of each other. Their brush with death had been cathartic for them all and would stay with them for the rest of their lives.

XV

On their return to Prague Julius and Nikolas felt a restlessness that was not assuaged by the normal routines and duties of army life. They found they were constantly trying to find new experiences to fulfill their lives.

They started to socialize a lot more, going to the theatre, dinner parties, and dances, as though trying to make up for the lost youth that had been dedicated to the army. They were always welcome wherever they went; a pair of young soldiers in uniform was always a desirable addition to any social event.

Lately several picture houses had opened in the city where you could go and watch moving pictures, mostly from America. Nikolas, especially, was enthralled by the sight of the black and white moving pictures on the screen in front of him accompanied by a pianist, which added to the excitement of the story unfolding in front of his eyes. Nikolas was known to go and see a moving picture at least three or four times, so captivated was he by this new invention.

Although still very dedicated young officers they began to understand that there was more to life than just being a conscientious soldier. Julius found himself becoming quite popular with the ladies, his good looks and obvious charms appealing to most females that he met. Nikolas too enjoyed the companionship of young women, although his shyness created a barrier around him. Julius tried to encourage his friend but it would usually take the added incentive of alcohol before Nikolas became comfortable in female company.

Their life in the barracks was still very much a learning process. Recruitment of non-officers was carried out on a territorial basis, and the army had sixteen defined areas. Julius' regiment was located in the South-western Bohemian district. Men of the Austro-Hungarian Empire were called for service from the first January of their twenty first birthday. These men were expected to serve for two years in the regular army and a further ten years in the reserve army.

Julius enjoyed being in the company of his men. He proved to be a popular officer, but he still noticed the large divisions between officers and privates, and also the great rivalry between religions and countries within the army. He

172

tried not to get embroiled in the constant arguments that flared up within the ranks, but it was hard not to get involved, and at times he found he had to take sides, something he hated to do. He began to learn what his father had meant by the fine line they all had to tread when dealing with so many emotive subjects.

His greatest joy was to get away from all the politics in the barracks and take Phantom for a ride. He had been overjoyed when the horse had appeared to recognize him when he had returned from the winter exercises, and with every passing week he felt he was achieving more and more with his mount. Phantom was the perfect horse for the many parades and escort duties that were required in the city. A tall, striking horse, Phantom drew everyone's eyes as they trotted by. The horse had learnt to behave obediently and had become a credit to Julius and the army.

Julius' other great love was to wander around Prague and discover all the joys that the city had to offer. From the magnificent Wenceslas Square, where he would often go on parade with Phantom, to the awe inspiring Prague Castle, including the famous St. Vitus Cathedral, where Julius and his company often performed sentry duty, he never ceased to be amazed by Prague's beauty and welcoming warmth that he had felt since first arriving in the city, almost a year ago.

Sometimes Julius would be sent to the Austro-Hungarian Army Headquarters, which were situated in a large, ornate building in the Loreto Square, opposite the Loreto, a building that housed a shrine to the Virgin Mary and several beautiful church treasures. Julius loved to hear the Loreto's bell tower sound its numerous bells as it struck the hour. Whenever Julius was sent to Army Headquarters he always felt an enormous feeling of patriotic pride when the majestic building came into sight as he climbed the hill towards it. He could see the standard of the Habsburg arms, the double headed eagle, flying above the entrance to the building, emphasizing the status and importance of the Imperial Army.

He would sometimes see Nikolas' father at army headquarters. Colonel Manz always stopped to talk to Julius, usually gruffly regaling another scrape that Georg had gotten into. Julius often went to the Manz household. He was always made very welcome and relished being a part of a family again. It made him look forward to the time when

173

Irmy, and then Mama, would come to live in the city. Irmy's marriage was drawing closer and Julius applied for leave to go to his sister's wedding. Despite his reservations, he was determined not to miss Irmy's nuptials and he had learnt from his mother that both his brothers were to attend. He was intrigued to see his elder brother after so much time and also to meet his elusive sister-in-law.

Nikolas had not mentioned Irmy for quite a while and so it was with some surprise that he offered to go with Julius into the city to help him buy a wedding present. The shopping did not take long as Julius had known that he was going to buy them a collection of Bohemian crystal glass. Bohemia was famous for its beautiful sculptured glassware and Julius made his selection easily. After arranging for the glassware to be delivered to Irmy's new house after the wedding, Julius took his friend out to dinner. Nikolas was very quiet and Julius could guess the reason. Feeling he needed to get his friend to talk he said, "you know you should have let me buy Irmy's wedding present on my own if it was going to upset you like this"

Nikolas looked up from staring into his beer stein with a grin on his face, "am I really so obvious? no, do not worry about me. If there is one thing I have learnt in the last few months it is not to dwell on things that might have been"

"What do you mean?" asked Julius

"Lying out there on that mountain, believing I was going to die, made me think about a lot of things. After that day, if Irmy had been unattached, I might well have told her how I feel, but she is engaged to be married and that is the end of the story. Our adventure taught me that if you want something, then you should pursue it, straight away, not prevaricate in any way, and have no regrets, for tomorrow you could be dead"

"I still do not understand where that leaves you and your feelings towards Irmy"

Nikolas turned to Julius and sadly said, "It leaves me absolutely nowhere, Julius, nowhere. Irmy is a closed book as far as I am concerned. She was what the romantics among us might call my first love, and there will always be a little part of her in my heart, but life does go on as they say. I am now determined to live my life as fully as I can, and with that in mind, is it not your turn to order me a beer?"

174

Julius could sympathize with Nikolas' feelings. The experience had changed his view on life, and the tenuous hold mankind has on it. Nikolas was right, life was there to be lived and living with regrets helped nobody.

Julius arrived in Kosice with the sad realization that this might be the last time he would be visiting the city where he had spent so many happy years.

When he arrived at his childhood home he was greeted by turmoil and panic as his mother rushed around trying to make sure everything was perfect for the wedding, which was to be in two days time. As Julius entered his home he was greeted by a hurried peck on the cheek from his mother and sister as they disappeared up the stairs muttering about dress fittings and veils. Julius dropped his bag in the hall and went into the sitting room to see if he could call for a maid to bring him a cup of coffee and something to eat, as he was hungry and thirsty after his train journey. He was pleased to find Franz sitting in the large chair by the fire, his feet resting on the sofa, reading a newspaper.

"If Mama catches you with your shoes on her brocade, it will be straight to your room with no tea, young Mayer"

Franz looked up from his reading with a wide grin on his face, "the state our dear Mama finds herself in at the moment I do not think she would notice if a whole herd of horses were stampeding through her sitting room"

Franz jumped up from his chair to embrace his brother, "good to see you little brother. I am really glad you are here. I have been surrounded by females for the last two days, females preparing for a wedding, you can imagine what that has been like"

"I was hoping to get something to eat and drink, I am famished"

"I would not hold my breath if I were you. The state of this household at the moment you would be lucky to get a glass of water. Cook has been baking for at least the last month by the look of the food in the kitchen, and still believes she will not be ready for the wedding in time and Mama has the other servants doing so many chores that I don't think they know if they are coming or going. I feel sorry for them. I had to take Mama and Irmy out for dinner last night, it was the only way I could ensure myself of having a decent meal"

Julius decided it was best not to even endeavor to call a servant but suggested to Franz that they go and find some peace and quiet, and food and refreshment at a local hostelry. Franz readily agreed to the idea and the two brothers left the house, glad to escape all the excitement of the wedding preparations.

Julius had always been close to Franz and they spent a very agreeable few hours discussing all the pertinent events of their respective lives since they had last seen each other. It had been over four years since they had last been together, but Julius felt immediately at ease with Franz, as though the parting had not been so long. Franz had grown up in that time. He was now much broader in the body, and there was a serious air about him, although to see these two men together one could not escape the fact that they were brothers. Viktor had told him that Franz was an exemplary officer and there was even talk of a promotion for him, which was excellent for such a young man.

When asked about Richard Beck Julius was careful in his reply, he did not want to prejudice his brother's opinion before he met his future brother-in-law. Richard and his mother were to arrive in Kosice with Papa that evening and they were to dine together at Richard's hotel. Franz had no more news about Karl than Julius had, except that he had been expected to arrive the night before but had not turned up. Julius hoped he would not let Irmy down, as he knew his sister would be most upset if not all her brothers were at her wedding.

Franz had heard about their escape in the mountains from Viktor and Julius was pleased when Franz did not press him too much on the subject, he still found it very difficult to talk about. Julius was gratified to find that Franz obviously liked Viktor and that he was a popular officer, "Mind you" added Franz, "I know where he gets his damned fool sense of humor from. Comes from sharing a room with an idiot like you for three years."
Julius looked at his brother with a mischievous look on his face "and what about this girl you keep writing to me about, would you not like to hear the sound of wedding bells too?" he asked unkindly, wishing to embarrass his brother. Julius was pleased to see the color creeping into Franz's face.
"I suppose I deserved that" replied Franz, "actually, and this is just between you and me, I would marry Gretha tomorrow, if she would have me" Julius was taken aback by his brothers show of emotion as he continued, "but she is still young and you must remember I am only twenty two, I

176

do not want to make the same mistake as Karl and marry before I am ready"

"Do you think that is the case, or more the fact that Karl married the wrong woman?"

Franz had obviously thought this himself as he answered, "that may well be true, we will soon know the truth when we meet the mysterious Frau Anna Mayerova ourselves, if they manage to arrive in time for the wedding"

As the hour was getting late the brothers returned to their house to be greeted on the doorstep by Mama, in a high state of anxiety.

"Where on earth have you two been? Papa is here and we have to leave for the hotel in ten minutes, I was beginning to consider that all my sons were going to let me down this evening"

Both her sons kissed her on the cheek, then rushed up the stairs, promising to be back down in ten minutes, washed and ready to accompany her for the evening. True to their word, though somewhat out of breath and Franz with a cut chin from a hasty shave, they both appeared in time to depart for the evening. Papa greeted them with his usual reserve, whilst Irmy rushed across the room to greet them both affectionately, with Mama warning her not to crease her dress before their departure. Irmy looked very pretty and positively glowed as her brothers showered her with the compliments she deserved.

The evening was a great success. Richard was accompanied by his widowed mother, a genteel lady who sat in virtual silence all evening, but who was very happy to be in their company and to quietly observe her surroundings. Julius was seated next to her at the dinner table, with Franz on her other side, and between them the two brothers kept her happily occupied throughout the evening. Julius had to admit that Richard thrived in the company of his sister. He became quite humorous as the evening progressed and Julius was gratified to observe him often watching Irmy with such a look of pride and love on his face that he really could not deny the man his happiness.

The fact that Karl was not at their table was politely ignored by Richard and his mother, but Julius could see that his absence upset Mama and deeply angered Papa.

Julius and Franz decided to walk home from the hotel and as they sauntered towards their house Franz said,

"Richard appears to be quite a nice fellow" he turned to observe his younger brother as he added, "I had the impression this afternoon that you were not taken with our future brother"

Julius stared straight ahead of him as he replied, "I cannot imagine what gave you that idea. I must admit that on first meeting Richard I found him a bit solemn and serious, but there is no doubting that he loves Irmy and that she loves him"

Franz raised an eyebrow in skepticism, "very well, but I still think you have your reservations about this marriage"

"I must admit I am worried about their age difference, but he is Irmy's choice and Mama and Papa approve of him"

"I do not see their age difference as being a problem. Personally I think any man that married Irmy would not meet with your approval" As Julius was determined not to be goaded into an answer by his brother, Franz continued, "you know you have always been very close to Irmy, you were always going to be jealous of any man that married her"

As they walked along Julius thought about his brother's statement. To a certain extent Franz was right, he would have been jealous of any suitor of Irmy's. He had realized that a long time ago, but he also reasoned to himself that Franz had been away from home for such a long time that he did not understand all the other factors that contributed to the whole picture. Franz did not know of the independence and freedom of spirit so prevalent in their sister and Julius did not want this to be suppressed by marriage at such a young age. He was pleased that after her marriage Richard was to allow her to study nursing, but he wondered how long he would want Irmy to work once it conflicted with her domestic duties, or when she had children. Franz also did not know about Nikolas. Although in his heart Julius knew that Irmy might never have been attracted to his friend, there was always the idea in his head of what might have been. Being honest with himself he knew that this was partly the reason for his hesitation in sharing his sister's happiness, and the reason he had not completely taken to Richard. He knew all these thoughts were folly and that Irmy would marry Richard and probably be very happy, but there was a nagging worry at the back of his mind for her.

Julius saw that Franz was still watching him intently. Wanting to appease his brother Julius said, "yes, I realized that myself some time ago, but believe me I have come to terms with it, and now all I want is for Irmy to be happy" and he meant it with all his heart.

Julius' memories of his mother on the two days before the wedding was with a list in her hand, continually checking and rechecking the smallest details of her daughter's marriage, much to the chagrin of the servants who were being asked the same questions at least three or four times in the day. Close at Mama's elbow would be the constant shadow of Danusia, nodding her head at everything Mama said or loudly clucking her tongue when some minor mishap had been revealed. Julius, Franz and their father tried to keep out of the way as much as possible, unless their mother happened to come upon them around the house, and then she would send them on copious errands around the city. There was still no word from Karl, and Colonel Mayer would no longer allow his name to be mentioned. Julius was glad his mother and Irmy were caught up in the wedding preparations or else his brother's absence might have been even more upsetting for them than it already was.

The day of the wedding dawned bright and clear. The house still appeared to be in chaos and Julius wondered if they would ever be ready to receive the wedding guests after the ceremony. Mama insisted that they all sit down to a family breakfast together and Julius was glad to see that one of the servants had tactfully taken away the sixth chair at the table so as not to emphasize Karl's absence.

Frau Mayer was beginning to show the strain of the last few days, becoming tearful as she realized that she was losing her daughter that day. Irmy had to rush round the table to comfort her and assure Mama she was not losing her, would they not soon be living together in Prague? Mama started to dry her tears but said she could not promise not to cry in church.

"Do not worry yourself Mama" observed Franz, "you will not be heard above Danusia wailing behind you" The whole family laughed, glad for the release of the tension but also at the truth of Franz's statement.

Julius and Franz went ahead to the church to receive the wedding guests on behalf of their family. Both looked very handsome in their full dress uniforms and as some of Irmy's friends arrived to take their places in the pews, there was much giggling and fluttering of eyelashes at the sight of Irmy's two handsome brothers.

St. Elizabeth's had thrown off her gothic gloom for the day as the sunlight shone down through the stained glass windows onto the large displays of flowers that were arranged throughout the church. All the servants had been allowed to come and watch the marriage and they took their places at the back of the church. Richard arrived with his mother and Professor Krebs from the hospital, who was to act as his best man. He looked very happy and Julius was pleased to see him taking the time to talk to Irmy's friends and the priest who was to perform the ceremony. Julius escorted Frau Beckova to her seat, and after making sure she was comfortable returned to the back of the church as Mama and Danusia arrived. Mama looked calm, if not a bit strained as she greeted her two sons. She was already looking tearful, but was trying to keep her composure as she smiled and waved at the guests. Danusia already had a trembling lip and her eyes were full of tears, Julius and Franz could not look at each other for fear of bursting into laughter as they recalled Franz's prediction at breakfast. Franz escorted his mother down the aisle to the front pew in front of the altar while Julius showed Danusia to her seat and then joined his brother to sit in the pew behind their mother.

Julius was on his knees saying his prayers when he felt a sharp elbow in his ribs and looked up to see Franz motioning with his head to the back of the church. He looked round and was startled to see Karl walking down the aisle towards them.

Julius was shocked by his brother's appearance. He looked painfully thin, his face was drawn and there were dark circles under his eyes, he had aged and looked much older than his twenty-six years. As he approached his brothers his mother turned and with a gasp of amazement hugged her eldest son after which Karl took his place alongside his brothers, shaking them by the hand. Julius stared into his older brother's eyes and felt unnerved, but he did not know why. He had little time to reflect on this, or the whereabouts of the elusive Anna, as the organ played to announce the arrival of the bride and her father.

Julius did not begrudge Danusia crying that day as he himself had a large lump in his throat as he watched Irmy

180

and Papa walking up the aisle. Colonel Mayer was resplendent in his uniform and he looked as if he was going to burst with pride as he walked with his only daughter towards the front of the church, nodding to acquaintances as he passed them on their slow march to the altar. Irmy was absolutely glowing; Julius would have sworn there was a light shining around her as she made the long walk to her marriage. Her dress was cream, swathed around her body as though it floated on its own. Her hair was threaded with pearls and she carried an enormous bouquet of cream flowers. She looked an absolute picture of happiness as she glided up the aisle on her father's arm. Julius stole a glance at Richard who stood transfixed with his mouth open as he watched the vision of his future wife walking towards him. Julius knew in that moment that whatever his own thoughts about Richard, he truly loved Irmy.

Irmy and Papa hesitated as their eyes alighted on Karl. Papa's face was a mixture of emotions as at first he regarded his eldest son with the joy of seeing him, then, as if remembering his past misdemeanors, gave his son a reproving, angry look. Karl appeared to ignore his father as Irmy beamed at Karl and would have interrupted her progress to give her brother a welcoming hug but Colonel Mayer checked her arm and indicated to her to carry on walking towards Richard. After father had carried out his paternal duties at the altar he turned to join Mama, but chose to ignore his eldest son as he took his place in the front pew.

The service was beautiful, and Julius believed even the hardest cynic could not but be moved by the sentiments of that day, though he noticed Karl did not choose to join in the devotions or sing any of the hymns chosen for the service. Danusia, of course cried so loudly that even Mama, red-eyed herself, had to turn during the service and give Danusia one of her stony looks to indicate that she should cry a little more quietly.

After the service everybody made their way to the Mayer house for the wedding breakfast. Karl was persuaded to join Julius and Franz in their carriage for the journey home although he seemed reluctant to talk to his brothers. The ride was very uncomfortable for all three occupants. Franz and Julius were bursting to know the circumstances of Karl's late arrival and the whereabouts of his wife. Both felt they could not broach the subject and Karl was not volunteering any information as he gazed out of the carriage window, trying to avoid looking at his younger brothers. Because of Karl's reluctance to speak to them any small talk seemed banal in the strained atmosphere of the carriage, so the journey was spent in total silence. As Julius raised his eyebrows in consternation to Franz who shrugged his shoulders in resignation, Karl turned round to look at them and they received a mocking hint of a smile from him as he returned to watch the passing scenery. Julius and Franz colored at being caught in such a way but in that fleeting moment Julius knew what had so unnerved him about his brother in the church, it had been his eyes. When Julius had looked into his brother's eyes they were like looking at a dead man's eyes, there was no life in them, no emotion, only sadness. So unlike the cheerful boy Julius had known in his childhood. Karl was a very troubled and unhappy young man.

When they returned to the house, Mama and Irmy embraced Karl and Irmy introduced him to her new husband. Karl talked amiably to his brother-in-law but Julius could detect a reticence and reserve in his brother, as though he longed to be away from the house. Papa greeted Karl with a perfunctory shake of the hand and Julius thought he caught his father telling Karl that he would speak to him later, and he noted that nobody broached the subject of his missing wife.

After the introductions and greeting of guests everybody sat down to the wedding breakfast. Cook had excelled herself and the meal passed with the bonhomie and pleasure of such a happy day. Papa made a welcoming speech which received a very gracious reply from Richard and everybody toasted the bridal couple. From his position at the table Julius could observe Karl, who was seated between the priest, an old family friend, and Frau Beckova. Most of the meal he sat staring at his food and when he did join in a conversation his contribution was minimal, although Julius noticed that he drank several glasses of wine. Julius had been seated between two of Irmy's friends, which no doubt had been at the instigation of his sister. They were very pretty girls and Julius enjoyed the trivial conversation that passed between them as both girls flirted outrageously and openly vied for his attention during the meal.

After the meal everybody went into the garden to allow the servants to tidy the dining room and for the guests to enjoy the late afternoon sun of the warm spring day. After a while Julius realized that Karl was missing from the company and went to try and find his brother. Instinct made Julius head for the nursery and as he quietly entered their old playroom he observed his brother, leaning on their old rocking horse whilst looking out of the gable-window, watching the wedding guests in the garden below. The watery afternoon sun shone through the window illuminating the dust that danced in the air, spreading a hazy mist over his brother. The window was slightly open, and the sound of murmured conversations and the occasional bursts of tinkling laughter could be heard from the happy party in the garden. Julius stood for quite a few moments watching his brother until he made a noise as if he had just entered the room.

"Hello, what are you doing up here..." Julius did not finish his sentence as he was embarrassed to see his brother quickly stand up straight and wipe his eyes as though he had been crying.

"Karl what is the matter, can I help at all?"

Karl looked at his brother and for an awful moment Julius thought he was about to laugh at him, but appeared to change his mind as he said bitterly, "I forget how old you are Julius, it is so long since I have seen you. Look at you, strong, confident, good looking, your whole life in front of you, you do not know how lucky you are"

Karl started to play with an old wooden toy which he had picked up and then dramatically threw it against the wall, where it smashed into little pieces. Julius strode across the room and grabbed his brother by the arms and shook him vigorously. Although younger than Karl he was now taller than his brother and much stronger as he held him in a vice like grip and compelled him to look at him, "what the hell is the matter with you? This will not solve anything"

Karl regarded him with a cynical sneer on his face, "what do you know little brother? you know nothing of life"

Julius felt his anger rise as he retorted, "for your information, *big brother*, I have been in the army for four years now, I am not the little boy you left behind all those years ago and I could probably give you a good whipping, which at the moment I think you deserve. Now are you going to tell me what is going on or shall I go back downstairs and rejoin the party, where I can have a much better conversation than the one I am having here"

Karl's sarcastic confidence left him as he sagged in his brother's arms and stared down at the floor. "Right" said Julius as he let go of his grip on Karl, "do not say that I did not try to help" and he strode off towards the door. Julius stopped as he heard his brother shout, "Wait" and turned to hear him appealing for him to stay. Julius pulled up two chairs and told Karl to sit down, he was still angry at his brother's attitude but wanted to help him, he was so obviously unhappy.

Looking haggard and tired Karl told Julius all about his disastrous marriage. "I was watching everybody down there, so happy, so optimistic about the future, just as I was on my wedding day. I loved her so much Julius, she was so beautiful, did you see the photographs?" Julius nodded, "I wanted to give her everything, and anything she asked for I would get for her, regardless of the cost. I knew I was getting myself into debt, but I really did not care, as long as she was happy, as long as it made her love me"

"Did you not stop to think that that you were buying her love?"

"That is easy for you to say, you have never been in love, you will understand when it happens to you"

Julius stopped himself remarking that if that was love then he did not want it, but carried on listening to his brother's story.

"When I had to ask Papa for money it was so shameful but I knew it was the only way out of my troubles. Anna just laughed and said it was my right as the eldest son. When I suggested she ask her father for help she just taunted me by saying it was my responsibility now to look after her, not her fathers. I suppose you know father paid off all my debts? Well he wrote to all my creditors, paying them, but indicating that he would not be doing so the next time, it was so humiliating, no one would give me credit any more. Eventually Anna would take no more, she could not live without all the pleasurable things of life and told me if I could not get more money, she would look elsewhere for them. What could I do? I was desperate. I wrote to Papa, but he would not help me, I even sold some of my valuables but it was not enough, Anna told me she did not love me anymore"

Karl put his head in his hands and rocked himself from side to side in his misery. Julius leant forward and tried to comfort his brother in his grief but could not find the right words to say. What could he say, certainly not what he was thinking. To be brought to such humiliation by the love for a woman was degrading enough, but to be this pitiable for a woman who obviously did not care for Karl at all, except for his money, was humiliating in the extreme. When Karl appeared to have recovered some of his composure Julius felt he had to ask, "And where is Anna now?"

Karl got up from his seat and starting walking impatiently round the room as if the truth was too hard to put into words. He went back to the window and looked out at the party below as he said, in such a low voice that Julius had to strain to hear him, "that is the worst thing of all, she has left me and has become the mistress of a colonel in my regiment"

Julius stared open-mouthed at his brother. "You do not mean that this is common knowledge in your regiment, and it is accepted? What of her family, what do they say?"

Karl returned to his chair and sarcastically replied, "come Julius, you know how civilized we must be, officers of His Majesty's Imperial Army. Of course everybody knows, even her family, who at least are scandalized by her behavior, but for the rest of them they all say nothing, pretend not to know and no doubt have a good laugh about cuckolded Mayer behind my back"

Julius had been rather scathing of his brother's attitude towards his wife, but now his heart went out to Karl. He knew his brother was right, it was a scandal, but one that would be ignored and swept under the carpet, such was the way of the army. He wondered how Karl could endure the shame of his position, it was not a scenario he would wish for his worst enemy. "Does Papa know of this? Maybe he could use his influence in the situation"

Karl looked up, "no Julius, I think I have caused Papa enough pain and distress don't you? I am a grown man, and I must sort my own life. I have applied for a transfer, I have even thought of leaving the army but it is the only life I know, what else would I do?"

Julius had to agree with him, the only life Karl knew was the army, his life was very limited in that respect. "You have to tell Papa, you owe him that much. Better to hear it from you than from a malicious rumor. He is not so unreasonable

185

you know, you might be surprised at how forgiving he can be"

"After the anguish I have caused Mama and Papa, I very much doubt that, but I suppose you are right, I have to tell him. He has asked to see me in his study later"

"Would you like me to come with you, I really don't mind"

Karl eyed his younger brother with a quizzical look on his face, "you really have grown up little brother, most people would think you were the elder sibling in this room"

Julius grinned, "not if they knew some of the scrapes I have got into over the years they wouldn't" Julius rose from his chair and Karl looked alarmed.

"Where are you going, you are not leaving?"

Julius smiled, "no, I am going down to get us some black coffee, you are going to need to sober up a little before you meet Papa, then I am going to bring your coffee back up here and whilst you sober up I am going to bore you with some of those escapades, all right?"

As Julius left the room Karl looked across at his brother and said, "thank you, Julius, it was good to talk to someone"

"It was my pleasure," replied Julius as he left the room in search of their coffee.

Karl had his interview with his father on his own. He never divulged what was discussed between them but when he emerged from his father's study afterwards he looked as though a great weight had been lifted from his shoulders. Julius told Franz what he had learnt from Karl. Franz was appalled at his brother's situation and angry at his treatment.

The day after the wedding Irmy and Richard departed for their honeymoon, it pleased Julius to think that it would only be a few weeks and he would be reunited with his sister in Prague. When they had waved goodbye to the newlyweds Mama went with Karl to see Frau Beckova who was still at the hotel.

After they had left the house Colonel Mayer summoned his two younger sons into his office. This was obviously to be a serious interview as Papa was sitting sternly behind his desk and two chairs had been strategically placed in front of him.

"Sit down, will you" as the men took their seats Colonel Mayer continued, "I think you know why I have called you in here. I presume you both know of your brother's predicament? good, then I will not waste my breath reiterating his past follies. I think you are both old enough, and I hope wise enough, to be privy to some decisions I have made in light of his news. I am sure you are aware that this is unlikely to be confined to Karl's regiment in Linz, but I hope if you ever hear any malicious stories about your brother you will address it with the quiet dignity I expect from both of you, is that understood?" both men nodded, "this family will not be brought down to the level of idle gossips. Karl and I have agreed that Mama and Irmy will not be told the full story of his marriage" Franz went to open his mouth in protest as Colonel Mayer continued, "Believe me Franz I have thought long and hard about this. We will tell your mother that Karl's marriage is at an end, as simple as that. That alone will cause your mother great distress, let alone the other sordid events, it is for her sake that I ask you to keep your silence about this, believe me"

"But what if Mama should hear the truth from someone else?" asked Julius, he understood his father's wish to save his mother any undue grief but he felt uneasy at the deception he was being asked to carry out.

"In Prague I think that is very unlikely Julius, but if that should happen I will assess the situation as I think appropriate"

Julius observed his father, in this situation he was the embodiment of a Habsburg colonel in the Imperial Army. Authoritarian, proud, whose every word *would* be the law. Franz and Julius realized there was no point in arguing with their father. He had made his decision and nothing would deter him.

"I am also going to try and expedite Karl's transfer from Linz, the sooner he leaves there the better. Although he could obtain a divorce from Anna on the grounds of her adultery he informs me that for the moment he is going to leave the situation as it is. I do not think your brother will be thinking of another marriage for a very long time. One more thing gentlemen, your brother needs the support of his family at this time. I know he has been very stupid, and I believe he knows that, but we must not judge him too harshly, let us hope he has learnt something from the past few years, and that you have too. Karl and I will tell your mother about the separation this evening so I would appreciate it if the two of you would go out for dinner and leave us alone. Your mother will need your support in the next few days, I do not know how she will take this news, it is a shame that she has to face this after the joy of the wedding"

Surprisingly Frau Mayer took the news of the failure of her son's marriage very well. As she told Julius the next day, "I have known there has been something wrong for a very long time, call it a mother's instinct, but I knew. I have to say I never really liked Anna, I never said as much, I thought it disloyal. I am not as outspoken as your sister am I Julius? But I am not so old-fashioned as to not realize that Karl is going to be much happier without Anna, his happiness, the happiness of you all, is the most important thing to me"

Not for the first time did Julius marvel at the insight of his mother. She was always the loyal Habsburg wife and mother, but underneath her domestic veneer Julius often thought there was a self-determining woman who saw far more than she would ever disclose. It was at times like this that Julius sensed where Irmy got her independent spirit.

XVI

The last few days of his leave were very enjoyable for Julius. He had spent the time getting to know his brothers again, it had been a long time since they had all been together and they had no way of knowing when they would see each other again. Karl had positively blossomed in the days after the wedding, as if sharing his misery had alleviated his pain. Mama and Danusia fussed over him making sure he ate three hearty meals a day, while Franz and Julius took him out to the local beer kellers where he confessed he had not enjoyed himself so much in years. Even the strain between Papa and Karl lessened as the days progressed and Karl started to lose his haggard and haunted appearance.

Papa travelled back to Prague with Julius. He was anxious to find a new house for Mama as he knew that she would be very lonely once the excitement of the wedding had subsided.

Back at the barracks Julius resumed his duties whilst helping Colonel Mayer look for their new family home. He had said little about the wedding to Nikolas, not wanting to upset his friend, but this was offset by his news of Karl. Julius had sworn his friend to secrecy over the affair and he knew he could trust Nikolas. It was a relief to tell the story to someone outside the family, though Nikolas was as shocked as his father and brother had been.

"Who would believe a woman could control a man to that extent, do you think we will ever be that silly over a female, I hope not"

"Who knows, I would never have believed it of my brother either. Anyway I am determined not to marry until I am at least forty"

"Just as well" observed Nikolas, "who could imagine any woman wanting to marry you!"

Papa found the perfect house for Mama. It was not as large as their house in Kosice, but as Colonel Mayer pointed out, with all her children having left home Frau Mayer did not need such a large house. The house stood in a quiet street on the outskirts of Prague. It was a terraced town house with four floors located not too far from Frau Beckova's house and Irmy and Richard's new home. Frau Beckova had advised Colonel Mayer on the right location for

189

the house and had obviously enjoyed herself, escorting him around and introducing him to his new home. Papa was pleased with his choice and told Julius he quite envied him his posting in such a lovely city. While in Prague Papa and Julius dined with Colonel and Frau Manzova and the evening was a great success, the two Colonels enjoying each other's company immensely. "I told you" observed Nikolas, "those two are carved from the same block"

Julius would not see his sister or mother settled into their new homes as shortly after his return to Prague he was on his way to Styria for summer maneuvers. Nikolas remained behind, as he was to carry out guard duty for the city during the summer. Julius found the Styrian countryside very different to the landscape of Salzburg, but no less breathtaking. He loved the sheer beauty of the countryside set against the luxuriant pastures that nestled beneath the gentle slopes above them.

He was soon ensconced with the regiment in their camp and assigned a young, spotty adolescent called Frederik. Julius tried to be patient with the young cadet, he remembered the experience of his first summer camp, but at times he thought he would scream with frustration at the mistakes Frederik made. Lying on his camp bed watching the young boy cleaning his gun made him wonder if he had been so green and inexperienced. He supposed he must have been and once more thanked Captain Schneider for his restraint and wisdom.

During his months in Styria he was able to see Franz and Viktor and had an enjoyable few days in their company. Viktor was well and happy, and the responsibility of being an officer suited him.

"No regrets about not going into the family business?" asked Julius one night as they ate a meal in the barracks mess.

"None whatsoever" replied Viktor, "I now know I could never have sat behind a desk in an office for the rest of my life. This suits me, it has its drawbacks and shortcomings as you know, but overall I am very happy here"

"Do you think Josef is happy?" asked Julius of his friend.

Viktor hesitated a moment before he replied, "I really do not know. Do you think Josef will ever be really happy in life? I don't think he is fitting into regimental life as easily as we are but I have always had the impression that whatever he did in life, Josef would manage to find something

190

negative to say about it. Please do not get the wrong impression, I really like Josef, I think he is a wonderful man, but that is how I perceive Josef's nature, and I do not think he will ever change"

"Have you heard of this fellow who lives in Vienna that everybody is talking about, the one who analyses everybody's natures and says why we are like we are?"

"Do you mean Freud?" answered Viktor, innocently.

"That's the fellow, well if ever you leave the army maybe you could apply for a job with him"

Viktor regarded his friend as he replied, "Do you know, sometimes I really miss Vienna and the three of you, but one thing I really do not miss is your awful sense of humor Julius"

By the end of three months Julius felt he had been able to teach young Frederik a lot about the training and logistics of the army. He had also learned a lot himself. The divisions amongst the Imperial Army still remained and Julius found it difficult to unite the different cultures amongst his men. It had seemed so easy as a cadet to believe that you could change the attitudes of men under your command, but the reality was that the animosity was so deep rooted, and so ancient, that it was impossible for these men to see how detrimental their quarrels were within a fighting army.

It was very different to be in charge of men on maneuvers. You had to make decisions, often very quickly and without a lot of thought, your decisions were made mainly from instinct and it was difficult to know whether a certain movement of men and artillery was correct or justified. A wrong assessment of a situation could mean the loss of lives in a real confrontation. Whilst he hoped he did not harbor the prejudices and lethargy of many officers he also realized that it was easy to criticize senior officers, as he had done when he was a cadet. Now he saw that they had often made decisions that in their minds they thought were the right ones at the time. It was difficult to tread the fine line between leading your men to a glorious triumph or a dishonorable defeat.

Julius returned to Prague in September to find Mama living in Prague and Richard and Irmy settled into their new house. He also found out from Nikolas that Irmy had started her nursing training.

191

"Your mother and my mother have become quite friendly and your mother appeared at our house in a fine dudgeon as Irmy had just informed her of her plans"

"Your poor mother, how did she react?"

"She sympathized with your mother, they see it as unthinkable that Irmy should want to be a nurse"

"I am really sorry that my mother intruded on your family Nikolas, what was she thinking of?"

"Do not worry yourself, my mother loves the intrigue. I think your mother just needed someone to talk to. I am afraid that Irmy finds the whole situation quite amusing"

Julius looked at his friend, "you have seen Irmy?"

"Do not worry, Julius, everything is well. Irmy held a dinner party when she moved into her new house and as her favorite brother was absent from the city she invited his best friend instead, along with my parents"

"How awful for you, why did you not refuse the invitation?"

"I decided as she was living in Prague now I would not be able to avoid seeing her and to be quite honest I think our first meeting was probably better without an over anxious friend looking over my shoulder the whole time. I cannot pretend it was an easy evening for me, but I think I behaved myself. I have seen Irmy since at my parent's house, so do not distress yourself. Richard is a very lucky man"

Julius could not decide whether this was said with sarcasm or not but he knew it must have been a very difficult evening for Nikolas, seeing Irmy so rapt in her new marriage. He could not blame Irmy for inviting Nikolas, she had no idea of his friend's affection for her, but even so he wished the evening had been avoided.

Bracing himself he presented himself at his parent's home. As he had predicted Mama talked incessantly of the folly of Irmy taking up nursing training until Julius felt beholden to point out that there was nothing Mama or Papa could do about the situation as Irmy was a married woman and now only answerable to Richard, who condoned his wife training to be a nurse. This subdued Frau Mayer somewhat, though she did add that it would not be long before Richard would be wanting a family, then what would happen to Irmy's nursing training? After that whenever she spoke about her daughter's nursing ambitions it was with a martyred look on her face and with an air of pained resignation.

In his army duties Julius still encountered a certain amount of hostility from Colonel Reichart, and although he was assured by other members of his company that this was not a situation especially reserved for Julius, he felt that the Colonel held a personal animosity towards him and wondered why. The situation was not improved when Julius, with Phantom, was picked to be one of the lead riders in a ceremonial parade in Wenceslas Square. The cavalcade was to take place at the beginning of December and the large military procession was to pass through the famous square in the middle of the city. Wenceslas Square was not in fact a square but a very long, broad, cobbled street, originally a horse market, but now lined with shops and hotels. At the top end of the square stood the magnificent National Museum that had been completed just over ten years ago. It was a great honor to be selected to ride in the procession, but instead of being pleased for his chosen men Colonel Reichart dismissed their achievements as an unnecessary waste of time.

Phantom was groomed until his coat shone and his mane and tail were brushed to perfection. The riders, including Julius, were in their full dress uniform, and as they all rode up the square on that cold December morning their hearts filled with the pride of the whole Imperial Army. There were crowds each side of the street who had gathered to see the spectacle, and Julius managed to spy Mama, Irmy and Danusia waving amongst the gathered populace.

Julius especially enjoyed Christmas that year. Although he was not allowed Christmas leave, it was still possible to spend the day with his family. It was wonderful not to have to travel on a long train journey to get to his home. None of the other male members of the family had managed to get leave for the festivities but he accompanied Mama, Richard, Irmy, Frau Beckova and Danusia to Midnight Mass on Christmas Eve. Although they did not worship there Mama insisted, as it was her first Christmas in Prague, that they celebrate Midnight Mass in St. Vitus Cathedral, within the castle walls. Julius knew the castle and the cathedral well as he had spent many a day and night there on guard duty. Whenever he entered the cathedral he always looked up at the magnificent vaulted ceiling, so perfect in its conception, and would marvel at the intricacies of such a structure, built more than five hundred years before.

Julius loved this building, it was the resting place of the old Kings of Bohemia, including that of Wenceslas. Julius would breathe in the history and atmosphere of the cathedral as soon as he walked through its hallowed doors, and on this very religious night that feeling was enhanced by the beautiful voices of the choirboys as they sang the Christmas service and the devout congregation celebrated the birth of Jesus.

Some weeks after Christmas Julius visited Irmy and as always Irmy was delighted to see her brother. Julius was pleased that since their marriage he had always been made very welcome whenever he had visited Irmy and Richard. He had worried that he might feel like an intruder on their marital bliss but they had always made him welcome as an honored guest. Their house was both elegant and welcoming, Irmy had had the rooms decorated in pastel shades of yellow and cream which gave the appearance of warmth and comfort, where sofas were covered in copious cushions and throws and the rooms were always filled with sweet smelling flowers. Julius always felt at ease in the sunny, spacious rooms.

Although Irmy was now training at the hospital Richard often worked long hours and Julius knew his sister sometimes felt the loneliness of her situation. She had left all her close friends behind in Kosice, and although she had started to make acquaintances in Prague, most of them were Richard's friends and a lot older than herself. That she loved nursing there was no doubt, whenever Julius visited her she would regale him with stories of her training. She enjoyed her work and Julius was pleased for her.

Irmy had received a letter from Karl and she showed it to her brother. Irmy was still oblivious to the full extent of Karl's story, and because of his promise to his father Julius decided there was no need to apprise his sister of the whole situation. Irmy had received the news of the end of her brother's marriage with the calm assertion that she was not at all surprised, she had never liked Anna since meeting her and to her mind Karl was well rid of his wife. Colonel Mayer had managed to hasten Karl's transfer and he had been posted to Vienna. Julius was not sure whether this was coincidence or Papa trying to keep a paternal eye on his wayward son, but either way Karl appeared to be loving Vienna. He had been assigned a desk job at Army Headquarters, and although Julius himself would have hated

194

the thought of such a confining job, Karl wrote that he enjoyed the change in duties and liked the political arena he found himself in. Julius was glad that Karl was at last starting to sound optimistic about his future.

Julius had wanted to see Irmy to specifically discuss their mother. He had become worried about Frau Mayer, lately she had appeared to be depressed and rather lethargic, but whenever he asked her if everything was all right she would always reply that she was well and he must not fuss over her. When Julius had related his concerns to Irmy she seemed uncomfortable as she said, "Do not worry about Mama, Julius. You must remember she has been through a lot in the past year, my wedding, the move from Kosice and the news of Karl's marriage, I just think it has all been too much for her, and women Mama's age, well, they do get a little depressed for no reason, it is just a stage she is going through. I also believe she is lonely. I am at the hospital and have my husband here, but I have sometimes felt lonely, think how Mama must be feeling. She has left all her friends behind in Kosice, and although Danusia and some of the servants have come here with her, I believe she still feels a little isolated at times. I do try and see her as often as I can, but the hospital and Richard demand a lot of my time. It is good to see she has become friends with Richard's mother and Frau Manzova, do you not think the Manz family are such nice people?"

Julius looked up to see if this was said with any guile, but knew it had been said in all innocence.

"I especially like Georg," continued Irmy, "he is such a loveable little fellow"

Julius snorted as he said, "I do not think Colonel and Frau Manzova would agree with you. That young devil causes them so much trouble, but you are right, you cannot help but like Georg"

"Do not tell his mother, but he arrived on my doorstep the other day asking if he could take refuge in my house" Irmy laughed "it seems he had got himself into another spot of trouble and did not want to have to go home to face his father"

"The impudent pup. What did you do?"

"It was very difficult to keep from laughing, he had such a pathetic look on his face, but I persuaded him that his best course of action was to go home and face his father. To stay here would only postpone his inevitable punishment. Do you know why I have such a soft spot for that little rogue, Julius? He reminds me so much of you at that age"

"I refute that emphatically," argued Julius, "I was never in as much trouble as he gets himself into"

"Yes you were, you were just never caught as often," laughed Irmy

Julius was approaching his twenty first birthday and he started to think about where his life was heading. He knew he did not want to be married for a long time yet, but he enjoyed the company of females and began to wonder if he would ever meet a woman with whom he could fall in love with.

Irmy would often invite him and Nikolas along to social events in the desperate hope of finding an escort for her brother. These soirees were very enjoyable and sometimes Julius had arranged to meet a certain girl again, but they had never left him with a strong desire to prolong a relationship. At one of her dinner parties Irmy had invited a new friend she had met since moving to Prague. Her name was Suse and Irmy had sat her next to Nikolas for the evening. The two had obviously been attracted to one another and since that evening had been on several excursions together. Julius was glad for his friend and hoped that Suse would at last enable Nikolas to forget about Irmy, but he was also a little jealous. He wished he could find a companion with whom he could share outings to the theatre or the moving pictures, someone he could walk with in the parks or take out to dinner, but despite all Irmy's efforts there was nobody who stirred any emotion in him and Julius hoped he was too much a gentleman to take out a young lady just to satisfy his own ego.

In June of that year Julius and Nikolas went to Vienna for an artillery and munitions course. He was glad to be back in Vienna again, even if it was in the sweltering heat of the summer. As usual the city was quiet as most of its inhabitants had left for cooler climes, but Josef was there and he arrived at their rooms the evening of their arrival. Josef had not changed, if anything Julius thought he had become more arrogant since they had last seen him. Josef said he had bad news for them, "I have been ordered to join summer maneuvers for a month, but I will be back before you finish here. Why do you not try and have a few days leave at the end of the course. You could stay with my mother and I, and we could look up some of our old haunts, what do you say?"

Julius was rather taken aback by this suggestion, he was in two minds whether he wanted to see Josef's mother again, but Josef had asked with such an appeal in his voice that they felt they could not refuse and Nikolas appeared to be quite taken by the idea. So it was agreed that at the end of their course they would stay a few days with Josef. After Josef had departed Nikolas observed, "he was very eager, almost too eager, do you think there is something ulterior to his invitation?"

"I really do not know," replied Julius, "but for now I do not want to worry about it. I think we should concentrate on the course, it is going to be very hard"

The course was very intensive and very difficult, but Julius and Nikolas thoroughly enjoyed it. Since joining the Horse Artillery Julius had felt himself a novice when it came to his knowledge of artillery, guns and ammunition. There were new innovations being invented the whole time, the most exciting of these was the improvement of breech-loading mechanisms. Before these improvements a gun would jump out of position during firing and after each round of ammunition had been spent the gun would have to be re-sighted. The new advances resulted in the gun remaining in position throughout its firing and therefore did not have to be re-adjusted after each round.

The course gave Julius an extensive knowledge of all weapons of warfare. Not only did it cover rifles, handguns, and automatic pistols, their range and firing power, but also that of the big guns, when best to use them, how to utilize their capacity and range. They discussed the transportation of heavy guns and their ammunition in warfare and which gun would suit which terrain. They were taught how to use a field clinometer, a device for laying guns. The range of a big gun was related to their inclination and elevation, once a soldier knew his range, usually from a map reading, a gun could be elevated to give the correct range, allowing for meteorological conditions, terrain variations and ammunition, amongst other things. The field clinometer was used to check the correct gun setting, and adjust it if necessary, for all these conditions.

Although he knew that with every month new inventions, new guns and ammunition were being tested by the military, Julius felt that by the end of the course he had an extensive knowledge of the movement and utilization of artillery for the army. Both Julius and Nikolas did well on the course and with their high marks were promised an annual revision so that they could keep abreast of all new artillery being used by the army.

At the end of such a taxing month Julius and Nikolas were looking forward to their stay with Josef. After leaving their temporary barracks they picked up a tram to the district where Josef's mother lived. As soon as they alighted from the tram they knew they were in a very expensive area of the city. All the houses were enormous, like small castles, and they had difficulty locating Josef's house as they found it to be hidden behind a high wall that could be only negotiated by passing through a large wrought iron gate.

As they walked up the long drive Nikolas let out a long, low whistle as the house came into view. They knew that Josef had a wealthy family but the extent of that wealth had never occurred to them until that moment. Julius had never seen such a fine looking house. Its front aspect was supported by several white stone columns which framed an enormous double fronted door, above which was a large stone carved coat of arms in relief.

As they approached the front door one half of it swung open as though their arrival had been anticipated. Not quite knowing what to do Nikolas stepped forward onto the front porch as a small, portly man stepped forward. He was dressed in full livery of green velvet frock coat and breeches, looking so much like a caricature that Julius and Nikolas found it hard to keep from laughing. He stood in front of them, his back ram rod straight, and though far smaller than the two men in front of him managed to look down his nose as he said in a very deep voice, "Lieutenant Mayer, Lieutenant Manz, you are expected, please follow me" and with that he turned on his heel and walked into the house.

The hallway they found themselves in perfectly complimented the outside of the building. The floor was laid with black and white squared marble tiles and from the hall rose a beautifully carved staircase which turned in a majestic sweep up to the next floor. The hall was decorated with enormous pictures and chandeliers that blended perfectly into their surroundings, anything small would have looked insignificant in this setting.

As Julius and Nikolas stood in the middle of the hall taking in the opulence of their surroundings two young boys, dressed in the same green livery, appeared as if from nowhere and took their bags from them accompanied by a solemn bow. On hearing a discreet cough Julius and Nikolas turned to see the butler motioning them to follow him. Trying desperately to refrain themselves from copying the little man's pompous walk they proceeded through several corridors and rooms before the butler stopped, opened a door, and announced them.

They were relieved to see Josef, lying on a large comfortable sofa listening to Bach's Brandenburg Concerto, whose melodious notes were emanating from a phonograph machine. On seeing them enter he jumped up to greet his friends.

"At last, I thought you two were never getting here, where have you been? well never mind, you are here now. Can I offer you some refreshment? I am afraid all I can suggest is a cordial or tea. Mama does not allow alcohol in her house, only with our meals, influence of my father you see"

Both Julius and Nikolas requested some tea and after Josef had given his order, rather offhandedly, the butler left the room.

Julius looked around the elegant salon. He worked out that he could probably place Mama's sitting room in this room about six times and still have space to spare. It was beautifully and richly furnished with large tapestries hanging on the walls and was dominated by an enormous fireplace with a black marble mantelpiece surmounted by a mirror, whose surround was carved in golden relief. On top of the mantelpiece stood a wonderful gold clock. It was decorated with golden cherubs who danced around the face of the clock and supported it underneath. One wall of the room was completely made up of large windows, which stood from floor to ceiling and were decorated with elaborate swathes and drapes of gold velvet. Beyond the windows could be seen an enormous and immaculately kept garden that stretched as far as the eye could see. Julius felt that he was in a palace, visiting royalty.

After they were seated Nikolas and Julius told Josef about their course. He seemed very interested and after some discussion said, "you know they are saying that the horse, and therefore the cavalry, will be outmoded in the

199

future with the popularity of the automobile. It is all the talk here in Vienna"

"I hope not," said Julius, "I realize that automation is playing an increasing part in our lives, but I would like to think there will always be a place for the horse in the modern army. For example, there are places that horses can take vital supplies or pull heavy guns where no automotive vehicle could go"

"I hope so," said Josef, "but they are also saying that with the advent of superior new guns and ammunition a soldier on horseback would be too easy a target and if that happens, where will the cavalry be then, or the horse artillery for that matter?"

"I cannot believe an army can exist without horses, but you have to admit that automotives are beginning to get as fast, if not faster, than horses and they can carry far more supplies than a mere horse" said Nikolas, "they have also proved that they can pull heavy guns, a task which only a large team of horses can do"

Julius looked at Josef, "is there really a worry for the cavalry Josef?"

"I have my fears I must admit. Of course the old guard in Vienna believe it will never happen, you know how people are about new inventions and progress. They believe things will never change, but for myself I think the automobile is here to stay and it will change everybody's lives in one way or another"

The conversation left the trio very subdued. Whilst Julius knew in his heart that what Josef was saying could well be true, he hoped the picture was not as black as he had painted it.

They were relieved when the door opened and the butler re-entered the room followed by three maids in green dresses and starched white aprons carrying silver tea services on silver trays. Nikolas and Julius were overjoyed to see one of the trays full of Viennese pastries, they had both been very hungry but manners had forbidden them to ask their host for something to eat.

After the butler had poured their tea he and the maids left the room. The pastries were delicious and soon the tray was empty as the three men sat back and relaxed while they drank their tea.

"My mother apologizes for not being here, but she had to go out this afternoon, you will see her at dinner tonight, I am afraid we will have to stay here to eat. I do not want to upset her"

"That is fine with me," said Nikolas, "to be honest with you I am so tired from the rigors of the last few weeks that a quiet dinner tonight and a long sleep seems a very attractive proposition"

Josef poured another cup of tea as he said, "I wrote to Viktor, inviting him to join us, but unfortunately he will still be on maneuvers until next month, which is a shame. It would have been good for us all to be together again"

"As long as the result was not as disastrous as our last meeting" added Julius

The three men sat silently in the luxurious serenity of their surroundings, the warmth of the sun enveloping the room as they lounged, replete from their tea and pastries, happy in their silence, all thinking of their lucky escape over a year ago now, and thoroughly content with their world.

Julius was shown to a magnificent bedroom resplendent with an enormous four-poster bed, hung with brocade canopies. He was sure at least four people could have comfortably slept within its starched linen sheets. Not for the first time did he wonder at the change in lifestyle that Josef had had to endure when entering the army. He looked out of his window and found his room was at the front of the house, facing the long drive.

As he was gazing out at the immaculate lawns interspersed with tall, regal, evergreen trees he saw a carriage, drawn by four gray horses coming up the drive. He knew instinctively that it was the Countess von Kutz returning home. He craned his neck to catch a glimpse of her as she arrived at the front door. Julius' view was impeded by one of the columns, but he managed to see one of the young pages rush out to open the carriage door and to see the Countess alight from her coach, though his only sight was of her swirling skirts and large hat as she walked into the house. Julius stepped back from the window, unnerved by the emotions that the sight of Josef's mother had stirred in him. He was not looking forward to dinner that night and his stomach felt like it was somersaulting as he descended the staircase to join his friends for dinner.

Julius had difficulty finding the right room. On his journey he had to ask at least two servants for the right directions as he had found himself lost. The servants of the household were very courteous and polite, but Julius was unnerved by their reserve and subservience. Whilst he realized that this was the expected behavior of servants in such a household, he decided he preferred the more intimate relationship that his family enjoyed with their servants.

Eventually he arrived at the right room and walked into a large sitting room, not as large as the room where they had enjoyed tea that afternoon, but still fairly extensive, and found Nikolas and Josef sitting deep in conversation with the countess. The countess was seated in a large wing backed chair and Julius felt his throat muscles constrict as he gazed at her elegant beauty. As she looked up at her visitor he was once again entranced by the beautiful blue eyes that had so enthralled him at the ball. The countess held out her hand to him as she said, "Julius, how lovely to see you again after all this time, it is wonderful to have you and Nikolas in my house. I hope you will have a very happy stay with us"

Julius muttered the expected polite answers, and then seated himself next to Nikolas on the sofa. The countess carried on with her conversation with Nikolas and Josef, who were animatedly talking about their activities for the next few days. Julius contributed little to the conversation, preferring to sit back and observe the countess, afraid to speak in case he made a fool of himself in front of his friend's mother. Josef kept trying to bring him into the conversation, obviously worried by his friend's silence, eventually asking Julius if he was unwell. Surprised out of his daydreaming Julius replied, "no not at all, I believe the hard work of the last few weeks are beginning to have its effect on me, I am just a little tired" Although everybody accepted this lame explanation, Julius kept finding Josef's quizzical gaze on him for the rest of the evening.

Julius was glad when the door opened and the butler announced more dinner guests. Earlier Josef had explained that they were to be joined by Count and Countess Donner who were old friends of his late grandfather. After being announced an old man, sporting the largest white handlebar moustache that Julius had ever seen, strode into the room. Behind him came a little mouse of a woman who tiptoed in behind her husband. Her character reflected her looks, for after being introduced by Josef's mother, she was not heard to utter another word all evening, leaving the talking to her husband, who more than made up for her silence.

Josef had said that their guest was quite a character, but neither Julius or Nikolas were quite prepared for the verbosity of the man as he commandeered the conversation for most of the evening, seeming to have an opinion on any subject that was raised, all of them controversial and highly disputable. The three friends were often to be seen looking from under their eyebrows at each other, trying not to burst into laughter, as the count propounded another outspoken and preposterous view. Several times Josef's mother was heard to say, "Ernst please, temper your arguments, you will have us all arrested" but even she was seen to be hiding a smile behind her napkin.

For all his pomposity Julius couldn't help but like the old rogue, even when his outbursts bordered on the treasonous, "I have to say young gentlemen, I am a very patriotic man, I love my Emperor, virtually the same age, you know, sort of grown up together. He has had a sad life, would not have wanted to be Emperor myself for any amount of money. Look at that son of his, he was raving mad, though no-one will admit it"

Julius ruefully thought that it would take one to know one, but diplomatically held his tongue, "if you ask me a good thing he took his own life, what sort of Emperor would he have made? would have been the end of the Empire I believe. You know at the time they said it was a shooting accident at Mayerling, but we all knew, we all knew" He stopped his discourse for a moment, staring in front of him, as if remembering all those years ago, then he shook himself, appearing to wake up and stared round at the table, for a moment unaware of where he was, "now where was I, oh yes" at this point Julius could feel Josef, who was seated next to him, shaking, trying to control a fit of giggles. He looked across the table at Nikolas who was staring intently at his plate, not daring to look up in case he joined Josef in his laughter. Only the countess was controlling her emotions, although there was merriment in her eyes, she was watching her dinner guest intently, trying to look as though she was absorbed in his conversation. "I have to say I am not sure whether we might have been better off with a madman than His Holiness Franz Ferdinand"

"Ernst!" cried Josef's mother, shocked at the religious title Count Donner, in his sarcasm, had given the heir to the throne.

"I am sorry Elisabeth, but that man will be Emperor to these young men one day, and God help them is what I say. He is a self-opinionated brigand with his modern ideas; no one likes him you know. We are too much under the influence of the Huns if you ask me. When he is Emperor he will give the Empire to the Kaiser, just you wait and see"

Although Julius reasoned they were the ramblings of an old man, he knew there was some truth in what the count was saying. Franz Ferdinand was unpopular in some quarters; Papa had often spoken of his misgivings about the man. He also knew that many people in the Empire shared the count's mistrust of the German influence in their country. That the Habsburg monarchy was very reliant on the German Kaiser, Wilhelm II, was seen by the populace with increasing alarm, not least in the army where it was an everyday topic of conversation. However Julius disagreed with Count Donner's assessment that Franz Ferdinand would be in collusion with the Germans. Franz Ferdinand's dislike of the member countries within the Empire were well known, but it was also known that he was wary of the Germans as well. It unnerved Julius to think of more division within the Empire. Even now countries such as Hungary and Bohemia and Moravia were petitioning for more autonomy for themselves, influenced by the leadership of such men as Karolyi in Hungary and Masaryk in his own country. If Franz Josef, and ultimately, Franz Ferdinand could not sustain a united Empire then things would be looking very bleak indeed.

After the Count had drunk what was probably the entire brandy supply of the household he said his drunken goodbyes and stumbled out to his carriage followed by his loyal wife, still tiptoeing behind him, smiling sweetly at Josef and his friends.

When they had departed Josef turned to his mother and laughingly said, "I do not know why you put up with that old scoundrel mother, I swear he gets worse every time we see him. The next time we hear of him, it will be locked up in jail on a charge of treason, and it will serve him right"

"Now Josef" replied his mother, "do not be so unkind. Ernst was your grandfather's best friend, and has always been very charitable to us and your brothers, do not forget that. Ernst Donner is one of the kindest men you will ever meet, if not a little eccentric"

"A little?" questioned Josef, his eyes raised to the ceiling, "well he is good entertainment, would you not agree?"

This question was aimed at Julius and Nikolas who were embarrassed by Josef asking them to comment about a friend of his mother's. Nikolas felt he should rescue the situation by replying politely, "well I found him very good company, his views are interesting, to say the least"

Josef laughed as he said, "well said, Nikolas, have you ever thought of joining the diplomatic service?"

Nikolas blushed as the countess added, "Josef, do not be so unkind, you are embarrassing your friend. Thank you for your kind words, Nikolas. I hope this evening was not too boring for you. I myself am always fully entertained by Count Donner, now I will retire and leave you to discuss what you really thought of our dinner guests. Goodnight, gentlemen"

After the countess had left the room Nikolas turned to Josef, "you are a lucky fellow, Josef, your mother is charming" Josef was pleased with his praise, and after another glass of brandy the three men also decided to retire. As Josef's bedroom was in a different direction to his guest's rooms Julius and Nikolas found themselves walking down the corridor to their rooms on their own.

"You did not tell me what a beauty Josef's mother is Julius, she is absolutely stunning"

"Is she?" replied Julius, trying to sound innocent, "yes I suppose she is. I probably did not think about it as she is Josef's mother"

"Personally I do not think that fact has anything to do with it. If I were a few years older, or she was a few years younger, I think I could quite easily find myself falling a little in love with the Countess von Kutz"

Julius stopped walking and faced Nikolas and said rather too vehemently, "that is a terrible thing to say Nikolas, that is Josef's mother you are talking about"

Nikolas seemed taken aback by his friend's rather violent reaction to his observation as he replied, "all right, all right, point taken. I was only talking hypothetically, not seriously you know. But I would still like to bet that there are more than a few men in Vienna that have fallen in love with Josef's mother"

Julius did not reply, but carried on walking towards his room. Nikolas walked behind him, and if Julius had turned round he would have seen a questioning look on his friend's face as Nikolas analyzed the conversation that had just taken place.

Julius, Josef and Nikolas left the house early the next morning and so did not see the countess at breakfast. They had decided to make an early start and visit all the old places that had so filled their lives for the three years that they had lived in Vienna. Josef told them their first stop would be a surprise and Julius and Nikolas were swept back to their cadet days as Josef took command and guided them through the streets of the city, just waking up from its early morning drowsiness.

This was the best time of day to be abroad at that time of year, before the heat started baking the pavements and the air grew still and lifeless. In the early morning the air was fresh and cool as the sun rose in the sky and the streets were busy with tradesmen, anxious to transport their wares before the heat of the day forced most people indoors.

It was soon obvious where Josef was leading his two friends as they walked the streets towards their old barracks. They were hardly questioned at the sentry post as they passed under the large arch that led into the main courtyard where they had started their army lives, so long ago. It was as if the years had melted away as they watched the all too familiar scene of horses being made ready for their riders, and the sound of a sergeant shouting his orders at young cadets as they desperately tried to keep up with an intricate marching drill. The three men stood savoring the sights and smells of their younger years, nostalgia overwhelming them for a while as their memories took hold of them.

They were nudged out of their reverie by Josef telling them they had an appointment to keep and they dutifully followed him as he walked towards their old barracks. As they walked through the doors of the West barracks they were overjoyed to see a familiar face, with the same wide, beaming smile and twinkling little eyes. Smid had not changed a bit as he shook hands with his former charges. There would be no informal welcoming hug in front of the cadets and officers walking through the foyer, but they all knew of the affection they felt for one another at that moment.

"Smid it is so wonderful to see you" said Julius pumping the little man's hand, "you look so well"

"Well that is because now I do not have to look after you young scallywags" he cheekily replied.

Josef informed them that he had arranged for Smid to have the morning off so they all retired to a local coffee house and spent a pleasant morning reminiscing over old times and catching up on all their current news. Smid drank so much coffee and ate so many pastries that Nikolas remarked if Viktor had been there as well the coffee house would have run out of supplies. It was sad when Smid had to return to the barracks, but with promises to keep in touch the little man waddled off down the street, back to his work. As they had no wish for any luncheon, they had all eaten so much at the coffee house, they spent the rest of the day walking round Vienna, seeing the sights and generally enjoying the warm summer's day.

That night Julius had arranged to meet Karl. He felt that he should see his brother alone in case he wanted to discuss things of a personal nature, so Josef and Nikolas were going into the city on their own that evening. Although Julius was not sure if either of them were a good influence on each other they parted in the city with Julius reminding them to not get too drunk as they did not have himself or Viktor to see them home that night.

Colonel Mayer was away from the city so Julius and Karl had decided to go out to a restaurant for a meal. Julius was amazed at the transformation in his brother. His face had filled out, he looked a lot happier and had lost the vacant look from his eyes that had so disturbed Julius at Irmy's wedding.

"Viennese life obviously suits you," said Julius to his brother after they had been seated at their table.

"Life away from Linz suits me," grinned Karl, "but yes I am enjoying myself here. I like the work, I have made some new friends and I love the city, I always have, ever since I was a cadet here"

"Do you not find the politics of army life here in Vienna rather stifling?" asked Julius and then proceeded to tell him of the meanderings of Count Donner. After he had repeated what the old man had said Julius was surprised to hear his brother reply, "Well although his facts are a bit warped, in essence his assessment of the situation is probably not far wrong. No one will admit to the turmoil within our government, or the dissent. The Habsburg Empire is run by old men, who will not listen to any reasoning or new ideas.

The Emperor is in his eighties, it is not known how much longer he may live, but where Franz Ferdinand is involved, many are saying better the devil we know, than the devil we do not. Many are suspicious of him but who knows, he may be the breath of fresh air we have been waiting for"

Julius was disturbed by his brothers assessment of the situation, especially when Karl added, "our main concern within the army is how far behind we are becoming compared to other armies"

"What do you mean?" asked Julius.

"Everyone has the idea that we are this bright, confident nation, a powerful force in world politics, sustaining a modern, well armed fighting force but I feel the reality is very different. The trouble is everybody believes in this fantasy but the truth is we are far behind other countries in our armament expenditure and manpower. Unfortunately when the army points this out to the government, they only want to believe in the myth of the great Imperial Army and do not see the need for further modernization and the outcome is that in the future we will be lagging behind compared to the armies say of Germany, France, Russia and Britain"

Julius was astounded by his brother's outburst but had to believe him. Karl now worked in the heart of the Army headquarters and there would be no reason for him to lie to his brother. Besides Julius could see by the fervor in his eyes that Karl utterly believed in everything he said.

"And what would happen in a time of conflict?" asked Julius wide eyed.

"For now, we would be a force to contend with, but if things progress as they are doing, in the future, God help us"

Karl could see he was dismaying his brother, so diplomatically changed the subject by asking after Irmy and Mama and their move to Prague. Politics were not mentioned again that evening, but Karl's words played on Julius' mind for a long time.

When Julius returned to Josef's house that evening he was informed by the butler that Josef and Nikolas had not returned home but that the countess was in her sitting room and would be pleased if Julius would join her in her salon. Although his thoughts were still in turmoil from the revelations of the evening manners forbade Julius refusing his hostess's request, though he was uncertain of his feelings at being alone with the countess.

As soon as he entered the room he knew he should have gone straight to bed. The countess was sitting, reading a book, but as he entered the room she laid the book down beside her and looked up to greet her guest. Julius had never seen her look lovelier, the subdued lighting of the salon added to the shimmering beauty before him. The countess was dressed in pale blue and the slimmer line of the new fashions showed off her figure to perfection. The blue of her dress enhanced the color of her eyes, making them look like deep pools of shining water. Julius suppressed a gasp as he was enraptured by the vision before him and desperately tried to maintain his composure in front of the countess. He was afraid to utter a word in case his voice did not come to him and was saved by the countess smiling at him and asking him to take a seat.

After he had chosen a seat, as far away from the countess as was diplomatically possible, she rose and asked him if he would like to join her in a cup of coffee to which he could only nod foolishly, feeling like a schoolboy back in the classroom. All he could hear going through his head was 'Julius control yourself, you are looking like an idiot, control yourself" Julius had never known a woman to have this much effect on him, and that the woman was Josef's mother made the situation even more mortifying for him. He realized that the countess was standing over him, handing him his coffee. He looked up to see the countess had a very concerned look on her face and she was talking to him. "Julius, are you unwell?" she asked, "you look very pale, did you not enjoy your dinner with your brother? please, may I get you a cognac? It may help you"

Julius quickly refused her offer, he knew he was acting like an adolescent boy, but the closeness of her, the smell of her perfume, of fresh spring flowers, the memory of which floated back from the ball, made it very difficult for him and all he wanted to do at that moment was to bolt for the door. The countess resumed her seat and after he had drunk some coffee and wishing he had accepted the cognac, Julius made a supreme effort to talk sensibly to Josef's mother.

"I am very well thank you," said Julius, in a voice that sounded very strange to his ears, "I think I am just a little tired from the past few weeks. It was a very intensive course and I feel the long hours we worked are catching up with me"

Julius took a deep breath, the room seemed to be spinning around him as he desperately tried to subdue the feelings that were welling up throughout his body.

The countess regarded him for a long moment before she said, "Well, as long as that is all, but if you feel unwell, do not hesitate to tell me so I may call my physician"

After another embarrassing silence whilst Julius tried desperately to think of something intelligent to say the countess asked, "I am pleased that I can talk to you on your own, Julius. I wonder if you could tell me, do you think there is something worrying Josef? He seems very distracted lately. I would not ask you to divulge any personal confidences you may have with my son, but I would like to know if he is unhappy"

Julius was glad to be distracted with the subject of Josef. He was surprised that the countess should think Josef unhappy and quickly told her that as far as he was aware, Josef had no great worries that he knew about. He wondered whether to tell her of Viktor's assessment of her son's character, but decided against it, he was not sure whether the countess would condone any adverse criticism of her beloved son. Julius decided to add, "but I do think, and I do not say this to vaunt my own popularity, or that of my friends, that Josef has not been as happy since finishing his cadetship. You yourself told me that he does not find it easy to make new friends. What we experienced in those three years together was something very special, something that we will never experience the like of again. I know I still miss those days, even though I still share my life with Nikolas and am once again surrounded by my family, it is often a regret that those times are gone.

My judgment would be that with all the changes in his life, Josef is still not settled or as happy as he was, and that he finds that a difficult thing to cope with. Did he tell you of his experience in the snow storm?" the countess nodded gravely, "that was something that is very hard to describe, or share with somebody who has not experienced such a close look at death. I think he may still be coming to terms with that as well" Julius stopped, in his confusion he was sounding like a babbling fool.

There was another uncomfortable silence as Julius was aware of the countess staring straight at him, her eyes never leaving his face. He felt himself redden under her relentless gaze and then wanted to run away in his embarrassment as she said "I would say that you are a wise and caring young man, Julius, and my son is very fortunate to be able to call you his friend, and I thank you for that"

Julius swallowed deeply, her praise and her attention was too much for him and he knew he had to leave the room before betraying his emotions to this beautiful woman. He rose, and feigning tiredness, took his leave of her and with a curt bow he left the room.

As soon as Julius reached his room he leant against his door trying to catch his breath. The effect the countess had had on him had been overwhelming. At that moment, if he had had the nerve, he would have run back down the stairs and fallen at her feet to confess his undying love for her.

He paced around his room for quite a while, clenching his fists, tormenting himself with thoughts of the beautiful woman whom he had been so close to, but who was so unattainable. Hot sweat trickled down his back as he observed his tortured face in the mirror. He poured some cold water from the pitcher on the dresser into a large bowl. Stripping to his waist he dunked his head into the icy liquid, throwing the water over his body, hoping to relieve the aching desire that coursed through his body. Reaching for a towel he thought he heard a knock on his door. As he turned from the dresser, rubbing his face with the towel he nearly fainted as he glimpsed an illusory figure in the half-light. Julius gasped as he realized it was the countess leaning against his closed door. She was dressed in a pale pink negligee, which perfectly complimented her skin, and her luxuriant hair was unbound, falling to her waist in gay abandon. Julius thought he was dreaming, he could not believe that the beautiful apparition before him was real. He was in a state of undress and foolishly tried to cover himself with the towel. Staring straight into his eyes the countess walked slowly towards him. Her beautiful eyes held his, and though she did not say a word, no words needed to be spoken. In the depths of those sad, beckoning, whirlpools of sapphire Julius could see the same desire as his.

Julius dropped the towel as she stood before him. Still with her eyes locked onto his, Julius took the countess into his arms and kissed her, it was a kiss such as he had never experienced before. At first he was tentative and circumspect with her, kissing her softly, holding her as though she was a piece of rare porcelain, careful that he did not scare her away. He did not want to break the poignancy

211

of the moment, in case this really was a dream and he was about to wake up. As he held the countess in his arms, he felt her hands curl around his neck and very subtlety her body started to move against his, and as he became aroused he found himself pressing himself against her lovely body as they swayed together in their passionate embrace. Julius thought he would explode as he felt the end of her tongue encircle his mouth and dart in and out, encouraging him to do the same.

Julius could contain himself no longer, he pulled her tightly against himself, not wanting to let her go as he tasted the sweetness of her and they both kissed with a frenzied passion that enveloped the whole of their body. The countess' hands caressed his back, and then suddenly she pulled herself away from him and Julius thought he would scream with the torture of losing her. Once again she looked up at him and held him in her magical gaze, still not saying a word and as Julius started to say something she put her finger up to his lips and smiled a soft gentle smile, full of sadness and expectation. "This is just for tonight, Julius, just for tonight" she whispered and she took his hand, kissed it and then led Julius to the large four poster bed, all the time her eyes held his and her eyes were telling him all the things he needed to know.

As she lay down on the bed her hair fell around her and Julius hesitated, not wanting to spoil such a lovely picture. He had always thought she was the most beautiful woman he had ever met, but now, seeing her lying in front of him, beckoning him with her eyes, he did not know if he dared proceed.

As if reading her thoughts she sat up again, reached up, and undid the buttons of his trousers. Julius closed his eyes, trying to contain himself before he exploded. He swiftly removed himself of his clothing and was pleased to see that his body had at last distracted the gaze of those lovely eyes. Julius pulled the countess up towards him and deftly removed her negligee, she was naked underneath. Julius gasped as he feasted his eyes on her body, her skin was luminescent in the candlelight, her slim figure belying her age, as did her wonderful voluptuous breasts. Julius picked her up and laid her carefully onto the bed. He buried his head in the beautiful perfection of her full breasts as she stroked his head and his hands found the warm, inviting wetness as he explored the inner secrets of her body.

Julius had never known lovemaking before that night. They made love several times, each time was as wonderful as before as they explored each others bodies, soared to new heights, then would lay in contented rapture, unable to keep their hands from each other, as though parting from one another would mean that the dream would be broken. Each time Julius feared it would be the final time, until he felt the stirring within him again as her hands would travel over his body and her eyes would plead with him once more. Eventually, as the dawn light seeped through the curtains and the birds could be heard singing their morning welcomes, Julius fell asleep, the countess in his arms, her beautiful hair lying across his chest, Julius thought himself the luckiest man that had ever lived.

Julius was awoken by the sound of banging on his door. He could hear Nikolas shouting to him, "Julius, it is nearly eight o'clock, you have overslept. Are you going to grace us with your presence today, or not?"

Julius sat bolt upright in his bed, his first thoughts were for the countess, but as he turned he realized that he was quite alone. He jumped out of bed and flinging on his dressing gown he opened his door slightly and peered out at his friend. Trying to retain some semblance of normality he said with affected cheerfulness, "I am sorry Nikolas, I think Karl and I had rather too much to drink last night. Look you go off with Josef and I will meet you for lunch if I am feeling better"

"Well, if you are sure" replied Nikolas, "so much for warning Josef and I about the evils of drink. Can I get you anything?" Julius assured his friend that there was nothing he needed but a few more hours sleep and with Nikolas promising to leave word of where they were to meet for lunch Julius thankfully shut the door on his friend.

He stood for a few minutes trying to collect his thoughts. He wondered for a while if last night had been a figment of his fertile imagination, but he knew it was not. His body was a testament to the night he had spent with the countess and he knew it had been very real. He was glad that he would not have to face his friends that morning. He needed the time to sort out his feelings and his mind. As he walked round the room he saw a letter with his name on it and he knew who had written it. He lay back on the bed as he read the hand of the woman who had lain with him with such ecstasy the night before.

'My dearest Julius, I do not know why I am writing this, but I feel I owe you an explanation for last night. I never want you to think ill of me, and I hope after reading this you perhaps will understand me a little better. Please do not think that last night was a usual occurrence for me. It was not and I do not think it will ever happen again. From our first meeting at the ball I felt there was something between us. It was a feeling in my body that I had not felt for a very long time, and I think it was the same for you, I pray that I was right.

My life has not been easy, and at times it has been very unhappy. I do not say this to gain your sympathy, more to explain myself to you. Something drew me to you last night, I do not know what, but I somehow knew that with you I would find a fulfillment that I have never known, with someone who would not judge me too harshly, who would understand the emptiness of my life. I think we both know that this will never, can never, happen again, but thank you for a wonderful night. When we meet again it must inevitably be as the mother and friend of Josef, but I hope you will always regard me with a little fondness in the future, Elisabeth'

Julius read the letter over and over again. A letter from a wonderful woman, a sad and lonely lady who was capable of so much love and affection but who remained here in her ivory tower in a loveless marriage. When the countess had entered the bedroom the night before Julius had known that anything they shared would be confined to those few hours together but still the letter filled him with sadness. Sadness for the life of the countess and sadness for a doomed love that he would never be able to share with anyone else in the world. As he lay down onto the pillows he turned his head and smiled bleakly as he buried his face in the linen that smelt of spring flowers.

XVII

Julius did not see the countess over the few remaining days of their visit which were spent in long bouts of eating and drinking with his friends. He did not even have to say goodbye to her as a message came from one of Josef's brothers that one of his children had been taken ill and the countess immediately left to stay with her sick grandchild. Josef came to the station to see them off on their journey back to Prague and Julius thought what a lonely figure his friend struck as he stood on the platform waving goodbye.

On their journey home Julius related to Nikolas his conversation with Karl. Nikolas was as disturbed as Julius by Karl's revelations and agreed with his friend that there must be some truth in what Karl had said, for he had no reason to lie and it was very similar to what Count Donner had said over dinner at Josef's house.

"I love living in Prague" added Nikolas, "but one thing I find frustrating is the lack of current news that we get there. When we do hear of anything it is usually weeks old. When we lived in Vienna you felt you were at the heart of all the army and government information"

Julius had to agree, not for the first time did he realize the limitations that they experienced by being posted in Prague.

In the Austro-Hungarian Empire the official language spoken was German, all business was conducted in German and all professional people spoke the language. Julius had spoken German since young as his parents were Austrian and he had only learnt to speak Czech and Slovak by listening to the servants and talking to classmates at school who spoke the languages, as had Nikolas. This disregard of the Czech and Slovak languages was resented by the Bohemian lower classes, who all spoke Czech and Slovak and regarded it as Austro-Hungarian autocracy that they should be forced to speak German in their own country. This was further exacerbated by the large number of Germans who lived mainly in the Sudetenland and were not welcomed by the Czechs. They had a natural aversion to Germans, who were regarded as a nation not to be trusted. Added to the antagonism of the Bohemian people was their distrust of the Austro-Hungarian Army, stationed in their cities. Whilst in Vienna Julius and Nikolas had enjoyed the respect that the army was held in in Austria, but it was very different in Prague. Although people were not openly hostile towards him Julius felt a certain amount of tension when he and fellow soldiers were around. Julius knew that this stemmed from the martial law that had been imposed in Prague in the winter of 1908, after Czechs had taken the side of the Serbs, when they had tried to incur civil unrest in the southern Slav provinces of the Habsburg monarchy. It had been a difficult time for the army, especially when some soldiers who had been imposing martial law had been Czechs themselves. Nikolas' father had spoken of the deep divided feelings his men had encountered in those worrying times, and ever since those dark days the Czech people still held a wary dislike for the Austro-Hungarian Army. It was a difficult time for all soldiers, with so much dissent within their ranks, not least the proliferation of Austrians who were posted to Prague and its outstations who only spoke German and therefore could not even communicate with the ordinary soldier. Julius worried that in the future Prague could fall even further behind and be seen as a mere outstation for the army.

When Julius and Nikolas returned to their barracks they had a joyous reunion with Phantom and Steel. Both men had become very attached to their horses and spent the next few weeks exercising them and reacquainting their mounts with the rigors of army exercises and parades which they had missed whilst they had been in Vienna.

Once back in Prague Julius and Nikolas settled down to their military duties. Papa was home on leave and Julius was pleased to see his father again, though he was worried to see his father looking strained and tired. Irmy was as ebullient as ever, obviously very happy in her marriage and nursing training. Nikolas had learnt on his return that Georg had stretched his parent's patience just once too often and was now to be sent to a military boarding school as his punishment. Nikolas went to see his wayward younger brother and came back to report that he had found a very repentant young man who had begged Nikolas to speak to their parents on his behalf to try and stop the transfer to his new school. Nikolas had dismally failed to persuade his parents against their chosen course of action, although he had to admit to Julius that he had not felt totally committed to his task, as he really did think that boarding school may be the best future for his brother, before he became completely out of control.

Julius told Nikolas about Georg turning up on Irmy's doorstep the year before. "The little devil" said Nikolas a broad smile on his face, "you have to admit the Manz boys have taste" Nikolas continued to escort Suse and seemed quite attached to her, but Julius still had the feeling that Nikolas would always have a place in his heart for Irmy, he just hoped it would lessen over the years.

The year was 1912 and Julius was approaching his twenty-second birthday. At times he would look around at his life, his friends and family and wonder just where he was heading. Although he knew he worried too much about things, thoughts of his future came into his mind with more frequency of late. Although he loved being in the army and enjoyed living in Prague, not for the first time did he think to himself whether he wanted to follow this same course for the rest of his life. Whenever he expressed his misgivings to Nikolas, his friend would always tell him he was thinking too deeply and should wait and see where life should happen to take him. They were both still young and inevitably in the future they would be promoted. They would then be sent to serve in different regiments in different places, he just wanted to run before he could walk. Whilst acknowledging the sensibility of his friend, Julius still had a nagging voice in his head, questioning his motivation and expectations. He would wonder where he would be in ten years time and was perplexed to realize he had no idea or even a hint of any ambition as to what he wanted to do in the future.

When he tried to discuss his worries with his father, though admittedly in a very vague way, Colonel Mayer had given him virtually the same reply as Nikolas, and so Julius had changed the subject for fear of offending his father. Only Irmy appeared sympathetic to his feelings, though even she added that maybe he needed some new interests, outside the army. Julius reluctantly admitted that the army had become his life, but he could not envisage doing anything else. Irmy suggested that maybe what he needed was a diversion for himself, in the shape of a female companion. Julius was shocked at her insinuation and found himself retorting, "I did not think to hear you of all people saying such a thing. After all you used to say about Mama trying to get you married all the time"

"Who mentioned marriage?" Irmy replied artlessly, "all I said was female companionship, you know some of us women can be very entertaining company believe it or not.

I presume you provide yourself with the other sort of female companionship?" Irmy laughed, "Julius you should see your face! Do you think a young lady does not know of such things, or is it just that one should not talk about them?

Julius' disapproval was partly due to his guilt of the night he had spent with the countess. Julius was also uncomfortable discussing such things with his sister, but he was really not too surprised. Irmy had always been outspoken and since her marriage he believed she had become even more so.

"All I am saying is you need a diversion from your army duties, to socialize more, go out and meet people who are not connected with the army. There is a big wide world out there Julius, and the trouble with army personnel is that they do not believe there *is* anything beyond the army. I should know, I lived with you all for long enough"

Julius thought about his sister's words and he knew there was some truth in what she said. Army life was very insular and many personnel were apt to live within their environment and disregard anything that was occurring in the world that was not relevant to the army regime. He determined to himself that he would take Irmy's advice and socialize, as much as his duties allowed, and patronize the arts more. He loved the theatre and the opera, but rarely went to either, so promised himself he would make more effort in the future.

As to female companionship, he agreed that the idea was very welcoming, but until he found someone who he could be completely at ease with he knew that he would not be able to fulfill his sister's wishes, much as he would have liked to. He shivered as an image of the Countess von Kutz once more materialized in his mind and he determinedly pushed it away as, with a sigh, he consoled himself with the knowledge that her image was becoming more blurred and he really did not think about her as much these days.

For a long time Julius had felt a growing respect for Richard since his marriage to Irmy. Julius could see that Richard loved Irmy, his eyes would light up when she entered the room and he would watch her as she moved around showing an avid interest in everything she said. In fact it was their compatibility that so impressed Julius, they would endlessly discuss things, each showing a lively interest in each other's opinions, but not afraid to contradict each other if they disagreed with anything that was said. They shared the same sense of humor and their shared interest in anything medical bought them even closer together. Julius would often watch the two of them together and envy them their marriage. He knew he had been wrong to question their betrothal, now their ages seemed of no consequence, indeed the more he got to know Richard the more he understood how liberal and young thinking the man was.

Some of his liberal ideas shocked Julius, who often felt the more senior of the two men when in Richard's company. Richard encouraged everybody to speak their mind, and even to question those in authority, believing that just because such men held senior posts it did not mean that they were constantly right in the decisions they made. Although Julius would have liked to agree with Richard he often speculated how Colonel Reichart would have regarded this view. In fact many of his and Richard's amicable arguments were about the army's attitude to its men and the way the army was run. Richard could not understand how Julius could work in such a regime, and Julius would spend many an evening trying to explain to Richard the long heritage of the army and the reasons for some of its practices, though he often found himself unable to defend his arguments and would ruefully submit to Richard's way of thinking. Julius was always amused to note that Richard never expounded his views in front of Papa, Richard may be a liberal man but he knew better than to incur the wrath of his father-in-law.

As the army was so often discussed between them Julius one day asked Richard if he could visit him at work, at the hospital, saying to Richard, "you seem to know so much about my work but I know nothing of what you do at the hospital"
Richard readily agreed to his request and Irmy was pleased that Julius was taking such an interest in Richard's work. Julius was genuinely curious about Richard's profession, but his tour of the hospital shocked and unnerved him. He decided he could never work in such a place himself, for whilst he acknowledged what a worthwhile job all the men and women did in the medical world, the hospital itself, though clean and well run, left Julius feeling nauseous and inadequate. The smell and the sight of so many sick people did not appeal to him at all. He could not bear the groaning of the ill patients or the vacant, trusting looks of the invalids as they lay pathetically in their beds. Most of all he was

impressed by the patience and duty of the nurses and doctors as they tended their patients, Julius knew he could never last for more than a day in a place like that and his respect for Richard and Irmy deepened.

Julius accompanied Richard on his rounds, as he visited his patients. Some were waiting for surgery, whilst others had already received surgery, Richard treated all with the utmost kindness and respect. It was a new side of Richard that Julius had not really thought about. He watched Richard as he moved from bed to bed, offering words of encouragement, explaining a medical procedure, chatting about their families, or assessing when they could return to their home.

Julius was especially struck by a little old lady in a side ward. She was very old, with sparse white hair, milky gray eyes and little gnarled hands that plucked nervously at her sheets as she spoke to Richard, who sat on the side of her bed. He chatted to her for quite a while, so softly that Julius had to strain to hear what he was saying. He took her deformed hands and stroked them as he spoke to her. When he rose from her bed he said very gently, "now you take care of yourself, and if you want anything do not hesitate to call one of my nurses straightaway, or if you want to see me just tell them and they will fetch me"
The old lady gave him a macabre smile that stretched the skin over the bones of her face exposing a toothless mouth, reminding Julius of a grinning skull.

As they left the room a nurse approached Richard and he asked Julius to stay with the sister who had accompanied them on the round as he had to hurry off to a patient, but hoped he would not be long. The sister was a middle-aged woman who wore a large starched cap and a brilliant white apron that rustled when she moved. She walked with her back perfectly straight and Julius reflected she would do justice to any marching drill. She had smiled on being introduced to Julius, but whilst accompanying Richard on his rounds had been very serious and had answered all his questions with precision and brevity. She turned to a notice board in the corridor and started to rearrange the papers on the board, as though to stand idly around was something this woman never contemplated. Julius felt it was good manners to talk to the sister, to break the uncomfortable silence.

"I wonder if you know my sister? she is training to be a nurse here"

The sister stopped her positioning of tacks and looked at Julius "of course, Herr Doktor Beck's wife, Irmy. I can see the likeness. She is going to make an excellent nurse, you must be very proud of her, and of Herr Doktor Beck"

Julius was pleased with her praise of Irmy and in the high esteem that Richard was regarded within the hospital. He had never thought before about the importance of Richard's work, but watching him he saw that Richard was a very good doctor. How wonderful it must be for him to be able to make someone better, to alleviate the pain of suffering, it made himself feel rather insignificant.

"Do you always work with Herr Doktor Beck, sister?"

"Not always, but I do like working with him, and I am not saying that because you are his brother-in-law" she made Julius feel as though he was standing before a very strict schoolmistress and his devilry took over as he said, "and how are the views of my liberal brother-in-law accepted in the hospital?"

Julius was rewarded with seeing the sister quite flustered by such a frank statement, then she recovered herself. She had obviously decided on candor as she replied, with the trace of a smile on her lips, "well, I have to say he certainly raises eyebrows within the hospital with some of his practices, but I for one support him whole-heartedly and his patients respect and revere him for the good doctor he is, which to my mind is what medicine is all about"

"What does Richard do that is so terrible? I thought he had a wonderful rapport with his patients"

"Oh he does" replied the sister vehemently, "he certainly does, but he does not like to adhere to certain rules in the hospital. For instance, he is always being reprimanded for sitting on the bed when talking to patients, that is strictly forbidden, and they say he spends too long with individual patients and that takes up valuable hospital time"

"I thought that was a good thing, look at the way he comforted that old lady, she was very content"

"Well that is a case in point. Frau Hennerova has an incurable illness, she has only weeks, maybe even days, to live, there is nothing left that we can do for her. The hospital directors want her to leave the hospital, but Herr Doktor Beck knows she has no family to look after her, and would be leaving to die alone, so he has insisted she stays here until she passes away. That sort of thing does not make him popular with the gentlemen who run this hospital, but he is very popular with the staff"

Julius pondered this, it was a side of Richard he had never seen before, and he realized that for all his passionate theories Richard had just as many battles with his superiors as any army personnel. He also appreciated what a compassionate man Irmy had married. He walked back down the corridor and watched Frau Hennerova, her little body hardly visible under the bedding, who was going to be allowed to die in dignity, whatever the cost to Richard.

Richard sent a message saying the emergency was more severe than he had at first thought and would Julius mind finding his own way home as he may be at the hospital for some time. The sister escorted him to the door, her apron rustling beside him as they negotiated the long corridors to the entrance to the hospital, "Well, Lieutenant Mayer, I hope you enjoyed your visit to the hospital, though I have a feeling the medical profession is not for you" Julius looked at the sister who had an eyebrow raised and a comical glint in her eye.

"Did I make it that obvious? I am sorry, I very much admire everything you do here, but I am afraid it would be the last place I would choose to work"

The sister at last allowed herself a little chuckle as she said, "do not worry yourself, most people have your reaction to a hospital and its workings, you are certainly not in a minority." He was rewarded with a wonderful wide smile from the sister as she added, "and I would like to sincerely say that I hope I never see you here again, in a professional capacity that is"

Julius smiled and shook the sister's hand. As he left the hospital he once again pondered his brother-in-law. Irmy had told him that Richard chose to work in the hospital, though a private practice would be more financially rewarding. Luckily his independent means allowed him to be able to choose where he worked, and he loved being a surgeon, so the hospital suited him. Julius knew they would never be close friends, as he and Nikolas, and even Viktor and Josef were, but the more he got to know him the more he liked Richard.

When Julius recounted his visit to Irmy, she laughed at what the sister had said to him. "Sister Jagerova is a fine nurse, very serious in her work, but very understanding,

222

she obviously liked you, I would never have believed she would be so open with a stranger. I must tell Richard that his plans did not go completely as expected"

"What do you mean?" asked Julius.

Irmy laughed, "Richard was worried by the effect you might have on the young nurses so he deliberately chose Sister Jagerova for his rounds that day as he did not think that she would ever succumb to your charms. Richard may be a gifted doctor, but his assessment of women is not always very good"

"The crafty devil, I did not think he could be so devious. I cannot imagine how he would think any of the nurses would be attracted to me"

"Oh Julius, enough of your modesty, you know exactly what affect you have on women. You may not display the same swaggering confidence of Josef, but it is there all the same, you just choose to ignore it. You do not know how popular I have suddenly become amongst the other nurses since they realized that the handsome visitor with Herr Doktor Beck was my brother"

Julius was heartened by his sister's opinion of himself, but despite all her encouragement he wondered whether he would ever find that certain someone to share his life with.

XVIII

In October of that year a rumor started spreading around the barracks of the outbreak of war between Turkey and Montenegro. The whole army was in a state of great excitement as senior personnel rushed around to try and find out if the news was indeed true and what this would mean to the Habsburg government and the Imperial Army.

Everyone Julius spoke to had a different version of the events in the Balkans, and not for the first time did Julius regret not being at the heart of politics in Vienna. He was sure that his father and Karl would know exactly what was going on at that moment, and thought of using the new telephone system, but did not know how to speak directly to his father or Karl. He reasoned that he would hear the news as soon as it reached Prague. Josef and his mother had a telephone installed in their house, but he knew contacting them would be futile, not least because Josef was probably at his barracks, and he had no desire to talk to the Countess, knowing the sound of her voice would only renew the feelings he had so long been trying to subdue. Besides, Julius thought enviously to himself, Josef was probably preparing for war at this very moment. By the time the call for mobilization came to Prague, the hostilities would in all likelihood be over. The Balkan countries were always fighting each other, this was probably just another of their petty skirmishes.

When news came several days later it became apparent that the conflict was growing as the Bulgarians, Serbians and Greeks had declared war on Turkey as well. By now the whole of the city was bracing itself for a call to arms but still no news came from Vienna for the mobilization.

As the days turned into weeks there was continuing news of heavy fighting in the Balkans, especially of heavy losses to the Turks, but the Imperial Army stayed in Vienna, despite the Austrian government threatening the Serbian government with several ultimatums.

One night Julius was having dinner with Nikolas' parents and although he knew it was wrong to ask Colonel Manz to divulge any covert information about the army's plans his impatience could hold him back no longer and after Frau Manzova had left the men to their coffee and brandies he asked the colonel for his assessment of the situation. The

224

colonel thought long and hard about his reply before he said, "I wish I knew Julius, I have had no official response from Vienna except to say that as of this moment in time the Imperial Army will not be drawn into the conflict. My own personal conclusion, and you must remember I am not privy to the policy making in Vienna, you would do better asking your father about that, but my personal opinion is that the government do not want to see the army drawn into this situation. They are content to sit back and watch the hostilities and let them sort themselves out. If in the end the outcome is not to their liking, then maybe they will take a firm hand with the warring factions, who knows. I know the government will not condone Serbia becoming a stronger nation, but let us see what happens"

With that Julius had to be content. Although he believed Colonel Manz's assessment of the situation had been a fair one he could not believe that the mighty powers of the Habsburg Empire were just going to sit back and watch countries like Serbia gain further power and lands, but that appeared to be what was happening.

As it became clear mobilization was not going to take place the barracks settled back into the routine of army life and at the beginning of December news was received of the ceasing of hostilities and that the Turks had requested a truce after the Sultan's army had been defeated. Turkey was left with few European possessions and a peace conference was organized in London for the following year. This was highly unsatisfactory to Julius. It was said that the Balkan states were dividing up the conquered lands for themselves and Julius wondered why the Austrian Government were not overseeing the peace talks instead of the British government.

The whole situation left nagging doubts in Julius' mind and Karl's warnings kept returning to him. He was pleased to find that Papa and Karl were returning for Christmas leave that year. At last he might be able to find out what really had happened in Vienna over the last few months, and certainly why the Austrian government had not wanted to intervene in the Balkan conflict.

Papa and Karl arrived home two days before Christmas. Franz had not obtained Christmas leave but had written that he would be able to spend the day with Gretha and her family.

Julius was shocked by his father's appearance, he looked very tired and much older, his hair having turned almost completely white. Karl looked well, but rather tired, dark circles under his eyes underlining the strain of the past few months. Julius was desperate to hear their news, but they were both tired from the journey and he sensed his father did not want to be burdened with army matters on returning home for some well earned rest. Frau Mayer was shocked by her husband's appearance and spent the next few days ordering her husband to rest and barring him from any exertion or discussion of army affairs. Julius could sense that Karl was also tired of the political intrigue but was so anxious to talk to his brother that at the first opportunity he took Karl off to a local beer keller and plagued his brother with so many questions that in the end Karl had to succumb to his interrogation, if only to quiet his younger brother.

"All right, I will tell you as succinctly as possible, but please, after that, no more questioning. I am here on leave, here to forget about work, you can be almost as annoying as my wife was, and that is saying something" Julius ignored the rebuke as Karl told him what had happened in Vienna over the past few months.

"Now remember, I do not know everything. I am not prey to all the confidential meetings within the government and the army, so I can only tell you events as I saw them, all right?" Julius nodded in anticipation, "the official version is much as Nikolas' father told you. The capital was in uproar when the news first came through, we all thought we would be at war within days, and I believe military action was contemplated but eventually the government decided against any intervention. Personally, I think they were worried more about the political outcome of intervention than the actual ethics of going to war"

"What do you mean by that?" asked a puzzled Julius.

"I mean that in the end it was not our government's decision to make, we are just not seen as a great political power in Europe any more. They may have given all the excuses they could think of why they did not mobilize the army. They did issue several ultimatums to Serbia which went unheeded, which previously would have precipitated a conflict, but without the support of Germany, which we did not have, I am afraid to say, we were not strong enough to act"

Julius swallowed hard at his brother's words, "you mean they dangle the strings and we dance like puppets?"

"I do not think it is quite as bad as that, it is just that it is no longer the situation where we can exist on our own, we have to answer to too many other nations now. Maybe by expanding the Empire we have in fact made ourselves weaker, not stronger. I know the government is determined to make their presence felt at the peace conference next year, but how important a role they will play we will have to see"

"Do you know what Papa's view is of all this?"

"Papa is a member of the old guard. With no disrespect to him, he is fiercely loyal to the Emperor and the army and has always lived with the belief in the invincibility of both, and that is his dilemma"

"I do not understand" said Julius.

"Look Julius, you and I are young, we have seen miraculous things happen in our short lifetimes, automation, telephones, even machines flying in the sky, we are more able to embrace new ideas, perceive events with fresh young eyes. We both have a loyalty to our country and our Emperor, but we both know things are changing rapidly within the army, things that we both probably do not like, but things that are happening, none the less. For Papa it is much harder. All his life he has been brought up with the Habsburg belief of absolute authority and respect and he will live by that to his dying day, but I believe, deep in his heart, he knows things are going drastically wrong, and trying to equate the two is very difficult for him. He has taken events very hard, he can see through the diplomatic rhetoric as well as any man and his heart is saddened. I can honestly see him retiring after this, I do not think he could bear to see the decline of his beloved army"

"Do you think there is a future for the army?" asked an alarmed Julius, scared at what his brother's answer might be.

Karl grinned for the first time that evening, "do not worry little brother, I do not think the army is about to be dissolved, or the Empire for that matter. No they will carry on for many years, believe me, I just feel we should prepare ourselves for a different army, with a more modern approach to suit these modern times. My only worry is that people in Vienna are treating this like some childish game. They are so incensed by the audacity and the increasing power of Serbia that they will do anything to try and exert their supremacy, just to teach them a lesson, to show they cannot deride the Habsburg Empire. To be honest when I see the old fossils that are in charge in Vienna I know it is time that things changed, it can only be for the better. I should not worry if I were you, this will not happen for many, many years, you will be a colonel yourself by then, and then it will be you the young officers will be calling an old fossil!"

Julius could not decide if he was comforted or disturbed by his conversation with Karl, but he was careful not to be contentious in front of his father during Christmas and often when he looked at Papa during his stay he could see the conflict within his father and he wished he could help him, but he knew his father was too proud a man to seek advice from his young son.

The Christmas festivities seemed to revive his father. By the time he was due to return to Vienna he was looking much happier with himself and more content. Julius had to at last agree with Karl that retirement from the army might not be such a bad thing for his father, something he thought he would never admit to. Irmy, Richard and Frau Beckova joined the family for the festivities, and Irmy was shocked by her father's appearance. Julius saw her take Karl to one side asking after their father's welfare and Julius was relieved to hear Karl innocently blaming age and probably overwork for their father's fatigue. Irmy spent the rest of the leave helping Mama and Danusia fuss over Papa, which he enjoyed, though Julius lost count at the number of times Papa hinted to Irmy how he would love to have grandchildren to which Irmy would always answer with a strained smile on her face and a glare at Julius laughing behind Papa's back.

Papa and Karl returned to Vienna after the New Year. Julius had told Nikolas what Karl had told him and both of them discussed the subject at great length, coming to the conclusion that though Karl may be right, they could not believe that the Empire now held such little influence on the European political front. It just did not seem right, but the more they analyzed the situation the harder it became to refute the possibility of the situation.

In May the peace conference was held in London. The conference was reported in all the newspapers, which they both perused over avidly, trying to ascertain the situation.

Since the amnesty of last year there had still been skirmishes in the Balkans and it was revealed that even before the hostilities had started last year the Balkan countries had drawn up a secret treaty, dividing the countries that they hoped to win in the ensuing conflict.

With the new treaty, Turkey lost most of its possessions in Europe whilst Serbia was granted large areas in Macedonia. Bulgaria and Greece also gained new lands. Through it all the Austro-Hungarian government played very little part and Julius reflected that Karl's appraisal of the situation had been fairly accurate after all.

The treaty did not create the harmony it hoped for amongst the Balkan states however, they still argued over lands that they thought rightfully belonged to their own particular country and the fragile pact was broken when another Balkan war was declared in June. This time there was no excitement in the barracks, as the army had now accepted their non-intervention in the hostilities and took a stoic acceptance of their position.

The fighting was shorter this time with Bulgaria now in conflict with Serbia and Greece, who were later joined by Romania and Turkey, and the Bulgarians were forced to an armistice by July.

Once again a peace conference was held, this time in Bucharest and the Austro-Hungarian people held their breaths to see how many more lands the distrusted Serbians would extract this time. There was outrage when Serbia once again gained more territory, however it was seen as a fillip to their national pride when at last the Austro-Hungarian government intervened and insisted that Serbia and Montenegro give up part of the lands they had occupied to establish the new independent state of Albania. The Serbs were further outraged when they were denied hoped for territories that would have given them direct access to the sea, these lands being given to the Greeks. The Austrian government had been alarmed by the emergence of a strong Serbian nation and the animosity between Serbia and Austria was elevated to new heights by the Habsburg intervention.

After the Bucharest treaty the populace believed that the hostilities were at an end and that the Balkan crisis had now been resolved, but if anything the bitterness between various countries was now deeper than ever before, simmering just below boiling point, waiting for the next crisis to reveal itself.

Somewhat mollified by the government's participation in the peace talks Julius began to regard the future with a more optimistic outlook. Whilst the troubles within his country and the army still remained Julius felt that with the Balkan hostilities over they could return to a normal life again.

During the upheaval of the past few months Julius' mother had been informed of the sad news of her only brother's death. Julius had never really known his Uncle Leopold. He was a somewhat reclusive figure, who had married but had never had children. He and his wife had lived in the southern Austrian town of Klagenfurt, and although Julius could remember visiting them in his younger years he had not seen his uncle for some time. His uncle's wife had died many years beforehand and Julius knew his uncle had suffered with ill health for some time and had been too ill to attend Irmy's wedding. Mama took his death very badly. She was a lot younger than her brother, but seemed to regard his death as an indication of her own mortality. She bemoaned the fact that she had not visited him more in his last years, although, as Irmy had pointed out, they had written to each other regularly, and so had kept in touch.

It was several months after his death that Julius received a letter from his Uncle Leopold's solicitors. It transpired that his uncle had left all his money to be divided between the three sons of his only sister. Uncle Leopold had been quite a wealthy man, and although his estate had been divided into three, it still meant that Julius had been left a sizeable inheritance. He had to read and reread the letter several times before he could grasp its contents, and although he knew he could not retire on such a sum he had the pleasant realization that he could look to a future with a lot more security, confident his nest egg would provide all the little extras he might want.

Karl wrote that he was using part of his inheritance to repay the money Papa had lent him to pay off the debts that he had accrued during his disastrous marriage. Julius was pleased at his brother's mature handling of his money, although Mama had hinted that she and Papa were not going to accept any money from their son, they were comforted by the fact that Karl's first thought had been to

230

pay them back. Mama had been very worried on hearing of her brother's benevolence that Karl would not be able to cope with having so much money and may have cause to stray again. She was even fretting that Anna would hear about Karl coming into money and would reappear to help him spend it. Julius felt this a little far-fetched but was intrigued to wonder just how his sister-in-law would have reacted if she had heard the news. Julius had enough confidence in Karl now to know he would never have Anna back in his life again, but when he told Mama this she only frowned and dismissed Julius as having no notion as to how being in love could affect a person. Julius bleakly reflected that he was not too sure how right his mother was about that.

Franz wrote in his usual ebullient way that now he was a man of means he had asked Gretha to marry him and they were to be married next year. Julius could not blame his brother, in fact he rather envied him, he had obviously been in love with Gretha for some time. He knew that were it not for the fact that it was difficult to support a wife on a lieutenant's wage Franz would have married her long ago. Julius wrote to Franz congratulating him on his engagement. He also wrote to Viktor, asking him if he could ask his father as to the best way he could invest his money, he reasoned that Herr Leitner would be the best person to advise him on financial matters. He had always admired Viktor's father since meeting him in Salzburg and remembered him as an urbane man with integrity.

With his increase in wealth Julius started to socialize more, always buying the best seats at the theatres and at the opera house, and he and Nikolas started to frequent all the best restaurants in Prague, something they could not afford to do before, and something they had missed since losing Josef's patronage in Vienna. Josef wrote congratulating Julius on his inheritance and jokingly added he could now send him the bill for all the socializing they had done when they were cadets. Nikolas still favored the picture houses, now growing in number, and he would drag a reluctant Julius along as well. Although Julius was fascinated by the sight of moving pictures on the screen before him he never found them as appealing as Nikolas who would go and see the same moving picture time and time again. Julius used to laugh at Nikolas saying Suse must be very fond of him because she accompanied him so many times to see the same film. Nikolas was still walking out with Suse, though when pressed he would never comment about his fondness for her. Julius was unsure whether this was because Nikolas was never a man to admit to his inner most feelings or the fact that he simply was not sure what his affections were for Suse.

Julius had known Nikolas for seven years now and in that time his respect for his friend had grown with the passing years. From the time they had met in the rail carriage on their way to Vienna Julius felt that Nikolas had never changed. Nikolas was a kind, genial man who was rarely enraged. He took an almost lethargic view of life and would only regard the good side of people and always reasoned that everybody had some benevolence in them, though he had to admit this was a difficult premise to argue when referring to Colonel Reichart. Everybody liked Nikolas, from stable boy to officer and in all the years he had known him Julius had never heard anyone say anything disagreeable about his friend. He often wondered what would have happened if they had not shared a room as cadets, had not become best friends. He really could not imagine it, as he now could not imagine his life without Nikolas being a part of it. He knew that he had been a very lucky man the day he had met Nikolas Manz.

There was much excitement within the city as a new statue was to be placed at the end of Wenceslas Square. It was to be positioned in front of the National Museum and had been designed by Josef Myslbek, a leading Czech sculptor. Everyone knew that it was to be a statue of St. Wenceslas, the former King of Bohemia who had lived in the tenth century, but nobody knew what it looked like and its arrival was awaited with eager anticipation.

Julius and Nikolas were ordered to provide the guard for the statue at its unveiling. They both felt very honored to be included in the escort duty as they knew there would be large crowds in the square to see the new monument. When Julius first saw the statue he was amazed, first by its size, and then by its beauty. The statue was cast in bronze and was an effigy of the saint on horseback and in armor, wearing a cloak and carrying a ceremonial pennant. Julius marveled at how lifelike the figure was, he was particularly impressed with the sculpting of the horse, which proudly stood, its right front leg and back right leg raised as though about to proceed majestically on his way, carrying its regal

232

mount. The statue was erected on an enormous plinth so that it stood high above the crowds of people, for all to see. On each corner of the plinth were four smaller statues of Czech patron saints, and all the figures had their backs to the National Museum building, facing towards the full length of the famous square.

The statue was greeted with enormous cheers and loud applause as it was shown to the populace. The city and its people were imbued with the excitement as they paid homage to their former king and saint. The day was declared a public holiday and Julius and Nikolas, their ceremonial duties dispensed with, joined the revelers in the city, ending back in the square in the modern Hotel Europa.

The hotel had become very popular since its re-opening a few years beforehand. It was decorated in the style which everybody was calling Art Nouveau, a new, and some thought brash, art movement. Julius was not sure whether he liked this new art form, feeling it was too modern for his rather conservative tastes, but it was proving to be very modish and he had to admit that he found the design of the Europa quite breathtaking, from its gilded edifice to the welcoming interior, with its large mirrors, painted paneling and sociable bars and restaurants. Everyone of their acquaintance seemed to be in the hotel that night and Julius and Nikolas spent the evening greeting old friends and drinking to new ones.

One evening Julius was lying on his bed trying to summon the energy to raise himself in order to go out. It had been a bad day and he was not in the best of moods. His company had been practicing for a procession that was to take place through the Prague streets the next week. The men had been doing well, their marching drills were very near perfection and they were standing to attention, waiting to be inspected, when Colonel Reichart appeared on the parade ground.

Whenever the colonel appeared around the barracks there was always an instant air of hostility and apprehension. Reichart proceeded to take over the inspection, spending a very long time walking up and down the columns of men, criticizing the very smallest breaches of uniform etiquette or commenting on the conditions of guns which Julius knew had been cleaned for hours beforehand. Julius and his fellow officers had to follow behind the colonel, looking straight ahead, for fear of

233

showing their incredulity at some of the trifling comments the colonel was shouting at the men. It was a very cold day and by the end of the inspection many of the men had blue extremities from the cold.

Thinking the inspection was over, Julius signaled for the men to be dismissed, but Reichart interrupted him, suggesting he might see the march past that the men had been practicing. Jaws dropped as they realized, stiff with cold and after hours of work, the men would have to go through their marching drills again. The result was a fiasco. Julius did not know at that moment who he was more annoyed with, the colonel for subjecting the men to the drill, or the men for giving such a poor show in front of the colonel. They had performed their march so well beforehand but were now reduced to making themselves look like cadets on their first day of recruitment. Julius knew that the presence of the colonel did not help, but even that did not excuse the chaotic appearance of his men, or the venomous tirade that assailed their ears as the colonel told them exactly what he thought of their performance.

After blasting the men he turned to the officers present and in front of the entire assembly embarrassingly castigated them on their complete lack of leadership and control. After orders that they were to stay on the parade ground practicing for at least another two hours the colonel marched off, leaving behind some very angry and disgruntled men. Although Julius did not agree entirely with all the colonel had said, he knew that in some respects his vitriolic harangue had some justification. After a stern lecture to the men the marching drill was extended for another two hours.

By the time Julius got back to his room he was cold and tired. He had missed Nikolas who was on night guard duty and he was due to go to Irmy's house that evening. Irmy was having another one of her suppers, which Julius knew was just an elaborate charade for him to meet another 'nice young lady' that Irmy hoped he would like. Irmy's matchmaking could be very tiresome at times, and tonight Julius did not feel that he was really in the right mood to act the charming and benevolent young man that Irmy had no doubt described to her friend. His bed was soft and comforting, and he would have loved to have stayed there but for the concern of Irmy's wrath, something he feared almost as much as Colonel Reichart's.

234

He had decided that a long soak in the bath might revive his weary body when there was a knock on the door and a young corporal entered asking for Nikolas.

"I am afraid Lieutenant Manz is on duty" said Julius and seeing the young man was in some sort of dilemma added, "can I be of any help?"

The young corporal, pleased to unburden his load replied, "there is a young gentleman at the door insisting he must see Lieutenant Manz. I told him that he was not allowed into the barracks, indeed I would like to know how he got this far, but he is very insistent. He looks very distressed, I even thought at one point that he was about to burst into tears"

"He has not by any chance got bright red hair, about so high, with a cheeky smile?" asked Julius.

"Well, I cannot say about the smile, I do not think he is in the mood to smile at the moment, but the rest of your description fits the young man perfectly. You know who he is, then?"

Julius sighed, "Yes, I know who he is, I will come down and see him" and reluctantly he postponed all thoughts of his bath and went down to the front door to find out what mischief Georg had been up to this time.

Julius was shocked by Georg's appearance. He looked scruffy, dirty and very thin and his blue eyes looked even more enormous than usual, staring out of his pale face. His face puckered into disappointment when he saw it was not Nikolas descending the staircase, but he managed an angelic Manz smile when he saw it was Julius. However the smile quickly disappeared when he saw the stern look on Julius' face.

"Georg what on earth are you doing here? why are you not at school? do not tell me you have run away? of all the stupid, idiotic things to do" Julius immediately regretted being so severe with the boy. Georg clutched at his hat nervously and as he looked up at Julius he nodded as enormous tears welled up in his eyes, making him look more pathetic than ever.

"All right, all right, Georg, do not cry, dry your tears, and we will see what we can do for you" said Julius, trying to mollify the young boy. He was sorry to have been so stern, but consoled himself that Georg had caught him at a bad time when he was not in the best of moods.

Julius tried to determine what to do next with Georg. Firstly he knew he must get changed, so after a quick word with the corporal who seemed happy to turn a blind eye to Georg being in his rooms for a while, he quickly marched Georg upstairs and into their room. Telling Georg to sit on Nikolas' bed, Julius proceeded to wash and change while he pondered what to do next.

"You are not going to take me back to school are you?" asked Georg in a small, tremulous voice, "please don't. You do not know what it is like there, I hate it. If you send me back there, I will only run away again" he said defiantly.

"If you talk like that I will" said Julius, "give me one good reason why you should not go back to the school. What do you think your parents are going to say about all this?"

"That is why I came here. I hoped after I had told Nikolas how terrible the school is and how unhappy I am there he might talk to Mama and Papa and persuade them to let me come back home. They listen to Nikolas, you know how persuasive he can be"

"I am afraid you are out of luck young man" said Julius, "Nikolas is on guard duty, and will be all night and you cannot wait here to talk to him"

Georg looked devastated at the news of his absent brother. Julius told him to have a wash while he thought about what he should do. He did have some sympathy for Georg, he was obviously desperately unhappy at the school, so unhappy that he had run away, despite the repercussions such an act could have. He did not want to march him straight back to Frau Manzova, as he knew her first recourse would be to immediately return him to his school. He felt that Nikolas would have probably agreed to Georg's request to speak to their parents, so in the absence of his friend, he reluctantly felt that it was now his duty to liaise for Georg, though he was not looking forward to the task. He looked at his watch, and realized he was already late for Irmy's soiree. Irmy, why had he not thought of it before? He would take Georg to Irmy's. She would know what the best course of action would be. She was a woman and women understood that sort of thing.

Irmy was shocked to see Georg and even more alarmed by his story. She did not appreciate her brother's reason for bringing him to her house, especially when Julius undiplomatically added his thoughts on her capability of handling the situation better than he because of her sex. However her compassionate nature took over as she berated Julius for not giving Georg something to eat as the

236

child looked half starved. She took him down to the kitchen so that cook could give him some food while she found out more about Georg's situation. Georg looked as though he had found his guardian angel as he followed Irmy out of the room, regarding her with almost hero worship with his big blue eyes.

Julius had been aware of a young woman in the room, had even been introduced to her on his arrival, but had not even listened to her name in the confusion of Georg's situation. Now that Irmy had left the room he turned to her and offered his apologies for upsetting her evening. The young girl smiled, "do you always pick up young strays in the street and bring them home to your sister?" she laughed,

"I try not to let it happen too often, Irmy gets upset if I bring too many"

They both laughed and for the first time Julius noticed how pretty his dining companion was. She was small and very dainty with a heart shaped face that held the most unusual, mesmeric, sparkling gray eyes, which complimented her shining black hair that was dressed on top of her head. When she laughed she displayed a perfect set of small white teeth. Her whole face displayed a merriment and devilment that appealed to Julius, but it was her eyes that captivated him, he had never seen such lovely eyes on a woman, apart from Josef's mother, and he preferred not to think about those.

"My name is Erika Lehmannova, we were introduced, but I think your mind was elsewhere at the time. I work as a volunteer nurse at the hospital, that is how I know Irmy and Herr Doktor Beck"

Julius started to chat to Erika who had seated herself on one of the sofas. He sat himself on a seat opposite her and spent a very pleasant few minutes chatting to Erika before Irmy returned to the room, dressed in her coat and hat and in a great hurry.

"I am really sorry about this Erika, I am going to see Frau Manzova. It is at times like this that I wish more people had a telephone, but I think it is better that I go and see Georg's mother in person"

Richard had had a telephone installed in the house so that the hospital could contact him easily, but the Manz household had not taken to the new invention, and, like

Julius' own mother, had so far resisted having one in their house.

"I have spoken to Georg" continued Irmy, "he is a very unhappy boy and I hope I can persuade Frau Manzova to change her mind about his present situation, but I feel I should see her straight away in case the school should contact her about Georg's disappearance"

"I am really sorry to have disrupted your evening, Irmy, would you like me to accompany you to the Manz's?"

"Do not worry yourself Julius, it will be better if I go on my own" said Irmy, "You did the right thing bringing Georg to me first. I think I can present the situation better than if you had arrived on their doorstep with Georg. Georg is eating in the kitchen with cook and then Martha has been instructed to give him a bath and put him to bed. I think it is better that he stays the night here, before confronting his parents"

"Would you like me to see Fraulein Lehmannova home?" asked Julius, confused by the abrupt ending to his evening.

"Good heavens, no. If it is all right with you Erika, and if you can stand my brother's company for a while, I have told cook to carry on with the meal. The dining room is ready for you and Richard is due home at any moment. I hope not to be too long, so I will join you later. Are the arrangements satisfactory to you both?"

Erika smiled in agreement, and Julius, who was feeling very hungry, decided that a meal shared with Erika Lehmannova was a very pleasing thought.

"One last thing Erika" said Irmy as she was leaving the room, "do not be taken in by Julius' charm. Remember what I warned you about him" and with a delighted laugh she quickly vacated the room.

Julius, feeling a little embarrassed, turned to Erika and said, "would you like a glass of sherry while we wait for Richard, you can tell me everything my sister has told you about me. Then I will refute everything she has said"

The evening was a great success, Julius found Erika a very enjoyable companion. Richard had called from the hospital to say that he had been delayed, so Julius and Erika began the meal on their own. They were enjoying their dessert when Irmy arrived and Julius found himself feeling annoyed that his sister had come home so early and had rather spoiled the ambience of a very agreeable evening. Irmy did not notice the significant looks that passed between her two guests as she related her audience with Frau Manzova. Georg's mother had been very upset with her younger son's antics, but after Irmy had explained everything to her she had calmed down somewhat and agreed to listen to Georg's story in the morning when Irmy was to take him home.

Whilst Irmy was telling Julius that she thought she had persuaded Frau Mayer not to send Georg back to his boarding school Richard returned from the hospital, looking tired and drawn. Irmy at once repeated the story to her husband, whilst she arranged for some food to be brought to him. Julius could still feel Erika's gaze on him, but noticed she had become somewhat subdued as soon as Richard had entered the room.

 It was now getting late and as he was on duty early the next morning, Julius excused himself, whilst offering to escort Erika to her home. He felt Irmy and Richard were both tired and Richard seemed relieved that he would not have to entertain his guests for much longer. As Erika lived only a few streets away from Irmy's house they decided to walk the short distance to her home.

The night was very cold, but there was a full moon and the stars were evident in the dark night sky. As they walked along their breath appeared in great clouds of mist and disappeared into the night air. Julius decided he liked Erika Lehmannova very much and was determined to see her again. Walking her home he tried to think of a way of approaching the subject of a further meeting. She appeared distracted so he asked her, "is there something wrong. You became very quiet at the end of the evening"

Erika carried on walking, but lifted her lovely eyes to his as she said, "no I am well. I had a lovely evening, it is just, ...I cannot tell you, for I know you will laugh at me"

"I promise not to laugh, and that is a soldier's promise" he smiled.

"Well please do not tell Irmy, but I am always a little frightened in Herr Doktor Beck's presence. He is a very nice man and well thought of at the hospital, but he always seems so austere to me. I have often wondered that Irmy........."

She did not finish her sentence and Julius could see her blushing in the moonlight as she realized she had said too much.

Julius smiled, "you were wondering how someone as lovely and effervescent as my sister could have married Richard, am I right? Oh Fraulein Lehmannova, do not look so pained, you should see your face at this moment, it is quite a picture. It is an honest question, and if you can keep a secret I will tell you something. When I first met Richard, I really did not like him very much, and I thought he was far too old and serious for Irmy. But over the years I have come to realize that they adore each other and are well suited. The more I have come to know Richard, the more I am aware that he is a very caring, honest and honorable man and whilst I know we will never be close, I respect him and know he will always look after Irmy. At first I think he may give the appearance of a dour, somber man, but I assure you Richard Beck is a lot deeper than that. I would say to you if you know Irmy at all well, you know that she would never have married a man who was boring or whom she did not love"

"I suppose not, I had never thought of it like that, you have given me a lot to think about Lieutenant Mayer, and I promise not to tell a soul your secret. I hope Irmy will invite me to her house to dine again. I nearly did not accept tonight as I was so worried about having dinner with Herr Doktor Beck"

"So why did you accept?"

Erika smiled a lovely, coy smile, as with her eyes lowered she replied, "the nurses at the hospital told me I would be insane to turn down the opportunity of dining with Irmy's handsome brother, so they pressed me to accept the invitation"

Julius laughed as he said, "I do not think I will ask whether I lived up to your expectations, I would be too afraid that I would regret your answer"

Erika looked at him slyly as she said, "I am sure you are well aware of what my answer would be, I would not have thought of you as a modest person"

Erika giggled as she suddenly turned up some stone steps, leaving Julius open-mouthed at her audacity, "This is where I live, thank you for a lovely evening, Lieutenant Mayer, and for walking me home, it was very kind of you"

"Julius" replied Julius, rather dazed.

"I am sorry?"

"Julius, please call me Julius, that is my name. I wonder if I may see you again, Fraulein Lehmannova, then you will not have to worry if you are invited back to my sister's house or not"

Now it was Erika's turn to be dumbstruck as she stuttered, "yes, I, I would like that very much, thank you. I hope I will see you again soon, and please, call me Erika. Goodnight. Julius" and she hurriedly entered her front door.

Julius returned to the barracks feeling elated, but disconcerted. He was not sure if Erika Lehmannova liked him or not. He decided, as he pulled up his coat collar against the icy wind that had started to blow, that he would never understand women as long as he lived, and thought that maybe that was their strongest attraction.

Julius was woken by Nikolas returning from his night duty. He told him about Georg and the antics of the night before.

"The stupid young fool. What is he playing at?" ranted Nikolas.

"Steady on Nikolas" interrupted Julius, "Georg was in a hell of a state last night, he is a very unhappy boy. You would have felt compassion for him if you had seen him. Let him tell you his side of the story, before you make assumptions. Irmy is taking him to your mothers this morning, your mother will do what is best for him. She has agreed to postpone Georg's return to boarding school after Irmy told her his story"

"I suppose I had better get round there this morning" said Nikolas, "this is all I needed after a night duty. Thank God Papa is away at the moment, I do not think he would be as understanding as my mother. Thank you for helping him last night, I am sorry if it disrupted your evening"

Julius smiled, "as a matter of fact it greatly helped my evening" and he proceeded to tell Nikolas about Erika Lehmannova, after promising Nikolas not to say a word to Irmy if he should see her that morning.

"Well I never" whistled Nikolas, "Julius has been caught at last. I knew a female would manage to captivate you eventually"

"I have not even taken her out yet, do not presume too much, Nikolas. She is just a nice young lady who I passed a very pleasant evening with. It has happened before you know"

"I know" said Nikolas, "but never before have you had such a lovesick, daft look on your face while you were talking about someone"

Julius ignored his friends teasing, but had to admit he still felt a warm glow of pleasure as he thought about the previous evening.

After his duties were over Julius returned to his room to find Nikolas lying on his bed, staring at the ceiling, looking very unhappy.

"You had better get dressed soon, or you will be late for duty" Julius reminded him.

When Nikolas did not respond to him he went over to his bed and looked down at his friend. He asked with some alarm, "is it Georg, what has happened?"

Nikolas wore such a bleak, despairing look on his face that Julius feared his friend had received some very bad news. Letting out a large, unhappy sigh and still staring up at the ceiling Nikolas replied in a low voice, "Georg is fine. The young scoundrel has persuaded Mama to let him stay in Prague and return to his old school and he promises to be the perfect son from now on, though how long that will last will be interesting to see"

Julius returned to his bed and sat down on its edge. Knowing Nikolas' moods he knew his friend wanted to say something, but was trying to pluck up the courage to speak. Suddenly Nikolas sat up and swung his legs over the side of the bed so he was facing Julius. He did not say a word but sat there swinging his legs back and forth, staring down at the floor, looking like a lost and lonely little boy.

"What is it Nikolas, we have always been able to talk to each other, can I help, is it Suse?"

Nikolas laughed, a pathetic contemptuous laugh, "if only it was, then my life would be easy" he looked up at Julius, "if I tell you something, will you promise that it will go no further than these four walls. I need you to promise me Julius"

Julius nodded, it was obviously a week for confessing truths after last night with Erika. Nikolas sighed again, then began to talk, still looking down, not able to look Julius in the eye.

"I cannot help it Julius. I thought I had gotten over her. I thought time would make it all go away, I thought Suse might help me forget her, but she hasn't" Julius, with a sense of foreboding, knew who Nikolas was talking about, Irmy.

"I knew today, as soon as I walked into my mother's sitting room and she was sitting there. So lovely, so full of concern for Georg, for my family. I wanted to shout, you could have

242

been mine, part of my family, you could have been sitting there as my mother's daughter-in-law, as my wife" Nikolas looked up at Julius, "do you understand, Julius?"

Julius nodded at his friend's imploring face, he understood only too well. He also understood that Irmy's concern was borne out of affection for the Manz family, but it was not the sort of affection that Nikolas craved for, and never would be, but how could he explain this to his friend without hurting him? He knew Nikolas harbored feelings for Irmy, but he had thought that over the years, and with the help of Suse, he had gotten over the love he had had for her, but it was evident that this was not the case. He could not think of what to say to Nikolas, because nothing he could say would help or console him. Irmy was a married woman, who loved her husband, and even if she were free it was not certain that she would ever have thought of Nikolas as anything more than a good friend, but how could he say that to his friend, who sat in such abject misery before him?

Julius was thankful that Nikolas did not seem to want a reply as he jumped up and pronounced he must get ready for his night duty. When he had washed and donned his uniform Nikolas said to Julius, "thank you for listening. I know there is nothing you can say, that there is no happy conclusion to all this, but it is good to know I can talk to somebody about it. Somebody who will not criticize or chastise me for my stupid thoughts. That is the best thing about you Julius, through all my stupid ravings about Irmy you have never judged me or told me to pull myself together, like so many other people would have done. I have always felt you had some sympathy for me and know what I am going through"

"I know" said Julius quietly, "I know, more than you realize, and I hope that is of some help to you my friend. You know I will always be here for you"

After Nikolas had left for his duty, Julius sat on his bed for a long time thinking about his friend. When he realized there would never be any conclusions to the thoughts that were racing through his mind, he retired and fell asleep where he dreamt of Erika Lehmannova and her beautiful eyes.

XIX

Because of the parade, Colonel Reichart ordered extra drill duties and rehearsals as he believed the men were not practiced enough. Julius noticed the men becoming more rebellious as the Colonel drove them harder. Whilst he sympathized with the soldiers and thought their treatment unjustified, his dilemma was not to show he was in agreement with them. As an officer he had to follow the commands of his senior officers, however much he disagreed with their orders.

The atmosphere in the barracks was becoming hostile, but the men reserved their animosity for the senior officers as it was apparent that the junior officers, such as Julius and Nikolas, were being punished as much as the ordinary men. Julius chose not to hear the mutterings of his men, mainly derogatory remarks about the colonel and usually alluding to his parentage, but he felt uneasy at the low morale that was prevalent.

Due to his extra duties, all leave and passes to the city were cancelled so Julius had to send a note to Erika, explaining his absence, and hoping she would understand. "She is learning very quickly what it is like to be escorted by a soldier" offered a gloomy Nikolas, who had cheered up somewhat since his meeting with Irmy, but who was not in a mood to sympathize with his friend, who was becoming impatient to see Erika again.

The procession on the day went perfectly. Julius could not have asked more of his men and even Colonel Reichart, on their return to the barracks, had to begrudgingly compliment them on their behavior. Julius had looked for Erika in the crowd, but had not seen her. He hoped she had been there, Phantom had looked his very best that day and behaved immaculately, something that Julius could not always rely on with such an unpredictable beast. It had cheered him to think that there might have been someone like Erika watching in the crowd, waiting to see him.

That evening Julius sent a note to Erika's house, requesting her company for dinner the next week in a restaurant in the city. He was pleased to receive a prompt reply, written with a dainty hand, accepting his invitation.

He dressed with care that evening and presented himself at the door of her house promptly at seven o'clock. A maid

244

led him into a tastefully furnished, large room where he met Erika's mother, a handsome woman who her daughter greatly resembled. Julius was touched to see Erika blushing as she entered the room, looking as lovely as he had remembered her. Julius had hired a carriage for the evening and he was glad to find that they soon settled back into the relaxed companionship that he had so enjoyed in Irmy's house. The evening was a great success, and when he escorted Erika back to her house he was rewarded with a delicate kiss before she left the carriage and waved goodbye from the door of her house. The evening was the first of many over the next few weeks leading up to Christmas.

Christmas was to be a large family occasion at the Mayer household. All the Mayer men had gained leave for the Yuletide, and as this was to be Franz's last Christmas as a single man everyone looked forward to being together again.

Papa, Franz and Karl all arrived the day before Christmas Eve. Julius was relieved to see his father looking better than he had done on his last visit home. Soon all three brothers were reverting to their childhood days, ribbing each other and playing silly jokes until their mother cried out in despair that her sons were never going to grow up.

Christmas Eve was spent with the Manz family. Mama had become close friends with Nikolas' mother, who had been a strong support for Frau Mayer in her first lonely days in Prague. The only blot on the festivities was the absence of Nikolas. Although entitled to Christmas leave that year, he had offered to work as he did not want to be near Irmy, or Richard for that matter. Julius knew he could not have borne seeing Irmy happy and radiant beside her husband. Georg of course was there, enjoying the attention of being the only child in the household and following Irmy around with determined adulation as he still saw her as his savior. Georg had returned to his school where he was supposedly being a model pupil, though Nikolas commented that he wondered how long it would last.

It was a very happy time, and after exchanging their gifts that evening they all went to St. Vitus Cathedral to celebrate Midnight Mass. The next day, Christmas Day, Mama declared that there was to be an embargo on any talk of military matters. Whilst she was pleased that her husband liked Colonel Manz she was driven to distraction by the fact that whenever the two men got together all they did was discuss the army. They would sit in the corner, talking very seriously and occasionally looking round to make sure no one was listening to them. Julius found this unnerving, as though they were discussing state secrets. He had asked Karl of the situation in Vienna, but he had dismissively said it had not much changed since last they had spoken. Karl was very pessimistic of the army's position, saying that the Balkans, especially Serbia was still a seething cauldron of discontent, and he would not be surprised if the government did not soon try to suppress the situation in some way. Franz dismissed Karl as being too politically motivated in Vienna. He still saw the army as the backbone of the Empire, and the Empire and the monarchy as the all-powerful nation it had always been. The diverse assessments of the two brothers led to heated arguments, with Julius frequently being brought in as the mediator. Privately, Julius longed to think like Franz did, but unhappily believed that Karl was nearer to the truth in his pessimism.

Franz disclosed that he had received orders to report for military maneuvers in Bosnia early next year. This statement left Karl looking stunned and horrified, and Julius noticed that Karl quickly asked his father for a private interview, after which they both left his father's study looking very concerned. When he asked Karl why the maneuvers so worried him Karl just shrugged his shoulders and said he was probably over-reacting to the news but added that he did not think that Serbia would take kindly to the Austrian Army being so close to them. Julius did not see what the trouble was, there had often been military exercises in the Balkans, but he was unnerved by his father's and Karl's reactions to them.

Julius spent time at Erika's house during his leave, she had a close family, with two younger sisters, who all welcomed Julius, and Erika met his brothers, who both took great delight in informing Erika of all Julius' past misdemeanors and shortcomings. He even found himself slightly jealous, an emotion he had never encountered before, when he heard Erika remark to Irmy, "How lovely to have grown up with three such handsome brothers" He was careful to watch Erika as she conversed with his brothers, especially Karl, who had now regained his roguish good looks. He was happy to note that although Karl tried to flirt shamelessly with Erika, she only regarded him with the same politeness that she bestowed on all his family, and kept her smiles only for him.

Looking back on that week with his family Julius could only remember one unhappy incident. All the family were gathered for dinner, including Richard and Irmy. They were discussing Georg and laughing at how Irmy had gained a shadow whenever he was around as he was so obvious in his adoration of her. Papa looked up from his plate and said to his daughter, "You are so good with children, Irmy, is it not about time that you and Richard presented your mother and I with some grandchildren. I would like that"

Afterwards Julius was sure that his sister's reaction had been one of absolute horror, but realizing that all eyes were on her the look quickly changed to anger, and scraping back her chair she wildly looked about her and then rushed out of the room. Frau Mayer stood up to follow her daughter, but Richard was quicker to the door, assuring Mama that it was nothing and he would find Irmy. The room was left in an awkward silence with nobody knowing what to say. The men carried on eating but the silence was broken by Frau Mayer rebuking her husband, "How could you have been so unkind to Irmy. How embarrassing for her. How could you have been so tactless?"

Colonel Mayer looked at his wife in complete astonishment. "But you said exactly the same thing to me when we were dressing this evening. That is what put the idea into my mind"

Frau Mayer looked at her husband reproachfully as she said, "I may have said it in the privacy of our boudoir, but certainly not in front of Irmy's husband and her brothers, I really do not understand you at times"

Julius looked down at his meal as he was tempted to point out to Mama that she had often brought up the subject of grandchildren, and many a time in front of anybody who was listening to her, but he knew not to cross his mother when she was in a mood, so remained silent. Papa looked out from under his eyebrows in a silent appeal to his sons on the complexity of women, but chose not to say any more.

Irmy and Richard returned to the room some time later. Irmy apologized for her rudeness and sat down to finish the meal with her usual good humor restored, but Julius was sure that Irmy had been crying and Richard looked very strained for the rest of the evening. Julius knew Irmy was determined to finish her nursing training, and wondered if Richard would have liked to have children now, after all he was not as young as Irmy. He hoped the subject was not causing any tension between the two of them.

On New Year's Eve the Manz's gave a party to celebrate the New Year. Nikolas could not avoid attending his own parent's party, so was a reluctant guest, although Suse accompanied him. Julius and Erika had been to the theatre with Nikolas and Suse and the two women had got along famously, so much so that they had attended a meeting together to hear Professor Masaryk speak. Julius and Nikolas had not joined Suse and Erika at the meeting as they were serving soldiers and could not attend what was ostensibly a political meeting. Both Julius and Nikolas had been interested to hear the girl's reactions to Masaryk's oration when they met them later. Masaryk had been a philosophy professor at the university in Prague. He was a popular figure in Bohemia, who was esteemed because he was truly independent of any Habsburg influence. Where other leaders seemed independent until offered lucrative government positions, Masaryk never succumbed to this bribery and thereby earned the respect of the people and, begrudgingly, the government. Masaryk was also unique in that although he passionately believed in the independence of his country, he still upheld a belief in the Habsburg monarchy and always talked about a united Habsburg Empire. When Erika and Suse met Julius and Nikolas after their meeting they had obviously been impressed by the man and by his oration. The only subject that worried Julius was Masaryk's call that there had to be a moral change within the Habsburg Monarchy and government in order to preserve itself as the situation could not remain as it was. Masaryk's words left Julius with a chill in his heart as he remembered virtually the exact same words spoken by his brother Karl.

The party was very enjoyable, although Julius noticed that whenever Irmy and Richard appeared close to them Nikolas managed to maneuver himself away from their presence. He hoped that nobody else noticed the coincidence, but as he knew he was the only person privy to Nikolas' confidences decided that nobody else present would have any notion of the emotional battle his friend must be waging within himself.

Just before midnight all the guests assembled in the Manz's large sitting room to await the New Year. Erika was on the other side of the room, talking to Julius' mother, who had taken enormously to Erika. This pleased Julius but he became rather tired that his mother thought Erika the perfect candidate for a new daughter-in-law. Frau Mayer took every opportunity of hinting at the possibility of such an event until Julius thought he was going to scream at her unending innuendoes. Irmy thought the whole situation highly amusing after all the years that her mother had harassed her with the hope of Irmy marrying. "Now you know how I felt" laughed Irmy mischievously as Julius wanted to disappear through the floor at another of his mother's embarrassing statements in front of himself and Erika.

Erika always took his mother's eccentricities with good humor, smiling sweetly but not replying to any of Frau Mayer's probing questions. Julius himself was ambivalent on the subject. Whilst he knew his mother's interest was aroused, as Erika was the only woman he had brought home to meet his mother, he himself was unsure of his feelings for her. That he liked her a lot was certain, but was he in love with her? that was another thing. The grim specter of the Countess was always in the back of his mind, playing with his emotions and creating unwelcome comparisons to Erika. He enjoyed her company, was at ease with her, he desired her, but not with the overwhelming feelings that he felt he should have if he had met his companion for life. There was not the thrill that he wanted to envelop him at the thought of her, and whilst he knew she had strong feelings for him, he was not sure he could reciprocate such a strong passion. He would have liked to have discussed his feelings with Nikolas but felt it was an undiplomatic subject to broach after Nikolas' revelations about Irmy. He had thought about asking Irmy's advice, but could not discuss his innermost feelings with a woman, so for the moment he decided to ignore his dilemma, enjoy Erika's company and see what fate would provide for him.

As the clocks began to chime the twelve bells to herald the New Year, Erika walked around the room and joined Julius. On the twelfth stroke of the clock's chimes everybody raised their glasses and welcomed in the New Year. Julius turned to Erika and they toasted each other, both staring into each other's eyes. Julius gaze never left

Erika's face as they drank their glasses of champagne, both reluctant to spoil their shared moment of togetherness, even though the room was full of noisy, happy people, all celebrating the new year.

"To us" said Julius.

"To us" replied Erika, "Happy New Year Julius. I hope this will be a momentous year. Full of happiness and love for everybody, and let us hope we will all achieve what we are dreaming of"

As Erika lifted her glass, Julius was unsure of her meaning, but was slightly unnerved to observe the deep warmth and affection in her lovely eyes.

"Happy New Year" said Julius, "and welcome to 1914"

XX

In February Mama, Irmy and Richard travelled to Styria for Franz's wedding. Although Papa was to join them there. Karl and Julius had been unable to obtain leave for their brother's wedding.

Mama and Irmy came back with high praise for Gretha, whom they had found utterly charming and who obviously adored Franz. Julius looked at the wedding photographs of his brother with some envy. Franz and Gretha looked so happy and contented that no-one looking at the picture could deny how in love they were. Their happiness projected itself out of the photographs. Julius was struck by the difference between these pictures and the ones taken at Karl's wedding. He was glad for his brother, Julius had always been close to Franz, and was delighted to see that his brother had obtained the partner he so richly deserved. On her return Frau Mayer was even more determined to see her youngest son settled into marriage, it seemed to be her only topic of conversation whenever Julius went to see his mother.

Julius had received orders to attend another munitions course in Vienna that summer. He was pleased to be going back to the city again, mainly because it meant he would be able to see Josef, but uncertain of his feelings if he should meet the Countess again.

Josef and Viktor still wrote regularly to Julius and Nikolas. Julius looked forward to the arrival of their letters, especially Josef's, which were always full of his dry wit and sense of humor. Josef's letters were long but very interesting, describing his social life in Vienna and his army career. Whenever Julius read his friend's letters he would wonder at the futility of being posted in Prague. Although he loved the city itself far more than Vienna, and enjoyed living near his family, Josef was much more aware of current events and army politics, as Karl and Papa were, and Julius felt he was missing out, that he was always the last person to hear of any news.

Viktor had written from Graz that he felt much the same as Julius, and it was evident that the dissent within the army was far more prevalent away from the Empire's capital than within it. In fact whenever Julius would mention in a letter to Josef of his concern at morale within the army,

Josef would always reply with some incredulity that Julius should believe that such a thing existed. Nikolas reasoned that although it was probably exciting to be in Vienna it did tend to give army personnel a very insular view of themselves.

In March the Austro-Hungarian Army announced that it was to start military maneuvers in Bosnia. At the same time it was disclosed that the heir to Emperor Franz Josef, the Archduke Franz Ferdinand and his wife, would make an official visit to Bosnia and its capital Sarajevo in June, where, as Army Inspector of the Imperial troops he would see how the preparations for the exercises were advancing. Many saw the Archduke's visit as highly provocative and as a warning to Serbians and their aspirations for autonomy from the Empire.

After his honeymoon Franz wrote that he would be joining the maneuvers in Bosnia, as was Viktor.

In May Julius and Nikolas travelled to Vienna for their course. Julius found the timing opportune. For several weeks now, ever since she had returned from Franz's wedding, his mother had been hinting of his attachment to Erika. Everybody seemed to think that their engagement was imminent and even Irmy had started to drop unsubtle innuendoes every time she saw her brother. Julius perceived these revelations with an air of despondency. All he could see before him was a long corridor of inevitability. Engagement, marriage, children, army and the prospect did not fill him with the elation and hopes for the future that it should. He knew this was because he was unsure of his feelings for Erika, but as the months progressed and Erika was becoming more and more affectionate towards him, he felt trapped, as if he was heading along a path prescribed for him by the people around him, rather than one of his own choosing. He had tried to discuss his feelings with Nikolas, but his friend did not understand his predicament. "No one is forcing you into marriage Julius. You must do what you think is right. Look at me, my mother is always asking about Suse and myself, but I just choose to ignore her interference"

Julius smiled to himself. Erika had told him that Suse would marry Nikolas tomorrow, if he would only ask her, but she kept her silence rather than frightening Nikolas away. Julius reflected this was typical of Nikolas. Although the most caring man in the world, he went through life sometimes oblivious of the most apparent situations under his own nose. Julius believed that Nikolas' circumstances were very similar to his own, he just was unaware of it. Julius felt a great burden of guilt, he did not want Erika to believe that he was about to ask for her hand in marriage and he did not want to hurt her feelings. He enjoyed her company and truly loved her, but he knew he did not love her enough. He felt that whilst he was in Vienna, he might be able to assess the situation calmly and decide on his true feelings on his return.

Vienna was quiet as many people had left the city, but Josef was still on duty and met up with them shortly after their arrival. It was wonderful to see Josef again, he looked more handsome than ever, his maturity sitting well on his shoulders. Once again Julius and Nikolas were invited to stay with Josef and his mother after their duties ended in Vienna. Although Julius was not sure of his feelings on seeing Josef's mother, he felt he could not refuse the invitation without proffering a valid reason, which at the time he could not think of.

The course was very interesting, artillery and guns were advancing in design by the day and the new information that Julius and Nikolas had to absorb sent their brains whirling as they concentrated on the intricacies of munitions, from small hand held pistols to enormous field guns. Julius had not realized how much he had needed this course. All his previous knowledge became superfluous to the new information that they were regaled with. It also made both Julius and Nikolas aware of how the Austro-Hungarian army was behind in the production of guns and ammunition.

Their course tutor, an irascible old Habsburg major, evidently took great offence at the fact that his pleas for modernization were ignored and so proceeded to regale his students on the army's shortcomings. He compared the advancement of guns available to the other European armies compared to their own, even announcing that the Habsburg armaments expenditure was drastically less than that of their neighbors, perhaps as little as a quarter of other countries. Whilst most of the officers dismissed the old man's ramblings as those of an old fool, affected by his lack of advancement in the army, Julius felt uncomfortable at his diatribes. False or not, his pronouncements were treasonous and alarming. The old man however was a good teacher, when he was not ranting and raving, and Julius and Nikolas learnt a lot during the course, not only about their own armaments and weaponry, but those of other armies.

Erika wrote often of how much she missed him and was waiting for his return to Prague, but Julius had to admit that he did not often think of her and hoped that this was because of the intensity and hard work of his course.

They saw Josef often and one night after a sumptuous meal in one of the finest Viennese restaurants, they sat back in their seats, replete with the good food and wine, and relaxed over their Pharisaer, a strong black coffee with cream on top, served with a small glass of rum. Josef was regaling them with the stories of his latest female conquests. Although Josef had a very cavalier attitude to women he had a very entertaining way of recalling his exploits so that one could not help but laugh at his arrogance and not take offence. That his stories were often filled with half truths there was no doubt, but it was also true that Josef had a dazzling affect on women, where his mere presence would have females behaving quite irrationally in front of him in order to catch his eye. Although Josef asked about Erika, Julius felt it was disloyal to discuss her in such company, so would always change the subject.

"So you have not found the woman of your dreams Josef?" asked Julius, "I cannot wait until a young lady steals your heart. And if she should throw it back in your face, I hope I am there to watch it. It will be a spectacular sight"

Josef laughed good-naturedly, "Even I would like to see that, no I think I am destined for greater things myself"

"What do you mean?" mocked Nikolas, "Do not tell me, they have found out that you are the bastard son of Franz Josef, and soon to be our new Emperor! no, I know, they have promoted you to general, the youngest general in the Imperial Army, just do not forget your friends in your new high office, sir!"

Josef ignored Nikolas' sarcasm as he became serious and said, "No I have thought about this a lot lately. Do you not think we were saved on the Grossglockner for a reason, that somehow we have been given a blessing from above to go on and maybe make a difference to this world?"

All three men were silent for a while, reliving that awful night on the mountain. Since then they had all had a higher appreciation of life, thankful for their situation, but saved for a special reason? the thought had never occurred to Julius and so he told Josef. Josef shrugged his shoulders and, with his seriousness gone, dismissed the conversation saying, "well you may think me stupid, but I honestly think that, and one day I will prove it to you"

The rest of the evening continued in idle conversation and the three men parted in good spirits back to their respective barracks. On the way home Nikolas asked Julius if he understood what Josef had been talking about in the restaurant. "Well I think I understood, but I cannot say I agree with him. I do not think it was divine intervention that saved us that night, but sheer good luck and Viktor. It all sounds a bit too deep for me and sounded very unlike Josef" "I agree" said Nikolas, then his face erupted into a wide smile as he added, "God help Vienna, Josef had a big enough ego before all this, the last thing needed was for him to believe he was destined for greater things!"

During the month of June the heat in the city was unbearable. The city sweltered and Julius and Nikolas found it difficult to concentrate on their lectures as they sweated in the close and stuffy classrooms.

Late in June Julius and Nikolas were sitting in the classroom trying to pay attention. The night before the two men had been out with Josef and had dined well and drunk a large amount of alcohol. The lecturer was a particularly boring man whose voice droned on in a constant tone making him sound like a honey bee, looking for some pollen. Sitting at the back of the classroom Julius rested his head on his hand, trying to pay attention. His head hurt from his drinking the night before, and with the heat of the classroom overcoming him he was drifting off to sleep. He woke with a start as Nikolas was digging him in the ribs.

"Shut up you idiot" hissed Nikolas quietly "You are muttering in your sleep"

Julius sat upright, trying to concentrate but within a few minutes he felt the weight of his eyelids pushing down over his eyes as he desperately tried to keep awake.

There was a crash as the classroom door was opened and a young corporal entered the room looking highly excited, his eyes wide as he whispered to the lecturer. Julius could tell the news was important and felt instantly wide-awake. The corporal dashed out of the room, off to spread his news and the officers looked expectantly at their lecturer who stood before them, deathly white and obviously shocked.

"Gentlemen, I have sad news for you" he began gravely, "Today, the heir to the throne, the Archduke Franz Ferdinand and his wife have been assassinated. I feel in these sad circumstances that classes will be ended for the day. Good day gentlemen"

There was a furor of mayhem and noise as the officers began bombarding the unfortunate lecturer with questions. The lecturer put up his hands as he tried to silence them.

"Gentlemen, please, I know as much of this as you do. I do know that the Archduke was visiting Sarajevo in Bosnia today, so I presume that is where he was when he died, beyond that I suggest we wait until we hear more official news, good afternoon" whereupon the man picked up his notes and vacated the room.

"Sarajevo?" shouted one of the officers, "That means those damned Slavs, it must have been them. The government will have to do something about them now. The Emperor will insist on it"

There followed several minutes of heated argument and analysis until they had exhausted all the outcomes possible in the situation and every Slav had been condemned to death in as many ways as they could think of. The group dispersed and Julius and Nikolas returned to their rooms, ruminating on the day's events.

"Do you think the situation could be serious?" asked Julius of his friend.

"I think it is as serious as the government and our Emperor wants it to be. Ever since the Balkan Wars several factions have been looking for an excuse to get back at Serbia, and unfortunately this may be the one they were looking for"

"I think quite a lot of people will be thanking the Serbs, the Archduke was not the most popular man in the country" said Julius.

"Well that maybe so" replied Nikolas, "but I have the dreadful feeling that the assassination of the Archduke is going to lead to some very turbulent weeks ahead, although I hope to God I am wrong"

But Nikolas was not wrong. The whole country was up in arms at the assassination of a member of the Royal family at the hands of a Serbian dissident. Over the next few days the circumstances of the murder became apparent through government statements and newspaper articles.

The events of the day in Sarajevo did not exactly cover the Habsburg officials in the city with any glory. It emerged that despite the anti-government feeling in the Balkans security for the royal party had been virtually non-existent and there had already been one attempt on the Archduke's life when a young Bosnian called Gavrilo Princip had shot Franz Ferdinand and his wife.

The next few weeks Vienna was in uproar and a showdown between Austria-Hungary and Serbia seemed inevitable. Julius' course continued, although lectures were frequently cancelled and haphazard as the military began preparing for a possible conflict. Rumors were rife within the barracks, every soldier had a different story to relate or a different opinion to extol on the future plans of the government and the army.

Everywhere was confusion and every time Julius tried to see his father Colonel Mayer would have to cancel their meeting. Julius decided this was not a good omen and by the second week of July arranged to meet Karl as he was desperate to receive some genuine news and not have to listen to the wild rumors that were circulating everywhere.

As before, Julius' reaction to possible action was mixed. He knew that most of his anxiety then had been because he was a young inexperienced cadet, but now he was a twenty four year old soldier who was trained for conflict and believed himself ready for it. He did not feel scared, but he still felt a sense of foreboding for the future, believing that his beloved army may not be as ready or as able for war as so many people believed.

Most of his fellow officers were jubilant at the news and preparing themselves for a glorious fight and Julius hoped they were right in their optimism. They were already saying that if they did go to war the conflict would be over in months, if not weeks. The entire city appeared to be attending Mass as the churches and cathedrals were packed, with citizens praying for a victory even before war was declared.

When Julius met Karl in his rooms he feared the worst. Karl looked tired and strained and told Julius he could only spare him a little time as he had to report back to Army headquarters within the hour. After offering Julius a drink Karl slumped into a chair and appeared to be gathering his thoughts as he said, "So, little brother, I presume you are here because you want to hear what is going on. I have never met anyone as tenacious as you" he looked at his younger brother and then asked, "do you want me to tell you the truth, or would you rather I put it in the veiled term of the diplomat I am so quickly becoming?"

Julius smiled, he could never imagine Karl as a diplomat, but that was obviously the role he was playing these days, "what do you think?" he asked.

"All right, honesty it is. You understand, I suppose, that however much we like to convince ourselves and the people of this country, we could not attack the Serbs without the backing of the Germans?" Julius nodded, he had understood that from the beginning, however much he had hated the idea.

"The Emperor and our government are hell bent on confrontation. Whether it is because of the sad loss of the Archduke, or just an excuse to start a conflict with the Serbs, I will leave you to decide, but I think you know the answer to that one. Last week meetings were held in Berlin and both the Kaiser and Chancellor Hollweg have promised to support us if there should be war with Serbia" Julius swallowed deeply, he knew in those few words that their fate was sealed, with the backing of the Germans he knew his country would have no obstacle to going to war.

"Are they not worried about the Russians, or even the French or British?" he asked Karl.

"To be honest I do not think they have even considered the French and British particularly. Russia is their big worry, but they are hoping the Tsar will be so disgusted by the royal assassination that he will not support Serbia and therefore not join the conflict"

"Do you think that is true?"

"I cannot say, Julius. The Russians have always supported the Serbs, but the Tsar must be shocked by the killing of a member of the Habsburg family, let us hope his shock lasts long enough to prevent him supporting the Serbs. The government is drafting an ultimatum for the Serbian government as we speak, with any luck that will scare them enough to accede to our requests and thereby avoid a confrontation. If not, then I think we will be at war"

"And then?"

Karl grimly laughed, "I am not all seeing Julius, I cannot foresee the future. I am just presenting you with the facts as I see them, after that, who knows. There is just one more thing I think you should know. If the Serbs do not

258

accede, then our troops have been primed to be mobilized at very short notice"

Julius did not understand, why was Karl telling him this. It was obvious that the army would be mobilized.

"You are not thinking little brother, which troops will they use, who are there, carrying out military maneuvers at this very time?"

Julius felt his blood run cold as the reality of the situation assailed him. He knew who was in Bosnia, Franz and Viktor.

Julius shared his news with Nikolas and Josef, swearing them to secrecy as Karl had told him in confidence. All around them soldiers were in a high state of anxiety, all predicting what would happen next, but Julius kept his thoughts to himself, worried now for his brother and his friend.

On the 23rd July the Austro-Hungarian government, with the backing of the Emperor Franz Josef, delivered their ultimatum to Serbia. Serbia were given forty eight hours to reply, and everyone waited with bated breath to hear their reaction to the news and to the reaction of the Russians, who were feared far more than the Serbians. The only Russian intervention was to ask the Austro-Hungarians to extend their time limit for the Serbian reply, but this was refused.

On the 25th July just before the six o'clock deadline Vienna received the reply from the Serbian government. In veiled phrases they agreed to most of the terms of the ultimatum except for one, which was the participation of Habsburg officials in the murder investigation of the Archduke that was to be held by the Serbian authorities. It was what the Austrian government had been hoping for. As the Serbs had not unconditionally accepted the terms of the ultimatum the Austro-Hungarian government severed diplomatic relations with Serbia.

Although the announcement was couched in diplomatic rhetoric the newspapers of the day perceived this as a prelude for war and the whole country prepared itself for the confrontation.

Julius at last managed to see his father the next day. He looked tired and unwell and Julius was once again shocked by his appearance. His father seemed to have accepted the inevitability of war, and spoke of it quite optimistically, though Julius felt that his father did not believe in what he was saying but was being the loyal Habsburg soldier.

259

Colonel Mayer was upset that he knew about the possible mobilization of troops in Bosnia, but Julius did not disclose his source. He told his son that seven army corps had been ordered to mobilize that day and with a heavy sigh he agreed that one of those corps did include Franz.

For the next few days' pandemonium reigned in the city. No one knew what was going on, least of all the military. Any semblance of normal barrack life had been abandoned as Julius and Nikolas tried desperately to find out if they should return to Prague, if their company was to be ordered into the conflict, or whether they were to stay in Vienna, no one seemed to know what they were to do. Finally it was decided that they should return to their regiment in Prague. This order was received with mixed emotions, although Julius believed himself to be at the centre of things in Vienna he felt he should be with his men if indeed they were to take part in the inevitable conflict. Here they were being treated as a nuisance, in the way, but at least in Prague they could prepare themselves for mobilization.

The night before they left Vienna they had dinner with Josef, who was as mystified as they were as to how events were going to turn out. "It is as though they are chickens who, after their heads are cut off, are still seen running round the farmyard" joked Josef, "I asked for leave to see you this evening, thinking there was no chance of being allowed into the city at a time like this, only to be waved assent as if they could not get rid of me quick enough. I really think they have as much idea as to what is going on as I have, which means very little. Personally I cannot wait. Lucky old Viktor, I say. He will no doubt come back covered in glory, if I know him"

The three men ate their meal with their usual good humor, but there was a somber edge to their joviality that evening. They did not know when they would see each other again and there was also the knowledge, left unsaid, because if they mentioned it, it might well come true, that one of them may not come back from a war at all. Through all the oratory, opinions and rhetoric of the barracks in the last few weeks, Julius had never heard one soldier admit that whatever the outcome, war would always mean injury and death to men.

Julius and Nikolas were preparing to leave for the station the next morning when there was a light knock on their door. Nikolas opened it to find Smid standing before them, a large smile on his face as ever, clutching two small boxes. They had seen Smid when they had first arrived in Vienna, but with the turn of events had not been able to see him again. Smid shuffled his way into their room, and with his face red with embarrassment, gave them each the small boxes that he had been carrying. When they opened them they found identical silver chains carrying a likeness of St. Wenceslas. "These are for you sirs. I hope you will always wear them and think of me. I bought them to bring you luck should you, well, should you find yourselves in battle. I hope you will not need them, I am sure you won't, but just in case. I understand he is your saint, so I thought he was appropriate"

Julius and Nikolas were so touched by the little man's kindness that they did not know what to say. The awkward silence was broken by Smid, "I had best be getting along, sirs, behave yourselves now, and none of your stupid heroics, promise me?"

"We promise" laughed Nikolas.

"Thank you, Smid. You should not have spent your hard earned money on us, but we do appreciate them. We will wear them always"

Smid smiled, "I think even Lieutenant Kutz liked his, I was not sure, you know how particular he can be"

Julius thought that Josef would have been very moved by the little man's kindness, he had always had a soft spot for Smid. Smid said his goodbyes, then waddled off down the corridor, turning round to wave at Nikolas and Julius as he went.

"He may not have all the money in the world" said Nikolas, "but there goes a true gentleman"

As soon as Julius returned to Prague he regretted leaving Vienna. Although their fellow soldiers were desperate to hear of all the events in Vienna, most of them seemed to regard the situation as just another Balkan skirmish that would be sorted out within days. The only advantage to this was that his mother and Irmy were not in a state about Papa, Karl or Franz as he had expected them to be, thereby lightening his burden of having to break the news to them about Franz. Papa had asked him to delay telling his mother and sister about his brother's mobilization until it was absolutely necessary. It was not thought that the troops would be in position until the second week of August, and he hoped by then that a diplomatic answer

261

might have been found and his wife would never have to know how close her son had come to fighting in a war.

All leave had been cancelled so Julius could not see Erika, though she sent him a note as soon as he arrived back at the barracks.

In the first days of August, Prague received the news that ships of the Austro-Hungarian Danube flotilla had bombarded Belgrade and that the Tsar of Russia and the Emperor Franz Josef had proclaimed the order for the general mobilization of their respective armies. Julius knew this was bad news. The government had hoped for the non-intervention of Russia, but these hopes were completely dashed as Russia declared its military support for the Serbs.

News in Prague was intermittent and unreliable but the barracks were in turmoil when it was announced that Germany had declared war on Russia and begun to mobilize its troops. What was even more perplexing to the populace was that Germany did not only attack Russia but occupied Luxembourg from where they attacked Belgium, a neutral country, as they made their way towards France.

The news was received with incredulity by the Austro-Hungarians. Julius could not believe it, within the first few days of August, 1914, because of Germany's aggression, the war had escalated to involve many European countries. Germany, with Austria-Hungary and Turkey hanging on to its shirttails, was now at war with Russia, France and Britain. As Nikolas murmured when the news was received, "It is as if they have opened Pandora's Box and now cannot close it"

The Austro-Hungarian Army in Bohemia made ready for war, but still no orders came for their mobilization. There was no news of Franz or Viktor, although it was known that many battles had been fought, some with heavy losses. The only way of getting any information was through official government statements, which were often very ambiguous, or through newspaper reports.

Mama had received a letter from Franz, but it had been written before the declaration of war, and Nikolas and Julius had received a letter from Josef saying his regiment had been ordered to Galizien, where heavy fighting had been reported. Josef's letter had been very non-committal and Julius wondered how his friend was really feeling at the thought of his first sight of battle. Frustration grew in Prague and many officers and soldiers became short

262

tempered and fractious at their inaction, but still no orders came from Vienna.

The greater part of the Austro-Hungarian army was sent to meet the Russian attack in Galizien, but the Russian army overran the Austrian forces and there were reports of the loss of over three hundred thousand men in battle. The Russians marched through Galizien and eventually reached the passes of the Carpathians and were only prevented from invading Hungary by the German victory further north at Tannenberg, in Eastern Prussia.

The reports from the Serbian front were no more encouraging and alarmed Julius as he thought of Franz and Viktor. There had been a large battle in September on the River Drina, which ran along the border of the two countries. Austro-Hungarian forces had invaded Serbia in the North where they were repulsed by a strong Serbian offensive, but the Austrian attack in the south of the country had been more successful, and they had made considerable advances.

All the accounts of the battles were reported in the newspapers, all stating an optimistic view of their army's activities. Julius and Nikolas heard some of the more genuine reports in the barracks, but these were not freely reported, as this was deemed bad for morale. They both agreed that Germany was taking over their army, and that they were now virtually under German control in all of their engagements.

In the middle of November, with rumors running wild about the successes and failures of the Austrian-German alliance, orders arrived from Vienna for the mobilization of Bohemian regiments, including that of Julius and Nikolas. In the summer of 1914 when war had been declared Italy had been a member of the Triple Alliance between itself, Germany and Austria-Hungary. Italy had managed to withdraw from the initial conflict by stating that, because of the Austrian oppression of Serbia, the terms of the Alliance no longer applied. Italy had always been uneasy neighbors of Austria, coveting their lands and there was a historic mistrust between the two countries. At the outset of war an Austrian army corps had been sent to the Italian border.

Wary of Italy's intention Vienna ordered Julius' regiment to the Italian/Slovene border to bolster the frontier guard and to build defenses and fortifications against a possible Italian advance. Mobilization would take several weeks to organize and the barracks began to implement the vast organization that was needed in order to prepare themselves for the Alpine slopes.

Julius was at first enraged, he did not want to spend the war on some sort of guard duty, if he was going to enter the war he wanted to fight to defend his country. Already there were descriptions filtering through of the harsh fighting on the battlefields of France and Belgium and on the eastern front against the Russians and Serbs and now they were to be sent to the mountains to act as mere defense guards.

Julius went to see Colonel Reichart. He was so furious that he asked to be reassigned to a fighting unit. Colonel Reichart listened to his protestations with a calm air and waited until Julius had finished to say, with a cold, malevolent voice, which cut through the air, "you are a trained soldier, Mayer, who will follow orders without question. We are at war, do not behave like a sniveling child who has had his toy taken away from him, now get out of my sight before I have you charged with dereliction of duty"

Julius was stung by the colonel's words, but on reflection realized that there was some truth in what his senior officer had said. He had behaved like a churlish child, but he had hoped for more understanding than the tongue-lashing he had received.

Mama was bereft at his posting, she was urgently waiting for news of Franz, but as none was forthcoming had resigned herself to the notion that no news was good news. Irmy said that Richard had volunteered to go to the front to work in a field hospital, but had been told that they had enough volunteers for the time being, but would maybe use him in the future. They are obviously expecting a large number of casualties thought Julius grimly. Meanwhile the hospital and its entire staff were told to prepare to receive wounded from the front, when the Austrian hospitals could no longer cope. Irmy had finished her training and was now a qualified nurse, but even she was wondering how she would cope with men wounded on the battlefront, something she nor any personnel in the hospital had never encountered before.

The preparations for mobilization proceeded, such an exercise was vastly different on paper than it was in reality. At every juncture a new handicap would appear, from the transportation of the horses to the movement of provisions, everything seemed to take longer than was hoped for. As a

264

Horse Artillery unit the movement of the horses was crucial to the company. All horses would be transported by train, and then by foot up into the mountains. The horses were essential, providing not only transport for men, but as load bearers and for pulling heavy ammunition. This was seen as especially vital for their destination, where automated vehicles would prove indispensable, but only for certain terrain. Up in the mountains the horses would come into their own, and provide the lifeline for the regiments.

Julius prepared Phantom for his long journey. The horses would have to be watched throughout the whole journey, many of them had never travelled by train, and if a horse became deranged within the truck the result could be catastrophic. In order to see to their feeding and watering, and to soothe them, the grooms travelled in the rail trucks.

A few days before they were due to leave for the Italian border Nikolas and Julius were at Prague station making sure Steel and Phantom were safely secured into their stalls on the train. The horses were to travel ahead of the main body of soldiers, so that they could help with the movement of essential equipment and be ready for their riders by the time they arrived. The sergeant of the horses who had become a firm ally of Julius since he had shown his expertise with Phantom came up to them as they patted their charges, waiting for the all clear to be given before the train departed.

"Don't you worry, sirs, we will take good care of them, they are like our children you know"

Julius smiled as he said, "I know that, you treat them better than you do human beings"

"Well they are far nicer than some human beings you know" the sergeant joked. The whistle sounded for the all clear, and with a last pat for their horses, they left the train and watched it leave the station.

"That will be us in a few days" said Nikolas, "after all the delays with our departure, I cannot wait"

"But don't you wish you were going to fight?" asked Julius, the reprimand from Colonel Reichart still very prominent in his mind. Nikolas had warned him vehemently against his course of action, and had been proved right. Julius now wished he had listened to his friend.

"Maybe" said Nikolas, "but with the war progressing as it is I think it very likely that we will soon be needed to bolster the Russian front. I do not think for a moment we will sit out this war on the Italian border. With the supposed casualties that they are reporting there is no way that we will not be needed there"

Julius realized the logic of his friend's argument and for the first time in weeks looked forward to travelling to Gorz with a great deal more optimism than he had felt before.

Julius and Nikolas were allowed two days leave before their departure in order to visit their families. Although Julius was sorry to be saying goodbye to Mama and Irmy, the visit was very strained. Mama was desperately trying to avoid mentioning any aspect of the war, but her anxiety at hearing nothing from Franz would suddenly envelop her and she would sadly talk about her son. Then she would realize she was not helping Julius who was about to leave her as well and so would try to make amends for her insensitivity. Julius found his mother quite exhausting and was worried for her welfare. Anything that he, Irmy or Richard tried to proffer as reasons why Franz had not written fell on deaf ears as she constantly thought the worse.

It was with some elation that, on the day before Julius left, Mama received no less than six letters from Franz, all written over the past few months. Mama became very excited whilst reading of her son's experiences, but the letters alarmed Julius. Franz did not describe any of the fighting or his conditions. If this was because of orders not to write too much in case letters fell into enemy hands, or to save Mamas feelings, Julius could only guess at. However, even in his very ordinary writings Julius could detect deterioration in his brother's attitude from the first letter to the last. It was nothing discernible, nothing that Julius could put his finger on. He had the overwhelming sense, whilst reading Franz's accounts, that things were not going well and had got worse as time progressed. Julius believed that the letters had been written by a depressed man. Mama did not seem to notice as she gaily read them over and over again, but Julius could tell by the way Irmy lifted her eyes towards him that she also could sense their brother's melancholy.

After Mama had left the room Julius and Irmy discussed their brother's letters and agreed that something was wrong, or at least that their brother was a far from happy man.

"Well at least he is still alive, as far as we know" said Julius, "that at least is a blessing"

266

Irmy sighed, "is that how we have to view things now, do not worry about his soul, at least he is alive? how many other families are feeling like we do? Just waiting for that terrible knock on the door. At least you are not going to the fighting, that is one thing we can be happy about"

Julius refrained from telling her of his discussion with Nikolas, he did not think Irmy would like to hear of the possibility of his going to the front as well.

On the last evening before his departure, Julius sat in his room reading his letter written by Josef's mother. For over two years he had kept the note close by him, reading and re-reading it until he knew the words by heart. Now he knew he must destroy it and with that knowledge he felt his memories of that night fading into the distance. With a heavy heart he read the letter again for the last time and then systematically tore it into little pieces and threw it onto the fire, watching the pieces curl up and blacken in the flames. He knew in the event of his death all his personal belongings would be looked through and read, and though he longed to keep her letter he owed the countess the dignity of taking their secret to the grave if he had to. Slowly he dressed himself for dinner and sadly made his way downstairs.

Mama had planned a dinner party for Julius and invited Erika along. Mama was a lot happier since her news of Franz and the dinner was very pleasant. Even Erika seemed to have lessened her fear of Richard as she entered into a lively discussion with him about the Czech attitude to the war. It was well known that the Czech leaders and many of its people were hostile to the war. It had been evident to Julius on the Prague streets where some citizens had turned away from his uniform as a silent objection to his participation in the conflict. When war had broken out Tomas Masaryk had left Prague for Western Europe and many people saw this as his protest to the war.

Richard and Erika's conversation was swiftly turning into a heated argument when Irmy said, "I think that is enough, we are here because it will be Julius' last night with us for some time and I do not want him to remember it as a falling out between two of the people closest to him"

Richard quickly voiced his apology, while Erika blushed a delicate shade of pink. Julius felt very uncomfortable. He hoped Erika's blushes were from the argument, but he knew it was more from Irmy's reference to a 'close friend'

267

Ever since Mama had told him of this dinner party, he knew that she, and to some extent Irmy, had expected him to announce, if not his engagement to Erika, then at least some form of long term commitment to the her and this he knew he could not do. When he had gone to Vienna he had realized that Erika was not the girl for him. Although he missed her, it was not the heart-wrenching void that her absence should have given him. He knew he had been more excited at the thought of seeing Josef's mother again than at the thought of returning to Prague and seeing Erika. Whilst the outbreak of war had perhaps colored his opinion he knew it was the right one. It was the thought of telling Erika that worried him the most. He did not want to hurt her, she would make someone a wonderful wife, but when he rehearsed saying this to her the words sounded like hollow, insincere platitudes that a gentleman would not say to a lady, but that is how he truly felt.

He was mortified when after dinner Mama made some excuse for her, Irmy and Richard to vacate the room, leaving Julius and Erika alone. They both stared at their coffee cups in the uncomfortable silence that prevailed until Julius decided he must speak, "Erika....."

"It is all right, Julius" Erika gave him a trembling smile as she looked at him with misty eyes, "it is all right, I know what you are about to say. I think I have known for quite a while now. I know I care for you far more than you could ever care for me" Julius opened his mouth to protest but she stopped him, "no, do not try to deny it Julius, I know you too well. I just always hoped that you might grow to love me in time, but I suppose I was deluding myself. I, I know this sounds contrived, but I hope we will always be friends and that you will write to me occasionally, I would like to know how you are getting on in this absurd war"

"Of course" replied Julius, not sure of what to say, "I really do care for you, Erika, it was just not enough, for me and most of all for you, I wish it could be different, I really do"

Erika rose from her seat and walked round the table to stand beside him, "I know" she said sadly, then leant down and gave him an affectionate kiss, "goodnight Julius, thank your mother for the dinner, tell her I hope to see her again soon" As she walked towards the door she turned round and said, "Look after yourself, Julius, please do not get hurt" and with tears in her eyes she left the room.

Julius sat for a while staring at the flickering candles thinking about Erika. It had taken all his strength and resolve not to rush from his chair and race after her, but he knew it would have been the wrong thing to do. He had made the right decision, he knew that, but it did not make him feel any better at that moment.

When Mama returned to the room she was shocked to find Erika gone, Julius was not up to answering her barrage of questions and was grateful to Richard and Irmy who skillfully diverted Mama from her interrogation for the rest of the evening. When Richard and Irmy left Julius saw them to the front door and followed them out onto the street where they were going to walk the short distance to their house. The night was very cold and cloudy and the skies looked heavy with snow.

"Are you all right Julius?" Irmy asked solicitously, and then surprised Julius by saying, "you made the right decision, if your heart was not committed it was best to let her know"

"How did you....?" stammered Julius.

Irmy laughed, "call it women's intuition, we know about these things. I liked Erika, I thought you were very well suited, and I am sorry she was not the one for you. Goodnight Julius, I shall see you in the morning"

Irmy was to accompany Mama to see him off at the station, but Richard had to work at the hospital. He said his farewells to Julius, with hearty backslapping and overtures to take care. As he took Irmy's arm he said to Julius, "you are right to wait, Julius. The right girl will come along, you will see. It may not be for a while. Look at me, it took me long enough" he looked fondly at Irmy, "but I think you will agree, she was well worth waiting for" and with a proud smile on his face Richard and Irmy walked off down the street.

Julius stood and watched them until they had turned the corner, he was heartened by what Richard had said, and felt better. He was right, it was better to not have than to settle for second best. He was still young, and for now all thoughts of his future must be stored away. There was a great war raging across Europe, and although for now he was not going to be an integral part of it, he felt sure that in the future he certainly would be.

XXI

As Julius left the house the next morning he was touched by the servants all lining up in the hall to say their goodbyes. Some of the servants he had known since childhood, having moved from Kosice to Prague with Mama, but even the newer servants appeared upset at his departure.

Danusia, of course, was in floods of tears, holding her apron to her eyes in her anguish. To Julius, Danusia had not changed since his days in the nursery. He calculated that Danusia must now be well into her fortieth years but she still possessed the large round, comforting figure, the permanently red cheeks and the warm, welcoming, innocent face that so endeared her to everybody. Mama had hinted that Danusia had wanted to accompany them to the station to see him off but Julius had recoiled in horror at the suggestion. He imagined her floods of tears and maniacal embraces in front of his brother officers and his men. Now as he gave her a last hug he felt churlish at his vehement protestations, but knew he had been right. As their carriage left their street the sounds of her wailing could still be heard as they turned the corner. Mama and Irmy were falsely bright, trying to keep their emotions in check for him. He was glad when they arrived at Prague station, and the mayhem and disarray that met them took their minds off the coming parting.

Everywhere was chaos and noise as it appeared the whole of Prague had come to the station to see off their friends and relatives. Everyone held posies of flowers, the traditional Bohemian gift to soldiers leaving for active service. There were tears and hugs as soldiers said their goodbyes and tried to find their seats on the train. Julius was saying his farewells to Mama and Irmy when Nikolas arrived at their side with his mother and Georg. Frau Manzova and his mother were close to tears as they greeted each other, both sharing in the loss of their sons. Irmy hugged Nikolas in greeting and gave him a posy of flowers. Julius noticed his friend flinch at the show of affection from Irmy and quickly jump back out of her arms. Irmy seemed not to notice as she greeted Georg, but Julius saw the bewildered look in his friend's eyes.

Julius shook Georg gravely by the hand as Georg told him how lucky he was. "I hope this war lasts for a very long time so that I can grow up and fight in it too"

"Georg" cried Frau Manzova, "that is a terrible thing to say. No one should ever wish to prolong a war. Think of all our brave men fighting on the Russian front. I am sure most of them wish the war was over now"

Julius saw his mother cringe at the mention of the Russian front as she thought of Franz. Julius rubbed the boy's mop of red hair as Georg rolled his eyes heavenward and mischievously winked at Julius and his brother.

It was time to board the train, to find their brother officers and see their men settled in. Julius hugged his mother and Irmy, and laden with flowers he and Nikolas located their carriage.

As the train blew its whistle and slowly steamed out of Prague station, hundreds of men hung out of the windows to obtain a last glimpse of their loved ones. Everyone on the station was waving frantically and most of the women were crying as some attempted to follow the train down the station platform.

Julius could see his mother and Frau Manzova waving furiously, tears running down their faces. Irmy was standing beside them, nobly trying not to cry, though her eyes filled with tears, as she comforted her mother. Georg could be seen running alongside the train, weaving in and out of the crowd, trying to keep up with his brother. His face was alive with a large smile as he enjoyed the excitement of the occasion. He was shouting something as he ran, but his voice was drowned by the noise of the train and the sounds of the people voicing their farewells. All Nikolas and Julius could do was smile and wave at Georg as he stopped at the end of the platform and stood watching them as the train travelled out of his sight.

The journey was long as they travelled through Austria and at last arrived at the border town of Gorz. Gorz was the capital of the Habsburg crown land of Gorz-Gradisca and was known as a noted cultural centre. Situated in Slovenia, the city afforded a perfect base for the Austro-Hungarian army to build their defenses against the threat of an Italian attack.

Since Italy's declaration of neutrality in August 1914 the Austrian army had started to plan a line that was the most suitable for defending their borders. It had been decided to

271

abandon positions that, though more advanced, were harder to defend and, keeping in the main to mountainous regions, to build permanent fortifications there in case of attack.

The border between the Austro-Hungarian Empire and Italy ran from the Adriatic Sea, through the plains below Gorz and then followed the Julian and Carnic Alps in a wide sweep round to the northwest. The Alpine mountains possessed formidable natural positions that would give the army superior defensive locations against the Italians. In the beginning the work had been carried out mainly by volunteers and territorial battalions and when Julius' regiment arrived in mid December, the building had already begun.

After being allocated their temporary quarters, Julius, Nikolas and their fellow officers were called to a meeting by Colonel Reichart. It was explained to them that their duties would entail the building of defenses along the whole of the border with Italy. This would mean the building of bridgeheads and fortifications on the plains, as well as building trenches and finding caves in the mountains. These would hopefully provide storage facilities and bombproof refuge if there was a conflict.

Nikolas was assigned to Tolmin at the base of the Julian Alps, to the North of Gorz, whilst Julius was to stay in Gorz to help supervise the fortifications there. Although Julius wondered to himself if such extensive work was merely a waste of time, he was glad at last to be gainfully employed. His only real misgivings was the cold weather, which was not conducive to the large scale of work that was needed over the next few months.

It was with a heavy heart that he said goodbye to Nikolas as he packed his bags ready for departure. Nikolas laughed at his friend's melancholy, "for goodness sake Julius, it is not as if I am going into combat without you. Look on the bright side, I am taking Colonel Reichart with me, at least you do not have the pleasure of his company for a while, you are the lucky one"

Julius knew Nikolas was right and he knew why he was feeling so depressed, but he did not like to voice his opinions to his friend, in case he laughed at him. Ever since he had known Nikolas was going to Tolmin, he had been afraid that when he received his orders to proceed to the Russian front he would have to go there on his own. He

272

wanted Nikolas to be there with him. It was not that he was scared of conflict, but he felt that in some way that Nikolas was his lucky mascot, and things would be all right if he were around. He knew his reasons were stupid and totally illogical, but he felt them all the same.

After Nikolas had left Julius found himself under the command of a Colonel Genner, a much older man than Reichart. Julius reckoned him to be near his father in years, but the old man was as fit as a man half his age. He had an instant rapport with the men under his command, and after Colonel Reichart, Colonel Genner was a breath of fresh air to the officers and men alike. Julius found his men working harder for the old warhorse than they had ever done for Reichart. Their greatest obstacle was the weather, as the lashing cold rain of December progressed to deep snow and ice.

Most days found Julius out with his men supervising the building and fortification work outlined by army engineers. Lorries and cars were used a lot; the pack horses being sent to the more mountainous regions. Julius would ride around on Phantom to the various sites, trying to encourage his men despite the freezing conditions, and giving a helping hand if it was needed. News came from Tolmin, Trentino and Carnic regions that work was progressing well, but the fortifications around Gorz and the Soca River were proceeding at a slower pace. This was mainly due to the vast amount of work that was needed in those areas.

Christmas 1914 passed by and was hardly noticed, the work becoming even more behind schedule because of the weather. On Christmas Eve the officers and men went to Midnight Mass at the Cathedral of San Spirito in Gorz. Prayers were said for the casualties of war and Julius fervently prayed that Franz, Josef and Viktor were not among them. He had heard little from his friends and family since arriving in Slovene. Mama and Irmy had written, but he had no news from his brother or his friends. Karl had written that he was still in Vienna, and that his request for a posting to the Russian front had been denied, although he hoped this would change in the future. Julius knew that Karl meant he would probably be needed soon to bolster the numbers of the army as large casualties were believed to have been suffered in the last few months, he just could not say so because of the censorship imposed on personal letters. Karl had written that he had not seen Papa for some weeks. Their father had been assigned a high level job within the Army headquarters in Vienna and this was taking up most of his time. 'Do not ask me what it is' wrote Karl 'you know our father; he would never divulge any information which he should not. I just hope that this is not all too much for him. The last time I saw him he had lost a lot of weight and was looking rather unwell'

Julius was alarmed by Karl's reference to his father's health, but reasoned it must be due to the pressures of work and the war. Everybody was affected by the enormity of the conflict, and worried about its outcome.

After Midnight Mass Colonel Genner invited his officers to join him for a glass of schnapps to celebrate the Yuletide. One of the young officers asked Colonel Genner the question they were all thinking about, when would they be sent to fight the Russians and the Serbs? Colonel Genner looked about the room at the men, all eager to hear his answer. His face puckered into a frown as he drank his schnapps. Staring into his empty glass he said, "so, that is what you are all waiting for, the call to arms" He shook his head sadly as he continued, "oh to be young again, so brave and so full of glory, I envy you. I do not know if, or when, they will send for you gentlemen. If you want my honest opinion, I do not think they ever will"

His statement was met by large gasps and protestations as several officers attempted to disagree with him. The colonel raised his hand to silence them. "Do not get so excited gentlemen, this is just a friendly discussion over a glass of schnapps is it not? You asked the question, I am only saying what I believe to be true. I have been in this region for a long time remember. I know the Italians, they did not declare their neutrality with the aim of keeping out of this war. It was merely so they could sit on the fence, something they are very good at, believe me. Let me put this to you. They have always coveted our lands near their borders, the Trentino, Istria, Trieste. What if the enemy offered them these territories in return for their support in the war?"

"But that is supposing they could win those lands from us, we would not let them" volunteered one young officer.

"Maybe that is so, waiving all those considerations aside, do you not think that that would be a very juicy carrot to dangle before the Italians? and do you not think that the Russians would like to engage a large force of the Austro-

Hungarian army here on the Italian border, rather than us augmenting a mighty force in Russia?"

"So what you are saying is that you believe that our building of defenses here is not merely precautionary, but could well turn out to be a battleground"

Colonel Genner shrugged his shoulders, "I am merely stating a supposition, gentlemen, but it is something for you to think about. I hope it does not happen, because out there is a very hostile landscape to fight a war on. Now if you will excuse me, I will retire and leave you all to argue the point, as I am sure you will. Remember we have an early start gentlemen, goodnight"

All the officers rose and saluted as the old man left the room. As soon as the door was closed there was a furious argument amongst the men as to whether the Colonel was right or not. Julius, in no mood for confrontation, soon excused himself and retired to his bed.

As he lay thinking about what the Colonel had said, he had the feeling that the Colonel was not merely stating a vague idea that had come to him. He believed that the old man knew more than he was admitting to. For the first time Julius began to seriously consider that his war could well be fought here on the border, against an Italian army, rather than on the Russian front. The thought gave him more than a little anxiety. Warfare here would be very different to the other fronts in this war. It would be dangerous and as much to do with the terrain and the climate as with the enemy. He wished Nikolas were here to talk things through, and with these unsettling thoughts whirling around inside his head he eventually managed to fall off to sleep.

After the New Year of 1915, the work proceeded laboriously. Tempers became frayed at the hard manual work expected of the men, and the cold temperatures and snow-covered terrain did nothing to soothe their nerves. News trickled in from the Russian front of some success for the German and Austro-Hungarian armies although these were countered with more reports of the heavy loss of life.

At the end of January Nikolas returned to Gorz, the work at Tolmin having been completed, and Colonel Genner requesting extra help. To everyone's relief Colonel Reichart did not return with his men, he travelled further north to oversee the fortifications there. Nikolas proclaimed himself happy to be back, if only to be rid of the hated Colonel. Reichart had driven the men so hard that Nikolas declared

275

that he had thought he would be witnessing a mutiny amongst his men if they had not returned to Gorz. He had gone up into the mountains and had enthused about the defenses built up there. "I tell you Julius, if we are attacked, there is no way they can get us off those mountains, the slopes have been made virtually impenetrable"

Work carried on for the next few months. A bridgehead had been completed at Tolmin and now they were building one at Gorz. As the days wore on the weather improved and by March the conditions were far more clement and the work became easier. Julius began to wonder if Colonel Genner had been right about an Italian invasion, as things were very quiet. From their elevated positions the Austrian army could easily see the Italians also creating fortifications on their border, but this was only to be expected. The men were getting more and more restless, eager to make their contribution to the war. Although the rumors were rife of Italian duplicity, the men were discouraged by the lack of any large armaments arriving in the area, let alone any formation of long-term camps for a large massing of troops.

Julius and Nikolas were out riding on Phantom and Steel one bright spring morning and they had stopped at a vantage point above the city. They had been sent on a daily errand which was to survey the plains below them and report any extra activities by the Italians that might be of interest. Julius looked through the field glasses that were strung round his neck and took a slow panoramic sweep of the scene before him. All he could see were the fortifications that were known about, there was no sign of any new activity from the Italian army.

"Do you think there is someone out there, looking at us, looking at them?" grinned Nikolas.

"If they have any sense there will be. Do you know it is quite depressing, I keep on imagining to myself what it is going to be like doing this until the end of the war. We will still be up here watching through our field glasses when the peace is signed"

"God, I hope not, I do not know if we can hold the men much longer. They are all complaining that they did not join the army to become laborers"

"I know how they feel" moaned Julius, "Sometimes I think this is worse than Prague, we are more cut off here than we ever were there, and that was bad enough"

The two men were silent as their thoughts returned to Prague, and then inevitably to their friends and Julius' brother. Nothing had been heard of them for so long that they both admitted to fearing the worst. The idea was quickly pushed from their minds as their steeds, impatient to be off, shook their heads and stamped the ground with their hooves, wanting to move on.

"Race you back to the camp" shouted Nikolas, and with a slap of the reins he and Steel raced off towards their encampment in the valley below. Julius watched him go, not wanting to join in the race, but delighting in his friend's madness as he galloped down the steep slope. The encampment was busy with its daily activities and the men looked like tiny ants as they moved around their canvas tents. The camps had been set up behind the town when the extra troops had arrived from the other regions. Gorz had not enough accommodation for so many men and although all the officers had accommodation in the town the majority of them spent most nights in the camps with their men.

Julius returned at a slow trot to the camp to find Nikolas handing Steel to one of the grooms. He had just dismounted when their batman, a young recruit called Hans, came running up to him. Hans had joined them when Nikolas had returned to Gorz, he was a very new, very young recruit, tall and thin, who reminded Julius of a young foal, so uncoordinated were his movements. Although Hans did not know the first thing about being a batman he was eager to learn and was forgiven the mishaps from his clumsiness because of his sheer enthusiasm and optimism. Not a very bright lad, he was always at hand when Julius and Nikolas returned to their quarters and had established a hero worship for his two officers. Julius and Nikolas had found out that this was because he had been severely mistreated by his father. He was so amazed that people could be nice to him that he repaid their kindness with devoted adulation. Nikolas watched with a frown on his face as Hans came running up to them breathlessly.

"Salute Hans, you know the rules, you will find yourself on a charge if another officer sees you" ordered Nikolas.

Hans' face turned bright red as in his embarrassment he came to an abrupt halt and hastily proffered a far from satisfactory salute. The salute was made worse by the fact that Hans had a letter in his hand that was now waving around his head.

Julius managed to smother a smile as he said, "All right Hans, what is so urgent?"

"Please sir, sorry sir, it's just that this letter has arrived for you, and I, well I have heard you talking about your brother from Graz, and that is where the letter comes from"

Julius snatched the letter out of Hans' hand and although he did not recognize the writer's hand knew that it was from Franz's wife Gretha. He held the envelope in his hand, wanting to open the letter but afraid to in case he could not bear the news that it held. He heard Nikolas curtly dismissing Hans and barely felt his friend's hand on his arm.

"Julius are you all right?" asked Nikolas, "would you like me to leave while you read your letter, I presume it is about Franz?"

Julius nodded his head as he turned from his friend and walked over to sit under the shade of a tree to read his letter. With shaking hands he released the paper and taking a deep breath started to read. 'My dear brother' wrote Gretha, 'I felt it best to write to you as soon as possible. I know how close you are to Franz and that you will be worrying about him. Please do not alarm yourself, your brother is alive, but he has been injured in battle. He stayed for a while in a field hospital, but I am happy to say he is now back with us and staying in the local hospital. Franz was injured at Przemysl at the end of last year. He suffered numerous shrapnel wounds in his back and legs. We will have to see after his period of recuperation whether this will be a long-term injury or not, no one seems to know at the moment. As you can imagine the thought of not playing a part in the war has severely depressed him. I hope that his melancholia improves with time and we will have our Franz back with us very soon. I am sure he would love some correspondence from you, if you are not too busy. He often talks of you and your childhood days with such warmth and affection. I would also add, and I hope this is some comfort, that he mentioned your friends, Viktor and Josef, and I feel that they were both well when last Franz saw them, I hope so. We will pray for you, as I am sure you will for us, your sister, Gretha'

Julius read and reread the letter, knowing that what it did not say said far more than what it did. He knew from the strained language of the letter that things were worse than Gretha had stated. He also knew that letters were being censored and that his sister-in-law would not be able to write the truth. However she had managed to convey to Julius that there were more things wrong with Franz than merely his injuries. He felt that there was some irony in Gretha's writing when she had said that Franz's depression was due to his non-participation in the war. He rather thought that it was somehow due to his participation in the war rather than anything else. Julius thought back to Franz's letters that his mother had received, when he and Irmy had thought that their brother was hiding something, Gretha's letter merely seemed to confirm that. Julius was lost in his wild thoughts when he felt a shadow loom over him and he looked up to see Nikolas standing before him.

"Is everything all right?" he asked with concern, "is the news bad?"

Julius proffered the letter to his friend. Nikolas took the letter, then sat down beside his friend in the shade of the tree to read it. Julius watched his friend's face run a gamut of emotions as he read the letter.

"Tell me what you think, Nikolas, I would like your opinion"

"I think Franz has been injured, as Gretha says, but I think she is trying to tell you that his injuries are more than just physical ones"

"I agree," said Julius, "though how much he is affected is hard to tell. Obviously Gretha could not say in her letter, so I suppose I will just have to be patient. The only way I am going to find out is on my next leave home, whenever that is, presuming Mama and Irmy have been told"

With that Julius had to be content, but his patience was not too exhausted as the next week Nikolas' father arrived from Prague and asked that Julius attend his quarters in the town.

Nikolas' father greeted Julius with his usual abruptness. Colonel Manz was never a man to waste time and before there was any chance for idle small talk he brought up the subject of why he had asked to see Julius.

"Your sister asked me to see you concerning your brother Franz"

Julius swallowed hard, although he wanted to know the truth about Franz he was afraid of what he was about to hear.

"Irmy thought it was best that you know the full extent of your brother's injuries, as it would be impossible for her to tell you by letter herself. As you know Franz was injured in battle and has severe wounding to his back and his legs. These, though severe, are now mending and even his leg, which was causing great anxiety seems to be healing well. Richard believes that it is possible that he will always walk with a limp, a small price to pay for one's life would you say? The worrying thing is the state of your brother's mind. I am afraid your brother is suffering from a depression brought on by his experiences of warfare. Evidently it is happening a lot, especially on the French and Belgian fronts. Men that are constantly under bombardment from shells and gunfire, as your brother was, are succumbing to an illness that affects their mind as well as their body. They flinch at noises, their speech is undisciplined and they are prone to horrific nightmares. To be honest, when you know what some of our men have been through, it is not surprising"

Julius assessed what Colonel Manz had told him and then asked, "Do you think he will get better?"

"I really do not know, Julius, I do not think anybody, even the doctors, know. Of course when your Mama heard of your brother's injuries she travelled to Graz. Your father was furious with her, but you know your mother, she would not be stopped, despite the danger. She arrived back a few days before I left and I can honestly say she was very heartened by her visit. I do not think it was a mother's blind optimism talking, I think she had really seen an improvement in Franz's condition during her visit. Obviously to be back in peaceful surroundings with his wife is going to help him and your mother says Franz's wife has been a wonderful nurse. I think all we can do now is give Franz time to recover. He is a young, fit man with an iron constitution, I am sure he will be all right. Your mother was not sure whether I should tell you, but Irmy and I believed the truth was better than you being stationed here not knowing what was happening to your brother. I hope we were right"

"Yes, sir, thank you sir, I am glad you have told me. I am happier now Franz's situation is clearer in my head"

As Julius returned to his quarters he was glad that he now knew the truth of his brother's injuries. Although he wished that Colonel Manz had had a more definite prognosis of Franz's condition, he felt that a heavy weight had been lifted from his shoulders.

In his anxiety to hear about Franz Julius had omitted to ask Colonel Manz why he had arrived in Gorz, but in the next few days it became very apparent. Colonel Manz had only stayed in Gorz for a few days before returning to Prague but it was obvious why he had come. News came through that the Italians were in protracted negotiations with the enemy. The Austro-Hungarian government in Vienna ordered the army to intensify their defensive work on the Italian border. To this end more troops began arriving in April and the work began to escalate, especially on the Soca front.

If Julius and his men thought they had been working hard before it was nothing to the work that was carried out in the following month. The men worked in shifts, working day and night. Heavy armaments began arriving and the artillery began placing the guns in strategic positions along the front. The fact that a lot of the reinforcements were new conscripts, quickly trained, and with little army experience did not help. By May two or three rows of wire entanglements were in place in front of most of Austria's strategic positions. Trenches were built into rocks and caverns, some lined with cement and all the bridgeheads had been completed.

On May 23rd 1915, senior officers were informed that Italy had declared war on the Austro-Hungarian Empire. The news was received with elation by most of the men, who had been straining at the leash for the past few months, eager to participate in a real fight at last. The army at the Slovenian front had now been augmented by Hungarian Honved troops, and Slovenians, anxious to defend their lands. Italy was a country ringed by mountains, at the start of the conflict Austro-Hungarian forces were in a good position as they held the mountain line. If battle did ensue it meant that the Italian army would have to fight their way up from the plains. The fighting would be difficult, if only from the terrain on which it was to be fought. Italy's main objective was to prevent an Austrian advance into the Trentino in the West, and to defend their lands around Lake Garda. They also wanted to push through the Austrian defenses and cross the Soca River towards Trieste in the East.

The first few weeks saw sporadic fighting as the Italian Army tried to advance towards the Austrian lines. The Italians attempted to attack the bridgeheads of Tolmin and

Gorz, but because of their position and structure and because the Italians lacked artillery of even medium caliber they made little progress. Their forces in the North achieved slightly more success in the area around the village of Caporetto/Karfreit on the Soca River. The formidable northern position of Mrzli was captured and lost four times until Italian troops eventually managed to partially occupy it after bitter fighting.

Even in the first few weeks of skirmishes there was loss of life, and for the first time Julius encountered the horrors of war. Protected by the bridgehead at Gorz Julius and his unit were secure and were engaged in siting guns onto the advancing Italian troops and laying down ammunition for further attacks. Other units though had many losses and daily reports came back of the terrible suffering of injured men and Austro-Hungarian soldiers being taken prisoner. Julius and Nikolas spent the days making sure equipment and arms were stowed and positioned properly and kept clean and dry so that they worked to maximum efficiency.

Every man carried a rifle, which could kill a man some distance away. The rifles used by the Austro-Hungarian Army were usually 1895 Steyr 8mm models, but this could vary from regiment to regiment. Each rifle had a bayonet fitted beneath the barrel, an effective weapon for close fighting. The bayonets were fashioned with a groove along its face, thus ensuring its easy removal from a man's body. Each rifle carried several bullets in a magazine for rapid fire and each soldier always carried extra ammunition. Some officers carried handguns; Julius had a 1912 nine-millimetre Steyr automatic pistol, which he carried in a holster around his waist. Soldiers were also issued with grenades which they carried into the attack. Julius had to make sure that all of his men carried their identity lockets that were hung from a string around their necks. In these were recorded the details of the wearer, essential in the event of capture or death. They contained the soldier's year of birth, the town, village or municipality where he came from, his political district and his country along with his army number.

The hardest task had been to transport the heavy guns into strategic positions in the mountains. Automated vehicles had been used up to a certain point, but after they had reached their limit, the army had to rely on natural horsepower to take the guns up. Julius was amazed as he watched heavy twenty five pounder guns being hauled up over sheer rock faces by the pulling power of a team of horses and heavy ropes.

Machine guns were thought to be the best defensive weapon. They had come to the fore in France and Belgium in 1914, and were a relatively new invention. However their potential was quickly realized and soon most of the armies were producing as many as they could. Although the Austrian army had very few, more were arriving daily as their production increased. A soldier manning a machine gun could prevent hundreds of men from advancing.

Julius' main occupation was the siting of the howitzer guns. These guns were more versatile than the field guns as they were usually of a heavier caliber and could lob their shells over an arched trajectory, at about a forty-five degree elevation. Julius believed that in their protected position at Gorz, and in the mountains, these guns were one of the most effective offensives against the enemy.

Towards the end of June it became obvious that the Italians were mustering their forces for a large assault. The fifth Austrian Army occupied a line from Mount Nevo to the coast of the Adriatic Sea, and the Italians attacked these lines. Even the new recruits with no army training could see how foolhardy the attack was by the Italians. Julius watched from his location on the heights above Gorz as the Italians attacked. They were in a hopeless situation, Austrian artillery had the advantage of their dominating position, whilst the Italian artillery had not enough guns to create an effective assault. As the Italian forces advanced they were bombarded by the Austrian guns, whilst the Italians who were operating from positions below had no observation points and were blind to their opponents.

The fighting was furious and deadly, Italian ammunition could not break the wire entanglement defenses. Through his field glasses Julius could see brave young soldiers who had reached the wire trying to cut it with scissors or place gelatin tubes, which had little effect. The Italian soldiers were like sitting ducks as Julius observed his first sight of the slaughter and destruction of war. Wave upon wave of men surged forward to their deaths under the barrage of Austrian artillery. Julius watched as the sound of shells rushed through the air, followed by a bright flash and clouds of gray smoke billowed into the air. When the smoke cleared it usually revealed a pile of bodies, covered in blood, and men desperately trying to crawl back to their lines, before their injuries took their lives.

The battle lasted for over a week. The fighting was chaos and pandemonium as wave after wave of attacks were repelled. As well as the success at Gorz and Tolmin where the bridgeheads had held, the Austro-Hungarian Field Marshals and Generals, who were never seen near any danger areas, could also celebrate the holding of Podgera to the North.

The loss of life was heavy and there were whispers around the camp of as many as ten thousand casualties, but officers were encouraged to dismiss these rumors as mere gossip. There was an endless procession of ambulances, automated and horse drawn, taking the wounded and dying to the field hospitals behind the lines. Julius had never seen so much blood and so many injuries, some making him want to vomit where he stood. He thought he would never be able to expunge the smell of cordite and smoke that hovered constantly in the air over the battleground.

The battle was Julius' first encounter with violent death. He would never forget the sight of bodies blown to bits by gunfire, or the desperate cries for help from injured and dying men, waiting to be helped. Even at night their cries echoed across the plain and into the hills, traumatic to all those listening to the pitiful sounds. Julius had to admit that the fighting had also stimulated him, death and injury were sickening, but the sheer excitement and noise of battle were something he had never encountered before. Even Nikolas had to agree with this as he rode into camp one day, covered from head to foot in soil and dirt, his uniform torn and grazes to his face. His eyes shining bright with excitement he recounted how a stray shell from an Italian gun had landed not three yards from where he had been standing. It had created a huge crater in the ground beside him, covering him with flying soil and dirt.

"You were lucky, my friend" said Julius, "maybe you should take care not to make yourself a sitting target for the enemy. Next time you might not be so fortunate"

Nikolas grinned, still elated by his brush with danger. He felt inside his tunic and pulled out his chain with the image of St. Wenceslas. "I will be all right as long as I am wearing this. Remember, Smid is looking after me"

284

Julius laughed at his friend's childlike faith in their erstwhile batman, and shook his head as he watched Nikolas dance off to his tent.

Several miles behind the front lines, safe camps had been established. Soldiers did not live at the front line for more than a week at a time. They would then spend another week in the support trenches and then another week in the reserve trenches behind the lines. This rotation was interspersed with being sent to the safe camps. Soldiers were sent to the camps so that they could sleep, change into clean clothes, take a bath and relax. These havens were usually set up in villages and towns far from the front lines.

It was with some surprise when Julius and Nikolas were informed by Colonel Genner, some days after their first battle that they were to be sent to the camp. Both men protested vehemently with the Colonel. The war had only just started for them, and they wanted to remain a part of it, but the Colonel insisted that they go. "You and your men have been here now for six months, even if you think you do not need the rest, your men do. We have enough men here and there is talk of reinforcements from the Russian front. Go, relax, and come back rested and better soldiers"

There was to be no more argument, and both men had to confess that on reflection a change of scenery did sound like a welcome change. The camps provided a haven of normality amongst ordinary people, who were eager to help the brave men defending their lands, and treated them like heroes. To this end there were even bordels in some towns that the men flocked to, they had been deprived of female companionship for too long.

It was only when they observed the fresh faces of new recruits arriving on their way to the front that they realized how jaded and tired they all looked. The men enjoyed the rest, they savored hot baths and new clothes, their old ones being filthy and lice infested. They spent most of the day relaxing, sleeping, playing cards, listening to phonograph records or reading books. Many men took the opportunity to write copious letters to their loved ones and friends. One thing that battle had taught them all was that life was very ephemeral, and the love of family and friends was very important. Julius wrote to every member of his family. His letter to Franz was especially difficult to write, not really knowing what to say to his brother, how to express his true

285

feelings without the censor blacking out his words. He also wrote to Viktor and Josef, hoping they would receive his letters and also a letter to Erika and Smid. The letter to Erika had been friendly and circumspect. She had asked Julius to write to her and at that moment he wanted all the friends he could, but he worried that his letter might be misconstrued as something more than it was.

It was with disbelief that Julius, Nikolas, their brother officers and the men were issued with new uniforms. In the middle of the greatest war for many years the Austro-Hungarian government had decided to alter the uniform from its previous 1909 issue. All the officers agreed it would be laughable if it were not so ludicrous. The old pike gray uniforms were replaced by a field gray uniform, which was to be standard issue to all ranks of both the Austrian and Hungarian armies. The new uniform was very similar to the old one, except that the tunic was cut looser and had a stand-and-fall collar. The special headdress for the horse artillery, dragoons, hussars and lancers was abolished. So were the red trousers for the cavalry, which had proved to be such a target in open warfare, and all mounted troops were issued with a field gray side cap.

At the camp some of the assault troops were issued with the German steel helmets despite some protestations, though they were promised Austrian ones in the future that had been commissioned into production. All ranks were indicated by patches and patterned lace on the collar of their tunics. Julius and Nikolas, as Second Lieutenants, wore a single silver star on their collars. The good thing about the uniform was that it was new and thus clean. At the front every man wore their uniform for the duration, during the day and at night when sleeping. The uniforms quickly became soiled, dirty and smelly, and were often infested with fleas and lice.

After two weeks at the camp, the orders came for their return to the front. All the men had not realized how tired they were, and most had spent their time in the camp sleeping. He was glad to be returning to the battle zone but Julius encountered mixed feelings. Whilst he did not believe himself afraid, he would often close his eyes and see the casualties of the last battle before him. Although knowing he did not want to die, it was obvious that now there was the possibility of death. If God did choose to take him he prayed that he would be able to die with dignity and quickly, he knew he did not want to be one of those men screaming for help on the battlefield.

On returning to Gorz they heard news of the Austrian army on the Galizien front. Large numbers of German troops, under the leadership of Field-Marshal Hindenburg, had been diverted to Poland to assist the Austrian troops. In May the combined German and Austrian forces had broken through the Russian lines at Gorlice and the Russians had been driven out of Galizien and had abandoned the Polish lands.

By June Przemysl had been retaken and the capital of Galizien was in Austrian hands. This was seen as a great victory and heartened the morale of the army, but it was with increasing uneasiness that the Austro-Hungarian soldiers observed the influence of the German army over their own. Perhaps more alarming was the realization that the Austro-Hungarian army could not survive without the Germans supporting them.

The Austro-Hungarian Army had now been reinforced by five new divisions as towards the end of July it was obvious that the Italians were mustering for a second attack. Battle reports had been coming in of several skirmishes within the northern mountain regions of the border. The fighting in those areas was very different to the plains and river assaults to the South. On the higher slopes the Austrian army had built strong barriers and fortifications that had been prepared in the months before the declaration of war by Italy. The terrain of the area did not lend itself to attacks by large masses. The fighting that did take place were sudden attacks by troops trained for the mountains, but in smaller groups.

In Gorz and Tolmin, with their solid defenses and bridgehead, the Austrian army prepared to meet the Italian attack. The fighting was hard, but the Austrians quickly realized that these attacks were only half hearted and it soon became clear why. The Italians, knowing how impenetrable these two positions were, had concentrated their forces further south, where they had had more success in breaking the Austrian lines. They concentrated their attack on the Carso plateau and attacked the heights of San Michele, which they then occupied.

The top of San Michele dominated the whole of the Isonzo/Soca plain. The Austrian army wanted to retake this important position and under the orders of General Boog eighteen battalions attacked the Italians. The Italians, exhausted by the concentrated artillery fire, were forced to retreat. General Boog decided after this victory that his troops should reform, descend the San Michele, and proceed to the Isonzo and drive the Italians out. This proved to be a grave error of judgment on the General's part. Austrian troops were repelled by an Italian counterattack and were decimated by Italian artillery fire. The attack was a disaster, resulting in the loss of San Michele and the lives of thousands of Austrian soldiers. It took five more days of heavy fighting before the Austrians regained San Michele, but a victory soured by such a dreadful loss of life.

When the news came to Gorz, where fighting was still muted, it was met with anger at the futility of the second attack by Boog. It had been a grave error by a senior officer that did nothing to increase the soldiers confidence in the officers under whom they served. Men were starting to mutter about so much loss of life for the gain or loss of such little territory. Julius could in some ways sympathize with the men. When he talked to them he tried to explain that this was the way of modern warfare. He could easily use the French and Belgian front as a perfect example. There had been horrendous loss of life in the first year of the war, but the trench lines there had barely moved.

It was not the only subject that he had to reason with his men about. He and Nikolas were well aware of the difficulties the army was having within its own ranks with men of so many different nationalities living in close proximity with each other. It was virtually an everyday occurrence to have to break up arguments or even physical fights between men, merely because they were of a different race or creed. There was also a lack of confidence in senior officers that was daily becoming more apparent. It was known that senior officers did not join the soldiers at the front, an historical fact. However in these modern times, the men were acutely aware of the lack of experience that these Generals and Field Marshals had of practical warfare, or of their men, the fiasco at San Michele with General Boog only highlighted this. Julius found it increasingly difficult to argue this point with his men, because in truth, he agreed with them, but as an officer he would never betray his true feelings. It was becoming a dilemma for him and one he discussed in his confession with Father Tomelski.

288

Father Tomelski had arrived at the front a few months beforehand. A young, intelligent Pole, with a kind open face, he had been a breath of fresh air around the camp. He was popular with the men and could just as easily share a risqué joke with a soldier as take tea with a General.

Nikolas and Julius had taken to him straight away and looked forward to Mass, a ceremony that had become especially important to them over the last few months. Never a deeply religious man, the war had given Julius a renewed calling to his faith and he found solace in his prayers and benedictions. This was increased when he watched the work of the priest, as he walked among the wounded giving them comfort in their pain, or when he was delivering the last rites to some poor soul. Julius could see how this young man's religious comfort meant so much to his men, and realized how important religion was to so many people.

Father Tomelski was never too busy to help anyone, even after hours of tending the sick and dying, his face gray with fatigue and sadness, the Father would leave his bed to write an important letter for a dying man to his family. Many of the men could not write so the priest would write for them, painstakingly writing in his bold copperplate script. Although most open within their confession, Nikolas and Julius were often joined in their tent by Father Tomelski where they would quietly discuss the worries they had about the war. Although a priest he had a mature understanding of warfare. He could always be relied upon to hold a stimulating discussion that would provide many thought provoking subjects for Nikolas and Julius to think about.

After the cessation of fighting in August Nikolas and Julius were ordered to report to Colonel Genner. The Colonel looked tired and drawn, but then so did most of the men after six months of fighting. As they entered his room he asked them to sit down and offered them coffee. The Colonel picked up his cup, then leaned back in his chair appearing to stare at the ceiling.

"Well, gentlemen, I must congratulate you. Your artillery fire seems to be working well, and you have only lost five men from your unit, not bad I think"

Julius received this statement with skepticism. He regretted the loss of the men, even if it was only five. Such a small loss was to be expected as they had not encountered real combat yet. Their task had been to provide artillery gunfire on to the attacking Italians. This had been done from very protected positions, but the loss of even five men was something he did not live happily with. The worst thing was to help their senior officers write to the families of the dead men. It seemed hypocritical to describe a person to someone, who would then write a sympathetic letter to his family as though he had known him well. Julius wished he could write to the families but this was not allowed. Colonel Genner ceased his perusal of the ceiling as he looked directly at them.

"This, gentlemen, is completely off the record and is not to be repeated, but tell me, just what has Colonel Reichart got against you two?"

The words hit Julius and Nikolas like a bombshell. The color drained from their faces as they looked at each other not knowing what to say to the Colonel.

"For myself I have found you both very able officers" the Colonel continued "but it seems you are not popular with the Colonel, can you explain this to me or have I missed something? Whatever you say will not go beyond these four walls, I assure you"

Nikolas decided to speak, "as far as we know, we have not done anything. If this is off the record sir, then all I can say is that Colonel Reichart has not liked us since the day that we joined him in Prague. Certain people seem to think that it is because we are the sons of Colonels and he thought of us as rather privileged. That is all we can think of"

Julius rolled his eyes to the ceiling at his friend's frankness, and waited to see how Colonel Genner would react to his outburst. Colonel Genner burst out laughing, a big booming laugh that was probably heard by the Italians down on the plain.

"That would be right. I think that just about sums up Colonel Reichart, and that is definitely off the record, gentlemen. But that does not help your situation I am afraid" He held up a sheath of papers as he said, "these are letters from Colonel Reichart, recommending both of you be moved up into the high mountains to assist our forces up there. He insists, and I quote, 'they are both well used to mountain warfare and are ably trained to survive in winter conditions' I see from your records that this is not an unfair statement, but I have to tell you gentlemen it is a very inhospitable assignment. You are going up there just as the winter weather approaches, it will not be easy for you. Combat in the mountains is very different to here in Gorz, but army headquarters have accepted Colonel Reichart's assessment and you leave as soon as possible and travel north to the Carnic Mountains"

Julius and Nikolas listened with stony faces. They knew they could not do anything about their new postings, but were far from happy about it. They had helped to create the artillery positions at Gorz and wanted to stay to oversee them. They also knew that Genner was right. They were going into the mountains at the wrong time of the year, where conditions would be atrocious and their thoughts travelled back to the storm on the Grossglockner. They both thanked Colonel Genner for his honesty and saluted their senior officer as they left the room.

"Try not to worry too much, gentlemen, I will try to get you back here as soon as I can. I at least think you are exemplary officers. Good day"

When they left Genner's room Nikolas' face was as black as thunder, "that bastard has got the last laugh hasn't he? If he were here I could easily strangle him"

Julius was alarmed by his friend's fury. "What is done is done, Nikolas. Who knows, this assignment could be interesting. You yourself said the mountains were virtually impenetrable, it will be interesting working out the logistics of armaments in that terrain"

Julius statement calmed Nikolas' mood as he turned to his friend and punched him on the shoulder, "only you could find something good to say about this, maybe I should strangle you instead"

Their departure was delayed as the army was waiting for reinforcements and there had been sporadic fighting in Plezzo and Tolmin. Forces were being redeployed from the Russian front as well as Landsturm mountain brigades to swell the support teams. The Landsturm was composed of men up to the age of thirty-nine who had previously served in the army. They were a reserve force who were expected, in time of conflict, to act as a line of communication and supply the troops, but in a non-combative role. There was also work to be done at the rear of the occupying army. So far the men had been adequately fed and clothed, but as the war progressed food was getting scarcer. This was partly because of the cutting of supply lines but also the need for more food due to the increase of men at the front.

291

To this end men were put to work to turn land behind the battle lines into arable lands where crops could be sown to feed the troops. The weather in September had turned very cold, especially at night which added to the deprivations of the men and did not help with the supply of food.

Julius and Nikolas found themselves kicking their heels, waiting to be given permission to leave. They were sad to be leaving their men behind and even Father Tomelski expressed his unhappiness at their going. "Who am I going to have my stimulating arguments with to occupy my evenings?" joked the priest.

"I tell you what father," replied Nikolas, mischievously, "if a Colonel Reichart returns to this camp, have a talk to him. He is a fair-minded man, open to new suggestions and ideas. I am sure you will spend many happy hours in sociable debate"

Julius had to warn the Father of his friend's teasing, he did not think that Reichart, a Protestant Lutheran, would happily take advice from a priest.

Hans had proved to be a problem. When he had learned of their reassignment he had openly wept and begged them to take him with them. Despite trying to persuade him of the harshness that they would encounter, of which he had no experience, Hans would not be swayed. He annoyed them so much with his endless request to accompany them that in exasperation they asked Colonel Genner if Hans could continue in their service. They felt sure the Colonel would not countenance such a move. Unfortunately they were wrong. No doubt weighed down with far weightier contemplations Genner acceded to their request with a wave of his hand and a summary dismissal. Hans was overjoyed and quickly made himself ready for the journey. Nikolas and Julius were issued with winter Alpine uniforms, white for camouflage, warm heavy clothing, lined boots and alpenstocks. At last at the beginning of October, with heavy hearts, Julius and Nikolas left Gorz and headed for the mountains.

XXII

The journey took several weeks. As they were travelling on their own they had to detour round the rear of the fighting lines, through friendly country, and the climb into the mountains was long and hard. They travelled on Steel and Phantom and behind them came Hans with a packhorse. Their route was between various camps behind the lines, most nights they stopped at these camps for shelter and food. On the nights that they did not encounter a camp they slept under the stars and ate their rations. To Julius it was a bewildering change from the battle zone. They passed through beautiful countryside and apart from meetings with men in uniform, one could almost believe that they were on a holiday trek. The weather was turning noticeably colder, it was unusually cold for the time of year and Nikolas and Julius were worried about reaching their destination before the snow fell.

When they came to the foothills of the Carnic Mountains their worst fears were realized. Already on the lower ground the snow had fallen, so they knew their ascent into the mountains would be long and dangerous. Because of their horses the first part could not be negotiated by the mountain funicular railway, although it had been kept in use for civilians and soldiers alike at the outbreak of war. The rail line was well behind enemy lines and so far the army had not seen the need to dismantle it in case of enemy advancement.

Their journey would have to be made on horseback and Julius and Nikolas hoped that their steeds would be able to negotiate the terrain. Both men had not foreseen such heavy snowfalls so early in the winter. Hans was entranced by his first view of the northern Alps. He spent most of the journey with a broad smile on his face pointing at the breathtaking scenery. As Julius surveyed the scene before him he found it very hard to connect the beautiful, peaceful vista before him, to the war ravaged lands around Gorz. Gorz itself had come in for some heavy bombing in the last few weeks and as they had left the city Julius reflected on how it had changed since they had first arrived. Most streets had been bombed and shattered buildings and rubble straddled the roads, so sad in such a beautiful city.

The journey was steady but slow. Julius had been worried about Hans' reaction to the difficult conditions, but they did not seem to bother him at all. He proceeded with enough enthusiasm for all three of them, did not seem to notice the cold, and reveled in the clean, bright air that could only be inhaled in the mountains. They knew they were climbing higher as the altitude started to grip at their chests, making their heads ache and leaving them feeling light headed. This did not trouble Julius and Nikolas too much, they knew the condition was only temporary and that within days they would once again be used to the thin air. The mountains seemed eerie, so quiet after the noise of battle in Gorz. The horses had to take more rests as the thin air started to affect them and Julius and Nikolas walked with their rifles at the ready, aware that the enemy could be anywhere.

At last they encountered a guard post, where a surly young corporal greeted them with raised rifle and told them to put their hands above their heads. After he had retrieved their papers from inside their coats, he apologized and saluted them as was appropriate to their rank. Julius told him not to worry when the corporal explained that there were enemy soldiers taking uniforms off dead Austrians and trying to infiltrate the camps. No one was to be trusted they were informed, even in uniform. While the corporal shouted orders for some men to accompany Julius and Nikolas to their camp, Julius asked him how the fighting was faring around these parts.

"It has definitely died down in the last week" the corporal informed them, "heavy snow and the bitter cold have not helped the situation. The use of firearms is restricted, with such heavy snowfalls we have to be wary of avalanches. I have never known it as cold as this so early in the winter and we are experiencing a lot of cases of frostbite, make sure you wrap up well sir, it will take you some time to get acclimatized to the cold"

After thanking the corporal Julius and Nikolas were escorted by a group of six men, who looked happy to be on the move instead of standing around getting cold at the guard post. The men moved quickly and quietly, obviously used to their terrain, and Julius and Nikolas, leading their horses, found it difficult to keep up with them. The sergeant in charge of the soldiers halted his men after Nikolas had asked them to slow down.

294

"Sorry sir" replied the sergeant with a smile on his face, "I forgot you're not used to conditions up here. We have learnt that you have to move quickly so that you are not a sitting target, you never know who's hiding behind a rock, aiming his barrel at you"

"Do you mean there are snipers around here?" asked Nikolas breathlessly, very red in the face with his hands on his hips, trying to recover himself. His breath escaped in short bursts and curled up into the sky in white swirls of air.

"Yes sir. Those Italians are a wily lot, though I have to say their Alpini troops are well trained. They are all over the place, they climb the mountains in ones and twos, hoping to pick us off. Of course we do it back to them, so all is fair in love and war as they say. They are doing exactly what we do, spying out our positions, noting munitions and troop movements, seeing what our defenses are, and if they manage to take a pot-shot at the enemy, then that's a bonus. Not a lot else you can do when the weather is so bad"

Julius was amazed at the man. He sounded as though he was talking about a playground game, rather than the fighting of a war. He decided to hold his tongue, no doubt the man was telling the truth. He was obviously an experienced mountaineer, his leathery complexion and knowledge of the land were a testament to that. Julius reflected that his war was going to be very different to the one he had been experiencing for the last few months.

The camp they arrived at was very similar to the camp they had stayed in above Heiligenblut. There were sturdy log cabins nestled into the mountainside and hidden by a vast wood of spruce trees, so that from a distance you would not know it was there. Even the smoking chimneystacks disappeared into the green foliage above them so that the enemy could not locate the camp. Skis were stacked up against the cabins and Julius felt a rush of excitement and nostalgia as he realized he would soon be skiing again.

After having their papers checked once again they installed their horses in the stable block. If they climbed higher into the mountains, as they knew they would have to, the horses would no longer be needed. The horses would be invaluable in and around the camp, and when they had to descend, but from now on their skis would be their main form of transport. After leaving Hans to unpack their belongings Nikolas and Julius went to report to their senior officer. As they walked through the snow, observing the constant activity around the camp they heard a familiar booming voice behind them, "well I never, they told me you were coming, but I could not believe it. So what have you two done wrong to get this posting?"

Major Hals had not changed at all, if anything he looked swarthier than ever, and he still maintained the larger than life persona that endeared him to everybody.

"Major Hals" cried Nikolas as he saluted his senior officer, "what are you doing here?"

"My boy, my boy, how quickly you forget" said Hals, with a twinkle in his eye, "How could the Austro-Hungarian army fight a mountain war without Major Hals? I am personal adviser to General Feldke, they seem to think I know something about these mountains"

Julius laughed at Hals' affected modesty. What Hals did not know about the mountains was probably not worth knowing.

"And where are your friends, von Kutz and the brave Leitner, I am surprised they are not here with you"

Nikolas told the Major that Josef and Viktor were on the Russian front. Julius noticed the fleeting look of dismay that crossed the Major's face at this news and knew that the Major was also thinking of the rumors of heavy casualties in Russia. After promising to meet later, Julius and Nikolas went to report to their new senior officer.

One thing that the Austrian Army got right was their appointment of the senior officers who they sent to oversee mountain warfare. The senior officers sent to the Alps all had long experiences of life in the mountains, loved the terrain, and recognized the drawbacks of the territory for their men fighting in such inhospitable circumstances. Such a man was Colonel Adler. Born in the mountains he could be described as the perfect Alpine leader. Julius and Nikolas immediately took to the Colonel. His men adored him, he was always fair, he loved the mountains and he understood them. In his early fifties, he carried the weather-beaten look of all mountain men, but when he spoke it was with the assurance and conviction of a man who knew exactly what he was talking about, a man who always told the truth, no matter how demoralizing it might be. He believed in telling his men the exact situation they were in and the consequences they might encounter and he never sent his men on any foolhardy missions that he did not feel had some chance of success. Julius realized over the next few weeks that the Colonel was also lucky in the steadfast support he received from General Feldke, helped by Major Hals' wise observations.

The first few weeks were spent acclimatizing themselves to their new surroundings. They skied a lot, having to brush up on their techniques, and encountering again the aches and pains of unknown muscles after a days skiing. They were briefed on the present situation, the positioning of troops and armaments, where defenses were built and the general tactics of the Italian army so far.

Listening to the other officers recounting their experiences it became clear that combat up here was necessarily carried out on a one to one basis, with small units going off for days, and sometimes weeks at a time. They had to fend for themselves, hopefully finding their own food, though this had been difficult since the snow had fallen. Julius knew that the most important thing was to watch your own back up in the mountains. You had to be constantly alert, apart from the fortified strongholds the slopes could be very open and one could be seen and heard from a long way off.

This was apparent one day when Julius had gone with a group of ten men onto the slopes. They were taking him to show the positions of the heavy guns and ammunition. Colonel Adler had realized, due to the course they had been attending when the outbreak of war had been declared, that Julius and Nikolas had the most up to date information on armaments of anyone in the camp. He ordered that Julius carry out a recce of all their gun positions and report back any improvements that might be needed. Julius was accompanied by a Captain Wesse, who was a brilliant skier. As they inspected the sites, Julius made notes in a small notebook in his cursory shorthand that he had learnt as a cadet. This was extremely difficult as he had to write in his gloves, it was dangerous to take them off in such extreme cold for fear of frostbite. Julius had wondered if he would be able to shoot a rifle with his gloves on, but a young soldier had morbidly told him that if he had the enemy in his sights he would find the trigger easily enough.

As they were returning to the camp after a long day they were skiing through a group of trees when Captain Wesse came to an abrupt stop and held up his hand for silence. Every man stopped as swiftly as possible, although Julius turned red as his skis clattered into that of the man in front of him. The captain motioned for a young soldier to hand him some field glasses. Julius wondered what the captain had seen, for as he scanned the horizon before him everything looked tranquil and quiet. The captain's perusal came to a halt at a dip on a far slope, shielded by some trees. Julius could still not see anything, but as the next officer in seniority he was handed the glasses and when he looked through them saw a small shining light and was certain that something dark had just moved in the midst of the trees. Julius dropped the glasses and nodded to the captain, who, with the use of sign language, sent half the men off with Julius to circumvent the valley below, while he himself took the rest of the men around the other side of the valley, to meet up at where they believed there might be enemy soldiers in wait. The men all side stepped back up to behind the trees and then noiselessly started their descent around the valley.

Julius felt an incredible awareness of mixed emotions as he carefully skied down the side of the valley. He could hear his own heart thumping as the excitement of the chase overtook him, but he also felt a weakness in his knees at the thought of a possible confrontation with the enemy.

It was easy to creep up on their foe, if there was anyone there they were in a deep depression of the slope; Julius and his men would not be seen until they had climbed up to the top of the ridge. When they arrived below the slope Julius could see their other party arriving. With a thumbs up, they all primed their guns and advanced into the hollow.

What they found took them completely by surprise. There, crouching with their backs to Julius' party, were two Italian soldiers, oblivious to the fact that to their rear were a dozen Austrian soldiers. They kept glancing from behind their refuge of the trees, looking up the slopes to where Julius had just come from. Captain Wesse pointed his rifle at the men and ordered them to raise their hands above their heads. They probably could not understand any German, but they knew enough to know they had been captured and so rose from their crouching positions with their hands above their heads. Two soldiers skied down to them and took away their rifles and roughly searched their uniforms for any further weapons. Satisfied, they nodded to the captain that the men had been disarmed. Ordering some of his men to stay on the edge of the dip and keep a lookout in case these men were not on their own, Captain Wesse told Julius, and the rest of their party, to follow him down.

Julius was amazed as he came to a stop in front of the men. In fact they were not men, but boys, probably not much older than Georg, both shaking in fear, and Julius was embarrassed to notice that one of them had soiled his trousers in his fright. One of the boys wore a pair of round spectacles that magnified his eyes, eyes that held so much terror that almost against his will Julius felt sorry for him. He guessed it was the spectacles that had been glinting in the alpine sun, and so had alerted the vigilant Captain Wesse. Seeing the two boys he realized that they probably thought they were going to be shot, after all if he were captured he would not put it past the Italians to shoot him. How would he cope with facing such a death, would he soil himself as the boy had?

One of Julius' men spoke a little Italian so he tried to find out what the boys were doing there. He discovered that they had been in a scouting party of about twenty who had been caught up in an horrendous storm a couple of days ago. During the storm they had become isolated from their companions, and when the storm had abated had found themselves totally lost, with no compass or bearings to find their way back to their camp. Julius could sympathize with their predicament, he knew what it was like to be lost in a storm. They had spent the last two days trying to find their way back to the Italian lines, with no success. Captain Wesse laughed at this and said rather unkindly, "stupid bloody Italians. They were heading straight for our lines, no sense of direction these Latins" all the men joined in the captain's laughter, and although they did not understand what the captain was saying the boys understood they were being laughed at.

The boy's hands were tied behind their backs and they had to be blindfolded as the captain pointed out that he did not want them to know the location of their camp. The Italians were then tied by ropes to the last skiers and dragged behind them back to the camp. The journey became very slow as several times the boys stumbled in the deep, powdery snow, when they were roughly hoisted up and pointed in the right direction. Julius knew they were being treated badly, but held his tongue as he saw Captain Wesse watching him.

"You may not like it, but if I told you what had happened to some of our soldiers at the hands of the Italians, you would think I am being very lenient"

Julius had heard the stories around the camp of the treatment of Austrian soldiers at the hands of the Italians, but how much was true, and how much was propaganda he could not be sure.

At last they reached their camp where they handed over their prisoners, who would be sent down the mountain to a holding camp. The two young boys looked relieved when they were told what was going to happen to them, obviously believing that they were to be shot by the enemy soldiers. Their faces erupted into large grins making them look even younger. Whilst Julius was writing out his report for the Colonel, Nikolas joined him.

"I hear you captured some prisoners. I did not realize that we were kidnapping children from the kindergarten now"

"You have seen them?" asked Julius.

"Oh yes. They are creating quite a sideshow for the men. It is their first look at an Italian for weeks" Julius started to rise from his seat.

"Do not worry yourself Julius, Major Hals has seen the men return to their duties. A detail will be here within the hour to take them away. Why so worried about Italian pigs?"

Julius was startled by his friend's language, but could not blame him. He hated Italians as much as any Austrian did, but the sight of the two boys had unsettled him. "I am not worried about them" replied Julius, "but think about it Nikolas, they are so young. Do you know what my first thought was when I saw them? I thought of Georg. They cannot be much older than him, they could be him in a few months time, and he could find himself in the same situation. I just hope he is treated as well, which is not really saying that much"

Nikolas was very quiet, realizing the truth of Julius' words, and he was still sitting on his bed deep in thought when Julius gathered up his report and went to Colonel Adler's office.

The winter months were spent in strengthening defenses or creating new ones, the weather was very harsh and fighting was spasmodic due to the terrible conditions. Heavy mists hung over the mountain most of the time and there were frequent snowstorms. Many men succumbed to the cold conditions, suffering from colds and influenza, some proving to be fatal. More men were lost to avalanches, the inhospitable terrain and illness than in combat over those winter months. Christmas and New Year passed with hardly an acknowledgement and many days were spent confined to their cabins due to the weather. The horses became restless with the inactivity, as did the men, and morale became very low. Communications were difficult, the only news coming from messengers who occasionally managed to get through the blocked passes and the lack of letters from loved ones increased the men's dissatisfaction. Food was beginning to run low and Colonel Adler had to admit to his officers that if the weather did not improve within the next few weeks the situation would become very grave.

Towards the end of January, the days became brighter and the men rejoiced in feeling the warmth of a cold, but bright sun on their faces. The men's humor improved as the weather improved, and with it the realization that fighting would once more begin. From further down the mountains could be heard the constant sound of the artillery bombardment as the two adversaries shelled each other's positions. Even when they were lying in bed at night Julius and Nikolas could hear the sound of the whistling shells and the loud explosion that followed when a shell hit a target. Julius wondered if he would ever forget the sounds of the relentless bombings, even when they stopped for a short while the noises still reverberated inside his head.

At the beginning of February, news came to the camp that reinforcements, replacements and provisions were arriving soon. This was good news, the food supply was getting short and Julius thought that if the men had to eat much more wurst and potatoes they would have a mutiny on their hands.

Julius was on guard duty one day when from below could be seen a large company of men, making their way up the mountain pass. The snow had melted enough to expose the brown earth on the passes below and spring mountain flowers were pushing their dainty heads through the snowy blanket around them that was diminishing daily.

Julius ordered his men on guard, as he had found out when he had first arrived, no one was to be trusted. The retinue made its way up and a young soldier was sent on ahead to present their papers to the guards. With everything in order, the men proceeded up the mountain, the officers on horseback, the men walking behind. Julius saluted the senior officer and ordered a detachment of his men to guide the company to the camp. It was as the men passed him that he saw a familiar face.

"My God, I am dreaming, if I had known you were here, I would have asked to have been assigned elsewhere. It is no good trying to hide from the war up here, Mayer"

Josef looked exactly as Julius remembered him, and so much like his mother at that moment that Julius felt a large constriction of his heart. Josef was still as handsome, with the same confident swagger and easy elegance, so evident as he slid from his horse to embrace his old friend. It was only up close that Julius could see the subtle changes in his friend. There was a long deep scar along Josef's jawbone, which Julius had to grudgingly admit, added a certain something to his friend's good looks, if that were possible. But it was in his face that Julius could see the difference. Josef looked tired, with deep lines etched into his face that expressed the terrible things Josef must have witnessed in fighting on the Russian front. His eyes held a wariness of everything around him, and had lost the warmth that they had always shown before. If one did not know Josef they would probably say they saw no difference in Josef von Kutz, but Julius could see it all too well.

There was no time for questions, so many that Julius wanted to ask, but Josef had to rejoin his company. With a promise to see him later he jumped on his horse with his usual cavalier attitude and proceeded on his way. After he had gone Julius realized that he had not told Josef that Nikolas was in the camp, but presumed he would find him soon enough. Julius spent the rest of the day in agitated expectation of his relief so that he could get back to camp as soon as possible.

When Julius returned to his cabin he rushed in the door shouting to Nikolas that Josef had arrived, only to find his two friends relaxing on the beds and sharing a joke. For a moment Julius was swept back to Vienna all those years ago. He almost expected Viktor and Smid to come through the door at any moment. After greeting his friend again he started to regale him with a barrage of questions, but Josef laughingly told Julius that he and Nikolas had been waiting for Julius in order to eat. He said he was starving and he would answer all his questions after he had had his meal.

They walked to the mess cabin where all the new and old officers were introduced. During the meal Josef was very quiet as the other officers in their company gave their account of the war. The officers were optimistic of the Austro-Hungarian advances so far, but Julius watched Josef as his face became darker as the meal progressed.

At last they were back in their cabin, where Julius ordered Hans to produce the brandy and Josef started to relax. Josef began by telling them about Viktor. He told them that Viktor had covered himself with glory and had been promoted to lieutenant, and that he was very much alive when Josef had left the Russian front. The news greatly cheered Julius and Nikolas. Josef was reticent to talk about his experiences in Russia but what he told them was enough to understand how terrible the war there had been. Josef was in the conquering army that had taken Lemberg in June and also present when the Russians had retaken it in August. That defeat had left a bitter taste in his mouth, and his account of the battles were both bloody and horrifying as Julius and Nikolas heard about the full horror of war. Josef portrayed a disillusioned man in a disillusioned army. When Nikolas had pointed out his was a very different story from the one that had been told over dinner by his fellow officers Josef merely sneered as he said, "but they are good loyal soldiers, who have been ordered to spread the patriotic word. Do you think any of us would be allowed to tell the truth? I am only telling you because you are my oldest friends, and I know this will go no further than these four walls. We are honorable gentlemen in an honorable army, did you not know?" he added sarcastically, "I know this is war, and the Russians are a vile, wild people, who employ ignorant peasants to soldier in their army, but sometimes I am afraid we have done things which are just as bad in the name of our beloved emperor. I have seen mass slaughters of defenseless Russians by our own soldiers as we retreated, brutality is not something confined to our enemy, believe me"
Julius thought of Franz, perhaps understanding more about his brother than he had before.
"At least things here are not so bad" observed Nikolas, staring into his glass, "too many men have lost their life, it is true, but at least we have been able to defend our borders with some success"
Josef laughed sarcastically as he answered, "My God, you have been too long in these mountains, have you not heard

what is happening down in the valleys? How long have you been here?"

With mounting dread Julius and Nikolas listened as Josef told them what he had heard in the camps on his way up into the mountains. After they had left Gorz the weather had worsened. There had been long periods of torrential rainfall. The rivers had flooded and the trenches had been transformed into torrents of mud under the beating rain. There had been heavy fighting on the Carso where losses had been high for the Austrian Army but worse for the Italians where some regiments had lost over half their men in the bitter fighting.

As the end of the year approached the temperatures had been lower than any man could remember and some nights had dropped to eighteen grades below zero. The men had tried to offset the terrible conditions by covering the trenches with sheets of metal, and wood, and some had tried to line their dugouts with sandbags. The situation was becoming so bad that the army had to order extra clothing, especially woolen garments and warming food. The woods behind Gorz and similar strongholds were stripped bare to provide heating as hundreds of thousands of men became exposed to the terrible weather.

Despite all these good intentions it was known that several thousand men, Italians and Austrians, had died in the winter months from exposure, disease and avalanches. Julius and Nikolas were grieved by Josef's revelations. They felt inadequate, having endured the last few months in the comparative safety of their position while down below so many of their fellow countrymen had died from the awful conditions they had been exposed to. They were somewhat consoled by Josef telling them that the campaign on the Austrian border with Italy was seen by the Austrian people as a success and was hailed as an indication of the great might of the Empire, this view evidently being propounded by the newspapers and the news reports screened by the picture houses. Nikolas asked Josef why he had been assigned to their mountain regiment.

"Do you know I have not the faintest idea, I wish I knew. They have directed some troops from the Russian front to bolster troops on the border, but why I am here in the mountains I do not know. Hardly my cavalry training I would think. I presume they are short of soldiers who have been trained in the mountains, though I cannot say I am upset by my posting. It is good to smell the clean fresh air, instead of the stench of dead bodies and the smoke of the battlefield"

Josef's company had also brought the much anticipated letters from home and for the next few days the men in the camp were seen with their noses in their letters which had accumulated over the past few months. Mama wrote that she was still worried about Papa, but was happier with regards to Franz's health, which was confirmed by a letter from Gretha with glowing references to Franz's improved health and a short, shakily written note from Franz himself which cheered Julius up immensely.

Karl wrote to say that he had at last been released for active service and was awaiting his posting. Irmy's letter was more alarming as she wrote, with the censor in mind, about conditions at the hospital. She told him that she was very busy and that the hospital was very full and that she was at work so much lately that she had hardly seen Mama. Her greatest worry was that Richard could be called to the front, and with the news of so many casualties Julius thought he would not be surprised if that was the case. Julius also received a letter from Erika, very friendly, but written with a certain reserve, as if she had found it a difficult letter to write. She wrote that against her parent's wishes she has applied for the position as an auxiliary nurse at a field hospital. She was not allowed to say where, but would be leaving Prague very soon.

Julius was shocked by the news. Although he knew there were many female nurses at the field hospitals, he was not sure he agreed with their presence there. He did not believe it was the place for a female, how could they cope with the horrendous sights he himself had seen on the battlefield? Working in the field hospitals could also be dangerous, many field hospitals had been hit by indiscriminate bombing, with fatalities amongst the medical staff. Julius had to reflect that it was lucky that Irmy was married to Richard, as he was sure, knowing her impulsive nature, that she would have volunteered to go to the front as well.

Nikolas was pleased with his correspondence. His mother wrote that his father had been assigned to Army headquarters in Vienna, although, like Julius, he had not had a letter from his father. Nikolas laughed as he read from his mother's letter. "It seems that Georg presented himself at the local recruiting station and told them he was old enough for active service. Luckily the sergeant used to be in my father's company and so recognized him. He marched Georg round to my mother's house where he was severely reprimanded for wasting army time. When will the little rogue learn? God if he could see the horrors of this war he would be hiding in the attic of our house rather than trying to join the army before he was old enough. Poor Mama, it is bad enough that I am out here, without having to deal with Georg" Suse had written him many letters. "Are you going to marry this girl?" asked Josef, regarding his friend with a mocking smile on his face.

"Do you know I had not really thought about it, but since you ask, yes I think I will. If this war has taught me anything, it is to appreciate ones loved ones and, if she will have me, I think I will ask Suse to marry me"

Julius regarded his friend in amazement. He had never thought of Nikolas marrying anybody, and he was not sure he was marrying Suse for the right reasons. He had never talked of love when discussing Suse, indeed had not even mentioned it when declaring he was going to marry her. Julius knew that Nikolas still held a place in his heart for Irmy, but would not have advised his friend not to marry just because of that. He truly felt that Suse and Nikolas were not a great love match, and wanted only the best for his friend. Without telling him about Irmy, Julius related his reservations to Josef when they were alone. Josef upset Julius by laughing at him.

"Oh, Julius, you never change, still the eternal romantic. Have you ever thought that there may not be such a thing as a 'great love' for Nikolas? That none of us may meet the partner of our dreams? Maybe Nikolas is not deeply in love with this girl, but that does not mean they may not live happily together for the rest of their days. Stop looking for perfection, Julius, it really is not there. You may let your life pass you by looking for it, and that would be a terrible waste. Believe me, I know"

Julius was tempted to ask Josef what he meant, but was hurt by his friend laughing at him so he changed the subject, but later he began to wonder if maybe Josef could be right. Was he too particular? Maybe he should have remained with Erika, after all they were compatible in so many ways. His thoughts troubled him, but after a long reflection Julius decided to forget all thoughts of love and his future. He was in the middle of a war, and he did not know how long it would last or if he would survive it. He would concentrate on defending his country and leave romantic notions for another time.

Julius' reunion with Josef was to be short lived. A few weeks after his arrival came orders for Julius to travel to the Trentino. He was sad to be leaving his friend so soon but was glad that he was returning to the job he had been trained for, the artillery. Nikolas was to stay in the high mountains and his frustration at Julius' posting was obvious. "Why have they sent you down, when I have to stay here, acting on guard duty again? There are rumors of a major offensive in the next few months and I will be stuck here"
Julius sympathized with his friend and was sad to be parting from him. Once again he had the notion of Nikolas as his lucky talisman and he would have given anything for Nikolas to be accompanying him down to the lower slopes. The months of inactivity had made everybody hungry for action, though it was noticeable that the men of Josef's company were quite happy to stay in their present positions. They had all seen enough of bloodshed and war to last them a lifetime.

It was sad to say goodbye to Hans, who was upset to see Julius going but was comforted by the fact that he still had Nikolas to look after. Colonel Adler thanked him for all his help and Major Hals came to see him and the company of men who were to accompany Julius to the battle zone.
"So you are going, second Lieutenant Mayer. I think I shall miss you. I told you I would see all your friends before the end of this war, I suppose you have no more news of Leitner?" Julius shook his head. "Well never mind, I am sure he will turn up. He was a survivor that one" and with comforting words he dismissed the men on their journey.

Nikolas and Josef came to see him off. There was much banter and laughter, but beneath it was an underlying sadness at the parting. Julius knew that his friends were watching him as he and his men threaded their way carefully down the slippery mountain passes, but he did not look back. There was a large lump in his throat and he knew the reason he did not look back was in case the sight of his two closest friends waving goodbye was too much for him.

When Julius arrived at the base camp the area was a hive of activity. The snow had disappeared from the lower slopes and it was obvious there had been a lot of work carried out during the winter months, strengthening the front. Julius found himself in quarters with seven other officers, and after he had stowed his belongings he was taken along to an officer's meeting to be briefed on the future advancement plans of the army. There had been heavy fighting from Plezzo to the sea, again resulting in heavy losses, with offensives, then counter offensives, but ultimately little ground lost and little taken. Julius reflected that it had been the same story for the last year and not for the first time pondered on the reason for it all. He was not the only soldier to be thinking this as the reason for the winter fortifications became apparent.

It had been decided that in the next few weeks the Austrian army were to launch a massive offensive from the Trentino through the plains towards Trento. The attack was to be supported by more than two hundred guns and over three hundred thousand men. If successful the army would be in an overwhelming position, being at the rear of the Italian lines that were attacking the Soca front. Julius was immediately set to work checking guns and ammunition, positioning them for battle and transporting them with the lines of advancing men. The thought of a glorious victory spurred the men on and for the next couple of weeks the whole camp toiled with the optimistic air of a conquering army.

Observing the plains before him Julius regarded the situation that was to come. The strategy was a good one, it was known that the Italian commander, General Cadorna, was concentrating his efforts on the Soca front, hoping to take Gorz and ultimately Trieste, the ultimate prize for the Italians. For the past few weeks the brigades and divisions on the Soca had been told to keep up the artillery fire and small attacks to keep the interest away from the Trentino front. There had also been localized attacks in the mountain zones where there had been bitter fighting. If the offensive could be launched as a surprise to the Italians Julius could see their ultimate success.

The evening before the battle Julius lay in bed talking to his brother officers. No one could sleep as the thought of tomorrow's battle occupied their minds. The fatalities for junior officers had been enormous in the first year of the war. Junior officers faced the most danger of all, they were supposed to lead the charge from the front, straight into enemy rifle and machine gun fire and it was well known that promotion was becoming much easier for junior officers who

308

survived the battle merely because so many other young officers were dying. Despite the knowledge of their situation all the officers knew their duty and what was expected of them. The night before a battle was especially hard, lying in their canvas tents, listening to the sound of the constant shell explosions, wondering if you would ever sleep in your bed again. Some officers hid their worries with forced cheerful banter, while others preferred to remain quiet, lying in their beds staring at their tarpaulin ceiling as they smoked a cigarette. Others read, or wrote what they hoped would not be last letters home to their families, and everybody prayed.

The next morning Julius was with his men ready for the signal to advance. Phantom was especially twitchy that morning, his ears drawn back and showing the whites of his eyes, he snorted through his nostrils and stamped the ground. Julius and his men were positioned just to the left of the main advancing divisions, their guns aimed on the enemy. Julius had made his calculations with his clinometer and the big guns were loaded, ready to be fired. At the rear could be seen some observation balloons. For the last few days observation balloons had been launched to observe enemy positions, these were simple inflatable bags with a wickerwork basket suspended underneath from within which one or two observers could look ahead over enemy lines, noting their battle strategy, looking for any unusual activity or spotting the accuracy of artillery fire. Julius believed that a balloon observer must be the worst job in the army, not only did you have to ascend up into the air, an occupation he did not really believe in, despite the increase of flying machines in the sky, but it was also highly dangerous. Up in the balloon, tethered to a rope from the ground, the observers were sitting targets for the enemy and were frequently shot down.

Senior officers delivered their stirring speeches of patriotism and then retreated to a safe distance behind the lines to observe the success or failure of their plans. The signal was given and the advance began. It was the first time that Julius had entered the front line of battle, all he could see was a mass of running men and horses as they ran down the plain towards their foe. Julius was occupied setting off the guns to provide a cover for the advancing soldiers. He observed where the shells landed and had to keep adjusting the guns to make sure their targets were accurate ones. The noise was overwhelming, the sound of running feet, horses and guns being pulled along were overshadowed by the constant barrage of artillery fire. There were the yells of the men as they advanced along the battlefield and the screams of the dying as they were hit by shells. Frequently Julius and his men had to dive for cover as shells hurtled towards them and landed on the battlefield. Julius had difficulty holding Phantom as the sounds of battle and the smell of blood sent him into a frenzy. The battle proceeded for several hours, with Julius and his men holding their positions to the rear of the field and siting their guns beyond their own soldiers and onto the Italian lines. Despite their rear position it was obvious that the artillery were a target for the Italian shelling. The artillery divisions were known to be dangerous assignments in battle as the enemy would always try to blow up the guns aimed at their advance parties, and several times the armory would have to be moved as the enemy would eventually pinpoint their position.

Late in the afternoon Julius was trying to help a soldier release a breech that had become jammed, a common occurrence on the bigger guns. The cry to warn Julius was too late as he looked up and watched in horror as a shell came through the air towards him. He knew he should fall to the ground but stood transfixed as the metal shell screamed through the air. Suddenly he was pulled to the ground and Julius found himself face down in the earth with a protective arm over him. The earth erupted around him and came cascading down over him and he thought he had been hit until he lifted his head and saw an enormous hole in the ground near him and his men. Julius looked round to see who his savior had been and found himself looking at a young corporal in his regiment. He was completely covered in thick black mud, his face was black and only his eyes and his teeth were visible as he gave Julius an enormous grin. "You all right sir?" he asked, the grin still wide on his face. Looking down at himself, Julius realized that he too was covered in mud and must look just as awful as the young corporal

"Yes, yes I think so" said Julius shakily, "Thank you, I...."

"Don't mention it sir. All in a days work"

In all the mayhem around him Julius had to laugh at the young man's cheek. His laughter soon halted in his throat as he looked around him. There was a heavy veil of smoke

310

and as it began to clear Julius could see bodies with limbs blown off, mutilated and covered in blood lying in terrible, twisted positions, all over the plain. Julius saw behind him a man dying as the stumps of his legs twitched and his eyes rolled around in their sockets until they stopped and turned heavenwards in their deathlike stare. Julius pulled himself up onto his knees and wretched, the vomit joining the mud that caked his uniform.

He hoisted himself to his feet willing his legs to give him some support as they felt so weak beneath him. He looked towards his guns, two were completely destroyed, the dead bodies of his men draped over their twisted metal, as though in death they still knew their duty to the artillery. Other men were discarding the dead bodies from the guns that were still working, throwing them aside and realigning the heavy guns towards the enemy. Julius looked in wonder, he knew they were right, the guns were the important thing, they could prevent even more loss of life, but the soldiers disregard for human dignity was an abhorrence to him, and one he knew he would never get used to.

Julius rushed to the guns, the shells still resounding overhead, as he tried to ignore the dead men around him. He detailed some of his men to reposition the artillery and a few to help the wounded. The noise was terrible, augmented by the wounded men crying out for help.

As Julius moved between the guns he was suddenly halted by a soldier reaching out and grasping at his riding boot. The man was lying pinned beneath a gun carriage. The man looked up at Julius, and although he knew he should be attending to the guns, he knelt down beside the man. The soldier was a young private covered in slimy mud. He was trying to say something and Julius knelt closer so that the man's mouth was next to his ear. He spoke so quietly that Julius could not hear him, he was having difficulty breathing, and his body became overcome with convulsions. The soldier closed his eyes and his twitching stopped. Julius thought he had died but suddenly the man's eyes shot open and summoning his last vestige of strength he reached inside his tunic and pulled out a letter. He looked Julius in the eyes, then breathing his last breath, died. Julius looked away, he could not look at the man, but before he left him he forced himself to close the staring eyes and pulled the letter from the man's grasp and placed

311

it inside his tunic. As he rose from the body a sergeant raced up to Julius and saluted.

"Are you the second lieutenant?" It was impossible to know Julius' rank from his mud splattered uniform.

"Yes" replied Julius wearily.

"I have just received orders on the field telephone, you are to advance. I cannot find any of your senior officers, I presume they are dead, these are your orders"

The soldier ran off leaving Julius bewildered and speechless. He did not know whether to laugh or to cry as he looked around him. The ground was covered in dead bodies, he did not know how many of his own men were dead, where his senior officers were and he had been given the order to advance.

Julius knew this was not the time to be shirking his responsibilities. Summoning up all his years of training, he rallied his men round, sorted out the guns and ammunition and prepared to advance to the co-ordinates he had been given. The guns were secured to the teams of horses and Julius jumped on Phantom and prepared to advance. The shelling had lessened, it appeared the Italians were retreating, but all the time Julius and his men were advancing they were still bombarded with mortar attacks and shell fire. Around them flares were being launched into the sky calling for help from the artillery or being used to send signals where communications were difficult. When Julius reached the assigned position he was met by another regiment, as depleted as his own, but thankfully with some surviving senior officers. One of the captains complimented him on his success in getting the guns to their positions and Julius gratefully gave the captain the command of his men and his guns.

The battle lasted many days, but the offensive seemed to be working, the Austrian army had passed Bolzano and had reached Trento. Julius had never felt so weary in his life. His first sight of real battle had been bloody and dangerous; he knew he would never come to terms with observing so much loss of life so close at hand. It was not just observing the artillery fire, that could knock a man off his feet and throw him into the air, but also the man-to-man combat he had seen. He had watched men fighting for their lives and ending other lives with a quick thrust of a bayonet, or a close shot with a rifle. He himself had looked into a man's eyes as he had shot him dead. He believed it

312

was something that no man should endure and something that he could never forget. Julius now understood the lines of pain etched onto Josef's face, he had seen battle, battles perhaps worse than Julius had observed over the last few days if that were possible, and he was not sure how any caring soul, whatever their nationality, could ever come to terms with that. He had accompanied the wounded as they had been transported by the stretcher bearers to the ambulances, watched as they writhed in pain, calling for their loved ones or pleading with God to end their misery. Julius had seen that even through their pain, for many their greatest joy was the relief of knowing that they may never have to go onto a battlefield again.

Several days into the battle Julius was supervising the arrival of much needed ammunition. Despite the loss of several guns to shellfire, the ammunition was still running low and on its arrival Julius was trying to get it allocated across the field as quickly as possible. He had just ridden down the lines to deliver the ammunition and was returning to his men when he saw the young corporal who had saved his life standing by a gun and waving his hands in the air. Julius brought Phantom to an abrupt stop and leaned down to find out what the young soldier was shouting to him. All Julius could remember of the next few moments was a bright flash that blinded him and the next thing he knew he was sailing through the air. When he hit the ground he lost all consciousness.

Julius must have been unconscious for just a few moments for when he opened his eyes there was still the pungent smell of smoke and burning flesh around him and the smoke was so thick that at first he could not see anything. His head throbbed and he could not see out of one eye, as it was filled with blood. He tried to raise himself up but could not so he painfully lifted his head and realized that lying beside him was the torso of his beloved Phantom. His beautiful, sleek, shiny body had been ripped apart and his mutilated coat was covered in thick oozing blood. Julius managed to raise an arm as he stroked his old friend's mane, knowing that his magnificent steed was dead and wishing to give his wonderful horse one final embrace.

Lying on the battlefield, unable to move, surrounded by his dead and dying comrades, Julius felt the tears that he wanted to cry for his beloved dead horse and wondered why, after seeing so much death and destruction of his

313

fellow human beings, he should now want to cry for a horse. Deep down he knew it was not just Phantom he cried for, but for all the death and destruction he had seen over the past few weeks. As he looked around him, Julius saw the body of the young corporal, his arm still stretched above him in that fatal wave, lying across a gun barrel. What he had been trying to say to Julius, he would never know and Julius felt sad for the young man who a few days earlier had saved Julius' life, but who now had lost his own life and who had caused the death of Julius' beloved Phantom.

Eventually Julius was tended by a medical orderly, denoted by the red cross on his arm. He was a young lad, who hardly spoke or showed any emotion, he was used to the horrendous sights of war, and was anxious to be on to the next victim and off the battlefield. The orderly carried a double haversack from which he produced a dressing and tended Julius' head. With a mighty effort the orderly had pushed Phantom to one side as he tended the wounds. Julius watched in some distress as the once magnificent beast was pushed and kicked out of the way, like a joint of meat at the butchers. The orderly checked Julius' legs, which were not broken, and told him he had a nasty cut on his head, but apart from that he thought there were no mortal injuries. Julius started to thank him, but the orderly was already away to his next victim. He was thrown onto a stretcher and run off the field to a waiting ambulance. Julius turned on his stretcher to catch a last glimpse of his wonderful horse lying on the battlefield, even in death, portraying the dignity that he had always had in life.

After being tended to at the dressing station Julius was transferred to a field hospital, wearing a large bandage around his head and suffering the worst headache he had ever had in his life. The doctors confirmed that all he had was severe bruising and a bad gash to his head that needed several stitches. Due to lack of medicines, the anesthetic was not strong enough, and Julius suffered the agony of feeling the needle and thread as they passed through his scalp. He could not complain, around him were men with the most appalling injuries being tended by tired, gray looking doctors, wearing aprons and clothes covered in blood, treating hundreds of patients lying on stretchers, queuing up outside the tents. Julius wondered if Richard was working in such a hospital and his heart went out to the doctors and surgeons working in such dreadful conditions as

314

he remembered the pristine clean, clinical atmosphere of Richard's hospital in Prague. Throughout his ride in the ambulance there had still been the constant noise of gunfire, and even in the field hospital work would suddenly stop as a shell exploded close by, causing the ground to shake and the lighting to flicker on and off.

After the field hospital Julius was taken to a hospital behind the front lines. He was transported in an automated ambulance which could carry six men at a time as their stretchers were stacked in tiers of three each side of the ambulance. All Julius could remember of the journey were the screams of pain from his fellow passengers as another large hole in the road was negotiated, the ambulance swaying from side to side, and the never ending noise of the shelling. At times he thought his head would burst until the painkillers the doctor had given him began to work and he drifted off into a hazy stupor.

At the hospital he was overcome with a deep depression. He mourned for Phantom, and he mourned for all the dead men lying out on the battlefield. He wanted to be rid of this damn war, but he also wanted to fight and bring about a quick and glorious victory for his country.

When he woke up in the hospital a nurse handed him a letter, thinking it was his. At first he tried to give it back to her but when she told him it had been found in his jacket, he remembered the dying soldier on the battlefield. The letter bore no address, so Julius reasoned that he would have to open it in order to find where to send it.

The letter had been written by the soldier the night before the battle had started. It was a bittersweet missive, written to his wife, telling her of his apprehension at the thought of the coming battle, how he loved her and hoped he would be seeing her and their baby son very soon. Julius lay back on his bed for a long time after reading the letter. He knew that the soldier's wife would never read her husband's last letter. He had not supplied an address and had merely signed at the end with his first name, Willi. Julius had no way of finding a Willi from all the thousands of fatalities that the battle had produced. Not for the first time did he thank God for his own salvation. He also reflected that he was glad he was not married or had children as he thought of the poor widow and fatherless child, left with nothing but memories of a poor soul who had given his life so heroically for his country

As the days progressed, his headaches lessened and his body began to hurt less. He protested that he was fit to return to duty but the doctors said he needed to rest his bruised body and his headaches were still causing them some concern. Whilst he was in the hospital he learnt that eventually the advance had lessened and the Austrian Army had stopped north of Vicenza. Julius was frustrated that the army had not advanced further but these thoughts were forgotten when he was told that he was to be allowed home on leave.

Julius could not believe it when he read his orders. He longed for the comforts and joys of home, but he felt his place should be here, fighting the war. He had sent a letter to Nikolas and Josef telling them of his exploits and he hoped that he was going to see them again soon, he felt in need of their company, but now here were his orders to return to Prague. Everyone kept telling him how lucky he was, but it was with a heavy heart that he packed his bag, ready to return home.

XXIII

The journey home was long and tedious. Julius was annoyed by the sympathetic stares of people as they noted his uniform and the large bandage that swathed his head, protecting the stitches in his wounds. He noted the somber attitude of his fellow passengers; they all had solemn, gray faces that reflected the two years of war that they had endured. This was borne out as he walked the streets of Prague on the way to his parent's house. The city appeared weary and solemn, as though a dark pall had descended onto its stately buildings. There was a noticeable absence of young men on the streets, all that were left were the old or infirm, who doffed their hats at his uniform as he passed them by. Julius noticed the black armbands that were worn by every other citizen walking along the streets. In the wearing of their sorrow on their sleeve they shared the tragedy of their loss with each other. To Julius it was a stark reminder of all the dead bodies he had witnessed on the battlefield.

As he entered his street he ran up the steps of his parent's house and knocked on the door. He had not been able to tell his mother of his homecoming. The mail was so difficult that a letter would have probably arrived after him, and he secretly enjoyed the thought of surprising her. When there was no reply Julius rapped the bronze lions head again and stepped back onto the first step to see if he could see anybody in the upstairs windows. He knew his mother must have lost a lot of her staff as they had been called up to fight or work in industry to help the war effort, but he felt sure that somebody must be in the house. When there was still no answer to his knocking Julius reluctantly walked down the steps and resolved to walk to Irmy's house.

When he arrived at his sister's house, he was consoled when a maid answered the door. He did not recognize the maid and when he informed her as to who he was she looked startled as she ushered him into the parlor. She informed him that madam had been working at the hospital all night, but that she would wake her immediately. Julius protested that Irmy should not be woken, but the maid insisted it would be all right and hurriedly left the room.

Julius walked around the room, happy to be back in familiar surroundings once more. This room had not changed at all, and he watched the afternoon breeze gently play with the lace curtains as the sun shone through the window. Julius reflected that sitting in this room one could almost forget the horrors of war and the terrible things that were happening across the continent.

He was jolted out of his reverie, by the opening of the door and Irmy entering with a look of dismay on her face. The first thing Julius noticed was how tired Irmy looked, ageing her beyond her years, but he put this down to the long hours she was working at the hospital. Her eyes did not hold their usual sparkle and there were deep lines down the sides of her mouth illustrating the harsh times she had endured. The second thing that Julius noticed was Irmy's dress. He stared in horror as he realized his sister was dressed in black, the color of mourning. Before he could ask her why, Irmy ran to him and enclosed her arms about him in an enormous hug, as though she could not bear to let him go. He felt her shuddering body and realized that she was crying. Gathering her hands in his Julius led her to the sofa, never taking his eyes off his sister, witnessing her abject misery. Although desperate to know the cause of her grief Julius let her cry for a while as he held his arms around her, wanting to protect her from her desolation.

Eventually she dried her eyes with a handkerchief and looked up into Julius' eyes. He was swept back to their nursery days, when she had fallen over, or been teased and her eyes would fill with tears and all her brothers would rush to console her.

"Irmy what is the matter?"

Irmy recoiled in horror as she observed her brother with such dismay on her face that Julius feared for her sanity. She could not find the words to speak to him, so she stood up and paced around the room.

"You mean you did not know? I thought you were here because you knew, that you had been given leave to come home to us"

"Irmy, you are not making sense, what is it I do not know? tell me"

"Oh, Julius" she cried, "I do not know where to start, I have such dreadful news. Everything is so awful, it is Papa. Papa died two months ago, in Vienna, it was his heart. They say he died in his sleep,.....oh Julius where were you?"

Irmy ran to Julius and fell into his arms and started to cry again. Julius sat staring at his sister's head, not being able to take in the news. Papa, dead? It could not be, he was still quite young, he had not looked too well lately, and Karl had said as much in his last letter, but dead? it was not possible. Julius sat for a long while in his sister's sitting room, watching the afternoon light play a dance on the chandelier crystals, holding his sister, as if by comforting her he delayed the realization of the awful truth. He watched the lights dance on the wall as he thought of his father. His rock, his inspiration, sometimes stern, always wise, a man who had never embraced or kissed his sons or ever shown any real outward forms of affection towards them, but despite this they all knew how much he had loved them. His father, the loyal Habsburg soldier, always principled, never deviating from his duty, who always saw everything in black and white, good and bad, honorable and dishonorable.

As Julius sat in his sister's house and watched the afternoon turn to dusk, his sister slept in his arms, her grief giving way to the welcoming sanctuary of sleep. Julius thought of all the things that had been left unsaid, all the things he would have wanted to say to his father if he had been there, but knowing it was now too late. He knew that it did not really matter, his father had known how Julius had felt about him and he knew his father would have been embarrassed if Julius had ever tried to voice his own feelings, but he resolved if he were ever to be blessed with a son of his own that he would make sure his son was told how his Papa felt about him, because one day, before you realized it, it might be too late.

The room was in darkness when Irmy woke up, still lying in Julius' arms. He had not wanted to move for fear of waking her, and he had been so engrossed in his own thoughts that he had not even noticed the darkness descending on the room. Irmy stretched and looked around as though not sure of where she was, "Julius? What time is it, my goodness why did you not wake me? I will call for Katya and we will have some food and something to drink" After the lamps had been lit, the room took on a warm cozy glow as Julius waited to hear the whole story from his sister.

"I am sorry about my outburst, Julius. It was not much of a homecoming for you was it? It was just so wonderful to see you, to be able to share the last few weeks with someone, I do not think I could have carried on on my own for much longer" Irmy managed a ghost of a smile, the first one

319

Julius had seen on her face since his arrival. He sighed to himself as he remembered the carefree Irmy of yesteryear, who always had a smile on her face, and a sunny disposition. How war changes everybody, reflected Julius, as he observed the woman in front of him, aged beyond her years, carrying so much grief and hardship on her shoulders. He was even more sorry for her as she related her story to him.

Richard had been called for service to a field hospital and had left several months ago. Due to army enlisting there was now an acute shortage of staff at the hospital, so her workload had increased dramatically. It was not that she minded the work so much, but she felt so much for the patients she had to tend. Bodies torn apart, blindness, loss of limbs, horrible disfigurements, but beyond their physical illnesses were the men's mental condition, of which she, the doctors and her fellow nurses, had no experience and found very difficult to bear. Julius was tempted to tell Irmy that he had seen all these injuries inflicted on the battlefield, along with the horrendous deaths that he had witnessed, but he didn't. He realized that Irmy needed to talk out her anguish and so let her carry on.

Her worry for Richard was obvious, as well as her worry for Julius and Karl, who had now been posted to the Russian front. Then two months ago had come the terrible news of Papa from Vienna. Mama had been inconsolable, nothing Irmy could say could help their mother's grief. She had shut herself in her room for several days and would talk to no one. Irmy had not known what to do. She would have liked to stay with Mama but the hospital needed her, and there was no question of her deserting her duty. Luckily for Irmy she had had the support of her mother-in-law, Frau Beckova and Nikolas' mother. When she had told them of her dilemma, and her obligation to her work, the two ladies had told her they would resolve the situation between them. They had gone round to see Mama, coaxed her out of her room at last, and persuaded Mama that she could not live on her own in her house. As she could not stay with Irmy, who was at the hospital most of the time, Frau Beckova had insisted that Mama stay with her, telling her that she would be welcome company. So Mama had closed up the house and was now staying with Frau Beckova, and Frau Manzova visited her as often as possible.

"I think my mother-in-law must be a saint" added Irmy, "I do not think Mama is the easiest guest at the moment, but I hope in time, she will get better, they say time is the best healer, I hope that is true" once again the tears welled up in her eyes and Julius could see Irmy's grief, a grief that had not been allowed to be acknowledged whilst looking after their mother. "The army said they would send a message to you and Karl, I presume you did not get it? I told Gretha of course, but she does not think Franz would be able to endure such news and so we have agreed not to tell him until Gretha thinks he is well enough, though she says he does very well and improves daily. Julius you do not think they would send Franz back to the front do you? Gretha seems to think that such a thing is a possibility"

Julius did not want to lie to his sister, but he could not tell her that he had seen men returned to the front that were not mentally capable of coping with battle conditions, so he told her that he thought Franz's' return to the army at the moment was highly unlikely and hoped to God he was right.

Dinner that night was a very subdued affair. Irmy seemed too exhausted to talk, and Julius was once again lost in his thoughts of the past and the future. He was to stay with Irmy and told her that he would go in the morning to Frau Beckova's house to see his mother. He knew he would have to sort out his father's affairs whilst he was in Prague, a task he did not look forward to, and the last thing his battle weary mind wanted to contemplate. Irmy had told him that Papa had been brought back to Prague and had been given a full military funeral. Julius was glad that his father had been given the funeral that he deserved, but marveled that he had had one at all. He reflected that if every poor soul who had died during the last two years were honored with a military funeral, they would still be conducting them for many years to come.

Julius felt weary, and so excused himself early, his head had started to ache again and his body yearned for a soft comforting bed. As he was leaving the room Irmy said, "Julius, are you all right, is your head hurting you? I could get you a draft to help you sleep"

Julius smiled at the concern on Irmy's face, the consoling nurse as ever, "no, I am well, really, I do not need anything to help me sleep, I am so tired"

"Julius" Julius looked at his sister as he noted the tremble in her voice, "is it as bad as the men say? they tell me things I cannot imagine, things you never read in the newspapers, are things really so terrible?"

Julius knew Irmy wanted to be reassured, wanted to believe that the situation was not so bad, that Richard and Karl would be all right, but he could not deceive her. He knew he could have lied to Irmy, but he had neither the heart nor the enthusiasm to betray the trust he knew his sister had in him. Julius sighed deeply, and looking his sister straight in the eye he said to her, "yes Irmy, conflict is terrible, it is like hell on earth. It is something I would not wish on my worst enemy, but it is something we all must come to terms with in our own way until this war ends, and let us pray to God that that is soon" with that Julius left the room and retired to his bedroom where sleep at last gave him a welcome escape from the dreadful reality around him.

The next morning Julius visited Frau Beckova's home. Frau Beckova greeted him with surprise and joy at his visit. "Julius it is so good to see you, your Mama will be overjoyed that you are here. I cannot think of a better tonic for her at the moment. I am so sorry about your father; he was such a fine man who will be missed. You have seen Irmy? how that child has endured the last few weeks I cannot know, her husband and brothers away and then the news of your father. I am not sure I could have coped with everything like she has. Your mother is upstairs, she has just returned from Mass. I will fetch her for you, but before I do, I would like a private word with you Julius"

Frau Beckova sat upright in her seat, twisting a white linen handkerchief between her gnarled fingers, as though reluctant to continue her speech. "I think you will find your mother much changed Julius. She may even shock you, but please remember she has suffered enormous grief these last few months and needs the love and nurturing of all her family at this time. She will get over this Julius, all she needs is time. I remember when my dear husband died....."

Frau Beckova was not allowed to finish her sentence as the door burst open and Frau Mayer came into the room and enveloped her son in an enormous embrace. Julius was startled by the vehemence of her actions and looked over his mother's shoulder with an enquiring glance at Frau Beckova. The old lady shook her head, and with a smile for Julius, quietly rose from her chair and diplomatically left the room, leaving Julius to talk to his mother.

It was several minutes before his mother released her hold on Julius and in that time he was startled to realize that Mama's hair had turned nearly completely white, and in his arms she felt thinner, and much frailer than he had remembered her. When eventually Mama stepped back to look at her son Julius could not believe the change in his mother. It was not just the loss of her lustrous hair, or the fact that his mother was now painfully thin, something she had never been in the past, but it was the fact that since he had last seen his mother, a year and a half ago waving him goodbye at Prague station, she had become an old woman. That her grief had brought about this transformation was all too obvious. Her mouth was transfixed in a downward droop and she wore no cosmetics, not even the rouge she habitually wore, but it seemed as if her whole body had succumbed to old age. No longer was there the proud stance and rigid straight back of a contented woman of mature years, it had given way to the stoop and lethargy of old age, as if she had lost interest in herself and, with it, life itself. Even her eyes were dull and lifeless, and the smile that she managed for her son was one of supreme effort on her part, which did not extend to her eyes. Julius tried to collect himself, to disguise what he was thinking, but found he could not.

"Do not look at me in that way, Julius, you were never one who could hide your feelings were you?" Frau Mayer walked to a chair, and even in her walk was the affectation of an old woman. As she sat down she said, "So you are here. What have you done to your head? Is it very bad?" Mama rambled on for several minutes, asking questions, but not waiting for any answers, as though not wanting any. She mentioned everybody, from Frau Beckova's kindness to an old friend in Kosice, but not once did she mention Papa. Julius decided he must broach the subject. Julius knew from Irmy that there were several things to be done about Papa's estate, things that Mama had refused to contemplate, or had kept deferring to a later date. Although Julius did not want to upset his mother, he did not know how long his leave was to continue and so felt he had better sort his father's affairs as soon as possible.

When Mama had paused for breath Julius said, "Mama, do you not want to talk about Papa?" Julius' mother sat in her chair for several minutes, not saying a word, just staring ahead of her, as though Julius was not in the room, and, still maintaining her motionless gaze she said, "no, Julius, I do not want to talk about Papa. He has gone, he has left us, what more is there to say? I am alone now, I have no-one" Julius was perplexed to realize that his mother did not speak with any trace of wanting sympathy but had spoken as if stating a mere fact. He wished she even had tears in her eyes, but his mother was dry eyed, with a steely determination on her face.

"Mama, how can you say that, you have Irmy, and Karl, Franz and me and many friends, we are all here for you"

Frau Mayer stopped staring ahead of her and turned round to face Julius. Regarding him with a stony stare she said, "No you are not. You and Karl are away, fighting this dreadful war, and who knows if you are coming back. Franz is a casualty, like me, and besides he is in Graz with his wife, and Irmy, well Irmy has Richard and that hospital, they are more important than me"

"Mama" cried Julius, "that is unfair and unkind. I cannot believe you mean those things"

"Oh but Julius, I do. I hate this war and I hate the army. I have devoted my whole life to your army. I saw it take my sons one by one, and now it has taken my husband forever, and what have I to live for now? To watch my sons die like their   father?"

Julius sat amazed at his mother's outburst. She was so bitter, so hard; it was a side of her he had never seen before. He had expected to find his mother beside herself with grief, not this acerbic woman who sat before him. He reasoned that maybe this was the way she was dealing with her grief, but this woman was so unlike the mother that he had known that he feared for her sanity.

There was the sound of knocking at the front door, and Nikolas' mother, Frau Manzova appeared in the room.

"Julius, how good it is to see you. You are injured, what happened to you? Have you news of Nikolas?"

Julius was glad of the diversion that Nikolas' mother had created from the uncomfortable scene he had been having with his mother. He was pleased to tell Frau Manzova the latest news of her son and to see her well. She had not heard from her husband, who was in Vienna, but she quickly changed the subject, as she kept a watchful eye on Julius' mother's reactions to their conversation. Coffee was ordered, and the next few minutes were spent in idle talk, waiting for their refreshments to arrive.

324

Frau Manzova told Julius that Danusia was also staying in the house, and Julius went off in search of his old nurse. Julius found her in the kitchen, on seeing Julius enter the room she leapt to her feet and enveloped him in an enormous embrace, as she cried loud and copiously that her little boy had been delivered back to her. After disentangling himself from Danusia, Julius was then subjected to further tears as Danusia wept for his father. Julius patiently let her cry her tears of grief as he reflected that he wished this was the way Mama had reacted to his father's death instead of the stoic detachment he had witnessed upstairs in the living room.

After telling Danusia to come and visit him at Irmy's house, Julius returned upstairs, where Mama and Frau Manzova had been joined by Frau Beckova. Coffee was a very strained affair, with Nikolas' mother and Frau Beckova trying to maintain a stilted conversation whilst Mama continued to stare straight ahead of her, refusing to be enticed into any conversation at all.

As Frau Manzova stood up to leave, Julius saw the opportunity to take his own leave, and with a promise to visit his mother on the morrow he bowed to his hostess and left the house with Nikolas' mother. Once out on the street Frau Manzova turned to Julius and requested that he return to her house with her. The walk was spent in idle conversation, mainly about Nikolas and Georg, and it was not until he was seated in the Manz's parlor that Frau Manzova divulged the real reason for wanting to talk to Julius.

"I know you are upset about your mother, Julius, we all are, but I would ask you to have a little patience. Your mother is not rational at the moment, but in time she may improve, she has to come to terms with your father's death, and at the moment she simply cannot do that"

"Do you think the way she talks about my brothers and I, the army, even Irmy, is her way of coming to terms with my father's death? It seems very strange to me"

Frau Manzova gave him a kindly smile, "I know this may be difficult to bear Julius, but in some ways your mother is probably just voicing an opinion she has had for many years. You are a man, so you may not understand, but I have been an army wife for as long as your mother, I feel her pain. Being married to a soldier is a very unfair life for a woman. Yes, we accept it, most of us know we are marrying our husband and the army, it is just the reality that is hard to bear. We are often apart from our husbands for long periods of time when we are left to bring up our children on our own. We travel around the country, not knowing where we are to live next, leaving our friends and families behind, it can be very hard at times. I know what you are thinking, and you are right, it is something we choose, because it is our duty and we love our husbands. The trouble is that when the one thing that was the central part of our existence has gone, in your mother's case your father, then the future, and the past, seems very hard to bear. Your mother is not the first woman to vent her anger and her grief at the army, and she will not be the last, especially in these times, when so many women are losing their loved ones and asking the question, why? All I ask is that you bear these things in mind when you think of your mother. She is not trying to hurt you, it is just her way of dealing with her grief. As I said, she may get over this, but she may not, and that is something you and your siblings may have to contend with in the future. Just never forget the mother you knew, she is there somewhere still, she has not really left you. I am sorry to be so candid with you Julius, I just wanted you to understand your mother's condition, or you may end up hating her"

After Julius had left Frau Manzova's house he decided to walk to his father's grave. He had a lot to think about. Once he had entered the graveyard he stopped as he looked at all the fresh new graves that had been dug, the graveyard had almost doubled in size since he had last been to the church.

It was some time before he found his father's grave, appointed with a new headstone, where the brown earth was covered in sweet smelling flowers. He noticed a fresh bouquet of flowers laid by the headstone, and read the note attached to them. The flowers were from his mother, obviously left when she had attended Mass that morning, as were most of the flowers on the grave, all accompanied by notes written in his mother's neat hand. Julius knelt down beside the grave, trying to compare the woman who had left such loving notes to the woman whom he had encountered that morning. All the notes began with 'my dearest Gotthold' and it was with some surprise that Julius realized that he had never heard his mother call his father by his baptized name.

The memories of Papa surrounded him as he remembered his childhood, hunting with his father, being scolded by him as he stood in front of his father's desk trying not to cry at his father's anger, family holidays where his father truly became a parent and not a soldier. He recalled his father's pride when Julius had entered the army, and remembered watching his father in the emperor's cavalcade on his first day in the army. He could picture him now riding by, his pride in his beloved army so obvious to see. He thought about his last meeting with his father when everybody had been preparing to enter the war. His father had looked tired and unwell and he had been shocked by his father's appearance. He wished he had known then that it was to be the last time he would see his father, and he reflected how many other families were wishing the same thing at this time.

Kneeling by his father's grave Julius hoped his father was listening to him and spurred on by the longing to talk to somebody, he sat there for a long time, telling him his fears, his anxieties, his experiences of war, of Mama, but most of all he told him of his love for him and the sadness of his death. He stayed by his father's grave for a long time, the tears falling down his face, as the grief he had had to suppress for the sake of his mother and sister could at last be displayed and he wept for the loss of a wonderful father and a remarkable man.

After drying his tears Julius left the graveyard and went to keep an appointment at the hospital where Irmy had arranged for one of the doctors to see his wound. The hospital had changed greatly since his last visit. As he passed by the wards he could see that they were vastly overcrowded. No longer were there patients with everyday illnesses, or little old ladies lying patiently waiting to meet their maker. The beds were full of soldiers, covered in bandages, displaying lost limbs and broken bodies. Julius was revolted by the macabre scenes in front of him giving him an unwelcome reminder of the hospitals at the front. As he walked down the corridor listening to the wails and screams of so much pain he wondered how his sister could work in such an atmosphere and then rejoiced that she did. He knew that people like Irmy could be these soldiers saving grace from a hopeless world.

Julius had not seen the extent of his injuries, but was not comforted by the grimace on Irmy's face as his bandage was removed. "Do not tell me," said Julius, trying to lighten the situation as he saw the distress on his sisters face, "you cannot find a brain in there"

Irmy managed a laugh as she replied, "Julius, we knew years ago there never *was* a brain in there"

The doctor declared himself satisfied that the stitches were well placed to mend his wound and that they could be taken out quite soon. As Irmy reapplied his dressings and bandages the doctor appeared more concerned with Julius' headaches. He told Julius that he could not recommend a return to active service for him until he was happier with his physical condition. Julius did not know whether to be elated or saddened by this. He knew the rest at home would do him good, but he also thought of his friends, comrades and men at the front that he felt he should return to.

Walking home with Irmy he noticed his sister was unusually quiet, and asked her what she was thinking about. "I was just thinking about you actually" said Irmy, "this afternoon was the first time I have treated a member of my own family. I was wondering what it would be like if I had to treat a loved one if they were seriously injured, I am not sure I could cope"

Julius knew she was thinking of Richard so he said, "there is very little likelihood of Richard being injured you know, he is there to treat the casualties, not become one himself" He did not want to tell her of the bombings near the field hospital he had been in, he felt it was best that she did not know.

Irmy attempted to shrug off her gloom as she said, "yes, I know you are right, Julius, I am just being maudlin. I cannot help but worry, oh Julius, in some ways I can sympathize with Mama. I hate this war; there is so much sadness and unhappiness. I realize that things have changed, and it scares me, I want my old life back again, but I know we cannot turn back the clock"

Julius took his sister's arm and walked home in silence, moved by his sister's plea. He had to agree with her, their old life seemed so wonderful now, so secure, so safe, but he knew that, whatever the outcome of this war, life was never going to be the same again.

The next few weeks Julius spent sorting out his father's estate to ensure that his mother would be well provided for in the future. After much persuasion his mother accompanied him to see the family lawyer and visit their

328

bank. Luckily Colonel Mayer, with his soldierly precision, had left his affairs in immaculate order, so the task was not too arduous, but it was the last thing Julius had wanted to do on his precious home leave.

Julius visited his mother daily, but his presence did not appear to improve his mother's disposition, and at times Julius would despair that she would ever get better.

Soon after his arrival Georg called at Irmy's house, desperate for news of his older brother. Georg had grown up in the years since Julius had last seen him. He was now as tall as Julius, and looked so much like Nikolas that when he had first walked into Irmy's sitting room he had thought that his dear friend had also managed to come home on leave. Georg still maintained his cheeky demeanor, the war had not curbed his youthful enthusiasm. He was desperate to join the army and was annoyed at the insistence of his parents that he continue with his studies for the time being. Julius tried to make him understand that war was not like any book he might have read, that the reality was far more inglorious than he could ever imagine, but Georg was not to be swayed and declared that he would be joining Julius and Nikolas in the not too distant future.

There was still no news from Karl or his friends and as Julius perused the newspapers his fears for them grew. Julius marveled that he was more aware of what was happening in the war from reading the newspapers or watching the screens of the local picture house than he ever was fighting for his life on the battlefront. The news reports were portrayed with a patriotic fervor to inspire their viewers, but Julius felt that they were far from the truth and it enraged him to watch such a bland display, hiding the horrific truth of warfare from the people.

He was interested to watch the news film from the French and Belgian fronts, again echoing glorious successes for the German Army and wondered how much of it was true or just merely gratuitous propaganda. He had heard that conditions there, though very different, were as horrendous as their own in Slovene, with casualties as high and the same stalemate conditions, with hardly any land gained after over two years of fighting.

Despite the patriotic posters that proliferated every empty space on Prague's streets, and despite the nationalistic fervor that manifested itself in vivat banders, mementoes of the war sewn by women to raise money for the war charities, or the postcards on sale depicting the brave men of the army fighting on the battle front, Julius knew that things were going dreadfully wrong for the Austrian government and the army.

The people were beginning to feel the effects of two years of war, food and essential items were becoming more scarce and luxury items were virtually a thing of the past. Frau Manzova had told him that Colonel Manz had written from Vienna to say that the food situation was worsening there, and the populace were beginning to let the government know that they were becoming increasingly unhappy with the situation.

The news from the Russian and Serbian fronts was even worse. At the beginning of June the Russians, under General Brusilov, had launched an attack upon the Austrian army and by the end of June the army was in full flight towards the Carpathians, having suffered a humiliating defeat at the hands of the Russian Army. During the offensive the Russians had regained much of eastern Galizien, and thousands of Austrian soldiers had lost their lives whilst over four hundred thousand soldiers had been taken prisoner and the Russians had commandeered a large number of Austrian guns.

The crushing defeat of the Austro-Hungarian army led to most of the Austrian commanders being replaced by Germans, a circumstance which caused outrage in Vienna, and greatly reduced the influence of the Austrian government in the war. Julius read about these events with a sickening heart, remembering his brother's warnings before the war started, which seemed now not to be as outrageous as when they had first been propounded.

Worse news was to come for the army at the beginning of August. The Italian commander, General Cadorna, had ordered an attack on the Soca front, and despite fierce resistance by the Austrian army, the Italian army had advanced and taken Monfalcone and Gorz, with a heavy loss of life to both sides. Julius could not believe it. That the Italians had managed to get past the bridgehead at Gorz, the bridgehead that he had spent so many months to build, was unbelievable. The Italians were now ensconced in Gorz as the Austrian army had retreated further back behind the Soca River, a circumstance that Julius found very hard to bear. With reports of more fighting to the south, where the Italians had also taken Mount San Michele, Julius was even

330

more determined to return to his men as soon as possible.

Finally the doctors gave Julius permission to return to Slovene. His stitches had been removed, and his headaches had lessened. Even his hair had grown back to its former length. With Irmy's tender loving care and lots of sleep, Julius felt better than he had done for years. When Julius received his orders to return to the front there also came a letter advising him of his promotion to full Lieutenant. Julius received his promotion with the skepticism it deserved. Whilst hoping he was an able officer, he had no allusions as to why he had been promoted. Too many young officers were losing their lives in battle, his elevation in rank was more to do with the lack of officers than his abilities. Even so, he was honored to hold the rank of Lieutenant and, observing the two silver stars on the collar of his blouson, hoped his father would have been proud of him.

About a week before he was to leave came news that Karl had been taken prisoner by the Russians. Julius had been dreading receiving such a letter, but with the news from the Russian front, he had to admit to himself that he was not unduly surprised. He worried for his brother, prisoners of war could be badly treated, though he did not voice this opinion to Irmy. She herself was devastated by the news, coming so soon after all her other worries. They both agreed that they would not tell Mama about Karl, it would not help her to know the true fate of her son.

In the few days that he had left of his leave, Julius promised Irmy that he would write to Papa's friends in Vienna, to see if they could ascertain any more news about their brother. Irmy appeared to collapse under the weight of so much intrigue with their mother, and Julius felt guilty about leaving her alone to shoulder so much of the burden at such a time. His sister looked exhausted, she insisted on keeping her hours at the hospital, as well as tending their mother, who was still intent in making Irmy the focus of her misery.

Julius went to see Frau Manzova and Georg. Whilst he knew Frau Manzova had worries of her own, with Nikolas at the front and still no news from him, he asked her if she would keep an eye on Irmy for him and explained her situation. Frau Manzova promised to do all she could and agreed that Irmy was taking far too much upon herself.

As Julius was talking to Frau Manzova Suse arrived to pay a call on Nikolas' mother. Julius had seen her a few times during his leave where she had incessantly asked him about Nikolas, and wanted to know every little detail of how Nikolas was faring. Not for the first time did Julius feel a pang of envy for his friend. He wished he had somebody at home, so desperate to hear about his welfare, so obviously in love with him. He knew Nikolas was considering marriage to Suse, and on reflection, Julius decided that his friend was making a wise decision and wished he himself had such a decision to make.

As he took his farewells of Suse and Frau Manzova, his hands full of letters for his friend, he was stopped in the hallway by Georg, who had followed Julius from his mother's sitting room.

"Do not worry about Irmy, Julius, I promise I will help to watch over her"

Julius could not help but allow a small smile to appear on his face at the young man's earnestness. Georg turned red, looking so much like Nikolas did when he was embarrassed, that a rush of affection for Georg came over Julius and he regretted laughing at him.

"Do not laugh at me, Julius" Georg cried indignantly, "You may think of me still as that young boy you used to know, but I have grown up a lot since then. I want to help Irmy because she has always been so kind to me. Do you remember how she persuaded Mama to let me leave that horrid school? I shall never forget that"

Julius calmed his young friend down with thanks for his concern, and with a farewell embrace, he left the Manz house to walk back to Irmy's. As he walked along the street the smile appeared back on his face as Julius reflected that Nikolas was not the only Manz male to fall a little in love with Irmy.

Before Julius left Prague at the end of August came the news that Romania had entered the conflict by declaring war on Austria. The next day it was announced that Germany had declared war on Romania, whilst Italy officially declared war on Germany. Julius read the news with a heavy heart, the conflict was escalating, and he could see no quick outcome to such a widespread war. It would also mean that the Germans would now feel they had a free hand to enter the war on the Italian front.

The news from that frontline was getting worse. The Italians had continued their advance, and were aiming to capture Trieste. The Italian troops had pressed forward to the Carso and had taken Tivol, to the north east of Gorz, and the present battles were being fought in dreadful conditions, the autumn climate of the region causing as many problems as the enemy.

As Julius left Prague he reflected on how his beloved city had changed. It still held its casual air of elegance, but it had lost its feel of gaiety and romance. Now it was enveloped in a gray, somber mist, that lay on its historic buildings like a shroud. This was enhanced by its people, who walked the streets with their heads bowed, grieving for lost loved ones, or worrying for relatives and friends fighting at the front. The people were enduring many hardships, with food becoming short and new clothing and amenities becoming a rarity. Their spirits were not lightened by the news of so many defeats and losses at the front.

As Julius walked to the station, watching the gray, sad faces of the passers by he wondered if they would ever be able to laugh again, to go back to those pre-war halcyon days, and realized they probably never would. As the train left Prague he looked out of the window, watching the familiar landmarks of the city disappear into the distance, wondering if he would ever see them again.

XXIV

Julius arrived at a base camp in a town behind the lines in the middle of September. The town was a picturesque, busy place, which in peacetime had probably been a very sleepy, comfortable place to live in. Now it was filled with army lorries, horse gun carriages, and the noise of the constant movement of marching men, which disturbed the once peaceful air of the Slovenian countryside.

The first thing Julius noticed was the lethargy and despondency of the men. They all looked gray and weary and Julius could see how the defeats of the past few months had affected everybody, and he felt ashamed at how well and fit he looked after his own leave.

Julius reported to the senior officer for his posting where he was told that there were two officers who had been asking after him. When Julius asked who they were the major merely smiled and directed him to the barracks to the north of the town. Julius had reasoned that Nikolas must have come down from the mountains, but was overjoyed on entering the room to find Josef and Viktor fast asleep on their beds. With a cry of joy Julius leapt on top of Viktor, pummeling him with his fists with the joy of seeing his old friend again, whom he had feared dead or injured after such a long time.

"Mayer, get off you stupid bastard," yelled the familiar voice, "I can see you have not changed, get off me before I break your neck"

Julius leapt off the bed, eager to speak with Viktor.

"I told you Viktor" said Josef's drowsy voice from the other bed, "he will never grow up, you can see that they have mere boys fighting on this front"

Julius was too overjoyed to see his friends to take any notice of their teasing and whilst he unpacked his bag they all caught up with each other's news.

Nikolas had gone home on leave, indeed he must have crossed Julius on his way back to the front. Julius was pleased for his friend, Frau Manzova would be overjoyed to see her son, and maybe Nikolas could talk some sense into young Georg about his obsession with joining the army as soon as he possibly could. Noticing Julius' black armband Julius had to tell them about his father. Josef and Viktor offered him their condolences and there followed an

334

uncomfortable silence, where neither of them could think of the right thing to say to help their friend in his grief.

Josef had come down from the mountains two weeks ago and was waiting for his next posting. Viktor had left the Russian front some months ago and had been home on leave and so had missed the disastrous campaign of the last few months. When he heard about Karl he went very quiet, but the look on his face told Julius what a dangerous position Karl was in. Viktor said very little about his experiences of the last two years, but like so many other soldiers, his face said it all. Gone was the round faced, spotty adolescent that had remained when his three friends had matured. It was now replaced by a thin, gaunt young man, with a face deeply lined by a misery that one could only imagine.

As Julius sat watching his two friends in animated conversation with each other he reflected how like so many other fellow officers they were. Soldiers who had encountered battle fell into two categories, there were the ones who wore their hearts on their sleeves, who could not cope with the horrors they had seen and there were the others, thankfully in the majority, like his two young friends here who preferred not to talk about their experiences, but who hid their true feelings with idle banter and forced bonhomie. Julius wondered which was the better course and wondered if they, like him, lay in their beds at night silently reliving all the horrors that they had witnessed before sleep gave them a welcome release from their angst.

It was with no surprise that Julius found that Josef and Nikolas had also received a promotion, although Viktor enjoyed arguing the point with Josef that he had received his promotion first. Josef and Viktor were troubled when Julius told them all the news he had gleaned when he had been at home. Like Julius they had been disturbed by the news that Italy had declared war on Germany as they too felt that German influence on their front would be brought to bear as it had in Russia.

The next few days were spent in idle relaxation whilst the three men waited for their orders to return to the front. They had years to catch up on and Julius was surprised to learn that Viktor was engaged to the elusive lady who had sent him lilac scented letters from Salzburg. When Julius asked him what had made him decide to get married Viktor had shrugged his shoulders and replied, "I suppose it was this damned war, it makes you consider how precious life is. I have been writing to Sonia for such a long time, seeing her when I went home on leave I realized I wanted her to be with me when this war ended. I knew then that I was in love with her"

Julius thought that this was the most emotional he had ever seen Viktor, and as he congratulated his friend, he once again wished that he had the same feelings for someone. As though reading his thoughts Josef looked at Julius and with a mischievous look on his face said, "oh I forgot to tell you, when Nikolas and I came down from the mountains we had to take one of our soldiers to a field hospital. He had slipped and broken his ankle. We met a beautiful young nurse there whom Nikolas said you were once involved with. I must say Julius, your taste has improved greatly with the years, she was lovely, why on earth did you stop seeing the girl?"

Julius turned bright red as he heard his friend talking of Erika in such a familiar way. He was also jealous at the thought of Josef inflicting his charms on Erika, as he felt sure his friend would not have missed the opportunity of flirting with someone so pretty.

Julius was desperate to hear how Erika was but could not bring himself to ask Josef about her. He did not have to worry too long, for the next day he received a letter from her, no doubt prompted by her meeting with Nikolas and Josef. It was a very non-committal letter, telling Julius of her experiences in the field hospital and how lovely it was to have seen Nikolas and to have met Josef, of whom she had heard so much. Of Josef she said no more, and Julius hoped this was due to a lack of interest on her part. Erika also enclosed a photograph that had been taken of her, her fellow nurses and some of their patients. She looked happy enough and Julius thought how lucky her patients were to be tended by such a lovely person. Julius placed the photograph inside his tunic, its presence cheering him up whenever he looked at it.

Julius was delighted to find that he, Josef and Viktor were all to return to the front together. Throughout their time at the safe camp he was relieved to see that Josef had recovered a lot of his easy charm that had seemed to desert him after his time on the Russian front. They had all been posted to the same area, to the rear of Gorz and the Soca River.

336

At the front Julius discovered that he was once again under the command of Colonel Genner. Genner too was showing the strains of war and did not greet Julius with quite the same verve as before. He congratulated Julius on his promotion and for surviving his posting in the mountains and Julius was relieved to find that he was to be posted back with his old regiment, working under a Captain Milic.

When Julius arrived at his quarters, he found young Hans once again in attendance. He had come from the mountains with Nikolas and had also been reassigned to his old regiment. When Julius asked him about his home leave, the young boy merely shook his head, stating he preferred to be here than at home. Julius received this information with some wonder. That the boy should prefer the hell of the front to his home was an indication of how unhappy his life must have been.

After leaving Hans to stow his bags Julius reported to Captain Milic. Milic was a Czech, not much older than Julius, who carried with him such an air of enthusiasm and optimism that Julius liked him straight away. After he had been dismissed Julius went in search of his men who were in the trenches, watching the Italian trenches that were just over the ridge from their position. All men were now issued with the steel Bergendorfer helmets, named after their Austrian designer, and these were worn at all times in case of shell and mortar attacks, which were relentless from both sides, day or night.

As Julius went amongst the soldiers, greeting old, familiar faces he grieved to see so few of his original men. All the new recruits were fresh-faced and very young, Julius reflected that this was how his original team of men had looked, and now most of them were lying in their earthy graves, making way for the arrival of these young lambs for the slaughter.

When Julius had arrived at the front, the effects of the last few months of fighting were all too evident. The trenches, hastily made after the retreat, were far from satisfactory. The morale of the men was very low, the loss of Gorz affecting them badly, and without the croplands growing around the city, which had been abandoned in the retreat, food was now becoming scarce.

To Julius' consternation the condition of the artillery was abysmal. Julius learnt from Captain Milic that during the battle for Gorz they had lost over thirty guns, over one hundred machine guns and a large store of hand grenades. Although they were making every effort to replace these guns as quickly as possible, it had not been fast enough and Julius found the artillery greatly depleted.

It was lucky for the Austrian Army that bad weather had caused a delay in the Italian advancement, for Julius was sure they could not have taken a full Italian attack at that time. The weather was atrocious, the rains fell for days on end, causing flooding and the disintegration of the badly built trenches. Many men became ill and they suffered what the doctors called trench foot, caused by the cold and the wet and the men never taking their boots off, causing their flesh to rot. If the rain did not fall then the land was covered with a thick hazy fog that lent an eerie feel to the landscape. Julius likened it to being in the dark, you could not see where you were going, lost all sense of direction and worst of all you did not know where your enemy was.

Julius enjoyed working with Captain Milic. He had a dry sense of humor, which appealed to the absurd in Julius and the two men soon found themselves working as a productive team. Captain Milic kept a very strict company, but his sense of humor was never far from the surface, playing practical jokes, keeping the men's spirits high and indulging in continuous verbal puns and nuances with his junior officers that endeared him to everybody serving under him.

The main job of the army in the area was to defend Trieste. Julius and his company were sent to help a vast army of soldiers who were building the strong defensive position of Hermada, which covered the road to Trieste. The conditions for building were horrendous, not only from the weather, but from the constant bombardments and skirmishes with the enemy. Day and night the men worked hard trying to build the fortifications, encumbered by having to carry their large packs and guns, wearing waterproof capes and hampered by the slimy mud that covered everything. At the end of each shift Julius found himself traipsing back to his camp bed, his puttees and uniform caked in mud, soaked through to the bone, too exhausted to wash, where he fell asleep to awaken in the morning to start all over again. The cathartic effect of his home leave soon disappeared and Julius felt as though he had never left the front at all.

Despite the hard work, danger and inclement weather, Julius found that the work helped his men. The physical labor diverted their minds from the last few weeks and all the men relished building a defense that would hopefully stop the Italian advance. By mid-October the fortifications were built and more guns and machine guns had arrived to bolster up the defense systems.

One day Captain Milic ordered Julius to take a detail of men along the front to help with a unit to the north of their position. After choosing ten men Julius began the march along the road. The road was very busy, many lorries, ambulances and staff cars for officers filled the road, along with the large amount of men marching to their various assignments and destinations. Overhead could be seen the naval aircraft, Lohners, who flew regular sorties from their base in Trieste. Their presence in the skies overhead had increased during the war, their main activities being gun spotting, the shooting down of enemy balloons or dog fights with their Italian counterparts.

The march was hampered by the fact that the road was being heavily shelled and every so often Julius would have to give the command for his men to take cover as another shell from the Italian lines whistled its way towards them. All along the way there were wreckages of burnt out cars and corpses of men strewn across the road showing the accuracy of the enemy gunfire.

After a couple of hours of hard marching Julius sighted their destination, the journey had taken longer than expected, mainly due to the dodging of shells, but Julius was glad that he had arrived at the town with no casualties amongst his own men. The traffic on the road had virtually disappeared and the shelling had ceased for the time being.

As Julius looked up he saw several small cars coming towards them and recognized them as officer staff cars with their drivers. His attention was drawn by a large report to his left and as he looked towards the enemy lines he saw the launch of a massive shell attack aimed at the road. With a yell Julius gave the command for his men to take cover and as they scrambled off the road he realized that the drivers, safely within the confines of their cars, did not know that they were about to be bombarded by a shell attack. Julius leapt from his position and started waving to the cars, trying to warn them of their imminent danger, but the cars were too far away and as they drove towards him in what seemed like slow motion, Julius ran up the road, looking like a madman, waving his arms about and screaming at the top of his voice. As the shells whistled overhead Julius dropped to the floor and covered his head with his hands as the impact of the ammunition blew the cars into the air, bringing them down to the ground with the deafening sound of crushing metal and then a deathly silence.

Julius looked up to see the swirls of smoke enveloping the twisted metal that were once motorcars. Although dazed Julius shouted for his men, who came running up the road to their lieutenant and they all ran to the wreckage to see if there were any survivors. The cars were completely destroyed, bodies that had been blown out of the cars lay twisted and deformed all over the road. Julius shouted to his men to move the bodies to the side of the road, and he noticed that some of the younger soldiers, after depositing their loads, proceeded to vomit into the verge. Julius ran to each car, hoping there might be survivors, but every car revealed the twisted, bloodied bodies of men beyond any mortal help. As Julius approached the last car he saw an arm sticking out of the metal and was amazed to see the hand twitch. Julius hoped that the owner was alive and desperately called to his men to try and get the man out of the car.

With their bare hands the men tore away the metal and although the man was badly hurt he was still breathing. He was trapped by one of the seats, but after wrenching the seat clear, Julius and his men set about trying to pull the man clear of the wreckage without causing him any further injury. Julius knew that they would have to be quick as there was no knowing when the Italians would send their next shell over, so with more speed than tenderness the man was pulled clear of the car.

He was barely conscious and his face did not betray any pain as he was laid onto the side of the road. Julius opened his first aid box that was attached to his belt. The man was covered in blood, and Julius tried to clean his face and body to ascertain exactly where his injuries were. As the blood was cleared from the man's face, Julius and several of his men looked at each other in astonishment. Lying in Julius' arms was Colonel Reichart. Julius looked at his men, knowing what they were all thinking. They had rescued their old enemy, who had never ceased to make their life a misery, who had probably been one of the most hated

340

senior officers, and here they were, risking their own lives to save his. The irony was not lost on Julius or his men, but Julius knew his duty and started to apply tourniquets to the worst of the Colonel's injuries. As the men covered the Colonel with their capes an ambulance arrived. Two orderlies jumped down from the vehicle and saw to the Colonel's injuries, giving him morphine for his pain. Julius remained at the Colonel's side and as Reichart opened his eyes, his eyelids fluttered as he tried to focus on the face of his former lieutenant. He opened his mouth to speak, but at first no sound came, then he said in a small thin voice, "I always knew I would end up in hell, and I always knew you would be there too Mayer"

A malicious grin appeared on the thin, broken face of the colonel as he coughed and dark red blood appeared and dribbled down his chin. Julius looked at the orderly who shook his head in resignation at the fate of the colonel. His eyes returned to Reichart's as the colonel tried to speak again. Julius could not believe the hate in the man's eyes as he looked up at him and said, "you and Manz always thought you were better than me with your airs and graces and your military families, you hated me and now you have saved my life, I suppose you are regretting that now" Reichart coughed again, this time the blood filling his mouth and gushing out over his chest. Julius looked away, revolted by the sight of the little man in the throes of death, but revolted even more by his spite even as he lay dying.

Julius heard the raucous bubbling in Reichart's throat as he struggled to say something more, but he had neither the strength nor the will to do so, and as Julius turned to look at the colonel once more, the colonel died, still with the look of hatred clouding his eyes. Somebody started to say a prayer, but Julius stood up and walked away from the hated man's body, too shocked to speak. It was obvious that his men felt the same feeling of revulsion, for as one they all stood up and followed Julius down the road. Julius turned to take one last look at the Colonel and stood and observed his body lying alone on the side of the road, left now even by the orderly who had started checking the other bodies for any sign of life.

As Julius and his men walked the last part of the journey into the town, all of them were silent, shocked by the carnage they had just observed and disturbed by Reichart's evil as he lay dying. In some ways it was not a surprise to

Julius and the men who had served under the colonel, they knew how hateful the man was, but to the new young recruits the colonel's vitriol had left them disturbed and they had begun to eye Julius with a curious fascination, as though the colonel's revelations had portrayed a lieutenant they did not know. Julius was aware of their curiosity and after consultation with his sergeant they decided they would try and explain Reichart's character to the men. The sergeant agreed to talk to them that night, believing it was wrong for an officer of Julius' rank to have to explain such things to enlisted men. Julius was grateful to the sergeant, but wondered what the sergeant would say, as he himself was still not sure as to the exact source of such venomous abuse from the colonel, and half wished that he could listen to the sergeant's explanation so that he himself might understand the colonel's hatred.

The scene on the roadside had unnerved Julius and as he entered the town he was overjoyed to see Viktor coming to greet him. After seeing that his men had beds for the night, Julius joined Viktor and told him of the days events. Viktor listened in silence as Julius tried to describe, as fairly as possible, how much the colonel had disliked him and Nikolas.

Viktor merely smiled at his friend, "Julius, you really must not take this so much to heart. Reichart was only here for three days, but he left with the intense dislike of every man in the town. The trouble with you is that you want everybody to like you, and when they do not, you cannot understand it. It would be a very dull world indeed if we all got on together would it not? You cannot say everybody got on together in Vienna. I only have to remind you of Josef, who was not the most popular cadet there has ever been"
Julius relaxed in Viktor's comforting words, but he was still upset to think that one of the reasons Reichart had disliked him was because he was the son of a Colonel and supposedly from a privileged background. Once again Viktor laughed at his friends naiveté, "but Julius don't you understand? Look at our class of cadets, we were all pretty much the same. Every one of us came from privileged backgrounds. Reichart was very much the exception, a man who had come up through the ranks from a lowly position, there are not too many of those about. When you think about it he must have been a pretty exceptional soldier to do that. More is the pity that he did not use his exceptional

342

talents to the good, rather than fostering a hatred for us poor mortals who he believed did not deserve our commission, just because our parents could use their positions or wealth to buy us into the army, and maybe he was not so wrong about that"

Julius turned incredulously to his friend, "what do you mean?"

"Admit it Julius, you were always the one lecturing us about how bad some of our officers were, how they did not have the right attitude towards their men, well maybe that has something to do with the way the army recruits its officers in the first place"

Julius had to smile at last. Only Viktor could pick up on Julius' youthful self-righteousness and throw it back in his face, and maybe he was not so far from the truth.

"The ironic thing" continued Viktor, "is that Colonel Reichart died too soon. The army cannot afford to be as choosy as it once was. Have you not noticed that the officers they are now rushing through cadet school in Vienna in less than six months are from several different walks of life? Very different to the type of soldier they recruited in our day. With so many casualties of war our officers will soon be more like the Reicharts of this world than you or I, and maybe that will not be such a bad thing, as long as they do not have Reichart's personality. You mark my words, after the war the Imperial Army will have a vast new breed of officers, and the likes of you and I will have to accept the changes"

There was a knock at the door and Julius' sergeant entered the room. He hesitated in front of Viktor, but after Julius told him to speak freely in front of Lieutenant Leitner the sergeant informed him that he had spoken to the other young soldiers and explained about Colonel Reichart's behavior. He added that he had been backed up by the other soldiers in the town who had no better impression of the Colonel than they did. Julius was relieved to hear it and after dismissing his sergeant felt happier about the situation. Although he knew that he did not need his men's approbation he felt that in some way the scene that day had reduced their respect for their lieutenant and he needed that, if nothing else.

Julius spent several days in the town, glad of Viktor's company. Viktor proved to be a popular officer, he was popular with his men and they worked hard for him. Julius'

343

men were detailed to help with the fortifications, necessary as the Italians had advanced close to the town in the last battle, and their steady bombardments shelled the town relentlessly whilst Julius was there. Julius was regarded as quite a hero after the story was told of his trying to warn the cars on the road to the town. He wondered if this was because he had tried to save people's lives, or whether it was because he had seen the death of the hated Colonel Reichart.

The bad weather continued, the downpours of freezing rain at least postponing the bombardment but bringing with it further worries. Viktor told Julius that their food supplies were getting very low, and promised ammunition was not arriving. Added to this there had been outbreaks of the dreaded typhus and cholera, deadly diseases, brought on by the terrible conditions the men lived in, where rats freely roamed the camps and most men became infested with lice and maggots, however hard they tried to keep up their personal hygiene.

The days passed quickly and Julius ordered his men ready for the return to the fortifications at Hermade. His farewells to Viktor were short and succinct. In the arena of war no one liked to admit that they might never see one another again, but everyone lived with the knowledge that that the likelihood was always present.

News of the attempted rescue of the officers had reached Hermade. On his return even Captain Milic had patted Julius on the back and declared the likelihood of medals for the men's bravery. Julius had to smile at the thought; Colonel Reichart would be turning in his lonely grave at the thought of Julius receiving a medal for trying to save his life.

When Julius returned to camp he found letters waiting for him from Irmy and Mama. The letter from Mama was very disturbing. It was written in such a dispassionate way, only talking about the weather and who had been to visit her, that it was like a letter she had sent to Julius when he had been in cadet school, not a letter to a man entrenched in a war that spanned a continent and produced thousands of casualties every day. Mama did not even mention the war, nor did she mention Karl, Franz or Irmy. After reading his mother's letter Julius decided that although the letter said absolutely nothing it spoke volumes as to his mother's the state of mind. This view was endorsed when he read the letter from Irmy. He knew that she would be loathe to worry him and therefore she did not dwell on her situation too much, but he could tell her circumstances had not improved since he had left Prague, he felt so sorry for her. She told him that she had received some letters from Papa's friends in Vienna and although they had been very cordial and very kind, promising to do all they could to find out more about Karl, she did not feel any confidence in their help in the future. Julius frowned as he read Irmy's letter. He realized that Irmy was pinning her hopes on receiving help from Vienna, but he knew there was very little anybody could do for Karl, except maybe pray.

Irmy's letter was not all bad news; she wrote that she had heard from Richard, who was well, but overworked. Franz had written to her and she felt he was improving and sounded optimistic about his future. Her last bit of news made him sit up. She told him that she had seen Nikolas, as Frau Manzova had made frequent visits and had been very kind to her, and she added that Nikolas had become engaged to Suse, which she thought was wonderful and so heart-warming amidst all the bad news they had had lately. It was typical of Irmy's romantic nature to add that she felt a personal involvement in the affair, as was it not she who had introduced Nikolas to Suse? Julius had to smile, Irmy still playing the matchmaker. Well he was pleased for Nikolas and Suse, he just hoped they would not rush into marriage, as he hoped he would be the best man at their wedding.

Towards the end of October news came that the Italians were advancing towards their position. They were pushing forward all along the front and were taking thousands of prisoners on their way. The bombardments from both sides increased and the Austrian Army braced itself for a huge attack from the Italians. Julius and his men were ordered to position themselves, with their guns, higher up into the Julian Mountains to form a protection for the soldiers fighting lower down the slopes.

The actual task of getting the big guns, especially the howitzers, up the slopes was a long and arduous task. Automated vehicles could only go so far, after that it was up to the horses or the pack mules to pull the large pieces of machinery and supplies up the mountainside. Several times a few hours of climbing and hauling were wasted as the heavy duty ropes snapped either with the weight of the

345

guns or from the jagged rocks cutting through the fibers. Sometimes this would also break the machinery and several discarded useless weapons littered the slopes as they made slow progress on their ascent. The rest of the equipment would be pulled up on sledges, or carried up by the men on their backs and ropes would be laid out on the mountainsides to assist the men in climbing the icy slopes.

Captain Milic, Julius and their men were ready for the assault when the main Italian army advanced towards them. The fighting was sporadic, the weather holding up any major advancement. The rain continued to pour down, turning to sleet in the cold October air. From their entrenched position higher up on the slopes the Austrian Army managed to hold back the Italian Army. The Italian commanders, knowing they would need a huge concentration of guns to take the Austrian positions, guns which they did not have, realized that their efforts would be in vain. This, coupled with the appalling weather conditions coming with the onset of winter, compelled the Italian Army to postpone any further advances and retreat to their original lines.

The cessation of fighting at the beginning of November came as a huge relief to the Austrian Army. It enabled them to organize new lines, strengthen existing ones and augment supplies that were running low. The main task of the officers was to improve the morale of the men. This was difficult with the non-activity that the pause in fighting brought. It gave the men more time to think about their position, to grumble about the lack of food and warm clothing as the temperatures fell as winter approached. It also gave the men time to ponder about what they were really fighting for.

Since the start of the war the different countries within the Empire had become more hostile than ever, it was well known that at home in their respective countries the independence movements were rising in popularity, with the people asking why their young men were dying in the name of an Empire which did not care about them. This was also prevalent within the army, with the different factions still holding deep divisions amongst themselves, especially at the front, where even the hardest fighting did not seem to create any form of unity. Many former citizens of the Empire were now fighting for the British, Russian and French forces. It did not help the Czech contingent within the army to know that at the outbreak of war several patriots had refused to fight for the Empire and large numbers of Czech partisans had left the country, the largest amount joining the Russian army. It was unnerving to think that in the fiercest fighting on the Russian front Czechs were fighting Czechs on opposing sides. The situation had not been helped when it was found that several Italian prisoners of war had been found to be Czech deserters including some officers. It was a delicate situation for all Czechs, especially the officers and Julius found the situation very hard to come to terms with or explain.

Towards the end of November came the distressing news of the death of their Emperor Franz Josef at the age of eighty-six. Although Franz Josef's death at such an advanced age was to be expected his demise was another crushing blow to the army's morale. Most men had never known another leader in their lifetime and the idea of change and the loss of his leadership brought despair to many of the men. Grown men cried as services in his memory were performed throughout the camps. Black armbands were worn and everybody saw his death as the end of an era, and an omen for the coming days. Soldiers feared for their future without their King and Emperor.

Franz Josef was succeeded by his great-nephew Karl. Not much was known of the man. Until the events in Sarajevo, which had precipitated the war, all eyes had been on Franz-Ferdinand as the heir to the Habsburg throne. Senior officers began to extol the virtues of the new Emperor, trying to boost the loyalty of their soldiers, but there were many discontented murmurings among the camps about the suitability of their new leader.

The last few months of fighting had taken their toll on the men. They had suffered the ignominy of a fierce Italian advance that had resulted in retreat which was seen as a humiliating defeat. This, followed by the news of the death of their Emperor, had not helped the mood of the men as they approached a winter that was proving to be the coldest in living memory.

The snow had fallen in early December and there were now reports of roads blocked by at least four meters of snow. Even on the lower slopes the men had heard the rumble of avalanches that echoed through the mountains, warning everybody of its deathly intent as men held their breath, listening to the horrifying sound of snow rushing its powerful course down the sides of the slopes. With the inactivity that prevailed in the bad weather came the realization that things were becoming worse. Food supplies were low, leaving men weak and easily prone to illness. Men were dying of many diseases, including influenza, that many found hard to fight in their pathetic conditions. It was becoming increasingly difficult to keep warm. Despite the heavy winter uniforms, the inactivity that trench warfare engendered meant that the cold affected even the most warmly clad men. For miles around the landscape was laid bare as soldiers cut down trees and retrieved any materials that could be easily burnt and thus provide some badly needed warmth.

Julius sat in his trench, trying to ignore the bitter cold that crept over his body. He had been writing a letter to Irmy and the extreme temperature hampered his ability to write. He would write a sentence and then quickly don his fur gloves over his woolen ones to ward off the onset of frostbite which was affecting so many of the men. His letter was taking hours to write, and as Julius sat in his huddled position, swathed in his great trench-coat, wearing the essential steel helmet, he looked around him at the dark, gloomy, freezing trench that had become home to so many men.

He raised a tin mug to his lips, drained it of its contents, and promptly spat it out again. What passed for coffee these days was a grainy, weak brew. Julius did not dare ask what it was made of, so far removed was it from what one would normally call coffee. Not only did it taste disgusting but it was stone cold. Although Hans had only brought in the coffee a few minutes ago the harsh temperatures meant that nothing stayed warm for very long. Julius longed to be back in his mother's sitting room, a fire burning in the grate as one of the maids bought in a tray of hot steaming coffee and a plate of heavenly pastries. His reminiscences bought a great wave of depression over him as he realized his circumstances and the futility of his daydreaming.

He shook himself out of his reverie and tried to pull back the cuff of his coat in order to observe his watch. His next tour of duty was due, when he would visit the men in the front-line trenches and observe them in their squalor and haplessness as the extreme cold not only claimed their weary bodies, but also their minds and morale. It was with sadness that Julius found himself joining the men in their despondency. Julius rose to leave the trench and he jumped as a rat ran over his boot and he tried to kick it away. He felt like an old man. He had sat in the cold for some time and his bones ached with the exertion of movement.

Suddenly his sense of humor returned for a moment as he reached for his rifle. He looked down at his enormous fur lined boots, his bulky trench-coat, enormous gloves and then looked up at the rim of his Bergendorfer, its strap digging into his chin to ensure it would not get blown off, and Julius laughed to himself. He imagined himself being challenged by an Italian soldier at this very moment and realized that he would no more be able to lift his rifle up at speed, than he would be able to walk at an even pace with his feet in formation, so big were his boots. He felt as useless as a newborn child, and the idea pleased his sense of humor so much that he began to laugh at himself, until he was laughing so much that tears ran down his face. Hans ran in to see if Julius was all right, startled to see the lieutenant crouched over in the middle of the trench seemingly laughing with no one but himself. At first Hans feared for Julius' sanity and tried to make him sit down to recover. Julius eventually pulled himself together and through his laughter assured Hans that he was not yet ready for an asylum and with a big grin on his face lumbered up the ladder out of the trench to start his inspection. Julius' fit of laughter did him the world of good, the depression that had been hanging over him for several days lifted for a while and as he toured the trenches with Captain Milic he felt better than he had done for months.

Just before Christmas Nikolas returned to the front, bringing with him all the news from home, as well as reports of the events which were sweeping across Europe. Nikolas looked well and healthy, and Julius was saddened to reflect that within a few weeks back at the front his friend would be looking as weak, gray and despondent as the rest of them. Nikolas was bursting with news, obviously happy in his engagement to Suse.

"I know I have done the right thing" enthused Nikolas, "and I know what you are going to say Julius. You know Irmy will always have a small place in my heart, but if this war has taught me anything it is to take your chances while you can, and I know now that I do love Suse"

Julius looked at Nikolas' shining face, and knew that his friend was truly happy, and was overjoyed for him.

"Well, congratulations, all you have to do now is find the right girl for me"

Nikolas looked at his friend and with an innocent look on his face said, "I thought you already had"

Julius felt himself coloring as he thought for one horrendous moment that Nikolas had found out his secret about Josef's mother. His face froze in astonishment, only to be relieved when Nikolas added, "I always told you, you should have stayed with Erika. Did you know Josef and I met her at a field hospital?"

Julius let Nikolas ramble on as his legs returned to their original state and his head had stopped throbbing at the thought of his indiscretion being known. The thought of the Countess still brought a lump to his chest and he tried not to think about her, but his feelings were always mixed. He did not know if it was a longing for her, or a feeling of guilt about the wonderful night they had spent together.

Julius accepted Nikolas' kind words of condolences regarding the death of his father. Colonel Mayer's death seemed such a long time ago that gradually the pain of his father's death was easing. Nikolas brought letters from home, with no more news of Karl, and told Julius that he thought the strain was becoming too much for Irmy and that he and his mother feared for her health. Julius was worried by Nikolas' account, but was glad his friend had been honest with him. He was thankful that Frau Beckova and Frau Manzova were being such a help to Irmy. Nikolas mentioned that Georg was often visiting Irmy, and even he had to agree with Julius that he thought his brother was a little besotted with Irmy.

"Mind you" added Nikolas, "at least it sometimes puts him off thinking about joining the army. He still seems very determined, despite my lectures"

"Do you think he will enlist?" asked Julius.

"To be quite honest, I think it will be very difficult to stop him. He is not the headstrong young fool he was Julius. Surprisingly enough he has a very intelligent brain inside that head of his. I have to admit he put forward a very good argument for joining the army, and you know if it was us in his situation, we would be the first ones knocking on the door of the recruitment office"

Julius had to agree, but knew if Georg had seen half the sights that he had encountered in the last two years he would be less in a hurry to play the hero and enlist.

Nikolas' accounts of events elsewhere were more optimistic. Towards the end of the year Falkenhayn, of the German army, had led the newly formed Austrian 9th Army against Romania with the German Field Marshal von Mackensen, advancing south of the Danube. Both armies had converged on Bucharest and the Romanians had retreated, leaving the Germans to take Bucharest in December, this left only Moldavia in Romanian hands. It was good to hear of Austrian victories after the disappointments of the last few months.

During his leave Nikolas' father had arrived in Prague on leave from Vienna. Nikolas was obviously worried about his father who had arrived looking old and exhausted, and both men were once again drawn to the parallels between their two fathers and were silent as they reflected the fate of Colonel Mayer. Nikolas had had long conversations with his father whilst he had been at home and Nikolas related that Colonel Manz feared that German intervention in the war with Italy would be happening sooner, rather than later.

"My father feels that now Italy has declared war on Germany they will bring their presence to bear as they have in Russia"

"God I hope not" said Julius, "though I have to say some of the decisions that have been made lately leave a lot to be desired"

"It would be the last thing we need," agreed Nikolas, "I suppose you noticed how bad things are at home? The people are becoming very disenchanted with our government and the army. The death of the Emperor has really lowered what little morale there was. Food is becoming scarce and everyone you meet has a member of their family who has either died or been injured in the conflict. Mind you, I have to say that our soldiers here are seen as heroes. It is reported that the Italians have sustained twice as many casualties as us and have hardly advanced their positions since the beginning of the war"

Julius snorted his contempt at his friends attempt to paint a rosy picture, "well, I suppose that is true, but that is true of all warfare now, look at the French and Belgian lines, they have hardly moved either for the past two years. That is nothing to do with heroics, that is the way war is fought in this day and age. Less movement but more casualties, and all such a terrible waste"

Nikolas looked up in surprise at his friend's sarcasm, Julius smiled at his friend "do not worry Nikolas I am not about to give up or surrender myself to the Italians, but you have been away too long, you have forgotten how hard it is here, I will ask you how optimistic you are in a few months time when you have been back fighting at the front, then tell me how you feel"

XXV

The harsh winter continued with a large loss of life due to diseases such as dysentery, cholera and typhus, which swept through the camps in the terrible conditions that continued through Christmas and beyond the New Year of 1917. Guards would be found frozen to death in the morning, or suffering from hypothermia and frostbite. Lorries and trains would not work, so vital supplies did not reach the front and the men were always hungry. They had started to kill rats to eat, despite being warned of the health hazard, but their hunger overtook their reason. Guns became iced up, and the dark uniforms of the soldiers made the men easy targets for enemy snipers.

The only relief was a few weeks in the safe camps behind the lines. Here the men rejoiced in the near normality of life, baths, rest, sleep and a chance to believe you were a human being once more.

Julius, Nikolas and their company were sent with Captain Milic to a safe camp in the New Year. Nikolas enjoyed serving under Captain Milic as much as Julius and their company was as unified as any at the front at that time. This was especially important to the Bohemian units as daily reports were rife of Czech soldiers passing over to the Russians in their thousands. They all hoped the rumors were unfounded, but could not quite shake off the fear that they were true.

In every camp brothels had appeared to cater for the needs of the soldiers. These were tactfully ignored by the authorities as they were seen as welcome diversions for the men who had been away from home for such long periods of time. The bordels were clearly defined, those for the ordinary soldiers, and those for the officers. There were worries as to the risks the men were taking in contracting diseases such as syphilis and gonorrhea but these were thought to far outweigh the needs of the men. Discretion was the order of the day if one visited the brothels, but no one blamed a man for seeking the solace of the warm body of a woman in such troubled times. The more lewd of the brothels would find their girls hanging out of the windows enticing the men in. Often these were common, highly rouged girls who always managed to make Julius and

Nikolas blush as they hid their smiles while the girls passed bawdy comments about private parts of their anatomy.

One day Julius, Nikolas and Captain Milic were making their way to the local brothel that was frequented by officers. The girls there were known to be clean, and although nothing like the houses in Prague and Vienna, filled a void for the men that they badly needed. As they entered the house Nikolas looked up the stairs to see a familiar face coming towards them.

"Viktor, you old roué! I suppose there is no point in asking what you are doing here?"

"A charming greeting I must say," laughed Viktor, as he embraced his friends. Julius and Nikolas introduced Viktor to Captain Milic, and, all thoughts of bodily fulfillment forgotten, they decided to return to Viktor's room for a particularly good bottle of cognac that he had been saving for just such an occasion.

"Well you may want to recapture old times" joked Captain Milic, "but I for one know there is a certain young lady upstairs who would be devastated if I did not visit her this very moment. So I am afraid gentlemen I will have to disappoint you, I am far too chivalrous to let a lady down" and with a dramatic bow and loud laughter the captain ran up the stairs, two at a time, to seek his partner for the afternoon.

"I like him" said Viktor, with a grin on his face "there is a man after my own heart"

The three men were delighted to be in each other's company again. Viktor had been at the camp for a few days and reported that Josef had gone home on leave. "Lucky devil" added Viktor, "I suppose he will be sampling the delights of Vienna or being spoiled by that beautiful mother of his"

Julius tensed at the mention of the countess as Nikolas added, "I do not think there are too many delights of Vienna to sample at the moment if what my father says is true. They are feeling the effects of the war as much as anybody else"

Viktor opened the bottle of cognac and with pledges of not mentioning the war again, the afternoon was spent in friendly reminiscences helped along by the excellent cognac. The next few weeks passed amiably enough, and the three friends, often joined by Captain Milic, could almost believe

354

they were back in Vienna, a life that was now a fond but distant dream to them all.

The weather did not ease for many months and even by March when the usual early flowers would have been pushing their colorful heads up towards the warming sun and the trees would be bursting into bud to herald the new springtide, the snow still blanketed the ground and there was little sign of spring arriving at all.

The cold weather persisted and back at the front Julius and Nikolas encountered the constant grumbling of the men, bored with the inactivity the weather caused, bad tempered with the freezing weather and lack of comfort, and demoralized by being perpetually on the defensive against the Italians. They were still very short of food and the deaths of so many men due to the conditions and disease did nothing to help the morale of the troops. The only advantage of the cessation of fighting was that it heralded the arrival of much needed troops and guns to bolster the beleaguered Austrian forces.

As April came the snows gradually began to melt at last. The mountains were still covered in thick snow and there was heard the noise of skirmishes coming from the higher slopes, but gradually as the snow melted it uncovered the brown and green lower slopes, which soon turned to slimy mud, as the thawing snow turned to streams of water which swelled the rivers into rushing torrents. Although the weather was warmer the men were soon wishing for the snow back as they tried to combat the constant mud and water that invaded their trenches and dugouts and which permanently covered their clothing, seeping into every orifice that was open to the elements. Soon the men no longer tried to wash off the mud, seeing it as a never ending task. With the spring came the realization that hostilities would start again. The men became more alert, anxious for action, mixed with the fear of what that could bring.

One day Julius was out at the dog pens watching the animals being fed their meager portions. The dogs had become an integral part of the army, being used to pull sleds carrying provisions over the snow, and to tow infantry guns with light ammunition. Some were also used for their sensitive noses to locate the wounded on the battlefield. Julius liked to come and watch the dogs, since the loss of

Phantom he had become wary of becoming close to another horse, although Nikolas still kept Steel close by him.

Julius had not been reassigned another horse. Thousands of horses had been lost in the battles, when a battlefield was observed after a conflict there would be many horses lying dead with the men. Officers were allowed the luxury of their own horses if they survived, but horses were now just taken from the compounds if and when they were needed. As the food situation worsened many soldiers, from both sides, would drag dead horses back to the camps where they would be used to supplement the poor diet of the men.

Julius liked the affectionate nature of the dogs who would always greet him with a friendly wag of their tails and a welcoming bark. Julius was talking to one of their handlers when he saw Hans running down the slope towards them, waving his hands in the air. Julius frowned, despite their best efforts, he and Nikolas had not been able to curb the natural exuberance of the boy and his departure from soldierly etiquette often left them in despair. They would frequently berate their batman and explain that with other officers he would have been up on a charge several times. These lectures did nothing to compose the boy and Julius closed his eyes as he watched Hans approaching and hoped that there was no senior officer watching such a flagrant breach of the rules.

Hans ran up to Julius shouting "Sir, sir" and then stopped before Julius, his hands on his hips, trying to catch his breath, great clouds of colored air issuing from his mouth, as his red cheeks puffed in and out. The dog handler looked on in amazement at the abandonment of the boy in front of him. The action irritated Julius as he said, "well I shall ignore the fact that you have not saluted me Private Lupac, even though I could report you" he looked warily at the dog handler, realizing he should not lose face in front of the private, but not wanting to be too hard on Hans, whom he genuinely liked, despite his inclination for flouting the rules, "hurry up man and catch your breath, I presume you have a message for me?"

Hans looked up at Julius' sharp words and suddenly remembered his position as he stood to smart attention and saluted his senior officer, his breath still coming in short bursts and his face redder than ever. At last he recovered some of his composure and he managed to say amidst large gasps of air, "Sir, Lieutenant Manz sent me to fetch you. He says there is urgent news for you" Hans looked sideways at the dog handler as he audaciously added, "he has been talking to Captain Milic on the field telephone, he seemed very excited by the news"

Julius rolled his eyes heavenward as the boy once more flouted the rules by talking out of turn to an officer but he was too intrigued to find out what the momentous news was to censure Hans again. Instead he strode off up the slope with Hans scurrying behind him.

When Julius entered their trench Nikolas was in a high state of excitement, "Julius you will never guess what I have just been told, you will not believe it, I am not sure that I do" Julius decided it must be his day for encountering annoying people as he patiently waited for Nikolas to tell him what was so amazing. "Well it must be serious," observed Julius, "I suppose there is little hope that everyone has surrendered and this war is at an end?"

"No, I am afraid not," said Nikolas, finally becoming sensible again as he sat down to face Julius, "Captain Milic has just telephoned me, Tsar Nikolas has been forced to abdicate and the Russians have withdrawn from the war! I really cannot believe it"

Julius sat down, he knew he had understood what his friend had told him, but he could not believe it either. The mighty Tsar abdicate, it was not possible.

"He cannot hope to have his little son rule the country, what is he thinking of?" asked Julius.

"No Julius I did not explain myself, the people made the Tsar abdicate, he and his whole family have been put under house arrest and it is the people who have taken over the country. It is the people who are now ruling the Russias"

Julius stared open mouthed at his friend, he just could not believe it. All his life he had been brought up to believe in the absolute power of the monarchy, that your king was the absolute leader, and now the great Tsar, who called himself the father of his people, was no more.

"But why?" stuttered Julius, "I do not understand. We know that many of the populace have been unhappy about this war, but to force the Tsar to abdicate, that is unbelievable?" Julius felt himself going cold as he thought of the implications for his own country. The death of Franz Josef had left a void that had not really been filled, could the same thing happen to the Emperor Karl? Julius shrugged off such depressing thoughts as he became aware of Nikolas talking to him.

"Julius, you do not seem to understand what this means. The great Russian army is no longer in the war. It means the Russians are no longer threatening the rear guard of the German army. It will make the Germans stronger, and hopefully release much needed troops to help us here, though let us hope it will be Austrian troops and not Germans. Maybe when you have been able to absorb all this you will begin to realize how these events might affect you personally"

Julius looked at his friend, his mind still racing with all the thoughts and implications that the news had brought him. "What do you mean, affect me personally, how can it?" asked Julius still feeling very confused.

"Captain Milic told me to tell you that with the withdrawal of the Russian Army there has come the widespread release of their prisoners of war. With any luck Karl could be on his way home as we speak"

Julius was shocked out of his thoughts as he grabbed Nikolas from his seat and started dancing with joy around their cramped quarters. He felt happy for the first time in ages, if Karl was on his way home, he knew he could not have heard more wonderful news. Since hearing of his capture Julius had never stopped worrying about his brother, knowing how he might be suffering under the Russian regime, and he had never dared to hope that he might see Karl again. Now he knew if his brother was still alive, there was a possibility that he would soon be safe.

News of the abdication of Tsar Nicholas II and the subsequent withdrawal of the Russian army from the war soon spread throughout the camp. The reports boosted morale as it was seen as an indication of the collapse of the enemy, but the realization that the people had forced the Tsar from his throne created unrest and mutterings amongst the men who started to compare themselves with the Russian people. It also caused dismay amongst the senior officers who started to see the crumbling of the institution of the monarchy.

The euphoria over the Russias was short lived. A few weeks later Captain Milic entered their trench with the somber news that the United States of America had declared war on Germany. Julius and Nikolas could hardly believe the news; it was as though they had been given a new toy only to have it snatched away again.

"I do not understand," said Nikolas, "I knew the Americans were unhappy about the sinking of the Lusitania, but that was over two years ago"

"It seems" said Captain Milic, "that our German allies have seen fit to tell our opposing forces that any of their sea going vessels would be blown out of the water if they were located in certain areas"

"The Americans would not enter this war because of a threat, I do not believe it"

"No, they would not" answered the captain wearily, "but they would if a German submarine had sunk six of their vessels"

The three men sat in silence for a long time as the implications of this news sunk in. They knew that with the might and money of the United States of America, the opposing forces were now stronger than ever.

In the month of June Julius received the news he had been waiting for. Irmy had written to tell him that she had heard from their father's friends in Vienna. Karl's name had been found on the lists of prisoners of war who were to be repatriated. She wrote that she did not know when this would be, but it was still the best news she had had for a long time. Mama was still not improved but Irmy had been boosted by the arrival of Richard on home leave, and with the news of Karl she felt much better and was sure Mama would rally soon.

Julius was not so sure as he read the letter he had received from his mother. He hated the coldness and lack of feeling in his mother's letters. It had almost come to the point where, when he held his mother's letters in his hand, he had no wish to open them as they left him with such feelings of dejection and gloom. He had also received letters from Erika, still at the field hospital. The letters were very friendly but still non-committal, none the less Julius looked forward to seeing Erika's neat hand on the paper, her letters giving him some welcome respite from the hazardous world he lived in.

One day Julius and Nikolas were lying on their cots discussing a letter Nikolas had received from Suse. They always read each other's letters out to each other. It somehow gave them a sense of much needed normality to hear of their loved ones and friends. Nikolas always took a long time reading Suse's letters to Julius. He left long gaps as he hurriedly read to himself any private or romantic notions that Suse had written to him. Julius always found this very entertaining as he watched his friend's embarrassment as he read of his fiancée's affections. Nikolas had asked Julius to be best man at their wedding, though as yet a date had not been decided. This was going to be harder than it sounded, Nikolas wanted his whole family to be there, which would be difficult with his father stationed in Vienna, plus the chances of them getting home leave together were very slim. Julius insisted his friend go ahead with his marriage, even if he was not there, but Nikolas had seemed hurt at the very suggestion.

"I could not be married without my greatest friend being there, it would not be right. I have discussed this with Suse and she agrees with me, if it means we have to wait, so be it. Let us face it, this war cannot last forever"

Julius had to doubt his friend's optimism but was very flattered to think he meant so much to Nikolas. As Nikolas was reading his letter from Suse he suddenly sat up and swung his legs over the side of the bed. "I do not believe this" he exclaimed, "what is the girl thinking of?"

Julius raised a questioning eyebrow at his friend, wondering what had so annoyed him in Suse's letter. "I cannot believe it" repeated Nikolas.

"What is the matter?" asked Julius, his curiosity aroused, "what can you not believe for heavens sake?"

"Suse has volunteered to work in a munitions factory. What is the world coming to?"

Julius had to hide a smile from Nikolas. He had often discussed the position of women working with his friend. He knew from long ago that although Nikolas admired Irmy he had never completely approved of her training to be a nurse. Nikolas was a very traditional man, who believed a woman's place was in the home, and though to a certain degree Julius had to agree with him, Nikolas was far more defensive about the subject than Julius could ever be. When Nikolas had come back to the front from his leave he had bemoaned the fact of how many women were now working. Even when Julius had pointed out that this was a necessity due to most of the male population away fighting at the front, he had not been able to convince his friend of the suitability of women working in factories, hospitals and shops, basically taking on the employment vacated by the men conscripted to the war effort. When Julius had deigned to offer the opinion that maybe this was a harbinger of things to come, that maybe after the war more women would want to acquire employment for themselves, Nikolas had dismissed the notion as ridiculous, women were not meant to work, and the men would then be back to take up gainful employment.

It was not an argument that Julius pursued, but maybe because he had grown up with Irmy and seen her determination to become a nurse against all the odds he did not think all women would be content to return home to their domestic duties after the war. He had seen too much when he had been home on leave. Most women whom he had met were enjoying the freedom that employment allowed them and as he observed them he had realized that they would not willingly give that up when the war was over. Despite Nikolas' protestations, Julius also knew many men would not be returning from the front and that labor would be in short supply at the end of the war, then working women would probably be needed more than ever. As Irmy had said, their country was never going to be the same again after this war. Too many things had changed over the past few years to be able to return to their old way of life.

The summer proceeded with skirmishes throughout the front, and, but for the constant bombardment of both sides, the lethargy of the past few months continued. Life, when there were no battles, could be very boring within the trenches and camps. Daily masses were still being led by Father Tomelski. Julius wandered if the father had ever been away from the camp, he appeared to be always present, tirelessly passing amongst the men, talking to them, hearing their confessions or, in the worst of times, giving men their last rites. The young priest seemed to have a boundless source of energy, but even he carried the haggard look of a man twice his age.

Following a meager breakfast the men would be given their tasks for the day, this could be anything from repairing the camps after a bombardment to cleaning their equipment and every day the men had to have a medical check. After the men had performed their duties, and if they were not on guard duty, they would sit around reading, smoking or playing cards. Often the sound of melodious folk tunes could be heard across the camps as the men reminisced about

361

their homelands. Many wrote letters home which would then have to be read by a censor. If the letters contained information that might upset the people at home, or be of use to the enemy, the censor would black out the offending lines. This would upset the men but they accepted the practice as a necessity of war.

Lately new cap badges had arrived to be placed on their uniforms, these were a circular badge of metal for the conscripted men and bullion for the officers. On them was the initial K for their new emperor to replace the FJI which had adorned the army headgear for such a long time. The replacement of the badges displayed a poignant significance for the men, as they discarded their old badges for the new one. Once again they were reminded of the changes that were affecting their lives.

In August the Italians once again attacked the Austrian forces on the Carso plateau, north of the Adriatic, in order to attempt to seize Trieste. Julius and his men joined the Austrian forces in their bombardment of the Italian troops. Italy had been slowly advancing throughout the summer and had gained a lot of ground but now the fighting had spread as far north as Tolmin with the fiercest fighting the area had known in a long time. The battle raged into September with a heavy loss of life. The guns on the mountains were effective, but their stationary situation made them prime targets and Julius' company lost many men and suffered countless injuries. During one such skirmish Nikolas was hit by shrapnel in the arm. His wounds were not too serious and after being treated by a doctor he was soon back at his post, the ever present smile on his face as he once again extolled the virtues of Smid's lucky charm.

In September the Italians attempted a major attack on San Gabriele, but were thwarted by a counterattack by the Austrian forces and were unsuccessful. By the middle of September the Austrian forces were on the brink of collapse. The battle lines had swung back and forth but eventually the Austrians had forced back the Italians but at a tremendous cost to themselves. They were very low on ammunition and their soldiers, despite the arrival of troops recalled from the Russian front, were physically and mentally exhausted. The Germans had seen enough. They could not allow the collapse of the Austrian army and decided to send troops to the Italian front.

362

The morale of the men had never been lower. After the fighting of the last few weeks every man had seen enough of war and bloodshed to last them a lifetime. To many the news of the German reinforcements was a godsend which they viewed as a beginning of the end of the war. As the troops attempted to clear up after the debacle of the past months they greeted the arriving German troops as saviors. All around the countryside lay the evidence of the carnage of war. Whole villages and towns lay in ruins, devastated by the constant shelling and bombardments. Large groups of homeless people roamed the country roads, refugees fleeing from the battle areas, their carts piled high with the few meager possessions that were all they had left, and with nowhere to go.

Nikolas' arm had become inflamed and his wound had become infected with pus. Although his injuries were slight Captain Milic had ordered Nikolas to get them tended as soon as possible at the field hospital and Julius had been sent with him. They looked forward to the diversion of a day at the hospital. They were both very weary and the loss of their men had affected them both.

As they rode through the outlying camps they were assailed by the noise of men trying to repair the damage of the last battle. Julius pointed out to Nikolas the vast graveyard that could be seen on a far off slope. Each grave of uniform shape, each one supported by a bleached wooden cross, each one portraying the death of another poor soul.

They both heard their names called and as they looked round Julius thought he was seeing a ghost. Walking towards him was a young man, with a shock of red hair and an angelic smile. He was dressed in the uniform of a cadet officer and Julius felt as if he was being swept back all those years ago, to Vienna, watching Nikolas on his first day of army life. Nikolas leapt off Steel and strode towards his young brother where, all military etiquette forgotten, he gave Georg a welcoming embrace. Then he thrust his brother from him and said sternly, "What the hell are you doing here? As if I have to ask. What does Mama think of all this? Of all the stupid things to do"

Julius by this time had dismounted his horse and now stood beside the two brothers. He noticed the smile and the twinkle in Georg's eyes as he took his brothers severe rebuke in good heart.

"Do not act so surprised Nikolas," he said to his brother, "you knew I would be here as soon as was possible, and by the look of things, you are in need of me"

Julius had to laugh at Georg's audacity, thinking he was here as the savior of the Imperial army. "I thought you said he had matured" said Julius, still laughing.

Nikolas smiled, "maybe I was mistaken, I hope not. He will learn, and very quickly, unfortunately"

They could not stay long, but they learnt that Georg had only arrived at the front a few days beforehand. He told them everyone at home was well, and gave them letters from their families. Julius was especially pleased to hear from Irmy. He had heard no more of Karl's release and was anxious to know of his progress. With a promise to visit Georg as soon as possible Nikolas mounted his horse and they rode off to the hospital. Nikolas was very quiet on the ride, and after having his wounds dressed, the ride back to camp was equally as silent.

"You know it is not worth spending your time worrying about Georg," said Julius, trying to placate his friend, "you knew he would enlist as soon as it was possible. I know it is hard, but brooding over him will not help"

"I know," replied Nikolas, "but he is so young, with no experience of warfare, just a stupid belief that he can win this war single handed"

"Come now, Georg is not a fool. He comes from a military family, went to a military school, he is not a complete unknown to army life. He will be fine, believe me"

Nikolas sighed deeply as he said, "I wish I had your optimism Julius, I really do" Nikolas carried on his ride in deep thought and he remained very morose and quiet for the next few days.

Julius was confused by the contents of Irmy's letter. He was overjoyed to read that Karl had at last been released but annoyed to find that his brother had chosen to travel to Graz to see Franz and Gretha rather than go to Prague to visit Irmy and Mama. Julius longed to talk to Nikolas about his misgivings, but found his friend too preoccupied with Georg, and so he discussed his doubts with Father Tomelski. The father listened in silence as Julius told him about Karl. The priest already knew about Julius' family, they had had many a discussion about Mama's condition and Irmy's uneasy situation.

"Now correct me if I am wrong" began the priest after Julius had finished divulging the contents of Irmy's letter, "but you are annoyed because Karl has chosen to go and see your brother in Graz rather than visit your mother, why is that?"

"Well" began Julius, unsure why the father needed to ask such a question, "I think that Irmy is having a very difficult time with Mama, and I think that Karl going home might help the situation"

Father Tomelski shook his head, "I am sorry Julius I cannot agree with you. You really have not thought about this. Firstly you do not know if Karl is even aware of your father's death, or for that matter, your mother's state of mind since that sad event. Secondly you also do not know if he is aware of the terrible burden that your sister is bearing in these unhappy times" Julius moved to contradict the father, but the father carried on with his speech, "Julius, your brother has been a prisoner of war for the last year, we do not know what he may have endured in that time. He now wishes to spend time with the one person he knows who can share with him all the evils that they have both known from this war. Franz and Karl will both benefit, if Franz's' wife has invited Karl to her home it is obvious that she feels that they can help each other through their troubled times. You or I cannot know what they have gone through, we can only guess, let them have their time together. As much as you think he would be of benefit to your sister and mother, I think you should think of Karl's needs first. Like so many casualties of this war, he may take a lot longer to get over this than even your mother or sister"

Father Tomelski rose wearily from his chair and as he watched the priest walk amongst his flock, offering a kind word here, encouragement there, Julius realized that he had been too quick to condemn Karl. He could not hope to understand what his two brothers had endured because of this war, and he prayed fervently that he never would.

At the beginning of October six German divisions arrived to bolster the Austrian Army. Their reception was mixed, the soldiers knew they desperately needed the support of the German army but their innate distrust of their ally continued. The situation was not improved when a large amount of Austrian senior officers were relieved of their commands and replaced by Germans.

The Germans decided that they must take the offensive in order to smash the stalemate that existed. The plan codenamed 'Waffentreue' was for two Austrian armies to attack the Italians on the Bainsizza Plateau, north of Gorz, and on the low ground near the Adriatic shore whilst the German 14th Army, which consisted of the six German divisions and nine Austrian divisions would force its way over and down the Julian Alps, through Tolmin and Plezzo, dispensing with the usual preliminary artillery bombardment and relying instead on picked storm troopers to smash their way through enemy lines. Troops would then follow on behind them to deal with any strong points still left in enemy hands. To this end the guns were mainly arriving by hand, the infantry arriving by marching through the night, taking no vehicles, but carrying their equipment, ammunition and supplies on their backs or by pack animals. It was hoped that this would prevent the Italians from knowing about the massing of the men and therefore they could be taken by surprise. Meanwhile a later offensive was planned from the Trentino in the north towards the south.

Julius and his company were ordered northwards to provide the rear guard for the initial troop's advancement towards Udine in the west. They proceeded up the Moistroka Pass near Tolmin, climbing up the twisting, serpentine roads that straddled the mountainside, to reach their base for the battle ahead. All along the steep, rough roads cut into the mountainside they encountered hundreds of men, horses and carts moving the supplies needed for the days ahead. In Tolmin itself the Austrian Army had managed to maintain the bridgehead which afforded a starting point for the offensive. When the plan was explained to the officers they all looked round in bewilderment. The plan was a bold one and there was a feeling of elation that at last their troops were to be on the offensive but whether the tactics would work, no one was sure.

Julius was somewhat skeptical of the fact that artillery bombardment was not to be used initially. Being an artillery officer he believed in the power and use of guns in open warfare, but he had to admit that the heavy guns did slow an advance down. He was glad he was not to be in the advance force, he felt they would be cut to shreds without the coverage of field guns to shield them. He was happier knowing that after the advance party he would then be using the guns that were already at Tolmin, and in the

366

slopes above, to destroy any Italian strongholds that had not been conquered by the 14th Army.

The day of 24th October, 1917 heavy rains fell from the sky and snow was falling in the mountains. The conditions did not augur well for the battle and Julius sat huddled under his cape, his men and guns at the ready waiting for the signal to advance.

The waiting seemed endless, as they heard the artillery explosions and gunfire coming from the plains below, but at last the orders came through on the field telephone. Captain Milic ran through the mud to his men. His voice could hardly be heard through the driving rain and snow, but the men knew the time had come. Men, horses, guns and support vehicles all swarmed down to commence battle.

The first surprise was the weakness of the artillery bombardment that met their advancement. Firing their guns at the few targets left for them, they soon crossed the Isonzo, where there were the evident signs of battle and even more amazingly the signs of a rapid retreat by the Italians. All around them were abandoned vehicles, piled high with supplies, hastily left behind as the Italians panicked at the sight of the advancing forces. Bodies lay everywhere, a testament of the ferociousness and effectiveness of the storm troops as they pushed there way to the west.

Before long Julius and his men walked into the village of Caporetto/Karfreit. The rain still fell heavily, but the men did not feel it as the euphoria of success overwhelmed them. Caporetto was a pretty village, dominated by a bell tower that lay nestled in a valley next to the river. The ravages of war had overcome the hamlet, and as Julius walked along its streets he was intrigued to observe the influence of its Italian occupation. Leaving soldiers to guard the guns Captain Milic, Julius and Nikolas assembled the rest of their men by the fountain that dominated the central square of the village. With rifles ready they were ordered to begin a systematic search of the houses. It was good to get out of the driving rain as they ran into the houses. In some they found groups of local people huddled together, shaking from fear at the arrival of these new soldiers. The wine store of the departing Italian army was found and Julius immediately placed a guard on it for fear of the men being tempted.

All the Italians were lined up and taken as prisoners, just a few of the thousands who were taken that day. After a company was left in charge of the village Captain Milic gave the orders for the advance and once more they were progressing across the countryside. All along the way they came across disaffected Italian soldiers rushing to give themselves up to their enemies. Many were young boys who were crying, telling the soldiers that they were being shot at by their own soldiers as they tried to desert. At one point the prisoners were outnumbering the advancing soldiers, as the Austrians had not envisaged such a total collapse of the Italian army.

As darkness fell the advance continued. Shells and rocket fire lit up the dark sky, the frequency of the victorious three green and then one white flare exploding in the skies overhead displaying the large amount of territory falling into Austro-German hands. Machine gun fire could be heard over the mountains and across the plains throughout the night. As Julius' company halted they prepared to strike camp. Their guns were positioned and they carried on the bombardment of the few pockets of Italian resistance that remained. The men were all tired, the terrain covered in the advancement had not been easy, but the joy of victory made up for the pain in their limbs.

For the next few days the rout continued, the misty conditions that followed the rain providing the element of surprise, confusing and disorientating the retreating Italian troops. Julius was amazed as he realized just how successful the battle had been, his own company suffering little loss of life compared to the thousands of Italians who lay dead or wounded in their path.

They kept finding large groups of people, soldiers as well as civilians, who had been attached to the various services that had augmented the Italian Army. Such had been the speed of the retreat these people were left behind and were wandering, bemused by their situation. Julius was astounded as he observed their prisoners of war. It was hard to believe that these wretched, broken men had been the force that they had been fighting against for the last two years. They sat on the ground, the rain lashing down, shivering in the cold, most staring into space, none of them looking at each other, empty shells of men.

On the last day of October, seven days after the start of the battle Julius and Nikolas were sitting in their temporary

368

camp, on the outskirts of Udine. Udine was in the middle of the plain between the Isonzo and Tagliamento Rivers that, until the last few days, had been the Italian general headquarters. They had been quickly evacuated by General Cadorna, the Italian commander, when he had heard of the Austrian advance and the Italian command had fled to Padua to set up safer headquarters there. The two friends were drinking a welcome cup of coffee that actually tasted like coffee. Over the past few days the men's elation had come not just with the feeling of victory as they overran and advanced towards their enemy but also from the retrieving of large quantities of supplies that had been left by the Italians in their hasty retreat. For the first time in many months the men were able to eat and drink well and their full stomachs increased their feeling of well being.

The advancement had been an uplifting experience for Julius and Nikolas. They both knew that with that success had come loss of life, but far less on their side than that of the Italians. However they had to admit that the sight of the demoralized and broken Italian soldiers had touched a nerve inside them on which they did not want to dwell too long. It was easy to look at those soldiers with contempt, but they both knew that only a few months ago those soldiers could well have been themselves and their own men.

Captain Milic walked up to them with a large smile on his face. "Gentleman, I have just had a meeting with the colonel which was interrupted by a very interesting telephone message. You will be pleased to know that as of now our armies have reached the Tagliamento River and as we speak are preparing to follow the retreating Italian army across that river to advance towards the Piave" All the men cheered as they reflected on the enormity of the Austrian-German advance. In the past seven days the Italians had completely lost any advances that they had made over the last two years.

After the men had dispersed Captain Milic sat down with his two lieutenants. "I have more good news for you two. It seems that the radio operator was a young man called Manz who especially wanted the Colonel to know his name, I cannot imagine why" Nikolas beamed, happy to hear that his young brother was well but not so happy to hear that he could well be near the front. Milic rose to leave them and as Nikolas and Julius jumped up to salute their senior officer he turned back and said, "Oh, one other thing, the operator also said that Mounts Kutz and Leitner have been sighted this very day. I believe the colonel is still looking at his map, trying to find them" without a trace of emotion the captain left them. Julius and Nikolas turned to each other, grinned and then embraced each other as they fell about laughing at the very unsubtle way Georg had managed to tell them that Josef and Viktor were very much alive and well.

The Austro-German Army advanced forward for the next few days towards the Piave River, the pincer movement of the Austro-German armies creating a crushing defeat for the Italians. The battle produced many stories of heroics and textbook strategy for warfare. All over the area, ground was retaken that completely nullified any previous Italian advances. In the south the Bainsizza Plateau, which had taken the Italians over three weeks to capture, was retaken within hours. Further north a Captain Erwin Rommel had managed to retake Mounts Mrzli and Matajur in just fifty-two hours, strongholds which had cost the lives of thousands of Italians and Austrians during the past two and a half years.

The phenomenal success of the battle was to be its undoing. Not realizing just how successful the advance would be or how quickly would be the sudden collapse of the Italian army, the army could not keep up its relentless pressure on the Italians. They had no back up or contingency plans for such a huge advancement and there followed a wild confusion of orders, which were often issued and then changed which led to conflict and arguments. It also saw senior army officers and divisional commanders issuing their own orders and soon there was hopeless chaos amongst the army.

The Italians managed to cross the swollen waters of the Piave River, consolidate their position behind its banks and then construct a defensive line. Unable to bring up reserves, and with a lack of munitions and men, the Germans called a halt in front of the Piave River.

Despite being unable to finally bring about a total defeat of the Italians the battle was seen as a great success for the Austro-German forces. During the battle Italy had sustained tens of thousands of casualties and over half a million more had deserted or been taken prisoner. Large amounts of Italian deserters had fled back to their homelands whilst the

Austro-German alliance had suffered far less casualties than the Italians. However the halt of the Austro-German armies had allowed the Italians to rebuild their defenses and their defeat instilled a steely resolve in the Italian soldiers defending the Piave River, who managed to hold their lines, despite constant bombardment from the opposing forces. With such a humiliating defeat the Italian commander, General Cadorna was dismissed and the Italian government asked for help from their French and British allies.

By the middle of November the situation had become a stalemate and the rumors of the imminent arrival of French and British reinforcements swept through the Austrian camps. Many of the men accepted the news with the cavalier attitude of a conquering army, but many more received the news with trepidation, knowing that their war was far from over.

As the fighting died out the exhausted Austrian-German armies held the Italian Army in front of the Piave River, whilst to the north the Austrian forces in the Trentino advanced southwards between the Adige and Piave Rivers through the Asiago Plateau to attack the Italian left flank. However this advancement was not as successful as the ones of the weeks before. The Austrian troops encountered long standing defensive positions holding troops who were not taken by surprise as they had been in the south. Initially the Austrians gained some advance, taking the town of Asiago, but although the fighting continued in that region it died out in January as the freezing weather once more spread its icy clutches over the armies at war.

XXVI

The freezing winter weather of 1917 allowed a lull after the frenetic activity of the past few months. Once again it enabled a beleaguered army, this time the Italians, to regroup themselves, receive much needed provisions and armaments, and also allowed time for British and French reinforcements to arrive, answering the call of their demoralized ally.

In the Austrian and German camps the news from the homeland was not encouraging. The men were alarmed to hear of protest strikes in Vienna against the government as well as widespread food shortages. The maritime blockades set up by the enemy, especially those of the British forces, were taking their hold. Food prices were rising and it was difficult to buy even the necessities of life. It was estimated that the average person was only receiving a quarter of the food that a person would need. In their hardship the German and Austrian people were becoming very enterprising in their use of 'ersatz' materials to supplement their everyday existence. Nettle fibers were used for making cotton; coffee was being made from dandelion roots and barley, whilst tea was made from raspberry leaves. Even boot soles were made out of wood because of the shortage of leather.

In her correspondence Irmy could only hint at the hardships that the people were bearing in Prague, but he could tell that things were very harsh. She was still working at the hospital and Richard had returned to the front. Irmy seemed to think that Mama was at last improving in her health, although it was proving to be a very slow and arduous task. Julius reflected that in her letters to him his mother still appeared as cold and remote as before. He had not heard from his brothers, but Irmy had added that Gretha had written to her to tell her that Franz had improved beyond all her expectations and that Karl's presence had been a boon to his recovery, both men taking strength from each other. Julius was delighted to read this and once again marveled at the perspicacity of Father Tomelski. Julius had also received a letter from Erika, full of her news, but Julius noticed an edge of weariness and sadness in her writing, and realized that the war was having its toll on her as well. She asked Julius to congratulate

Nikolas on his engagement to Suse and added that she hoped that she would be in Prague when the happy event occurred.

Soon after the battle to the Piave River Julius and Nikolas had both received notification of their promotion to captain. Although again they were both not unduly surprised at their elevation it was with some pride that Julius observed the third silver star on his collar. Julius would soon be celebrating his twenty eighth birthday, quite a young age to achieve the rank of captain, and not for the first time did he wish that his father was still alive to have seen his son promoted.

The double promotion was both a blessing and a drawback for Julius and Nikolas. Both would now be in charge of their own units and so would have to part company from each other. Julius especially found this upsetting. For a long time he had regarded his friend as his lucky charm, and now they were to be separated, but he also knew he would miss Nikolas' company, his humor, his wisdom, and most of all, in this time of such death and destruction, he would miss Nikolas' sense of honor. The blessing was that now they would not be part of the same unit they could both apply for leave together so that Nikolas could be married at last. Home leave was very rare, but Captain Milic had applied for them and they had received the news that they could both return to Prague in July, pending any further developments on their front. Nikolas was ecstatic and the preparations were made for a July wedding in Prague.

It was welcome to at last look forward to something happy, rather than only looking forward to endless months in the trenches, and the possibility of further battles. The Italians may have been routed, but everyone knew that the British and French had arrived and the euphoria of their victory had given way to the realization that the war should and could have been ended in one stroke were it not for their disorganization at the end of the battle, a fact repeatedly discussed amongst the men. Now the Italians were regrouping with renewed vigor and many were wondering if the war would ever end.

Julius was assigned his new company of men. He was pleased to see a few seasoned veterans amongst the very young faces that were now dominating their weary army. Hans was to remain with Julius. At first he had been distressed at having to choose between Julius and Nikolas, a fact which caused much merriment between the two men, who did not know who would be the winner, the person who Hans stayed with or the person who was leaving him behind. They still thought highly of Hans who continued to retain his childlike enthusiasm whatever the circumstances, but his military abilities had not much improved despite the hours of tuition from Julius and Nikolas. In the end the situation had resolved itself with Nikolas finding that his company's former captain had been killed and his batman was still in residence at his new camp. Nikolas' company was stationed in the north on the Trentino and it was with a heavy heart that Julius said goodbye to Nikolas as he began his journey north in the freezing winter conditions.

Julius was to stay in the camp by Udine. He spent the next few weeks getting to know the men and officers in his new company. Most of the new recruits were very young and painfully lacking in any military training. This was also true of his officers, only his lieutenant, a young man called Zizic, had been in the army for more than three years, the rest were all raw recruits drafted into the war.

The weather did not help the situation. Julius would have liked to be giving the men even some basic training for the warfare they would inevitably encounter in the next few months, but the terrible winter conditions prevented the carrying out of even the most basic exercises. Julius had to be content with talking the men through their duties whilst they grumbled about the cold and the terrible conditions they lived in.

The Bohemian units were especially uneasy at this time with the news from home that the Bohemian members of the Reichsrat had demanded a sovereign state of their own for the 'historic boundaries of Bohemian lands and of Slovakia' This caused much confrontation between the various companies with Austrians taking exception to the Czechs and Slovaks demand for an independent homeland coupled with the rumor that hundreds of Czechs were deserting daily. Julius himself knew of several Czechs that had deserted within his own regiment but he could not believe the numbers that were being discussed amongst the men. He himself was ambivalent as to the question of independence for his country. Julius had been born in Bohemia and now regarded himself as a Czech, but his parents had been Austrian and he had been brought up with absolute respect for his Emperor and country, as a citizen of the Austro-Hungarian Empire and a loyal soldier in its army. However he knew that feelings were strong amongst many of his fellow countrymen, remembering the rallies before the war held by Masaryk, and he knew many Czechs wanted autonomy for themselves. Whether this included a complete break from the Empire Julius was not sure. He knew that Masaryk had always campaigned for an independent state that was still allied to the Empire, but Julius worried that since the outbreak of war this view had altered. Now, talking amongst his men, it was obvious that most Czechs would welcome a complete break from the mother country. The prospect worried Julius, and added to his difficulty in leading a united company in a war in which many men wondered what and who they were fighting for.

The terrible weather continued, making any chance of conflict untenable. Though the conditions were horrendous the Austro-German army was bolstered by the success of the last few months and the Italian provisions left during their hasty retreat meant that the men were much better fed than in previous winters. The stagnant months allowed Julius to survey the modern equipment and guns that the German divisions had brought with them. Julius realized that they had been fighting for nearly three years with vastly inferior equipment compared to the Germans and with far smaller numbers than those commanded by their allies. Julius began to wonder just how different this war might have been had the Austrian army been equipped with the guns and ammunition supplied to the Germans. It was a theory that Julius was discussing one night with Viktor. Since the cessation of fighting Julius had managed to see quite a lot of both Viktor and Josef. After they had reached the Tagliamento they had both returned to the camp at Udine and Julius was meeting them frequently. Viktor too had been promoted to captain, although Josef remained a lieutenant, a fact which he took in good humor.

"Let us face it" he told Julius one day, "I was never going to be a model soldier like you three. I am very proud to have achieved this rank already, what is the saying, 'promoted to the level of ones incompetence'

Julius had to laugh at his friend and although he searched Josef's face to find any trace of bitterness there he found none and concluded that Josef was happy in his role of lieutenant and did not want the added responsibility of being a captain. Julius thought he had better not point out that with so many casualties of war he would wager it would not be long before Josef was adding another star to his collar. Viktor believed that Josef's somewhat apathetic demeanor at this time was a lot to do with his disenchantment at the treatment of the cavalry since the beginning of the war. The Austrian cavalry had found that they could not be employed in trench war and as the war had progressed much of the cavalry had been dismounted. Although some units were retained in a mounted role for escort duty, the vast majority of the remaining cavalry force was placed into dismounted units as more mechanized transport took over the role of the horse. This created resentment amongst the cavalry who saw their role diminish as the war progressed.

Julius often received letters from Nikolas, who wrote to say that he was settling in well and he always mentioned his wedding with such an animated hand that Julius began to feel quite excited about his friend's forthcoming nuptials. Georg had also returned to Udine and even after his encountering the horrors of his first battle still managed to remain as cheeky as ever.

When Julius had discussed Nikolas and Susie's' wedding with him Georg had merely dismissed the occasion wondering why his brother should want to tie himself down at such a young age. He for one was never going to marry, or if he did, not until he was very much older. Julius chuckled at the young man's lack of romanticism and hoped he would be around when Georg fell in love for the first time, so he could repeat the words the boy had uttered in his naive adolescence. Georg did not even seem bothered that he would not be able to attend his brother's wedding. "Good heavens, I am glad I am missing it" he told Julius with an air of bravado that Julius did not altogether believe, "I would have to sit there all day, on my best behavior, whilst all my relations would be telling me how much I had grown and it would be my turn next, and other such inane observations" Georg smiled broadly as he had added, "do not worry Julius, with my not being there it means that instead they will be telling you it will be your turn next, and asking you if you have a young lady and all those embarrassing questions we all hate" Julius turned red at the thought of it and for the first time he began to wonder if going to Nikolas' wedding was such a good idea after all.

Over the next few months the weather started to turn warmer and the army began to prepare itself for battle. All along the front there were minor skirmishes and as Julius prepared his company he thanked God for the presence of Lieutenant Zizic, who proved to be a more than able soldier who pulled the company into shape and earned Julius' lasting respect. Julius wondered if he had been such a good lieutenant for Captain Milic, he hoped he had been. He often recommended Lieutenant Zizic to his superiors, lamenting the fact that it would probably mean a swift promotion for the able officer, but realized as good a soldier as Lieutenant Zizic deserved to be a captain, a job in which he would surely excel.

Towards the end of April 1918 came the orders for Julius and his company to proceed north and join the army on the Trentino. Julius was pleased that he would be seeing Nikolas again but was sorry to be leaving Viktor, Josef and especially Georg to whom he had become very attached.

The men looked forward to the diversion of transporting themselves and their provisions to the north, and as the weather had improved the journey would not take long. Julius had not heard from his family for a while, the frequency of mail becoming worse as the war progressed but he had felt easier in his mind lately, knowing that his two brothers were safe from the perils of war, and that Richard was in a comparatively safe position in his field hospital. Irmy was his greatest worry but her latest letter had been more optimistic than her previous ones and he did not allow himself to worry too much about Mama, he would keep his reservations to himself until he saw her in July.

Julius arrived at the base camp in Trentino in the middle of May. Despite some worrying moments, caused by Italian snipers along the way, the journey had been uneventful. His men had worked and marched well together and on their arrival on the Trentino he felt they were a more cohesive force than the one that had left Udine. Everywhere there was talk of the imminent offensive which everyone knew must be soon after the inactivity of nearly five months. It was known that the Italian army had been augmented by the British and French forces and that the Austrian and German troops were still not at full strength after the fierce battles of the year before. The coming months would be very different to the previous battles; Italy was not likely to allow another rout such as the one they had experienced at Caporetto/Karfreit.

It was over two weeks after he had arrived at the camp that Julius met Nikolas again. He looked well and the office of captain sat well on him. After catching up on each other's news Nikolas explained the situation for the army on the Trentino. He expressed concern at the readiness of the Austrian troops for full battle but it seemed that an offensive had been planned for an attack southwards from the Trentino and a second attack from the Piave front at the same time which was to take place in the next few weeks. "We have been instructed to launch an artillery gas bombardment on both fronts. It seems that a lot of the Italian gas masks are faulty and we are to use that to our advantage, plus the smoke will act as a screen for our advance"

Julius digested this information for a while. Gas bombardments had been used before, but it was something that Julius disliked. The sight of a man choking and screaming from a lethal dose of the gas was a terrible sight and one that Julius would prefer never to have to encounter again. He had read that mustard and chlorine gas had been used extensively on the battlefields of France and Belgium with horrific effects, where many believed it was better to die than to live with the after effects of an attack.

In the middle of June Julius and his men made ready for the battle. Julius had spent most of the day preparing his men, many of them nervous because they did not know what they would encounter the next day. Julius and Lieutenant Zizic tried to bolster their men with a confidence they did not really feel. They knew that the Italians were backed by the British and French forces and that their own army was not ready for a full-scale battle.

Tired and dejected Julius knew he should find his bed for the night as they had orders to muster for battle at sunrise the next morning, but he knew he would not sleep and something compelled him to ride along the front to Nikolas' company to seek him out.

He found Nikolas in his tent seated at a table, writing. Julius stood for some moments watching his friend who was unaware of his presence. Nikolas was crouched over the desk, trying to write in the semi-darkness illuminated only by a small oil lamp. A rush of affection swept over Julius as he regarded Nikolas, his truest friend for so many years, and he was reminded of how many times he had seen Nikolas in this same position, crouched over his papers, at cadet school, in Prague, and now here in the theatre of war. Julius shook himself, telling himself that it was his tiredness that was letting him indulge in such maudlin sentimentality.

"So I am not the only person who cannot sleep tonight," announced Julius as he pulled back the flaps of the tent.

"Julius" cried Nikolas as he leapt up and greeted his friend with an enormous cherubic smile on his boyish face, "I was just thinking of you"

"Good thoughts I hope" replied Julius.

Nikolas laughed as he said, "I was just writing to Suse and I was telling her all our news. What are you doing here? Can I get you a cup of coffee?"

Nikolas summoned his batman who swiftly appeared at his senior officer's command. He was an older man who, after receiving his orders, deftly saluted and left the tent.

"Slightly more efficient than poor Hans" observed Julius.

"Very much so" chuckled Nikolas, "Jan could even be compared to Smid for his efficiency. I think I have definitely been the lucky one where batmen are concerned, don't you?"

"Maybe so" conceded Julius, "but perhaps you do not have as much fun"

The two men sat in silence as Nikolas' batman brought in their coffee. Julius looked around at his friend's living quarters. On the desk was a charming picture of Suse, Julius imagined it must be nice to wake up to her smiling face every morning. He still had his picture of Erika, but he kept that on the inside of his blouson, the only photograph he displayed was the one of his family, taken so many years ago when everyone had been so young and carefree, a time that seemed a lifetime away now. After the batman had departed Nikolas sat back with his coffee and regarded his friend. "You have not told me why you are here, Julius. Is something troubling you?"

Julius tried to think of a sensible answer for his friend but could not find one. "No, well that is, I do not think so. It is just that I have had the strangest feelings today, as though there is a cloud above my head that does not go away, I cannot really explain it. I do not know why I feel like this, apart from the obvious of course, but then I have never felt like this prior to a battle before"

379

Nikolas smiled at his friend, "maybe it is the added responsibility of going into battle as a captain, you know how seriously you take yourself"

Julius had known Nikolas too many years to rise to his friend's teasing and so instead returned his smile as he said, "perhaps you are right. I know you all believe I think too deeply about things. Anyway, being here with you has lightened my spirits already, you know you are my lucky charm"

Both men laughed and started to discuss the battle tomorrow. After finishing his coffee Julius rose to leave, knowing he should be back with his men and getting some sleep before the morning. Nikolas walked out with Julius. The clear night sky was littered with hundreds of twinkling stars and there was a warm breeze that danced with the burning campfires. A perfect evening in an imperfect world.

On an impulse Julius suddenly turned to Nikolas and embraced him in a bear like hug. As Julius stepped back Nikolas was regarding his friend with a quizzical look on his face, "are you sure you are all right Julius?" he asked with concern on his face.

Julius smiled, "yes I am fine" replied Julius, "just getting a little sentimental in my old age. I will see you tomorrow Nikolas, remember to keep out of the way of any stray shells"

"I will do my best. Do not worry about me, I have too much to look forward to to do anything stupid, besides you forget, Smid is looking after us"

Julius raised his hand in mock despair at his friend's optimism and then mounted his horse to start the journey back to his camp. Nikolas stood watching Julius for a long time with a worried look on his face before returning to his tent to finish his letter to Suse. Julius felt better for having talked to Nikolas but he still had a strange sense of foreboding that would not leave him until at last he managed to fall asleep in the early hours of the morning.

At six o'clock the Austrian army was ready for their attack. Julius went amongst his men, checking equipment and guns, talking to them, trying to imbue them with some confidence. Many, especially the younger ones, were shaking with fright, while others stood with their eyes burning, straining to be allowed to start, to attack the hated Italians.

As Mass was said Julius prayed that the end of the war would be soon. He knew he was weary, he had seen enough of death and defeat and even triumph to last him a lifetime. Now he just wanted victory for his country and for the fighting to be over.

As he once again checked the positioning and trajectory of the guns under his command he made ready to launch the shells as cover for the advancing forces in front of him. He had looked for Nikolas but had not seen him that morning, he was not unduly surprised. Nikolas' company was a few kilometers to the east of his position, and he knew at this moment Nikolas would be checking and rechecking just as he was, waiting for the order to begin their advancement.

At last the command came through and the soldiers prepared themselves. The charge began and as the guns were ignited Julius watched their ultimate destination to see if the guns had to be moved in order to be sure that the opposing forces were the true targets. Julius and his officers called out the orders for the movement of the big guns and the men scurried around to move the huge weight of guns to comply with their officer's orders. Several times the breeches would stick and the men would hastily try to get them moving again, a dangerous job which could often cause a soldier to lose his hand.

After about an hour the battle seemed to be going well and Julius received his orders to advance the guns. Hurriedly the heavy loads were hitched to the teams of horses who would pull them to their next destination. All around there was the sound of shouting as men bellowed to be heard above the deafening noise of the shells and machine gunfire which constantly bombarded the battlefield. As Julius advanced, shouting his orders to his men, they trampled over bodies of soldiers and horses that lay all over the battlefield. No one could stop to think of the dead men they were riding or running over. Advancing troops were especially vulnerable without the backing of the field guns so the priority was to get the guns to the next position so as to protect fellow soldiers and yourself as quickly as possible.

Julius soon realized that this battle was being fought with a violence and a tenacity he had not seen before. By the afternoon the army had succeeded in occupying large tracts of Italian trenches but at a huge cost in soldiers and weaponry. Despite their retreat the Italians had started to counterattack and their shelling was increasing. Julius ordered his men to take cover behind the discarded trenches and from this defense they continued their bombardment. The fighting was strenuous and determined, already Julius had lost more than a third of his men and guns.

With Lieutenant Zizic's help Julius managed to muster his remaining forces, but they could not raise anyone on the field telephone and Julius knew that if he did not receive fresh orders soon he would have to make a decision as to their next move. The Italians could be seen to the south and they looked to be driving the Austrian forces back. Julius decided to carry on the bombardment with the men and guns he had left, though he was not sure how effective this would be.

After giving Lieutenant Zizic his orders, Julius set about working out the position of his guns. The view through his field glasses was not encouraging, the Austrian soldiers were still retreating and suffering huge losses as they did so. At last the guns were ready and Julius was relieved to see them hitting their targets, but then one of his men ran up with the news that their ammunition was running low. Julius' heart sank; he had to make a decision as to whether to hold their ground and risk the guns being taken or retreat in the hope of joining up with another artillery company.

He had decided to stay for another half hour when he heard the rumblings of horse's hooves above the roar of the bombardment and looked behind him to see a company racing over the terrain towards them with field guns in tow. Julius could have jumped for joy but his elation knew no bounds when he saw Nikolas ride up, jump off his horse and run towards his position behind the trench.
"Why do I always have to get you out of trouble Julius" he asked with a grin stretching from ear to ear.
Julius quickly told Nikolas of their position and they decided that as Nikolas' company had arrived with more guns and ammunition, they would hold their ground to create a defense for the retreating army and hopefully hold the Italians until reinforcements arrived. Their officers were told of the plan and quickly the men set about positioning a line of guns aimed at the Italian soldiers and their weaponry. The strategy started off well with the guns scoring many

382

direct hits, but it soon became clear that the Italian guns had located their situation and soon shells were beginning to land precariously near their position.

After losing two more guns Julius and Nikolas decided to retreat further back into some low lying hills which would afford them more shelter from the Italian barrage. Once the order was given the men quickly hitched up the guns to the horses and retreated to the hills. The maneuver worked well with only the loss of two men as shells continued to rain down on them until they were out of range for the time being.

Once in more defensive positions the men set to work again on the guns and the task was made easier by the fact that they were spared too many attacks, the hills giving them the much needed protection they required to give them time to set up the guns. By now more artillery divisions had arrived along the front and once Julius and Nikolas' own divisions had started their bombardment again, the onslaught was diverted by so many more guns being used.

While rushing to re-sight a gun Julius passed Nikolas, "it is good to be working with you again Julius" he shouted, "this is quite like old times" Julius smiled and then ran on to reposition the gun. The wheel of the gun had become stuck in a crevice of the hill and Julius helped two of his men try to lift the heavy gun round. This could only be achieved by brute force, so he put his shoulder to the wheel and with his feet bolstered against a rock he heaved to against the large gun. He thought he heard a shout but could only look up in amazement as he saw Nikolas running towards him and then a bright flash in the sky.

Julius thought all the wind had been sucked out of his body as he felt himself being lifted up into the air and then he dropped heavily against the face of a rock. An excruciating pain began to race through his body as though it were on fire and he started to shake all over. Men came running up to him and he began to feel nauseous as he looked down at his legs and saw them deformed and twisted under his body, lying at impossible angles. His left leg looked particularly bad as he observed the bones protruding from the skin below his knee. His left arm was pinned under his body and he found he could not move it. He longed for the blessed relief of unconsciousness to relieve his pain but it did not come, instead he found himself surrounded by men crowding round him. He closed his eyes as his head started to spin and only opened his eyes when he realized that Lieutenant Zizic was speaking to him. His lieutenant was leaning close to him, the concern obvious on his face. Julius tried to speak, but all he could manage was a strangled croak as he said to Zizic, "get the men back to their guns, you must defend this hill, or you will all be dead. Send one man for the medics, everyone who is able must get back to the guns"

Zizic nodded in comprehension and as Julius closed his eyes again he could hear the able lieutenant issuing the orders and he could sense daylight again as the men all returned to their posts.

Endeavoring to ignore the pain that was torturing his body Julius tried to prevent himself from passing out. Although he would welcome the escape from the hell he was experiencing he had remembered Irmy telling him that you should never let a person suffering from shock pass out or go to sleep. He realized that the horrendous pain was slowly leaving his legs and this worried him even more. To keep his mind off his torment Julius tried to think about Irmy, Mama, Franz and Karl, anything to keep his mind occupied. He started to think about Vienna and cadet school and Nikolas......Nikolas!

His eyes shot open as he remembered the last moments before the shell had landed. Nikolas running towards him, Nikolas pushing him out of the way, so where was Nikolas? Julius tried to pull himself up with his right arm, the effort and the pain it brought bringing him out in a cold sweat until he did think he would pass out. Eventually he was sitting upright propped up against a rock and he looked around at the mayhem that lay around him. The gun he had been trying to move was smashed to pieces, lying over it were the bodies of the two men who had been helping him and there, lying on the ground beside it, was Nikolas.

Nikolas was lying with his back to Julius, but from his position he could see his red hair was matted with blood and his body lay misshapened and badly injured by the shell blast. Julius could not tell if Nikolas was alive or dead. Julius screamed, "Nikolas" but the sound was no more than a strangled whisper. With every muscle straining and with a superhuman effort Julius started to drag himself along the ground, pulling himself along on his one good arm. He never thought he could feel such agony, and he had to keep stopping before the pain made him pass out. Eventually he reached Nikolas and cradled his head in his lap, his one good arm supporting his head. A young soldier came running up to them and then stopped short as he looked at Julius and saw the tears in his eyes and the bewildered look on his officer's face. Nikolas' eyes were closed, all color drained from his face and his lips were blue. Julius looked down at the remnants of Nikolas' body. One of his legs had been blown away, leaving a stump of sinew and muscle, there was a gaping hole in his chest and his uniform was covered in ruby red blood. Julius rocked Nikolas to and fro as he tried to give him comfort. The tears fell down his face as he looked down at his friend. Julius nearly jumped as Nikolas opened his eyes, lifted up a hand towards Julius, gave him one last cherubic smile, then, as his eyes turned heavenward, Nikolas Manz breathed his last breath.

As the young soldier stood by respectfully, Julius cradled the body of his friend, the tears still falling down his face. With great care he wiped Nikolas' unharmed face and stared at the familiar features that even in death held the innocent, kind look that had endeared him to so many people. Julius felt inside Nikolas' tunic and found the chain of St. Wenceslas that Nikolas had set such store by and took it from his friend's neck, placing it carefully into the pocket of his blouson. When the medics arrived they found Julius still holding Nikolas and were amazed looking at his injuries that the captain had not lost consciousness. When they tried to release his hold on Nikolas' body Julius would not let go and they were met with such a look of venom that they left Nikolas lying with Julius whilst they tried to tend his wounds.

Julius felt very tired and longed to fall asleep, to wake up and find this was all a dream, but he knew there was something he had to do. He beckoned to one of the orderlies to come close to him. With the man's ear very close to his mouth Julius began to speak as loudly as he could, to make sure that the soldier could hear what he was saying above the continuous noise of the battle. Summoning the little strength that he had left Julius ordered "you will take the captain's body on a stretcher to the dressing station with me"

As the orderly began to object to this plan Julius pulled him with his one good arm to make sure the soldier was looking into his eyes. "Forget your bloody orders. *I* am ordering you to take Captain Manz back to the dressing station with me, do you understand?"

The medic, still staring at Julius, slowly nodded, afraid of the manic, determined look in the badly injured captain's eyes. He had no wish to argue the point on the battlefield with shells exploding around them and the Italians advancing towards their position. As the stretcher-bearers arrived he ordered them to take both captains to the dressing station behind the battle lines. With a shrug of his shoulders he ran off to tend his next casualties, all thoughts of the strange captain immediately forgotten.

The journey to the dressing station was horrendous. With the gunfire sounding closer by the minute the orderlies had no time for the niceties of manners and quickly hauled Julius onto the stretcher, causing him to find his voice at last as he screamed with the unbearable pain. He thought he would pass out but with extraordinary willpower he fought himself back to consciousness. He knew he had to stay awake to ensure that Nikolas was taken back behind the lines with him. With extreme effort he raised his head to see Nikolas being put onto another stretcher. He could see the orderlies shaking their heads, wondering why they had been told to put Nikolas onto a stretcher, when the captain was so obviously dead. However their misgivings were put aside as they obeyed the orders the medic had given them and at last Julius and Nikolas were lifted up to begin their journey. The orderlies ran with their charges over the rough terrain where every movement seemed to tear Julius' body apart.

At the ambulance Julius once again pushed his pain to the back of his mind as he looked around to make sure Nikolas' body was put into the ambulance with him. He was lucky, there was too much activity for the drivers to notice whether their passengers were alive or dead as they were indiscriminately pushed into the back of the vehicles. Once again during the journey Julius struggled to remain conscious and he had never felt such joy seeing the doors of the ambulance flung open and he hoped that very soon his mission would be over and he could abandon himself to whatever fate awaited him.

As the stretchers were taken out of the ambulance Julius reached out and grabbed the side of Nikolas' stretcher, determined he would not be separated from his friend in the mayhem that unfolded before his eyes. As far as the eye could see Julius observed rows and rows of wounded men laid out on the ground, all waiting to be seen by the medical staff in the tents painted with red crosses at the edge of the area. Julius tried to close his ears to the screams and cries of the injured men about him. He himself, although in great pain, had no inclination to cry out, he was determined to carry out his plan, and that knowledge kept his mind steady and focused, and detached from his pain.

Julius was laid down on the ground and with his hand still firmly gripping the pole of Nikolas' stretcher the orderlies laid his friend next to him. With great effort Julius turned to look at Nikolas, who had now lost all color and wore the macabre pale mask of death. A medic proceeded up the line towards Julius, inspecting the injured men, attaching labels saying 'yes' and 'no' At last he came to Nikolas and Julius gripped his stretcher tightly, he had got this far he would not be prevented now. The orderly attached a 'no' label to Nikolas and then a 'yes' one to Julius as Julius stared up at him, and even smiled to make sure the orderly was well aware he was alive.

After the medic had carried on up the line Julius, with great effort, leaned across to his friend and ripped off his label and then put his own label saying yes in its place. The strain was beginning to tell and Julius' head was spinning, but he was rewarded for his effort. A few minutes later orderlies came up the line and started to take away all the bodies with the 'no' labels, these were the soldiers who had not survived the journey from the battlefield. When the orderlies came to Nikolas they were amazed to see his 'yes' label but shrugged their soldiers and moved on to Julius. "Where is your label?" they asked.

Julius waved his one good arm around to show he had no idea, but the orderlies were satisfied that he was a definite yes and carried on up the line, too busy for any further thoughts of Nikolas. Julius started to relax, his plan was working, now he only needed one more element to succeed. Julius lay for what felt like hours waiting for his turn to be carried into the medical tent, the scene around him one of pandemonium and chaos. The noise of the battlefield could be heard in the distance above the cries and screams of the injured. Every so often large clouds of foul smelling smoke would appear, blocking the view for a while until it dispersed to once again display the horrors of the brutality of war.

Julius was never to know how he managed to maintain consciousness for such a long time, but ever after he was always firm in the belief of mind over matter for he knew it was the only thing that kept him conscious that day.

As the time drifted on he began to fret, and then, just as he was giving up hope, he saw him. Coming towards his section was a priest, the cross hanging from his neck glinting in the evening sun, like a marvelous omen to Julius. At one point Julius thought that the priest was going to walk past him, but Julius called out to him and despite all the noise around them something made the priest stop and turn to kneel by Julius. In a whisper Julius told the priest what he wanted of him. When Julius had finished, the priest looked down at Julius' horrendous injuries and with tears in his eyes, anointed Julius with the sign of the cross and said "Bless you my son" With that he rose from his position beside Julius and walked round to kneel beside Nikolas' body. Julius' hand was still clasped around the stretcher pole and at long last he relinquished his hold. The priest anointed Nikolas with oil and with Julius whispering the prayers with him he began the service of blessing for Nikolas Manz.

When the service was over the priest returned to Julius and asked him if he could do anything else for him. Julius shook his head and whispered, "No father, not yet, I think there are other people who need you more than me"
With that he closed his eyes and at last welcomed the warm embrace of oblivion that he had refused to accept for the past few hours.

As soon as Nikolas had died in his arms Julius had known he could not have left his dearest friend alone on the battlefield, could not have left him to be just another body discarded in retreat. Nikolas Manz deserved more than that. He deserved to be buried in a proper grave and to be welcomed into heaven with the blessings of his church. It was something Julius had had to do, not just for Nikolas and himself, but also for Georg, Frau and Colonel Manz and for Suse. It was the last thing he would do for Nikolas and he hoped his friend would have been proud of him as he was proud of Nikolas, because for the rest of whatever life he had to live, Julius knew that Nikolas had sacrificed his own

life for his, and for that he would never be able to repay
him.

XXVII

Julius could never recall what happened to him in the weeks after Nikolas' death. When he finally lapsed into unconsciousness it was a blessed relief from his pain and the anguish of his friend's death. Several times he experienced the sensation that resembled swimming underwater and desperately trying to scramble himself up towards the surface. He could see blurred images of various people talking to him, as if they were above him and he was looking at them through the water, but each time the images would become misty, then fade, as he would feel himself sinking down again towards the oblivion of his unconsciousness.

Eventually Julius forced himself above the waterline and with a great effort opened his eyes to the eerie specter of a darkened room lit by only a single candle that threw ghostly dancing shapes above his head. Julius closed his eyes again, wondering where he was. He knew that at least he was alive, but his body felt disturbingly detached from his head, heavy and remote. When eventually he did reopen his eyes, he started to peer into the gloom around him. There were tubes hanging from his body, and his left arm was encased in a heavy white plaster. By raising his head slightly, which made him feel as though hundreds of red-hot needles were attacking his brain and his eyes, he could see that his lower body was encased in a large frame that supported the bedclothes above his legs. Julius shut his eyes again as with sudden clarity he remembered his last battle, his injuries and, worst of all, he remembered Nikolas.

For some time he lay in the bed, hoping that it had all been a horrendous dream, but in his heart he knew it had all been very real. The door to his room opened and light flooded in as he listened to someone entering his room. He was aware of the person checking his tubes and then knew that he or she was raising the bedclothes from the cage that enveloped his legs. He was not sure he wanted to encounter anybody at that moment, but his curiosity overcame him and he was met with the shadowy view of a woman wearing a large white hat standing at the bottom of his bed. Overcome with excitement Julius said "Irmy?" but his euphoria was short lived as the woman walked into the candlelight and, although his vision was blurred, Julius could

390

see it was not Irmy. The nurse was considerably older than his sister and the disappointment that it was not Irmy overcame him and he felt the tears welling up into his eyes.

"Captain Mayer, at last you have joined us" The nurse had a beautiful voice that calmed Julius down and he opened his eyes to see her smiling face beside him, "I will fetch the doctor for you, he will be so pleased to see you have woken up"

The nurse quickly left the room, leaving Julius with such a feeling of desolation that he closed his eyes and prayed for the sanctuary of his previous oblivion, but it did not come. Instead the room was flooded with light again as Julius observed a doctor march into the room. The doctor wore a white coat and Julius was swept back to his visit to Richard's hospital in Prague and once again he was seized by such a longing to see a familiar face that he thought he would break down as the doctor pulled up a chair to sit beside him. The doctor was an elderly man with white hair and spectacles that were perched on the end of his nose. At first Julius found it hard to focus on the man's face but eventually his features became sharper as he started to talk.

"Captain Mayer, I am Herr Doktor Sachs, I have been tending you since you arrived at the hospital" Julius ignored the doctor and stared up at the ceiling, his mind was racing with a jumble of thoughts as he tried to concentrate on what the doctor was saying to him, "you have been at our hospital for nearly four months, lapsing in and out of consciousness" Four months! Julius could not believe that he had been here for so long. "You are in Austria, in the Empress Elisabeth Hospital" Julius listened in disbelief as he realized he had been transported to an Austrian hospital, the situation just did not seem possible, but why had they not taken him to Prague? As if reading his thoughts the doctor continued, "you could not be sent to a hospital in your homeland as your condition was diagnosed as too dangerous for such a long journey. As it is this was the nearest hospital you could be sent to that was free from danger" When Julius still showed no reaction to the doctor's statements he stood up from his chair and replaced it against the wall, "I think this is all a little too much and too soon for you, I will leave you to rest and we will speak again tomorrow" Julius wanted to scream that he had been resting for the last four months but he was glad the doctor was going. He was tired of his heartiness and just wanted to be alone to sort out his feelings.

For the rest of the night Julius lay staring at the ceiling, sometimes drifting off to sleep, but always waking up to continue his meandering recollections and always he would come back to thoughts of Nikolas. He tried to think of his future, but could not contemplate one, and every past memory brought him back to Nikolas and the terrible feelings of guilt that started to envelop him as he tried to come to terms with the fact that he had lived whilst his friend had died.

Over the next few days he was visited by so many people that he lost count of who they were. All of them were very kind and were concerned for his welfare but he grew frustrated as no one would give him an honest answer to his questions. It took him a few days before he realized that this was a concerted effort by the staff to shield him from any harsh reality that he may not be able to cope with.

Several times a day nurses would tend to the wounds in his legs, give him bed baths, or turn him to prevent bedsores. Julius would try to engage them in idle conversation that he hoped would eventually lead to one of them telling him his situation, but every time they would skillfully avoid answering any direct or indirect question that he tried to ask them. No one was inclined to tell him the extent of his injuries, although they all took frequent looks under his cage, nor were they forthcoming with any prognosis of his condition.

The other subject they would definitely not talk about was the war. Whenever Julius asked about how the troops were faring he was told that he did not need to trouble his mind with things that no longer concerned him, he was not likely to be rejoining his unit for quite a time and the important thing was to get better. Julius despaired at all the asinine answers but lying stationary in his bed he was unable to do anything about the situation and in the end resorted to stubborn silence as a protest to their treatment of him. His depression deepened and in the end all he could resign himself to was hopefully recovering as quickly as possible in order to leave the hospital to return home. He was asked if he would like to talk to a priest, but he knew he could not face confessing to a stranger all the doubts and guilt that he had been experiencing, his feelings towards his religion began to waver as he reflected on a God who could bring so much death and destruction to so many people.

One day he did venture to ask if he could write to his sister. The nurses brought pens and paper and with great difficulty and with appalling handwriting he managed to scribble a few lines to Irmy. The nurses did offer to write the letter for him, but he declined, believing that they would not write what he truly wanted to say. He had received letters from Irmy and Mama since he had been at the hospital, many written whilst he had been asleep, but even these he felt had been written with a certain reserve, and he had a suspicion that his sister was fully aware of the hospital's reticence to be honest with him and that she was complying with their request.

As the weeks progressed and Julius' health began to improve Herr Doktor Sachs at last appeared to be mellowing in his attitude towards Julius. One morning, after having inspected his legs under the cage, the doctor pulled up the chair again and sat down next to his bed. Julius had been reading a book, and still annoyed at his treatment by the medical staff, proceeded to rudely ignore the doctor sitting beside his bed.

"Captain Mayer, I know you think you are being badly treated, and that we are not being totally honest with you, but I do assure you we have your best interests at heart" Julius ignored the doctor and pointedly carried on reading his book.

"So Captain Mayer" continued the doctor, "why are you so hostile towards us when you know that your welfare and recovery is the most important thing to us?"

Julius let the book fall as he turned his head towards the doctor, "because I am not a child, Herr Doktor, and I do not like being treated like one"

The two men stared at each other and the doctor appeared to be making a decision as he said, "so you think you are being treated like a child, I assure you it is not our intention to do so"

"Maybe not, but that is what it feels like" replied Julius, "tell me doctor, why will you not tell me what has happened to my legs, whether I will ever walk again, what is happening in the war. Why all the secrecy?"

The doctor sat back in his chair, "there is no secrecy captain. You must remember you have come through a very traumatic and disturbing journey. The decision was made that too much information too soon would be too great a shock for you"

Julius regarded the doctor for a long time before he bitterly replied "Doktor, I have been fighting in the war for the past three years. I have seen death and destruction that you can never dream of. Oh yes I know you will say that you have seen horrific injuries, but you have never seen them inflicted on a human being in front of your eyes, seen man kill his fellow man. Have you watched your best friend, his body blown apart, die in front of your eyes? Now do not tell me I cannot face reality doctor"

The doctor stared at Julius for a long time before he said, "Very well captain. As you are probably aware your arm was badly broken in two places, but that was the least of your injuries. Your legs were badly broken and mutilated by shrapnel and required extensive surgery. Your right leg fared better than your left leg. As you are probably aware after surgery your right leg was placed in plaster up to your hip and we hope to remove that plaster soon. Then we will know how well the bones have knitted. It is your left leg that is our greatest concern. Due to the extent of the injuries to your leg we could not place a plaster on it, in fact at one point you were very close to losing it, I am afraid that an amputation was contemplated. However thanks to the excellent surgeons that we have in this hospital we think we have saved your leg. Your inactivity of the past few months has helped in the healing process, but such wounds are open to infections and we have to be very careful with them, hence the constant inspections. Even if your leg wounds heal well, it will take months of constant exercise to renew the wasted muscles in your legs, before we know if you will ever walk properly again, if at all"

Julius swallowed hard as he asked, "and the prognosis, doctor? An honest one please"

"Honestly? I cannot say. Time is the great healer and you will have to be very patient. You are young and extremely fit and in the end a lot of your recovery will be up to you. Is that what you wanted to hear, Captain Mayer?"

For the first time since arriving at the hospital Julius smiled, "perhaps not, but at least I now know the truth, thank you doktor"

"I am sorry that you think we mistreated you, but your health was our prime concern. I see now that I was somewhat misguided, but I still maintain you were not ready for the truth"

As the doctor rose to leave Julius closed his eyes, but when the doctor had left the room Julius opened them again as the tears streamed down the sides of his face and fell onto his pillow. He had wanted to know the truth but now facing up to that truth he felt scared and alone. He had thought himself so brave and rebellious, but now he knew the doctor had been right and at that moment he felt like a lost little boy, desolate, and petrified of the future.

After their conversation a new relationship began between Julius and Doktor Sachs. The doctor started to explain the realities of Julius' injuries to him and also told him of the hard work which would be needed over the next few months to enable Julius to walk again. He even sent the nurse who would be helping him with his rehabilitation to explain to him just what would be involved. The nurse introduced herself as Nurse Muller, she was a middle-aged woman with a sharp, hard face and a little twisted mouth that trembled as she spoke to Julius. She was plainly put out at having to spend her precious time talking to Julius when, as she explained to him, his exercises would not be starting for a while yet. However she told him just why and how the exercises would develop and by the end of her consultation Julius felt more scared than ever. It was going to be a long and very hard road to recovery and it was obvious that Nurse Muller would breach no slacking from any of her patients. As she marched out of his room, Julius lay back and decided she would have made a very good sergeant major.

Despite the black picture the nurse had painted for Julius he felt all the more determined that he would work as hard as possible, the better his health became the sooner he could go home. He often thought of Prague and wondered how his family was faring. He longed to know how Viktor and Josef were and hoped Georg had stayed away from any danger. Then he would stop and wonder how Georg, Nikolas' parents and Suse had taken the news of Nikolas' death. He wanted to tell them how bravely Nikolas had died, and thinking of their grief made his feelings of guilt return. Would they ever forgive him for being the cause of Nikolas' death? He knew he should not think like that but the notion was never far away and the thought of it constantly gnawed at his troubled mind.

395

His contemplations were completely diverted one day when Doktor Sachs once more took the chair from the wall to sit beside Julius. Doktor Sachs had taken to visiting Julius often for little talks, and although the doctor had been far more open with Julius he still declined to mention too much of the outside world. Julius could tell by the grave look on the doctor's face that this occasion was to be different. He became alarmed as he believed the doctor was about to tell him some bad news about his legs, and so he was quite relieved when the doctor started discussing Julius' life in the army.

After a few minutes the doctor began to talk about the real reason for his visit. "Captain Mayer, you are becoming quite a nuisance to my staff with your endless questions which I am sure you are aware they have been instructed not to answer" the doctor smiled kindly at Julius as he said "personally I do not think you are ready for more shocks but my staff are at the end of their tether with you. I have to ask you captain, in your opinion, are you prepared for this? and before you answer that question I will tell you the news is not good, not good at all"

Julius searched the doctor's face and saw a great sadness there and he was not sure whether he was ready for more bad news but knew he would have to face the future sometime and the sooner he started the better.

Later that afternoon Doktor Sachs returned to Julius' room with a pile of newspapers, without a word he placed them on the table beside Julius' bed and then left the room. Julius' first thought was to reach out and grab the first newspaper but then he stopped suddenly, afraid of what he was about to read. After staring at the pile for a few minutes Julius haltingly reached for the first paper and began to read. As he read his dejection grew and in bitter rage he began to throw the discarded papers around the room as he snatched the next one off the pile.

The newspapers had been published in the last few months and as he read Julius realized that his life was never going to be the same again. The battle he had been injured in, in which Nikolas had given his life, had been a disaster. Both the armies on the Trentino and Piave fronts had been bloodily repulsed and by the beginning of July the Austrians had had to rapidly withdraw their troops back to their original lines.

The last battle had been staged at the end of October on the Piave at a place called Vittorio Veneto when the Austrian and German armies were completely routed and were forced into a full retreat. Julius read with fear and astonishment how the Austrian army had completely collapsed and many regiments had mutinied and marched off to their homelands, attacking any officers who challenged them. Soldiers on leave had refused to return to the front and there were riots at home with the people in uproar at the collapse of the army and angry with the appalling conditions which they themselves were suffering.

On the 3rd of November 1918 an exhausted Austro-Hungarian army had signed an armistice. The Italian army took hundreds of thousands of soldier's prisoner as the Austro Hungarian army fell to pieces and soldiers began to try to get back to their national home as best they could amidst the confusion and chaos.

The empire was no more, every people of the empire had abandoned the Habsburgs and had established their own national state. In his own country Julius read that Masaryk and his national council had been recognized by the British and French governments and on the 28th October Masaryk had been proclaimed president and was trying to join the Czechs and the Slovaks into a united state. With the desertion of the Czechs the heart of the empire had begun to crumble as at the beginning of November Karolyi, the new leader of Hungary had ordered all Hungarian troops home to their new independent country.

The Germans, with all her allies defeated and her own army fast retreating had to sue for peace and on the 9th of November the Kaiser and his family had fled to the Netherlands.

A few days ago, on the 12th November the Emperor Karl had refused to abdicate but in the face of defeat had left Vienna and gone into exile.

Julius lay in his darkened room for a long time. So this was what it was all about. This was what he had been fighting for, risking his life for, for the past three years. This was why Nikolas had given his life, why millions of soldiers had died. For nothing, absolutely nothing. He had not fought for a new country, he had fought for the Empire, an empire which was no more, gone. It was all for nothing. As he lay reflecting on the past few years an even bigger anger grew within him. What now? He had a new country, but no army, no employment and he began to feel real fear, the fear of an unknown and uncertain future, with no place for Julius Mayer.

Julius woke up to find Doktor Sachs standing beside his bed. The newspapers had been cleared away and the doctor was observing him with a worried look on his face. "I am sorry Captain Mayer, I thought it was too soon for you"

"Herr Mayer doktor, did you not know there is no more army, you can hardly call me captain now"

The doctor sat down and tried to gather the right words to say, "You are still a captain, at least in this hospital. The world may be in uproar and we do not know what will happen in these uncertain times, but you will always have your rank"

"Just no army" replied Julius bitterly.

"What can I tell you? I am not a military man, I cannot explain things to you, but this I do know, every soldier fought bravely, defending his country, you must never forget that. For now no-one seems to know what is happening, so I suggest that you and I agree that we will work really hard and get you well as soon as possible so that you can return home to your family fit and healthy, what do you think?"

"Or maybe as a cripple, then I will be very useful"

"Captain Mayer at times you have exasperated me beyond even my renowned patience, but I have never thought of you as a person who gives up easily and I do not wish you to prove me wrong now, is that understood?"

Julius was surprised at the harsh tone in the doctor's voice and he reluctantly nodded his head.

"Your recovery starts tomorrow, I suggest you get a good night's sleep because tomorrow morning you start your rehabilitation exercises with Nurse Muller, and that will take your mind off things, believe me, goodnight"

The doctor briskly left the room, leaving Julius once more to his thoughts as his depression deepened. As so often had happened in the past few weeks the longing to talk to Nikolas overwhelmed him, and his despair returned as he realized he would never be able to confide in Nikolas again, laugh with him, argue with him and that void stretched before him leaving him feeling angry, lonely and very guilty.

Although his right leg was still in plaster Nurse Muller arrived bright and early and started working on Julius' left leg. Julius thought he was going to die as the nurse ruthlessly manipulated and massaged his tender leg until he thought he could take no more. No amount of screaming or pleading would stop her, as she took a gleeful delight in Julius' pain. Even the foulest of swear words that he hurled at her did not put her off as she started the slow process of building up the wasted muscles of his leg. When she had finished she washed her hands in the sink and as she was drying them she stood by Julius' bed. "I have heard every swear word, every expletive known to man in my time, so none of your language is going to put me off, and may I say the worst language always comes from the officers. I will see you well Captain Mayer, believe me, and you will not put me off my task, whatever you may think"

She left Julius to his thoughts as his leg continued to throb and send shooting pains through his body. It was quite a while before Julius realized that it was the first time that he had felt any sensation in his leg and despite his pain the fact cheered him up tremendously.

Nurse Muller arrived promptly every morning to inflict her sadistic torture on Julius. At times Julius felt that if he had been mobile he would have cheerfully punched Nurse Muller in the face, such was the pain that she happily put him through. He started to call her Attila, after the murderous leader of the Huns, which she seemed to accept with no offence whatsoever, but which always brought hidden smiles from the young nurses who assisted his tormentor.

As Christmas 1918 approached Julius could not shake off his depression. The news of the collapse of the Empire had affected him greatly, as he faced the prospect of a future with nothing to look forward to.

He longed to find out what had happened to Viktor and Josef, but there was still no word of them and he feared the worst. Irmy had written to say that she had tried to find out about his friends for him but with everything in such turmoil and with communications virtually non-existent due to the chaos that had ensued at the end of the war she had been unable to find out the fate of his friends. Irmy's letter had been far more open than before, perhaps because he had written to her to tell her that he now knew the fate of the army. She was relieved at last to be able to tell him all the news which she had previously had to withhold. Karl and Franz were fine. Franz was now going to work for Gretha's father on the family farm, his condition vastly improved with the knowledge that he would not have to return to the war. Karl had gone to live in Vienna. He was unsure of the future of the army and was now trying to find employment with the help of the many friends he had made in that city. Irmy was happy with this arrangement, Karl had always loved Vienna and she was pleased that he was taking a positive attitude towards his future. Richard had returned from the front at the beginning of December, very tired, but had immediately started working again at the hospital, as they were desperately short staffed and the wards were overflowing with the casualties of the war, which was the main reason neither of them could travel to Austria to see him. Added to this had been an outbreak of a particularly virulent strain of influenza that was sweeping across the continent. The epidemic had increased the need for hospital beds as people began to be hospitalized adding to the strain on the medical staff. She herself was still working hard whilst Mama remained at the long suffering Frau Beckova's house. The arrangement was working well although Irmy wrote that their mother was still very bitter, despite the fact that her three sons had survived the war, something which Irmy believed she should be very grateful for.

Georg had returned unscathed from the front. Like thousands of other soldiers he had simply made his way home after the collapse of the army. Irmy wrote that he was, not surprisingly, a much more serious young man than he had previously been, who was finding it difficult to come to terms with the death of his adored older brother. Irmy added that the Manzs were stoically accepting the death of their son but that Frau Manzova especially had taken the news of her son's death very badly. She had sent Julius her love, and had thanked God that at least he had been spared. She obviously did not know the circumstances of Nikolas' death and Julius knew, with a heavy heart, that one day he would have to tell Frau Manzova about her son's death. He wondered then if then she would be thanking God for Julius' reprieve.

Julius could tell that conditions at home were still very bad for everyone. Irmy said that with their new independence and their new leader the people of Prague were looking to the future with an optimism that had not been present over the past few years of the war. Already people were dismissing the war and talking of their great new country that they could rule themselves without the oppressive hand of the Habsburgs. Irmy had added that she hoped they were justified in their confidence as she believed it would take a long time to eradicate the ravages of war from the hearts and souls of the people.

After reading his sister's letter Julius lay in his bed staring at the ceiling. Outside he could hear Christmas carolers heralding the Yuletide as snow softly tapped at his window. Julius shivered as the snow brought back memories of the many months spent living in its thankless environment at the front. Once again the feeling of loneliness enveloped him and he longed to be back in the warmth, comfort and love of his parent's sitting room, exchanging Christmas presents on Christmas Eve before going to church for Midnight Mass. All that was gone, it would never come again. Julius shut his eyes, hoping that the welcome comfort of sleep would, for a few hours at least, give him an escape from his miserable existence.

Christmas came and went, and despite the jollity and encouragement of all the doctors and nurses Julius could not join in with their festive celebrations. Doktor Sachs seemed concerned with Julius' depression and hoping to cheer him up told him that his plaster would be coming off his leg in the next few days and that he would then be moved onto an open ward. The doctor had thought that this news would help Julius but instead it filled him with such fear and dread that it brought him out in a cold sweat. Julius could not be sure why he felt so anxious but the thought of having to talk to and discuss events with fellow officers was unbearable. He had come to like his solitude, with only the doctors and nurses for company, people who never discussed the war and who never asked him anything personal about his experiences. He knew, being a soldier himself, that all the other officers would want to talk about the war, his part in it, what battles he had fought in, things Julius did not want to remember, he just wanted to be left alone. Doktor Sachs noticed his reticence and despite many discussions in order to encourage Julius, Julius still maintained he did not want to be moved. Nurse Muller continued with her ministrations and the day arrived for Julius to have his plasters removed.

It was a wonderful feeling when the plasters were cut off, not least that it relieved him of the terrible itching that he always had. Julius was elated that at last he could sit completely upright, feel his arm and look at his legs. After a brief look he wished that he hadn't. The legs he surveyed did not look like his, they were painfully thin, with livid scarring all over them that accentuated the white skin around his wounds. His left leg was especially bad, with the scarring travelling the whole length of his leg. He could see two large scars on his lower leg and remembered the sight of his bones piercing through his skin as he had dragged himself towards Nikolas. The memory made him shut his eyes and the surgeon, thinking he was upset at the state of his legs, said, "your legs may not look particularly well to you Captain Mayer but we are inordinately pleased with your progress, their recovery is better than we had anticipated"

Julius smiled dutifully, not sharing the doctor's optimism. The surgeon informed him that now that his plaster had been taken off he would be able to be taken around in a wheelchair. The surgeon thought that Julius would be overcome with joy at this statement but once again Julius felt the panic rising at the thought of leaving the security of his room. Later that afternoon a nurse arrived with two orderlies, who deftly picked Julius up and placed him into the wicker chair. It was nauseating to feel so helpless, like a baby, and Julius began to feel his stomach churning as the door was opened and he was propelled into the corridor outside.

Julius was only in the wheelchair for about an hour, but when he got back to his room, feeling light headed and very tired he had to admit his first outing into the outside world had not been so bad. The nurse had taken him through the wards on his floor and he encountered rows and rows of beds all filled with injured men. Some of their injuries were horrific, so horrendous that Julius had to steel himself to look at their mutilations. The very badly injured lay still and silent, lost in their misery, while others moaned and shouted in their pain.

Those officers who were mobile had all come up to him, introduced themselves, saluted and shaken his hand. He noticed several card games taking place, some patients were reading and in a room off the ward men were smoking as they listened to a gramophone record playing in the corner of the room.

The experience did him good as Julius realized he was not the only person with injuries, not the only person left without a livelihood, not the only person confused about the future. In the few conversations he had the war was not even mentioned. Everybody seemed more intent on discussing the fiasco of the war's ending and the futures for themselves and their respective countries.

When the orderlies laid him back in his bed, Julius was so tired that he fell asleep straight away and when he woke up he did so with a renewed vigor, maybe his isolation had made him more maudlin than he should be and for the first time Julius began to look forward to his move.

Two weeks later Julius was relocated onto the ward. Although he missed the privacy of his own room he enjoyed talking to fellow patients and joining in their conversations. Although most of the patients were Austrian, none of them took exception to the fact he was Czech, everyone recognizing that they were united in the loss of their army which gave them all a common bond. It was by tacit agreement that no one talked about the war if they did not want to. There were a few officers, imbued with a bravado character, who wished to remember the conflict, but in the main everyone kept their thoughts to themselves, not wishing to dwell on the disastrous past of their army. It was only in the dead of night when a few patients, full of the alcohol illicitly smuggled in by the orderlies who were handsomely paid for their efforts, would start to relive the battles.

Julius always detached himself from these conversations, he had enough negative feelings of his own to have to listen to those of other men. He had started to buy some brandy from the orderlies, but this he persuaded himself was only for medicinal purposes. Since leaving his room Doctor Sachs had been reducing his dosage of painkillers until at times, especially after Nurse Muller's visits, Julius felt he could bear the pain no more. Despite his pleadings the doctor would not increase his medication, explaining that he did not want Julius to become addicted to them. Julius did not care about addiction, he just wanted to relieve the pain and he found that the brandy dulled the edges of his torment and allowed him to sleep. Whether the medical staff knew of the orderlies' indiscretions was not clear, if they knew they turned a blind eye to it.

Julius was now allowed to spend a large part of his day in his wheelchair. He enjoyed the freedom this afforded him, especially to leave his bed and have a change of scenery. He joined in the endless card games that were played to pass the hours away. Julius played bridge, he had first been taught the game by Josef at cadet school in Vienna and had enjoyed the intrigue and intricacies which the game offered. Now he started to play every day and became quite an adept player, taking pleasure in the camaraderie and idle conversation which always accompanied a game.

One day Julius was wrapped up in blankets and although the weather was quite cold a young nurse took him for a walk in the grounds of the hospital. Julius felt his heart bursting with joy as he surveyed the clear blue sky above him as the cold air stung his face. Snow lay on the ground, though the paths had been cleared and Julius marveled at all the ordinary things he perceived as so wonderful. Birds flying in the air, large drops of water falling onto the snow as they melted off the branches of the trees, looking at the prints of the birds and animals in the virgin snow. Julius breathed deeply as the cold air was sucked into his lungs, hurting his chest and making him feel light headed. The young nurse who was with him looked at him with concern and asked him if he was feeling unwell.

Since he had returned to the ward one of the main topic of conversation amongst the patients was the young nurses. Julius sometimes wondered how the young women put up with the endless flirtation, teasing and jokes that they were subjected to. He would think of Irmy and wonder if she was spoken to like that, and he supposed she was. All the nurses took the bantering in good heart, he thought some openly enjoyed it, and it was only when a brash young man overstepped the mark, which wasn't often, that he would be rebuked for his rudeness. The other patients would often make fun of Julius who never joined in the flirting, a picture of Irmy and Erika never far from his mind. Not wishing to appear churlish Julius would ignore their teasing, especially when they would remark on his popularity with the nurses. When Julius ventured to offer that the reason for this was perhaps because he was polite and respectful they would all laugh at him and call him 'pretty boy'. There were quite a few surreptitious liaisons between patients and nurses and Julius wondered how many of these were borne from loneliness amongst the men who longed for a little warmth and affection after the long cold years of the war.

For the next hour Julius had a very pleasant conversation with his companion, he asked her about her family and then he told her about his, leaving out the events that were still too raw in his heart to repeat to a stranger. Instead he mostly talked about Richard and Irmy which seemed to interest the nurse as she asked about their hospital and the work they were doing. Julius thoroughly enjoyed the company of the young woman, just to talk in idle conversation was very pleasant.

As the nurse pushed Julius back to his ward she said, "I have really enjoyed our talk Captain Mayer, it explained a lot about you"

Intrigued Julius asked her what she meant. "Oh it is just that the other nurses and I have noticed that you treat us differently to the other young men, you are more circumspect, I suppose. Now I understand why, with your sister being a nurse I suppose you look at us differently, it makes a refreshing change"

"Do you mind the teasing from the men?" asked Julius.

"Good heavens, no, you get used to it. They are never rude and we know how to handle the ones that sometimes are, it is all part of our job. Do not worry about us captain, we are tougher than you think"

Julius found himself laughing, he was sure they were, women were certainly changing and he was not sure how comfortable he was with that.

Julius' physiotherapy continued, but did not become any easier. Just when Julius thought he was coping with Nurse Muller's exercises she would introduce new ones that would rack his body with pain and cover his body in perspiration. However Julius did begin to see some progress and he started to look forward to the sight of the orderly coming to collect him for his morning sessions, if only to relieve the boredom of hospital life.

The hardest thing was to fill the day. Julius could only read so much, write so many letters, play so many rubbers of bridge. He loved to be wheeled out to the grounds where he could sit and watch the passers by or read a book with the fresh spring sun warming his face. However this was not always possible as the effort of getting him out into the gardens meant that an orderly or a nurse had to be taken from their duties and the staff was stretched as it was. The nurses said that the influenza epidemic was now stretching across the whole of the European continent. The virus was

405

affecting everybody, medical staff as well were starting to catch the dreaded disease. Julius had read in the newspapers that thousands were dying from the illness, some likening it to the casualties of the war. Julius, not for the first time, pondered on the theory of divine retribution but held his tongue as the doctors and nurses tried to cope with their increasing workload.

XXVIII

One gray morning Julius was lying on his bed reading a book. Outside the rain was lashing against the windows and the skies were dark, even though it was early afternoon. The somber skies darkened his own mood and, not wishing to join in any of the communal activities taking place at the far end of the ward after lunch, Julius had gone to lie on his bed to read a book.

He had drunk rather heavily the night before and was alarmed to realize he had finished a whole bottle of brandy. He had to admit that some days were better than others, but yesterday had been a particularly bad one with Nurse Muller berating him for not trying hard enough after a very tough session, followed by the death of a patient in one of the end rooms. Julius always hated it when someone died. The screens would be pulled around the bed as nurses and doctors gathered round. The nurses would always leave ashen faced as a priest arrived to administer the last rites. Julius especially hated to see the priest. The sight of the father filled Julius with such mixed emotions that he always wanted to flee from his presence. He experienced feelings of guilt because he had not attended a service or given confession since he had arrived at the hospital, but also the sight of the priest always brought back memories of Nikolas, memories Julius would rather forget.

Julius' head ached from the excesses of the night before which had not been helped by being served a cold lunch. All the men had complained whereupon the sister, a dragon of a woman who commanded her ward with an iron will, had given them all a stern lecture on how overworked her staff were. She had been so scathing in her speech that they had all felt like schoolboys back in the classroom. His mood darkening further, Julius had retreated to his bed. He was desperately trying to keep his eyes open as they involuntarily kept closing whilst reading his book when he heard some whistles from the end of the ward and a few of the men saying "hello, looking for me?"

Julius continued trying to keep his eyes open as he attempted to focus on the page in front of him.

"Hello Julius"

Julius thought he was dreaming as he turned to look at the owner of the familiar voice, but he wasn't dreaming.

Standing at the end of his bed stood Erika, looking as lovely as he had always remembered her. She had a broad smile on her face and her eyes sparkled with fun. From the end of the ward some of the men were calling, "trust pretty boy to know her" "don't keep her all to yourself, remember us poor mortals" Julius and Erika grinned at the harmless banter. Julius pulled himself up into a sitting position as Erika brought a chair to his bedside. Julius took her hands in his and studied every detail of her face. She was hardly changed, a few small lines around her eyes but still the same Erika. Julius thought he would cry with the nearness of someone so dear to him. It made him realize just how lonely he had been. They both tried to talk at once until Julius said that Erika should begin. Julius sat back and relaxed in the pleasure of watching her face as she talked to him.

Erika had been transferred to a hospital within Austria after the collapse of the army. She had been working there treating the war wounded until last week when her transfer back to Prague had come through. She was going to return home until she received a letter from Irmy, telling her about Julius and where he had been hospitalized. Irmy had told her she had been worried about Julius and as Erika was not far from his hospital would it be possible to visit him sometime? If Irmy had been there, Julius would have kissed her, he could think of no better tonic than the vision that sat before him now. Erika was leaving for Prague in two weeks, she had taken leave as she wanted to spend some time with Julius before she returned home, if that was all right with him. All right with him? Julius was ecstatic.

That afternoon they talked of everything, their experiences of the war, the terrible ending, their new country. Eventually they even talked about the one subject Julius was dreading, "Erika, did you know about Nikolas?"
Erika dropped her head and nodded, "Suse wrote to me, I am so sorry Julius, I know how much he meant to you, to everybody, you could not help but like Nikolas, he was that sort of man"
Julius nodded and Erika prudently left him to his thoughts until he said, "would you mind very much if we do not talk about Nikolas just now. I do not think I could face it at the moment, the memories are too painful"
Erika looked at Julius as she said, "of course, I understand, but maybe sometime you should talk about it, it might help,

I am always ready to listen you know" Julius nodded but he knew it was too soon for him.

The hospital seemed to take a very lenient view when it came to Erika's visiting hours. She endeared herself to all the staff, even the dragon matron, and was always willing to help around the ward. She also helped Nurse Muller with her sessions. At first Julius had been embarrassed at the thought of Erika seeing him, not only as a patient but also at seeing his unsightly legs. Erika noticed his reticence and laughed at him, "honestly Julius the sights I have seen over the past few years I am sure I will not be shocked, besides it will be useful to watch your treatment. I can pass the information on to Irmy, you will still need help when you get back to Prague you know"

Julius found himself upset by her reply, she had not included herself in his life back in Prague and that troubled him. All the other patients in the ward were envious of his beautiful visitor but whenever they would ask Erika to reveal any indiscretions about Julius or would allude to any closeness between the two of them Erika would merely laugh and tell them that she and Julius were just very old friends which would be greeted with jeers of derision by the men.

A few days after Erika's arrival Julius was lying awake in his bed, it was the early hours of the morning and Julius was finding it hard to sleep. He was tempted to get the brandy out of the cabinet by his bedside but since Erika's appearance at the hospital he had tried to abstain from drinking, preferring instead to enjoy Erika's company, if only for the short while that she was with him. Julius lay listening to the noises of his fellow patients as they tossed and turned in their beds, snored, or quietly called to love ones in their sleep. Through the stillness of the night could be heard the occasional scream of someone in pain, but mostly the air was still, with only the rustling of the trees outside the window disturbing the eerie silence of the ward. At the end of the room there was a door ajar from which radiated a soft lambent light and where sat the nurse on night duty ready to heed the call of any of her patients.

As a door opened near Julius' bed she bustled out of the room to meet the two orderlies who had brought in a new patient on a stretcher. Julius watched in the half-light as the man was lifted onto his bed as the nurse fussed around him trying to make him as comfortable as possible. The nurse started whispering orders to the two orderlies and Julius' senses became suddenly alert as he strained to listen to what they were saying. Holding his breath, so that even his breathing did not impair his hearing, Julius tried to heed what the two men were saying to the nurse. He was sure he had heard correctly and the excitement that enveloped him sent the blood rushing into his head as he absorbed the implications of their conversation.

As the nurse and the orderlies left their new patient to his sleep Julius tried to remember their conversation, word for word, and convince himself that he had heard correctly. The nurse had told the two orderlies to go down to the stores to get her some bandages as the new patient's dressings needed to be changed. The orderlies had started to grumble, as they generally did, but then one of them had said, "well we cannot do it straight away, we have to help to turn von Kutz on the third floor. We have very strict instructions about him" The nurse had dismissed their excuses with derision, but had allowed them to go as long as they fetched the new dressings afterwards.

Julius lay on his bed, digesting the information he had heard. Von Kutz, could they mean Josef, was it possible that he was here in this hospital? He knew that there were other von Kutzs in the world, but Julius clung to the faint hope that it could be Josef. He was still turning this possibility in his mind when the orderlies returned with the new bandages. He thought at first that he would ask them outright who the mysterious von Kutz was, but something made him stop. He had a better idea, orderlies would probably want to be paid for the information, and they had had enough money from him for their illegal alcohol. No, he would wait until morning, Josef was not going anywhere, and then he would ask Erika to find out if the von Kutz on the third floor was indeed Josef. Highly excited at the prospect of his friend being in the same hospital Julius found it hard to sleep, but eventually his eyes closed as the sunrise started to creep through the shutters of the hospital windows.

The next morning Julius, despite only sleeping for a couple of hours, was wide awake and anxiously waiting for Erika's visit. She chose that morning to arrive later than usual and Julius started to fret that she would not appear at all. The orderlies turned up to take him to his session with Nurse Muller and still there was no sign of Erika. Nurse

Muller was in an unusually bad mood that morning and his exercises turned into a nightmare as she pushed him as hard as she had ever done before. All the time Julius was thinking of Josef and the rigors of the morning passed over his head as he waited for its end and then hopefully he would be able to persuade Erika to help him. He knew he was clutching at straws, but ever since he had heard the name von Kutz last night he had an inexplicable feeling that the patient on the third floor was indeed Josef. The thought filled him with an optimism he had not felt for a long time and he had an overwhelming desire to see Josef, talk to him, because he would understand Julius' nightmares as no other person, apart from Viktor, could. He was taken back to their last drunken night in Vienna, when they had pledged to always help each other. Well now he desperately needed Josef's help. Maybe Josef could lift the cloud of guilt and despair that constantly hovered over Julius, that always stayed with him, even since Erika's arrival. He wanted to be absolved and he thought that only Josef or Viktor could do that, for only they would really understand.

After the session Nurse Muller's bad mood had lightened as she bestowed a rare smile on Julius and told him that due to his progress she was thinking of recommending to the doctors that Julius should begin to learn to walk, initially with the aid of crutches. Normally Julius would have greeted this news with the excitement it deserved but that morning Julius' thoughts were elsewhere and he merely thanked Nurse Muller and impatiently asked the orderlies to take him back to the ward as quickly as possible.

When they wheeled him into his ward Julius was overjoyed to see Erika talking to one of the nurses and, dismissing his helpers, he wheeled himself at breakneck speed down the ward towards Erika. Grabbing her hand and trying to pull her away he pleaded "Erika, come quickly, I must talk to you in private"

A cross look shadowed Erika's face as she said, "Julius, please, do not be so rude, I am talking to Nurse Wollrum. I will be with you in a moment"

Julius, oblivious to Erika's scolding, was almost shouting, as he pleaded "Erika, please, this is more important than your idle conversation. I have to talk to you right away, it is very important"

Erika looked angrier than ever, but her face softened as she recognized the urgency in Julius' manner, and knowing him not to be an ill mannered man, she excused herself from the nurse and wheeled Julius back along the ward. Once back at his bed Erika demanded, "what is this all about Julius? I have never seen you so rude"

Julius looked around them and aware that several of the men were observing them hurriedly said, "I am sorry, I can explain, but please, will you ask if you could take me for a walk in the grounds, it is more private there and I do not wish to be overheard"

Intrigued by his secrecy Erika decided to hold her questions and went in search of the matron to request her permission to take Julius into the grounds. Julius fretted whilst she was gone but was relieved when she returned, covered him with blankets and took him out into the gardens.

"Why on earth were you so late this morning? I needed to talk to you urgently" Julius asked unkindly. Erika stopped his wheelchair and moving round to face him said, "I do not know what has got into you this morning Julius Mayer but if you carry on talking to me like that I will go back to my hotel and leave you stranded here, do I make myself clear?"

Erika stood defiantly with her hands on her hips, her face suffused with anger which made her gray eyes sparkle and her cheeks glow a rosy red. Diverted fleetingly from his preoccupation with Josef, Julius thought he had never seen Erika look lovelier and felt terrible for talking to her so rudely. Giving her what he hoped was a suitable look of contrition Julius said "I am sorry, please forgive me. Did you know you look beautiful when you are angry?"

Erika dissolved into laughter as she ruefully shook her head and said, "and did you know you look like a pathetic puppy when you use that stupid look Julius, all right I forgive you. Now I will walk you to that bench seat and then you can tell me what you are obviously bursting to say"

It was a bright, warm spring morning and Erika had to shield her eyes from the shining sun as Julius animatedly told her about the overheard conversation from the night before. When Julius had finished he could not tell Erika's reaction as her hand still shielded her face. She was quiet for a few moments as her hands dropped to her lap and Julius could tell she was trying to find the right words to say to him. Eventually she turned to face him with a troubled look in her eyes. "Tell me Julius, why are you so desperate that this von Kutz is Josef, you do realize it could be a total stranger? Von Kutz is not a very remarkable name"

412

Julius gave her a quick and easy reply, "but if it is Josef it would be wonderful. I do not know what has happened to him, or Viktor for that matter, to know he is alive would mean so much"

Erika continued to watch his face intensely, unnerving him, as though she was willing him to be truthful and his blood turned cold as she said, "so if Josef was alive, it would be one less death to blame yourself for, and someone who could relieve your feelings of guilt. Am I right, Julius?"

If Julius had been able to, he would have fled from Erika's presence at that moment, but he remained rooted to the spot, astounded at her insight, grieved at the truth of her statement. Still Erika stared at him as she said, "Well Julius am I right?"

Julius heard a foreign, false sounding laugh escape from his mouth as his voice faltered, "no of course you are not, what on earth are you talking about" but he could not meet her eyes as he picked at the fringes of the blanket that covered his wasted legs. Erika grabbed the arms of Julius' wheelchair as she said "Look at me, Julius, I am not a fool, I have seen too many men like you in this awful war. Ever since I arrived here you have only managed to mention Nikolas' name once. Stop blaming yourself for his death Julius. Nikolas has gone, but you have to go on living, but not living with this guilt until it destroys you"

At that moment Julius hated Erika, hated her for seeing through him, hated her for voicing what he felt deep inside, hated her for being right.

"How can you lecture me" shouted Julius in his anguish, "you do not understand, you cannot understand, nobody can"

"Except Josef" said Erika softly.

Julius hung his head, deflated by his outburst "Maybe, I do not know, but I know he can help, I am sorry but I cannot explain it to you"

Erika took his hand and raised Julius' chin so that he was looking at her, "I am sorry too, I am sorry if I was unkind, but I thought I could help, I can see I was wrong. I will find out about your mysterious von Kutz for you, but you must understand that it is very likely that he is not Josef and if you do find out it is him you may be disappointed, he may not be your answer. I honestly believe that the only person who can help Julius Mayer is Julius Mayer, and I hope *you* will see that that is true as well, before it is too late"

Julius and Erika sat in silence for a long time before Erika wheeled Julius back to his ward.

Two days later Erika arrived to see Julius with a troubled look on her face. Julius had just woken up from his afternoon nap and was expectantly waiting for Erika. For the past couple of days she had had more difficulty than she had anticipated finding out the true identity of the patient on the third floor. She had reported to Julius that this von Kutz was treated with secrecy and there was a great deal of reticence from the medical staff to deal with any enquiries as to his identity. It had intrigued her and she had become as determined as Julius to find out if it really was Josef. Erika sat down beside his bed, looking weary and uneasy.

"Are you all right? asked Julius solicitously. Since their discussion in the garden, their relationship had tangibly changed, a circumstance that upset Julius, who took every opportunity to try to regain the trust that they had once shared.

"Yes, yes, I am fine. I have good news and some strange news and I do not know where to start, it is all so confusing"

Julius swallowed hard, restrained by the look on Erika's face to ask her to tell him her news as quickly as possible.

"Now I do not want you to get too excited Julius but I am almost certain that the patient on the third floor is Josef"

"What do you mean, I do not understand, is it or is it not Josef up there?" demanded Julius.

"Julius please" replied Erika wearily, "I am finding this very hard to explain to you and if you resort to your bullying tactics again I will most certainly leave"

Julius noticed the tired lines around her eyes and realized that gathering the information for him had been difficult for her. Regretting his words he refrained from speaking again as she told him her story.

"I have spoken to so many people in this hospital that my head is spinning, largely due to the fact that no-one will tell me anything. From the few bits of gossip and scraps of information I have been able to glean from unguarded conversations I have been able to find out that the patient on the third floor is a Lieutenant Josef von Kutz" Julius' heart sung as he took in the news. It must be Josef, it must be. "And that is all I could gather as to his actual identity. However I think the rest of the mystery surrounding him points more to betraying his identity than anything else.

Von Kutz has his own private room, evidently paid for by his very wealthy family who live in Vienna. He receives priority medical treatment, with strict instructions that only his medical team and their staff are allowed to see him, something which everyone adheres to, evidently bolstered by a huge benefit donated to the hospital by his family. Now that does sound like the von Kutzs, does it not Julius?"

Erika had finished with a triumphant smile on her face which turned to dismay as Julius asked his next question, "Erika, I must see him, you must arrange it for me"

"I am sorry Julius, this is where our mystery deepens. No one, but no-one, will tell me the extent of his injuries, but one thing everybody is sure about is that Josef will not receive any visitors. It is not just his family's wish that he has no visitors, evidently it is his own as well"

"Do not be silly, Erika, he will see me, I am sure. You know what Josef is like, he is just being his usual arrogant self. He has probably sustained an injury and does not want anybody to see him until he has regained his good looks, but if he knows I am here, then that would be different"

Erika sighed and continued to look worried as she said, "I do not know, Julius, I think there is more to this than I can find out. Anyway, we shall soon know, I bribed one of the orderlies, at great expense I might add, to take a message to him. I have told him that you are here and that you would like to visit him. We will see what his reply is soon I hope"

"Erika you are an angel. What can I say to thank you?"

Erika shook her head and chewed miserably on her lip as she replied, "I would not get too excited, Julius, you have not had a reply yet. I do not want you to be upset if Josef refuses to see you. It seems he has become somewhat of a recluse up there in his room and he may not want your company"

Julius laughed as he said, "that will not happen, believe me. I know Josef too well, we have been through too much together, I cannot wait to see him again"

Erika continued to view the episode with an air of despondency and none of Julius' optimism would deter her from her gloom.

Julius waited three days and still he had no word from Josef. He could not believe that his friend had not replied to him. He started to think of all the reasons that Josef had not received Erika's message. He became convinced that the orderly had pocketed the money and had not delivered the note. Every time Erika visited him he would regale her with his disappointment at having no answer and continually urge her to find out from the orderly whether his message had been delivered.

Erika started to lose her patience with his continuous obsession about the message until she said, "Julius, please, you must understand, the orderly is taking a great risk delivering my message. With the rules surrounding Josef's' room he could lose his job if this intrigue is uncovered. He may not even have had the opportunity to deliver my note yet, think on that and in the meantime please do not make my life a misery with your constant preoccupation with Josef. I leave for Prague the day after tomorrow and I do not want to leave having lost my patience with you"

Julius was suitably chastened by Erika's outburst and realized he was being unreasonable towards her. He had not known that she would be leaving so soon and was upset to think of her going. He made a supreme effort to not even mention Josef's name in her presence but the thought of him was never far from his mind.

The next evening, the day before her leaving, Erika had said goodbye for the night and had left to return to her hotel. A few minutes later Julius was surprised to look up and see Erika chatting to the ward nurse and pointing towards Julius. For a moment he became excited as he felt sure she had come back to take him to see Josef, but as she walked towards him and he saw the grim look on her face, his hopes were quickly dashed.

Erika sat down slowly, "I have just seen the orderly who took my message. I am sorry Julius, there is no easy way to tell you this, Josef refuses to see you. He would not say why, just that he will not see anybody, not even you"

Julius swallowed hard, trying to prevent the tears that he could feel welling in his eyes. It could not be true, why would Josef refuse to see him? Josef would not desert him, would he? When he did not say anything Erika worriedly looked at him as she said, "Julius, are you all right?"

Julius nodded and managed a weak smile for Erika's benefit as he said, "thank you for trying. Would you mind terribly if I asked you to leave me now. I feel very tired" The words sounded inane to his ears, but he wanted to be left alone. Erika rose from her chair, "of course, I understand. I will come to see you in the morning, my train does not leave until the afternoon. Are you sure you are all right?"

Julius nodded and as Erika left the ward she kept looking back over her shoulder, as though assuring herself that he was all right. Julius waved to her, but as soon as she was out of sight he rolled over and watched the tears mist his eyes as he stared into space.

He could not believe Josef would not see him and as he lay in his bed that night, the blessed sanctuary of sleep eluding him, he tossed and turned as his mind raced with his tortured thoughts. As he fell asleep he had come to a conclusion, the only reason Josef would not see him was because he had heard the circumstances of Nikolas' death, and he too blamed Julius. Julius could not bear the burden of such guilt, and as the empty bottle of brandy allowed him to fall asleep at last, he vowed that in some way he would see Josef, tell him what had happened, tell him the truth, and nothing and nobody was going to stop him.

The next morning Erika came to say goodbye to him. He was determined that she would not know how disappointed he was at Josef's refusal to see him. He greeted her with a joviality that he did not feel and when she asked him how he felt now that he had had time to think about things he told her that he was resigning himself to the fact that he would not be seeing Josef.

Erika watched him with a disbelieving look on her face, but whatever she really thought she chose to keep to herself as she proceeded to talk of other things. She told him she had been to see his surgeon to discuss his return to Prague as early as was possible. "You will be pleased to know that they are to start you walking on crutches at the beginning of next week. The doctor has explained to me all your treatments and I have a letter for Herr Doktor Beck and Irmy outlining everything for them. The doctor was very impressed with Herr Doktor Beck's credentials, and feels sure that if you are going to Prague to be consigned to his care you could be home very soon. Do you not think that will be wonderful Julius?"

Julius nodded and smiled in assent, all the time thinking of what he would have to do before he left the hospital. "The doktor was concerned with your journey home, but when I told him that I was sure Irmy would come to accompany you back to Prague, he was more than happy with the arrangement. I only hope I have said the right thing, every hospital seems to be stretched to their limits, what with their war wounded and now this flu epidemic, but I am sure the hospital will be able to spare Irmy for a couple of weeks" Erika drifted on with her conversation, but Julius only heard half of what she was saying, his mind was elsewhere, far away from the complexities of his journey home.

Erika rose to leave, she had a train to catch and suddenly Julius came to his senses as he realized that this was their last time together, at least for a while. Julius asked Erika to sit down again and as he took her hand, he looked into her eyes, causing her to blush and look down into her lap. Julius did not know what to say to her, but the thought of her going was greatly upsetting him and he knew he had to say something.

"You do not know how good it has been to see you Erika" he began, "I was really at a low ebb and you have done me more good than any medicines could have done. I know you came because Irmy asked you to, but I appreciate the fact that you are here none the less" Julius paused, not knowing what to add, as Erika said, "do not be silly Julius, I wanted to see you, we will always be friends I hope"

Julius looked at her lovely face and found himself saying, "and maybe we will be more than friends again one day?"

Erika withdrew her hand from his as she sadly said, "no Julius, I think not. You made a decision about me a long time ago and I do not think your opinion has changed since then. I know you are lonely and hurt and I think so much of you, but I am not the solution, believe me. I would love to be closer to you but it would not be right. I would only be second best and I think I deserve more than that"

Julius could see the tears in her eyes and his heart went out to her, but he knew she was right. He had spoken in an unguarded moment, without thinking, words which would have been better left unsaid, and now he was sad to think he might have hurt Erika again. She was right, she deserved more than that.

"I am sorry Erika, I did not mean to hurt you, I would never want to do that"

Erika put her hand up to his cheek and through her tears smiled her lovely smile as she said, "I know Julius, I know. You are very troubled at the moment, but you must come to terms with your torment, before it tears you apart. Promise me, when you are ready, please talk to someone, you

418

cannot bottle everything up like this, it is not doing you any good"

Julius nodded as Erika gave him a last kiss on his lips before she left him. She never looked back and although several of the patients waved to her or called out their goodbyes she did not acknowledge them as she left the ward. Julius sat staring after her for a long time. At least in one thing he could do as she asked. She wanted him to talk to somebody, and he knew who that somebody was.

The days after Erika left were very lonely and empty for Julius. He missed her smiling face entering the ward each morning, he missed talking to her about his loved ones and their home, but most of all he missed her company. Josef's refusal to see him had dealt him a huge blow and he wished that Erika was still with him to share his plans but reflected that she would not be pleased with the measures he had decided he was prepared to take in order to see his old friend. There was no one he could talk to. Although he had created many friendships amongst his fellow patients on the ward they were not of a nature that he could disclose his innermost feelings to any of them. He missed Nikolas and knew some of his reticence to make friends was a knowledge that he was afraid of becoming close to anybody again after Nikolas' death.

He continued to take part in the daily activities of the ward, watching his fellow patients prepare for the future in their differing ways. Men who were coming to terms with their injuries, men who weren't. Men who lay lifeless on their beds all day wrapped in their own hopeless misery or those who strutted about the ward with a false bonhomie and a brightness which betrayed their unconscious fear of what they would do with the rest of their lives.

Julius watched with envy as more and more men were discharged and his ward became less crowded as only those men with long-term injuries were left. Julius longed to go home and he took heart from the half remembered conversation he had had with Erika about his possible return to Prague. He was determined to work hard to enable him to walk again, but he was equally determined that before he left he would see Josef.

The transition to walking on crutches was far harder than Julius had ever imagined. He had thought that he would haul himself up and then with the aid of the crutches walk across the room. The reality was very different. To start with just getting up and onto the crutches took all his energy, but once there he felt how weak his legs were as they would not support his body, and then the floor seemed to jump up towards him and he felt faint. His head swam and he landed in an inelegant heap on the floor. Once again he was raised by the orderly to start the process all over again.

It took him more than three days to master just raising himself onto his crutches and then he had to re-educate himself as to how to walk. It was as if his legs had forgotten how to work and he had to concentrate really hard as he willed his legs to proceed one after the other in an ungainly shuffle. Julius had never felt so frail or so feeble in all his life. He felt useless, with orderlies and nurses having to rush to help him at his every move. Julius became bad tempered with his slow progress. When told he would be walking on crutches he had imagined he would be going for long walks by himself after the first week, but by the end of the second week all he had done was just about master how to put one foot in front of the other, and that often had to be done with the assistance of a nurse. Added to that was the discomfort of sores which had developed in his armpits and on the palms of his hands as he got used to holding the crutches.

After the sessions Julius would arrive back in his ward, wet through with perspiration and so tired that he had barely lain down on his bed before he was asleep. The only thing that kept him going was the thought of getting up to the third floor to see Josef. Erika had told him the name of the orderly that she had bribed and he kept looking for him but every time he saw him it was when other people were around. Julius became more and more frustrated, his spirits were lower than they had ever been and he started to find increasing sanctuary from his pain and disappointment in another bottle of brandy.

One morning Julius woke with his usual headache from too much drinking the night before. He refused breakfast and was just receiving a particularly stern lecture from the matron about the folly of not eating when over her shoulder he saw Feltz, the orderly Erika had told him about, arriving onto the ward. He strode up to the matron who turned on the unfortunate man and demanded to know what he wanted. Feltz shrank back as he told her he had come to collect Captain Mayer to take him to Nurse Muller.

420

"You can tell Nurse Muller that Captain Mayer will not be coming for his session this morning, he is not up to it, would you not agree, Captain Mayer, a lack of energy shall we say?" The matron gave Julius a baleful stare, willing him to disagree with her. Julius opened his mouth, then closed it again. He had to think quickly, this may be his only chance to talk to Feltz on his own and now he had jeopardized that chance with his stubborn willfulness. Smiling what he hoped was his most beguiling smile Julius said, "Matron, I am sorry, I realize I was stupid to refuse to eat my breakfast, I promise, on my honor, I will do so in the future"

The matron pulled herself up to the full extent of her statuesque frame, folded her arms and regarded him for a few moments before she said, "very well Captain Mayer, I will forgive you this time, I hope you mean what you say and do not forget I have your word of honor on this. Please remember captain, we are here to help you, your health is important to us, and lack of nutrition will not help your recovery, do I make myself clear?"

Julius nodded meekly and then was overjoyed as the matron turned to the orderly, "very well, orderly, you may now take Captain Mayer"

The matron strode off down the ward, obviously happy at the success of exercising her power over Julius.

The orderly helped Julius into his wheelchair without a word, but as they left the ward Julius decided to seize the moment, as he did not know when the next one would arise.

"Your name is Feltz, is it not?" Julius asked, trying to sound as if he was making polite conversation.

"Yes, sir" replied the orderly, as he pushed Julius down the corridor.

"Feltz, I believe you did a favor for me a few weeks ago. A young lady asked you to find out if I could visit Lieutenant von Kutz on the third floor, am I right?"

Julius felt the progress of his wheelchair waver for a moment before he was pushed on down the corridor, the orderly saying nothing. Julius twisted in the chair, trying to look at the orderly's face, but the man was staring straight ahead of him, refusing to look at Julius.

"Damn it man I am not trying to get you into trouble, no-one else will know of this I promise. I just hoped you would help me again, it could mean an awful lot of money to you"

This time the man's eyes flickered briefly onto Julius' face and then continued staring straight ahead of him.

Julius thought he was getting nowhere until a soft voice above him asked, "how much? how much are we talking about" Julius breathed deeply as he told the man the obscene amount of money he was prepared to give him in order to get to see Josef. He had thought about this a lot and he knew that it would take a large amount of money to bribe someone to help him in his plan, but he did not care how much it was, such was his determination to see Josef. The man gasped at the amount, but said no more as they had arrived at Nurse Muller's room. Once he had delivered Julius into the care of Nurse Muller's assistants Feltz left the room but not before giving Julius a long stare. Julius spent the whole session wondering if all his plans had come to nothing. He had given Feltz the bait now all he could pray for was that he would find the money too irresistible to refuse.

Julius was disappointed to see another orderly come to collect him to take him back to the ward. The rest of the day he spent lying on his bed deep in depression, wondering if he would ever get to see Josef.

The next morning Julius' spirits rose as Feltz again appeared at his bedside. Once out in the corridor, Julius started to ask him if he had considered his offer, but all the orderly did was to cut him off mid sentence and roughly growl, "not here, later" That was all he would say, and with that Julius had to be content, but he was not dissatisfied with the man's reply. He had not dismissed his offer and was interested in at least hearing what Julius had to say, now all Julius had to do was convince the orderly to help him. Feltz came to collect him after another grueling session and as they returned to the ward Julius found his route change as he was pushed off into another corridor where Feltz opened a door and wheeled Julius into a large linen store cupboard. Making sure he had closed the door securely Feltz turned to Julius and roughly asked, "you mentioned a lot of money yesterday, just what do I have to do to earn it?"

Julius swallowed deeply, he knew this might be his only chance and he had to convince Feltz to help him. "Not a lot, really. All I want you to do is get me up to the third floor, take me to Lieutenant von Kutzs' room, and then afterwards take me back to my ward"

422

Julius stared straight at the orderly as the man let out a skeptical chuckle. "Oh, that is all is it? You must be mad, I would lose my job if they found us. Anyway, no-one sees that one, something strange there I reckon"

"You mean you have not seen the lieutenant?" asked Julius amazed, "then how did you get my message to him?" Julius had the dubious feeling that this man had pocketed his money without even delivering his message to Josef, but he did not want to antagonize the orderly, he needed his help. "Oh he got his message all right, I just got one of his staff to deliver it to his lordship that's all" The orderly boldly returned Julius' stare and Julius found himself believing the man.

"Why do you call him his lordship?" asked Julius.

"Well he must think himself above others, stuck up there, refusing to see anybody. Why do you want to see him anyway?"

"That is my business Feltz, now do you want the money or not?"

Feltz scratched his bristly chin as he contemplated Julius' offer before replying, "I am tempted and I suppose we could do it at night, if we are very careful, less staff about then you see"

Julius heart was turning somersaults as he hoped the orderly was coming round to accepting his money. He needed this man's help, the lack of progress he had made with his crutches had convinced him that the only way up to the third floor was in his wheelchair, and for that he needed assistance, let alone actually finding Josef's room.

Feltz was obviously still pondering the situation as he said, "all right, I think I might be able to get you up there. I will work out how and try to contact you, but if not just be ready to go when I come and get you. Now about the money, I want it at the time I take you"

"Agreed" said Julius, who would have agreed to double the money if it would just give him the chance to see Josef, "but I will give you half when we go up, and the other half when I come back to the ward" Julius did not relish the thought of being stranded on the third floor, something he felt this old rogue was quite capable of. Feltz began to protest at Julius' lack of trust in him, but relented when Julius upped the price a little.

"Now I suggest you take me back to the ward before they start to wonder where I have got to"

Feltz took Julius back to the ward and left him without another word or even a backward glance. Julius felt elated. After making arrangements for a bank draft to be sent in order to get the money issued, he spent the rest of the day in a pleasurable rubber of bridge and went to bed that night feeling better than he had done for a long time.

Julius' feeling of elation soon turned to one of frustration as the days turned into a week and still there was no sign of Feltz. He realized that the moment would have to be right but after Feltz had appeared to accept his offer the feelings of anticipation had been so high that now, a week later, Julius' depression was beginning to return. He no longer sought the solace of a glass or two of brandy as he had decided that he could not afford to drink at night in case the orderly came to fetch him. He wanted his mind clear for his meeting with Josef.

His physiotherapy continued and he was heartened by the daily awareness of the strength returning to his legs. He also had the encouragement of the nursing staff who would motivate him by ensuring him of the possibility of his soon returning home. This, coupled with a letter he had received from Irmy, only strengthened his resolve that he had to see Josef as soon as possible.

In her letter Irmy had told him that Erika had returned with his medical records from Doktor Sachs and that Richard, in consultation with his medical staff at the hospital, had agreed that Julius should soon be ready to return to Prague. Irmy had written that they were still very busy coping with the flu epidemic but that thankfully, with the warmer weather, fewer patients were being admitted. She also wrote that due to the hospital being full it had been decided that Julius would recuperate at Richard and Irmy's house, as she and Richard could look after him. Julius wondered if this was what Richard and Irmy wanted, they must be very busy and the thought of a further burden in their home was probably not a welcome prospect. However he reflected that he would enjoy being back in civilized surroundings once again. He had had enough of hospitals to last him a lifetime, and the thought of not having to adhere to the strict regime of hospital life filled him with an optimism he had not felt for a long time.

He had not received a letter from Mama for over two months now, and thought it odd that Irmy had not mentioned her in her letter. He presumed that as he was to stay with Richard and Irmy that Mama must still be staying with the long-suffering Frau Beckova. He knew his last few letters to Mama, written a few weeks ago, had been short, circumspect and merely dutiful and wondered if this had offended his mother, maybe that was the reason she had not written back to him. He resolved to write her a long letter that day but was forestalled by the arrival of a letter bearing a Salzburg postmark and written with the unmistakable hand of Viktor. Julius tore open the letter anxious to hear news of his friend. The tears welled up into his eyes as he read the letter, written by Viktor with his usual good nature and charm. It was so wonderful to hear from him, to know he was alive and safe.

Viktor wrote that, like Georg, at the end of the war he had made his way back to Salzburg. He did not dwell too much on his reminiscences of those dark days, skirting around them as if the memories were too hard to confront so soon. However the rest of his letter was cheerful enough. He had returned to Salzburg in the December of last year, and in the April of this year had married Sonia. Viktor, a married man! it did not seem possible. Viktor had tried to find out what had happened to his friends, but with communications so muddled after the ending of the war, this had proved very difficult, but at last he had received a letter from Irmy, telling Viktor about Julius and of course Nikolas. Julius' heart contracted with pain as Viktor wrote of the sadness of their friend's untimely death and went on to remember all the good things about Nikolas and all the times they had shared. Once again Julius felt the guilt creeping through his soul as he wondered how Viktor would react if he knew how Nikolas had died.

Julius sat up with a start as Viktor continued, 'as to Josef's whereabouts I am afraid I have not been able to find out where he is. I received a very strange, terse letter from his brother, saying that Josef had been injured, but was now recovering and he would ask him to contact me when he had made a full recovery. He did not tell me where he was and made it quite plain he had no intention of telling me his whereabouts. It is all very strange, Julius, do you not think? Well at least we know he is alive, and after the events of the last few years we should be thankful for that. I am sure Josef will contact us in his own good time. Do you think the war could have affected him like your brother? I suppose the von Kutzs would not like that fact to be known amongst the upper echelons of Viennese society, though from what I hear the upper echelons of Viennese society have other things to worry about at the moment' Julius reflected that this was probably true. Although no longer interested in current affairs since the damning day when he had learnt the fate of the army, and indeed of Europe, he was still privy to the daily conversations of his fellow patients and was aware of the broader issues of the day.

The war may have ended, but the suffering was still continuing for many people. Soldiers were returning home, not as war heroes but as men the populace would sooner forget about as they were too much of a reminder of their defeat. The ordinary citizens were still short of food and basic materials and the economy was in disarray.

The aristocracy, too, were adrift in the chaotic times of the aftermath of the war. Bereft of a royal figurehead they were desperately trying to find a role in life that would fit in with the new world that was emerging at the end of the great conflict.

In January there had been a Peace Conference in Paris and in May a Peace Treaty had been signed in the Hall of Mirrors in the Palace of Versailles. Germany and Austria were now independent republics, with both countries having to give considerable territories to the new independent state of Poland which caused great resentment, especially in Germany. Slovakia was taken from Hungary and had been united with the Austrian lands of Bohemian and Moravia to form the new country of Czechoslovakia, under the leadership of Masaryk. Hungary also lost Croatia and Slovenia to Serbia and Montenegro and these countries were united to form the new state of Yugoslavia. In the Baltics the states of Latvia, Lithuania and Estonia also received their independence and in the Middle East the Arabs were deeply angered when the British promised to allow Jews to set up a 'national home' in Palestine.

At times Julius felt he could not keep abreast of all the vast changes that were sweeping across Europe. The old Empires were gone, Germany was all but contained under the constraints of the treaty and everyone started to breathe again with the thought that there would never again be a war fought like the one that had taken place over the last four years. Even Julius, dismayed at the loss of his army and unsure of his own future, felt that if anything had been learnt over the past four years it was the futility of war

426

and with that knowledge at least everyone could be sure that their own children would not have to endure the misery of another war across the continent.

Julius was dismayed when Herr Doktor Sachs arrived at one of his sessions to tell him he had received a letter from Richard and that Irmy would be arriving to take him back to Prague in two weeks time. The doctor was surprised at Julius' lack of enthusiasm at the news and, after sending the orderly away, pushed Julius out of the treatment room. Instead of taking him to his ward the doctor took Julius out into the grounds. Although it was early June, the sky was filled with angry gray clouds, which reflected Julius' mood. He knew the doctor had brought him out into the gardens in order to talk to him, but his mood blackened as he had no desire for the conversation. He was too worried at the thought of Irmy arriving without his having seen Josef. He was even tempted to ask the doctor outright if he could arrange for him to see Josef, but he knew this was futile. There was too much secrecy surrounding their very benevolent patient to expect any of the staff, let alone the good doctor, to help him. Besides, he did not want anyone to know of his connection with Lieutenant von Kutz, it would bring unwanted attention upon himself.

The doctor sat on a bench after he had placed Julius' chair in a position where he was sitting directly opposite the doctor. Over the months Julius had come to admire and respect Herr Doktor Sachs. He knew him to be a good, caring doctor, with an unnerving capacity to understand his patient's anxieties, even when they did not divulge their inner feelings to him.

Julius tried to avoid looking at his face as the doctor said, "Captain Mayer, I must say I am surprised at your reaction to the news of your going home. Tell me, was I wrong to say you were ready for this?, because if you believe you are not, I could write to your sister and brother-in-law suggesting that you stay with us for a while longer, would you like me to do that?"

Julius stared at his lap for a long while, not knowing what to say to the doctor. Part of him wanted to ask the doctor if he could stay, to make sure he would see Josef, but another part cried out to return home, back to Prague, amongst his loved ones. Although he knew his future was uncertain, lately he had thought more and more of Prague and longed to return to its familiar cobbled streets and elegant

427

buildings, to breathe its air, to get some normality back into his life. When Julius did not reply the doctor continued, "I know the thought of going home may be a bit worrying for you. Many people find the sanctuary of the hospital welcoming and are afraid to enter the outside world again, especially when their future is so unsure, but you know you are luckier than most. Soon you will be back to your former robust health, which is more than can be said for thousands of your fellow soldiers, and you have a family to return to who are fully able to give you the treatment and recuperation as excellent as that which you have received here. Or maybe you are still worried at the reaction you will receive from the friends and relatives of your dead friend?"

Julius jerked his head up and clenched his fists to control his temper. He was angry at the audacity of the doctor, but also angry at himself as he knew the doctor had touched a nerve which he had been suppressing since he had heard that he was going home. He knew one of his greatest fears would be confronting Nikolas' parents, Georg and Suse and having to relate to them the circumstances of Nikolas' death. He wondered if he would have the courage to be honest with them, to face their resentment, but he knew he would have to tell them the truth, if not for his sake, then for Nikolas' and the thought of it filled him with a dread that would not disappear.

"Captain Mayer, I, I am sorry" stammered Doctor Sachs, obviously shocked by the hostility apparent on Julius' face, "I would not have mentioned this if I did not feel that you needed to talk to someone. Your lovely young friend Fraulein Lehmannova was worried for your welfare, and only told me in the strictest confidence in the hope that I might understand what you have gone through. She said you would not talk to her of the circumstances of your friend's death. Would you like to talk to me now, perhaps it might help?"

Julius' anger melted away as he looked into the kind face of the doctor. He knew the man was only trying to help him, and for a fleeting moment he was tempted to unload his burden of guilt but the moment disappeared and Julius felt his mind close again to the doctor's offer of help. No, he would wait and talk to Josef. Josef would understand, Josef knew Nikolas, they had shared a very special life, and together they would help each other. He knew in that moment what he would do, he would go home with Irmy, but if Feltz did not help him, he would make sure he visited Josef by whatever means that were necessary before he left the hospital.

Regaining his self-control Julius smiled at the doctor, "Do not worry about me doctor. You are right, I have a lot to be thankful for, hopefully I have a future, which as you say is more than can be said for an awful lot of people. I am worried about having to console my friend's family, but I know it is a duty I will have to perform, and hiding here will not make it any easier. Please do not worry about me, I am a survivor, who knows with these legs I may go on to be a circus acrobat!"

Doctor Sachs let out a great roar of laughter at the absurdity of Julius' statement and seemed content that his patient was in a stable frame of mind. Julius himself, with the momentary return of his whimsical sense of humor, felt quite elated. He had made a decision and nothing was going to deter him from that course. He was going to see Josef and after that he would go home to Prague and then decide on his future, whatever it was.

Two nights later, in the early hours of the morning, he felt someone shaking his shoulder and as he roused himself out of his slumber he was suddenly very awake and alert as through the gloom he realized it was Feltz standing by his bedside. The man put a callused finger to his lips intimating that Julius hold his tongue as he helped Julius into the wheelchair that he had brought with him. All the time Feltz kept a watchful eye on the office at the end of the ward where the night duty nurse could be heard moving about the room. Warily Feltz wheeled Julius out of the ward, Julius was not bothered if any of the sleepless inmates in his ward watched them as they departed, he knew they would keep quiet and not alert the nurse. His only worry was if the nurse found him missing from his bed. As if reading his thoughts Feltz whispered as he wheeled him down the corridor, "don't worry, she's just made her rounds. Creature of habit that one, if nothing goes wrong she'll not make another round for an hour. That's how long you've got" An hour did not seem long enough to Julius, but he did not complain. He was on his way and he was not going to jeopardize this chance of seeing Josef.

The hospital was eerily quiet in its gloom and Julius was sure that the noise of his wheels, which sounded extremely loud to him in the surrounding silence, would alert someone to their escapade. Feltz pushed the wheelchair at an alarming rate, but as they proceeded to the rear of the hospital building he eased the pace somewhat as he became less nervous, pushing Julius through a maze of corridors into the less public part of the hospital. Eventually Feltz stopped at a large grilled door then walked round to face Julius.

"Got my money?" Julius handed the man an envelope containing half the money as they had agreed. Julius was annoyed to see the man open it roughly and quickly count it, as though he did not trust him. The man smiled a lopsided grin displaying a foul display of yellowing and crooked teeth. "Good, now this is one of the service elevators, there should be nobody about up there at this time of the morning, but if our luck doesn't hold, pretend to be asleep and leave me to do the talking, understand?" Julius nodded. "I will take you to the room, but I can't wait outside, it would bring attention to you if they saw me loitering about in the corridor. I will come back for you at three o'clock, make sure the corridor is clear before you come out" Julius nodded and looked at his watch. His time with Josef was decreasing with every minute and he was impatient to get there.

Feltz pulled open the gates and pushed Julius inside then turned a large handle as he closed the gates behind them. Julius could not believe the horrendous noise the elevator made as they ascended. He feared that the whole of the hospital would be there to greet them when they stopped, the noise had been so great. Feltz must have noticed the worried look on his face as he chuckled, "sounds loud but no one is in this section at this time, we should be all right"

Far from being comforted, Julius was relieved when the elevator shuddered to a stop and Feltz opened the doors. The silence of the hospital returned as Julius was pushed through another maze of corridors until Feltz stopped outside the door of a private ward.

"Here we are" he whispered, "don't forget, three o'clock" Julius nodded as he stared at the door in front of him. The enormity of what he was doing dawned on him and as he turned to watch Feltz striding off down the corridor he was almost tempted to wheel himself after him.

He was suddenly filled with a strange sense of foreboding as he looked up at the door. Summoning up all his courage he reached up and turned the brass handle. His

430

body was covered in a cold sweat as the door slowly creaked open and he propelled himself into the dark, forbidding interior of Josef's room.

XXIX

Julius peered through the gloom. As his eyes became accustomed to the darkness he saw a bed on the far side of the room illuminated by a single candle that cast ghostly shadows across the ceiling as its small flame flickered in the breeze from a half open window. Julius wheeled himself into the room but came to an abrupt stop and clasped his hand over his mouth as the foulest stench overwhelmed him, so foul that he began to retch. He had smelt the nauseous odor before, but never had it been so strong as in the confines of this room. It was the smell of putrid, rotting flesh, of gangrene.

Julius had seen gangrene many times during the war, the first indication of the mortification of decaying flesh was common amongst wounded soldiers. It was the smell that engendered the greatest fear in every man. In this room, although masked by hospital disinfectants, the smell pervaded the chamber like a harbinger of death and for the first time Julius wondered if he had been right to come.

He shivered, the open window made the air chilly and damp. Julius felt the stillness and coldness travel over his body whilst the shadows on the ceiling danced above him like ethereal spirits warning him to depart. Julius' senses told him to leave and he would have fled at that moment, but the silence was broken by the sound of someone breathing heavily. The hairs on the back of his neck stood on end as an unfamiliar guttural voice echoed around the room as the occupant of the bed spoke. "I knew you would come, Julius, I knew you would not stay away. You are a fool, why could you not have left me alone?"

The speaker gasped in tortured breaths, as though the effort to speak was using all his energy. Fascinated, but at the same time appalled at what he might find, Julius approached the bed. As his eyes met the horrific scene in front of him Julius wept. The tears ran down his face as he came face to face with the ultimate horror of his worst nightmare.

Lying on the bed was Josef, but not the Josef that Julius had known. Not the handsome, debonair man, strong of body with the perfect face and a shock of blonde hair that always fell carelessly across his deep blue eyes. The shell of the man before him had a body which had been blown

432

apart. Josef had no legs and only one arm, his stumps swathed in bandages. His left arm had been amputated at the elbow and there was evidence of the onset of disease which seeped through the whiteness of the dressing. His right arm was badly mutilated whilst his remaining hand had only three fingers, and his chest, carelessly covered by a flimsy blanket, showed a network of stitches and tubes, but it was Josef's face that shocked Julius the most. The once beautiful features were hideously disfigured. The only remnants of his hair sprouted out of one side of his head in wispy tendrils. The rest of his scalp was bald showing a skin livid with bright red scars. One of Josef's eyes was missing, leaving a large empty socket surrounded by scars that ran down the side of his face. The side of Josef's mouth was missing, cut away to display his teeth and gums like some macabre skeletal mask. As if in some whimsical act of hate the other side of Josef's face remained as a remnant of his former good looks, providing a perverse glimpse of the beauty that had once been Josef. From all parts of his body tubes protruded and there was one hanging out of his throat which produced an eerie hissing noise every time Josef breathed.

Julius tried to say something, but the words would not come, the tears still streamed down his face as he reached out and took hold of Josef's remaining hand, trying not to flinch as he held the deformed limb.

"Josef I am so sorry" he whispered. Josef had been staring straight ahead of him but now he turned his one good eye towards Julius.

"Sorry for what?" his voice hissed and gurgled and Julius watched with an eerie fascination as the tube vibrated with his voice. "Sorry to see me like this, I suppose. You should be sorry that I did not die, that would have been better"

Julius was shocked by his friend's words, but, and he hated himself for thinking it, maybe it would have been better for Josef to have died rather than to be like this. Not knowing what to say, all thoughts of his prepared speech for Josef forgotten, Julius desperately tried to think of some words of comfort for his friend, but none came. How could you comfort a man, especially a man like Josef, who had sustained such terrible injuries.

"I hear your family are making sure the hospital are seeing to your every comfort" the words sounded foolish, but they were the only ones that Julius could think of to say. Josef uttered what Julius presumed to be a contemptuous laugh, but which instead sounded like the cry of a trapped animal and caused his whole body to alarmingly convulse.

"Still the same old naive Julius" said the tortured voice, so unlike the mellifluous tones of the old Josef, "they are not paying them to look after me, they are paying them to keep me hidden up here, so that I am not a source of gossip, so no-one will pity the noble von Kutzs because their son looks like a circus freak. Do you know where they are sending me from here?" Josef's one eyed stare bored into Julius, defying him to look away, "they are sending me to a sanatorium, kilometers away from Vienna, where no-one will know me, where I will not be a burden upon my family, where I can go whilst they wait for me to die"

"Josef, I cannot believe you, your mother would never treat you like that" Julius argued vehemently.

Josef returned to staring at the ceiling, as though the effort of his speech had tired him too much. He was silent for a while until he said, very quietly, "I wish I could believe you Julius, but for the last two months I have had no word from my mother, and no promise of a visit. Does that sound like someone who cares?"

Julius' heart went out to his friend, to be so lonely and afraid, and now it seemed even his mother had deserted him. He could not believe it of the Countess. She had adored Josef, there had to be an explanation, but he could not think of one to comfort his friend. Julius was jolted out of his reverie by the sound of Josef's tubes moving as he prepared to say something.

"What of Nikolas and Viktor, how are they?"

Julius swallowed deeply as he said, "Viktor is back in Salzburg" he did not add that Viktor was now married, he did not think Josef would want to hear of their friend's happiness, "and Nikolas, I do not know how to tell you this Josef but Nikolas died in the same battle in which I was injured and...."

Julius was just about to tell Josef the circumstances of Nikolas' death when he was devastated to hear Josef say, "Lucky Nikolas, would that I could have been as fortunate"

The anger welled up inside Julius as he exclaimed, "how dare you say that Josef, it is a terrible thing to say"

"Is it? tell me Julius, on your honor. Who is the luckier, Nikolas, or me, living this hell on earth from which there is no escape, no reprieve, where the only thing I can pray for is death, even though they insist on keeping me alive"

Julius did not know what to say. He knew his friend was right, but he could not agree with him. Nikolas was gone from them but at least Josef was alive, with a brain which obviously still held the capacity to be its controversial self, and he told Josef so.

"Julius, what good is a brain, when your body does not work, when the sight of you repulses people, when you cannot do one thing for yourself without help? I always believed we had been saved on the mountain for some special purpose, now I know it was all a lie. Tell me what do you think I am going to do with the rest of my life. Marry, have children, go to my club occasionally, attend the opera?"

Once again Josef fell back into his pillows as the effort of speech tired him, he closed his eye and Julius watched as tears fell down one side of Josef's face. There was nothing he could say or do. He was tiring Josef, upsetting him, he decided he should go but resolved to come back and see him again. Now he knew where he was he would try to get up here on his own. Just as he was about to tell him he was going Josef opened his eye and not looking at Julius said, "Do you remember, all those years ago, when we went out to dinner after we had finished our exams?" Julius nodded as a great sense of foreboding came over him, "do you remember what we promised each other?"

Julius answered slowly, "well we were all fairly inebriated, especially you and Nikolas as I remember, I think we were pretending we were the Three Musketeers or something"

Josef did not join in with his attempt to lighten the conversation as he said, "you know very well what we said that night Julius, we promised that wherever we were in the world, whatever we were doing, we would always look after each other if we needed help" Julius watched his friend as he gasped for air, Julius started to say that he ought to go, but Josef held his hand tight as he looked intently at Julius, "I want you to help me now, Julius. I am asking you to honor that promise" Julius felt the cold of the room circle around him as his head started to swim, but nothing had prepared him for what Josef said next, "I want you to bring me a gun, Julius. I want you to find me a gun and bring it to me here"

435

Julius' thought he was going to vomit, as the bile travelled up his throat. He knew why Josef wanted a gun, he wanted to end his life, he wanted to commit suicide. Julius' mind reeled, not only was it a mortal sin, but he would be aiding a man in taking his own life, something he knew he could not do. Julius stared wide-eyed at his friend as the enormity of the act dawned on him. "Josef, I cannot, it would be wrong. Nothing is as bad as that. I will get you help, I will contact your mother. You can come to Prague with me, anything but that Josef, anything but that"

"I do not want anything else Julius, my life is at an end, and I want it to finish now rather than later. Can you not smell the disease, Julius? and it gets worse every day. Do you know what they are saying now? That they are going to operate on me again to take off more of my arm, to stop the disease spreading, but what is the point? I cannot go on living like this. I know you think me shallow, but the only thing I had to recommend me were my looks, and I have not even those now. What sort of life is there for me, you must understand that"

"Josef, I do, and you know I would do anything for you, but not this, you cannot ask this of me"

"But I can Julius, we all made a promise, a promise I am now asking you to keep"

"But it was a promise made in jest, in a drunken moment, we were not being serious"

"Well I am being serious now. I need your help Julius, you are the only one who can help me, please, I am begging you"

Julius regarded the wild look in Josef's eye and heard the pleading in his voice, but he knew he could not help his friend, not to take his own life, he could not. He would not be able to live with himself or his conscience. "I am sorry Josef but I cannot do this, I wish I could, but I cannot"

Violently Josef pushed his hand away. "Then go" said the strained rasping voice, "we have nothing more to say"

Stunned by the hatred in Josef's broken voice Julius wheeled his chair backwards, looked at his friend, and then decided to leave, he would return another time when hopefully Josef would be calmer. Josef was staring again at the ceiling, but as Julius made for the door his tortured voice once again echoed around the room "Julius, I will never forgive you if you do not do this for me, get out of my

436

room and do not bother coming back unless you are willing to help me."

Julius never knew how he got back to the service elevator. He remembered wildly wheeling himself down endless corridors, banging into walls and almost tipping himself up, totally unaware of his surroundings. His vision was obscured by the tears of anger and dismay that filled his eyes as the sound of Josef's last tortured words raced around his head, repeating themselves in accusation and hate. Instinct must have guided him to where Feltz stood idly waiting to return to collect his charge. The sight of Julius so distressed obviously unnerved the orderly as he tried to calm Julius down.

"You all right, sir, things not go well, what happened in there?"

Julius ignored his questions as he ordered Feltz to get him back to his ward as quickly as possible. Feltz said no more as he pulled back the doors and pushed Julius into the elevator, but eyed him warily as Julius closed his eyes and the blessed noise of the elevator descending took him away from the hell he had encountered. Julius sat in his chair shaking, his whole body trembled and his head pounded as he tried to make sense of his meeting with Josef. Nothing he could imagine had prepared him for what had just happened. Since knowing Josef was in the hospital, even with all the secrecy surrounding him, it had never occurred to Julius why Josef would not have wanted to see him. In his arrogance he had not stopped to think that there might have been a valid reason for Josef's isolation, even when Erika had remarked on the strangeness of the situation he had not considered the reasons for them.

As Feltz at last delivered Julius to his ward, he gave him his envelope, then waved the man away, and he scampered off, glad to be able to leave his distressed charge. Julius looked around the ward, he did not care if the night nurse discovered him, but she was still at her desk in her room. Julius hauled himself onto his bed, pulled the covers over him and accepted the comfort of their warmth. He was still shaking, he could not still the trembling of his body, and although he felt exhausted the welcome relief of sleep eluded him as he thought about Josef. He knew he had to do something, but he did not know what. His mind went through all the possibilities, but he found no answers in his meandering reflections. Time and again he came back to

Josef's request to find him a gun. He knew he could not do what Josef asked of him, but remembering Josef's pleadings and picturing his terrible injuries, part of Julius wished he could do this one thing for his friend. Although he had always regarded suicide as a mortal sin and a coward's way out he reflected on Josef's poignant picture of the life that stretched out before him and he wondered were he in Josef's position whether he would not himself long for the chance of an early release from a living hell. He resolved to write to Josef's mother and he would write to Viktor. Julius could do little lying in the hospital, but perhaps Viktor could offer more practical help. He may not be able to help Josef in the way he had asked but perhaps between them he and Viktor could do something for their friend, he deserved that at least.

Julius did not sleep that night, his mind too full of Josef, and when the nursing staff tended him the next morning, they were shocked by his appearance and told him to stay in bed and rest for the day. This suited Julius admirably, he had no wish to talk to other people and the peace of a day's rest would maybe help him come to terms with the debacle of his meeting with Josef.

For most of the day he dozed fitfully in between writing letters to the countess and Viktor. Writing to the countess was very difficult and several times Julius screwed up the paper and started once more to write his letter. In the end, in an effort to be as unemotional as possible, Julius realized he had written a cold, factual letter, but he did not care. He wanted Josef's mother to understand the seriousness of the situation, to help her son, he could not believe she would abandon him, and he was honest with her about his meeting with Josef. To Viktor he wrote the facts, not about Josef's talk of suicide, but of his situation and all that Josef had told him. After he had written his letters he felt slightly better, as if by actually doing something he had helped relieve some of the burden. After making sure that his letters would be mailed immediately Julius at last fell into a deep sleep.

Over the next few days Julius became aware that he was retreating into a shell where he could be alone with himself, where he could afford himself the privacy of pondering his situation, where unencumbered he could try and work out what he would do next for Josef. He knew the hospital staff were worried about him, but he could not cheer himself up

438

for the benefit of them or his fellow patients. They all tried to bolster him up with careless chatter and light hearted conversation, but Julius was withdrawing more and more from their circle, happy with his own company, their existence seeming insignificant compared to the tormented life crumbling away on the third floor.

Every day he looked for the mail, a stupid pastime as he knew there was no chance of any replies yet, but he longed for their responses, perhaps with an answer to his dilemma. He still went for his exercises every day, the thought of being able to help Josef spurred him to try even harder. He was progressing well, becoming quite adept on his crutches and spending long sessions on two parallel bars, walking up and down with their support until he was told he would soon be able to start walking with the aid of walking sticks.

He knew his disinclination to talk or join in with any activities on the ward worried Doktor Sachs and the nursing staff, but he did not care. He had other things on his mind. Doktor Sachs had told him that Irmy was arriving next week.

He still had not had a reply from Viktor or the countess and if he did not receive a letter from either of them soon he would have to make a decision himself. He had thought over and over again what he should do, he knew now he could never supply Josef with the means to commit suicide. He would have to live with that knowledge for the rest of his life, and much as he wanted to help Josef he knew he could not bear the burden. Besides, he truly believed that when Josef heard his plans for the future he would not want to contemplate suicide any more. The idea had been mooted when he was with Josef. Although it had been said in the heat of the moment, his plans had grown over the last few days and Julius was sure he could persuade Josef to agree to it.

Josef was a wealthy man, and although it looked as though his family would shun him and their responsibility, Julius was not about to. He would take Josef back to Prague and with the help of Richard and Irmy he would create a home for Josef, with all the help and care he would need for the rest of his life. Julius himself would always be on hand to help his friend and at least Josef would know he was surrounded by people who loved and cared for him. He knew at first Josef would object, but he was sure he could persuade his friend that it was better than spending his

439

days in a sanatorium. Spurred on by his plan Julius prepared to go back up to the third floor again to see Josef before Irmy arrived. He thought he could remember the route when Feltz had taken him, all he needed was the opportunity to make sure he had a chair for the journey. Although he was getting stronger every day he was not sure if he had enough stamina to go on his crutches. He realized, against his better judgment, that he needed Feltz's help again.

As luck would have it two days later Feltz came to take Julius to his physiotherapy. The man was a consummate actor. He treated Julius as though he had never met him before, but Julius noticed that the man could not look him in the eye. On the way Julius once again asked Feltz for his help, but the man's reply left Julius stunned as he said, "well I am always willing to take your money sir, but I am afraid this time I cannot help you. His highness left the hospital two days ago, and before you ask, I don't know where. Nobody seems to know, likes his secrecy that one"
Julius thought he was going to pass out as he was wheeled into Nurse Muller's room. He could not believe it, Josef had left the hospital and he had no way of knowing where he had gone. He had left thinking that not even Julius cared for him and that fact hurt Julius most of all.

One look at Julius' white face and distressed condition and Nurse Muller sent him straight back to the ward. Feltz was obviously worried about the affect his news had had on the young officer and he quickly wheeled Julius back and left him without another word.

Julius lay in his bed for the next two days, unwilling to talk to anybody, to eat anything, lying in the oblivion of his misery, knowing he had let Josef down. He should have gone to see him sooner, he should have told him of his plans, so many things he should have done and now it was all too late. Julius did not think he could bear living with his conscience and his only solace was his never ending bottle of brandy.

The only motivation for Julius to leave his bed was when he received a visit from Herr Doktor Sachs. He knew he was to receive another lecture but realized the error of his ways when the doctor informed him that Irmy was arriving in a few days time and if his present lethargy did not improve he would be forced to tell Irmy that Julius would have to remain in the hospital for the foreseeable future.

440

There was one thing Julius had decided lying in his bed and that was that as soon as he returned to Prague he would start trying to find out where Josef had gone and when he had recovered all his strength he would bring him back to Prague as he had promised himself he would. He had written again to the countess asking where Josef had been taken and he had also written to Viktor, asking him if he could try to find out where Josef was. Julius started to eat again and resume his exercises and although he still kept his solitary existence he at least gave the pretence of returning to his normal self in preparation for his journey home.

Julius thought he had never been so happy to see anyone as when Irmy walked down the ward towards him. He had not seen his sister for nearly three years and the sight of her made him want to weep for joy. Irmy was now twenty-eight years old, a year younger than her brother. She still retained her beauty, but Julius could see that the previous years had been hard and difficult ones for his sister. Her prettiness was still there but there were telltale lines around her eyes and mouth and her eyes had lost the sparkle and verve of her youth. Irmy ran the last few steps to her brother and hugged him in a tight embrace for several minutes. When at last she relinquished her hold on him Julius could see the tears in her eyes as she smiled and said, "Oh Julius it is so good to see you again"
Irmy wheeled her brother out into the hospital gardens as his friends on the ward called out, "not another beauty pretty boy, how do you do it?" Julius could not help but give them a wry smile, they were obviously unaware that Irmy was his sister.

Once out in the gardens Irmy and Julius sat and discussed recent events and mutual acquaintances, both aware they were avoiding saying what they really wanted to talk about. At last Irmy summoned up her courage as she said, "I saw Herr Doktor Sachs before I came to see you, I wanted him to give me an assessment of your progress, it seems he is worried about you"
Julius tried to look unconcerned as he shrugged his shoulders and said, "Really? I do not see why"
Irmy looked at her brother as she said, "I think you do Julius, you never could look me straight in the eye when you were lying to me, and it seems you have not changed"

Julius looked up to see his sister smiling at him and he found himself relaxing and returning her smile. It was good to have her near him again, good to feel at ease, to have someone to talk to. "All right miss know-it-all. I have had a few things that I have had to sort out, but I am sure everything is going to be all right. You are here now and I am going home, that is all that matters"

Irmy fidgeted with her gloves, deliberating on what to say next, "Erika told me you were having difficulty coming to terms with Nikolas' death. Does that have something to do with your unhappiness?"

Julius squinted up at the sun and watched some birds fly past as he tried to decide what to say to his sister. "A little, it is too complicated to talk about now, please do not persist with this, it is something that I first have to understand myself"

"You know you will have to see Frau Manzova on your return? She is desperate to see you. She is trying to act as though she has accepted Nikolas' death, but I do not think she has. She needs to know how Nikolas......well you know. Maybe talking to her will help you as well"

Julius reflected that this was nothing further from the truth, but he could not say this to his sister, it would have been revealing too much of how Nikolas had died. Instead he merely nodded in appeasement and tried to change the subject. "Now tell me all about Richard, and Mama, what of Franz and Karl. I have had letters from them but nothing from Mama for months now, I suppose I have offended her again in some way?"

Julius was startled to find Irmy bursting into tears and as he held his sister's hands through her tears she said, "Oh Julius, it seems that I am always the bringer of bad news to you. Mama passed away over two months ago, it was the influenza, so many people have died of it since the end of the war. She just seemed to give up, she has never been the same since Papa died, I think she just lost the will to live"

Julius was speechless, how much more bad news could he hear? Poor Mama, so wretched at the end of her life, torn apart by the loss of her beloved husband. Julius remembered the terse, offhand letters he had written and felt guilty of his treatment of her.

"Why did you not tell me?" he asked.

"Herr Doktor Sachs thought at the time that you were not well enough to take such news, and then as time went on we agreed that it would be better if I told you myself. Are you very angry with us Julius?"

Julius was angry, but at the sight of his sister so distressed he had not the heart to remonstrate with her and instead held her in his arms as she cried her tears. She had had to withstand so much during the war, it must be so terrible for the people left at home, worrying about their loved ones at the front, waiting every day for the dreaded telegram, but Irmy had had the added onus of dealing with the death of both her parents along with her work at the hospital, he wondered how she had withstood the strain for so long. His anger subsided as he realized she had only been thinking of his own welfare and he tried to stem her tears by asking about the other members of their family.

Franz was very well, recovered from his experiences and now helping to run Gretha's father's farm and loving the outdoor life. Karl had bought an apartment in Vienna and had found employment in an office and was happy, his experiences of being a prisoner of war not forgotten, but hopefully well behind him now. Richard was back at the hospital working with the remaining war wounded and with the influenza epidemic. Here Irmy faltered in her account as she remembered Mama so Julius quickly asked her about Frau Beckova and Danusia. "Frau Beckova contracted the influenza, but she is a remarkable lady, she must be at least seventy years old, but she fought the illness and is now fully recovered, as hale and hearty as ever. As for Danusia, well she managed to avoid the epidemic. Of course she is devastated by Mama's death, quite what she will do now I am not sure. At the moment she is staying with Frau Beckova, they suit each other very well, but I think when our life is back to normal I will ask her if she would like to live with Richard and I, we owe her that at least"

Julius nodded his head, although he was deep in thought. Whilst he realized Danusia would probably want to stay with Richard and Irmy, especially if they were to have children, she might be getting a little too old to be able to care for young infants. He wondered how she would feel about caring for a severely disabled young man. She would be ideal as a companion and carer for Josef. Julius was shaken out of his daydreaming by Irmy saying to him, "are you listening to me Julius? are you tired, would you like to go back inside?"

Julius waved away her concerns as she told him that Colonel Manz had retired with the disintegration of the army, and that Georg was attending the university and was planning to become a lawyer. Julius could hardly believe his ears. Georg, naughty, headstrong, loveable young Georg a lawyer, it just did not seem possible.

"You will find a very changed young man from the Georg you used to know" said Irmy, "Nikolas' death has affected him greatly, and his observations of the war have done much to curb his youthful enthusiasm. It is a pity in a way, I did not think I would ever say this, but sometimes I long for the spirited little devil that was Georg instead of the somber young man he is now" Irmy sighed deeply as she added, "the war has changed so many people, and I can find none of them changed for the better" Brother and sister bent their heads in agreement as they both reflected on how things had changed over the last five years.

As Julius spent his last few days in the hospital, his thoughts kept returning to his mother. He could picture her when he was young, returning from school, she would be in the nursery waiting to share afternoon tea with her children. He remembered her standing on the station platform in Kosice, seeing her three sons leave her, knowing she was losing them to the army which had so dominated her all her married life. Julius wished he had been more aware of his mother's feelings in those days, had understood how difficult life must have been for her. He tried to push away the image that kept appearing in his mind of the embittered woman whom he had encountered on his last leave in Prague, when he had heard of his father's death. He had tried to offer her comfort, but by then it was too late, too much had happened to allow his mother to return to the warm, caring woman he had known. Instead he preferred to remember the woman who had had such pride in her sons, the elegant woman with whom he had danced at the Ball. He talked of his feelings to Irmy, asking her questions about their mother's death.

"Do not blame yourself Julius, I do not think any of us really realized the true extent of Mama's feelings until after Papa died. I do know that it is something I must have felt as well, somewhere deep inside myself, because from a young age I knew I did not want to marry a soldier. I knew I could not

444

have endured the long separations that Mama and Papa suffered. Richard may work long hours at the hospital, but at least he returns to his house every evening. Mama was very ill towards the end, but even during her feverish ramblings she still spoke of the love and affection that she felt for all her children. Believe me, despite her attitude after Papa's death, the old Mama was still there, buried deeply maybe, but she never stopped loving us you know" Irmy stopped for a moment, obviously upset as she thought of her mother's last days, "I am afraid that at the end she just lost the will to live. I have seen it happen many times, especially with the war wounded, men so badly injured that they no longer wish to remain in this world"

Julius thought of Josef and spurred on by the need to talk to someone, and knowing that Irmy would listen with a sympathetic ear, he told her about his meeting with Josef, though he did not mention Josef asking him for a gun. Irmy listened attentively, even when he told her about his plans to bring Josef to Prague. When Julius had finished Irmy took him in her arms as she said, "Julius, I am so sorry, after all you have endured to have found Josef like that. It must have been awful"

"You will help me, please Irmy, you and Richard must help me"

Irmy hesitated then smiled, "of course we will try and help you but there are some things you must understand first. Now I do not want you taking umbrage when I say what I have to say, but I believe you would want me to be honest with you, am I right?"

Julius nodded, the relief of sharing his burden had made him light headed, and he knew whatever Irmy was about to say would not deter him from his course.

"I have worked with so many men like Josef and I have to say many of them are very similar. To us the answers seem so simple, but it is never that easy. What you must understand is that victims like Josef do not think like us. We would think, well thank God he is alive, he has a life in front of him which he should make the best of, but I am afraid many amputees and badly injured patients believe the opposite. All they want is to die, or at least be left alone, so they do not have to face up to the realities of the difficult life they have ahead of them. They see no golden days ahead of them, only misery and despair. To be able to understand their anguish you must try to think like them"

445

Julius listened to his sister, puzzled by what she was trying to tell him, "What are you saying to me Irmy?"

"What I am trying to say is that you cannot live Josef's life for him. What you feel is right for him, may not be what he wants. Tell me truthfully, when he told you what the future held in store for him, did you not think, however fleetingly, how terrible his life is going to be, that maybe it would have been better for him to have died out there on the battlefield?"

"Irmy that is a terrible thing to say, I cannot believe, that you a nurse, who tends the sick, can say such a thing"

"Actually I did not say that Julius. I was asking you if you did not think of such a thing, and you did not answer me, which means that the thought did cross your mind"

Julius fell into an indignant silence, not wishing to confirm his sister's truism.

"I know you want to help Josef, and I think your sentiments are well intentioned. Obviously not all patients are like Josef, but if Josef's injuries are as terrible as you have described to me, then the Josef who I briefly met will have great difficulty coming to terms with those injuries. All I am saying is that if you find Josef and manage to persuade him to come to Prague, then do not expect him to thank you for it and prepare yourself for some very upsetting times because in my experience with situations like the one you are proposing the patient begins to hate his benefactor for the very reasons why he is trying to help him"

Julius was about to argue his case when Irmy kissed him on the cheek and added, "you are too kind for your own good Julius, but if you are determined to pursue this plan of yours then I promise you that Richard and I will help you all we can"

With that Julius had to be content. Irmy had not dismissed his idea out of hand and that gave him heart for the venture.

When the time came for his departure Julius felt quite sad to be leaving the people who had been so kind to him for the last year. He had asked Irmy to buy presents for the nursing staff and they all blushed as he left them all with a kiss on their cheeks. "The old Julius returning I see" said Irmy under her breath as they climbed into their car which was to take them to the railway station. Even Nurse Muller seemed upset to see him go and he was surprised to see the matron come to the hospital entrance and wave goodbye. His last view of her was her standing on the hospital steps, her arms folded majestically under her ample bosom as she shook her head at his departing car.

Saying goodbye to Doktor Sachs had been especially hard. Over the past months he had developed a very special relationship with the doctor. Julius began to regard him as a father figure and was grateful for his wisdom and common sense which had seen him through some very difficult times. When Doktor Sachs had arrived on the ward to say goodbye they had both fallen about laughing. Not wishing to wear his army uniform Irmy had brought some of Julius' old civilian suits with her. Julius had not realized how much weight he had lost until he had donned one of the suits. He looked reminiscent of a clown as the cloth of the suit hung in great swathes of material around his body. The only way he could keep his trousers up were by fastening a belt around his waist and pulling it in as tight as possible. Irmy saw the funny side as well but lamented that they did not have time to have a suit made for him before they left for Prague. Julius could not care a less.

He was sad to be leaving the friends he had made at the hospital but his longing for home had grown even more since Irmy's arrival and now he was eager to begin his journey, however strange he looked. It had been decided that he would make the journey on crutches and use his walking sticks, on which he was now quite adept. Most of the journey did not involve too much walking and Irmy could always obtain assistance if they needed it. Irmy had a wheelchair waiting at home which she had borrowed from the hospital.

"Well, my boy" Doktor Sachs had said, "I cannot say that you have been the easiest of patients, but you will do. I am happy to think that you may behave better for your sister than you did for some of my staff" Doktor Sachs smiled to show he had been teasing Julius, then he whispered, "I do not think you will misbehave as much with your sister, do you?" Both men smiled knowingly at each other as they both looked at Irmy who was chatting to the matron at the end of the bed. It was obvious, even with his short acquaintance, that Doktor Sachs had already obtained the measure of Irmy.

Julius looked fondly at the doctor as he said, "I do not think I can thank you enough for all you have done for me. Thank you for your patience and understanding, without you I do not think I would be here today"

Herr Doktor Sachs shook his head slowly as he said, "I think you would have been, captain, you are a survivor. Now all I ask is that you go from here, fully recover your health, and enjoy life. You are a young man who has so much to look forward to, and you are very lucky, there are many young men of our country" here the doctor stopped as he realized his mistake, "sorry my country, and your country, that have not been as lucky as you"

Both men smiled and as Julius rose and shook the old man's hand, he hoped that one day he would be able to carry out the doctor's wishes, but for the moment he felt as much a victim as the next man. He knew it would be a long time before the memories of the war would ever leave him.

To be out in the world again was wonderful. Even the ride to the station filled Julius with wonder as he perceived people going about their business, following the normal daily routines of their lives. At the station Irmy busied herself seeing to the stowage of their baggage and guiding Julius through the station on his crutches. Julius found it very exhilarating, but was unnerved to find people watching him with his disabilities. Julius was glad to be at last seated in their compartment, away from the staring eyes. Irmy noticed his anxiety and told him to forget his reception. "I am afraid a lot of people want to forget about the war, especially the end of it. It seems if the war is not mentioned it will all go away, if only that were true"

Julius laid his head back onto the seat and closed his eyes, wishing those people could have seen a battlefield, the mutilated bodies, the men crying out in pain, the barbarism inflicted by both sides in the name of war, then they would know war could not be forgotten, should not be forgotten, if only to prevent such a nightmare ever happening again.

After his initial upset, Julius enjoyed the journey. The train was to take them to Vienna, where they were to transfer onto the train to Prague. At first Julius had been excited at the prospect of seeing Vienna again, but Irmy told him that they would only have an hours wait at the station before they caught the night train to Prague. Irmy apologized to Julius but the arrangements had been made before she had known about Josef. Julius had wondered whether he might have visited Josef's mother if they had stayed in Vienna. On reflection Irmy argued that this would

448

not have been such a good idea. It would be better to wait until they had found out about Josef's situation first. Julius was going to need all his diplomatic skills to persuade the von Kutzs to agree to his plan and at the moment, physically at least, Irmy did not feel that Julius was up to clashing with Josef's family, especially his father. Julius saw the sense in this, he knew he would have to be patient and wait until Viktor or even the countess gave him news of Josef, but the anxiety still worried him as he thought of Josef lying alone somewhere thinking that even Julius had deserted him.

The other reason that Irmy had not contemplated staying in Vienna was that Karl was not there as he was visiting Franz in Styria. Irmy had shown Julius photographs of Franz and Gretha on their farm and with them had been a letter from Franz telling Julius that as soon as he was physically better he was to come for a holiday to the farm, the pure air and farm life would be a wonderful tonic for him. Julius looked for a long time at the photographs. He envied his brother, happy with his wife, their smiling faces shone out at him and he was determined that once he had sorted his life out he would go and visit them.

"Maybe if Richard cannot leave his work you and I could go to Graz, I would so love a holiday and to see Franz and Gretha again" added Irmy.

Julius smiled at his sister, much as he knew she would love to visit Franz and Gretha, he knew she had only offered to accompany him out of the kindness of her heart, and because she knew it would make sure that he did indeed take the trip. His heart went out to her, thankful for her kindness and love.

The journey home gave Julius and Irmy the chance to get to know one another again. Julius' recollections of the journey were of the constant conversation between his sister and himself as they caught up with all the news of the last three years. Irmy tried to explain all the events that had led up to the independence of the newly formed state of Czechoslovakia until his mind reeled with the complexity of it all. Irmy's observations were optimistic however, she related the positive feelings of the people in Prague as they experienced life under their new democracy. Julius' feelings were still ambivalent, one moment he had thought himself an Austrian, but now he was an independent Czech allied with the Slovaks. It was all very confusing and not for the

449

first time did he wonder just what and who he had been fighting for for the past four years.

Irmy diplomatically did not talk about Nikolas' death, she seemed to sense that the subject was still too upsetting for her brother, instead she tried to discuss the future with him. Until he had left the hospital Julius had chosen not to think of his future, save one that involved Josef, but he realized after talking with Irmy that he would have to think seriously about what he was to do next. He knew his bank account was quite healthy, Viktor had written that four years of army pay and his inheritance monies had created a fairly large sum, but this would not last forever and Julius discussed with Irmy what he should do next.

The subject frightened him, here he was a young man, twenty nine years of age, with no experience whatsoever apart from thirteen years in the army, an army which no longer existed. Irmy had once remarked that army life was very insular, and Julius now pondered the truth of her statement. The army had been his life, he knew nothing else, so what was he to do now? He knew in the future, if he was to maintain a decent standard of living he would have to gain employment, but what? His talks with Irmy did not alleviate his anxiety. She told him that it would be many months before he would be fit for any employment and he was more than welcome to stay with Richard and herself indefinitely. Although Julius knew that his sister meant every word he had no intention of intruding on her for any longer than was necessary.

Irmy brought up the difficult subject of Mama's house. Evidently it was to be sold, but Franz and Karl had agreed that if Julius needed the house for himself, then the sale could be postponed. Julius was touched by his brother's generosity, but he knew they would need the money from the proceeds of the house as much as he would in the future. Besides, the house was far too large for him alone, and he did not think he could bear to live there, watching for the ghosts of Mama and Papa. "Well it is your decision, we just thought you may need the house if you were thinking of settling down in the future"

Julius was not sure what Irmy had meant by this, but he did not pursue the conversation. Several times Irmy had brought up Erika's name and Julius had pointedly ignored her attempts to find out his true feelings for her. Erika had made it very plain that she was just his friend, and he could

450

not envisage being close to a woman for a very long time. He had too many emotional feelings to contend with, without sharing them with another person.

Vienna station had hardly changed. Before boarding for their train Julius and Irmy had lingered in the coffee house on the station where he had often sat with Nikolas and Viktor as they waited for their trains taking them home from cadet school. There was still the hustle and bustle that he remembered from his youth, but regretfully Julius noticed that somehow the people looked shabbier, with a lethargy that illustrated their disappointments of the past years. The Imperial days had gone, leaving behind a confused and defeated nation trying to pick up the threads of their former lives.

Julius was happy when they were at last settled into their carriage and he could watch the departing city of Vienna as it swept by his window. He had been disappointed with his glimpse of the city, being in the hospital had sheltered him for too long and he knew now he would have to face up to the stark realities of post war life.

XXX

As the train pulled into Prague station Julius stood at the compartment window, supported by his crutches. He had pulled down the window even though it was a chilly day and was excitedly telling Irmy that he could smell the wonderful air of his home city. Irmy shook with laughter, and even their fellow travelling companions were seen to smile as Irmy retorted that she was not aware that Prague smelt of the coal fire and steam that was swirling round their carriage and pervading their compartment through the open window. Julius did not care, he had never felt happier, he was home at last.

Three years had been a long time, but to Julius Prague had not changed at all. The station still held its magical welcome and here there was a marked contrast to the station in Vienna. The people were smiling and straight away Julius noticed the positive attitude of the people that Irmy had told him about. Irmy asked him to wait in the carriage whilst she sorted out their luggage. Julius sat down and watched the scene in front of him, close to tears at the realization that tonight he would be sleeping in a bed in Prague.

Julius turned as he heard someone enter his carriage and was overjoyed to see Richard walking in. Like everyone Richard's face showed the strain of the war, but he looked well, carrying a little more weight than before, which suited him. He immediately sat down next to Julius and smiled a wide smile as he shook his hand.

"Julius it is so good to see you" he said as he pumped his hand, "At last Irmy will be truly happy, now she has you back under her wing and we are going to make you as good as new, mark my words" Julius once again warmed to this remarkable man who was displaying the greatest joy because his wife was happy.

Julius pulled himself up onto his crutches and was pleased to see that Richard did not offer him any help. It was very noticeable, since sustaining his injuries, that people wanted to help too much, feeling that the invalid was incapable of doing anything for himself. With his innate insight Richard left his brother-in-law to raise himself onto his crutches whilst he busied himself collecting their belongings together.

452

Outside the station Julius was led to a motorcar, which was being looked over by several people. "Richard, is this yours?" exclaimed Julius, "I never thought you would have succumbed to all these modern inventions"

Irmy laughed as she said, "It is his pride and joy, he loves it. I would like to learn to drive it as well, but he will not teach me"

"Quite right" replied Julius, "Driving an automobile is not for a lady"

Richard laughed as he said, "I think you are heading for a fall with that argument m'boy. No, my main worry is that these contraptions are not reliable enough, I do not want Irmy stranded in the middle of nowhere if it should stop, that is all. Automobiles are becoming very popular, there is a shortage of horses since the war, and many of these have been bought to take their place"

Richard was not wrong. On their journey home Julius saw many automobiles on the road, far more than before the war. He was also interested to see the attitude of pedestrians as they ignored the metal machines and several times Richard had to stop suddenly as someone walked in front of them into the road.

Julius looked in wonder about him, he could not put his finger on it, but Prague had subtly changed. The fashions were certainly different, particularly for the women. Their dresses and coats were far more slimline than before, with dropped waists that gave the women very different shapes than the nipped in waists and voluminous skirts of his mother's day. Julius found this rather unnerving and at the same time quite appealing.

Several times Julius asked Richard to stop as he saw another landmark that he remembered. Poignantly Richard stopped beside the statue of St. Wenceslas at the top of the square. As Julius sat looking up at their patron saint in all his splendor, it seemed a lifetime away when he had ridden in the cavalcade with such pomp and pride to mark the statue's unveiling.

At last they were home and as Julius struggled out of Richard's automobile the door was flung open and Danusia ran down the steps to greet him. Julius found himself smothered in her ample embrace and was only prevented from toppling over by Irmy shouting, "Danusia, please be careful, Julius is not very strong yet and he has had a tiring journey"

Danusia sprang back from her embrace, tears streaming down her face, as she fussed around Julius, trying to arrange his crutches for him, running in front of him and he thought he really would fall over. This time Richard saved him by passing Danusia a valise and telling her to take it into the house. Richard smiled at the departing rotund figure as he said, "she means well you know, she has been so excited for the last few days. She took your mother's death very badly, your coming home has cheered her up considerably"

"I know" said Julius, "I promise to be kind to her when I get into the house, if she does not knock me over first!"

The next few weeks flew by as Julius began to get used to being home again. Irmy proved to be a harder taskmaster than Nurse Muller and made sure that Julius did his exercises every day as well as massaging his legs for him. Julius found this rather disconcerting and when she first told him to undress he had acted very coyly and had sheepishly asked her to leave the room. Irmy had stood with her hands on her hips and a stern look on her face as she lectured him, "Julius Mayer, I cannot believe you are being so childish, I am only asking you to remove your trousers, not take all your clothes off. I have seen a pair of legs before. Believe me with some of the sights I have seen since beginning my nurses training, the sight of my brother without his trousers will be nothing. We really do not have time for this, unless you want the onus of having to travel to the hospital every day for your massages, we will proceed with them here. Do not tell me you were like this with the nurses in the hospital?"

Julius blushed as he said, "No, but that was different, they were not my sister"

"Julius for heaven sake, stop thinking of me as your sister then, and start thinking of me as your nurse. If you do not take your trousers off soon I will arrange for Erika to come here and give you your massages"

Julius returned his sister's challenging stare. He knew she was sure that he would be even more mortified at the thought of Erika ministering to his legs in the privacy of Irmy's home and so with a deep sigh he started to unbutton his trousers. He was pleased to notice that at least Irmy deigned to feign an interest at something outside the window so that his embarrassment was not wholly complete. Julius was pleased that Irmy, on seeing his legs,

454

was quite optimistic about his progress and he noticed that his scars were becoming less livid and less noticeable than before.

After the first few days, Julius was used to his sister tending him. She had a delicate touch and was far more relaxing than Nurse Muller had been. With Irmy's constant ministrations and the contentment of being home Julius progressed rapidly over the next few weeks to a point where he hardly used his crutches and instead walked with two walking sticks.

Irmy kept him to a strict regime, making sure he walked every day, carried out his exercises and had a healthy diet of well-cooked food, something he had missed in the hospital. Irmy had told him that although there was still a shortage of some supplies the situation was improving, and she made sure the Beck household only had the best of everything. Irmy was also lucky in her domestic staff. She had managed to retain her cook throughout the war and had also employed two new maids at the end of the conflict. As had been predicted women who had enjoyed their employment during the war were loath to give up their new freedoms and were disinclined to return to mere domestic duties which had led to a shortage of domestic staff everywhere. Irmy's cook was first class and was happy to be able to cook for someone who so obviously relished and enjoyed his food as Julius did, unlike Richard and Irmy, who often would return late from work at unsociable times and then just pick at their food.

When Julius had returned to Prague he had told Irmy his intention of having some new suits made, but she had urged him just to have one made for the time being and he was glad to have taken her advice. He started to put on weight with the help of Irmy's cook, and within a few weeks his first suit was beginning to feel very tight.

On his return Julius' only anxiety had been that he knew he would have to face Nikolas' parents but he was spared the dreaded meeting when Irmy told him that Frau Manzova had not been well and so Nikolas' father had taken her to a spa resort, in order for her to recover her health. Julius was relieved to hear that the Manzs would not be returning to Prague for some weeks.

Julius was sitting reading a book in Irmy's sitting room one day when he heard the sound of the doorbell ring. He looked up as the door opened and in walked Georg. The sight of the young man, looking so like his brother made Julius gasp and he felt his heart tightening as the grief of Nikolas' death once more swept over him. Julius tried to jump up to greet his young friend but Georg motioned for him to stay seated as he advanced towards him and shook his hand. Julius had the overwhelming feeling that Georg had wanted to embrace him, but something had held him back. Julius was upset to see a sadness and somberness in Georg's eyes where once there had been such spirit and fire.

After summoning Irmy's maid and asking for a cup of coffee for his guest Julius tried to engage Georg in conversation, but the talk was stilted and uneasy, so much so that against his own wishes Julius asked, "Georg, what is the matter, are you trying to avoid what you really want to talk about, do you want to talk about Nikolas?"

Georg sat looking miserable and his face reddened as he said, "I wanted to come and see you Julius, and I knew you would want to talk about Nikolas, but do you mind if we do not? I know it would help you, but I really do not think I can talk about him at the moment, do you mind awfully?"

Julius wanted to laugh out loud and shout for joy. Ever since Georg had walked into the room he had dreaded having to tell him the truth of his brother's death, and now he did not want to talk about his brother at all. Julius knew it was a coward's way out, but he was thankful none the less.

After assuring Georg that he was perfectly happy to accede to his wishes Georg started to relax and Julius began to see a trace of the old Georg coming to the surface at times. He told him about his life at the university, about his ambition to become a lawyer. When Julius asked him why he had decided to become a lawyer Georg merely shrugged his shoulders and said, "I do not know really, the law has always intrigued me and I knew I had to do something"

Julius nodded, wondering how many other young men were like him and Georg, their livelihood taken away and now trying to find a new objective for their lives, thousands he supposed.

The afternoon passed pleasantly enough, there was some mention of the war but Julius could see that Georg did not want to dwell on the past so he told him about his brothers and Viktor. He also mentioned Josef in passing, but did not tell Georg the full extent of his injuries, Julius had

456

the feeling that Georg did not want to contend with such realities at the moment.

At last Georg rose to leave, promising that he would return to see Julius. With a hint of mischief Julius said, "It is a pity you cannot stay until Irmy returns, she will have been sorry to have missed you"

Georg looked at Julius and a large smile crossed his face, an angelic smile that once again caused Julius to pause at the memory of his dead friend, but at the same time it made him happy, because for a fleeting moment he was reminded of the Georg he had known, the mischievous little boy who has crashed into his mother's living room so long ago, when Julius had first met his friend's little brother.

"Very funny, Julius" chuckled Georg, "I think I am over my schoolboy crush now" his face clouded over again as the old Georg was lost once more, "too much has happened since then, it seems a long time ago"

Julius' heart went out to the young man as he made a decision, "I know you do not want to talk about Nikolas now, but if ever you do, you know where to find me. I understand how you feel you know, you are not alone. Everyone keeps telling me to talk about everything, that it will make things better, but I know I cannot, not yet, but I am always here to listen, maybe we can help one another"

Georg did not say a word as they walked towards the door, he turned to Julius, and this time they embraced. As he left the room Georg whispered, "goodbye Julius, and thank you"

Julius returned to his seat with a heavy heart. He had meant what he had said to Georg. If he had asked him to tell him about Nikolas he would have told him. He would have to one day he knew, but deep down he was glad that it had not been today, not yet, he was not ready.

Out of the pocket of his jacket he pulled out a sepia photograph and stared at it for a long time. It had been taken in the mountains. He and Nikolas stood with their arms around each other's shoulders, both laughing heartily as though they had just been told a very good joke. They stood in front of one of the timber huts, knee deep in snow, looking as if they did not have a care in the world. Julius traced the outline of the cherubic smile of his friend with his finger. A day did not go by when he did not think of Nikolas, when he did not blame himself for his death, when he did not ask God why he could not have been taken instead of Nikolas. Julius sat staring at the photograph as the

457

afternoon light dwindled to a shadowy dusk and even when he could no longer distinguish the forms on the card, he still sat clutching the precious memento of happier times.

Julius was dismayed when he did not receive a reply from Viktor or the countess, but his life was so busy with Richard and Irmy that the waiting did not seem so onerous as when he had lain in his hospital bed waiting for the mail to arrive. Julius had a steady stream of visitors, Danusia visited him daily and at times drove him to distraction as she fussed over him, wanting to see to his every whim. Whilst he knew her heart was in the right place, her attention became annoying until he began to wonder if proposing her as a carer for Josef had been such a good idea. Irmy did her best to protect him from Danusia's excesses, but at times she was seen to be trying to hold back her laughter behind Danusia's back as Julius pleaded with his eyes for an escape.

Danusia had obviously been deeply affected by the death of Frau Mayer. She talked of her continually and although Julius joined in with her reminiscences of his mother, he became aware that he was developing a very detached view of the death of his parent. Perhaps it was his battle to regain his health or just the acceptance of so many deaths over the last few years but he could not summon the tears he knew he should be crying for the loss of his mother. He confided his fears to Irmy who encouraged him to accompany her to Mass occasionally. Julius dutifully went to church, but the outing gave him no solace for his guilt.

He realized that because of the last few years he had lost his faith in a God who could inflict the horrors of war, the death and mutilation of so many men. He could not defend a God who had taken his best friend and who had so maimed another and he declined any further invitations from Irmy to accompany her to church. To her credit she did not try and persuade him otherwise, although Julius knew that she secretly hoped that one day he would once more know the benefit and comfort that the church could give him.

Erika often came to see him and sometimes they would go for a walk together, Julius insisting on using his walking sticks. Erika had greeted Julius with all her old warmth despite the fact that Julius knew he had greatly upset her in the hospital. He tried to make amends and before long they had fallen back into their old camaraderie. Julius was grateful to her for all her help, especially at the hospital, but he knew now they would only ever be friends, nothing more. This exasperated Irmy, who had obviously hoped their time together in Austria would have reunited Julius and Erika, and Julius and Erika found a perverse pleasure in teasing Irmy about their friendship until one day she threw up her hands in disgust and said, "very well, I concede defeat. I am not interested in the two of you any more and I will not interfere. I just do not understand you" Irmy had flounced out of the room, leaving Julius and Erika shaking with laughter and it was noticeable that from that time on Irmy accepted the fact that he and Erika were just good friends and that they were content with their situation.

Julius had to start accepting his new country. On the surface, nothing much had changed. Although the Czech language was certainly more prevalent, German was still universally spoken and the landmarks and road signs still bore their German names. It was strange to send mail with 'Posta Cesko Slovenska' written on the stamps and there was a new currency, where one hundred haleru equaled one koruna, but apart from that life did not seem to be much altered.

Once, when he had gone into the middle of Prague with Erika he had asked her if she would mind walking up to the Loreto Square to see the old Imperial Army Headquarters. The walk was hard and several times the steepness of the road and the cobbles caused Julius to stumble. Erika supported him as at last they crested the hill and came face to face with the old building. During his time with the army in Prague Julius had often climbed the hill to the headquarters, the large building always flying the Empire's flag. The flag was now gone, replaced with the flag of his new country, but the stone carved Imperial double headed eagle still presided majestically above the building's entrance. It seemed a lifetime ago when he would climb this hill and see the royal standard and be so proud to be a Son of the Eagle.

They stopped and sat down on a bench on the opposite side of the square to the building. Julius and Erika sat there for a long time, Erika diplomatically remaining silent as Julius sat staring at the edifice in front of them. Even this relic of the old Empire was shabby and forlorn. Where once there had been soldiers marching and constant activity, now all was quiet, a last remnant of the Austro-Hungarian Army neglected and forsaken. Without saying a word, Julius rose from his seat and started the long weary journey down the hill, hanging on to Erika's arm. He did not look back, he had seen enough.

Later, as they sat in a coffeehouse, Julius started to discuss his future with Erika. He had told her about Josef and she had been shocked at the news of his horrendous injuries. At first, after disclosing his plans to look after Josef, she had been as apprehensive as Irmy had been of such a large undertaking, but when she had saw how determined Julius was she had agreed to give him any help he needed. His plans for Josef were largely theoretical at the moment as he had yet to find out where his friend was now living, but he knew he also had to decide what he was going to do about his own future. He knew his army career would not help him.

Ever since leaving the hospital he had become more and more aware of how ill equipped he was for any future outside a military life. The mere fact that he had been a soldier in the Austro-Hungarian Army aroused derision in some of the people he met. Czechs were even more passionately nationalistic than before and now looked upon the partisan soldiers and those soldiers who had defected to fight with the Russians, as the heroes of the war. At the same time soldiers like Julius, who had fought for their Imperial dictators, were treated by some with contempt and dismissed as a past embarrassment. Julius found this treatment very hard to bear and it depressed him that all the Bohemian soldiers who had given their lives for their country and Emperor were now seen as foolish, deluded people, who did not deserve the name of hero. Happily this attitude was not true of all Czech citizens, most realized the huge sacrifice that all young men had made for their country, in whatever army they had fought and many would stop Julius in the street, or tip their hats in recognition of a war-wounded veteran.

Erika advised him, as Irmy had done, not to worry too much about what he was going to do, suggesting that he reach full health again before he began to think about his future. Julius knew she was implying that they did not know if he would attain his full health, and this might affect any future profession that he was contemplating, but he knew he was regaining his health rapidly. Although some days were easier than others and he still tired quite easily, he

460

could feel a strength returning to him that he had not felt for a long time. He was still often in considerable pain, but he realized that, either because his body was used to pain and could endure it better than before, or because the pain was less than it had been, it was a pain that he could now live with. He still enjoyed several glasses of brandy at night, but these were taken surreptitiously in his room, away from prying eyes. He knew he was still probably drinking too much, but the alcohol helped him sleep when sometimes the pain proved too much or his nightmares returned. No doubt his medication had enabled him to endure the worst months of his pain and he knew that now, with fewer pills, he should start to face life without seeking refuge in a bottle of alcohol, but he had yet to face that moment of truth.

Julius had been in Prague for two months and he was upset that he had not received a reply to his letter from the countess. Viktor had written a cheerful letter, telling him that he was now working for his father at the family bank, a situation which greatly pleased his family and his new wife, but of which he was not so sure. As he wrote 'I know I am fortunate in that I can find employment so easily, as you wrote Julius, military life did not equip us with a great deal of opportunities for the outside world, but I do feel this was the one thing I never wanted to do, one of the reasons I joined the army in the first place. Well, never mind, I am finding my employment quite interesting. My elder brother is a senior partner with my father, so I am given the task of visiting our more affluent clients, and endowing them with the 'Leitner personal touch' as my brother calls it, such is commerce. Actually I am finding it quite diverting, and it means I can travel around quite a lot, which suits me admirably as I cannot bear to be holed up in my office at the bank all day, which I am sure would eventually drive me insane. Too much of the outdoor life over the last few years I think.

Soon I am being sent further afield, in a few weeks I am travelling to Vienna to visit some of our clients. I am determined to visit Josef's mother whilst I am there, because I am afraid despite frequent enquiries made by myself, the mystery of Josef's whereabouts remains just that, a mystery. I am hoping by making a personal visit I can persuade Josef's family that all we want to do is help, I hope so anyway. I also thought I might try and find out what has happened to Smid, I would like to know if the old

461

boy is all right. Anyway I will keep you informed and will let you know as soon as I have any news regarding Josef. Who knows, on my travels I may one day visit Prague, my father still has some clients in your country who do not mind banking with mere Austrians!' Viktor finished his letter by sending his regards to Julius' family and sending him best wishes for his health from Sonia, his wife, with the hope that she would have the honor of meeting him one day. Julius was cheered by Viktor's letter. He was certain that Viktor's presence in Vienna would ensure that he would be able to find Josef's whereabouts. He felt envious of his friend with his wife, his employment, the freedom to travel about, and he hoped that sometime in the future he might have the opportunity to aspire to the same things too.

Julius did not receive a communication from Viktor for the next three weeks, and he began to worry that his friend had had to cancel his trip to Vienna, but he felt sure that Viktor would have written to him if that had been the situation, he knew how much Julius was relying on him for news of Josef. The weather started to turn colder as Prague prepared to brace itself for the onset of winter. Outside the days were frequently wet and windy and the leaves on the trees began to turn to their beautiful autumnal colors, allowing the city to take on a golden glow before the austerity of winter finally pervaded her streets.

One morning Julius carefully descended the stairs, desperately in need of a cup of coffee. He had been out drinking the night before and was now regretting his actions as his head felt like there were a thousand mallets inside his skull, all hammering to get out.

He had woken up fairly late and when he had entered the dining room had encountered Richard sitting at the table reading his newspaper. His brother-in-law had peered over his newspaper and after taking a few moments to look at Julius had observed, "I have to tell you Julius, the combination of your pills and alcohol will do you no good whatsoever"

Although at that moment, feeling as he did, Julius would have to agree with Richard, he was not about to give him the satisfaction of being right. His situation was not eased by Irmy entering the room, looking bright and cheerful, and saying, "Good heavens Julius, you look absolutely terrible" he was just contemplating whether trying to gain some sympathy by telling her that physically he felt unwell when she continued, "not that I have much sympathy for you, alcohol and your medication are not the wisest of partners"

Feeling outnumbered and devoid of any sympathetic understanding from his family Julius sat down at the table and sulked over his cup of coffee.

With an impish grin on her face, Irmy asked, "No breakfast today, Julius? You are sure I cannot tempt you with a nice softly boiled egg or some speck?" Julius' stomach turned somersaults as the thought of the greasy food made him feel nauseous. Richard laid his paper on the table and Julius knew he was about to receive a stern lecture as Richard took off his spectacles and started to clean them with his handkerchief, his face a picture of concern as he sat trying to choose his words. "I know you will think I am being harsh with you Julius, but as your doctor, and as your brother-in-law, I have to say that your drinking is not good for you. I realize that in the hospital drink was often a welcome release from your pain, but it is most certainly not the answer, especially not whilst you are taking the medicines that you have been prescribed"

Julius slumped in his seat, he should have known that Richard would have known about the illicit alcohol which was prevalent on the hospital wards.

"My other worry is how addictive alcohol can become, especially when it is drunk in large quantities" continued Richard, "alcohol will not help you restore your health Julius, it will only hinder it" Julius remained silent, he was about to argue with Richard that he was not drinking a lot, but he knew that a day did not go by without having at least a few drinks, and that, perhaps unkindly, he had included Danusia in his deceptions by persuading her to bring him a bottle of brandy when she came to visit him. He had instructed her not to tell anybody and with her undying adulation of her former charge had thought nothing of deceiving Irmy and Richard in carrying out this small thing for Julius. He had also, as his mobility improved, begun to go out by himself for the evening to one of the local hostelries and enjoy more than a few drinks with anyone who cared to drink with him.

Several times he had returned home very much the worse for wear, but he thought he had been quiet enough not to arouse the suspicions of Irmy and Richard, but he had obviously not been circumspect enough.

463

He sat at the breakfast table, aware of the concerned gazes of Irmy and Richard as they waited for an answer from him. Julius swallowed hard as he said, "I am sorry if I worried you or if I have disrupted your household, I promise I will try to look after myself in future. I can contain my drinking, it is really not a problem and thank you for your concern, both of you"

Irmy rose from her seat and put her arms around her brother's shoulders as she said, "you know we only have your best interests at heart, Julius, because we care for you so much, and I know you will be careful about how much you drink from now on"

Irmy at least seemed content but Julius was unnerved to look up and observe Richard watching him with a decidedly skeptical look from behind his glasses.

Later that morning Julius was lying on his bed as he tried to rid himself of the fearful headache that was still pervading his head when he heard a knock on his door. Expecting one of Irmy's maids to enter the room he was greatly surprised and overjoyed when Viktor walked in, looking very affluent as befitted a banker.

In some ways Viktor had not changed since Julius had met him in Vienna, over thirteen years beforehand. True he was no longer the spotty, somewhat nervous adolescent he had once been. Over the years he had matured into a stocky, broad man who walked with a dignity and grace that had endeared him to all the men he had served with, but Julius could still see glimpses of the young man, who had so nervously ventured into the army all those years ago. Viktor was now sporting a rather austere black moustache, which although Julius thought it aged his friend somewhat, nonetheless suited the elegant suit and overcoat that he now wore.

Julius leapt off his bed to embrace his friend, bombarding him with so many questions that he did not give Viktor the chance to answer any of them. "Viktor, why did you not tell me you were coming? what a wonderful surprise. Why did the maid not take your coat? here let me take it from you. How long have you been in Prague? what do you think of my city? How was Vienna? You have good news for me I hope?"

Viktor held up his hands in submission, "Julius, let me catch my breath, so many questions"

464

For the first time Julius was alarmed to notice that there was no jollity in Viktor's demeanor and his face did not break into its usual smile and an inner sense told Julius that his friend was not here on a social visit, but was the bringer of bad tidings. Feeling immediately subdued Julius took his friend's coat, and as he sat on his bed he bade his friend be seated in a chair beside the bed. Once he was settled Viktor allowed himself a first smile, but with quickening dread Julius noticed it was merely a smile of comfort which overshadowed a deeper sadness.

"Julius, I had to come and see you. What I have to tell you I could not tell you in a letter, it would have been too cruel of me"

Julius could not bring himself to look at his friend, for he knew what he was to say next. "I am truly sorry to have to tell you this Julius, but Josef is dead"

As though in slow motion Julius slipped off his bed and limped to the window. He stood looking out at the autumnal leaves that were falling from their branches onto the wet gray street outside Irmy's house. His room was warm and cozy, heated by a roaring fire in the grate but Julius felt cold and numb as if the life had flowed out of his body.

Still looking out of the window, unable to meet his friend's eye Julius at last managed to find his voice and with a coarse whisper he asked Viktor, "How did he die?"

With his back to his friend, Julius could perceive a moments hesitation in his reply as Viktor said, "his family said that he died of his injuries sustained in the war"

Julius turned to Viktor and looking directly at him said, "but that is not true is it Viktor?"

Viktor returned his stare with a look of amazement on his face, which he quickly hid as he said, "How did you....why would you say that?"

Julius limped across the room and grabbing another chair sat down to face Viktor, "tell me the truth Viktor, Josef took his own life, I am right am I not?"

The blood drained from Viktor's face and he appeared to collapse in his seat as he said, "I do not know, truly I do not. I am so confused since my trip to Vienna I do not know what to think"

Julius could see that the stress of his trip to Vienna had upset his friend and he was now concerned that he himself had added to that distress. "Just tell me what happened in Vienna, Viktor, I need to know"

465

Viktor settled himself in his chair, relieved to be able to discuss everything with Julius, "when I got to Vienna the family would not see me at first. I knew they were fobbing me off with excuses and in the end I was getting rather angry at their treatment of me. I resolved I would find out where Josef was. I knew there was little chance of gaining any respect from the odious father, so I wrote to Josef's brothers, and in no uncertain terms I told them their silence would not stop me in my determination. In fact I told them that if they did not tell me themselves I would have to resort to progressing with other means, which could mean talking to all sorts of people in Vienna, which may have proved rather embarrassing to their family"

Julius had to admire Viktor's tenacity, he did not know if he would have had the courage to stand up to Josef's family in the same situation.

"Well the threat worked" continued Viktor, "for by return of post I had a letter from Josef's elder brother requesting that I meet him at the family house. I must say I was very apprehensive, I had rather resorted to bully boy tactics and I did not know how I would be received. Although I am not sure I particularly liked Josef's brother, he had neither the looks or charm of Josef, I found him a decent enough chap, a bit full of his own self importance which I found strange after recent events, but there you are, some people are never going to let go of the old Imperial legacy. Anyway, when I told him that you had in fact seen Josef at the hospital and why we were interested in finding him he was obviously shocked that we knew the extent of his injuries, and though I could not be sure, rather moved by what we wanted to do for our friend. That is when he told me that we were too late, that Josef had died three weeks ago and had been buried in the family crypt in the grounds of their house. But do you know, all the time he was telling me this the man could not look me in the eye and I had the unnerving feeling then that he was not telling me the whole truth. As I took my leave he said, 'Tell Captain Mayer that we thank him for the concern that he showed for my brother. He was very lucky to have been able to call you both friends' and do you know I think I detected some sadness and even a little envy in his speech. A very rum fellow, very rum indeed"

Viktor sat in his chair for a moment, pondering what Josef's brother had said before he continued, "anyway, maybe I would have not thought too much more on the subject, but as I was being shown out of the house their butler, do you remember the little chap who always looked as if he had a nasty smell under his nose?" Julius nodded, "well, as he was helping me on with my coat, he looked around to make sure he was not being overheard, then he said, 'they did wrong by Master Josef, their treatment of him was reprehensible, he did not deserve that. He may have been a bit arrogant and vain but deep down he had a warm heart, and thank God he is free from his pain now, even though it was the wrong thing for him to do, but they could not even forgive him that, they are just pleased to be relieved of the burden' I thought the poor man was about to break down as he continued, 'I am sorry sir, take no notice of me, I am just an old fool being very stupid. You know, Master Josef thought a lot of you and your friends, at least he had your friendship, because God knows he did not have much else that was fortunate in his short life' It was not until later that evening that I really thought about what the little man had said, and then I started to wonder what was 'a wrong thing for him to do'

Over the next few days, whilst doing business on behalf of my father, I met quite a few people who had known or had contacts with the von Kutz family, and it was then I discovered that there was a rumor going around Vienna that Josef had committed suicide, mainly because his family had shunned him, but that the family had hushed it up to avoid a scandal and to make sure that Josef could be buried in the family vault, rather than in unconsecrated ground. They preferred the story that Josef had died a war hero, rather than someone who had taken his own life. Until today I have tried to dismiss these rumors as just scurrilous gossip, but how did you know he would have attempted suicide Julius?"

As the flames of the untended fire began to diminish and the room started to grow dark from the gathering dusk of the autumnal afternoon for the first time Julius related to Viktor the events of that fateful evening when he had visited Josef.

When Julius had finished Viktor sat in stunned silence for quite a while, taking in the full extent of the ending of Josef's wretched life. Eventually he said, "it was very unfair of Josef to ask you to help him to end his life Julius, what a burden that must have imposed upon you, especially as it

467

was in lieu of a stupid oath we made to each other on a drunken night so many years ago, why did you not tell me all of this before? Do not tell me you see this as some burden of guilt, you must not. Do you not see, Josef was only talking in his anguish and his pain, he would not have blamed you"

Julius felt himself plunge into to the depths of despair as he replied, "you were not there Viktor, you do not understand. Josef meant every word, I can hear that terrible voice accusing me now, and it is something I cannot forget. I should have helped him, at least he would have been with a friend at the end, instead of being frightened and alone"

"Julius stop this now. I will not listen to such idiocy. I know you well enough to know you could never have persuaded yourself to help Josef, just as you are feeling such guilt now, think of the guilt you would be carrying if you had been a party to Josef's death, you would not have been able to live with yourself"

Something stirred in Julius' befuddled brain and he said, "What I do not comprehend is why Josef's mother did not help him. She adored Josef, I am sure she would not have allowed the family to disregard Josef, it is something I will never understand"

Julius was distressed to see Viktor's face take on a somber mask as he said, "my God, I am so sorry Julius, I did not tell you, the Countess died from the influenza epidemic at the beginning of this year. Josef's brother told me they had been advised not to inform Josef as the shock would have been too great for him in his weak condition"

Julius thought he would faint and he felt in danger of being physically sick as he realized the awful fate that life had put before him. How much more grief and sadness could he take? He tried to remember the countess as she had been on the night she had come to his room, but her face would not come to his mind. Maybe they should have told Josef, perhaps the shock would have killed him and he could have joined his mother in hopefully a happier place than either of them had endured on earth. Then another thought leapt into his mind, "Oh my God Viktor, do you know what this means? all those months Josef lay maimed, frightened, alone he believed that even his adored mother had deserted him, if only he could have known the truth. He died thinking the only person on this earth who truly cared about him had abandoned him because she could not face the realities of

468

his injuries, how could his family have done that to him?"
Startled by his vehemence Viktor said, "you cannot blame them completely Julius, they thought they were doing the right thing, they did not know of Josef's true state of mind"
"They might have if any of them had bothered to visit him" argued Julius.
"That may be true, but we cannot live on maybes. What is done is done, it will not bring Josef back"
Maybe not thought Julius, but what was also true was that Josef had gone to meet his maker not only believing that his beloved mother had abandoned him but that also he, Julius, had done the same, and it was this circumstance that Julius did not know if he could live with.

Viktor continued to try and show Julius how wrong he was to bear any guilt over Josef's death, but despite all his protestations, Julius ignored the well-meant advice of his friend.

Viktor had to leave to catch his train to Salzburg and Julius was relieved when Viktor reluctantly took his leave. Viktor left Julius sitting in his chair and Julius was not really aware of his friend leaving the room, he was so wrapped in his own somber thoughts. Julius rose from his chair and went to look out of his window. It was some minutes before he saw Viktor leave the house and climb into his hansom cab. Part of him wanted to run out and grab Viktor, beg him to stay. Viktor was his last link to his past life, but as he watched his friend depart he wondered if even Viktor would understand or even forgive Julius. He felt that in some way he had caused the deaths of his two best friends and part of him wished he was with them, at least he would be released from the hell where he now found himself.

Viktor's news had been the final straw, he had lived too long with the guilt of Nikolas' death and now he had to live with the fact that he had been too late to help Josef. He wondered how Viktor would have reacted if he had told him about Nikolas as well. He knew his friend would have supported him, told him he was stupid to feel such guilt, but he knew all the words in the world would not relieve his suffering and as he looked into the future he felt its bleakness and loneliness enveloping him, with no respite from the burdens that he carried.

He heard a light knock on the door and without turning round knew that it was Irmy entering the room. "Julius, are you all right? Viktor told me about Josef, I am so sorry. Can I do anything to help?"

Whilst Julius knew that his sister's only thought was for his care her solicitous words grated on him and he wanted to shout at her to go away, but he found some self control as, without turning to look at her he said, "no, I am fine. If it is all right with you I would just like to be left by myself for a while"

Julius could feel Irmy hesitating as she said, "of course, I understand, but I am just downstairs if you need me"

With blessed relief Julius heard his door shut quietly and he knew he was alone. He shut his eyes, trying to stem the tears that had come to him, then he walked to the side of his bed and from the cabinet he pulled out a bottle of brandy and sought the only solace that he knew would help him.

XXXI

Julius could never really remember his life over the next few months. Whenever he tried to recall the time after he found out about Josef's death it was in distant flashes of a life that belonged to somebody else, not to him. That he sank into the depths of depression and selfishness that even he did not think possible was evident. He started to lose interest in himself and in his life and abandoned any resemblance of his former existence that was possible. Most evenings would find him in the local hostelries of the city, where, fortified by his continuous imbibing of alcohol during the day, he would abandon himself to the oblivion that his heavy drinking afforded him. Several times he would wake up in the morning in the bed of some prostitute or obliging woman, not having the slightest idea of how he had come to her bed, or indeed even where he was. He would often arrive back at Irmy and Richard's house mid morning, unshaven and dirty, ignoring the disapproving looks of the servants as he pulled himself up to his room where he would fall onto his bed to sleep off his dissolute behavior of the night before.

Most of the time Richard was at the hospital and so happily did not see his unorthodox homecomings but when he did he would never say a word but would give Julius a baleful stare as they passed one another. Even Irmy adopted the attitude that Julius was to be treated carefully through his troubles but at times she would remonstrate with her brother about his behavior. Depending on his inebriated state Julius would either brush aside her lectures or merely tell her she could not possibly understand what he was going through and to leave him alone. Although Julius knew he was upsetting and hurting Irmy, he carried on with the persistent pursuit of his own self-destruction.

Several times Irmy had confiscated the bottles of drink in his room and she had reduced Danusia to tears with her scolding when she had caught her smuggling in a bottle to Julius. Julius simply did not care, his only thoughts on the incident were that he had lost a convenient source for obtaining alcohol, nothing more. Besides, it did not really matter, with his mobility so much restored he was quite capable of buying his own alcohol now, which he did, frequently.

471

When Erika visited Julius she rebuked him for his disregard of his personal hygiene and health. He rarely bothered to shave these days and his drinking had started to have an affect on his appearance. Julius, who was enduring yet another horrific hangover just waved her criticisms away and told her she did not know what she was talking about. Julius' visitors became less and less as he continued to sink into the depths of his own despair.

One day he received a rare visit from Georg. Georg found Julius lying face down on his bed as, although it was mid morning, Julius had only just returned home and was still imbued with the alcohol from the night before. He had not even been aware of Georg entering his room until he felt a tap on his shoulder and he had opened a red, bloodshot eye to his visitor. As always when he first saw Georg he thought Nikolas had returned to him, and in his befuddled state he could almost believe that it was indeed his friend standing beside his bed. "Nikolas?" Julius murmured.

"No, Julius, it is Georg, are you all right?"

Julius tried to raise his head and the effort was too much as he slumped back into the pillow.

"What has happened to you Julius?, look at the state of you, what is wrong?" Julius did not like the patronizing tone in Georg's voice and the last thing he desired at that moment was a lecture by a young pup, even if he was Nikolas' brother. He murmured an expletive and in no uncertain terms told Georg to go away.

Georg's voice was incredulous as he said, "Julius, I have never seen you like this before. Erika said something about your present state, but nothing of this"

Julius had had enough, something inside him snapped and he sat up on his bed, his head spinning, and once more swore at Georg as he told him he was not prepared to be preached at by a boy just out of diapers who should know better. Julius could see Georg's face redden and if he had been sober enough he might have noticed the determination and resolution on his face that had always been prevalent on Nikolas' face on the rare times when he had been incensed with anger.

Julius was not prepared for what happened next as Georg seized him by the lapels of his jacket and yanked him up from his bed. Even if Julius had been sober, in his physically weakened condition he would have been no

472

match for the strong and powerful Georg, but in his intoxicated state all Julius could do was hang from the tight grip that Georg held him in as they stared at each other, nose to nose.

"I do not know what the matter is Julius, I am not even sure I care, but you are not going to solve your problems like this. You are a disgrace to the uniform you used to wear, and if it were not for the affection I knew my brother had for you I would give you a good hiding for what you just said to me" Georg's eyes narrowed as he said, "do not ever speak to me like that again, or I may not be able to answer for my actions"

With that Georg threw Julius roughly back onto the bed, picked up his hat and walked towards the door. "Do you know I always admired you Julius, but now all I can think of is how life is so unfair, that you are here and Nikolas is not. Do you think he would have wanted to see you in this condition?" Without another word Georg turned on his heels and walked out of the room, slamming the door behind him.

For a long time Julius lay on the bed, his clothing crumpled and his pride shattered, as he realized what a pathetic figure he must have looked to Georg. His parting words rang in his ears, repeating themselves over and over again until he fell into a troubled sleep. When Julius woke up he asked Irmy's maid to run him a bath and for the first time in several days he bathed and shaved himself. Sobered up, he presented himself in the dining room that evening and although the conversation was very stilted between himself, Richard and Irmy, they chose not to question him about his reformed state but Irmy was seen to smile for the first time in a very long time.

His rehabilitation was not to last. Although he tried very hard to face up to his problems, in his temperate state Julius found it hard to cope with life. After a few days he began to reassess his conversation with Georg and in his fragile state of mind began to see Georg's words as a damning indictment of himself, that he was alive and Nikolas was not. Georg was right, it was unfair and his fault and once more he turned to the bottle for an escape from the realities of the world.

It was the beginning of December, outside the streets were covered in white frost as winter approached. Snow had begun to fall very lightly, giving the streets a romantic air as everyone prepared for the Christmas festivities. Julius now hated the snow, it brought a harsh reminder of the terrible winters at the front, when all he had desired was to be home for Christmas with his loved ones. Julius thought the situation ironic, here he was with the life he had so often dreamed of whilst sitting frozen in his trench and yet now he wished he was a thousand miles away, away from Irmy and Richard's accusing eyes, away from his despair and hopelessness. No one came to visit him any more, not even Danusia, he had abused all his friends just once too often. He could not blame them, he did not even like himself. He had not spoken to Georg since the debacle of their meeting, although he knew that Georg still came to see Richard and Irmy. From his window he had seen him walking up the steps to the front door. Several times he had sat in his chair waiting with bated breath to hear the knock on his door but it never came. He could not blame Georg, he only had himself to blame. That was the trouble, he only had himself to blame for everything. Even Irmy did not come to his room any more. They would see each other in passing in the house, but she did not bother to seek his company.

One morning Irmy opened her door to be met by the sight of a constable supporting her half comatose brother, who was murmuring a song to himself as the policeman explained to Irmy that Julius had been found wandering the streets that morning and was not carrying any monies or identification with him. Irmy ushered the man into her house asking how he had managed to find her. The policeman explained that Julius had managed to slur an address, but that was about all he could ascertain from the young man. With grateful thanks Irmy called Richard's valet to take Master Julius up to his room and put him into his bed. The valet, who had no great estimation of Julius, roughly took him upstairs and unceremoniously dumped him onto his bed before leaving the room.

When Julius awoke several hours later he was surprised to find himself in his bedroom as he had no recollection of the night before, nor what had taken place. As he lay on the bed, his head spinning, Irmy entered the room carrying a tray laden with cups and a pot of steaming coffee. Julius felt most unwell but the look on Irmy's face prevented him from commenting on her presence in his room. Without saying a word Irmy poured out two cups of coffee and after handing one to Julius she picked up her own cup and proceeded to sit down on one of the chairs beside Julius' bed. Irmy did not say a word as she sipped her coffee, but merely looked at Julius over the rim of her cup. Julius still felt quite drunk and his sister's silence began to unnerve and anger him.

"All right Irmy, stop playing your games. Say what you have to say, get it over and done with and then please leave, I have not the stomach for one of your lectures today"

Irmy put down her cup as she said, "Julius do you know how you arrived home today? No I thought you did not, you were far too drunk as I recall. You were brought home by a member of the local constabulary, who had found you wandering the streets, like some vagabond, with no monies, what on earth happened to you?"

Julius tried to search his mind as to what had happened to him the night before but for the life of him he could not remember. He knew he had had his wallet with him when he had left the house last night and there had been quite a lot of money in it but where he had mislaid it he had no idea. His sister's questioning was tiresome, all he wanted to do was close his eyes and go back to sleep. "I have no idea, little sister" he answered sarcastically, "but who cares, I am here safe and sound am I not?"

Julius saw the look of anger that crossed Irmy's face as she replied, "Julius, this cannot go on, I have had quite enough of your behavior of late. I have tried to be understanding, to tolerate your misdemeanors, but today was the last straw. To return to this house with a policeman, what must the servants have thought?"

"Ah" said Julius, Irmy's sanctimonious tone annoying him, "now we have the truth. You do not care about *me*, it is your precious reputation you care about. How you will look in front of your servants, and think Irmy, what if any of your neighbors saw me this morning. What a scandal for poor Herr Doktor and Frau Beckova"

Irmy jumped up from her seat, and with her hands on her hips stood defiantly in front of Julius, "how dare you say that Julius, you know me better than to think that of me, but I cannot endure your profligate behavior for much longer. Just look at you, you are destroying yourself. You have alienated all your friends and if you carry on like you are, you will lose even my support. I have tried to help you Julius, but you seem determined to push everybody away. For God's sake stop wallowing in your own self pity, sort yourself out and get on with the rest of your life or one day you may wake up and find you have lost everything"

Because Julius knew that Irmy was telling the truth, he found her words even harder to bear, and though he heard the terrible words come out of his mouth and knew they were deplorable things to say, he could not stop himself.

"Oh stop being so sanctimonious Irmy. You always were a pious prig, but you could be as unkind as the rest of us. Look how you treated Nikolas, do you know how unhappy you made him?" As soon as he heard the words come out of his mouth Julius knew he had been wrong to say them, but his mouth seemed to run away with him as his mind screamed at him to stop.

Irmy had turned quite ashen as he continued, "you knew how much you meant to Nikolas, toying with his emotions, when you knew he had lost his heart to you. Flaunting Richard in front of him just to hurt him more, did you enjoy yourself?"

Irmy's eyes glazed over as her mouth fell open, "Julius that is a terrible thing to say, how can you say that of me. I.. I.. of course I had an idea that Nikolas harbored some feelings for me, but that was when we first met and I thought it was only a boyish crush. I never knew it was more than that. Why are you saying these things to me?"

"You are accusing me of causing misery to so many people. I just wanted to show you that I am not the only one. You may feel happy to lecture me, but maybe you should look at yourself, before you comment on the behavior of other people"

Julius could see the tears welling in his sister's eyes but he could not stop himself hurting her, taking a cruel delight in her discomfort.

"If...if Nikolas ever harbored any feelings towards me I can assure you I was totally unaware of them, and I can hold my head up high Julius, despite the cruel things you have said, for I know I never encouraged him in his feelings towards me and would never have done so.

Nikolas was one of the finest men I have ever had the privilege to know, but I can say with my hand on my heart that I never felt any more affection for him than that of a good friend, and if Nikolas were here today I swear he would agree with me"

Julius placed his hands over his eyes, his head ached and he was angry as he knew he was losing the argument with his

476

sister, and for some unknown reason that fact made him angrier than ever.

He looked up at Irmy, she looked so hurt and defenseless, just as he remembered her in the nursery when one of her brothers had teased her and made her cry. His instincts told him to rush to her, hug her and ask for her forgiveness but he was too angry, too bitter to do the right thing. Instead he stood up to face Irmy, "go away Irmy, run to your husband, run to your lovely life, your lovely house, where everything is so wonderful and nothing ever goes wrong"

He could see that Irmy was becoming angry as well as she said, "you think only of yourself Julius, you have become a selfish, bitter man and I cannot say I like you very much anymore"

Julius was now completely enraged, he did not want to hear criticism of himself. "Get out of my room if I am so odious to you. Just go away and do something useful with your life. Why do you not use your energy to do something worthwhile? Why do you not stop playing the saintly little nurse and provide Richard with some children, I am sure that is what he truly wants, or would that interfere with your precious life?"

Julius stepped backwards as he saw the expression on Irmy's face. She could not have looked more shocked if he had physically slapped her across her face. He thought for a moment she would faint as the color drained from her face and tears flowed down her cheeks. Without another word, Irmy turned and ran out of the room, slamming the door behind her. Julius rocked on his feet, his anger so intense that he picked up the coffeepot and hurled it at the closed door. As he stood watching the brown liquid and coffee grains fall slowly down the timbered door he felt ashamed of his treatment of Irmy. Her reaction had been so forceful and bewildering that he tried to recall just exactly what he had said to her, but the process was too much for his brandy soaked brain and with a large sigh Julius dropped onto his bed and fell into a deep alcohol induced sleep.

Julius woke up to hear his door open and the noise of the coffeepot being pushed along the floor by the opening door. Julius' head ached and his eyes hurt as with apprehension he raised his head to see Richard entering his room. Julius quickly closed his eyes and feigned sleep, hoping that Richard would go away. The last thing he needed was a confrontation with his brother-in-law. He reasoned that Richard was here because of his treatment of Irmy. He tried desperately to remember what he had said to her, but his head ached too much and the exertion of thought was too much for him. As he lay on his bed he could hear Richard picking up the pieces of the coffeepot and replacing them onto the tray on the table. Then he could hear him lighting the gas lamps around the room before he seated himself in the chair by his bed. Julius kept his eyes closed, hoping Richard would go away.

"I know you are awake Julius and I am not moving from this chair until you talk to me, and believe me I am a very stubborn man, I will wait here all evening if I have to"

Julius knew Richard was a man true to his word. With great effort he opened his eyes, they felt as if they had been filled with sand and the light of the room hurt him so much that he quickly closed them again.

Not wishing to look at Richard Julius kept his eyes closed as he said, "I know why you are here Richard, I know I was beastly to Irmy, just tell her I am sorry, I was just a bit under the weather, you know how it is"

"It is not for me to carry your apologies to Irmy, that is something you must do yourself, though I have to tell you that I am not sure if Irmy will receive you at the moment. Your sister is very upset and I am not sure a mere apology will help" Richard's tone made Julius at last open his eyes and sit up. It was stern yes, Julius had expected that, but there was a sadness in it that perplexed him. Julius swallowed deeply, his mouth felt as though it was lined with fur, and he desperately needed a drink, "did she, did she tell you what I said to her?" Julius had been looking down at his lap but he looked at Richard as he replied, "yes she did, everything. I think you know what you said was very wrong. However that is not why I am here, that is something that you must sort out with Irmy yourself, I am here for a different reason, though your treatment of Irmy has prompted me to talk to you"

Julius knew that Richard was being very serious as the doctor held Julius' gaze with an unwavering stare that defied Julius to look away from him.

"I am sorry to have to say this to you Julius. I have always admired you and held you in great esteem, not least for the great affection you have always shown for Irmy, but I must ask you to leave my house as soon as possible, I am afraid you are no longer welcome to my hospitality"

Julius stared at Richard with his mouth wide open. The man could not mean it, Irmy would never let Richard throw him out of the house.

"Since you have been living under my roof I have tried to bear your insupportable behavior, but enough is enough. I think today has proved that we can no longer help you. Whenever your behavior was questioned Irmy and I would always try and make excuses for you, you were badly injured, you had lost two of your closest friends, the war had affected you, but I am afraid that now we have run out of excuses. What really annoys me Julius, and I suppose I speak from a purely professional stance here, is all those months when the medical staff at the hospital worked for you, willing you to get better, performing miracles with your treatment, saving your leg when others would have recommended an amputation, all that and you choose to throw it all away. You do not deserve their dedication and you do not deserve your family or your friends. They have all supported you, but I am afraid there is nothing left to recommend you and I would ask you to leave my house at your earliest convenience"

Julius had listened to Richard in stunned silence. He did not know whether to cry or hit the fellow. He could not mean what he said, and Julius began to feel his anger rising again as he said, "you just do not understand, do you Richard? Call yourself a doctor, you have no comprehension of what I have been through, no understanding of what I endured, if you did you would not speak to me as you have. How dare you speak to me like that?"

Whilst Richard had been talking to Julius he had appeared calm and composed, but for the first time that he could remember Julius saw Richard really angry. His face turned bright red as he leaned menacingly towards Julius, "that would be right. Julius Mayer, the only man who experienced any great tragedy, who saw any loss of life, who wept for a close friend, only Julius Mayer you understand, nobody else. Good God man, we all endured the most horrendous experiences during the war. I saw men die, screaming for their wives and children, young boys crying for their mothers, men whom I desperately wanted to survive but who I could do nothing for but comfort them as they met long and painful deaths. You think you are the only one who grieves, who carries those memories with him?"

Julius remained in a sulky silence, shamed by Richard's words, but Richard took his silence as recalcitrance so he grabbed Julius by the arm and with a strength that surprised Julius he dragged him to the bedroom window.

Outside snow was falling lightly on the pavements and people were scurrying by, anxious to be out of the cold wind that whipped past their faces. Pulling the lace curtain aside Richard pushed Julius to the window as he said passionately "look out there Julius, look at those people. Ordinary people conducting their ordinary lives, but I would wager if you stopped any of them and asked them at least every other person would be able to tell you some pitiful tale of their grief or hardships because of the war. They would tell you of loved ones killed, lost on the battlefield, perhaps buried in an unmarked grave somewhere. Others would tell you of terrible disabilities, lost limbs, men that will never be able to work again, who have no future to look forward to, but have they given up? no they are carrying on with their lives as best they know how. You are not the only one to harbor such grief Julius, you are just one of thousands, maybe millions across our continent. As those people down there are getting on with their lives, so must you, or why did you fight for your country? why did all those men die? why did Nikolas and Josef die? to see you waste your life and destroy yourself?"

When Julius still did not say anything Richard led him to the tallboy in the corner of the room. On top of the tallboy stood an oval mirror and Richard positioned Julius' face in front of it, "tell me Julius what do you see?"

Julius looked and was appalled as he looked at himself, probably for the first time in weeks. His hair was unkempt, his face unshaven, his eyes were puffy and swollen and underneath them were large black bags, Julius knew he looked years older than he was. "I will tell you what I see Julius" persisted Richard, "I see a failure, a weak man who cannot bear the pressures of life. A man who has given up. Do you think Nikolas or Josef would agree with me if they were here? You know they would. I did not know Josef, but I am sure Nikolas would be appalled by your behavior"

Julius felt utterly defeated as Richard's words sank into his brain. He had never felt so miserable as he realized that Richard's opinion of him was probably what all his family

480

and friends thought of him, and he knew that they were right. As if sensing Julius' utter dejection Richard led Julius to the bed and he once again sat down in his chair.

"Julius I have to tell you that what I said earlier about you leaving my house, I meant every word. Irmy and I have discussed this and have decided it is our only recourse. Please believe me we know you are harboring a grievous secret that you will not share with us, but whatever it is, it cannot be so bad that you are prepared to destroy yourself over it. I urge you to take a good long look at yourself. Despite your behavior you know we would still be willing to help you, all we want is for you to get better, but if you will not help yourself then I am afraid we are no longer prepared to help you either. Promise me you will think about this. Please, before it is too late"

Julius nodded as he sat in a dreamlike trance, he felt as if his body was floating around the room, as though he was in the middle of a terrible nightmare that hopefully he would soon wake up from.

"I am going to leave you now, I think you need to be alone for a while, I will look in on you later, you might benefit from a sleeping draught"

Julius again nodded and Richard rose from his chair. As Richard reached the door Julius looked up and in a small frightened voice said, "Richard, I know I have to tell her myself, but please tell Irmy I am sorry, I did not mean to upset her"

Richard nodded and he appeared to hesitate before he said, "I do not know if I should tell you this Julius, but I think you should know in order to understand Irmy, if you are ever to be reconciled to her again. A few years ago Irmy was told that she would never be able to bear children. Knowing Irmy as you do you must realize how much this means to her and indeed how much the prospect of never having children of her own has affected her"

Richard left the room quietly as Julius sat on his bed absorbing all Richard had said to him and remembering his awful words of that afternoon. In his despair the tears started to stream down his face. He cried for Nikolas and for Josef. He cried for all the men, deprived of a future by the futility of war. He cried for the loss of his friendships and he cried for Richard and Irmy in their childless misery, but most of all he cried for himself.

When Richard looked in on Julius later that evening, he found his brother-in-law fast asleep, lying on his bed. In his sleep Julius had lost the tortured look he had borne of late and once again Richard was reminded of the man he had come to care for over the years. He reached for the quilt and placed it over Julius' body as he stood looking down at him, shaking his head. He had not liked being so severe with Julius, but his patience had been tried once too often and when he had heard how Irmy had been treated his anger had known no bounds. Even in her distressed state Irmy had at first been horrified when Richard had insisted that Julius must leave their house, but she could not defend any of the arguments that Richard had put to her and in the end had yielded to her husband's wishes. They had tried everything to rehabilitate Julius, but he seemed intent on destroying himself and Richard was not going to let Irmy watch her brother's descent into his own destruction. He hoped that Julius had at least listened to some of what he had said.

Once more he looked down at Julius' sleeping face. What had Julius experienced out there that was so hard to bear? Why would he not talk about it, what could have happened that was so bad? Richard sighed, the war may be over, but there were still many casualties, not all physical ones, who had since been forgotten. Richard extinguished all the lamps, and with a final check on Julius, he picked up the coffee tray and left the room.

Julius slept until late the next day. When he awoke his mind was clear and he realized he had not had a drink for at least a day and a half. The events of the day before crowded into his mind like some terrible nightmare, except that Julius knew it had not been a dream. He lay in bed thinking about what Richard had said, he knew Richard had been very serious about his leaving their house. The thought scared him, not least as he pondered where he could go, and then he knew he had nowhere to go. He had upset too many people to ask them to accept him into their homes. Maybe Franz and Gretha would allow him to stay with them, but he doubted it, especially after they had been informed of his behavior. He knew that Richard had been right in almost everything he had said, but it did not help him. Richard's lecture had not solved anything except to make him realize what a worthless person he was and now he was being asked to leave the only sanctuary he knew.

482

He had to do something for himself, but what? Well he would have just a little glass of brandy and then decide.

Over the next few days Julius did try to behave himself. He stayed in his room reasoning that if Irmy and Richard saw that he was not going out into the town they might think that he was trying to reform. Every time he tried to think of his future he became more depressed, and although he did reduce his drinking, he still managed to consume quite a few glasses a day, topped up from the various bottles he had hidden around his room. He knew that he should apologize to Irmy but the thought scared him too much as he was unsure of her response to him. With everything he had done of late his treatment of Irmy was his greatest regret. She was the one person he would never wish to hurt and he knew he had said some cruel and unkind things to her and he was frightened that she would never be able to forgive him.

One morning, one of the maids brought a letter into Julius' room. Julius noticed with apprehension that even the maid observed him with a contemptuous look on her face and quickly scurried out of the room as soon as she had delivered his letter. The postmark told him that the letter was from Vienna and after having read its contents Julius sat staring into space for a while. The letter was from Josef's solicitor informing him that Josef had left him a bequest in his will. That is all the letter said, apart from the fact that the solicitor would be writing again in the next few weeks with the full details of the bequest. Julius tossed the letter onto the floor and reached for a bottle of brandy. He knew he did not deserve anything from his friend and the fact that Josef had remembered him broke his heart. The alcohol started to take its effect as Julius passed out once more into the oblivion he so desperately sought.

When Julius woke up, it must have been night time because the curtains were closed and the lamps were lit. As he opened his eyes he was aware of someone in his room and as he turned his head he found Viktor sitting beside his bed. Viktor looked very somber indeed as he said, "good evening, Julius"

Julius looked at his friend as he said, "If you have come here to give me another lecture Viktor, you are too late, I have had enough lectures in the last few days to last me a lifetime, I do assure you"

Viktor bent down and picked up an empty brandy bottle, "and I see you listened attentively and realized the errors of your ways. Very intelligent, I must say"

"I suppose Richard and Irmy summoned you here to try and reform the bad boy. What did they tell you, what a hopeless case I am, what a great disappointment?"

"You should be thankful that they care enough about you. Actually I was on my way to an appointment and I thought I would use the opportunity to come and see you. It seems it was just as well that I did. I would never have believed it had I not seen it with my own eyes, what has happened Julius? If I had thought that the news of Josef's death would have affected you this much, I would not have told you in the first place. I knew you were upset, but I thought I had managed to persuade you how stupid you were to blame yourself. I presume that that is what this is all about"

"If only it were" whispered Julius, his head was aching again and he felt stripped and devoid of all feelings. He was uncomfortable with Viktor, of all the people left in the world Viktor probably knew him better than anyone else. Viktor had always been the strong, reliable one with common sense enough for all of them. How could he tell him about Nikolas? but he had the feeling that Viktor would not leave this room before he had heard exactly why Julius had progressed along his long path of remorse and guilt.

Viktor sat waiting for Julius to carry on, and as though reading his friend's mind he said, "all right I will be honest with you, Irmy has written to me, but I think she was rather economical with the truth. You look much worse than I expected, but she did not ask me to come, I am truthfully here on business"

Viktor sat back in his chair and with an air of finality he crossed his arms as he said, "and I am not moving from this position until you have talked to me Julius, and remember I can be as stubborn as the next man. I am going to sit here for as long as it takes, believe me"

Julius looked at his friend with affection. For the first time in a very long time, Julius felt some emotion pluck at his heart, as if it was telling him it was time to let go, time to give in and confess to somebody, and he was glad Viktor was with him.

It took Julius a long time to tell his story. He walked endlessly round the room, not daring to look at Viktor, and to his credit, his friend listened in absolute silence as Julius poured out his story. The relief of talking about it was immense, he knew Viktor could not absolve him, but to know someone shared his anguish meant a lot to him.

After he had finished his story Julius went and stood by the fireplace, staring at the numerous shapes and colors that the flames made as they curled and danced up the chimneystack. He was unnerved by the silence from Viktor and for a moment was frightened that his friend was so appalled by his story that he too would desert Julius. With dread he turned round to face Viktor who sat with a look of absolute amazement on his face. It was not the reaction Julius had expected, nor was he prepared for what Viktor said next.

"And this is the guilt you have been carrying for nearly a year and a half? This is why you have been crucifying yourself? For Gods sake Julius I sometimes thought you could be an idiot, but I never took you to be a fool"

Julius reeled from his friend's criticism and Viktor must have noticed the shock on his face as he leapt up from his chair and placed his hands on Julius' arms. "I am sorry I did not mean to upset you, but you must see, this is madness"

Tenderly Viktor placed Julius in a chair where he sat too stunned to speak. Viktor stood looking down at his friend, trying to find the right words to say to Julius and eventually he sat down with him.

"Julius, think on this, would Nikolas have blamed you had he been in your position? If it had been his life at risk, would you have not done exactly the same thing? Life is full of so many 'what ifs' that if we spent our life trying to resolve them we would never have a life to live at all, do you not see that? What I am trying to say is yes, it is tragic that Nikolas died, but not tragic that he died saving someone's life. He died heroically, he died leading the life he loved, he died saving his best friend, do you not think that is a wonderful thing? It is not how he died, but it is the way he died that you must remember and you should be celebrating that fact, not treating it as though it was some terrible catastrophe, and what you did afterwards was just as heroic, Nikolas would have been so proud of you"

Viktor observed Julius and was pleased to see some flicker of life in his eyes that had been absent before. He continued, determined that his friend should be relieved of the terrible burden that he had carried alone for so long.

485

"Tell me Julius, and I want you to think about your answer and to be totally honest with me. Knowing Nikolas as you did, would he have acted any differently if it had been someone else there that day? If it had been say a general, or a mere ammunitions boy or even that damn horse of his, would Nikolas not have done exactly the same thing for them as he did for you?"

Slowly, Julius nodded his head, a flicker of a smile on his lips.

"You know he would, but it just so happened that he saved you, something he would have wanted to do. An act of bravery which I know you would have performed in the same situation, and I hope and believe we all would have carried out if the situation had been the same for us. Julius I am not saying that for the rest of your life you will not sometimes think of that day and remember it with some sadness or regret, but it is time to lessen the guilt, to understand that in some ways it was a joyous thing that Nikolas did for you, and to remember that he would not have wanted you to be living like this, rather I think he would have been appalled. You have to move on, do something with your life. If not for yourself, then for Nikolas and Josef, otherwise why did they and millions like them die, was it all for nothing?"

The tears fell down Julius' cheeks as Viktor rose from his seat and hugged Julius and the two men sat in silence for a very long time.

After Julius had recovered himself somewhat Viktor called Irmy's maid and asked for a meal and some coffee to be sent to Julius' room. The two men both realized that they had done enough soul searching for one evening so their meal was eaten accompanied by idle talk, mostly from Viktor. He told Julius that he had found out that Smid had moved to Styria and was living with his sister, quite close to where Franz now lived. Viktor also informed Julius that he was to be a father sometime next year as his wife was now pregnant. Julius thought the news was wonderful and congratulated his friend, once again feeling a small pang of envy at Viktor's luck.

When the meal was ended and cleared away, Viktor rose and Julius began to feel a sense of panic at his friend's leaving. Viktor smiled at Julius' concern for his departure, "I am afraid you do not get rid of me that easily, my friend. No, Irmy has kindly invited me to stay with her so I will only be in the next room. I have business in Aussig, to the north of here, but I am sure I can defer my visit for a few days. I am going to telephone them now. In the meantime I suggest that you think about what we discussed this evening and then I would recommend you get a good night's sleep. We have a lot of work to do tomorrow" another broad grin crossed Viktor's face as he left the room saying, "just think of tomorrow as the first day of the rest of your life"

Julius was puzzled by what Viktor had said about 'a lot of work' but his brain was too tired to ponder Viktor's cryptic message. The day had made him very tired, but he felt relieved and almost happy, a sentiment he had not felt for a long time. He carefully prepared himself for bed, a luxury he had not experienced for a while, and with a contented mind quickly fell asleep, the astuteness of Viktor's arguments ringing in his ears. He slept very soundly without even realizing he had not even thought about having a drink all night.

Viktor threw back the curtains bright and early the next morning. The winter sun streamed through the windows as Julius dived under the covers protesting at his rude awakening.

"There is no use moaning at me Julius Mayer, you know I can be a very hard taskmaster. I suppose you have not even seen this time of morning for quite a while, but it is quite delightful. Certainly makes the city look beautiful, not as beautiful as Salzburg of course, but I suppose we will have to differ in that belief"

Viktor continued chatting breezily as he placed a breakfast tray on Julius' lap and then sat down to watch him eat it.

"You are not joining me?" enquired Julius as he looked warily at the coddled egg that stared aggressively at him from the tray.

"Good heavens no, I have been awake for over an hour already. I had my breakfast with Richard and Irmy and have even conducted some business before waking you up"

"I suppose you gave Richard and Irmy a full account of our conversation last night"

Viktor's smile disappeared from his face as he said, "Julius, you know I would not repeat anything that you have told me in confidence. All I said was that we had talked a lot and that I thought that our conversation may have helped. Was I right, has it helped?"

Julius looked at his friend as he sipped his cup of coffee. He wanted to be honest with Viktor, but he did not know what to say. "Yes it helped more than I can say......"

"Why do I feel there is a large 'but' at the end of that sentence" interrupted Viktor.

Julius smiled at his friend's forthrightness, "it is not a *large* but, it is just that it is not that simple. I know everything you said was completely rational and although the doubts are still there I have to say they are considerably eased"

Viktor leaned forward, "Julius I told you last night, I am not asking you to forget, you never will. All I am asking you to do is to put the whole thing in perspective. You really should not feel guilty, Nikolas and Josef would not have wanted you to either"

"I know" said Julius, "I think I just need some time, that is all"

"Exactly" said Viktor, looking cheerful again, "now, I have to go into the city on business. By the time I come back I want to see you bathed, shaven and trying to look at least a little more like the horribly attractive man you once were, if that is possible"

Despite Viktor's joking Julius still looked a little downcast as Viktor said, "there is just one more thing I think you should know, did you receive a letter from Josef's solicitor by any chance? Good, so did I, it seems he remembered us both in his will. Whilst I am gone just look at that letter again, I think there is something in it that will cheer you up"

As soon as Viktor left the room Julius jumped out of his bed to retrieve the letter from his bureau. At first he did not understand what Viktor had meant, but as he read it again a smile began to spread over his face and he started to dance around the room in a comical frenzy. God bless Josef! God bless Viktor! Why had he not seen it before? Josef had not blamed him. His will had been written in the sanatorium *after* he had left the hospital. Including Julius in his will could only mean one thing, that Josef had understood and forgiven Julius for not helping him. With gay abandon he ran out onto the landing and shouted to Irmy's maid to draw him a bath. The maid ran up the stairs to see what all the commotion was about to find Master Julius running around in his nightshirt calling for a bath. As she said later to cook, Master Julius had finally lost his marbles and it would be the asylum for him next, and none too soon neither.

488

When Viktor returned from his business in the city he found Julius, bathed and shaven, looking clean and spruce in a smart suit. Although Viktor knew that Julius would have to endure weeks of rehabilitation to even begin to look like the old Julius he had known, the transformation from the man he had encountered the night before was remarkable. It was not just Julius' appearance that had improved but his overall demeanor that had changed. Julius walked with a determined spring in his step and his eyes no longer held their haunted misery that had so perturbed Viktor. Viktor tried to hide a smile as Julius strode around him, awaiting his approval, like a young boy before his first day at school.

"I presume reading Josef's letter has helped you?" laughed Viktor.

"Do you know, I was so low in my cups when I read that letter that I did not even notice when Josef had written his will, but it has made me realize a few things"

"Oh yes, and am I to be a party to these revelations?" asked Viktor.

"Well it is very hard to explain, but I suppose it made me realize that it is very easy to look at something and straight away think the worst, as I did when I read that letter. But there are always two sides to every tale and although I do still feel guilty about Nikolas, I remembered what you said, about would I have done the same thing, and do you know I would like to think I would have. If I had seen any of you in danger I know I would have done anything to warn you"

"That is what I have been trying to tell you. I know it has been hard for you, but it is time to take a more positive stance. Josef always said you thought about things far too deeply and it seems he was right. What he said to you was said in his misery and his pain, he did not mean it, and if he did at the time I would wager he regretted it as soon as you left his room. Just like you did not mean the things you said to Irmy, but you said them nonetheless, even if you regretted it later"

Julius nodded and sighed, "you do not know how much, and I do not think she will ever forgive me"

"Nonsense, Irmy loves her big brother. She just wants you to get better, to stop drinking for a start, and that is where we are going to begin"

Viktor started to stride about the room, opening cupboards and looking under the bed while Julius watched him in astonishment.

"Viktor what the hell are you looking for?"

"Aha, number one" called out Viktor as he came out from under Julius' bed, looking triumphant and holding a brandy bottle above his head. In amazement Julius watched as Viktor proceeded to find all his secret hiding places for his bottles of brandy and to his mortification Viktor managed to find seven bottles hidden about the room.

"Any that I have missed? and you had better be honest with me"

Julius shook his head, "you seem very adept at finding secret hiding places for bottles of alcohol, is there something you have not been telling me Viktor?"

Viktor chuckled as he said, "no, no nasty skeletons in my wardrobe, or bottles for that matter. We had a very nice old Major in command of our unit in Graz. Old boy he was, near retirement. Trouble was he liked the odd tipple or ten. My captain and I, who had a soft spot for the old codger, realized that if he had been caught being drunk on duty, as he often was, it would have been a dishonorable discharge for him and no pension. So as much as we could we covered for him, which also meant occasionally searching his room for all his hidden bottles. I suppose you know this, but people like the old Major are ingenious with their hiding places, it became quite a game for us to find all his secret caches. Anyway, I have decided to remove all temptation from your path. This is not going to be easy Julius, but I am determined that you conquer your reliance for alcohol. You do know it is just a cowardly escape from facing up to your responsibilities don't you?"

"I thought you had finished with your lectures, Viktor, and yes I do know how stupid it is, you forget I live in the same house as a doctor and a nurse, I have been told often enough"

"Good, and now my next question is, do you want to give up the drinking? because the only way you can is if you want to"

Julius sighed again, it sounded all very well in theory, and he did want to change, but he did not know if he was strong enough.

"I am staying for six more days, how about we try now and see how you fare? If things look promising then after I am gone I am sure Richard and Irmy will help you"

Julius was not so sure about that but Julius could not refuse Viktor, he owed him that much.

Content with Julius' assurances Viktor then proceeded to sit down with Julius and between the two of them they wrote out a list of tasks that Julius felt he should carry out. Some were personal targets, such as fitness, eating properly, exercise, but it was the other list that Viktor wrote down that unnerved Julius the most. It was a list of apologies, so long that Julius began to tremble at the realization of how many people he had offended or hurt over the last few months. Top of the list was Richard and Irmy, a daunting enough task in itself, but then Viktor proceeded to write down amongst others Georg and Erika, and even added the servants, which Julius baulked at.

"Just call this a path to fulfillment for you. I am not saying go and see all these people today, but over the next few weeks, when you feel up to it and when you feel the time is right, I think you should talk to them, just tell them how sorry you are. As you cross off the names on this list I promise you will feel happier within yourself. I know you Julius, you are an honorable man and deep down you know this is right"

Two of the names on the list especially worried Julius, that of Frau and Colonel Manz. Viktor informed Julius that they had returned to Prague last week and had asked that Julius visit them. Irmy had told them that he was indisposed but he could not defer his visit forever. Maybe not, thought Julius, but he hoped their meeting would be later rather than sooner.

The next few days were very difficult for the two men. Viktor remained stalwart throughout as Julius endured highs of elation and lows of depression whilst his mind swung between many emotions as he struggled to convince himself that he must throw off the great weight that he had been carrying for so long and look forward to a happier future. His moods were not helped by his lack of alcohol. At times he would beg Viktor for just one glass as he trembled all over and perspiration poured from his body. But Viktor was too strong for him and would not give in and was content to suffer the onslaught of his friend's spectacular mood swings.

They went for long walks into the city, Viktor eager to visit all the sights he had heard so much about from Julius and Nikolas. Viktor made sure that Julius ate well, and had lots of sleep, often sitting by Julius' bed whilst his friend tossed and turned, experiencing the nightmares that had never really left him since the end of the war. Julius would wake up drenched in sweat, staring wildly around, looking for his demons, until Viktor would relax him once more and he would drift off to sleep again. All this time, Julius never saw Irmy or Richard. He was not displeased about this, he was not yet ready to face them, and Viktor seemed to understand this, never pressing his friend to do anything he did not want to, but Julius guessed that Viktor was telling them exactly how Julius was faring each day.

After the fourth day Julius began to feel that he might one day return to being the Julius Mayer he once had been. He and Viktor talked non stop and for the first time Julius could talk freely about the war, even talk about Nikolas and Josef without stopping himself with the feelings of guilt that had always come to him before.

On the morning before Viktor was due to leave to travel to Aussig, Julius started to feel moments of panic at his friend's leaving. He knew Viktor had to go, he had deferred his business for as long as he could, but he would have done anything for him to stay.

"I think you know what you have to do today" Viktor smiled at his friend, "it will not be so bad, and you cannot do this on your own, you need their help"

Julius nodded but he dreaded seeing Irmy and Richard. It was with some trepidation that he walked down the stairs and knocked on the dining room door. Irmy and Richard were having breakfast and as he opened the door he saw Irmy begin to rise, then check herself as she remained in her seat. Richard looked much sterner as he observed Julius over the rim of his spectacles.

"I, I wonder, if I am not disturbing you that is, if I might have a word with you both"

Richard gestured to a chair at the table and with his legs feeling like jelly Julius walked towards his inquisition.

It was the hardest interview he had ever had, he felt that Irmy with her unstinting generous spirit, would have forgiven him anything, but Richard conducted the conversation for both of them and it was apparent that he was still very wary of his brother-in-law's good intentions.

Julius did not explain the reasons for his behavior, he felt he had talked of them enough with Viktor, and the wounds were still very deep, but he explained how he had been feeling over the last few days, how Viktor had helped him, and how he was determined to get better and then he appealed to them for their help. Irmy agreed immediately but Richard was intent on questioning his motives as he said, "you know it is going to be a very difficult struggle for you Julius and I hope you meant every word that you said to us. I think you know I cannot, will not, tolerate any more of the behavior that we have witnessed from you over the last few months, but I am willing to give you the benefit of the doubt and both Irmy and I will do everything in our power to help you, if that is what you want. If you think you are straying from the path you must tell us immediately. Honesty is everything in such a case as this, do I make myself clear?"

Julius nodded knowing his hardest task was ahead. "I know you think me shallow and irresponsible, but I would like to apologize for what you have had to endure during the last few months, I know words are pretty useless, but I do mean that most sincerely. Richard I am sorry for what I said to you, everything you said was true at the time, I know that now. How you put up with me I will never know, I realize it was only because of Irmy rather than any affection that you may have had for me in the past, but I hope some day in the future, you will come to regard me with some esteem again"

For the first time that morning Richard smiled, "my esteem for you is already growing by the mere fact that you are sitting here in front of us today my boy. Whatever I said to you in the past was only said in the hope that you would see the folly of your ways, not out of a dislike for you, please believe me"

Julius turned to Irmy who was watching her brother with a nervous look on her face, "Irmy I do not know what I can say to you. You are the dearest thing in the world to me and that I should have been so unkind to you is unpardonable. I just hope that in time you will find it in your heart to forgive me and understand that I only said all those terrible things from the depths of my despair and from the depths of a brandy bottle"

Tears were in Irmy's eyes as she reached across and held Julius' hands tightly as she looked into his eyes, which were also touched with tears. Julius rose to take his leave, "I hope I will see you both later, but I have suddenly realized there is something I must do today and if I do not do it now, I fear I never will"

When Julius left the room he stood against the closed door for a moment with his eyes shut. He knew he was

493

happier than before he had entered the room, he felt that there had been some mutual understanding between them, but he wiped his brow with sadness as he knew that before his behavior of the last few months Irmy would have leapt up to hug him in her warm embrace instead of just holding his hands in forgiveness.

Viktor was waiting in his room, anxious to hear how Richard and Irmy had received Julius. "Fine, fine" was all Julius would say, his mind was intent on other things. "Viktor I have a great favor to ask of you today. I wonder if you would accompany me to see Nikolas' parents"

Viktor looked amazed as he said, "What on earth has brought on this change of heart? Of course I will, if that is what you wish"

"Whilst I was with Richard and Irmy I realized I would have to face Nikolas' parents sometime, and the thought scares me to hell. If you came with me I know you would not let me lose my nerve. If I wait until you have left Prague I may never summon up my courage again"

Viktor agreed and they left the house soon afterwards and set off for the Manz's house.

When they arrived at the familiar front door Julius stood looking up at it for quite a while, and with a quiet determination he turned to Viktor and said, "I know you are going to lose your patience with me Viktor, but would you mind very much if I went to see the Manzs alone?"

"Of course" agreed Viktor, "are you sure about this?"

"Yes, I know I have to start doing things by myself and this is one of them. I thought I could not do this without your help, but now that I am here, I think it would be better if I saw them on my own. Do you mind awfully?"

"Of course not. I will meet you later at Irmy's house, is that all right?"

"Perfectly" answered Julius as he climbed the steps towards the front door. He turned round to see Viktor walking off, but turning round to watch Julius.

"Goodbye Viktor" grinned Julius, "I promise I will ring the doorbell and enter the house"

Viktor then waved as he carried on up the street as Julius rang the bell that he had rung a hundred times before, but never with such a feeling of trepidation.

494

XXXII

Part of Julius had hoped that the Manzs would not be at home but he was informed by their maid that they had both just returned to the house. Julius waited in the hall as the maid went to inform her employers of his presence. Julius looked nervously around the familiar room, the sweat beginning to appear on his brow, as his anxiety enveloped him. He did not have to wait long before a door opened and Colonel Manz strode into the hall.

To Julius Nikolas' father had hardly changed at all. He still walked with the confidence and assurance of a senior army officer and for a moment Julius was visited by memories of his own father. Nikolas had always said the two men were very much alike, none more so than today as Colonel Manz strode towards him and began to pump his hand effusively.

"My boy, my boy, it is so good to see you. Thank you so much for coming to see us. Frau Manzova will be overjoyed by your visit"

Julius did not know what to say he was so overcome by the passion and warmth of the colonel's welcome, it made him feel very humble and he regretted putting off his visit for so long when it had obviously meant so much to Nikolas' parents. As he thought of what he must tell them, his spirits fell, but he knew it was something he must do, they both deserved to know how their son had died. As Colonel Manz led Julius through to the sitting room he bombarded him with questions as to his health, noting that Julius still used a walking stick and then asked after the health of Richard and Irmy.

Outside the sitting room door Colonel Manz stopped and before entering the room bent his head and said to Julius in a conspiratorial whisper, "do not be too shocked by Frau Manzova's appearance, she has not been well you know, but I believe she is on the mend" the colonel smiled at Julius as he said, "and seeing you will be a great boon to her, believe me"

Julius could not have felt worse at that moment and he started to regret visiting Nikolas' parents.

Nikolas' mother sat in a chair near a roaring fire. She had lost a lot of weight, and she looked tired but her eyes still held the mischievous twinkle that her two sons had inherited. The cherubic Manz smile lit up her face as she held out her hands in greeting to Julius. Julius crossed the room and bowed to Frau Manzova as he took her hands in his.

"Julius, you do not know what a tonic you are for me. As I am sure you have been told I have been unwell. I am afraid I caught the influenza, and it is not until lately that I am beginning to feel myself again" Frau Manzova paused as she contemplated what she had just said, "but I know I am lucky, look at your poor Mama. I am so sorry, Julius, it must have been very hard for you, after your Papa and of course..."

Here Frau Manzova drifted off into her own memories as she thought of her son. The colonel, realizing there was an embarrassing silence, strode across the room and invited Julius to sit in the chair opposite Nikolas' mother, beside the blazing fire. Glad of the diversion Julius accepted the colonel's offer of a cup of coffee, and the time was spent in idle talk of mutual acquaintances until the maid brought in their refreshments. As Julius sat with the colonel and his wife he began to wonder if they would ever mention Nikolas, they broached every other subject except that of their son. Julius could not decide whether he was happy with this situation or not. Whilst he did not want to discuss Nikolas' death he thought that Nikolas' parents had wanted to see him in order to talk to him about their son.

After they had finished their tea Frau Manzova said, "I am so sorry that we have not seen you before now Julius, but it seems that we kept missing each other. As soon as you returned to Prague, the colonel took me to a spa to help me improve my health, and I must say it was a wonderful diversion, and then when we returned Irmy said that you were indisposed, I hope you are recovered?"

Julius enjoyed Irmy's explanation of his condition as 'indisposed' but wisely did not inform the Manzs of their misconception. Frau Manzova asked Julius about his stay in the hospital and his rehabilitation and he spent the next few minutes telling them about his treatment and explaining why he still was in need of a walking stick, although he felt that soon even that would not be needed. The colonel and his wife listened in rapt attention and Julius began to feel perplexed as to where their conversation was heading. As if sensing Julius uneasiness, and although earning himself a reproving look from his wife, Colonel Manz said, "I

496

understand Suse has not visited you since your return to Prague Julius. Please do not be upset with her. Nikolas' death affected her greatly, and I think she finds it difficult to talk about him to anyone, I am afraid she has hardly visited myself or Frau Manzova, though I understand Georg visits her occasionally. It is very sad"

Julius noticed Frau Manzova staring into her lap, playing with the fringes of the shawl that was draped around her shoulders, and when she lifted her eyes to his they were filled with tears. Poor Frau Manzova, thought Julius, she had been looking forward to her son's wedding when she would have heard of his death, and poor Suse, her wedding dress probably now lying in a box in a cupboard, never to see the light of day. Julius' feelings of depression began to cloud his mind again as he became aware of Frau Manzova talking to him. "Julius, I know words are not enough, but I want you to know that the colonel and I will always be grateful to you for the friendship you gave our son, he was very fortunate the day he met you and I think you know how much he thought of you. The friendship that you both had is very rare and I am so happy my son was honored to call you his friend"

The tears were still in her eyes and Julius wanted to shout at her to stop, she did not realize how wrong she was, but he did not know what to say. Summoning all his nerve he said, "Frau Manzova, Colonel, there is something I must tell you, it is about Nikolas' death. You see there is something you do not know..."

"Oh but we do, Julius, we do. We know everything" smiled Frau Manzova.

Julius began to feel frustrated as he tried to say, "no, I am sorry, but you do not know what happened that day, it is something I have had to live with for a long time, and I feel it only right that I tell you everything"

"Julius, please, do not upset yourself" said Colonel Manz, " it is not necessary"

Julius felt his hands curl into fists as he tried to make Nikolas' parents understand, "it is necessary, believe me..."

"Julius" Colonel Manz interrupted, "I think we should explain. After Nikolas' death we received a long and wonderful letter from a Captain Zizic, I believe he was your lieutenant at that time?" Julius nodded, unsure of what the colonel would say next, "and he told us everything that occurred that day"

497

"What exactly did he write?" asked Julius, knowing that the Manzs could not know the whole truth.

"It was such a wonderful letter" sighed Frau Manzova, "not only giving us all the details of the battle, which the colonel appreciated, but also how Nikolas lost his life running to warn you of an impending shell, why what else is there to tell?"

Julius stared dumbfounded at Nikolas' mother. Amazed, not only at her reaction to her son's death, but the way she had made it sound as though she was describing a shopping trip, or a ride in the country.

"And, and you do not mind?"

"Mind what?" asked Frau Manzova looking as mystified as Julius did.

"You do not mind that Nikolas lost his life saving mine?" Julius thought his voice did not sound like his own as he tried to hide the shock that he was feeling.

There was a long pause as Frau Manzova stared at Julius and then turned round to look at her husband. Then Frau Manzova leaned out of her chair and took one of his hands in hers, "Oh my poor boy, I had no idea that this is how you have been feeling, did you think that we would in some way blame you for Nikolas' death?" again she looked across at her husband as if seeking his guidance and then she said, "Julius, Nikolas was a soldier, like his father and his grandfathers before him. He died in the service of his country, we could ask no more of him than that. That he died heroically, helping his men and his friend could only make us more proud of him, if that were possible. Captain Zizic told us he was running to warn you and several men trying to turn a gun, but that was typical of Nikolas, and I would not have expected any less of him. He also told us that, even though you were horribly injured, you dragged yourself to his side and that you were with him when he died. That action alone has helped me so much Julius, to know he was not alone when he died"

Julius stared, his mouth wide open and at that moment he could have leapt from his seat and hugged both Nikolas' mother and father for their kindness and understanding.

Frau Manzova looked kindly at Julius as she said, "you know you are very like your mother at times Julius, she would often find the negative side of things instead of seeing how positive things could be"

498

Julius reeled somewhat at the criticism of himself, it was what Richard, Irmy and Viktor had been saying to him all along and now even Nikolas' mother seemed to be agreeing with them. He felt he should still be honest with them as he said, "I cannot lie to you and I have to tell you I have not passed a day when I have not felt guilty about how Nikolas died. Perhaps if I had not been there he might have been with us here today"

"I know nothing we can say will help you Julius" said Colonel Manz, "but please believe me you cannot hold yourself responsible. I am very proud of my son and you should be too. It is of absolutely no use wanting him here today, though I wish to God that he was, he has gone from us, let us just be happy to celebrate his life not his death"

"Has Georg read Captain Zizics' letter?" asked Julius.

"For a long time I do not believe that Georg could come to terms with his brother's death, he would not talk about him or even mention his name and he refused to even read the letter from Captain Zizic. However a few weeks ago I persuaded him and I think it has helped him to reconcile himself to Nikolas' death. I hope so"

Nikolas' father sighed deeply, it was obvious that Georg's reaction to his brother's death had troubled them and Julius regretted not helping the young man more than he had.

Colonel Manz looked earnestly at Julius as he said, "I know you were not going to tell us either about your service to our son after his death, but what you did for him, taking him from the battlefield to receive the blessings of a priest was the greatest act of kindness I have ever known and one I know that my wife and I can never thank you enough for. We are forever in your debt, Julius, we do not know how we can ever repay you"

Julius sat stunned, he did not know what to say. Was he in a dream, a dream that at last released him from the living hell he had endured for so many months?

He was distracted by Frau Manzova who said, "Julius are you all right? you look as if you are about to be run over by a train. If you are wondering how we know of your gallant actions, the priest into whose care you gave Nikolas wrote to us as well. He was so moved by your act of loyalty to your friend that he wrote to us about you. We were so proud. He wrote that Nikolas must have been an exceptional man to have engendered such devotion from his friend, and I would like to think he was right. He was right was he not? Nikolas was exceptional"

Julius looked at this kind woman, knowing that it was a statement that did not need an answer. Nikolas had been an exceptional man and Julius made an oath to himself that in the future he would not let his memory down. He would live his life as Nikolas would have wanted him to. He would look forward with optimism and hopefully happiness, all the things that Nikolas and Josef could not now experience but he could and he would not waste it again as he had done in the past.

From the pocket of his waistcoat Julius pulled out a silver chain upon which hung a likeness of King Wenceslas which he placed into Frau Manzova's hand. "I want you to have this. Nikolas was wearing this when he, when he died. I know he would have wanted you to have it"

Frau Manzova stared down at the chain in her hand, then looked up horrified as she said, "no I could not take it. I am sure Nikolas would have wanted you to have this for yourself"

Julius smiled, the first genuine smile that he had smiled for a long time, "no, I think you should keep it, besides I do not need it, I have more than enough memories of my friends to last me a lifetime, that is all I need"

Whenever Julius was to look back at his meeting with Nikolas' parents he would always say that the encounter was what really started to change his life around. True he had had Viktor's stalwart support for the last week, without him he would never have visited the Manzs in the first place, but up until that time he had been promising to change his ways in order to please Viktor, Irmy and Richard. It was only after leaving Nikolas' house that he knew he wanted to change for himself and began to truly believe that he could.

That afternoon instead of returning straight away to Irmy's house he had gone for a long walk around the city he loved so much. He marveled at the beauty of the buildings and the pure joy of a cold winter's day that had his nose frozen and his ears tingling despite pulling his hat down onto his head. At one point he sat down on a bench and took a childlike joy in watching young lovers walking by, mothers scurrying past with their children and old people, shuffling along the streets, their wrinkled faces displaying a lifetime of emotions. As he sat there, the cold beginning to

500

numb his weary limbs he realized that he wanted to be like them. He wanted to be a lover, a parent, and one day grow old and gray, having experienced all the laughter, happiness and even sadness that made life so worth living. He wanted a future and he knew how lucky he was to be sitting, cold but happy, on a bench in a square in Prague on that wintry December day.

When he returned home he opened the door to be met by Viktor, dressed in his evening clothes, rushing down the hallway, "Julius are you all right? We were worried about you, we telephoned the Manzs and they said you had left them ages ago. Where have you been? What happened?"

Julius smiled at his friend as he slapped him on the back and said, "so many questions, Viktor. I am sorry I troubled you, I have been having a wonderful time"

Viktor looked suspiciously at Julius as he said, "you have not been drinking have you?"

Julius laughed at his friend, "oh ye of little faith. No my friend I am merely intoxicated with life, it is wonderful, do you not think?"

Viktor continued to look perplexed as he said, "I would like to know how your interview with Nikolas' parents fared, but we do not have enough time. Richard and Irmy have invited us to dine with them as it is my last night here. I am afraid I accepted on your behalf, I hope you do not mind"

"Not at all. I will quickly change and meet you downstairs, then I will tell you everything that happened today" With that Julius climbed the stairs humming happily to himself leaving Viktor with a bemused look on his face.

That evening was one of the happiest evenings that Julius had experienced for a long time. With Viktor's help he explained as much as he could to Richard and Irmy about Nikolas and Josef. They both sat listening with dumbfounded looks on their faces. It was Irmy who spoke first, "I just cannot believe you kept all this to yourself, why on earth did you not talk to us? You know we would have helped"

"I know, I know" sighed Julius, "It sounds so easy now, but I think once I started to blame myself for Nikolas' death I just could not get the thought out of my mind and it just seemed to grow and grow"

"And now?" asked Richard, "What has reconciled you?"

Julius went on to explain in some part it was his treatment of Richard and Irmy, when he had been so unkind to them,

501

"but I have to confess that a lot of it was due to Viktor, who proved to be the truest friend a man could have, and I would like to propose a toast, to Viktor Leitner, thank you"

As Richard and Irmy raised their glasses of wine and Julius raised his glass of water Viktor was seen to blush deeply but there was no doubting the triumphant grin on his face as he acknowledged the credit he deserved in bringing about Julius' rehabilitation. Julius went on to describe his interview with the Manzs' and even Viktor appeared amazed by the story.

"Poor Suse, and poor Georg" observed Irmy, "I knew he was not coping with Nikolas' death at all well but I did not realize how grave the situation was"

"No and that is one young man I definitely owe an apology too" said Julius, then looked at Viktor smiling over the rim of his glass, "I know, as well as several other people, I have not forgotten"

Viktor left early the next morning. He had a train to catch to Aussig and as Julius watched him depart he felt sad to be saying goodbye to his friend, but he knew he could now cope, in fact he felt quite rejuvenated to be once again on his own and he set his mind to planning what he was to do in the months ahead.

His first mission was to find Georg. He had expected a difficult scene, but he was met by a young man seemingly abashed by Julius' presence. He told Julius that he had read the letters from Captain Zizic and the priest and then started to apologize profusely for his behavior towards Julius when they had last met.

"You did not say anything that I did not deserve at the time" replied Julius, "I think it is you who should be accepting my apologies do you not think?"

Georg looked a little shocked as he said "what you did for Nikolas, I want to thank you, it was very brave, it meant so much to my parents and me for that matter, to know, well you know, just to know"

Julius nodded, he knew all too well now. "Why do we not forget our differences of the past and agree to be friends again. I am sure Nikolas would have wanted me to keep an eye on his wayward younger brother"

"Not so wayward now" grinned Georg, "but yes I would like that. I suppose I could call you an honorary brother, I think Nikolas would have approved"

502

"I think he would" agreed Julius, "and so will Irmy, she always wanted a lawyer in the family"

It was very close to Christmas, the snow was falling heavily outside the window, and Julius stood at the window of Irmy's sitting room, watching the snowflakes fly about in the air as they started to cover the city in their white panoply. Julius loved the way the snowfall brought a silence to the surroundings, where the blanket of snow even deafened the horse's hooves and the wheels of the automobiles. He still could not say he liked the snow, it still brought him painful memories, but as he stood looking out of the window he felt at ease with himself and happy.

The last few weeks had proved cathartic for him. He had nearly finished all the tasks on Viktor's lists, even apologizing to the servants, which had caused Irmy's maid to get very flustered and blush before she ran out of the room. Julius did not understand her but Irmy laughed as she said, "you have never really understood women have you Julius? You do not realize you have gone from a terrible ogre to Frau Beckova's handsome brother again. You have confused the poor girl, she is probably discussing you with cook at this very moment and coming to the conclusion that you are very strange, very strange indeed" Irmy left the room laughing to herself whilst Julius reaffirmed his suspicions that he would never understand women.

Suse had been more difficult. The Suse he met was very different from the Suse he had known. She was painfully thin, with dark circles under her eyes and her face was a mask of dejection and misery. Their interview had been strained and he had left her with the feeling that he had not helped at all. They had talked at length about Nikolas, but to his dismay Suse had talked as though she was discussing someone who was alive, as if Nikolas was merely away somewhere and about to return. She did not ask Julius about Nikolas' last days or his death and Julius, feeling it was something she did not want to discuss, did not broach the subject. Before he left her he told her that if ever she needed someone to talk to, he would always be there for her, but he left her house feeling very sad for Suse. She had to come to terms with Nikolas' death in her own way, as he had, but he wished he could have helped her more.

Apart from visiting various people Julius made a determined effort to make amends for his behavior to Richard and Irmy. Although they treated him as they always had, he was aware of a barrier between them. He had hurt them both very much and he wished he could turn back the clocks, if only to erase the terrible anguish he must have given them both. He often accompanied Irmy on her Christmas shopping expeditions into the city and they both took a childish delight in watching all the Christmas celebrations and Irmy helped him choose presents for Richard and the Manzs. He also bought gifts for Viktor and his wife, Karl, Franz and Gretha. He enjoyed buying extravagantly, his coffers were very healthy, especially after hearing from Josef's solicitor that both he and Viktor had been left a handsome legacy from their friend and Julius had received a beautiful pair of diamond and sapphire cufflinks that he had once seen Josef wearing and had commented on how much he admired them. Julius knew he would treasure the links more than anything, they were a personal memory of his friend and Josef's giving them to him meant more to him than money.

On one outing to the city on his own Julius had bought Irmy a beautiful pair of emerald earrings in an exquisite setting, which he knew would look wonderful on his sister. He had winced at their price, but knew Irmy deserved more than Julius could ever give her and was happy to think of the delight on Irmy's face when she opened them on Christmas Eve. Julius' benevolence knew no bounds that Christmas as he marveled at the joy of buying for others. He even remembered the staff at the hospital, and sent a silver pen set to Herr Doktor Sachs and gifts for the nursing staff.

It was whilst he was standing at the window waiting for Richard and Irmy to join him for dinner that he was aware of someone entering the room and he turned to see Irmy's maid, blushing as she always did these days whenever he encountered her. She dipped a little bob of a curtsey as she said, "Sir, it is Herr Leitner on the telephone, he wishes to speak with you" Like most people the girl had a mistrust of the telephone and made it quite plain she did not enjoy talking into the new contraption. Julius smiled as he said, "thank you" and he walked to follow her out of the room. The maid turned on her heel and ran out of the door like a frightened rabbit as Julius went into the hallway and picked up the telephone, holding the earpiece to his ear and speaking into the mouthpiece.

504

"Viktor, how are you? It is good of you to call. Are you back in Salzburg?"

Viktor's voice crackled along the line, "I am fine thank you. Yes I returned home a couple of days ago, wish I had stayed away longer, Sonia has me helping her with the Christmas celebrations" Julius could hear the laughter in his friend's voice and envied him his domesticity.

"The reason I wanted to talk to you Julius is that I have a proposition for you. Now do not say anything until I have finished what I have to say, all right?" Julius foolishly found himself nodding his head to the telephone as Viktor continued; "you know I went to Aussig after leaving you? My father is banker to a family there who have quite a few business concerns, but their main enterprise is the local coalmines, which they own. They are looking for a new manager in the New Year and I offered your name to them"

"What do you mean, you offered my name?" said Julius, feeling confused.

"I told you not to interrupt" laughed Viktor, "I just want you to think about this Julius. They are a very nice family, who seem to be well liked by their employees. Aussig is only a two hour train ride from Prague and you said yourself, even with Josef's money and the profits from your parent's house, you need to find yourself some employment. This is a perfect position for you, with generous remuneration, and the town is very nice. Herr Weiss said he would be only too happy to find you accommodation and staff for you should he employ you.

Now I do not want an answer straight away, think about it during the Christmas festivities. The position is not available until at least April of next year. They have a manager now who has been with them for over fifty years, but he is about to retire so you would train under him for a couple of months and then the position would be yours. What do you think?"

"I think that you have not told me yet what exactly I will have to do as 'manager' with this company"

"Well, basically manage" answered Viktor, whose attempt at light relief was lost on Julius, "your main task will be the transportation of the coal by rail to all their customers in your country, Austria, Germany, Poland, even the Russias, you have to arrange all that. The company offices are situated by the railway station, and that is where you will work. But do not worry too much, they will train you. Herr

505

Weiss wants someone he knows will be reliable and conscientious, and that is why I immediately thought of you"

Despite Viktor's attempts to bolster him up Julius felt the panic begin to rise in him as the thought of taking on such a responsibility dawned on him. He heard Viktor's distant voice saying, "I have to go now Julius. Please think about this. It is a wonderful opportunity for you. If you agree Herr Weiss wants to see you in January. You can visit Aussig, see if you like it, and see if he likes you. It is not definite you know, but you could go and see what you think of the place" Julius heard the final click of the phone and as he replaced the handset a million thoughts were running through his brain.

At dinner that evening Julius related his conversation with Viktor to Richard and Irmy. He still felt very confused, if not a little terrified as the thought of finding employment at last dawned on him. He tried to relay some of his fears to them, not least the fact that he was so ill prepared for work after being in the army for the last fourteen years. Irmy at first dismissed the idea as ridiculous, saying that Julius could not possibly leave Prague, this was his home, how could he even think of such a thing? Richard however was more pragmatic in his assessment of the situation. "I do not think you should rush into any decision at the moment, Julius, but I do not think you should dismiss Viktor's proposition without thinking about it. You have been offered what looks like a very good position and as you have said yourself, you are not exactly blessed with an abundance of opportunities when your whole life up to now has been in military circles. True, you would have to leave Prague, but Aussig is only a two hour journey away, you could easily come back to Prague every weekend if you wanted to. Please believe me I am not trying to wish you away from here, but this could be the new start you have been looking for. As Viktor suggested, think about it over Christmas, you do not have to make a decision straight away. You should at least travel to Aussig to see what the place is like. You may find you like the place, but equally you may hate it, you will never know unless you go there to see it. I must also add that at the least you owe it to Viktor, he has recommended you and you would be letting him down if you did not at least go and see what your employment entailed. I do not think Viktor would have proposed you if he did not think that the situation would be right for you"

Julius pondered Richard's words for the rest of the evening. Part of him did not want to leave Prague, was scared of the unknown life that beckoned him, but as he lay in his bed that night he had to admit to a feeling of suppressed excitement, of something new, of a fresh challenge for him. He had no idea what he was to do with his life and he felt that maybe fate was playing a part for him. As he drifted off to sleep he made a decision, Richard was right, he owed it to Viktor to at least go and see the place. He did not have to take the position if he did not like it, and equally Herr Weiss might take one look at him and decide he was totally unsuitable. For the moment he would not worry too much. He would celebrate Christmas and the New Year and then he would travel to Aussig.

Julius enjoyed Christmas immensely. Across Europe people were beginning to throw off the shackles of the Great War, as they now called it. The years of austerity were being blown away and the young people especially were expressing a new freedom and frivolity that they had been denied for so many years of their youth. Even the fashions dictated the new air of optimism. Women's hemlines were raised and they began to adopt a more streamlined, boyish silhouette to their clothes, the discard of their corsets symbolizing a discard of their suppression as women became more independent and demanded a more equal footing with their male counterparts. Although this bemused the older generation, Julius found this new attitude refreshing, although he was still alarmed by the attitude of some young women, whom he believed went too far in their behavior.

Although still in mourning for their mother and their friends Irmy decided to hold a party in her house to celebrate Christmas. She declared it was time to stop thinking about the past and to look forward to their future.

Julius thoroughly enjoyed himself, Irmy had invited several of the young nurses from her hospital and with his renewed health Julius reveled in their flirtatious natures. At times he was shocked by their behavior and speech but subdued his inner feelings when Georg told him he was being old fashioned and laughed at the somber attitude of an 'old' man. Next year Julius would be thirty years old and he had to admit to himself that at times, especially with the

507

experiences of the last few years, he did feel very old, however he did not want to be told this by a youthful Georg, as this made him feel even older.

Erika came to the party looking lovelier than ever accompanied by a nice young man who paid her rapt attention all night. Julius' reaction to seeing Erika with another man were mixed. He had to admit he felt a little jealous, but knew they would never be more than good friends, especially after his treatment of her over the past few months. Erika had graciously accepted his apology and they had renewed their friendship as though nothing untoward had ever happened. As Julius watched her laughing with her new beau he was happy for her, and he himself fervently hoped that one day he might find a companion to share his life.

Julius went to Midnight Mass with Irmy, Richard, Frau Beckova and Danusia on Christmas Eve. He had no inclination to go but went to please Irmy. He could not talk to her about his loss of faith, he knew that she would tell him that he needed the church now more than ever, but too much had happened to his loved ones and friends to let him believe in a God that had caused so much suffering and heartache to so many people. His memories of the war were too brutal and too sickening to reconcile himself to a religion that could absolve men of such heinous crimes as those he had witnessed over the past few years. As he knelt in the church the service did not touch him at all and with a sadness and regret he realized that he might never feel the same about his church again.

Christmas and New Year passed and in the middle of January Julius boarded the train that would take him to Aussig. He was just going for the day, to talk with Herr Weiss, and see if he would be interested in the job. Viktor had been overjoyed when Julius had agreed to go and he knew he had done the right thing, if only to please Viktor. As the train pulled into the station at Aussig Julius' heart was in his mouth and he felt very nervous.

When he left the station he came out onto a large, elongated square and opposite he could see the large sign of E & J Weiss, colliery owners and coal merchants, denoting the offices of Julius' prospective employers. Viktor had told Julius that the offices would be easy to find. They afforded a prime site near to the station where most of their produce was exported from.

As soon as Julius met Friedrich Weiss he liked him. He was a tall, dark man, with warm welcoming eyes and a generous smile. Julius was surprised to find him to be not much older than himself. He was dressed in a very expensive dark suit and walked with the easy elegance of a man of influence. He greeted Julius with a strong handshake and bade him sit in the seat before his desk. Herr Weiss immediately put Julius at his ease and before long the two men were discussing their mutual acquaintance, Viktor, before talking about Julius' possible employment.

Weiss was very interested about Julius' time in the army and his participation in the war, but Julius was pleased that he did not ask him too many questions, Weiss seeming to sense that too many private questions would have made Julius uncomfortable. Instead he enquired as to Julius' health as he had noticed Julius' stick. Julius quickly told him that he did not think it would be too long before he would no longer need the use of his stick, to which Weiss held up his hands and said, "it is no matter to me. Using a stick will not affect your work, believe me" As Weiss explained the job to Julius, he became quite enthusiastic.

When he had heard about it from Viktor his first reservations had been that it was an office job. Although Julius knew he could not afford to be fussy when it came to procuring some employment, the thought of being cooped up in an office all day had horrified him, but as Weiss explained, he would be expected to travel all over Europe to their clients as well as visiting the railways and their officials whilst organizing the transportation of the coal. The job sounded interesting and as Julius was taken around the offices and introduced to the staff he began to believe that he would quite enjoy working in such an atmosphere.

His last introduction was to a very old man, who sat hunched over his desk. His hair was snow white and worn unfashionably long and on his head he wore a black skullcap which denoted his religion. Weiss told Julius that this man would be training Julius in his job before he retired. The old man shook Julius' hand and looked him up and down with watery, intense eyes assessing the young man before him. He merely grunted at Julius and returned to his work. Leaving his office Weiss smiled at Julius as he said, "do not take too much notice of Jacob. He has worked for us for a very long time, and is very good at his job, but he is not getting any younger and resents the fact that we have asked him to retire. One would think he would be glad of the rest, he is over seventy now, and he knows we will take good care of him in his retirement. You will learn a lot from him, there is not much he does not know about this business, but we need to expand and the workload we envisage would be too onerous for an old man of Jacob's advanced years. The end of the war has opened up great opportunities for us and we need people like you to help us to realize that potential"

When they were seated back in his office, Weiss poured Julius a cup of coffee and as he handed it to him said, "well Herr Mayer, what do you think? do you think you would like to work for us?"

Julius was shocked by the man's directness as he answered, "surely it is I who should be asking whether you think I would be suitable for you"

"Herr Mayer, or may I call you Julius? Julius, you can have no better recommendation than that of the Leitner family, who have been our bankers for many years now. We are looking for someone intelligent, reliable and conscientious, and I think you fit all of those descriptions. Herr Leitner has told me a lot about you, and on our short meeting I would have to say that everything he told me has turned out to be true. I know you are inexperienced, but that is what appeals to me" Herr Weiss paused to smile, "it means we can train you to our way of doing business, not a bad thing for us, believe me"

Julius did not know what to say, not least did he wonder just what Viktor had said about him. Herr Weiss took his hesitation to be uncertainty as he added, "I think you have been made aware of your salary, and I hope you find that reasonable. How would you like it if we agreed to a six month contract to begin with, then if things do not work out, should you not like us, or we do not like you, then we are free to go our separate ways. What do you think?"

Julius thought this was more than generous and said so. He decided he would take the position and he would see if he suited this life and in six months he would know whether this was to be his future. After all, with Weiss's handsome terms, he really had nothing to lose. The two men shook hands and Julius agreed to start his employment with E & J Weiss in April. Herr Weiss offered to walk him back to the station and as they were leaving the office he turned to Julius and said, "I observed in Jacob's office that you did not even seem to notice his yarmulke, his skull cap. Did you realize that this firm is owned by a Jewish family?"

Julius looked at Friedrich Weiss not quite understanding the question, "No, but should it matter?"

"To some it might, believe me "

"Well I am afraid I am very ambivalent about religion sir" replied Julius, "besides as a lapsed good Catholic boy, I think I am hardly one to lecture or ponder other people's religions"

Herr Weiss let out a thunderous laugh and slapped Julius on the back as he said, "Herr Leitner said I should be careful of your strange sense of humor, now I see what he meant. I think we will suit each other very well Julius. Welcome to the company"

As Weiss walked Julius to the station he told him about the history of the company and how his family had become benefactors to the town as the business had grown. Although he did try to concentrate Julius had to admit later that the whole conversation went over his head as he mulled over the enormous step he had just taken.

Once he was on the train heading back to Prague Julius tried to remember the interview that had just taken place but all he could really recall was how much he had liked Friedrich Weiss and that he had felt at home in Aussig. From the little he had seen of it it had appeared to be a prosperous, clean town and Herr Weiss had said he would arrange accommodation and staff for him by the time he arrived in April. Everything seemed arranged and Julius felt at last settled in his mind. His past was behind him and he had a future to look forward to. That it was an unknown, uncertain future only excited him more.

The next few months were spent in ensuring he was back to full health and sorting out his affairs before his departure. Although there was no time to take his planned trip to see Franz and Gretha he had promised to go and see them in the summer, when the mines closed down for their annual holiday. He also hoped that at the same time he would travel via Vienna so that he could visit Karl, and everybody appeared happy with these arrangements. Saying goodbye was very hard, especially to Nikolas' parents and Georg, but he knew he would be back in Prague often. It was only his promise of returning for the weekend at least once a month that had appeased Irmy when he had told her that he had decided to move to Aussig.

With his trunks already sent on ahead Julius stood on the platform of Prague station on a cold April morning awaiting the train that would take him to his new life. Irmy was already crying as she said, "it seems I am always saying goodbye to you on this station. It is just not fair"

"Irmy it is not as if I am going to the other end of the world. As I keep telling you, Aussig is not so very far away. You will see, I will probably be so homesick that I will be back to see you next weekend, and then you will be moaning that you are never rid of me"

Richard diplomatically said he would go and check the times of the trains as Irmy wiped her tears and managed a weak smile for her brother.

"Oh Julius, you have been through so much lately, we all have. I do not think I can bear to see you go. With you going it seems like all my family have deserted me now"

Julius knew she was thinking of Mama and Papa as he said "I know, but you know I am not so very far away if you need me, and besides you have Richard, you are a very lucky woman"

"I know. It is just sometimes, sometimes I wish things were the way they were before, that Mama and Papa were still here with us, that we were all together and happy like we used to be"

Julius pulled Irmy to him and gave her a hug, "I know" he whispered in her ear, "but it is no use wishing things that cannot be, I should know that"

As he pulled back from their embrace Julius looked down into her eyes, "Irmy you are the dearest, most precious sister a man could ever have, without you I do not know where I would be. You know how sorry I am about everything"

Irmy lowered her eyes, they both knew that it was not only Julius' behavior they were talking about but the great sadness that Irmy could not talk about, her inability to have children, "I know" she whispered and Julius could sense her deep misery.

As the train pulled into the station Richard returned to them and Julius found his seat in the carriage. Leaning out of the carriage window he held Irmy's hands as he said to Richard, "Thank you for everything Richard. I know you will look after her, do not let these new ideas that the young women are trying to regale us with influence Irmy too much. She is strong willed enough as it is"

512

Irmy laughed through her tears, happy to hear her brother teasing her. Julius shook hands with Richard and as the train pulled out of the station he stood leaning out of the window watching Irmy crying as Richard put a caring arm around his wife's shoulders. Julius stayed watching them until they disappeared from his view and then he took his seat in the corner of the carriage.

As the train left Prague Julius sat watching the familiar landscape disappear from his view. He felt sad at leaving Irmy, but he knew it was for the best. Although he knew he had been forgiven for his past misdemeanors, ever since their argument there had been a barrier between them that he could not define but was always there. He had said some cruel things to her that could never be forgotten and she deserved to get on with her life without being burdened with having to look after her big brother. That Richard and Irmy's marriage would survive her barrenness he was of no doubt. Richard adored her and Julius had realized that Irmy's infertility affected her far more than it did Richard.

Sitting in the carriage he was reminded of his train journey of nearly fourteen years ago when he had been leaving home to join the army. On that fated journey he had met a young boy who would become his closest friend until his untimely death. So much had happened since then, but Julius knew his life had been enriched by meeting Nikolas and he would not have changed anything about his life even if he could, and the only pity was that Nikolas was no longer with him. He looked around his carriage at his traveling companions. No young man with an angelic smile and bright red hair today and yet he felt very much as he had done all those years ago, that he was starting a new life, a new adventure. Who knew what he might achieve or whom he might meet in the years to come. All he did know was that he was going to enjoy his life, make it worthwhile, and never forget the sacrifices that Nikolas and Josef and men like them had made for him, and for so many others.

Julius sat back in his seat and made himself comfortable for the journey, speeding through the countryside to his new life and hopefully the things he truly yearned for, some peace, happiness and love.

www.ingramcontent.com/pod-product-compliance
Lightning Source LLC
Chambersburg PA
CBHW080856020726
47502CB00008B/2258